To the Most High God who guides me and loves me

La Rose
Le Baton Chronicles

Book III

Claudia Helena Ross

BLAME HELENA
Books and Media

Blame Helena Books and Media
San Diego, California

www.blamehelenabooks.com

Blame Helena Books and Media ISBN: 978-1-947549-90-6

Cover art by Claudia Helena Ross. Photo - Evergreen Plantation-8050
by Michael McCarthy https://www.flickr.com/photos/msmccarthy-
photography/4594235420

25C09R19

www.blamehelenabooks.com

Printed in the United States of America
10 9 8 7 6 5 4 3 2 1

Prologue

arachiel lifted his head up toward the heavens, waiting with patience for a change he knew would come. It had to come. It could not, not come. Throughout eternity, he'd watched her sepals retreat into its furled corolla, parched by the heartache and pain seeping from within. The pain of her soul caused its ends to brown and curl. The petals of the corolla, hardened by grief and tanned in the midday sun, took on the mantle of the crackled sepals, twirling themselves together even tighter.

Each petal within shielded its neighboring comrade as much as possible; however, failing to do so, leaving a sizable portion of the petal exposed. Yet, the exposed area of each petal didn't wither in the heat of the sun. Instead, they mutated into a leathery existence, each melding with the exposed petal of its neighbor into a cohesive, weathered shield, protecting the one who dwelled within their fortress.

Sealtiel hovered high above the closed bud, misting it with his golden atomizer. The leaves seemed to welcome the moisture; however, the droplets of water beaded on the leathery petals, mixing with the dehydrated nectar locked within, creating a glaze which further hardened the membrane. The one whom the bud protected rolled around within, her movements causing the petals to protrude and then retract.

"Our Rose! She absorbs the love of God within the depth of her grief. She be well," Sealtiel said.

Barachiel opened his eyes. He'd lounged upon one of the Rose's lower leaves for an unknown number of days, waiting for her to awake. He nodded, agreeing with his brother's words. Barachiel had grown tired of the Rose's sulking. She needed to get over it. All was not lost.

"*Mon Frère*, you should harbor mercy in your heart for our Rose." Raguel appeared on a neighboring leaf. "She is a tender flower and doesn't endure betrayal well. She is accustomed to the unconditional adoration of *mon Dieu*." Raguel freed an adjacent leaf of the Rose's bush, entangled with its neighbor.

The Lord's sun beamed down upon him, highlighting the gold and bronze colored barbs and barbules, creating the iridescent hue of his magnificent wings. His brown skin turned to gold under the glow of heaven.

In a rare moment of vanity, in preparation to give his praise to the Most High God, Raguel adjusted his tunic adorned with the Ark of the Covenant levitating above the Ethiopian lands. In most instances, Raguel found Barachiel to be more concerned with the appearance of his tunic, but not today. Raguel knew the Rose's pouty state of self-pity distracted his brother.

Sealtiel landed on a leaf beside Raguel's and placed the atomizer on a nearby leaf, above his head. Taking the left side of his mustache, he wound it on his left hand, until he reached the end. He smiled, grasping the tendril's end with his fingertips, twirling it mercilessly into a fine thread.

While twisting the tip of his mustache, Sealtiel watched Raguel adjust his tunic. He'd never concerned himself with his appearance. He knew he always looked perfect, except for his five-foot long mustache. The left side was maybe three inches shorter than the right. He needed to stop twirling it.

Releasing the frazzled tendril, Sealtiel adjusted the sleeves of his emerald, iridescent silk robe. His tailor had constructed the garment in a heavy weave. It never wrinkled. His new garment was an improvement over the tunic he'd worn for an eternity. He'd needed a change. Yet, he'd chosen to maintain the scene embroidered upon it of his Chinese homeland, depicting a jade altar suspended above the countryside, with a sunburst radiating around it. The open tomb of the Lord Jesus floated above it all, granting hope and salvation to the Most High God's creation.

Sealtiel exhaled, satisfied with his appearance. Barachiel's failure to comment on his new look surprised him, but he let it go. Silence from Barachiel always proved to be golden.

Raguel gazed up into the sky, shielding his eyes from the sun. "She is well. A little compassion from you would strengthen her, Barachiel." Extending his arms, he gave her praise, love and support.

Having grown weary of waiting for the Rose to arise, Barachiel stood upon the leaf he'd reclined upon since she'd sequestered herself. The sun, disapproving and foreboding, took refuge behind a visiting cloud, a phenomenon rarely observed in the garden by the holy.

Extending his wings, Barachiel glided down to the base of her bush. Thorns catapulted toward him from the enormous stalk as he sailed to the garden floor. Raguel and Sealtiel joined Barachiel at his side. Barachiel drew his sword.

"You cannot do this thing," Raguel said. "You would strike down her bush?"

Barachiel swung his sword against the stalk, but a brass thorn deflected his strike. "She cannot sulk forever. She has all of heaven fawning over her, and for what?" Barachiel positioned his sword at the base of the stalk. "Isn't this the way of the Rose and the Prince Seed? Must we all continue to endure their never-ending drama of love and hate for each other?" Barachiel swung again, this time making contact.

The gash oozed a thick milky substance.

Thorny roots sprang up from the earth, capturing Barachiel, Raguel, and Sealtiel, pulling them to the ground. Now on their backs, the three found themselves trapped within the roots of her bush. Sickle shaped thorns soared out from the trunk of her bush and descended upon them, prepared to behead them.

The bud topping the bush opened, revealing a blood red blossom, unfurling its petals streaked with crimson. The one sheltered within arose from her crouched position and stood upon the blossom. Filled with vengeance and indignation, she unveiled herself before Creation. Her bare breasts heaving upon her chest, the Rose's tightly curled hair expanded and grew into a massive round orb. Roses blooming upon thorny vines from her kinky mane trellised down one thousand feet to the earth, encroaching upon her helpless captives.

The Rose smirked, the lines of face converging into a central point of rage. "You should learn to allow me my rest, Barachiel." Her vines encapsulated him, tightening around his throat, overshadowed by the sickle-shaped thorns of her roots. "I have much to think about. Many issues concern me. You would strike me when I am weak?"

Barachiel's throat closed. He couldn't speak with his voice, yet his spirit rebelled, refusing to be quiet. Her roots, thorns, and vines could neither bind nor silence his soul. *You only have one thing on your mind, ma Reine. Your Prince. You cannot weep forever. You must move on. You have not lost the love you seek.* Barachiel choked, a well-placed throne piercing his throat.

Raguel could never understand Barachiel's need to antagonize the Rose. Sure, they all knew she would get through her cycle of heartache. The Rose realized this fact as well. Yet, Barachiel could never resist the need to jab at her, as if pointing out her fatalistic behavior, instigated by the Prince Seed's repeated rejection throughout the centuries, would make her stronger somehow.

Raguel's own compulsion to intervene and to prevent Barachiel and Sealtiel from acting out their recurring roles in the Rose's saga amazed him most of all. Why couldn't he stay out of it? And yet once again, they all found themselves bound to the Earth, entangled in her roots and thorns, while the bare-breasted Rose stood atop her war blossom prepared to slay them all.

"Well, if this has occurred, then one more should join us to complete the act," Raguel said, comforting himself. He twisted within his prison.

The Slave walked across the bramble web of roots and thorns, nursing her ebony babe. She pulled the babe from her tit. The baby yelled. "C'mon boy," she said, hushing the child. "Your charge needs you. I'se gotta let you go." The

Slave pointed up.

The babe considered the one staring down at him, filled with rage and indignation. He smiled and gurgled. The Slave sat the babe upon Raguel's chest, encased in thorny roots. "Look after my boy and his seed."

"You know I will, Sarah," Raguel said. He watched her flash into a star and vanish.

The babe grew upon Raguel's chest. Once the babe had become a boy, he toddled over to where Barachiel lay imprisoned, dead. The boy reclined upon him and grew strong, until he became a man. "Papa, what is it?"

You must reason with her.

"Why me? What can I do?" The babe, once a boy, and now young man, waited in innocence to hear Barachiel's instructions from the realm of the Spirit.

You are her Protector. The Rose will listen to you.

Now the Protector of the Rose, the man, once a boy, searched the sky. Spotting the pinnacle of the bush in eternity's ethers, nearing the threshold of Heaven, he spied a woman standing atop an open blossom with vines streaming from her enormous kinky coif, hurt and enraged.

Wriggling within their prisons, Raguel and Sealtiel watched the young man begin his ascent up the bush, climbing the thorns instead of the leaves. The grip of the roots loosened. Raguel and Sealtiel freed themselves; however,

Barachiel remained bound. Raguel and Sealtiel stood back from the bush to find the Protector standing on a hardy bract extended to the left of the war blossom. They watched the young man talk to the Rose.

Raguel saw the Rose's lips move. The Sisters, her attendants, came and robed her and then cut away the vines of war from her hair. Each sister, taking one of her arms, glided the Rose down to the lake of Eden. She bathed. Raguel heard his Rose cry out in grief.

He could feel the pigmentation of his skin fade, the cloud of heartbreak draining the color and life from him. A cold air permeated the atmosphere of the temperate garden. The birds flew away en masse. The animals fled the Rose's presence.

Raguel returned his attention to the lake, but the Rose was gone. Hearing whimpering, he witnessed his Rose upon her blossom filled with defeat and self-pity. The petals of her flower drooped, limp and drab.

"You must go on, my Rose. Release it all and go on," the Protector said.

The Rose stood before her Protector, empty inside. She turned her eyes toward Heaven. Raguel watched life return to her. "God strengthen me," he heard the Rose say.

Raguel scanned all around him, finding all the vegetation of New Eden depressed from her lack of joy and love. The vegetation shuttered. In an instant, the greens, reds, blues and yellows returned to the plants, causing the vegetation to spring up in the rejuvenation of love.

"Love lives in spite of those who claim to love us, but reject us all the same. We must love ourselves, for the Most High God loves us without condition." The Rose straightened her back, her face still wet with tears. "What can any man deny us?"

Raguel embraced the Rose's words. He knew all would be well, as it had been throughout eternity.

Life returned to Barachiel's corpse. His shackles crumbled, and he sat up from his thorned box of torture gasping for air. Barachiel watched his son, the Protector, stand at the right of the Rose upon his now golden bract. "May you always have the Rose's ear and keep her safe," Barachiel said, but he knew his son would falter after a time.

PART I

Chapter 1

New Orleans, Louisiana. August 29, 1963.

"My arm has fallen asleep, I have a crook in my back from this rickety swing, the flying vermin are attacking me, while my grandmère is fast asleep, drooling on my chest." Julian Charles Chamberie heard buzzing in his left ear. Was it a mosquito or a goddamn bee? With his free hand, he swatted at the insect. In his imagination, the insect mocked him, laughing. It flew away.

A dove swooped down on him. "Go away!" Julian flailed his free arm at the creature. It chirped and retreated to the upper branches of the live oak tree. Two of the bird's comrades took up the arms of their friend and dove on him. At the last moment, the creatures aborted their attack.

"Go." The flying rats departed, leaving Julian in peace. Silence pursued, allowing Julian to release his anxiety brought on by the wildlife of New Orleans' Garden District.

Julian adjusted and grimaced, attempting to balance the

dead weight of his sleeping grandmère. "No one can stop me from leaving. It's simple. I will call the captain and arrange a flight for later today. I can arrive in D.C. by late tonight. I can hold Jannette in my arms."

Yet, he knew he couldn't do it.

In some way, his grandmère's tale entranced him. He had to hear the end. It was a like a late-night movie. He would watch a flick to lull him asleep. However, his need to know what happens compelled him watch the bad story to the very end. His grandmère's story wasn't any different.

His grandmère gurgled and grunted. She shifted onto her back somewhat, her head resting in the puddle she'd left upon Julian's soaked shirt. Her body relaxed. She snored.

He shouldn't have returned to the house from the Hotel Monteleone two days before. He should have stayed and followed through with his plans to commit the ancient woman to a nursing home and auction off the contents of the Chevalier Mansion of New Orleans. Yet, he'd allowed the old woman to sweet talk him with her stories. He'd fallen prey to her love. Sucker.

Now he was trapped. He couldn't leave.

Julian sighed, considering his predicament. His 116-year-old grandmère, Lela Chevalier Roberts, felt more like his daughter than his elder. Who could ever walk away from their child? His throat tightened with emotion, sensing at some point in his unexplainable existence he'd done so.

Detecting a movement in the corner of his eye, he followed it to find the rose bushes had blossomed. There had only been leaves a few moments before. The fragrance enchanted him. Since his childhood, he'd relished the scent of roses.

His great-grandmère's garden offered a wide variety of roses, each fragrance marrying with the other, swirling into an olfactoric concerto of intoxicating pleasure for Julian. Sometimes, the whiff of a single rose variety would break away from the pack, choosing to be admired for its unique fragrance. It would catch a little breeze and soar into Julian's nostrils, giving him a galactic rush and high.

Throughout his life, his great-grandmère had worn rose scents as the strong middle note, perched atop a musky end note. Julian recalled each perfume she'd worn throughout his childhood. Just as many people never forgot a face, he never forgot a scent. He'd always had a keen sense of smell. Julian didn't need to see a person enter the room. He knew whom they were based on their pheromones mingled with their perfume or cologne.

With care, Julian planted his right foot in the earth beneath the swing, pushing it back, and then releasing it. He could feel additional tension leave her body as the swing traveled forward and then back again. A stream of cool air

lined the humid atmosphere, the hot New Orleans day surrendering a few degrees to the anticipated coolness of the
evening yet to come.

Julian leaned into his great-grandmère a bit, cuddling
her like the daughter he'd never had. Julian thought of his
girlfriend Jannette, back in Washington, D.C. What a joy it
would be to have a little Jannette running around one day.
Or maybe they would have a son. He would make the boy
strong, encouraging him to embrace his inner genius and not
to take any shit off anyone.

He sniffed his great-grandmère's neck, and then her hair.
Chanel 22. Julian twirled his great-grandmère's platinum curl
between his fingers.

His great-grandmère grumbled in her sleep, snuggling
deeper into Julian's chest. Maybe she dreamed of her dead
husband. Her fingernails sunk into his chest. Dammit, even
in her sleep, his great-grandmère listened to his thoughts.
She needed to go to bed instead of using his shirt as a pillow
case. Julian lifted his great-grandmère's head. "Ugh! Slobber?"

Looking across the yard, above the boxed hedges, Julian
spotted people standing in the solarium. He didn't want to
yell for them, because he might wake his great-grandmère.
On second thought, he realized an atomic blast wouldn't
awake her. "Theo!"

A few moments later, the tall, cocoa brown handsome man with gray hair left the solarium, entering the area under the pergola, over-run with rose vines as old as the mansion. Theo shielded his eyes to protect himself from the late afternoon sun. "Keep your voice down boy 'fore you'se wakes up Ma'Dame. Whatcha want?"

Julian squirmed in his grandmère's death grip. "Come and get her. I'm tired of being her pillow," Julian said. "She has ruined my shirt. Look at this big wet spot. Besides, I need to go to the bathroom."

Theo walked over and stood above him, glaring. "She gonna wake up soon. I ain't disturbin' her rest." Theo returned to the house.

I hate him, Julian murmured in his heart. He didn't understand Theo's purpose at the mansion. Hell, why were any of the household staff there? Only the chef, Mario, seemed to have a defined role.

Julian still hadn't decided if he should commit her old ass to a nursing home or not. Theo, Sissy, Isabel, and Suzette still hung around, fawning over her and attending to her every need. He knew they only wanted her money. Yet, it was more than that. These four people, without any blood ties, seemed to be devoted to her.

Lela released a loud snore and held him tighter. He felt a warm liquid seep through his shirt. "Goddammit! What the hell? Such a lady." He removed his handkerchief from his pants pocket with his left hand and placed it beneath his great-grandmère's drippy mouth. The things he had to endure.

Accepting he wasn't going anywhere soon, Julian relaxed on the swing, cuddling his great-grandmère in his right arm, protecting her from harm. Julian leaned back in the swing and closed his eyes.

What did his great-grandmère's stories have to do with his mamère? He only wanted to know why had his mamère died. Why couldn't his great-grandmère just tell him instead of going through all the drama? Julian already knew the truth. It was his fault. His mother had died because of him.

Her tales swirled in his mind like a hurricane. But in a strange way, Julian felt as if he'd played an active role in the great-grandmère's stories somehow. Julian's eyes popped opened, feeling his great-grandmère stir upon his chest.

She snorted and continued her nap. Tears ran from her eyes, shut tight. She winced. "But Toussaint, you… Jamie."

"Toussaint?" What did Uncle Toot have to do with any-thing? Julian remembered his adopted uncle as a jovial man, but even as a child he could see the man had a dark side. Recalling his great-grandmère's tale and remembering the documentation regarding Toussaint's birth in *La Rose Family History*, Julian realized Toussaint was probably involved in some very significant way.

A fox ran from the bushes and sat on the garden lawn. He seemed to laugh at Julian. The fox groomed his lush tail and then rush away. "Foxes in New Orleans?" He'd never considered the animal as indigenous to Louisiana. But hell, why not? Every other animal in creation called the garden home. Why not foxes?

"Oh God," Julian said. His great-grandmère emitted a few guttural noises. She cleared her throat, snored, and then coughed, all at once. She stirred upon his chest, moving her head from side to side. She seemed to consider if she should awake and return to the land of the living. Although disgusted, he patted her arm with his right hand. After a few moments, Lela opened her eyes.

"Jamie?"

Julian remained silent, allowing her to regain her wits. He'd learned over the past couple of days to give her few minutes to find her bearings. After fifteen minutes, she sat up beside him.

Lela scrutinized the garden, disoriented at first. "This is 1963," she mumbled. Lela stretched and then turned to her left, finding her great-grandson beside her. "Have we been here all night?"

"It's late afternoon Thursday, Grandmère," Julian said. "It is still today."

Lela adjusted her Cartier watch on her wrist and squinted. "So, it is. I apologize, darling. I didn't intend to drop off on you like that."

Julian nodded, but said nothing.

Lela stood from the swing, appearing every bit of 116 years old to Julian. However, once she stretched and patted her cheeks, encouraging the circulation of blood throughout her ancient veins, she appeared refreshed and younger, as if in her late fifties.

"I am not ancient. Methuselah was much older than me. He is ancient." Lela patted her forehead with the back of her hand. "I'm only 116 years old. I'm still a young lady."

It's a trap, Julian thought to himself. He didn't comment.

"See, you're learning," Lela said with a sly smile. She walked over to the bar cart and poured herself a glass of water. She was still tired. When had she fallen asleep? She remembered. She'd been telling him about Jamie and Hanzel.

"I'm not going to think about that right now," she said to herself. What was the point? She had to focus on Julian, not her dead husband. She sipped her water. "Your shirt is a mess. Did you spill your drink while we napped?"

Lela watched her great-grandson's face converge into a snarl. She realized she'd napped upon him. So what, if she'd drooled on him? "Like you didn't throw up on me a thousand times as a child. Did I chastise you, boy?" Julian diverted his eyes. Good, she'd shamed him. The drool would dry, unlike the vomit and pee he'd gifted her with as a child. He would get over it. "What did Mario make for dinner?"

Julian inhaled deep. His stomach grumbled, returning to life, smelling the savory aroma wafting to the garden from the kitchen. "It smells like rack of lamb with potatoes and pearl onions, yeast rolls, and French onion soup."

Lela raised an eyebrow, surprised. She'd forgotten her great-grandson's keen sense of smell. "Do you think it's ready?"

Julian closed his eyes, savoring the sweet smells of dinner. "He's taking it out of the oven now. However, the roast must rest for few minutes."

"*Bon*. Let's go in and prepare for dinner."

Julian took his great-grandmère's arm and escorted her inside. He helped her up the grand staircase leading to the second floor and then opened the door to her suite. Lela patted his cheek before going inside. Wasting little time, he ran down the hall to his room, stripped off his saliva-soaked shirt and hopped in the shower.

Lela sat at the table, waiting for everyone to arrive. One by one, they all trickled into the dining room as Mario wheeled in the serving cart. She snickered when Julian entered, freshly showered and wearing a clean shirt. So what, if she had drooled on him? She deserved the right to drool on her children while she slept. "Bow your heads," Lela said, and then blessed the table.

Mario removed the lid, revealing the succulent leg of lamb to the applause of the diners. He carved the roast, serving each of them.

Julian sliced into his lamb and inserted it into his mouth. The meat melted on his tongue. His teeth were useless for this meal, but he chewed anyway, allowing the juices to permeate his taste buds, heightened by the fragrance of the lamb which invaded his nasal passages. He thought he would shout out. Mario was an excellent chef. Once Mario had served everyone, he prepared his own plate and then joined them at the table.

The pointless chatter of his great-grandmère's maid, Suzette, played on in the background of Julian's wandering mind. Tuning her out, his attention fell upon a portrait over the fireplace, behind the head of the table. It was of his great-grandmère and Uncle Toot. He found it to be strange. In the portrait, his great-grandmère sat in a red velvet chair holding a bouquet of blood red roses cradled in her arms. Uncle Toot stood behind her in the portrait with his hands on her shoulders, guarding her. "Why did you have a portrait made of you and Uncle Toot?"

Lela placed a buttery sautéed carrot in her mouth. "It's

as you have surmised. He is my protector. We had a portrait made."

"Is?" Julian said. "Uncle Toot is dead."

Lela nodded and cut a slice of the roasted lamb.

Julian considered the sinister expression Uncle Toot sported in the portrait, dressed up with a smile. "How is he your protector?"

He asked! Lela rejoiced in the Spirit before the Most High God, as always. She resisted the urge to jump up from the table and clap her hands in the presence of the Lord. Once again, she had triumphed over evil. Julian had expressed his desire to learn truth about himself and his family, in accordance to the rules stipulated by Mammon and Lucifer. "That is, well was, his role in my life."

"What does he protect you from?"

"Satan's minions."

Julian choked on his roasted potato wedge. He coughed it up into his napkin. Mario left his dinner, refreshed Julian's water and then returned to the table. Julian gulped the water, soothing his burning throat. "You need to resume your nap, old woman. You're delusional." Everyone fell silent around the table. What, had he blasphemed against God?

"Blaspheme? Almost. I'm not quite delusional yet, *mon fils*," Lela said. She dabbed the corners of her mouth with the hem stitched napkin and replaced it on the table beside her place setting, considering it. "Suzette, how old are these linens?"

Suzette placed her fork next to her plate and thought for a moment. "We've had them since the birth of Monsieur Julian," Suzette said, scowling at the young man.

"Well, remind me to shop for more. I've grown tired of this set."

"We have the linens embroidered with rose motifs," Suzette said.

Lela nodded, recalling the pattern. "Oh yes, I'd forgotten. Well, we should bring those out for a while, but I still would like to freshen up our selection."

Suzette nodded.

Lela exhaled, remembering her point. "And as for you, young man, Toussaint always looked out for me, even before I knew him."

Julian sipped his red wine. A boy appeared in the mirror of the glass, alerting him to danger. He could feel everyone at the table watching him, yet he couldn't break his gaze from the image on the glass. It faded. "Oh, did you tell me that? How he warned your father the first time Hanzel tried to hurt you?"

"I'm not sure. Perhaps," Lela said.

Julian considered the matter further. "It happened at La Rose Plantation. You told me Uncle Toot lived with you at the plantation."

"Yes, this is true."

His esophagus having recovered from his near choking, Julian stabbed a potato with his fork and placed it in his mouth. The rosemary engulfed his senses. His mind raced, thinking of the plantation with a renewed, unexplainable interest. It was all he could think about. Yesterday, he could care less about the place. Now, interest in their bastardized homeland surged within his heart, blossoming into a new obsession. "Where is the plantation? Didn't you say it still stands?"

Lela studied her great-grandson. "Well, yes. It does."

Julian swirled the Cabernet in his glass. "Have I ever been there?"

Lela thought back over the years. "Within your recent memory? I don't believe so."

Freak. She was hiding something. "Oh."

Everyone sat in silence, watching Julian. They'd all stopped eating. He felt a bit uncomfortable. "Well, maybe we can go there before I leave. It's not far, is it?"

Lela eyes misted. "No, it's forty-five minutes to an hour away." We can go tomorrow, if you're not busy."

Julian nodded and stuffed the last morsel of lamb into his mouth.

The family sat in awe watching Julian. He seemed so excited, talking to Lela. Mario arose from the table and cleared the dinner plates. He returned moments later, serving the pâté foie gras. After refreshing the wine, he took his seat. He, along with the others, sipped wine and enjoyed the pâté while Julian rattled on about La Rose, asking Lela a thousand questions.

Julian escorted his great-grandmère to her room. He kissed her on the cheek and walked away.

Lela lingered in the doorway for a moment, considering her words. "I would like to ask you a favor."

Julian stopped and turned, facing her. "What, Grand-mère?"

Lela blushed. "I want you to keep an open mind about your great-grandpère James. He was a good man, a great man." Lela patted his hand. "He would have loved you very much."

Julian frowned and turned to leave. He was tired. "Maybe."

Lela grabbed his arm, stopping him. "No, not maybe. He would have admired you a great deal. At least I believe so." Lela left the doorway of her room to embrace her great-grandson, who towered over her. Had Jamie been as tall as Julian? No, he hadn't. Julian inherited his height from his father, Robert Chamberie.

"It's fine, Grandmère It doesn't really matter," Julian said.

Lela patted his cheek. She stood on the tips of her toes to kiss him there. "I suppose you're right. I only ask you this." Lela returned to the doorway of her room. It was late. She'd eaten too many sweets and drank too much wine. She felt her age. Averting a slight swoon (she hoped Julian hadn't noticed), Lela grabbed the rose embossed door knob for discrete support. "Make no judgments until the end. Darling, I still have so much to tell you." Lela bit her lip, full of meekness. "Do you have pressing engagements back in Washington, D.C.? Do you have time to listen to me?"

Julian's heart broke. She was just an old woman who wanted someone to listen to her before she died. But, why did he have to be her ear? Yet deep down, he desired to be the one. "Yes, Grandmère. I have time."

Lela released a brilliant smile, full of the hope and promise of the prophecy yet to be fulfilled. "Bon. I will meet you downstairs in the morning at eight o'clock sharp." Lela rose up to the tips of her toes once again to kiss Julian. He stooped a bit, meeting her half way. Lela entered her room and closed the door.

Julian stood outside her room listening to creepy Suzette help his great-grandmère prepare for bed. God, Suzette was old as hell, just like his great-grandmère. She needed someone to help her old ass. Julian let it all go. He had learned in his few days there to allow the old women to do as they pleased.

He walked down the hall and entered his room. Julian sat on the bed, thinking of all his great-grandmère had told him. Without warning, he felt exhausted. Julian mustered the energy to strip off his clothes and jump into bed, falling asleep with thoughts of his girlfriend Jannette. He could smell her, although she was a thousand miles away. Even when she wasn't with him, she was. Julian closed his eyes.

Chapter 2

New Orleans, Louisiana. August 30, 1963.

The hot, slick, smoothness of her mouth surrounded him. He wished to cry out, but he couldn't. He rolled over and gazed into her eyes, a lion prepared to take the throat of his prey.

The clanging of the Liberty Bell roused him from his sleep. Julian opened his eyes. "Hello," he said, answering the phone with a deep and raspy voice. He tried to normalize his breathing, but was unsuccessful. He could smell her.

"Hi, honey."

Little slut. "You should stop doing that."

"What?"

He didn't feel like playing games with her. His girlfriend was a witch of some sort. He knew what she liked and when she liked it. Somehow, she had the ability to telepathically transport her desires to his mind and flesh in a way he didn't understand. He always knew when she awoke in the morning, because he would awake too, in every sense of the word.

"What, are you horny?"

"Julian, what kind of question is that?" He listened to her gather together her items required for the day. "I'm dressed and ready to go to the work at the library."

Julian couldn't understand why she kept her bullshit job in the Howard University stacks. He had plenty of money. Why couldn't she just stay at home, fuck him, and spend it? She had some sort of irrational idea about earning her own money. Dumb whore. Most women would kill for such a set-up, but not her. Julian knew she had to be screwing someone at work. As soon as he returned to D.C., he would handle it. But for now, he didn't wish to kill the last vestiges of his incredible wet dream. "What time did you wake up?"

"Seven o'clock."

Julian didn't care if she was one hour ahead of him in Washington, D.C. He knew what she'd done. "Oh really? What did you think of when you woke up?"

"You, as I always do," Jannette said a little above a whisper. She allowed a discrete moan of satisfaction escape her. "Yes, you did cross my mind. Anyway, when are you coming home?"

Julian knew he'd more than 'crossed her mind.' He allowed his imagination to roam, reconsidering her statement on how she'd 'thought' of him. God, he was still hard. "I'm not sure. My okie-doke, house Nigger grandmère wants me to visit the family plantation today. She's nuts. Who wants to return to the place of their captivity?"

The receiver crackled.

"What?" His arousal abandoned him.

"Maybe she wants to teach your insensitive, hard hearted ass something, Julian." Jannette fell silent for a moment. "Every day, we have researchers come into the library, searching for a lead on where they came from. You're fortunate, for you have a sane, cognizant, 116-year-old grandmother who was actually a slave, who remembers what it was like to be a slave, and has all the family history in her recollection, as well as the records, lands, and well, everything to back it up. There are so many Afro-Americans who would kill for such a legacy, laid out on a silver platter for them. But you don't care. All you can do is to call her names."

"Jannette…"

"Good bye, Julian," Jannette said. "And trust me, your sleep will be undisturbed tomorrow." She slammed down the receiver.

"Motherfuck!" Why did he keep her smart mouth ass around? He could have any woman he wanted, but for some reason, he chose to torture himself with Jannette. Maybe he was some sort of masochistic psycho who got off on her tongue lashings. But at the same time, he loved it about her. She truly could care less that he was fine and rich. In a strange way, she seemed concerned about his soul.

His soul was fine. He wished Jannette would shut up sometimes and do as she was told.

With the euphoria of making love to his girlfriend having evaporated in the noise blasting from her mouth, Julian left the comfort of his bed for the shower.

His life was going to hell hanging out with his great-grand-mère. Julian hadn't checked the markets since coming to New Orleans. Before his arrival, he'd purchased 100,000 shares of United Utilities, on the advice of his monpère. How was it doing? What if he needed to dump it? But somehow, he couldn't concern himself with it all. His great-grandmère had bewitched him.

Yes, Julian was convinced his great-grandmère was some sort of witch. How did she do the things she did? How, as a centenarian, could she appear as a young, vibrant woman? In fact, everyone in the house seemed more youthful and agile than him, and he was only twenty-four years old. The phenomenon boggled his mind.

Julian went to the library and checked his datebook. Nothing pressing, just reminders of tasks he needed to complete before the end of the third quarter. He needed a secretary. Why should he concern himself with such mundane tasks such as keeping his own calendar? But where could he find a secretary competent enough to complete tasks with the same level of quality and accuracy as he would?

"Oh shit." Julian heard the clock chime seven-thirty. He knew his great-grandmère preferred to take her breakfast at seven o'clock. He rushed to the terrace.

Mario had placed a small, ornate, gold plateau on the white wrought iron table filled with fruit and golden bowls filled with nuts, dates, and figs. Nothing could be simple. Maybe one of his ancestors had stolen the piece from Versailles. Julian found sausage and bacon set before his great-grandmère, along with a pitcher of juice. She hadn't touched any of it. Julian watched her finish her Eggs Benedict with extra hollandaise sauce. As he approached the table, she grabbed a slice of bacon and snacked on it. "*Bonjour, mon cher,*" Lela said.

He admired his great-grandmère in her canary yellow dress, accented with an extravagant yellow diamond pendant necklace, cascading down into the scooped neckline of her dress. His great-grandmère still had a nice rack for such an old broad. One would think her cleavage would have shriveled up by now, but they were still plump. Julian grimaced and then turned away. *I'm a freak for checking out my grandmère's chest.*

"It is our way, darling. Members of this family not only take pride in their own appearance, but in their relatives' as well," Lela said. "At times, it goes a little further than that."

Nasty. Julian sat in his chair. Mario prepared Julian's meal from the buffet set before them, a simple plate of sausage, bacon, eggs, and honeydew melon. Julian averted clapping his hands together in joy, spotting the fruit. He always enjoyed completing his breakfast with melon, for it cleansed his palate after ingesting greasy foods.

The singing birds in the live oak tree grated on Julian's nerves. The abrasive concerto of chirping sounded more so like nails scraping a chalk board. He wished they would stop.

"Do you still wish to go to the plantation today, darling?" Lela sipped her mimosa, light on the orange juice. She awaited his reply with an arched eyebrow.

"Do I have a choice?" Julian crammed eggs into his mouth. They were the best eggs he'd ever tasted.

Lela replaced the fluted glass on the table. "You always have a choice, darling. It's up to you." Lela reached down and massaged the back of her leg. Had a mosquito dared to nibble on her? "You should listen to your girlfriend, but it's your choice."

Julian choked on the bacon he'd begun to swallow. "What do you know about Jannette? How do you know I talked to her?"

A bird flew into the semi-enclosed terrace and landed on the arm rest of Lela's chair. She stroked the back of his head. Filled with mischief and playfulness, the bird chirped at her, fluttering his wings. Giving Lela his grand finale of staccato chirps, he flew away from beneath the pergola to the top of the live oak, rejoining his friends. "I'm not sure. I just asked a question."

Julian surveyed the yard as he ate. Every plant shuddered, and then bloomed in a blink of an eye. Grandmère was in a good mood. "I'm going."

Lela placed her fork on her empty plate, victorious. "Good. I think you will learn a lot." Sissy approached the table and stopped behind his great-grandmère's chair. "I'm ready, darling." Sissy pulled out the chair and assisted Lela from the table, escorting her inside.

"You're leaving me?"

When Julian had first arrived at the mansion, Lela had to move heaven and hell to influence the boy to spend the night. Now, he couldn't bear for her to leave him alone to finish his breakfast. "I wish to go inside to complete my preparation for our trip, but I can stay," Lela said. "Sissy, ask Mario to send me another Mimosa please."

Julian removed his handkerchief from his pocket and wiped his brow, waiting at the curb for his great-grandmère. Theo eased the gold painted 1963 Fleetwood Special to a stop before him. Julian couldn't believe his great-grandmère had purchased a new car. Exiting the car with his chamois cloth in hand, Theo wiped down the pristine vehicle, making the finish gleam in the sunlight.

"Theo, what are you doing?"

Julian turned to find his great-grandmère standing on the porch of the mansion.

Theo removed his hat and wiped his brow with his jacket sleeve. "I'm polishin' up the car."

Placing her hands on her hips, Lela's handbag dangled from her right wrist. "I don't want to take your car. I want to take my Eighty-eight."

Theo replaced his hat on his head and frowned at her. "Ma'Dame, it's gonna git too hot to ride wit' the top down," Theo yelled back. "Besides, my car has air conditionin'. You'se remembers what happened the last time we drove 'round in all this heat wit' the top down on your Eighty-eight."

Julian knew his great-grandmère didn't own the car. "What happened?" he asked.

Lela pursed her lips. "Nothing, boy. Stay out of grown folk's conversations."

"Naw, Ma'Dame. He should know," Theo said, grinning.

Lela cut her eyes at Theo. "Nothing. I just took a nap in the back seat."

Theo began to laugh, slow and steady, his deep sultry

voice floating across the front yard. "Yessum Ma'Dame, you'se took a nap aw'rite. Your heat stroke put you right to sleep." The guilt and desperation of the day took hold of Theo's heart once again.

"You was talkin' the same mess you'se talkin' now. Lookin' all pretty in your sun hat. Battin' your eyes at me, and tellin' me you'd be fine. We got out on that road to La Rose. The temperature had soared up to almost a hundred degrees. We'se came to a li'l ole shade tree, so I'se pulled over outta sun. I'se couldn't git the top up on the car. So, we'se was stuck out there on Route 51 with no water. That was my fault."

Theo fanned himself with his hat. "Thank the Lord, Dr. Jerry Barry had been drivin' by. He stopped and treated Ma'Dame right there on the side of the road. He put some little drops under her lip. Once Ma'Dame came to, me and Dr. Jerry got the top up on that old Eighty-eight.

"Doc sho' did give you what for Miss Lela, riding 'round in the heat like that." Theo thought for minute. "Nope, for some reason, he never put the blame on me." Theo scratched his scalp, and then put his hat on. "I'se don't reckon I've driven her 'round in that '53 Olds since."

The hairs stood on the back of Julian's neck. "Dr. Jerry? Is he the same doctor who treated me for my allergy attack the other day?"

Theo started laughing again. "What? You'se ain't talkin' 'bout when your tongue swelled up in your mouth?" Julian nodded. "Boy, that wasn't no allergy attack."

Lela crossed her arms beneath her bust and flushed red with indignation. "Theo, come and get my things and stop talking so much," Lela said. Suzette, Isabel, and Sissy, now standing behind Lela on the porch, chuckled.

Julian opened the door and entered the cool vehicle. So, his tongue swelling hadn't been an allergy attack. He really couldn't figure why such a thing would happen anyway. He tried to remember what had happened right before he choked on his tongue. Oh, yeah. He'd told Suzette she appeared to be every bit of ninety-seven years old. Well, she did. Not really, once he thought about it. She was just mean to him. But yes, his tongue had swollen as soon as he'd uttered the words.

Julian looked out the window at his great-grandmère. She seemed so sweet and kind. Fraud. Grandmère had a temper and he knew it; however, she camouflaged it well.

He settled into the plush leather seats, watching his great-grandmère wave goodbye to Isabel and Sissy as if she would never see them again. Theo held her by the arm, escorting her down the stairs and then the walk. Once they reached the car, Theo opened the rear door, granting Lela entrance. Suzette took the passenger seat. At last, Theo entered the car and pulled away from the curb.

Grandmère never made a move without the old, pasty face, red headed biddy, Suzette. Julian ignored whatever Suzette had just said under her breath in French. He assumed she'd cursed him for one thousand years.

Julian couldn't believe the State of Louisiana had decided to invest in its infrastructure. While cruising down old Route 51, Julian watched the continued construction on the new Interstate 55. He'd read articles about how one could travel from New Orleans, through Memphis and into Chicago along the road in two days, if determined. No more two-lane travel, contending with trucks and slow drivers. Each direction now enjoyed two lanes, making passing slower vehicles less dangerous. However, Julian never drove long distances. He always chose to utilize his father's jet. He didn't have the patience for extended travel by car.

Theo grunted.

Fuck you, Julian said to him in his heart. He returned his attention to the road. They passed through Hammond, the home of Southeastern Louisiana College. Forty-minutes later, they rolled into a small town named Independence. Route 51 followed the railroad track. Once outside of Independence, they stopped at small country store. "Why are we stopping? I don't see a plantation here," Julian said.

Theo frowned at the boy. "Wake up, Ma'Dame. We'se here."

Startled, Lela raised her head from where she rested it against the window. "Where are we, Theo?"

"Velma, right outside Independence."

Lela removed her Cartier compact from her purse and powdered her face. "I want a cool drink. Take me inside, Julian."

Julian considered the little store. "Feel like getting lynched today, Grandmère?"

Lela frowned at the boy. "Nothing will happen. This is Annie Capace's store. We'll be fine. Then we're going to walk down the road a bit," Lela said. "This land belongs to my former gardener, Doug Harris. He died many years ago, but I like to check in on his grandson James from time to time. He may not even remember me. He was a little boy the last time I saw him. In any case, it's nice to drive by the house and remember Doug."

"How long before we arrive at La Rose?"

Julian's impatience aggravated Theo. The boy couldn't enjoy life's ride, forever focused on realizing his destination. "'Bout fifteen to thirty minutes. We'se ain't got long now," Theo said.

Chapter 3

Eternity. St. Helena Parish, Louisiana.

Although he never cared for lawn maintenance, Jerémèy decided to edge the front lawn near the entrance of the home. He was almost finished, but somehow found himself disappointed the tedious task had now come to an end. He made a few, final snips.

Henri IV had taken landscaping to a whole new level. Leaning on his rake, Jerémèy turned his attention toward heaven, remembering the grandeur of it all. The *grand allées* bordering several different *parterre de gazons* had impressed him so. He'd decided to install gardens at the Chevalier Chateau in France, rivaling the *châteaux* and royal palaces. The chateau still felt like a prison, which it had been when constructed at the turn of the millennia. In any case, he'd desired for his queen, his *coeur* and *femme*, to feel at home. All her friends, as well as courtesans, lived in beautiful chateaux. He'd decided she would as well, if he had anything to do with it. So, he'd enlisted the help of his 16th century friend,

Claude Mollet.

Monsieur Mollet had been happy to sketch plans for Jerémèy, especially after he had smoothed over a concern which had arisen involving Mollet and one of the Henri IV's courtesans. Jerémèy recalled the day in the drawing room at Saint-Germain-en-Laye, finding Mollet close to tears. Jerémèy had assured Mollet he would fix the problem and he had, with surprisingly little effort. He remembered drinking cognac with the king, perhaps they had been playing cards. In any case, *le bon Roi Henri* went into a rant convicting Mollet as a rake, in more ways than one.

Jerémèy had shrugged it off, saying something to the effect King Henri should consider the source of his intelligence regarding Monsieur Mollet's activities. The matter dissipated, at least for Mollet. "Did someone die?" Jerémèy wondered. "Humph. I cannot seem to recall." He could only remember King Henri emitting a strange little laugh, one-third snort, one-third sneer, the last third covering the other two with a jovial, 'it does not matter' smile.

"Yes, I'm sure someone died." He hadn't cared, for it wasn't Monsieur Mollet. Before the year's end, Jerémèy had received the plans for the Chevalier Chateau. He loved the gardens so much, he had the plans modified and installed at La Rose Plantation, over one hundred years later.

Arising from his knees, he surveyed the curving lawn, accentuating the circular drive. For the front of the plantation, he'd designed a simple landscape, focusing on the manicure of the lawn, some shrubbery, and a modest parterre bordering the home. Up until recent years, he had always maintained a simple, miniature parterre de gazon in the center of the circular drive, depicting a rose. However, with the advent of the Rose Bowl, he'd reconsidered. But what would he institute instead? Jerémèy scratched his temple.

He'd showcased his formal gardens at the rear of the plantation house, in the East. The grand axis of the garden went on for a mile before meeting seven other axes at a central point. A fountain sat at its center, with a diameter of two thousand five hundred feet.

His mind drifted back a couple of centuries, when he and his slave Basso had first arrived on the virgin land from his Virginia plantation, La Pivoine, in the late 1700's. La Rose was an untamed wilderness, full of poisonous snakes, alligators, wild cats, and other animals, unwilling to surrender their home to humans. He remembered instructing Basso to pray to God Most High, requesting his favor and benevolence on their joint venture. Jesus listened, and the wildlife submitted and retreated.

It amazed Jerémèy how God always listened to the petitions of his children, loving his little ones with all his heart. Jerémèy had made it his mission to fulfill God's desires for his children. Yet, Jerémèy always encouraged Man to ask God for his desires; for it was their Heavenly Father's desire and joy to grant them their wishes.

Jerémèy stretched. Finding no one around, he released his wings and stretched them. He needed to visit the Groom and Prune; his feathers were a mess. Walking as a human always took its toll on his heavenly physique, causing his feathers to become flat and matted while concealed. Hearing the front door of the mansion open, he felt a breeze.

Lawrence walked out beneath the colonnade and unfurled his wings. Jerémèy could see the stress on Lawrence's face. The Keyholder always tested him.

Jerémèy walked over to his tool cart and grabbed a cloth. Wiping his shears clean, he replaced them in their compartment. He skipped up the granite steps to the shaded colonnade and stood beside Lawrence. Jerémèy flexed his wings and then relaxed, lighting a cigarette. He wished for a cognac.

"Hold out your hand, mon Frère," Lawrence said.

Jerémèy did as he was told. A drink appeared within his grip. "*Merci*, mon Frère. From the reserves of our Sun King, I'm guessing?" Jerémèy allowed the mellow liquid to permeate his senses.

"*Oui*, mon Frère. Our Rose and her Keyholder have returned."

Jerémèy nodded in agreement. It was a special day. He

glanced down the hill, but had yet to see the car turn the bend. He knew they were nearby. It would only be a few moments before they arrived.

Lawrence watched Jerémèy inhale the tobacco deep into his being. "How is he?"

Jerémèy exhaled. "Oh, you mean Julian?" Jerémèy took another puff and then extinguished his smoke. "The same, but not as angry this time," Jerémèy said. "Well, at least he isn't filling the cemeteries with his enemies, as of yet."

Lawrence snorted. "Give him time."

Jerémèy allowed his mind to drift back through the centuries, coming to rest in 1819 when his son, Augustus Chevalier, returned to the plantation from boarding school in New Orleans. "How long has it been, Lawrence?"

Lost in thought, Lawrence didn't hear his brother at first. He wasn't sure what Jerémèy spoke of, but then he located his brother's place in the Spirit. "Lawd, well let's see now. He was born in 1801. He returned to La Rose from school in 1819, something like. What year is it now?"

"1963."

"It seems like only yesterday," Lawrence said. "Lordy, it's been 144 years," Lawrence said.

Jerémèy nodded. The Lord did everything in perfect numbers. "Do tell? And when did Toussaint send Augustus back to the Lord?"

"Oh, that was in 1875."

"Astounding!" Jerémèy said. "Eighty-eight years. Only the Most High could plan in such a way. It is divine."

A strong breeze fanned the leaves of the live oaks and weeping willows, intermittently lining the drive. At least the leaves didn't wilt and fall from the trees with the approach of their evil one. Lawrence fanned out his wings, allowing the wind to aerate his feathers. "And now Augustus has returned. He will be here any second now."

Jerémèy aligned an errant feather on Lawrence's wing, blown askew by the winds of rage cast forward with the approach of their little evil one. "Yes, he comes, but against his will, as always." Jerémèy reconsidered his words. "Well, not like before. I think he returns more so out of obedience to the Rose and the Holy Wife."

Lawrence turned to his brother. "Sammie's here?"

"No, mon Frère. She isn't with him. He has yet to marry her, but they're 'living together' at his home in Washington, D.C." Jerémèy said. "But don't fret, he plans to do so."

Lawrence rolled his shoulders and wings to release the mounting tension. He didn't understand the current generation's need to 'live together.' There had always been some sort of commitment ceremony throughout the ages.

One of the grounds keepers swept the main drive as another stepped onto the porch to do a final sweep and tidying up. Still another appeared to polish the gold doorknobs as another worker gave the windows a final polish. "Lawd, what is it with this generation shackin' up? Why don't folks just get married like they're supposed to?" Lawrence furled his brow, unable to understand the practice.

"Man believes we're entering the Age of Aquarius, mon Frère. It is a time of free thinking, loving and living," Jerémèy said.

Lawrence scowled at the future, observing the shamelessness of man in the Spirit. Gomorrah would have gasped in shock of man's behavior in the current age. "Folks done lost their minds." He heard the intercom buzz in the house. Soon, one of his men opened the front door. "They'se at the gate, Larry."

"Thanks, son," Lawrence told him. Lawrence and Jerémèy stood in silence, watching the road. "I guess we should conceal ourselves," Lawrence said.

"You are correct," Jerémèy said. They returned to their normal stature, appearing as normal men: Jerémèy five-feet nine-inches, Lawrence seven-feet five-inches. The atmosphere stood still, the air silent. "The wildlife still fears him," Lawrence whispered. They continued to wait. At last, they spotted the Cadillac as it rounded the corner, and then begin its ascent up the hill. "I'se knows you'se done interacted wit' the boy," Lawrence said. "Did he knows you?"

"No, he never does," Jerémèy said, sadden.

"Are you'se gonna let him knows who you is this time?"

The Cadillac had nearly reached them. "What would be the point?" he said. "The time has yet to come." Jerémèy descended the steps and grabbed a rake leaned against one of the home's columns. "I'm the gardener. Who am I that he should know me?" Jerémèy winked and took his place with the rest of the staff in line along the drive, prepared to receive the Rose and the young master.

La Rose Plantation. St. Helena Parish. August 30, 1963.

JULIAN LOOKED AT his Rolex watch. Eleven o'clock. They had spent an eternity at the Capace's store. The lady who owned it had offered him candy. What the hell? He wasn't an eleven-year-old. Then, they had to walk down the road and visit with the Harris family on their little farm. Mrs. Katie had set out strawberry wine and food for them, and then showed them pictures of her goddaughter, Mr. James' niece, who'd moved to Chicago. The niece had sent a letter, telling the family she would marry soon. Who cared? He was ready to go. His grandmère had given him a dirty look. He left the hot, stuffy four-room house and sat out on the porch and watched Mr. James young nephews ride their new bikes. Finally, they'd said their goodbyes and departed around ten-thirty that morning.

They could have arrived at La Rose in fifteen minutes, but Theo drove so damn slow. Julian wished to hit him on the back of the head. Maybe then he could figure out how to use the gas pedal. Julian had to admit it had been a scenic ride. He was happy they'd beaten the freight train once they left the Harris' home. God, it would have delayed their trip another two hours, waiting for the train to pass.

They sat in the car outside the gate for five minutes. It took forever for someone to answer the buzzer. They waited another five minutes for the gate to roll open. Gaining admittance to the plantation was like receiving clearance to enter Fort Leavenworth or some sort of nuclear silo. Theo raced in, accelerating to one mile an hour.

Yet once they entered, the land amazed Julian. There were so many different trees, heavy laden with fruit and nuts at the end of August. The fields yielded a variety of different crops, primarily cotton. He suspected they grew sugar cane somewhere on the land, but he wasn't sure why he believed this to be so. Hell, it was Louisiana. Who didn't grow sugar cane?

As they drove on, he noticed more crops, such as corn, tomatoes, strawberries, tobacco and some other crops he didn't recognize. However, the size of these fields didn't compare to the land utilize to raise cotton on the plantation.

He considered the small, abandoned plank shacks lining

the road. Had slaves lived there at one time? As he considered them further, they seemed to have been businesses, shuttered long ago. Yes, he was sure of it. Some of them still had faded, hand painted marquees in French. *Patisserie*, he deciphered from the weathered sign above the rotted door. Why would one need a patisserie in the middle of nowhere in Louisiana?

"You're great-great-great-grandfather, Emmanuel Chevalier, operated many small businesses along this road in the early 1800's. This wasn't always a closed road. The slaves ran the businesses, and he gave them a small cut from the profits," Lela said.

Julian laughed under his breath. "He was a 'good Massa,' huh Grandmère?"

Lela understood the source of his cynicism. "Actually, yes. He saved a lot of our people from a life of misery and heartache they would have typically endured on other plantations throughout the Deep South. He found me, I mean, he found Musafa, later renamed Minnie, when she first landed in Virginia. Emmanuel brought her to La Pivoine, after having endured the Middle Passage. The voyage had nearly killed her. The slimy men..." Lela patted her forehead with the back of her gloved hand, regaining her composure. "He later brought her here, with about fifty other slaves."

Lela removed the gloves from her hands, for they had

grown warm. Her eyes fell on the passing cotton fields. She spotted workers amongst the crops. She'd just paid thousands of dollars for farm equipment. Why were they out there tending the crops by hand? She realized they enjoyed the work, in some way, renewing and invigorating their bond with the land. Lela frowned. They'd better use that new combine during harvest time. The contraption had cost her a fortune.

"In any case, paradise ended for the slaves here once Emmanuel's son, Augustus Chevalier, took over. The latter generations endured the same hardships most slaves of this nation endured, if not worse. As I've already told you, Father was a cruel man."

He needed a break from his grandmère after being in the car with her all day. Her 'Good Massa, Bad Massa' sagas irritated him. There weren't any good slave masters. If you owned slaves, you were evil. One didn't hear Jewish people talking about good concentration camp guards or of kind hearted German friends.

"Have you ever heard of a man named Schindler?"

"What?" Julian said. Goddammit, she was reading his thoughts again.

"You thought about the Jews holding no one of German descent in high regard for helping them." Lela removed her sunglasses and cleaned them with her handkerchief. She put them on and admired a sassafras tree as they passed, a bit away from the road. "Your Aunt Leelee had spoken of him while living with us during the World War II in New Orleans. She'd received word from some of her cousins trapped in Europe who'd worked for him. He saved many." She watched her great-grandson fume in silence.

"Do you believe everyone forced to exist under wicked governments and regimes are evil like their rulers? Do you believe all people agree with the actions and the mentality of the masses? Is that what you're thinking?"

Julian continued to look out the window. A river ran through the land. Flamingos? He didn't think flamingos were indigenous to Louisiana. All sorts of fowl relaxed along the river bank, gorging themselves on fish.

Much to his surprise, the animals seemed to take notice of them. Alligators glided across the water and left the river. In ranks, the prehistoric beings approached the road, marching in time to their syncopated gait. In fact, every creature left the river and its bank to line the road, opening their mouths wide as the car passed.

Chirps, tweets and roars from the wildlife filled the air. Julian turned around on the seat in time to see the creatures return to the river once their car had passed. Amazed, he sat forward on his seat. Through the windshield, he found snakes hanging from the willow trees lining the road, and then recoiling themselves around their respective branches once they passed. "What the hell?" Julian said a little above a whisper. "They act like they know who we are."

Lela nodded to the animals, acknowledging their praise. "Not really, but they know who I am."

Rounding the bend, Julian spied the mansion on the hill. He stopped breathing; his heart beat fast. He'd seen this house before. Sure, he'd seen pictures of the plantation house in the book documenting their family history. Yet, he knew he'd been there before. He'd seen this house before with his own eyes. The columns, he remembered the columns, the sweeping porch and the balconies. He spotted a third floor, just visible from the road.

The house had been constructed in a perfect square. It rivaled any Greek or Roman temple, the perfect columns spaced evenly apart, surrounding the perimeter. Julian could spy two stories beneath the roof line. Knowing his grand-mère, Julian wouldn't have been surprise if the house was aligned with the sun or some secret, unknown constellation, which on specific dates and times of the year, unlocked the gateway to the mysterious galaxies and uncharted worlds.

The home had to be his grandmère's key to her witch-craft, along with the other witches who probably occupied the land. Perhaps there was a starry constellation, the Rose, for which the house had been constructed as a pagan temple. The house had to hold the key to the universe.

"No, darling. You hold the key. It is hidden in your home in New Orleans," Lela said.

Julian turned to his grandmère, who seemed to nap with her head leaned against the window. Hell, she'd been fully awake three seconds ago. Witch.

As they approached the mansion, Julian craned his neck to peer out the windshield. Two figures waved feathered fans at them. He blinked. He saw one man in the distance, standing on the porch of the house, alone.

After a few minutes, the Cadillac stopped before the mansion. The young, freakishly tall Black man standing on the porch descended the steps. He knocked on his grandmère's window. Lela opened her eyes and smiled. "Good Lord," she said as the man opened her door.

He extended his hand, assisting Lela from the car. He hugged her tight, refusing to let her go. "Miss Lela! Lord, you'se a sight for sore eyes."

Lela wept in his arms. "You can't be that happy to see an old lady like me," she said.

"You'se ain't no older than me," Lawrence said.

Lela tapped him his arm. "Stop telling tales. Only God knows how old you are."

Julian got out of the car. Remembering Suzette, he walked around to the passenger door and opened it. He extended his hand to help her out.

She growled, but then smiled at him.

With a little work, she swung her legs out the vehicle, placing her swollen feet on the ground. The long car ride had caused her legs to stiffen. She stretched, and then walked over to the smiling man clutching Lela in his arms. "Bonjour, Monsieur," she said.

"Lawd, you'se still fine with all that red hair."

Suzette blushed. "How have you been, Monsieur?"

"I'se aw'rite for an old man." Lawrence turned to the house. "Nanette," he called. Soon, a curvaceous young woman stepped out of the receiving line before the front steps of the home. "Take Miss Suzette to Miss Lela's rooms. Miss Suzette wants to git Miss Lela settled in." Nanette nodded and went indoors, followed by Suzette. A number of young men exited the front door of the home to unload the car.

Lela grabbed Julian's hand and guided him over to where Lawrence stood. "This is my great-grandson, Julian Charles Chamberie."

Lawrence considered the young man, amazed. "This him?" Lela nodded. "Welcome, Massa Julian."

"I'm not your master," he said. "You're not a slave. You're free, in case you didn't know."

Lawd he's just the same. He just done moved to the other side of the road. "I'se been free since the Lord created me," Lawrence said. "I'se serves 'cause I choose to, not 'cause I'se has to."

House Nigger. Julian removed his handkerchief from his pocket, wiping his brow. It had to be at least one hundred degrees. "Who are they?"

Lawrence nodded and smiled with pride. "They'se the staff who keeps this place up."

"Grandmère, are they your slaves?"

Lela wanted to hit the boy. "No. They live here and are paid to keep this plantation going." Lela gathered her patience. "But yes, they are descendants of the slaves who once worked here."

Julian approached where they stood at attention, surveying each one as he walked the line. He stopped before one woman and peered into her eyes. "Why is she here?"

Oh God, he recognizes her. "Look at me Julian," Lela said. *That was long ago, let it go. She isn't whom she once was. Li'l Sis has changed.*

Her friend hasn't. Julian sneered at the woman. He resisted the urge to spit on her. He felt comforted, knowing she'd sensed his hatred.

Without warning, Julian lost interest in greeting and meeting the servants. He turned and left them standing in the oppressive noonday heat, unacknowledged. He could hear his grandmère thanking them for their service and loyalty.

The house. Ignoring the receiving line, he could only focus on the ornate, gold encrusted Cypress doors of the house. The doors' leaded glass windows entranced him, which encapsulated images of angels with swords, entangled in roses, warring against one another.

Home. Hell. Julian felt his body, mind, and spirit sinking into the marshy earth beneath his feet, although he stood on a stone paved drive. Emptiness and hatred embraced him. He couldn't love those who worked the land, who lived there. Why should he? They hated him. The slaves only tolerated him because he could destroy them without a second thought, without retribution. Each and every breathing organism on the land belonged to him. Power surged within Julian's soul, sprinkled with a heavy hand of callousness. "Let's go inside. It's hot."

Lawrence considered his disenfranchised staff, who stood before him with downcasted hearts. "Ya'll can go," Lawrence said to them. Lawrence watched them leave. As he listened to their thoughts, he heard their souls voice disappointment in the cold reception they'd received from Lela's great-grandson.

Once the last servant left, Lawrence walked over to the awaiting party. He patted Julian on his shoulder. Julian flinched, scolding him with hard eyes. Lawrence sighed. "Follow me," Lawrence said, leading everyone indoors.

Following the group into the house, Julian stopped and slapped the back of his neck. "Goddamn mosquitos," he said. "What the hell?"

Lawrence stopped and turned to face Julian. "Watch your mouth, boy."

Julian felt his chest become tight; his heart stopped beating. Much to his misfortune, he locked eyes with Lawrence, finding an authority and judgment within his eyes which shattered his soul. Sure, his grandmère could give him a dirty look, shaking his soul, but he didn't truly fear she would demolish it. He knew Lawrence could, if he so desired. After a moment, Julian watched the judgment and destruction ebb away from Lawrence's hard glare, once again becoming meek, humble, and welcoming. "Let's git in outta this heat."

Lawrence opened the large, heavy Cypress doors with ease, stepping aside to allow them all to enter. After Lela and Theo entered, Julian stepped across the threshold. The intricate mosaic glass tiled floor, depicting a rose with sword like thorns, entranced him. His head, controlled by an invisible puppeteer, turned to grand foyer and hall before him. The breath left his body.

Gold

Every architectural detail in the house had been accented with gold. Julian knew gold when he saw it. In fact, he'd always possessed the uncanny ability to identify gold. Even the best fakes never fooled him. He had no doubt there was little gold gilding, but solid gold, inlaid into the walls, ceiling moldings and the skylight. Gold also had been used as paint, highlighting the twists and turns of the Corinthian columns supporting the second floor. The statues and busts were made of gold. "This cannot be," Julian said.

"What?" Lela asked, removing her hat and handing it to a maid, who then disappeared with Lela's garments to some hidden closet.

"Grandmère, everything in here is made of gold."

Lela assessed the interior of the house through her grandson's eyes. She'd always believed the ornamentation to be constructed of another metal, maybe brass. "Really? I never noticed," she said. "Lawrence?"

"Ma'am?"

Lela blushed. She loved it when he called her ma'am. "Is it true?"

Lawrence finished directing one of the houseboys on to which rooms to take what luggage. "What's that Ma'Dame?"

"Is everything here constructed of gold?"

He considered the room. "I'se don't rightly know. Well, not everythang, I'm guessin'." Lawrence left them to direct the staff.

"Humph," Lela said, after admiring the room for a few moments. She dismissed it. "Well, maybe so Julian." Lela yawned. "I'm going to my room for a while."

Lela searched the second floor for Suzette. However, she spotted Nanette leaving her father's old room. Nanette glided down the stairs and stood before her, filled with admiration. "I'se done heard so much 'bout you, Ma'Dame. I'se honored to meet you."

Lela embraced the child and kissed her on the forehead. "Who is your kin, child?"

"Nicka."

Lela smoothed down her kinky hair. Well, I guess you're my great-great-niece; however, I can't tell you for sure to what degree." Confusion contorted Nanette's face. "Nicka was my sister."

"For really?" Nanette said. "What was she like?"

Lela's smile faded, her face falling slack. She appeared as a centenarian for a few moments, but then she harnessed her emotions, returning to her youthful appearance once more. "I'm afraid I never knew her, darling. My father, Augustus Chevalier, sold her off when she was young. Once the war ended, she returned here. I think my Aunt Sarah found her somewhere in Mississippi. By that time, I'd left the plantation. I didn't return to the States until the 1890's." Lela thought for a moment. "I remember visiting the Parish office, probably about taxes on this land. However, I don't think I returned to the plantation until maybe the teens or the twenties. I'm not sure."

Suzette descended the stairs and joined the group in the foyer. Lela clasped her hands together, recalling a task she wished to complete while visiting. "Suzette, we should hang the portraits in the salon."

"Oui, Madame," Suzette said.

"Gal, whatcha up to now?"

Lela blushed. Lawrence always made her feel like a special little girl. "I want to hang the portraits we had made."

"Well for sho'. We'se can do that," Lawrence said. He left to instruct the staff.

"What portraits, Miss Lela? Nanette asked.

Lela patted the child's hand. "Once my father died, Lawrence hired a Negro photographer named Solomon Philippe to come out here to take pictures of the former slaves still living on the plantation. In the 1920's, I then hired a photographer name Dorothea Lange to photograph those still living," Lela said.

"Wow, for really?"

"Yes, darling. We have many photos from the project, as well. I will ask Lawrence to bring out the photo albums before I leave." Lela patted Nanette's cheek. "Have you ever seen pictures of your folks?"

"No, Ma'Dame."

In her mind, Lela sent a mental picture to Lawrence, reminding her to show the books to the children. She could see him smile in his butler's office. "I will show you before I leave."

Lela gazed into the Nanette's eyes and then hugged her. "My Lord, won't you prove to be a great blessing to the family," Lela said. "You will hold the hand of the King."

"A king? Who me?"

Lela searched the child's eyes, finding a lack of self-worth dwelling within. "You are a princess yourself, but you don't know it yet. Who better to hold the hand of a king?" Lela watched Nanette's eyes fill with tears. "There is more for you in this life than working on this plantation. I promise you, my darling." The young girl nodded. Lela kissed her on the forehead. She had the prettiest dark brown skin. She reminded Lela of her mother. "I won't keep you. I will see you later."

Tired of listening to his grandmère bestow blessings on the worthless employees of the plantation, Julian wandered away to the far side of the grand hall. He toured the portraits, crests, and coats of arms which lined the walls, unimpressed. He stopped before an oversized portrait. He considered the petit pompous man depicted within, standing next to a huge horse.

The artist had crowned the little man with an oversized

powdered wig and red heeled shoes, surrounded by hunting dogs on a sprawling lawn. A mansion, presumably La Rose, loomed in the background on a hill. "Asshole," Julian muttered. The man in the portrait mocked Julian with his eyes. Julian could hear the man laughing at him. He read the brass plate beneath the enormous portrait. 'Emmanuel Chevalier, 1805.' "You're no savior of mine," Julian said.

He knew the man in the portrait and despised him. Julian desired to tear down everything the petit man had built. Julian would make the little man's fortune his own. Julian would prove the man a liar.

Hearing weeping and good will on the opposite side of the grand hall, his grandmère's words broke through the spell of the peculiar man in the portrait. He turned to find a lower being standing before his grandmère, the object of her praise.

Julian rushed over to where they stood, placing himself between his grandmère and the young girl. "Her?" Julian stared the woman up and down, a little more than a turd on the ground, in his opinion. "What king's hand will she hold?" Julian sucked his teeth. "An ignorant little Nigger bitch like her may clean his toilet, but never hold his hand."

Silence reverberated across the room, all standing in shocked awe, staring at Julian. "What the hell ya'll lookin' at?" Julian glared at them, prepared to whip them all for their insolence. "Get ya'll asses back to your chores."

The staff stood still. Lawrence rushed into the foyer. Augustus. The man standing in the mist of them all didn't resemble his former master a great deal; however, the hatred flowing from his soul was undeniable. Lawrence turned to Madame Lela, waiting for her reply.

Lela faced her great-grandson. "You will not enslave us again," she said. She walked toward him.

"Madame," Suzette called to her.

Lela stopped before Julian, coming nose to nose with him, her soul locking with his. She grabbed his throat with a death grip uncharacteristic for a 116-year-old woman. Julian turned blue. Lela trembled.

Suzette ran and grabbed her arm. "*Madame, s'il vous plaît!*" Paralysis commandeered Suzette's body. She collapsed.

Lawrence ran to where Lela stood choking her grand-child. "Ma'Dame, look at him. He ain't your Daddy." Lela trembled, hearing Lawrence's words. "It's his being in this here house. His soul is attemptin' to become one wit' the spirit of Augustus once more," Lawrence said.

Mortified, Lela froze.

"Ma'Dame, you'se gonna kills him."

Awakened from her rage, Lela found her hands around her great-grandson's throat. She gasped and released him, allowing him to fall to the floor. "What?"

Lawrence kneeled next to Julian and checked his pulse. He placed his hand above his nose. His breathing was shallow, but he was breathing. "He's alright Ma'Dame," Lawrence said. He ran his fingers through his close shorn salt and pepper hair. It was going to be a long visit.

Lela kneeled next to her great-grandson, taking him in her arms. "Julian, darling?" Julian didn't move. Had death claim him due to a momentary flare of her temper? "Awake darling, it's Grandmère." Julian lay motionless before her. Lela kissed him on his lips, breathing life into him. "Awake, my love."

Julian's eyes fluttered. He sat up and found everyone staring at him. His throat hurt. He stood from the floor and wiped his eyes. He stared at his great-grandmère, dazed and betrayed. She had tried to kill him. He'd never believed she'd desired to kill him until now.

He found Nanette standing near the staircase, crestfallen. Had he really said such cruel things to her? He didn't even know her. Why would he say such things? She incited repulsion in his soul. "Sorry," Julian said to her under his breath.

"Let's go to your room, Julian," Lawrence said. He patted the young man on his shoulder.

Lawrence ascended the grand staircase, its golden balusters emblazoned with angels intertwined and imprisoned in the brambles of rose vines. Julian followed him, incapable of understanding all that had happened.

The paralysis left Suzette's body. She stood, light-headed. After a few moments, she regained her wits. "Madame, are you going to be able to stay in this château with him?"

Lela smirked. "You mean plantation house?"

"It does not matter!" Suzette raised her voice at her mistress for the first time in years. "You nearly killed him. You *wanted* to kill him," she said. "Madame, he is no longer *tu père*. Yes, you are more powerful than him now, but he is the future! You cannot kill him."

Tears filled Lela's eyes. "I love my child. I do not wish to kill him." Lela turned to each of them, pleading with her eyes. "I saw Father," she said. "Didn't all of you see him too? Couldn't you hear his words?"

Everyone remained silent, staring at the floor. She could hear their thoughts, but no one would say anything. They'd all witness the spirit of Augustus in her great-grandson.

Lela had lost control. God, she knew better. Satan would not compel her to stomp out her own seed.

Lela sighed, wiping the tears from her eyes. She refused to accept the truth of what had just happened. "Julian would never say such things about Nanette. To call her a *Nigger?*" All the servants remained silent.

Julian had to release the past, as well as she. Maybe she

shouldn't have bought him to the plantation. She'd hope he would gain understanding and learn from the past, not degenerate into his former self.

Determination arose within her. "I will stomp Augustus out of his soul before we leave La Rose. I will set my great-grandson free." She cast her gaze upon the mosaic rose in the center of the grand hall. "God will set him free." She turned and left them. Lela climbed the stairs and entered her father's room.

Julian stood from his chair near the fireplace in Emmie Sue's room. He couldn't understand why he hadn't been allowed to stay in his own bedroom. Why had Lawrence assigned that little Nigger bitch to sleep there? He should have killed her back then, but he couldn't do it. In fact, for many years, he had no desire to murder his child. He'd loved her more than anyone could ever know, even though she was a Nigger. She hadn't looked like one. Still didn't. Passin' little Nigger. Strengthening his resolve, he refused to allow Lela to take control of him, no matter what she did to prove herself worthy of his love.

"I need a bourbon." Julian left the bedroom and went downstairs to his library. He stopped at the buffet, finding a floral arrangement upon it. "Where's my liquor?" He scanned the room, but couldn't find any, not even a golden bar cart. He remembered the stash he kept in Sammie's cabin. He left the mansion.

Julian felt drunk as he walked out the front door. He turned to shut the heavy cypress door; however, before he could grab the knob, the door closed by itself. "Spooky ass house." He descended the stairs. "I should've gone through the kitchen."

The mansion had to be two blocks long to the south. He rounded the corner and walked to the rear. His head hurt. "Where am I going?" Finally, clearing the southwestern corner of the mansion, Julian spotted the kitchen house. Sammie's house. He could feel himself grow hard with desire for her. It had been sometime since he'd enjoyed her.

Julian opened the door, finding the house empty except for a lone, high-back spindle chair. "Jannette?" Jannette was in Washington D.C. Why would he expect to find her in a shack behind his grandmère's plantation house?

Scuffing the rough-hewn cypress plank floor with his shoe, he spotted a small black pebble lodged between the floorboards. He bent down and tried to dislodge it with his finger, but only succeeded in breaking his nail down to the flesh. It bled. He stuck his finger in his mouth and sucked the blood, dulling the pain.

"Oh yes!" Julian reached into his trouser pocket and extracted his pocket knife. Opening it, he positioned the blade between the floorboard and the object. With a little work, he managed to dislodge the stone. Julian picked it up. The object wasn't a rock, or was it? He smelled it. "A coffee bean?"

You belong to me

She pitched the beans, striking him in the center of his forehead, scalding him

Julian ran his fingers through his hair. His soul and spirit swirled within him, blinding him.

She reached into her apron pocket and fiddled with the beans, loving him

Julian shook his head. Jannette didn't like coffee. In fact, she hated it with a passion. He dropped the bean in his pocket. The shack shifted. He steadied himself. He was losing his mind.

Julian fled the cabin. He ran, unable to stop. He came to a garden gate. His head was heavy. He felt drugged. The coffee bean. Falling to the ground before the weather worn barrier, he lost consciousness.

After a few moments, he opened his sleep laden eyes. Julian's gaze fell upon a white-washed shack inside the fenced garden. A crude cross had been mounted above the shack's simple door. The wave of intoxication passing, Julian managed to stand. Taking a few steps, he opened the gate and entered the garden.

Walking to the right of the building, Julian opened another diminutive gate, separating the church grounds from the graveyard. He entered. His head cleared. What day was it?

Walking through, Julian read the granite stones. Most of the stones had a single name on it with a year. Nat, 1815. Sarah the Slave, 1875. There were at least two hundred graves. He stopped. He died.

Sammie, 1863

The text which followed seemed to have been added after the original inscription.

La Mère de la Rose

Julian collapsed to his knees. "Sammie?" He couldn't stop crying. "Sammie," Julian said, wiping his face. "Why am I crying? Who is she?"

Julian calmed himself. "Sammie." He remembered his grandmère's story. She'd told him Sammie was Augustus' slave. This was his great-great-grandmother's grave.

"Yup. Sho' is Massa."

Julian jumped to his feet. He scanned the grounds, but found no one. Calming himself, he turned to Sammie's grave, finding a man before him. He screamed. He recognized him. "Lawrence, what the hell you doin' out here, boy?"

Lawrence sighed. "What did you call me?"

Julian searched his mind. Why was he saying such things? He never used derogatory slurs toward Afro-Americans, a self-fulfilling bondage implanted in the psyche of the Black race by the White man. First, he addresses the house girl as an ignorant Nigger bitch and now he'd called Lawrence a boy. "I'm not feeling well. I'm not myself."

Lawrence patted his shoulder. "You'se right and wrong 'bout that," he said. "Why doncha c'mon in the house, Julian? Have yo'self a cool drink. You'se can git sumpthin' to eat. Dinner should be on the table by now."

Exhausted, Julian nodded and followed Lawrence back to the mansion.

Julian sat at the table as Nanette served the first course. He couldn't look at her. He couldn't say sorry, either. It had surprised him he'd apologize the first time.

Well, he hadn't been wrong. She was an ignorant Nigger bitch. "Did you spit in my food, gal?"

Nanette said nothing, continuing with dinner service.

Sitting in her father's chair at the head of the table, Lela scowled at her great-grandson sitting at the opposite end. "You—" Lela stifled herself, noticing Lawrence standing along the wall with his finger to his lips, signaling for her to hold her tongue. Lela let it go and ate her soup.

Lawrence presented Julian with the carving knife, once it came time to serve the main course. He removed the lid to the serving platter.

"Roasted pig?"

"Yessuh. You'se likes pig, suh," Lawrence said.

Burning with hatred, envy, and jealousy, Julian carved the pig with precision and without mercy. He wished the animal to be the one whom he hated, the one who had humiliated him.

He remembered his grandmère's story. "Marion."

Lela choked on her Malbec, nearly spitting it out on the table. "I want to return to New Orleans right now, Lawrence." Lela arose from the table. Lawrence escorted her from the dining room.

In the foyer, Lawrence stopped her before she could go upstairs. "Ma'Dame, he's gotta process this and let it go."

Lela turned red with anger. "I will not allow him to mutate into his former self, into Augustus. He's pass that now."

Lawrence enveloped her within his massive arm span. She melted, tired and exhausted from trying to raise her great-grandson. "We'se never git past who we is, Ma'Dame," Lawrence said. "We'se just let thangs go, but they'se still in us." Lela wiped away her rebellious tears. "Give him a chance to work some thangs out, Ma'Dame."

Lela returned to the dining room.

Chapter 4

La Rose Plantation, St. Helena Parish. August 31, 1963.

Julian covered his head with the pillow, but it didn't help one bit. The constant crowing of the rooster inundated his senses, snatching him from his dreams of Jannette. God, he missed her. He'd considered flying her out to Louisiana just for sex, but he refused to make the call.

He didn't want her to meet his family. In fact, Julian wanted to keep Jannette as far away from them as possible. Grandmère would love Jannette; hence, the reason he needed to keep them apart. He didn't need his grandmère fucking up Jannette's head. Case closed, Jannette would stay in Washington, D.C. He would have to attend to his own cravings while stuck in Louisiana.

After taking the edge off his lust and desire for Jannette, Julian left the feather bed and headed for the shower. The soft bed hadn't bothered his back, much to his surprise. Maybe the mattress had been constructed with some sort of sub-support. He really didn't care, glad to have enjoyed a good night's sleep.

While drying his hair with the plush terry cloth towel, Julian entered the dressing room. He found linen slacks and a short-sleeved shirt, along with a cardigan, on the mahogany valet accented with gold fittings. "What the hell?" He was twenty-four years old and had been dressing himself for a long time. Why would the staff feel the need to decide what he should wear for the day? Julian removed the heavy starched shirt from the valet. He had to admit he kind of liked it. He slipped on the shirt and slacks.

Once he'd finished dressing, Julian left his suite of rooms. The faint aroma of bacon met him at the top of the staircase. Breakfast! He stopped for a moment at the railing, regarding the grand hall. His head catapulted upward, gazing upon the huge dome constructed of leaded glass, which dominated the ceiling. It even had an oculus like the Pantheon, except it had been covered with stain glass depicting a rose (of course).

Julian returned his focus to the grand hall. He admired the gold and glass mosaic floor, inlaid with the most beautiful rose he'd ever seen, encased in a golden framework.

The blood pooled around the head of the woman lying in the center of the rose.

Julian shook his head. He felt prickly and exhilarated, as

if he'd finally obtained a long-held desire. *Justice*. His wife was dead.

"Spooky ass house." Julian ran his fingers through his hair, still damp from his shower. He stopped before the bifurcated staircase, gazing into the grand hall. "This place reminds me of the Opera Garnier," he muttered. He descended the stair on his left and then paused on the generous landing.

Inhaling deep, he descended the ornate central stair. He could see his guests in the grand hall below, waiting for him to join them. They all beheld him in awe, unable to deny him as the master of the plantation, as master of the Parish and the state of Louisiana, both slave and White. They hated and feared him.

Tinkle

Arriving at the bottom of the staircase, Julian shivered and grabbed hold of the golden angel mounted upon the newel post. An electric current stung his hand, causing him to jerk it away. He surveyed the now empty grand hall, finding himself alone.

"This is 1963." His eyes filled with billions of tiny stars, he examined his now sweaty shirt, slacks and cardigan. He wasn't wearing some ancient tuxedo. Julian blinked hard, clearing away the starry host lodged in his eyes.

His stomach growled. Ages had passed since he'd last

eaten.

Captured by a flicker of light, Julian stopped on the stair and turned around. It twinkled. He walked up the stairs.

The polished mahogany steps entranced him, boasting a deep, blood red carpet runner, held in place upon each tread with a brass rod. It twinkled. Julian sat on the steps, entranced by the object. He stroked the carpet rod. Gold. Fully extending his hand, he placed his palm upon the metal. It wasn't solid gold.

"You are correct, mon fils."

Julian jumped, almost falling from his perch on the edge of the step. A man stood at the bottom of the staircase wearing pristine white shirt and slacks, protected by a full length white apron of sorts with a bib, suspended from his neck. He'd secured the apron neatly at his waist.

"Your great-great-great-grandpère decided gold would be too soft, so he overlaid each brass rod with an inch of gold. There is an employee here at La Rose. His sole task is to attend to the gold accents and objects of this plantation house. He has been trained on how to clean the objects without stripping away the gold.

"Monsieur Emmanuel — he is your great-great-great-grandpère in case you are unaware of your ancestry — developed the process. The world would kill to know it. In any case, the gold is in the same condition as it was the day

Monsieur Chevalier installed it. Oh, what year was it? Maybe 1799? No, perhaps 1809. The mansion was completed in 1809, just prior to young Master Augustus' arrival as a child. I believe your family lore dictates he arrived here at eight years of age."

Julian raced down the stairs and stood before the young White man with a light tan. He hadn't believed there were any White people left on the land. The man appeared older than him, perhaps in his mid-thirties. "How do you know all of this? Are you related to the Chevaliers?"

The man grunted and snickered all at once. "Everyone in the Parish is related in some way or another, Monsieur."

Julian stared at the man. "Who are you?"

The man adjusted his ascot. "I'm the gardener here. Well, one of them. It's my task to attend to the roses."

Julian scowled and suppressed his distrust of the man. "The roses are outside. Why are you in the house?"

The man raised an eyebrow. "Should servants stay out-side, Monsieur?" The man laughed, inserting his hands in his trouser pockets. "Perhaps I should remain in the yard with… Oh now what noun did Monsieur Augustus use? Oh, yes." He paused, savoring the insult from long ago. "'Nig-gers,' I believe he said. Should I 'Stay out in the yard with the rest of the Niggers,' Monsieur Julian?"

Julian stood before him, dumbfounded.

The man took pity on the boy. "I apologize for my crass language. Just one of Monsieur Augustus' persisting quotes around the plantation. But that is ancient history."

The man walked over to the pedestal drum table in the middle of the foyer, near the front doors. He rearranged the roses within the crystal vase, assuring maximum exposure for each flower. He removed his pruners from his pocket, clipping away a few leaves. He scooped them up and then scanned the area for a waste can. Finding none, he placed them in his pocket.

The gardener returned to the staircase. "If you must know, I cut roses for Madame's room this morning. I brought them in and gave them to Lawrence. Madame must always have fresh roses in the house." He looked behind him, considering the roses on the drum table. "I bought the ones you see before you as well."

"Why? Did she request them?"

"No, but heaven has commissioned it," the man said.

"Heaven?"

The gardener patted Julian's right shoulder. The hate, bitterness and resentment trapped within the child's soul surged into his hand. "I rebuke you, Satan. Leave him."

Julian stared at him, unable to speak.

The gardener turned to leave. "I won't keep you from your day." Stopping before the newel posts adorned with angels, the gardener considered the statue. Much to his chagrin, he noticed smudges on the ornament. He frowned.

Removing his handkerchief from his pants pocket, the gardener wiped away a smudge he'd noticed upon the three-foot-tall golden angel with its wings spread and sword extended, ready for war. He then examined the angel on the opposite newel post, finding smudges upon it as well. He wiped it down.

Once satisfied, the gardener replaced the cloth in his pocket. "I noticed breakfast has been served. You should go and eat before it grows cold." The man bowed to Julian and walked to the right of the central staircase, disappearing to the rear of the house.

Julian stood at the base of the grand central staircase, facing the closed, front doors. For a moment, he found himself in a garden he'd never seen before. He blinked and found himself standing on the stair. The gardener's comments confounded and baffled him.

Although breakfast called him, he couldn't tear his focus away from the red roses in the crystal vase atop the large kingwood and tulipwood drum table in the center of the foyer. Not even in France had he'd seen a table as grand as the one before him, adorned with ormolu mountings and fitted on legs with roaring lion heads for feet. Yet, the table paled in comparison to the roses. The roses filled Julian with a sense of euphoria and angst, leaving him torn between the present and another world he could neither grasp nor conceive.

Julian took his place at the head of the dining room table. Four people stood against the wall on either side, awaiting any need which may arise during the meal. Lawrence appeared at Julian's side with a covered, silver baroque tray. He sat it on the stand next to where Julian sat.

Julian nodded. Lawrence removed the heavy lid, revealing an eggshell colored china plate trimmed in twenty-four karat gold, loaded with eggs, bacon, potatoes, and a variety of sautéed vegetables. He placed the meal before Julian. Unable to control himself, Julian wasted little time delving into the meal.

Once Julian consumed his breakfast, the house servant Nanette served him fruit, consisting of grapefruit, pineapple, cantaloupe, honeydew and a mound of strawberries. He stared at the woman. "I know you. Where have we met?" Nanette returned to her place along the wall with the others.

Dumb Nigger. Hunger trumping his curiosity, Julian devoured the fruit. As Lawrence poured his coffee, Julian noticed something. "Where's Grandmère?"

Lawrence fetched the silver service containing the sugar and cream, placing it before him. "Ma'Dame was up early. She's somewhere outside wanderin' 'round on this here place."

After adding a bit of cream (no sugar), Julian gulped down the hot coffee. Much to his surprise, it didn't scald his tongue, but filled him with warmth and energy. The coffee had a funny taste. He didn't know if he liked it or not.

"It's chicory," Lawrence said. "You'se used to like it."

Julian nodded. Before the coffee, he'd wished to return to his room after the heavy breakfast. Somehow, it all coagulated in his stomach, providing him the fuel needed to face his day. "Where did she go?"

Lawrence stared at his little evil one. "I'se guess if you'se go out on the land and walk it a bit, you'd find her, Mis'sur."

Julian dropped his napkin on the empty plate, ready to leave. He'd grown tired of the okie-doke household staff. It was 1963; these people were no longer slaves. Didn't they realize it?

"We'se knows it just fine, Mis'sur," Lawrence said. "We'se love our Rose and we stay on here to serve her."

"What?"

Lawrence pulled out a chair, taking a seat to Julian's right. "Lets me explains sumpthin' to you," he said. "The folks you'se see here workin' on this place ain't slaves. They'se knows they ain't. They'se rich in their own right. Ma'Dame done blessed them. She done shared the wealth she got from the old Massa' wit' the chil'ren of his slaves," Lawrence said.

Figures, Julian thought to himself.

"They'se continues to work on this here place of their own free will, to glorify God and his Rose. It's a joy to serve the holy." Lawrence stood from his chair and smoothed the lapels of his tuxedo. "This here is these folks blessin', a reward for their ancestor's toil. But you'se cain't see it. They'se could go anywhere they wants to in this ole world. For some reason, they'se chooses to stay here, doin' the work of their ancestors.

Lawrence watched Julian frown, for he didn't understand the blessing. "They'se don't have to pay to live here on this land. We'se takes cares of ourselves on this here place. We'se don't buy nuthin' from the outside. We'se raise our own vegetables, our meat. We'se makes our own clothes and trades the wares we make here wit' each other. We'se even exports some of it to other countries, generatin' more wealth."

Julian stared at him, amazed. "Where do they live?"

"On this land," Lawrence said. "Some of the younger folks live in li'l ole townhouses a little less than twenty miles east of the main house. The older folks have homesteads here and there, scattered throughout the property. We'se got over 3,500 acres here. We'se built some roads throughout this here place over the years. Folks builds where they'se wants to."

This is Grandmère's land.

"Yessuh, it is," Lawrence said, responding to his thoughts. "But this here is heir property. We'se all shares in it."

The arrangement was a hornet's nest, from a legal standpoint. Eventually, someone would want to make a claim on a portion of the land. "What if someone wants out?"

"We'se buys them out. They'se leaves here for a while, but they always come back. They'se buys back in. We'se don't shut nobody out."

Julian considered the utopia his grandmère had created. He had to admit it was an ideal community. He could see a future where trust and honesty didn't exist.

Julian's glance locked on the portrait hanging on the wall at the head of the table. The man attired in 15th century French fashions snarled at him. Julian shivered, for the man in the portrait resembled the gardener he'd encountered on the stairs. He couldn't wait to leave the plantation house and all its ghosts. Yet, at the same time, it all felt familiar to him.

"I'se done seent it too, Mis'sur. The time's comin' when folks can't love each other and work together for the common good," Lawrence said, standing from the table. "Well, we'se gonna worry 'bout it when the time comes." He walked to the door.

The bussing staff came in and cleared the dishes. One of the servants presented a dish to Julian, upon which lay a steaming hot towel. He picked it up and cleaned his hands. "Do you have any idea where Grandmère may be?"

A sad grin appeared on Lawrence's face. Julian the boy, whom he'd had the pleasure of observing in the Spirit from afar, now addressed him. "Go out back and walk out yonder there for a piece. You'se gonna finds her there." Lawrence smiled at him and left.

The clock chimed. Half past six o'clock in the morning. Julian left the table, headed for the front door. He stepped outside and inhaled, taking in the morning, dew soaked air. He descended the granite steps and walked a quarter of a mile, finally reaching the mansion's edge. He turned the corner and continued, coming to the old cook house, after fifteen minutes. His heart constricted. He walked past it, resisting the urge to enter. His lover no longer resided there.

Continuing on, Julian came to what had once been a community square of some sort, now filled with shuttered shops. Leaving the little town behind, he walked down a gravel path lined with a variety of ground coverings and low shrubs with flowers growing up behind them. Sunflowers and yellow-gold zinnias crowned the bordering plants. He'd never seen such large zinnias.

In the distance, he spotted a wrought iron fence to the right of an old, one room building, which appeared to have been a church at one time. "I think I was here yesterday."

Within the confines of the inner fence, he could see a woman on her haunches, attending the earth, cloaked with a large, white straw hat. After fifteen minutes, Julian arrived at the gate. He opened it and entered.

Julian stopped before a young woman. Sure enough, she wore the straw hat which he'd spied some ways off, encircled with a band of white roses. She lifted her head. Julian found the brilliance of the starry host lodging in her eyes. The young lady, in her twenties, was magnificent. She'd been blessed with the face of heaven, toasted by the sun. Where had this young White girl come from? He took a second look and froze. "Grandmère?"

"Help me up, darling."

Julian blinked his eyes and beheld his grandmère, appearing as a sixty-year-old. He helped her up from the lawn. Confused, he kissed the old woman. Julian peered over her shoulder and noticed a tombstone in the little garden she tended. "Grandmère, who's buried here?"

She managed to smile, brushing the dust from her dress. "My maman. This is Sammie's grave."

Julian's body became rigid. Somewhere in the dark, in the past, he sat upon the barren plot of land drinking bourbon, cursing her, kissing her tombstone, loving her.

"Julian?"

"Yes, Grandmère?"

"Let it go."

Why was he crying? He didn't know the woman in the grave. Julian stooped down and rested his head on his grand-mère's shoulder.

She patted his back. "Augustus killed his love out of ha-tred for himself." Julian sobbed harder. "But *notre Seigneur* always gives us a second chance, *n'est-ce pas*, mon fils?" Lela kissed him and smoothed his hair. "Stop crying. Your joy has returned to you."

The grief left him as quickly as it had accosted him. The humidity of morning engulfed him. The overwhelming fra-grance of abelia attacked his sinuses. Julian feared he would suffocate and pass out. He removed his handkerchief from his pocket and blew his nose.

Julian wandered away, walking the graves. All the graves in the row had motifs of roses chiseled upon them. "What's with the roses, Grandmère?"

"What?"

"The roses?"

"Oh. These are Barachiel's children. All his children who have returned to the Lord are buried here, except for Sylvia and Augustus. Augustus is in his crypt in the Chevalier Cem-etery. Sylvia is buried in Mississippi, at the Olive Branch." Lela inhaled deep, missing the aunt she'd never known. "I'd considered having her exhumed and brought here, but she had built her life there. There she should rest."

Julian read the names on the tombstones engraved with a rose. Sammie. Sarah the Slave. Sallie. There were four markers without names, only roses. "What do you mean by 'the ones who have returned to the Lord?' Shouldn't they all be dead by now?"

The sun's rays intensified. Lela could feel her age accosting her, causing her to wrinkle and the ligaments in her joints to shrink and grow old. *My parasol.* Lela searched around for a bit, at last finding it before her mother's tombstone. She knew she couldn't bend over to fetch it. She reached.

Sensing his grandmère's distress, Julian followed the path of Lela extended hand with his eyes. He retrieved the white eyelet lace parasol and opened it, shielding his grandmère from the early morning sun.

Her facial muscles relaxed, causing the lines of age to disappear. Having regained control of her façade, his grandmère appeared as a forty-year-old. He watched her release the stress and oppression of old age.

Regaining her strength, Lela walked the graveyard. Julian followed her with the parasol. After touring the graves of her relations, she doubled back. Lela stopped and kneeled before her mother's grave once more. She remained silent, staring at the grave site.

"Emmanuel is Augustus' father. That's what the book

says," Julian said.

Lela leaned forward and kissed her mother's tombstone. Wiping away her tears, she stood without warning, facing her great-grandson. "Yes, you are correct," Lela said, dusting off her white eyelet dress. Why she always insisted on sitting in the dirt while wearing white she couldn't understand.

"You said Barachiel was their father?" Julian adjusted the parasol, persistent in his effort to shield his wandering grandmère from the sun.

Lela appreciated Julian's effort to keep her covered as she walked about. Julian could be a good boy when he wanted to be. "Yes, that's what I said. Why is this confusing to you?" Lela spotted a weed near her mother's tombstone. She reached for it. Lela snatched the weed away and then sat, folding her legs to the side.

Julian's eyes locked on the grave of Sarah the Slave. He hated her and her progeny. He could feel Sarah's hatred for him radiating from the plot of soil, seeking to destroy him for all time. He shivered. Anger and aggression surged within Julian, and then it was gone.

Struggling a bit, Lela arose and stood before Julian, intertwining her arm in his. "That's Toussaint's maman."

"Uncle Toot?"

"Yes."

Julian thought for a minute. "Well yes, I guess he would

have been a slave, but he never behaved as if he'd been one."

Lela stooped and patted the earth, reassuring Creation and her ancestors who'd gone on to be with the Lord. "Yes, it's true. But Toussaint was a slave, very much so. Yet, his mother shielded him quite a bit. However, Sarah couldn't always protect her husband. But, she would always give her brother hell for his attempts to mistreat Teddy."

Julian's mouth fell open. "Brother?"

Lela wished Julian would pay attention. "Listen to me boy," she said. "I keep telling you Sarah and Augustus had the same father, Barachiel."

Lela removed her hat and fanned herself. "What time is it, Julian?" Lela put her on hat. She burned.

"Half past seven o'clock." Julian couldn't believe the time. It seemed as if he'd just eaten breakfast. He never had a firm grasp on time when talking to his grandmère.

A strong wind surged from nowhere, blowing Lela's hat from her head. Soon the wind subsided, allowing the hat to come to rest on the lawn. Julian peeked beneath the parasol and screamed. Lela's face had become deeply lined and care worn, seeming older than her 116 years. He scooped her into his arms.

"Julian, darling," Lela called to him, losing her wind. She inhaled the life of the land. She gasped, but then regained control of her being. "One day, within your lifetime, in fact, within a few years, this land will pass away." Lela labored to raise her hand to wipe away her tears, but she managed to do so. "Our heritage will be lost, but not really."

Julian stood with his grandmère in his arms, withered into a mummy. Lela surveyed the graves and inhaled, absorbing what remained of life in the land. "I will not be buried here with my people, but in a land you visited in your youth. When the time comes, I will be moved to our holy land where I will rest until the Queen Bea mounts her steed and rides. I will be with her. I am her."

Julian stared at his grandmère in disbelief. "What are you saying?"

"You don't understand now, but one day you will. Once the Lord has condemned you, slain you, and returned life to you, you will understand. But that will be for a time yet." Lela's eyes filled with tears. "Yes, my love. It will be for a time yet to come." She laughed through her grief and joy. "You have much to endure before the time of my glory comes upon the Earth."

Crazy old biddy. He wanted to run with her to the shelter of the mansion, but he stood still, allowing her to speak. She grew lighter, her weight leaving her. He wanted to hear her dying words. Besides, nothing could be done to save her now.

"Perhaps," Lela replied to his thoughts, "...but it is so.

In any case, it's not important now." Lela considered her mother's grave once more. "Maman, it is well." The smell of ham roasting upon the hearth filled her nostrils, wafting through time.

"Oh God!" Julian ran at top speed for the mansion. Why had he stood there, allowing her to talk? "Please, don't die." Reaching the front of the mansion, Julian ascended the granite steps, struggling to manage the dead weight of his expired grandmère. He kicked the front door. He should've entered the mansion through the rear.

Lawrence opened the door and relieved Julian of Lela's lifeless form. Lawrence took her into the parlor and laid her on the sofa. With tears in his eyes, he crossed her hands upon her chest. Lawrence smiled at him meekly. He left the parlor and closed the door behind, leaving Julian with Lela.

Julian flushed red, witnessing his grandmère in repose upon the sofa. Defeated, Julian left the parlor as well, unable to stay in the room with his dead grandmère. He walked down the hall and entered Augustus' library, poured himself a drink, and sat at the desk. He submitted to his torment, the past now unified with his present.

He tried not to care or to wonder about her. It didn't work. He abandoned the neutrality of the library for the parlor. Julian had to see his grandmère once more. He stopped in the now open doorway, confronted with Lela lying in repose.

Julian couldn't endure his grandmère lying on the sofa. Why hadn't Lawrence taken her to her room? Did he want to torture them all, forcing them to view his grandmère? Julian wished to leave the room, desiring to escape the reality of her dead body.

Suzette rushed in and fell to her knees at the sofa. She wailed, mourning her mistress. It was the most pitiful sound Julian had ever heard. She seemed to have lost her mind. Her grief mutated into rage. "You are to blame, young man. You could not see she was ill?" Suzette collapsed upon Lela's breast.

Julian stood before them, unable to speak. It wasn't his fault. Lela had gone out on her own accord. Then the wind had blown away her hat, leaving her exposed to the sun. The sun had killed her, not him. He couldn't deny his role. He shouldn't have allowed his grandmère the opportunity to utter her last words. He should have rushed her back to the mansion without delay.

He went to the bar and poured a shot of bourbon. He hated bourbon, but he'd acquired a love for it since arriving at La Rose. His drink of choice was scotch, Glenlivet in fact. Julian tossed back the liquid. It soothed and comforted him all at once, dulling love and igniting indifference within his heart. Grandmère was old. Her time had come.

Lawrence entered the parlor and knelt beside Suzette. "Ma'Dame just fine ya'll. Doncha worry none." Taking a small vial from his pocket, he placed a few drops of the liquid inside his grandmère's bottom lip. After several minutes, her mouth moved. She moistened her lips, taking in the liquid. "See? She's aw'rite," Lawrence said. He picked her up from the sofa and carried her upstairs to her bedroom. Suzette followed them, ranting commands to the gathering staff.

Once he heard her bedroom door close, Julian sat on the sofa. His nerve endings continued to twitch and fire from the adrenaline pumping through his body. He couldn't understand what had just happened. Had his grandmère died? She was fine one moment, and then in the next she had withered in the sun. "I need to get out of here." Julian left the parlor to clear his head.

Chapter 5

La Rose Plantation, St. Helena Parish. August 31, 1963.

Julian strolled the grand hall, admiring the furnishings. As he considered them, flashes of people and events appeared before him. Faces. He felt anger, jealousy and hatred. At the far wall of the grand hall, he observed a maid in formal attire. He felt love, pain and regret. "This is a mind fuck."

He walked past the grand staircase, beneath the colonnade, finding the walls lined with portraits. They were much smaller than the ones in the parlors, dining room and grand hall. He stopped and looked around. "Where's the kitchen?" Why was he concerned with the kitchen? "Jannette," he said.

Walking beneath the grand staircase, he continued to the rear of the house. There were no doors or furnishings, only continuous walls accented with wainscoting. He spotted light outlining an object. "Maybe it's there." In the darkness, he arrived at a simple pine door. He turned the knob.

The door opened to the splendor of La Rose's gardens.

Perhaps it was a servant's door. Where was the primary exit? There should have been huge French doors topped with palladium styled transoms, opening to the gardens. At least, that what he'd imagined.

Julian walked across the terrace and turned around, facing the mansion. The rear façade had been constructed as a solid wall without windows. The only opening was the pine door, which had closed. There were no other avenues of re-entry via the rear of the mansion.

Julian rubbed his head. The bourbon was making him crazy. He walked toward the pine door. "What the hell?" The pine door had disappeared. He knocked on the solid wall. Had there ever been a door? Julian walked to the full span of the terrace, finding nothing.

Giving up on finding an entrance, he walked over to the railing of the terrace, facing southward across the sprawling French garden. Leaning over the edge of the railing, he found the mansion had been construction on the side of a hill, a few stories above ground level.

With no other options, he returned to the center of the terrace, facing east. His feet searing hot, he jumped back to find inlaid into the terrace floor a macabre glass eye within the midst of a starburst, staring back at him. He stooped down and touched the mosaic. It wasn't glass, but diamonds. Who uses diamonds for a mosaic? Wings extended from the left and the right of the eye, becoming one with the star. The eye glared at him, its lids narrowing to slits, causing its golden wings to flutter. "Fuck!" Julian jumped back. The inanimate eye, with its static wings mortared into the terrace, stared up toward heaven, unaware of his presence.

He walked around the menacing eye. His shins burned. Even passing near the eye was like passing an active volcano.

Reaching the safety of the balustrade, Julian admired the majesty of the gardens. He'd never seen such a garden in America. As a child, he remembered visiting somebody, with his parents, who lived in a palace of some sort in Brussels. Jonathan Chamberie, that was his name. He'd always believed him to be a distant relative.

In any case, Jonathan had a garden such as the one Julian now beheld. He remembered running down crushed gavel paths, and then along less prominent *allées* betwixt manicured trees. Julian had encountered small gates during his expedition, leading to secluded gardens. Whenever he would enter one of the gardens, most times he would find an old man sitting there, reading. Julian would ask each old man he'd encountered, "Who are you?" Each old man would reply in French, "No one, *mon prince*. I am here reading. Play."

He would leave one garden and then open another gate and enter. He remembered every garden at the Chamberie palace flaunted a variety of white flowers: white roses, camellias, stargazing lilies, many different lilies. He would stand in the garden's center and inhale deep, identifying each scent within.

Drunk with the flowers' perfume, he'd noticed in one of the gardens two *petite*, pale White women sitting side by side on a white marble bench. He hadn't noticed them when he entered. They wore white eyelet lace dresses, with their stark white hair flowing down to the green grass. One crocheted, the other tatted lace. Julian had asked, "What are you doing?"

Simultaneously, the women had turned their heads to face each other and then returned their gaze to little Julian. "Do you not know, mon prince?" Seeing he didn't, they answered in unison, "Preparing robes for your son."

Julian had found their response so funny, he'd fallen upon the plush, green grass and rolled around, holding his stomach. "I'm a little boy. I don't have a son!" His laughter spent, he sat up in the grass, finding himself alone. At that moment, his mamère had burst into the garden, crying. She'd been searching for him everywhere and hadn't been able find him. Finally, she'd heard his laughter, leading her to his concealed location.

A dove flew overhead, calling to her mate. The bird's song catapulted Julian into the present. He rubbed his arms, but couldn't warm up. Within a few seconds, he began to sweat.

Standing at the head of the stairs, Julian removed his cardigan. He hung it from the wing of an angel mounted on the granite parapet. Julian descended the steps, leading to the grand axis of the garden.

As he walked along, he could appreciate the dedication and work required to maintain the gardens. His grandmère had to employ an army to care for it all. In the distance, he spotted a fountain, maybe a mile away. After a half-mile, a statue of an angel came into view. The angel was enormous, perhaps half the height of the Statue of Liberty. He should have been able to see it from the road leading up to the plantation, at least from the terrace.

He walked harder and faster to reach the fountain. As he approached, he heard the voices of ladies as they splashed and frolicked about in a pool.

The path declined down a diminutive hill. He could see the shadows of additional statues, though cloaked by the trees. The laughter grew louder, water splashing up with every dalliance. Julian reached the edge, accented with trumpet vines shaped into topiaries, guarding either side of the entrance to a circular area. Silence pounded his eardrums.

"I can't believe this." Winded, Julian stood before an enormous fountain, at least one-half mile in circumference.

He found himself unable to conjure words. He'd never seen such hedonistic, sensual, and at the same time, pornographic figures as those in the fountain.

The female statues had been created in a variety of erotic poses. They awaited a sprinkle from the leering nude angel holding a pitcher above his head, smiling down on the bathers as he determined which he would enjoy next.

Julian had never seen a male nude statue with such an enormous penis. Who created stuff like this? It was like watching a porn flick set in ancient Greece, an orgy trapped in stone. Julian was surprise the sculptor hadn't made the angel's enormous 'Peter' a spout too.

It would have sent the wrong message

Julian turned around, but found no one. He returned his attention to the angelic statue. It seemed to smile at him, challenging him to a game of 'my pecker is bigger than your pecker.' Julian adjusted himself. "Don't bet on it," Julian said before catching himself.

The sun had to be getting to him. He sat on the edge of the fountain and scooped some water from within, splashing it on his face. Julian spotted a drinking fountain near the parterre bordering the eastern edge of the fountain. He walked over to take a sip. Once refreshed, he considered the depth of the eastern axis.

It seemed to go on forever, bordered at the horizon by

pine trees the size of redwoods. Julian turned west and faced the house. He could see the terrace and windows on the rear of the house. Windows? It had been a stone wall when he left. His stomach began to growl. He started back. Reaching the over-sized topiaries constructed of trumpet vines, Julian turned to take another look at the fountain. All was still within. "Perverts."

Yet, he couldn't leave the fountain. He returned to its edge and sat near a sculpture of a voluptuous woman doing an incomplete backbend, maintaining the painful arch. She extended her arms over her head, holding a small pitcher from which water streamed into the fountain. Julian found himself to be disturbed and excited all at once, her supple breasts and aroused nipples jutting toward the heavens. Beads of liquid, cast in stone, gathered in the upper area of her thighs. Julian resisted the urge to investigate further. He avoided the ecstasy upon her face. The artist had left nothing to the imagination.

"Children couldn't have played here." Julian dipped his fingers beneath water streaming from the contortionist's pitcher. He splashed the water on his face, and then dried himself with his handkerchief. "It's too damn hot." Glancing to his left, he spotted a door in the distance along the axis leading north from the fountain.

Julian left the fountain, led by a force he couldn't see

with his physical eye. After one-half mile, he came to an allée leading northwest to a bosquet. Continuing onward, he came to a shaded area. Julian lost sight of his invisible guide.

The bleached tree branches created a lattice work soaring up twenty-four feet, canopied over by the vines. Julian walked further, until he came to a parterre bordered by an allée intersecting his path. Julian turned north and walked for a few miles until he came to the *palissade* wall, covered with ivy. Soaring upward, the ivy shoots became entangled in the overhead canopy of trees. He shivered and then relaxed, enjoying the coolness in the mist of the garden. French moss trellised down from the tree branches.

One strand of moss twined itself around a branch of the live oak tree, disappearing behind the palissade of box hedges. "Looks shady over there." He walked along the allée, the cool air blowing through his hair. He heard a hinge creak. A little green door, set ajar, granted him entrance to a concealed space.

Julian could only imagine the number of secret gardens which lay hidden across the plantation. The perfume of the Four o'clocks drugged him. Intoxicated by the flower's perfume, Julian staggered to the swing suspended from the branch of the live oak and collapsed upon it.

After a time, Julian awoke, finding a pitcher of ice water on the tall, round table in the corner of the garden. He left the swing and poured a glass. A scent laden breeze engulfed him. Drinking his fill, Julian returned to the swing and slept.

Dark as midnight, he extended his hand to one stand-
ing in the midst of her blossom of despair.
Searching the Earth below, she beheld the man of
midnight. She accepted his hand.
They floated away.

Julian sat up in the swing, finding his grandmère asleep in his arms. He tried to remember what had happened. He'd carried his grandmère back to the mansion, dead. The fountain. He had drunk a glass of ice water. Yet now, his grandmère was with him. When had she joined him?

Julian felt his grandmère's tears upon his chest, soaking his shirt. "*Je suis désolée,*" she said, gurgling in her sleep. Julian patted her shoulder. Not again. Why couldn't she sleep in her bed? He was not her pillow. He decided not to complain, for he could be working on her funeral arrangements instead.

Gingerly, Julian shifted his grandmère and leaned her against the high back swing. Her head rolled back. He placed one of the swing's toss pillows behind her head. He kissed her on the forehead and stepped outside of the gate.

Julian regretted drinking the water. He would have to walk for miles before reaching the mansion. He walked down the allée, leaving the bosquet. Julian stopped.

"This is impossible." He'd traveled miles from the house. Now, the house was less than a block away. He turned around and walked back to the garden door. Opening it, he found his grandmère sleeping. He closed the gate and returned to the walk leading out of the bosquet. Julian stood in the unforgiving Louisiana sun, working it over in his mind. "I know how far I walked."

He recalled a childhood book his mamère would read to him, *Alice in Wonderland*. "I am definitely not Alice." He felt like he'd taken a bad 'pot' induced trip down the rabbit hole. He hadn't smoked marijuana since college. Maybe if he had some weed now, it would straighten out his thoughts.

He returned to the garden to awake his grandmère. She snored hard, sprawled out on the swing. She'd tucked her legs beneath her body. Maybe her feet were cold. It would take fifteen minutes for him to wake her up. "I'll let her sleep."

Leaving the garden, he traveled southwest along the little allée. Reaching the terrace steps of the mansion, he found twelve sets of French doors standing open across the rear façade of the mansion, allowing the breeze to billow into the mansion, blowing the white sheer curtains into the large salon. Each door had been crowned with palladium windows and surrounded by sidelights. Julian didn't find the little pine door through which he'd exited that morning. He entered the mansion, in search of the nearest restroom.

***

Leaving the bathroom, he passed Suzette in the hallway, putting towels away in the closet. La Rose had its own staff, why was she doing it? "I had a weird dream just now," he confessed to her.

Suzette raised an eyebrow, surprised the boy had spoken to her. "What is that, mon fils?"

"I dreamed of a woman who lived in a rose bloom. She was upset and had closed her blossom around her. A Black man came and talked to her. She listened to him and left her bloom."

Suzette dropped the towels. Julian picked them up and placed them on the bureau inside of the linen closet. "Mon fils, you dreamed that?" Julian nodded. Suzette considered what to tell him, when she realized something. "Where is Madame?"

"She's asleep on the swing in a private garden off the fountain," Julian said.

Suzette bolted down the hall. Confused, Julian ran after her. "Theo," Suzette cried. Julian could hear his heavy footsteps thundering somewhere deep within the plantation house.

Suzette burst through French doors leading to the gardens. Running down the small allée leading to the bosquets, Suzette pointed to her left at one of the doors within the wall of boxed hedges. "Is she there," Suzette yelled.

"Yes," Julian called out, trailing her by several yards. How could an old woman run so fast? Suzette threw opened the garden gate. Out of breath, she stopped short. Theo stopped behind her. Inside the garden where Lela slumbered, they found a man sitting beside her on the swing, stroking her hair. Theo charged the man, drawing his revolver.

A silver dagger appeared in Suzette's hand. She threw it, landing the weapon in the man's chest. He disappeared.

Lela opened her sleepy eyes.

Theo holstered his weapon and grabbed Suzette, attempting to calm her. She had turned blood red, giving her hair an orange appearance. Julian ran to Lela and sat with her on the swing, taking her in his arms. "Grandmère, are you alright?

"Yes, mon fils. Why do you ask?" Lela yawned.

Suzette turned to Julian. "Never leave her unguarded," she said. "*Comprenez-vous?* Do you understand me, mon fils? You are never to leave her unattended outside of the house, especially if she slumbers!"

"C'mon now Sue. The boy didn't know," Theo said.

Lela rubbed her eyes, wiping away the sleep lodged within them. "What's the problem?"

"Your enemy was here, Madame," Suzette said.

Lela yawned and stretched. "He cannot harm me."

"She was aw'rite, Miss Suzette. I had my eye on that ole rascal," Lawrence said, appearing before them. Julian gawked at him in amazement. Who appeared out of thin air? But then, Julian realized it was the way of his family.

Startled, Suzette squirmed within Theo's bear hug. "Where did you come from?" She scowled, brushing it all off. "Oh, never mind."

"Let's go on back to the house, Miss Sue," Theo said. He released her and left.

Suzette labored to suppress the vengeance raging within her French blood. She followed Theo, but stopped and returned to her mistress. "Why give him the opportunity, Madame? Hasn't the devil been granted ample opportunities to destroy you throughout the centuries?" Suzette turned on her heel and left.

Lawrence released a sad chuckle. Suzette sure was sexy when enraged. He suppressed his unclean thoughts and returned his attention to the situation at hand. "To be such a li'l ole thang, she ain't nobody to mess with, huh?" Lawrence laughed, attempting to soften the mood. Julian sat in the swing, clutching his grandmère, his face stoic.

"Son, it's aw'rite. Don't pay Miss Suzette no mind. Thangs are different here. I'se here. Ma'Dame's enemy has no power here." Lawrence walked over to Julian and tousled his hair. "Doncha worry, son." Lawrence left the garden, closing the gate behind him.

Julian rocked the swing while holding his grandmère close, overcome with guilt. "I'm sorry, Grandmère. This place is like a fortress. I didn't consider it dangerous to leave you alone." Julian turned red, choked with emotion.

"Darling, you've done nothing wrong," Lela said. "Suzette is overprotective. She can be very reactionary. There's nothing he could have done to me anyway. It wouldn't have been allowed." Lela took Julian's hand in hers. "Besides, you need to know he is real."

He swallowed the lump in throat and nodded.

"It's alright darling. You may ask," Lela said.

"Who was he?"

Lela smirked. "He is the devil, Mammon. He has pursued me since the beginning of time." She ignored his incredulous expression. "Why the surprise? You asked." Lela patted his hand. "He's part of the reason for me explaining all of this to you. You will understand before you leave Louisiana, mon fils."

Julian let it go. His family was crazy. His grandmère was alright and the intruder hadn't harmed her. That was all that mattered. "I had a dream, Grandmère."

Lela smoothed her dress, chuckling within. "You, Reverend King, and your dreams," she said with a smile. She smoothed his hair. "What did you dream, mon cher?"

Julian blushed. She always made him feel like an adored little boy. "I dreamed of a Black woman who lived in a rose blossom atop this towering bush," he said. "A Black man led her from within. She seemed sad, but released all and followed him."

Lela's face fell slack. She hadn't wished to revisit the time, but she could now see the Lord wouldn't allow her to escape it. "Oh, my darling. My love will never forget. Correction. I cannot forget."

Julian stared at her, confused.

"Your Uncle Toot."

"Oh." He wasn't sure what Uncle Toot had to do with anything, but he kept his comments to himself. Julian recalled all she had told him. "What happened with you and my great-grandfather?"

Lela began to cry without warning. "Darling, hell had just opened its door for me," she said. "Perhaps that's why I diverted the course of my story. The time following Jean Charles' death still troubles me, until this very day."

Lela placed her arm around her great-grandson, shielding him from all evil. "Well, I'll have to start at the beginning."

"Beginning?"

"Well, yes. I must start at the beginning if you're to understand. I'll begin with Toussaint." Lela reclined into her great-grandson's arms. She exhaled, and then inhaled, allowing the spirit of the past to enter her.

Julian wished to spit. Nothing could ever be simple. "I don't need to know the intimacies of Uncle Toot's life."

Lela patted his chest. "You could learn a lot from Toussaint."

"Yeah, like what?"

Lela continued staring into the past. "Uncle Toot overcame quite a bit to achieve all he did."

"By digging holes and tossing dead bodies in them?"

Lela popped Julian square in his smart mouth. "I apologize darling. I'm not sure what came over me."

Julian burned with anger, but he said nothing. After a few minutes, he repented. "I'm sorry, Grandmère."

Lela took pity upon him and gathered compassion in her heart for her child once again. She patted his thigh. "Toussaint took great strides to educate himself. My Aunt Sarah encouraged him to do so, along with his father, Theodore. We called him Teddy. Uncle Teddy was so proud of Toussaint! He would always say, "I'se a slave, but my son will be a Prince before God's throne."

Lela sat up on the swing, leaving the comfort of her grandson's embrace. She crossed her arms beneath her bosom and then patted her elbow, remembering her uncle. "In any case, Toussaint somehow educated himself.

"Once freedom came, a White man came to see him."

Lela strummed her right index finger against her chin, trying to remember. "No, I don't think that's right. It wasn't after the war. Maybe during?" She turned to Julian for assistance, but he didn't remember. Why would she expect him to? Augustus hadn't known about the visit. Lela closed her eyes and aligned her thoughts.

Julian isn't Augustus anymore. Her mind hopscotched through the decades. She couldn't keep her story straight. Lela inhaled, and then exhaled, ordering her thoughts. "I guess it really doesn't matter. The truth will come out in the wash." Lela considered her disinterested great-grandson, frowning as he sat next to her. She ignored him.

A small table materialized beside the swing with a glass of water atop it. "Thank you, Lawrence," she said. Lela sipped from the glass, refreshing her palette.

Lela leaned back in the swing, inviting her little wicked one to recline upon her chest. He accepted her invitation and took his rest. Lela gazed into the treetops.

PART II

Chapter 1

La Rose Plantation, St. Helena Parish. November 7, 1841.

His cries soothed her, causing the pains of child birth to slip away. Releasing the position of birth, Sarah began to fall backwards, no longer able to maintain the squatting position. Sammie tighten her grip on the slippery being in her hands. Still attached to his mother, her downward motion almost jerked the child from her sister's hands. "I'se got him," Sammie told her.

After the eternal fall, Sarah rested upon her small, hay mattress, exhausted.

Teddy kneeled and kissed his wife's sweat drenched brow. She'd survived. For a reason he didn't understand, Teddy had feared she would die during the never-ending perils of childbirth. She wasn't a spring chicken anymore.

He walked over to the table and remove an ancient knife from its sheave. His father Basso had given it to him before he died. Teddy had been cut with it, and so had his daughter, Missy. Now, the time had come for his son.

Sammie sat on her knees at the mouth of her sister's womb, holding the blood and mucus covered boy to her chest. Teddy kissed him. "Bien'vue, mon fils," he said. Taking the sharp knife, he liberated the babe from the clutches of him mother's womb. The child bled. Reaching into his pocket, Teddy removed some twine he'd found at the butcher's that morning and tied the cord off. Teddy scooted across the floor, reaching for an old tarp. He placed it beneath his wife to catch the afterbirth, once she delivered it. He concealed Sarah's private area with the old sheet. He'd had the sheet since Emmanuel was master. They'd enjoyed a few comforts back then. They now used the sheet during childbirth alone.

Smiling down on her new nephew, Sammie kissed him. She arose from the floor and placed the child in a galvanized pan to wash him.

Teddy opened the door of their cabin to release the smell of childbirth. The scent always amazed him, a mix of so many odors. It reminded him of Sarah's smell when she had her monthly visitor. Yet, there was something else mingled with it, like the aroma of wet iron. There was also the smell of death or bad meat. The odor wasn't repugnant, but present all the same. He could smell some yeast mingled into the bouquet. Childbirth smelled like life and death to him. Women possessed within their womb God's holy design of seed time, growing time, and then at last, harvest time.

Missy ran into the cabin through the open door. She must have been next door playing with the neighbors, Teddy figured. She'd wanted to stay and watch the birth of her brother, but he felt she was still too young. But that wasn't the real reason. He didn't know how the birth would go. Anything could go wrong, and he didn't want his young daughter to experience the heartbreak of childbirth.

Spotting her aunt at the worktable, Missy ran to her side. She stood on her tippy-toes to get a better look, but the table was too high. She could see her aunt washing something. She could hear crying. She pulled on her aunt's skirts.

Sammie bent down and kissed her niece on the forehead, taking care to hold the precious babe in her hands above the water in the galvanized pan. "Wanna help me?" Missy nodded yes. Sammie propped the newborn up in the pan. Without warning, she lifted her niece onto the rickety cane back chair.

Missy stood in silence, beholding the child for the first time. The pale babe lying in the galvanized tub amazed her.

"Take this here ladle and spoon some water on him."

Terrified, Missy followed her aunt's instructions, watching in wonderment while Sammie bathed her brother, washing away the fluids of his former home. "That's e'nuff. Let me git him ready 'fore he catches cold." Sammie hoisted

Missy from the chair and placed her on the floor.

"Where's Maman?" Searching the shack, Missy turned and found her mother lying half on the straw mattress and half on the floor. She ran over to her and jumped on her, showering her with kisses.

"Careful, Missy! Your Maman ain't feelin' good," Teddy said. "She just done birthed your brother."

Missy looked back at her father, her eyes welling up with tears. Facing her mother, Missy peered into her eyes seeking her approval, forgiveness and acceptance. Missy kissed her again. "Is that my brother Auntie got in the pan over there, Maman?"

Sarah nodded, unable to speak.

Sammie removed the child from the galvanized pan and dried him. She wrapped the infant in one of Teddy's old shirts, repurposed into swaddling. She stood before the family with the child in her arms.

Missy sat up from her mother's breast and clapped her hands, squealing in joy. "He's an angel, Maman!"

Teddy sat with his wife and daughter on the hay mattress. "Baby, he's fine! Just fine," Teddy said to Sarah.

Sarah worked her dry tongue within her mouth, attempting to quench her thirst.

With the baby in her arms, Sammie poured some water from the cracked, ceramic pitcher into a tin cup. She handed the cup to Teddy. Lifting Sarah's head, he placed the cup to his wife's lips, allowing her to sip.

Sarah took in some of the water and gasped. She'd panted and yelled for hours in her efforts to bring forth her son. Sarah rested her head against the thin mattress. She continued to pant, infusing her body with the oxygen it craved. After a few moments, Sarah caught her breath.

Sammie came over and placed the newborn in Teddy's arms. He wept as he rocked the baby, bouncing him just a bit. His tears splashed down upon the child's forehead.

Sarah coughed, but found her voice. "Whatcha gonna call him, Teddy?"

Teddy kissed his little one on the forehead and then both cheeks. Considering the boy, he wondered if he'd created the child without the aid of his mother. The babe was his spitting image.

He grinned, thinking of the night he and Sarah had made Missy. Teddy could feel her spirit and soul riding on his sperm into Sarah's body. He'd watched Sarah's eyes when his seed landed inside of her. Her body had contracted around him. She'd gasped, sinking her fingernails into his back.

Now that he thought about it, he hadn't experienced the same phenomenon when they conceived Toussaint. He remembered Sarah returning home from one of her 'trips.' They made love, the most intense lovemaking they'd ever enjoyed. Yet, he didn't remember his seed leaving him and taking root inside her. Perhaps it was just a one-time thing with Missy, since she was a girl.

In any case, he couldn't deny his son. Even now, he could see himself in the child as he gulped in his first few breaths of air, beginning his life's journey upon the Earth. Even Missy didn't resemble him to such a degree. Once she grew older, he could see himself in his daughter, but not as he could with the boy.

He kissed the child again. He couldn't stop. "Toussaint," he said. He'd heard the name once before, a freedom fighter for Africans on some island far away. "He's all holy to me. He's gonna lead the Lawd's people one day." Teddy wept a little, unable to believe the Lord had blessed him with the child.

Tears filled Sarah's eyes, attempting to conceal her deception. Teddy loved the boy with all his heart. But the Lord had allowed it. She could see in the Spirit Teddy would never find out Toussaint's true paternity. She let it go, receiving reality as it had manifested itself. The boy was hers and Teddy's son. Although a newborn, no one could deny Teddy as the child's father. The son was the mirror image of his father.

"I'se goin' outside to tell the folks." Kissing her once again, Teddy stood from the little mattress and placed the child in Sammie's arms. Kissing the child once more, he then ran outdoors. Sarah listened to the whooping and hollering of the slave community which surged into their home, welcoming the child to the Earth.

Sammie sat on the edge of her sister's bed. "He's hungry," Sammie told her. Finding her sister too weak to move, Sammie guided her sister's full breast into the child's mouth. Toussaint suckled.

Third Dimension

Sarah closed her eyes, allowing her life's milk to flow into her son. The milk would make him strong.

Yes, he's strong. Is he not?

Sarah opened her eyes. *Go away.* Her eyes darted over to her sister and her daughter. They couldn't see him. "Whatcha doin' here, Barachiel?"

Barachiel walked over and tickled the suckling infant beneath his chin. "Magnificent!" He wiped away a tear, filled with pride. "I've come to welcome our son. Shouldn't a father be present at the birth of his son?"

"Teddy's here."

Barachiel scanned the one room house. "Is he? Where?"

Sarah was too weak to bring him to his knees. She tried to muster her power, but baby Toussaint whimpered. Sarah figured the flow of her milk slowed when she focused her energy on incinerating his father.

Barachiel laughed at her feeble attempt to destroy him. Her concerns for nourishing her child had trumped her desire to kill him. "Well, my darling, you've always brought me to my knees, dare I say? A mother's love for her son weakens her ability to exact unfounded vengeance upon the sire of her son, *n'est-ce pas?*"

Toussaint began to whimper, his little hand grabbing his mother's free breast, while clutching the breast he suckled. "My, he is a child after his father's heart."

Sarah glared at him, holding her child close.

Childbirth and motherhood had dulled his daughter's sense of humor. He held out his hand and an object materialized. "Keep this for him," Barachiel said.

Sarah watched a key hover above her. Without warning, a gold box appeared above her and her son. An unseen force shot the key into the box. The box's lid slammed shut and disappeared. "Barachiel…" Sarah searched the room, only to find her sister and daughter present. Sarah surrendered to the comfort of sleep, exhausted.

Chapter 2

La Rose Plantation, St. Helena Parish. November 25, 1841.

Sarah arose from their little mattress to her knees. The rooster would crow in a few hours, and she wanted to get it done before the sun rose. She could take him, but was she strong enough to travel? She lay down again, wondering what to do.

Sarah's stirring jarred Teddy from his rest. He squirmed and then awoke, stretching upon the sparsely stuffed mattress. He made a mental note to go out and find some hay. Little Missy's mattress could use a re-stuffing as well. He stretched again, and then rolled over to kiss his wife and son. "What gots you'se troubled this mornin', Sarah?"

She wasn't sure how to explain it to him. "I'se wanna git Toot circ'sized."

Teddy sat up in bed. Sarah always told him about wild things the Good Lord would tell her. He always trusted the Word she received from him. "What's that?" Teddy had never heard of the word. His groin began to throb.

Sarah patted his hand. She knew her husband wouldn't take the suggestion well. On instinct alone, he'd clutched his pecker before he heard what she had to say. "It's what they did to Abraham, Moses and the Lawd Jesus. When the Lawd Jesus was a babe, they cut away the skin coverin' his privates."

Teddy clutched himself. "Woman, whatcha talkin' 'bout?"

Sarah took him in her hands and showed him.

"You'se ain't doin' that to Toot."

Sarah stared down at her son, unable to figure out how to convince her husband. "You'se would deny the Lawd from consecratin' our child?"

Teddy sighed. Why did she have to bring the Good Lord's name into it? He couldn't believe the Lord would want him to mutilate his son. Yet somehow, he felt it was true. He could remember a few stories from Sunday meeting where the preacher had mentioned the practice. He remembered going to the outhouse after one of those sermons to check and make sure still had all his parts.

He delved into his wife's eyes, filled with dread. He could see she wouldn't go against him if he didn't want to do it. "You'se knows I'se wouldn't go 'gainst the Good Lawd," he said. Sarah said nothing else.

Sarah possessed knowledge of things he could never know or understand, and he loved her for it. She was the only slave on the plantation who didn't work in the fields or anywhere else, and Master Augustus couldn't make her. Once or twice, he'd found Sarah arguing with their Master, staring him straight in the eye. What Negro looked White folks in the eye? But Sarah did. "Aw'rite. If'se you'se thanks it's best, let's do it."

Sarah kissed him. "You'se wanna travel wit' me?"

Never had she invited him along on one of her adventures in all the years they'd been married. "I'se don't know," Teddy said.

"It'll be aw'rite. You'se gotta come."

Teddy rubbed his bearded chin. "What 'bouts Missy?"

"She's comin' too."

"Aw'rite." Teddy got out of bed and put on his clothes. Sarah woke up Missy and dressed her. Next, Sarah clothed Toussaint in a little shift, and then wrapped him in his burlap blanket. It had a flower shaped patch sewn on the center. Teddy hadn't noticed it before.

The family stood in the center of the room. "Teddy, you'se takes Missy's hand." Sarah took his, holding Toussaint in her free arm. They vanished.

Teddy admired the grand building, awestruck. "Lawd, is we'se in heaven?"

"Not really," Sarah said.

Missy ran around the room, staring at the beings present. "Git ova' here gal!" Missy ignored her mother's cries, enchanted by the nice men and women. Some patted her head. She smiled at them and moved down the row of pews. She came to two dapper men sitting together. One smiled at her, filled with the love of heaven. The other frowned, but then allowed a cold smile to creep upon his face. "You're mean," Missy said to the man.

"You are correct, *ma fille*," the nice man said.

Missy stared at the two men. She didn't know what to do. The nice man tweaked her chin. "Do you have a piggy bank?"

Missy wagged her head no. "What's a bank?"

The nice man nodded. "Ask Papa and Maman to get one for you," he said, reaching into his breast pocket. "Put this in it."

Missy eyes bugged open. "Merci, Mis'sur!" She ran down the aisle to rejoin her parents.

The man with the cold smile frowned. "She's a slave."

The man with the nice smile watched as she ran away. "For now." In the Spirit, he saw his brother's plan for the child. He wept for her.

Missy returned to her parents, out of breath. "Maman, Maman! The angels are here," Missy said.

Sarah gawked at her daughter. She hadn't believed the child could see, but apparently, she had some sight. "Whatcha got in your hand, gal?"

Missy displayed her toothless grin. "The nice man over there gave me a coin!" She handed it to her father, who stared at the gold coin, amazed. "He said ya'll gonna git me a piggy bank to keep it in."

Sarah saw Barachiel sitting to the rear of the sanctuary. She saw Mammon sitting next to him, who smiled at her and licked his lips. Fear and rage arose within her heart. She wished to slay him in the presence of the Lord.

Toussaint whimpered in her arms. "We'se git you one ma fille, doncha worry," Sarah said, glaring at the devil. She pulled Missy close to her with her free arm, and then bent down and kiss her on the forehead. "Let your Papa hold it for you, aw'rite?"

"Yessum, Maman." Missy handed the coin to her father.

Sarah returned her attention to Toussaint, asleep within her arms. She bounced him, encouraging him to sleep a while longer. She would deal with Heaven's and Hell's folks later. Sarah silenced her mind and heart, allowing the Holy Spirit of the Lord to overtake her.

Teddy beheld the cathedral, filled with people he didn't know. Many of them were enormous, their knees jammed into the backs of the pews before them. Some scowled at

Teddy's son, seeming to curse him, while others wept, crying tears of joy.

Forgetting the strange beings who filled sanctuary, Teddy turned his attention to the lofty, vaulted ceilings, decorated with different scenes from the Bible. He couldn't read, but he recognized the pictures, depicting stories he'd been told by the preacher since his childhood. He saw Moses being pulled from the river. Another scene illustrated Pharaoh's daughter holding the child in her arms. Next, the artist presented Moses as a man, a leader of Egypt.

In the adjacent ceiling vault, the artist painted Moses killing the Egyptian, and then in the next scene Moses fled Egypt, escaping into the wilderness. Teddy scanned ahead, finding Moses having returned to Pharaoh's throne room, telling the king to let his people go. *My son will liberate our people*, Teddy said in his heart.

Yes, he will, my son. Yet, not as you understand

Teddy felt his flesh become alive with the Holy Spirit. He picked up little Missy and jumped around. He found himself facing Missy's 'nice man' who had given her the coin. The 'nice man' smiled at him, filled with kindness and mercy. Had he spoken to Teddy without words?

The observers who loved the Lord shouted and rejoiced.

Sarah closed her eyes and then opened them. A man dressed in all white, with skin blacker than midnight, appeared before the altar. "Sarah and Theodore, bring forth the child," he said.

Sarah and Teddy approached the altar. Toussaint yawned in his mother's arms.

The High Priest, Melchizedek, took the child from his mother and lay him upon the altar. A petit man appeared at the priest's side. Teddy didn't like the little White man. He resembled Missy's 'nice man' sitting in the pews, but Teddy wasn't sure. "Who'se you?"

The petit man lowered his head. "I'm your son's patron. I'm his friend."

Teddy turned to Sarah for understanding. She stared straight ahead, refusing to look at her husband. "Sarah?" She gave him a curt nod, indicating all was well. Teddy let it go.

"Dearly beloved, the Protector of our Rose has returned to Earth from the Lord." The observers fell silent. Melchizedek continued. "Today, we consecrate him, in the tradition of his father Abraham, to protect *le Mère* of the king, Le Baton."

Teddy stared at the altar, dumbfounded. It was true. He'd had a dream once while working out in the fields of La Rose Plantation. He hadn't even jumped the broom with Sarah yet. He'd prayed to God, "Lawd, I'se don't mind sufferin'. Just make my son a king so he ain't got to do this."

Once he'd prayed the words, a sunburst appeared in the

sky, blinding him. For a time, Teddy had passed out, or so he'd figured. Next thing he knew, the water boy was standing over him with a ladle in his hand. He'd given Teddy a drink and his senses returned to him. At that time, he'd shaken off his sun sickness and went back to work.

He'd hoped back then the Lord had heard his prayer. Now he knew for sure, he had. Returning to the present, Teddy listened to priest pray in a tongue he didn't understand. Teddy wiped away his tears while holding little Missy in his crook of his right arm.

"I, Melchizedek, who blessed Abraham, bless this child." Picking up a blade older than time, Abraham's blade, the High Priest of Salem held it up before the Lord, praying in murmurs. "Remove his dress." Two albino women with white hair appeared on either side of the priest. They removed the child's clothing.

Taking the child's penis in his hand, he cut and then cauterized him.

Teddy lost consciousness.

His wife and infant son slept next to him. Teddy arose from bed and looked out the window. Maybe it was fourth watch of the night. Curious, Teddy returned to the bed and lifted his son's little shift. He found him to be cut and swollen, but nearly healed. "It happened." Teddy lay down beside his wife. Something hard was in the bed. Fishing around, he found a coin. He smiled and fell asleep.

La Rose Plantation, St. Helena Parish. August, 1842.

SARAH RAN TO the well. With no time to turn the crank, she yanked the rope, dropping the bucket to the bottom as fast as she could. Hearing the splash, she pulled up the bucket with her hands and poured the contents into her water bucket. She broke into a lopsided run for home, trying not to spill the water.

She dropped the bucket at the front door, causing the water to splash out. She rushed in and scanned the one room shack. She didn't see him. Sarah rushed over to the mattress, pulled back the burlap covers and searched the bed. Toussaint wasn't there. "Lawd!" She searched the room, but couldn't find the child anywhere.

A little window surrounded by clouds appeared before her. She searched the Spirit, but couldn't find him. "Well, he's still on this here Earth," she said, trying to calm down. "Boy, show yo'self!" Nothing. Panicking, she turned to leave the cabin, prepared to search the plantation for her wayward infant. Giggling distracted her.

Her eyes ricocheted up to the corner of the ceiling. "Boy, whatcha doin' up there?" Her boy giggled and gurgled, hovering close to a rusty nail which had missed the stud, anchoring the tin roof to the house. "You'se git' from 'round there right now!" Sarah hadn't experienced these sorts of challenges with Missy. She had taken after her father, Teddy. However, Toussaint had taken after his and *her* father.

A breeze flowed into the shack through the open door, releasing from its spirit a finely attired man. He scolded the child floating near the ceiling with his eyes. "That will do, Toussaint. Come down."

Toussaint considered the two, trying to reason within his young mind what to do. His father furrowed his brow. Beings levitating to his left and right caught Toussaint's eye. He clapped his chubby hands together, finding his little friends floating with him, giggling. The cherubim fluttered their wings and then flitted around the small cabin. Toussaint pursued them.

Sarah watched in horror as her son chased the mischievous cherubim. "Ya'll git on!"

Crestfallen, the cherubim hovered in a group away from their infant friend. Barachiel patted his foot. "Return to the Lord, now." They didn't move. "All of you, at once!" They left, fearing Barachiel's wrath.

Near tears, Toussaint returned to his corner near the rusty nail. He began to talk in a language Sarah couldn't understand.

Anger surged within Barachiel, listening to his infant

son. "Do not back talk your mother, Toussaint. She has told you what is right. Come down this instant."

In obeisance to his father's voice, Toussaint floated down from the ceiling and came to rest on the hay stuffed mattress, kicking his chubby legs.

"Lawdy, he ain't even a year, and he's flying around?" Sarah pinned him down on the bed with one hand while she changed his diaper with the other. She'd found them on one of her excursions to a distant plantation house.

"I must say, he's much like his father, and nothing like your husband. Yet, he's the mirror image of your husband."

Sarah ignored Barachiel, tucking Toussaint into bed. "Look boy, Maman is tellin' your li'l ole tail to stay in this bed. If I'se catch you'se flyin' 'round, I'se gonna git your foot."

Toussaint laughed at her, knowing in his nine-month-old mind she'd do no such thing.

"Go easy on him, Sarah." Barachiel extracted a cigarette from his breast coat. Striking a match on the bottom of his boot, he lit it. "You weren't any better. As Mamie would say, you gave her 'fits.'" Barachiel exhaled and then laughed, remembering his child as a little girl.

Sarah didn't wish to remember being his daughter. Toussaint kicked his legs, enjoying his fresh diaper. "Doncha mess it up, boy," Sarah said as she propped him up on the straw mattress.

"And you'se the one who'se should go easy on him, Barachiel," Sarah said. "You'se makin' him grows up in bondage, when he should be free." Sarah listened to the Spirit and her countenance sank. She'd hoped her child would grow up to be like her. "His gift won't last none."

Barachiel grew solemn, observing in the Spirit the path of his son's life. "Perhaps not. As an infant, he's not spiritually blocked. He has just returned to Earth from the bosom of the Most High God; his spirit and soul are still connected to him. But yes, his ability to move through dimension and time as we do will diminish."

Barachiel kissed his son's forehead. The infant fell asleep. "I'm not sure why he will lose the ability to travel. Your gift persisted." Barachiel bent over and lifted the child from the mattress, rocking him in his arms. Toussaint opened his sleepy eyes. Barachiel peered within, witnessing the child's glorious future as a man and as the Protector of the Rose. "He will mature into a mighty man and will do great things. His current existence as a slave will strengthen him. He will do well. Do you not believe this?"

Sarah wiped away her tears, glimpsing her son's future in the Spirit of God. "He will. But I'se won't see it."

Barachiel kissed her forehead. "From Earth, no."

***

A light surrounded the crown of her child's head from ear to ear. It amazed her. No one could see it but her. She ran her fingers through the light, warming her hand like invisible feathers. Her boy was getting big. He was almost two years old.

Sarah's covert, 'relocation' missions had decreased since Toussaint's birth. Many of her people had been forced to languish in bondage without her to assist them in their journeys to freedom. Many had been caught by their owners, and then either killed, beaten, tortured or sold off.

She had to do something. Harriet Tubman had yet to come to age; her anointing hadn't come upon her to lead the people out. Once Harriet received her anointing, Sarah planned to go into a semi-retirement of sorts, attending only to special cases. In any case, now that Toussaint was older, he could endure a few hours without her.

"Take him with you."

The voice she despised filled her ears. "You'se should takes him wit' you."

Barachiel materialized next to her. He walked out to the front porch, lit a cigarette and then sat in the chair. Since Toussaint napped, Sarah joined him, sitting beside him in her high back rocking chair. She loved her rocker.

She'd come into possession of the chair while on a mission in Virginia, assisting a family of slaves in their escape. They'd almost been captured, lugging their grandmother's chair with them on their journey. Once she'd convinced them to accept her help, she transported the group to Les' home in Canada.

Most times, Sarah would return home immediately following a relocation. On that occasion, she'd tarried behind overnight. Les had been whining she never spent time with him, saying she would 'dump and run.'

After breakfast, she chatted with the patriarch of the refugee family. He'd explained to her his grandfather had made the chair for his grandmother once they'd started courting. His heart wouldn't allow him to leave the chair behind. They'd figured they could manage, but the journey proved to be more arduous than any of them could have ever imagined. As a thank you for saving them, the patriarch had given it to Sarah.

"Ah yes. Their master had been a neighbor of mine at La Pivoine Plantation in Virginia. A cruel man. A pig. He suffered a most unfortunate death."

"How'se that?"

Barachiel arched his brow. "If I remember correctly, he stumbled off a ridge and fell into the river bed below, impaling himself on a sharpened cane of some sort protruding from the river. No one found his body until many weeks later. I suspect it took a bit of time for him to die."

Sarah shook her head. She knew Barachiel had something to do with the man's cruel death. He wasn't any better than his son, Augustus.

"Your brother never learned how to manage the art of meting out judgment." Barachiel exhaled, the smoke forming little pictures of things to come. Sarah studied them, seeing all. The smoke dissipated into the humidity of the afternoon.

A little lady materialized on the porch, strumming her guitar. "Le Baton," she began to hum, filling all the souls around them with the Spirit of God. Her locked hair flowed above her head, forming a make-shift Menorah. Each time she uttered the name, Le Baton, the tips of her dreaded hair glowed.

"Got's you'se a band now, Barachiel?"

He laughed. "Should we not sing the Most High's praises?" He discovered smiles on the faces of the downtrodden slaves who passed by, attending to their chores. Although they couldn't hear the cherub's tune with their natural senses, their souls did. Their faces brightened. "They seem to enjoy thr psalm."

"Le Baton," the lyricist sang, strumming her guitar.

A light from heaven shined down upon them. Sarah released her irritation, basking in the glow of God.

Barachiel pitched his spent cigarette out into the road. He loved the little cherub's music, spurring him to lean back in the high-back chair. He relaxed and closed his eyes, savoring her music. After several moments, he spoke. "Your brothers and sisters are languishing in bondage. When do you plan to return to work?"

Sarah glanced over her shoulder through the open door into the cabin. There was no movement on the bed. "Toot still too young."

Barachiel nodded. "He isn't a normal child. Take him with you. He's a big boy now. You may find him to be of assistance."

Sarah placed her corn cob pipe in her mouth, lit it and considered his words. "Aw'rite, I'se tries it."

The chair rocked and hit the wall of her cabin, vacant. The songstress had vanished. Toussaint wailed. Sarah went indoors to attend to her son.

La Rose Plantation, St. Helena Parish. Winter, 1843.

THE VOICES OF the oppressed awoke her not long after midnight. She could hear dogs barking, pursuing the fugitives. She arose from bed and put on her dress, her straw hat, and then placed her corn cob pipe in her mouth. She lit it and inhaled.

The smell of tobacco awoke Teddy. He yawned. "You'se

goin' out tonight?"

"Yessuh. For a bit."

Teddy sat up in bed, wiping the sleep from his eyes. "You'se takin' Toot this time?"

Sarah screwed her lips, conflicted. Without his knowledge, Teddy had testified to Barachiel's words. Two witnesses. Sarah conceded. "You'se thank I'se should?"

"Yup."

Sarah bit her lip. She wanted Teddy to see her work and the gift God had granted her. She wished Missy to know she had a greater purpose in life than being some White man's slave. However, she worried about placing her entire family in harm's way. But then she strengthened herself. She felt God's loving reassurance rising within her, knowing he would protect them all. "You and Missy wanna come too?"

Teddy didn't know how to respond. Sarah had never invited him and Missy on one of her outings before. "You'se wants us to come?"

"Doncha wanna sees what I'se do?"

Teddy jumped up from bed, pulling on his pants and shirt. As Sarah dressed their son, Teddy rushed over to Missy's pallet. "What's wrong, Papa?" she asked in a groggy voice, heavy laden with sleep.

"You'se wanna go out wit' your Maman?"

At first Missy didn't understand, but then she remembered. Her mother traveled. Of course, she wanted her to tag along! Missy threw back her covers, jumped up and put on her good shift dress and shoes she only wore to Sunday Meeting. They were a little tight, but she cherished them. None of the other slave girls had shoes.

With everyone dressed and ready, Sarah held Toussaint in her arms. She prayed to the Most High God and his son, Jesus, for a safe journey. She smiled, receiving his love and promise that they would be fine. "Ya'll grab hands," Sarah said. They disappeared.

The Mississippi Delta was a hard place. The White folks living there had no compassion for either their slaves or free Negroes. Sarah could hear the dogs barking in the distance. Missy clung tighter to her father.

Sarah peered out into the Spirit, spotting the escapees running through the tall brush, terrified. "Lawd, they'se too old to run!" She reconsidered her words. "Lawd, you'se knows, not me."

Toussaint leaned over and whispered into her ear, "God can do all thangs, Maman."

Sarah kissed little Toussaint's forehead. He was right. Nothing was impossible for God. Jesus' blood covered all who accepted his gift.

Sarah realized everyone still held hands. Relaxing her

flesh and surrendering to the Spirit of God, she felt her family leave the ground, floating upward. She considered the trees around her. Finding a high, sturdy branch, Sarah landed her family there, out of harm's way. Teddy guided Missy to sit next to him. Toussaint left his mother's shoulder, floating over to his father shoulder, coming to rest there. He laughed. "Shush, boy," Sarah said in a hushed tone. Toussaint obeyed, covering his mouth with his hands.

Sarah floated down to a lower branch. The family watched from their respective perches in the tree. Soon, the escapees came into sight.

"Ya'll gone on ahead. I'se old. You'se gotta save ya'll selves. Help my grandbabies," the older man said.

The young woman and her husband stopped and waited for their parents to catch up. The husband ran back many yards. He grabbed the old folks' arms and pulled them along. Reaching the group, the husband let them go. They all huddled together, catching their breath. The daughter and husband wept. How were they all going to make it? Their little ones had run ahead, hiding amidst the trees and tall grass.

The daughter hugged her parents. "Ma and Pa, we'se ain't leavin' ya'll," the young woman said. "We'se leaves as a family, or we'se all stay," the daughter said. Her husband nodded in agreement. The daughter's husband looked over his shoulder, trying to figure out how far the slave catchers were behind them.

The old woman kissed her daughter and her son-in-law. "Let's us be. Ya'll go on 'head and find freedom."

Toussaint appeared on Sarah's shoulder. "Ain't it time, Maman?"

She nodded and sighed, but thanked God. At two years of age, Toussaint's ability to move in the Spirit had waned a great deal, but his gifts were still better than most folks. She'd felt him will himself to move a few moments before, but had only just manage to transition. She grimaced, dispelling Barachiel's declaration from her mind. "Hold on, boy."

Sarah floated down from the branch with Toussaint upon her back, leaving Teddy and Missy in the tree. She landed with ease, careful not to buck Toussaint. "All ya'll gonna be free," Sarah said to the refugee family.

Startled, the runaways jumped, believing they'd been caught. In the darkness, the young woman watched a woman with a child sitting on her back walk out of the shadows. "Who'se ya'll?"

Sarah lit her pipe. Toussaint giggled. "The Lawd done sent me here to help ya'll." The old folks started praying. Sarah could hear the barking dogs, now disoriented by the sound of the old folks' prayers. Sarah listened to the sound of their barking veer away to the East and the West of where the band of refugees stood. Their masters followed them.

The Spirit of the Lord concealed the refugees from the enemy.

Fear reclaiming them, the old folks stopped praying. Sarah beheld, in the Spirit, the dogs regroup and pick up the scent of the escapees once again. The vicious animals bolted in their direction, less than one-half mile away. "That way," the runaways heard the slave catchers call out. The dogs ran through the brush and tall grass.

Sarah searched the darkness, ascertaining the direction of the sound. She turned to the young woman, taking her hand. "Doncha fear. Isn't that what the Good Lawd done taught us?" Terror stricken, the runaways managed a unanimous nod in agreement to Sarah's words. They bowed their heads. The grandfather wiped away his tears. Sarah knew the runaways couldn't help their fear, but they would learn in the future to trust God. "We ain't got much time. Join hands."

Toussaint clutched his mother's neck tight. Sarah brought forth Missy and Teddy, floating them both down from the lofty branch to the Earth.

The young mother scanned the darkness, frantic. "My'se chil'ren."

In the Spirit, Sarah spotted the children hidden in the brush. "C'mere babies!" They rushed to her from their hiding places. "Ya'll take each other's hands." With the children, Teddy and Missy to her left, the parents and grandparents to her right, and little Toussaint on her back, Sarah united them all. "Lawd, strengthen me to transport all ten of us."

Paradis, Quebec, Canada. Winter, 1843.

TOO FAR OUT. Sarah sighed, considering the mounds of snow and ice. Why couldn't she ever hit her spot? Only the Lord knew. She considered the tormented souls of her weary refugees. "I'se knows it's cold and ya'll bare-footed, but we'se can make it. We ain't far now." Silent, the group nodded and followed their savior like little sheep after escaping the jaws of wolves. Sarah led them through the icy, snow caked roads of frozen Quebec, Canada. The moon illuminated the way.

The snow packed path opened into a cleared road. She could feel the confidence and determination of her followers grow. After a few yards, the road spilled out into the square of a homestead.

Sarah heard her brood gasp, taking in the massive, snow covered lodge with smoke billowing from the home's several chimneys. "Lawd, what is this here place," she heard the grandfather say. Running ahead to the party, Sarah stopped at the front door. She gave the pass: three raps, then five, and finally seven.

He sat at the fireplace beneath his bear-skin coverlet, reading his book. Yet, he couldn't concentrate. He put the book down and closed his eyes, allowing the serenity of God to soothe him. Maybe he should go asleep. He heard the alarm at the door and smiled. Finally, she'd arrived. When would he learn to have confidence in the Lord's Spirit? It had yet to fail him, after so many years.

Les Hicks arose from his chair and went to the door. He peeked out the curtains. Sarah. He'd had a feeling she would show up that evening, so he'd made some preparations, just in case. Les could always sense Sarah's arrival with refugees. His concern had spiked when they hadn't arrived a few hours before, but then he took comfort in the Lord. He knew the little brood would be safe.

Sarah always seemed to overshoot his homestead, materializing miles away at times. Usually, the Lord would reveal their location to him, pointing him in the direction where Sarah and her brood had landed. He would take the sleigh to meet them.

Yet on this night, the Lord had shut his eyes to the location of the groups' landing, allowing them to walk for whatever reason. The Lord knew best. Les comforted himself, knowing they'd only traveled a short distance, if the Lord hadn't sent him to fetch them. Sarah never could hit her landing mark. Only once could he remember her landing in the clearing before his home. She'd had a wounded refugee with her, at that time.

He opened the door. From the shadows of the forest surrounding the house, he watched the chilled survivors approach the house on Sarah's signal. After an eternity, they reached the front door covered with the frost of Quebec's night air.

"Ya'll home now," she said, guiding her little band of refugees inside.

Sarah loved Les' home in the woods. It took her breath away each time she visited. Constructed of lacquered logs, he'd adorned the home's interior with a variety of fur rugs and wall tapestries. She guessed they helped knock down cold drafts. She could see their father's influence in the construction and decoration of the home, lit by chandlers constructed of antlers. Most of the furnishings had been upholstered in a variety of tanned hides, velvets, and damasks fabrics. Yet the formal furnishings, such as the buffets, secretariats, gaming tables, and other furnishings, had been constructed in European workshops.

She lifted Toussaint from her shoulder and placed him on the floor. A dog ran over and licked him. Toussaint laughed, levitating, and then sitting on the animal's back. Spooked, the dog ran around the room. "Git down boy!" Sarah told him. Toussaint returned to the floor and the dog trotted away, coming to rest by the fireplace. He kept a watchful eye on the boy who could fly.

Sarah removed her wrap and handed it to the servant. "Les, how's you, boy?" Sarah stamped her feet on the rug and shook the snow from her dreaded locks of hair. Les hugged Sarah, glad she'd made it to his safe-haven.

Toussaint jumped up from the log planked floor and explored the home, seeking rest near the warmth of the fireplace. Les smiled, watching him toddle along the way. He could fly better than he could walk, that was for sure. "This your boy, Sarah?"

Sarah smiled down on the mischievous child. "Sho' is." Sarah watched her son toddle toward the fireplace. "Git away from that fire, boy."

Les emitted a slow, easy laugh, rejoicing in the boy's rebellious, exploratory nature. "Let him be. He ain't gonna hurt hisself." Les studied the man and young girl who didn't seem to be a part of the runaway band. The Lord unveiled their identity to him. "The Lawd is good! I know this ain't your husband Teddy. And this fine li'l ole thang must be Missy."

Sarah smiled with pride. "This them. I'se told you I'd bring them here one day. This here's the day."

Teddy shivered, now out of the cold and standing in the warm, comfortable home. "How you'se doin' suh?" Teddy shook Les' hand, a bit bashful. What Negro owned a fine house and lands such as this? It reminded him of Master

Augustus' hunting lodge in Mississippi, but much grander.

Les couldn't believe the blessing of the Lord. The day had finally come when he had the pleasure of meeting his brother-in-law. *Toussaint looks just like him*, he wondered in his heart. He saw Sarah frown. He let it go. "It's a pleasure to meet you after all these years, suh," Les said. "Sarah done told me a heap 'bout you. She thanks the world of you."

He patted little Missy on the head, who clung to her father's leg. "Yup, sho' do. Sarah always braggin' on you suh, tellin' folks how fine, smart and strong her man is," Les said. "I don't reckon none of us mortals can measure up to you." Les laughed, watching Sarah blush. After all these years, his sister was still sweet on her husband.

Teddy took his bashful wife in his arms. He kissed her on the forehead. "I'se the lucky one. Ain't no man gots a wife as fine as my Sarah."

Everyone in the room laughed, filled with warmth for the couple. Les put his arm around his wife. "She's fine aw'rite," Les said. "But ain't no wife as beautiful as my Lucy."

The wives broke out into laughter. "You'se right, but ya'll menfolk needs to quit shuckin' and jivin' us womenfolk," Lucy said. Everyone laughed. "Ya'll just tryin' to stay on your womenfolk's good side." Lucy winked at her female comrades. "I'se thanks we'll lets ya'll win. What ya'll say, ladies?"

"Amen," said the young runaway woman.

Sarah nodded in agreement. She realized something. "What's your name child?"

She cast her eyes to the floor. "Massa called me Gal. That's what they'se all calls me."

Sarah walked over to the old lady sitting in the chair near the fireplace, warming her feet. "Ma'am?"

She glanced up at her from the fire. "Yessum, honey?" She grasped Sarah's hand and patted it, grateful for all she'd done for them.

Sarah became shy, feeling the old woman's praise. "What did ya'll call your daughter when she came outta you?"

The old lady wept, releasing the first wave of captivity from her soul. "I'se called her my Giddy Joy. She was so happy. That there gal laughed all the time. She laughed until 'bout her third harvest, when her soul figured out ain't nuthin' to laughs 'bout."

Sarah grimaced and nodded, understanding. She returned to young woman, staring down at the floor. "Doncha ever cast down your eyes again, child. You'se understands me?" The young woman nodded. "Well, how'se 'bout we'se calls you Joy?" Sarah said. "You ain't never gonna knows sufferin' like that again. You'se free."

The woman's heart filled with happiness. She'd been named. "Baby, what you'se thank," Joy asked her husband.

He kissed her. The children squealed in disgust. "You'se

always been my joy."

Everyone clapped. "What's your name, suh?" Les asked Joy's husband.

Remembering his manners, he removed his worm ridden straw hat from his head. He walked over to the fireplace and tossed it into the flames. "Don't need that no more, I'se reckons," he said to the group surrounding him. He returned to his wife and clutched her in his arms. "Mammy done named me Ben. She wasn't my real mama, but she looked after and nursed all us chil'ren on the plantation who didn't have no folks." His face melted, the memory of his youth returning to his mind. "My mama got sold off 'fore I'se could 'member. I'se don't even 'member what she looked like," he said.

"So, Mammy raised us. Don't even knows her real name. Guessin' she didn't have one no way." Everyone stared at the floor. Ben sighed. "Perhaps the Good Lawd will show me even more favor and brings Mama back to me." Everyone stood around in silent agreement. "This here is Molly, my little girl, and Mar, my son."

Raising himself up on all fours, Toussaint focused his concentration and stood up from the floor on his chubby, sturdy legs. Once he found his balance, he walked over to the fireplace.

"Stop boy."

Toussaint scowled at Les and toddled away at a wobbly

gait. A ledger on the table commandeered his attention. He levitated, floating over to the chair, but not quite landing on top. Using all his strength, Toussaint held on tight and then pulled himself on top of it, winded.

Grabbing hold of the table top, the child hoisted himself up. Toussaint opened the book and flipped through. They all watched him move his finger up and down the columns, checking the math. "He's a whip," Les told Sarah.

"So you say. He needs a whuppin'."

"His father won't allow it." Les remembered himself, watching Teddy turn his attention to him. He'd said too much. "Well folks, I'se know ya'll tired. We have a little cabin on this here place where ya'll can rest." He watched fear rise in the refugees' eyes. "Don't ya'll worry none. This here place is as safe as heaven. Cain't nobody finds ya'll or git to ya'll here." He winked at them. "On this here place, ya'll got angels watchin' over ya'll. They ain't gonna let that ole devil touch ya'll." He could see them all exhale, relieved. They believe him.

Having said his peace, Les led the escaped family out the door and across the grounds to the guest house. In preparation for their arrival, Les had instructed his servants to put some water on the hearth.

"Lawd! Look at dese here rooms, Mama," the grandfather said to his wife.

The grandmother took it all in, amazed. "Well, the babies can sleep wit' us. Ya'll chil'ren can sleeps ova there," she said to her daughter and son-in-law.

Les took the grandmother's hand in his. "Ma'am, this is all for ya'll. Ain't nobody else sharin' this place wit' ya'll." The old lady sobbed before him. Les turned to the grandfather. "After ya'll done rested a few days, I'se take ya'll to town. We just finished a li'l ole house there. Ya'll can stay there as long as ya'll want. Once you'se gits on your feet, you'se can move on."

Ben stood before him, not knowing what to say. "That's mighty kind of you, suh." Les nodded, acknowledging his thanks. "What's this town called, suh?"

"Paradis."

His guests settled around the room as the servants brought in four copper tubs. They filled them with hot water in minutes, or so it seemed to the liberated family. "Well, I'm gonna go on back to the house. See ya'll in the mornin'." He and the servants left, pulling the door tight behind them.

"Who'se first?" Joy said, filled with laughter. The children ran and jumped into their tub.

Each family member bathed behind the privacy of screens. Joy bathed her children, and then jumped into bath herself. She'd never enjoyed a bath. She always drew the water and heated it for the master's wife, but never one for herself. She didn't wish to leave its comforts. Soon, Joy drifted off to sleep, until her husband awoke her.

Clean and safe for the first time in their lives, the family retired to their rooms and climbed into their clean, soft beds. Unable to sleep alone, Mar and Molly left their rooms and crawled into bed with Ben and Joy, falling asleep in each other's arms.

Peace and silence floated throughout the small cabin. Joy. The grandparents wept together. They praised God for answering their life long prayers for liberation and happiness. "Papa?"

"Yeah, Ma," the grandfather said, wiping his eyes.

"The Lawd was right in namin' our baby Joy. She done been just that, ain't she?"

He gripped her tight, smelling the lye and bleach in the sheets which they lay upon. "Sho' has been Ma. God done blessed us fo' sho'."

Sarah sat on the leather upholstered antler chair, watching her little boy run around in a circle before the fireplace. "'Bout five more minutes, Lawd." The boy dropped to the floor. Three minutes. Sarah laughed and left her chair. She knew his little tail was sleepy. The boy was stubborn, just like his father, Teddy. Sarah grimaced but suppressed her negative thoughts.

Taking the fleece throw draped across the back of the couch where Teddy and Missy slept, Sarah shook it out and then placed it over her sleeping little boy. He whimpered, the last vestiges of his soul resisting rest. "You'se out like a light, boy. Doncha try and fight it." Toussaint surrendered his will upon the bear skin rug before the fireplace, sound asleep.

Sarah considered her family asleep before her. The Good Lord had blessed them! What slaves traveled around the world on the wind of God, helping others escape bondage? She praised and thank the Lord.

Too excited to sleep, she went to the armoire and selected a raccoon coat with a matching hat. Sarah found it difficult to adjust to the frigid temperatures of the North. After ensuring she'd button the coat up to her chin, she pulled her fur cap down snug on her head. Feeling inside the warm pockets, she found what she desired. Fur mittens! She pulled them on.

Fully covered, Sarah stepped outside the lodge, closed the door behind her and trudged through the plowed compound. Coming to a secluded path, she turned, her booted feet sinking into the fresh snow. The walk proved strenuous. With each step, she pulled her feet out of the deep snow. She had a vision of webbed feet. Snow shoes! She should have put on snow shoes. Too late to turn back, she continued along the path.

Sarah walked a mile down a crystallized, snow encrusted path. The fine ice crunched beneath her booted feet like the fragments of broken crystal tumblers on the floor of Augustus' study. Her flesh tingling from the arctic breeze which cocooned her, Sarah came to a bench in the clearing. Someone had plowed a circular path around the outer edge of the area. The snow must have been twelve feet high within the clearing's center. The area must have been a garden in the summer months. In the center of the clearing, she spotted stone breaching the top of the snow. A fountain?

She couldn't understand how folks could live in the freezing cold. Yet it was freedom, so she figured folks managed. Brushing the snow away from the bench with her fur mitten hands, she sat in the chill of the night. Sarah gazed upon the stars of heaven. A half-moon hung low in the sky. She lit her pipe and slouched a bit, relaxing.

After a time, Les materialized before her. "Hey gal," he said and sat beside her. She hadn't realized he could move through time and space as she did. She exhaled and laughed a little. He was her big brother. Why shouldn't he be able to do so? They had the same Mammy and Pappy.

Les shook his head, listening to her. Why did she always underestimate him? Sarah had always been their father's favorite.

"I'se always cherished you. Don't that mean nuthin'?"

Les studied the bright half-moon in the sky. Change was coming, but he couldn't figure out when. Traveling upon a moon beam ricocheting down to the other side of the Earth, he saw the man he admired and smiled. "How's our brother, Claude?"

Sarah tapped out her pipe on the side of the bench, replacing it within her apron pocket hidden beneath her coat. She grunted in disgust. "I'se don't know him."

Les said nothing, admiring the half-moon still in view. It would soon drift out of view, moving on to bless unknown locales with its majesty. "You may not know him, but Toussaint will. He'll bring up your son, training him in his profession. Toussaint will bless God and men."

Les picked up a stick, submerged in the snow. He dug it into the frozen snow on the bench where they sat, dislodging the glacier from the space between him and Sarah. "You'se remembers him, Sarah. He was 'round on La Pivoine 'fore you'se left." Sarah held her silence, focusing on the moon. "Claude is a mortician now, in Paris."

"Paris?"

"Yes." Les threw down the stick. Piercing her spirit through her eyes, he could see she did know Claude. "You'se done been to Paris, ain't you?" She said nothing. Gazing into the Spirit, he could see Sarah materialize within Claude's parlor. She lit her pipe and faced him. She'd uttered the word 'brother' and then dematerialized into the atmosphere.

Sarah retrieved her pipe and tried to light it again. Spotting the spent tobacco in the snow, she remembered she'd finished. She felt her breast, but the tobacco pouch wasn't there. She'd left it at the house in Louisiana. "Damn." Sarah sighed. She couldn't lie to her brother. The Holy Spirit wouldn't allow her to do so. "I'se suppose you'se right."

Les nodded. "I am." He bent over and scooped up a handful of snow and made a ball. He pitched it. It soared upward, until neither of them could see it any longer. "You're gonna have to let Toussaint go with Papa for a time, but not for a time yet to come." He watched Sarah's eyes fill with tears. "Toussaint needs to gits his learnin'."

Sarah nodded, suppressing her guilt. She'd had a dream a few weeks before, which revealed her boy as a grown man in a fine suit. Filled with defiance and hoping for a different outcome, she wiped away her sorrow from her eyes. She wanted to keep her boy near and raise him up proper. But alas, she knew his father would take him. It couldn't be avoided.

She wished she'd remembered her tobacco pouch before leaving Louisiana. Les had always been a goodie-goodie, never indulging in tobacco. He craved meats and hardy foods instead. Considering how he ate, he should've been as big as a bull.

"I'se gits my exercise and stays in good shape."

Sarah said nothing, nicotine deprived and irritable. Les kissed her on the forehead and disappeared.

It began to snow.

Sarah arose from the bench and returned to Les' home. She awoke her family and gathered the sleep laden group against their will. They all joined hands and left.

Teddy sat up in bed, yawned and coughed. The air was thick and heavy with heat and humidity. He remembered. "Why didn't we stay?" He remembered touring Les' barn and admiring his grand stallions. Les thrived in freedom. In the dream of an alternate reality, he'd been a free man.

Sarah awoke and sat up on the hay stuffed mattress. Teddy needed to re-stuff it. He'd been saying for a month he would do it.

Angst radiated from him. She placed her hand upon his. It was true. He doubted if their journey had been real. "It was real, baby." To prove it, Sarah extracted a nearly melted icicle from beneath the covers and placed it in Teddy's hand.

The sliver of ice melted in his hand, wetting the bed. Teddy wept, his dreams melting away with the icicle. "And to answer your question, we'se couldn't stay there 'cause we'se got our work to do here."

Sarah left the bed and built the fire. Extracting a match

from the cast iron box on the wall, she lit it. Getting down on her hands and knees, she blew into the kindling until it caught fire. Teddy still hadn't fixed the bellows. She'd acquired the ancient vessel from one of her refugees who'd liberated it from their former master as repayment for their years of unpaid labor.

Once the flames raged in the fireplace, Sarah hung a pot of water on the cast iron tripod. After fifteen minutes, the water boiled. "Water's hot. Go on and gits washed up," she said to Teddy. After he finished, she awoke the children and bathed them in preparation for the day which lay before them all.

Chapter 3

La Rose Plantation, St. Helena Parish. August 31, 1963.

Two birds raised a raucous in the tree's mid-branches. Without warning, the creatures vacated the live oak tree. Julian shielded himself, in anticipation of a barrage of droppings as they flew over him, but the creatures held their fire.

Julian jumped up from his seat. "Let's go back to the house, Grandmère."

Lela nodded, allowing him to lead her away.

Leaving the garden, Julian became disoriented. He couldn't find the shortcut he'd taken earlier. Turning right and then walking southwest along the allée, he ran into a dead end. "I know I came this way earlier, Grandmère." Lela said nothing. The couple searched for another way out. Finding it, Julian and his grandmère walked the path for one-half mile. Julian felt relieved when he spotted the fountain in the distance.

Reaching the fountain, he gaped at the angel amid the

bathing women. The statue sported a sinister, slimy grin. He'd hoped his grandmère hadn't noticed the statue's enormous penis, but he figured she'd seen it many times before. Julian blinked and found the stone angel leering at the bathing maidens in loving (rather lusting) admiration, once more. "Ass," Julian said.

"What did you say, darling?"

"Nothing, Grandmère." After another forty-five minutes, the pair arrived at the grand terrace. Julian extended his hand, inviting his grandmère to sit upon the sofa. She sat, shivering. Julian stepped inside one of the open French doors. "Suzette!"

A few moments later, Nanette appeared. "Miss Suzette's upstairs. Can I'se help you wit' sumpthin'?"

The urge to say something offensive surged within him, but this time Julian caught himself. He couldn't understand why he hated her. He inhaled deep and suppressed his disgust for the young woman. "Tell her to bring Grandmère's wrap." Julian watched her disappear into the darkness of the mansion.

A few moments later, Nanette returned. "I'se cain't find her, Mis'sur."

Julian's burrowing stare turned to flint. "Try harder." Nanette hurried away, just averting a run. Julian gave chase and caught her by the arm. He should fire her. She served no purpose in the mansion. "Can't you do something as simple as finding Suzette? Her old ass can't move fast. You should check the closets. She may be hanging upside down in one of them to avoid the sunlight."

"Don't talk about Miss Sue like that," Nanette said.

Unbelievable. Now Nanette defended Suzette. Were they all members of the same coven? "Watch your mouth. You don't tell me what to do. I'll send you back to your shack in Mississippi to pick cotton," Julian said.

Nanette stood before him, mortified. Julian's blood chilled in his veins and shivers radiated throughout his body.

"Adjust your tone," Suzette told him with a snarl, appearing from nowhere. "You are not her master. You do not possess slaves here. You will address Nanette with respect." Suzette spat at his feet. "You cannot send her to *le magasin*, let alone to Mississippi, Monsieur."

Fear raptured Julian's soul. Suzette had turned 'kissed by the Grim Reaper' white with rage. Guilt descended upon him. He couldn't understand his need to degrade and berate Nanette. Yet, he couldn't apologize. "You may go, Nanette," Julian said. She raced away, covering her face.

With an abrupt turn, Julian set out for the terrace, but Suzette grabbed his wrist before he could escape. "What is your problem, mon fils? Everyone here loves you, but you behave as an ass. Why is that?"

"Maybe it's just who I am."

Suzette considered his words. "You are correct. You are an ass. But listen when I tell you, your grandmère isn't the only one you should fear. Continue on your current path, and I may disobey my mistress for the first time in decades." Suzette tightened her grip on his wrist. She could see the boy suppress his urge to cry out. "Like your great-great-grand-père, I enjoy snatching out tongues too." She released him.

Julian hurried from the salon and returned to the terrace. He sat beside his grandmère, rubbing his bruised wrist. He pulled down the cuff of his sleeve to conceal it. "Julian, what's wrong with you?"

He picked up the crystal goblet on the end table, misted by its cold contents. A wet ring remained on the glass table top in its wake. Taking a sip, Julian leaned back on the sofa and inhaled deep. "Nothing."

Lela searched the Spirit, but it was veiled. She let it go. A short time later, Suzette exited the mansion and walked across the grand terrace to where they sat. She wrapped the shawl around Lela's shoulders. "I'm fine," Lela said. "Why did you bring this to me?"

"Monsieur ordered Nanette to find me and bring it to you. He said you were cold and required your shawl."

Lela faced Julian who seemed to be distracted by something lingering in the morning glories, having just closed their blossoms for the afternoon. "Thank you," Lela said to her. Suzette frowned at Julian and returned indoors.

Lela let it go. She didn't have the energy to involve herself in every battle Julian incited. She had decided a couple of days before to pick her battles. Lela removed her hat and fanned herself. It was getting hot. Correction, it was already hot. "Let's go to the dining room," Lela suggested. "Lunch should be ready by now."

Julian watched Suzette bring out *croquet-madames* on a baroque, solid silver platter. A figure passing in the hallway caught Julian's attention. His grandmère's chef, Mario? He hadn't traveled with them to the plantation. Amazed, he watched as Mario directed the serving staff. Yet, he never heard him speak. Thinking back, Julian realized Mario always seemed present, but he'd never heard the chef speak.

Julian watched his great-grandmère clap her hands with glee, drooling as a servant placed two of the delicate sandwiches upon her bone china luncheon plate with baroque silver tongs. She grabbed a sandwich and took a hearty bite, a little of the egg yolk running from the corner of her mouth. *Such a lady.* However, with stealth quickness, she grabbed her napkin and removed the excess. *Little piggy.* It surprised him she didn't weigh a ton, considering how much she ate and drank.

Lela dabbed the corners of her mouth with her napkin after scarfing down both little sandwiches. Stretching across the table to the serving tray, she grabbed two more. "Why does my eating habits concern you, young man? I'm an old woman. I'm free to eat as I please," she said with a raised eyebrow. "Besides, as your mamère would say, 'I am fabulous as I am'."

Julian didn't reply, biting into his sandwich. It was unbelievably good. No wonder his grandmère had gobbled down several of them.

"I don't gobble," Lela said.

"You should eat in front of a mirror, and then you would know," Julian said. Once they finished their snack, Julian thought about something. "Grandmère?"

Lela sipped her Malbec. "Yes, Julian?"

"Are we Creole?"

"What?"

"Are we Creole?" He watched his grandmother stare at him in confusion, not understanding the inspiration behind his question. "While I attended Morehouse, my frat brothers would ask if I was Creole, after I told them I'd grown up in New Orleans. Heck, I didn't know! I'm not sure why I'm asking you this now," Julian said. His focus fell upon his empty luncheon plate, afraid he'd offended his 'there is no color, everyone is equal' grandmère in some way.

Lela reached across the table and placed her hand upon his. "It's fine to ask, Julian," Lela said. She leaned back in her chair, directing her attention to the ceiling's mural as she considered it all. "I'm not sure. I don't have a great deal of understanding regarding the Creole community," she said. A window opened to her in the Spirit.

She searched the past, seeking truth and revelation. Lela sighed, beholding all the Lord wished to reveal. "Well, I would say yes, as far as your father's side is concerned. Your grandparents, Antoine and Mary Philippe Chamberie, were Creole. So yes, you are." Lela considered the matter more. "Your ancestor is Jacques Chamberie. I believe he was French, but his family lived in Brussels, Belgium. They were bankers." Lela leaned forward and sipped her Malbec. "He is related to Jonathan Chamberie. How? I'm unsure."

Julian nodded, listening. "But aren't you Creole too?"

Lela shrugged. "I never considered myself as Creole. I'm French and Negro, or Ghanaian, as I later learned. I suppose some may judge me to be so." Lela studied her great-grandson. "Why do you ask?"

"I was just wondering," Julian said, taking a sip of water.

Lela nodded. The boy had cloaked his thoughts. He was learning. She concealed her pride in the growth of his supernatural abilities, after only a few days. "Does your identity or self-worth hinge on whether you're Creole?"

Julian sat his water glass on the table. "No, of course not," Julian said. "I just wanted to know."

Lela left the head of the table and walked over to where her great-grandson sat. She patted his cheek. "Don't allow racial elitism to define you."

Julian spat out his water. "What?"

"Don't allow people, well society, to define you or to put you into a box, to either elevate or discount you in accordance to your pedigree. It's a dangerous game." Lela poked him between his eyes just above his nose. "Allow the world to respect and fear you because of what lies within your spirit and soul, mon fils," she said, first pointing to his head and then his heart. "You're a savvy and intelligent man. Your soul is more lasting than your racial makeup. Remember that," Lela said, smiling at him.

Julian nodded and grabbed another sandwich from the platter. "Grandmère?"

Lela returned to the head of the table and sat. "Oui, mon cher?" Mario came in and cleared away the luncheon plates. The bussing staff followed him, removing the wine glasses. Julian snorted. Mario rarely bussed the table, always sending the staff to do so. He wondered why he'd left the kitchen? Maybe he wanted some daylight. Mario cast his blank, emotionless eyes on Julian and then frowned. Had he heard his thoughts? Mario lifted the tray stacked with dirty dishes and left without saying a word. Julian continued to wonder if he could talk. As long as the strange man didn't spit in his food, he didn't care.

"I assure you, Mario speaks. At least he talks to those worthy of engaging in conversation," Lela said.

Julian ignored her. Was she trying to say he wasn't worthy of conversation with the cook?

"Mario is a chef, not a cook. And yes, that is what I'm saying," Lela said. She could see the insult on Julian's face, causing her to burst into laughter. The servants set the table with tumblers and snifters to serve them stronger spirits. Once the server poured her drink, Lela nodded, thanking him.

"What was it with Uncle Toot?"

Lela took a sip of brandy from the snifter. "I'm not sure what you mean, darling."

Julian fiddled with the edge of the hem-stitched table cloth, attempting to sort out his concerns. "Uncle Toot was different, Grandmère. He seemed to know things he shouldn't." Julian shuddered, remembering him. "He had the ability to rape a soul with a glance, the same as you; however, he didn't try to hide his abilities." Julian caught her looking away. "Grandmère?"

Lela reached across the table and took her child's hand in hers. "Uncle Toot is different, well was." Julian said nothing for once, waiting for her to continue. "He's very much like his father."

"Teddy?" Julian waited for her to continue, not understanding. She sipped her wine. He thought about the book she'd written detailing everyone's genealogy. A glimmer of white light striking his peripheral vision caused Julian to glance over at the large, gold-gilded buffet against the wall. The book. He knew it hadn't been there before. No need for him to wonder where it had come from after life with his grandmère over the past few days.

Retrieving the book, he opened it and flipped through its pages as he returned to the table. He reached the section he sought: *La Famille de Bailey.* Above Toussaint's name were his parents.

"Teddy was his father."

Lela snorted. "Yes, Teddy raised him. However, he was not his father."

La Rose Plantation. St. Helena Parish. 1846.

AFTER A MORNING of gathering hay and restuffing the family's mattresses, Teddy moved on to his next chore, sweeping the porch. He'd tired of his wife nagging him. Sarah had told him he didn't do his chores around the house. He'd told her she didn't carry her weight all the time either; however, he couldn't think of anything in particular. She'd smiled at him, victorious.

He dug the broom into a corner of the porch. The broom had worn down; he needed to make a new one. While he swept, his thoughts drifted to his son. Teddy couldn't deny the boy was different. The child wasn't suited for life as a slave, that was for sure. Toussaint had a mind for money. He'd buried the family's fortune of fifty cents, along with the gold coin the 'nice man' had given Missy at Toussaint's ceremony to fix his privates when he was a baby. "There's my'se proof she forgets stuff too," Teddy said to himself, remembering Sarah hadn't found a piggy bank for Missy. He couldn't wait to remind Sarah about her lapse in memory.

Once Toussaint had buried the coins, he'd told him, "Papa, this ain't nuthin' compared to what God got set up for us." Teddy wanted to remind his son they were slaves and didn't own anything, but he held his tongue. The boy knew more than him.

The smell of meat cooking on the hearth drifted out to the porch. He rubbed his stomach. His wife's skills in the kitchen never ceased to amaze him.

The night before, on Saturday evening, he'd enjoyed an evening of fun with Linus, the new butcher and smoke house keeper for the plantation. Linus' papa had died around the last harvest, so the overseer had appointed him to the position.

Arriving before the other fellas, Linus took Teddy into the smokehouse. He shaved off a sliver of ham he was prepping for Master Augustus' Sunday dinner. Teddy popped it into his mouth. "Lawd! This sho' is good!" The slice of heaven melted in his mouth. Linus' daddy sure had taught him well. He'd heard his smoked goods were the best in the parish. The rumors were true.

"It's the Lawd's doin', not mine," Linus muttered in a grunt, a little embarrassed by Teddy's praise. He wrapped the meat in burlap and hung it by the door. Sammie would pick it up early Sunday morning.

That night, they sat out back of the smokehouse with Tiny the Cooker. He cooked moonshine, made wine and beer, and distilled other spirits for the plantation. Master Augustus sold the surplus to the townsfolks.

Tiny always skimmed some off the top to sell or trade with the slaves. He kept a few jugs for his own personal use, two of which he'd brought to the gathering. "Ya'll gotta 'scuse this here brandy. It's still a teenchy bit green, but it's good." The men didn't care, downing the brandy in two hours.

Fred the Weaver fell off his stool. "Lawd, Aggie gonna cuss me out good," he said, sprawled out spread eagle in the dirt. All the men laughed, knowing his wife would do just that. She'd cussed him out for lesser offenses. But being drunk? She would have a fit. The next morning, he would be expected to go to Sunday meeting. They all knew she would give him a tongue lashing for smelling like a drunk in the presence of the preacher.

"Yup, you'se gonna catch some hell for this here shit, Fred," Teddy said. All the men whooped and hollered. Teddy lit his pipe and leaned back on the three-legged cane back chair. He'd almost fallen over, but kept his balance. He started thinking about the ham Tiny had allowed him to sample earlier. "Linus, I'se give you'se two bits for half that ham you'se done let me taste earlier."

All the men laughed and ridiculed him. "Man, you'se ain't got one penny let alone two bits," Linus said.

"If's I'se give it to you, you'se gonna give me half the ham?"

"Brother, I'se gives you the whole thang."

"He's bullshittin'," Tiny said. He poured another round. All the men passed out, except for Linus and Teddy. Linus wavered on his chair.

"My'se offer stands, Linus. You'se want the two bits for the ham?"

Linus peered into his drink, watching it whirlpool to the bottom of the cup. Somehow, he refocused on Teddy. He believed he would fall off his chair. "I'se done told you I'se give you the whole ham."

Teddy closed his eyes. "Take your pointer finger and dig down below your right foot as far as you'se can digs."

Steadying himself, Linus leaned over and dug his finger down into the hard earth. "Ain't nuthin'…" Before he could finish his statement, he hit something. Dropping from the chair onto his hands and knees, he dug into the soil and extracted a silver coin with a woman's head on it. He turned it over betwixt his fingers and found a bird with its wings spread. "Good Lawd! I'se ain't never seent this much money!"

Teddy stood from his chair and stumbled toward Linus. "It's yours." He patted his friend on his back.

Linus managed to stand and went to the smokehouse. He returned a few minutes later, filled with humility. He extended his arm with a ham swinging from it. "Here, Teddy. Take the whole thang."

Teddy accepted the ham from his friend and slung it over his shoulder. "Whatcha gonna tell the overseer? What 'bout Massa's dinner?"

Linus wiped a tear from his eye. "I'se figures that out later."

After breakfast, Teddy sat out on the porch of their cabin with his wife and son. He belched. "The Lawd's gonna git you for belchin' like a pig," Sarah said.

"I'se had to let go of the oink. Now I'se done."

Sarah waved him off, suppressing her laughter.

Folks hadn't lied about the quality of Linus' smoked meats. Sarah had only cooked a few slices of the salted meat, having simmered it in water first to release the excess salt. Then, she placed the meat in the cast iron skillet (which he'd found soaking in a tub outside the cookhouse a few years before) and fried it for a few minutes, making the edges crispy, but soft and tender on the inside. He'd even found some eggs to go with the meal. Sarah had rustled up some grits. God was good.

Once finished, Sarah returned the remainder of the ham to its burlap sleeve, wrapping it with care. She then placed it in a bucket. She went outside and buried the ham out back somewhere. Their family would eat good on Sundays for months to come.

His stomach full, Teddy left his chair and grabbed his fishing rod from the corner of the porch. Relishing the anticipation of a day of solitude, reflection and prayer, Teddy skipped down the two steps leading from their cabin. He noticed Toussaint sitting on the porch near his mother stacking twigs, building a structure of some sort. He took pity on his son. "You'se wanna go fishin' wit' me, boy?"

Little Toussaint's eyes lit up. "Yes, Papa!" Toussaint jumped up from where he sat and grabbed his junior cane pole from the corner of the porch. He shot off the porch and ran down the little road. Teddy winked at his wife sitting in her rocking chair, smoking her corn cob pipe. She blushed and looked away. He returned to the porch and kissed her hand. She kissed him on the cheek, blessing him.

Teddy left the shade of the porch and walked down the road. Toussaint had run several yards ahead. "Slow down, boy," he said, but the child didn't seem to hear him. Teddy laughed and wagged his head. The boy would be alright.

As he passed his neighbors, Teddy tipped his hole ridden straw hat. He passed Miss Bits house. She sat on the porch, rocking her straight back cane chair. He couldn't figure out how she did it without tipping over. The old lady grinned at him, flaring her tattered skirts into a half curtsy from where she sat.

Old flirty. She'd been trying to get with him for years. A few years back, he had to be upfront with her. He'd told her Sarah was his wife. He could tell he'd hurt her feelings, but she nodded, accepting his testimony. She'd seemed to respect him more, because he'd told her the truth. He felt a little sorry for her. Back then, he'd prayed she'd find a love. But who? There was no one on the plantation available to love her, at least not out in the open.

Once he reached the river, Teddy searched for the crates he'd hidden in the brush. "They'se should be 'round here,' he said, pushing back the vegetation. "Here they is." The cat tails had grown up between the wooden planks of the crates. With a bit of work, he liberated the crates from the mighty plants. Teddy carried them to the river's edge and sat them in the mud.

Unable to wait for his father to arrive, Toussaint had already cast his line into the water. Teddy sat on a crate, releasing his cares and burdens. He cast out his line.

Toussaint, following the example of his father, sat on the smaller crate beside his father. His father crossed his legs. Toussaint crossed his legs. Teddy rested his elbow on his knee, to better support the weight of the pole. Toussaint followed suit. Teddy removed his hat, scratched his head, and then slapped it back on his head. Toussaint found his head itched too, so he removed his hat, scratched his head, and then slammed the hat back on his head, nearly crushing it. Teddy smiled. He couldn't do anything without the boy mimicking him. He scanned the water, searching for ripples from fish breaking the surface.

The morning sun light shined on the river, making it sparkle. Toussaint loved the yellow light of the sunrise. It made the gray river seem blue. His father lit a cigar. He wondered where he'd found it. Toussaint spotted another one in father's fishing basket. He reached for it.

"You'se still too young, boy."

Toussaint bowed his head, ashamed.

Teddy offered an alternative. "Why doncha take you'se a swig from the jar?"

Toussaint eyes lighted. His father hadn't offered to let him drink from the jar before. Filled with reverence, he removed the jar from the fishing basket. Screwing off the top, Toussaint took a little swig. The white clear liquid burned his lips. How did folks drink such a concoction? However, he held his peace, not wishing to appear as a child before his father.

He took another swig and then replaced the jar in his father's fishing basket. The sun rising in the morning sky grew hot, making Toussaint tired. He needed water. Toussaint wished to lie down on the shore. He took off his hat. Why was it so hot?

Teddy snickered to himself but said nothing, taking in the beauty of the Tangipahoa River in the morning sun. God had blessed him, even in bondage. What slave went fishing with his son every Sunday morning? He'd never been studded out, fathering new chattel for his master. He'd never been sold off, like many of his friends and the sons of his friends.

He couldn't understand why he and his family enjoyed such favor from Master Augustus. The master had never taken his little Missy. Teddy couldn't think of one bleeding virgin on the plantation Augustus hadn't violated, but he'd never taken his Missy. He praised God for his goodness.

Teddy rubbed Toussaint's knobby head. He'd just shaved it that morning before church. "You'se sleep boy?"

Toussaint sat up straight on his crate. "Naw, suh."

Teddy hid his amusement. Yes, he was blessed.

"What you laughin' 'bout, Papa?"

Teddy patted him on the shoulder. "Nuthin' boy."

Both of their lines became taunt. "Look Papa, we'se both got sumpthin' on the line!"

Teddy helped Toussaint draw in his catch, and then he drew in his own. "I'se reckons you'se right, boy."

Chapter 4

La Rose Plantation, St. Helena Parish. June, 1846.

Missy submerged the white bed sheet into the hot water and lye. Toussaint sat in the dirt, watching her work. Why did she have to work? She was only about five years older than him. Toussaint imagined his sister going to school and learning how to sew. Well, she knew how to sew. Maybe she could learn something else.

Yet, she didn't launder items for their family, but for the evil man who lived in the big house. Why did everyone work for him?

"He owns us."

"Whatcha means by that?"

"Just what I'se said." Missy removed the sheet from the cast iron cauldron. She rinsed it in a large galvanized wash pan. With much effort, Missy wrung out the sheet and hung it on the line behind her. "He owns everything on this here land, as far as your eye can see. We'se his property, whether we'se likes it or not."

Toussaint dug out a rock embedded in the soil. He pitched it out to the road. "Not me," Toussaint said. "Mama told me so."

Missy placed another sheet in the pot. Taking the bellows, she stoked the fire beneath the five-foot-tall cast iron pot. The coals glowed red, receiving the air the blower offered. "Then I'se guess it's so."

Sarah materialized a few feet away from her children. She walked over to them. "Get up outta the dirt, boy."

Toussaint hopped to his feet. "Maman!" He ran to her, clutching his mother's legs through her old, worn out skirt. She patted his head and then took his hand, walking a bit further over to where her daughter toiled.

Sarah concealed her pride in her daughter's work and her passion for it. What if their family had been free? Based on the quality of her work, Sarah had no doubts Missy could have her own laundry business. With a discerning eye, Sarah inspected the sheets Missy had laundered. "That's good. Real good, gal."

Missy beamed with pride. "Merci, Maman. I'se did them likes you'se learns me to."

Sarah nodded. She pointed at a minor stain Missy had missed. Missy nodded and submerged the section of the sheet into the pot of steaming lye water. After waiting a few moments, she extracted the textile. Filled with zeal to produce a superior product, Missy scrubbed the sheet with the brush on top her hand, contorted into a painful fist, scarred and cracked from two years of working with hot water and lye. Five minutes later, she presented the sheet to her mother, the spot now gone. Sarah smiled and kissed her child. "You'se done did good, chile," Sarah said.

Missy inserted the towels into the pot and stirred it with the long wooden paddle, encouraging the items to release the dirt trapped within its fibers. Sarah took her son's hand and led him away, leaving her daughter to her work.

Sarah found Toussaint to be bright, considering he was only five years old. He didn't possess the mental acuity, rather submissiveness, for plantation life. Although his father worked in Master Augustus' fields and gardens, Sarah understood her son couldn't do so for very long. He possessed an analytical and calculating mind. Sarah intended to nurture the gift God had given him.

Teddy had cultivated the boy's manual skills, teaching him the finer art of landscaping. Teddy worked as one of La Rose's gardeners, having graduated from the fields for a time. However, the overseer had ordered Teddy to return to the fields.

Teddy had begun to teach the boy how to put down the dead. With the overflow of victims from the Shed, Augustus could no longer dispose of them all in the remote areas of the Tangipahoa River.

In fact, St. Helena Parish had become known for its fat buzzards and crows. Folks joked the birds were so fat from feasting off Augustus' murders, they couldn't fly more than ten feet off the ground. They said the scavengers, birds and gators alike, sat on the banks of the river waiting to feed on the bodies the Sheddahs tossed out there. Some folks said the predators had grown lazy and no longer prowled for an-imal carcasses, for Augustus had ruined them with human flesh.

Slave folks forbade their children from playing in re-mote areas near the river. The stench was incredible. The river bank was littered with bleached white bones and skulls, and crawling with all types of critters and insects waiting to gorge themselves on the Shed's harvest.

A few months before, St. Helena's sheriff sent a team of deputies out to the river's edge to investigate Augustus' ac-tivities there, due to the soaring number of folks turning up missing around the parish. What they found out there gave some of the men nightmares for weeks. Instead of arresting Augustus for the murders, the sheriff had told Augustus, "Clean that shit up out yonder by the river." That's when Augustus commissioned Teddy to go out to the river every week and recover whatever he may find, despite the corpse's state of decomposition.

It amazed Sarah the law never came after her evil brother. But then she figured when one man's enormous fortune funded not only the local bank, but several banks in New Orleans, the Floridian parishes, the State of Louisiana Treasury, and God only knew where else, folks weren't interested in putting him away for a few White trash murders. The authorities always looked the other way, demanding a small payment in gold from the vaults her brother maintained on the plantation. She'd visited his vaults a few times, without her brother's knowledge, of course. However, she knew the true keeper of the vaults. It wasn't Augustus, but the Lord.

At first, the recovery and burial of the corpses traumatized Toussaint. The child would awake screaming in the fourth watch of the night, telling her he was covered in eyeballs or entrails. Once, he'd awaken and told her he'd dreamed he had a knapsack full of arms, their bloody, scarred hands grasping at his throat.

Sarah would complain to Teddy, telling him not to take Toussaint anymore. Teddy would listen to her concerns. Once she finished pleading with him, Teddy would take her hand in his own and say, "I'se don't understand why the Lawd has me takin' that boy down there either, but I'se knows its makin' him strong." Sarah would say no more, holding her peace.

La Rose Plantation, St. Helena Parish. August, 1846.

TOUSSAINT WOKE UP. The journey had made him dizzy. He would close his eyes and then open them, feeling as if he'd been in an unsettled rest. The sensation tickled, like a chill.

He examined where they'd landed. It was a one room shack, containing a chair and a straw stuffed cotton sack mattress. A woman lay on the mattress with a babe at her breast.

With great effort, he floated, more so tumbled, down from his mother's back. He didn't remember having to jump down before. He remembered flying like the birds. Maybe he was too heavy now. Sitting on the floor, he waited for his mother to speak. Toussaint watched the dark-skinned Negro woman stir on her pallet.

Soon, the dark brown woman eyes fluttered, finding Sarah standing over her. She yelled. "Hush, chile 'fore somebody hears you," Sarah said.

Filled with fright, the girl looked back and forth between the two. "Who'se ya'll?"

"I'se here to help you. You'se wanted the Lawd to saves you, right?" The girl nodded. "Well he done answered your prayers. Git up off that mat and let's go 'fore somebody comes."

The girl jostled her baby. "I'se can't leave without Jam."

Sarah reached into her apron pocket and removed her pipe. "He ain't coming back. If you'se wait on him, you'se and your child gonna die in bondage." Sarah placed her corn cob pipe in her mouth. She struck a match on the bottom of her shoe, and then lit it. Sarah puffed long and slow, finally exhaling a cloud of smoke. "Whatcha wanna do? You'se wanna save you and yours?"

The girl wept, considering her nursing baby. What would become of the child if she didn't take a chance and seek out freedom? "I'se wanna save my baby."

Sarah nodded. She extended her hand to Toussaint. He tried to levitate and float to her back, but he couldn't fly anymore. He stood up and walked over to his mother.

Sarah felt bad for her son, but she would talk to him later. "C'mon gal," she said. "What's your name, child?"

"Yella."

Sarah stared at her in disbelief, but she didn't have time to question the dark brown girl on why she'd been name 'Yella'. She probably didn't know anyway.

Yella grimaced, raising herself up with her child in her arms. The baby was about eight days old.

Sarah relieved the new mother of her child, taking the infant in her arms. She smiled at the babe. "You'se ain't never gonna feel the whip." The baby opened his eyes for a moment. Stretching and wriggling, the child gurgled and then returned to his rest.

Sarah stretched her hand to the child's mother. "Take hold of me."

Having returned to the fields without the opportunity to heal after childbirth, she gathered her strength. She winced, the pain overcoming her. She felt blood escape her. Yella collapsed on Sarah, grasping her around the waist.

"Toot, grab on," Sarah said.

Hanging his head, Toussaint clutched his mother's leg.

Paradis, Quebec, Canada. August, 1846.

IN THE SAFETY of Les' home, Yella rested in the rocking chair. Sarah placed the child in her arms. At once, the baby stopped crying and fell asleep, at peace in his mother's embrace. Brushing aside a dreaded lock of hair which had escaped her kerchief, Sarah kissed the woman on her forehead. "Ya'll gonna be safe now," she said. Yella nodded, drifting off to sleep.

Les handed his servant a note. "Give this to Dr. Clairmont." The servant nodded and left.

"You'se sendin' for the doctor?"

Les felt Yella's forehead. "Yeah, I thank she got an infection. She has a fever." Closing his eyes, he examined her internally. "Yup, she does. And a bad one too. I guess that's why the Lawd sent you to fetch her. He still has plans for her. She wouldda died on that place where she was workin'."

Sarah consulted the Spirit. "You'se right, Les. The overseer didn't care if she lived or died."

Les nodded. He noticed Toussaint sitting by the fireplace. "He done calmed down a heap since he was last here."

Sarah guided Les to the far side of the room. "He's upset. He cain't fly no more."

Les heart filled with sadness. "Yeah, I reckon he is. I know I would be. I wonder why?"

Sarah wiped away her tears. "I'se guess the Lawd figured he don't need it."

"Guess so." Les hugged his sister. He wanted her and Toussaint to say awhile, but he knew they couldn't.

"You'se right, brother. Too much goin' on right now."

He patted her hand. "I'se knows it. Maybe next time you'se can stay awhile. Bring Teddy and Missy too."

Sarah nodded. She didn't want to leave, but she didn't have a choice. "C'mon, Toot," Sarah said. "I'se see ya'll in a while. Aw'rite, Les?"

Les tipped his hat to her.

Toussaint raced from his favorite place on the floor near the fireplace and grabbed his mother's hand. He closed his eyes, bracing himself for transit. His body tingled, a current raced through him. This time he felt like a ball of mud tossed into the river. He came apart, into a hundred pieces. Then, someone scooped him out the river, and formed him into a ball of mud again.

Toussaint opened his eyes. They'd landed in the square of La Rose's Slave Quarter. He turned his gaze to the ground.

"What is it, boy?"

Toussaint looked up at his mother. "I'se can't fly no more, Maman."

Sarah stooped down. "Why you'se reckon that is?" Toussaint shrugged his shoulders. "I'se tell you why. You'se done outgrown it. You'se don't need it no more."

Toussaint wiped away his tears. "You'se and *Oncle* Les can still fly and ya'll old."

"Old?" Sarah laughed and then let it go. "Yessuh, we'se can still fly. We'se gotta save folks from bondage. We cain't walk up to folks and lead them out. So, the Lawd lets us fly."

"I'se wanna save folks too, Maman!"

Sarah kissed her child. "And you'se will. But the Lawd wants you'se to do it diff'rent. You'se okay wit' that?" Toussaint nodded. "Good. Trust God." She stared into her son's eyes. "What else troublin' Maman's baby?"

Toussaint gritted his teeth and balled his fists. "Maman, why don't we leave this here place and lives wit' Oncle Les?"

Sarah licked her finger and wiped the sleep from his eyes. She then smoothed down his eyebrows with more spit.

Toussaint squirmed, but she didn't care. He was her baby. She could cover him with spit if she so desired. "'Cause the holy one is here. We'se hafta stay here wit' her."

Toussaint nodded, understanding his mother's words. He could feel the presence of one so holy, God wept when she wasn't in his presence. Someone caught his eye. "Who'se that?"

At that moment, a woman with child walked through the square at the breaking of dawn, headed for the smoke house. She wasn't showing, but Toussaint could see the child in her belly. A short time later, she left with a ham slung over her shoulder. Toussaint couldn't take his eyes off her. "Tante Sammie!"

Sarah bent over and whispered into her son's ear, "You'se her child's protector and guardian. You'se guard the Lord's Rose." Toussaint searched his mother's eyes, seeking understanding. "We'se cain't leave 'til she does, baby. God Most High done anointed you to watch over her." Sarah kissed him. "He wants you'se to walk wit' her. You might spook Tante Sammie's baby ifs you can fly."

Toussaint smiled the biggest smile Sarah had ever seen. "Yes, Maman!"

You're good, Les said to her in the Spirit.

Sarah led Toussaint home and put him in bed.

Chapter 5

La Rose Plantation, St. Helena Parish. August 31, 1963.

Julian stood from the table and stretched. His lethargic body had stiffened from sitting at the table for hours while drinking too much scotch. Suzette entered the dining room, pretending to order the buffet. She left, throwing him a dirty look as she passed him. Julian had tired of the witchy woman, always lurking around his grandmother. "What about the gazebo, Grandmère? Can we go there?"

Lela considered the alternative. The structure was in a cool area on the northern side of the gardens. She could endure the heat for a few hours. "Alright."

Julian took his grandmère by the arm and led her outside to the terrace. The two crossed the lawn to the luxurious, screened in structure. It had to be as old as the house. Painted all white, the pillars, which supported the pagoda style roof, had been carved into majestic warrior angels battling dragons. The lattice work amazed him. It reminded him of a gazebo he'd seen as a child in either China or Japan. He couldn't remember where, with any certainty. His parents had taken him everywhere.

Leading her within, Julian found a small fan plugged in, circulating the hot, humid air. Who'd wired the gazebo for electricity?

"Toussaint updated the gazebo in the 1940's while your Aunt Leelee lived with us. She'd come to the States to escape the war in Europe." Maybe she'd already mentioned her stay to Julian. The boy seemed irritated. That wasn't it. She'd heard his thoughts and had responded to them. Oh well, to all of it.

Lela sat in the plush chair at the white wrought iron table, adorned with cupids with their bows drawn, taking cover in the rose vines, spindling up the table legs.

Her heart filled with joy, recalling some of the happiest days of her life when her old friend had lived with her after so many decades of separation. Julian sat behind her on the settee, crossing his legs. Lela twisted in the chair, so she could smile at her great-grandson. "In fact, darling, Toussaint completed several upgrades on the plantation."

"I never considered him as handy."

She couldn't understand the boy's animosity toward his uncle. "I never said he did it himself. He contracted out the work."

"Figures." Noticing the peaches on the table, Julian

grabbed one and bit into it. The nectar was too sweet, intoxicating him. The perfume of the fruit relaxed him, causing him to doze a bit. He resisted the urge to sleep. He thought of Jannette.

"Why do you dislike your uncle?"

Julian indulged another bite of the succulent peach. Had he ever enjoyed a peach so sweet? "I like him, Grandmère. Why would you say that?"

Lela said nothing.

He bit into the peach. He had to admit he did hold a latent disdain for Toussaint, but not always. Julian had only begun to despise the man once he left New Orleans. "He sent me away."

"What?"

Julian twisted his face trying to understand the unfounded belief. "Grandmère, I can't explain it. I always believed he was instrumental in me leaving New Orleans. I didn't want to go." Julian's throat knotted with emotion. "He always wants to send me away." Why would he think such a thing? He tossed the peach pit into the waste can. "This is foolish."

Lela arose from her place at the table and sat with Julian on the settee. She extended her arm to her child. He placed his head upon her bosom, ingesting the perfume of roses. Tears coursed down his face and came to rest upon his shirt, giving it a polka dot appearance.

Lela kissed her great-grandson's brow and held him tight. There was so much he didn't understand. Lela hadn't believed Julian remembered the circumstances surrounding his departure. "Darling, Toussaint was a complicated man. He could make hard decisions. You may not understand this about him, but I wish to explain it to you, if you like." Julian nodded. "It may take a bit of time, though."

"I have time, Grandmère."

Lela's hand glided down his back and patted his behind, as she had done when he was little. She could feel the tension leave his body. "Toussaint was a special man, as I've told you. With age, you will find it can take time for mortals to learn to manage the gifts God has blessed them with. The mind is a battlefield, attempting to manage the lies of Satan which are at war against the Word of God."

Lela scowled, thinking of those in the past who'd tried to destroy her. Leaves fell from the tree, cascading off the roof of the gazebo, and then sauntering down to the lawn. Julian didn't seem to notice them, but Lela did. Her temper had intensified in her old age.

"Toussaint had become an old man by the time he learned to manage his gifts and his temper. Yet, he could always 'see' and acted upon his sight. It may take most people their entire lives to trust their vision, but it came naturally to him." Lela throat became dry. A snifter of brandy appeared on the rattan end table next to the settee. "Thank you," she said.

"For what?" Julian sat up from her breast and scanned the gazebo. They were alone.

"Pardon, mon cher. I wasn't talking to you." She patted her great-grandson's knee. "Toussaint could be a difficult man. He didn't get along well with others. He never had the desire to do so, because he trusted no one straight off. With Toussaint, trust had to be earned." Lela tapped her finger against the arm of the cast iron sofa. "However, there was one he trusted. No matter what people may have said about him, Toussaint trusted him."

"Who was that?" Julian asked.

"Stank."

La Rose Plantation, St. Helena Parish. September, 1847.

FEAR, ANGER, AND desperation mingled with fate weren't hard to spot in the eyes of another. Nicka's eyes showcased the terror with clarity. Trader Jans grabbed the chain suspended from her spiked collar and padlocked it to the u-shaped bar inside the wagon. Nicka moaned, continuing to plead to Sarah with her eyes for help. The child had been gagged with an iron ball; yet, it hadn't subdued her tortured, muffled screams.

I'se gonna looks after your boy. Doncha worry, Sarah whispered to the child's soul. Lord, her child was only three months old. Nicka continued to weep and moan, causing her to clamp down on the iron ball in her mouth. Trickles of blood ran from the corners of her mouth.

God, why do you allow Augustus to live? Sarah figured the Lord had his reasons, but his wisdom didn't quell her anger. Besides, who was she to question the Most High?

Sarah smelled burning hair. She grabbed her locks cascading down from the left side of her head. Identifying the smoldering locks, she twisted the ends of dreaded hair betwixt her fingertips. She had to squelch her rage; otherwise, she'd be bald and Nicka would still be sold off.

Augustus had been drunk when it happened. Who became so drunk they don't know they're fucking their own flesh? At the same time, Sarah couldn't judge. She was no better. At least she hadn't been villainized and sold off like poor Nicka. The girl was only a baby.

Sarah had whispered to Augustus's mind to sell her to the same plantation in Mississippi where Sylvia had been sold. He'd listened, although she could see he believed the idea to have been his own. Sylvia would look after her. In fact, Sarah had already visited Sylvia once the baby had been born, to tell her to watch out for Nicka's arrival.

Tears continued to stream from Nicka's eyes and blood from her mouth. Nicka turned her attention from Sarah to the man standing over her in the wagon. Sarah followed her gaze.

Barachiel

Slumping over, Nicka slept. The spike from her collar stabbed her shoulder blade, but it didn't awake her.

"Giddy up." Trader Jans pulled away.

Barachiel took a seat beside Nicka on the wagon bed. He smiled at Sarah.

"Thank you," Sarah said to him without her voice, mouthing the words instead.

He tipped his hat to her. The wagon descended the hill and then onto the main road, taking the child away.

Sammie placed the little boy in the basket where Lela had once slept. These days, her little Lela traveled strapped to her back. Her little one was too busy to sit in the basket anymore. One day, Sammie had been taking the Dutch oven off the fire. She turned to find Lela had escaped her basket and had crawled across the table. Sammie almost dropped the hot pot on her foot, in her dash to catch Lela before she fell off the edge. She'd caught her just in time, too.

Sammie extended a green bean over her shoulder. A little hand grabbed it. She could feel her little girl's slobber on her neck. Giggles. She was still young and innocent enough to giggle. "Maman wants her baby to giggle for the rest of her days." Sammie shook her head, knowing her child wouldn't. Being a Negro slave girl in the South didn't afford many moments for giggling. But her baby could giggle for now. That's what counted.

Movement in the basket caught Sammie's eye. "Look, Lela. Somebody done woke up." Sammie sat her bowl of beans on the table and stood from the bench, leaning over the table to check on the child. He was awake and not crying. He had cried all morning. Sammie could do nothing to console him. "You'se seems peaceful e'nuff now."

"Cause his Mama's at peace."

Sometimes Sammie hated it when her sister appeared out of nowhere. Terror arose in her heart. "What? Did Augustus kill her?"

"Naw, your evil ass man was nowhere to be found. He had the overseer out there to supervise the transfer."

Sammie could never figure out if she loved or hated Augustus. She hated him for the most part these days. "Well, li'l Stanley settled down 'bout an hour ago," Sammie said.

"That's 'bout the time Nicka passed out in the wagon and Trader Jans took her away," Sarah said.

Stanley batted his little arms and legs. Without warning, Stanley stiffened his body. He then closed his eyes half way and grunted a bit, twisting his face up, tight. His small frame went lax.

Sarah and Sammie covered their noses. "Lawd have mercy! Boy, what you'se just do in there?" Sammie picked up a rag and fanned it about, in her feeble attempt the clear the air of the foul odor. Baby Lela twisted her face, her eyes fixed upon the baby in the basket.

Sarah held her breath, struggling to speak without ingesting the foul air. "Li'l ole stank tail," Sarah said, picking him up from the basket. Baby poop leaked everywhere. During her next excursion, she made a mental note to 'find' some cotton cloths she could use as diapers. "Well, you'se mine now. I'se guesses I'll be the one cleanin' you up, huh?" Sarah kissed the baby. It was nice to have another baby. Since Toussaint was six years old, he wasn't fun anymore. "Yup, guess I'll raise the devil's baby."

"Doncha call him that. He's Lela's daddy too."

Sarah snorted. "Then somebody needs to cut the devil's dick off, so he can stop redeemin' hisself wit' these li'l ole angels he keeps makin'. That motherfucka is overdue for hell."

Sammie waved Sarah off, shaking her head. Sarah walked out the back door with her little darling stinking up his basket and everything in its wake.

La Rose Plantation, St. Helena Parish. August, 1857.

HE RAN FASTER. He had to get home. He pushed himself even more. Stank crossed the lawn and ran up the stairs to the plantation house. He didn't have time to run around back. This news wouldn't wait.

Sitting in the butler's office, Lawrence turned from his whittling, glancing out into the Spirit. Stank. He sat the partially carved rose twining about a sword on the small table, shaking his head in disgust. Augustus had turned the ten-year-old boy into his little spy and handy man around the Shed. The other slaves had ostracized the child because they knew whatever Stank heard, the master heard.

Stank didn't only spy on the slaves. He proved gifted in gathering the secrets of the White folks in town. The men on the front porch of the general store took little notice of the boy, chatting freely about their romantic and business affairs. Bad things would always happen following one of Stank's reports.

Lawrence watched in the Spirit Stank running at top speed across the front lawn. The child had news about something; that was for sure. Hearing him knock, Lawrence left his butler's office and opened the front door.

"Is Massa Augustus home, suh?" The boy stood before him with his head bowed and his cap in his hand.

"He's in his li'berry, son." Lawrence watched the boy cross the foyer to the library. He stopped before the door and knocked. "Who is it?" Lawrence heard Augustus ask.

"Stank, suh."

"Get in here little Niggah and tell me what you found out.

La Rose Plantation, St. Helena Parish. September, 1857.

LELA BLUSHED. HE bowed to her and left. She smiled, sniffing the camellias. What Negro gave Camilla's to their intended? Lela clutched her flowers close, returning to the little kitchen house. She walked in, finding her Aunt Sarah sitting in the chair while her maman stirred some collard greens simmering on the hearth.

Aunt Sarah smiled at her. "Them some pretty flowers, gal," she said, removing her pipe from her pocket and lighting it. She took a couple of puffs, filling the house with smoke. "Where you'se git them?"

"I picked them from the garden."

Aunt Sarah placed her pipe on the table and walked over to Lela. She grabbed her by the arm, placing her face nose to nose with hers. "Gal, as long as you'se stay Nigrah, doncha lies to me ever again." Lela began to cry.

"Doncha chastise her like that, Sarah!" Sammie rushed over and clutched her weeping child in her arms. Horrified at the vibration she received from the child's flesh, she beseeched the Spirit for understanding. Sammie held her at arm's length, peering into her eyes. "Lela, tells your Aunt

Sarah the truth. Where you'se git them flowers?"

Lela wept harder. "My friend gave them to me."

Sarah frowned at her. "Give them to me." Lela handed her the flowers. "Go on back to your room over at your daddy's house." Lela ran out, leaving the door open.

Sammie returned to the collard greens. She stirred them with vigor, and then slowed, until she dropped the spoon in the pot. She reached in to grab it, scalding herself.

She cried out, hyperventilating. For some reason, she'd hoped for a different outcome for her daughter. Her eyes swollen, Sammie stared at the floor. "She's just a li'l gal. How? Augustus barely lets her outta his sight. Only time she is outta his sight is when she leaves the big house and comes here." Sammie's eyes skated about in the Spirit, searching for an answer. "Who is he? When did he gits the chance?" Sammie collapsed to the floor, wailing.

"Cain't nuthin' be done 'bout it now, Sammie. Ain't no sense in cryin' 'bout it."

Accepting the reality of Sarah's words, Sammie nodded, wiping her eyes with her apron.

Sarah stood from her chair and placed her pipe in her mouth. She hugged her sister and then left the cabin. Sammie returned to her cooking.

They were his eyes. Stank was sure of it. Yet, his eyes

didn't resemble human eyes, but those of a wicked god, hell bent on punishing his subjects for the smallest infraction.

Franky hadn't really done anything. How was he to know? But once Stank thought about it, how could Franky not have known? He had kissed her, and not just an innocent peck on the cheek. He'd kissed her like grown folks kissed each other. He'd watched him kiss her like she was his intended, out back near some bushes surrounding the Quarter. What had Lela been doing out there anyway? Observing the pure rage contorting Augustus' face, Franky must have done more than kiss her.

While eavesdropping on the older boys near the smokehouse, Stank had heard talk about what grown folks did to each other. Franky had been there with them, bragging about Lela. Franky hadn't known he was there, listening. He'd started talking about how the white Nigger girl was now his wife. Stank had ran to the mansion to tell Augustus. He now wished he'd kept the news to himself.

For months, Franky had talked to Toussaint and Stank about his love for the White Negro girl who lingered in the shadows of the mansion. Franky had told them that after leaving the fields, he would race to the mansion in hopes of watching Lela make her journey to the kitchen house. On the days she failed to appear, Franky had assumed she'd slept somewhere in the mansion. But maybe twice a week, he would spot her.

Stank wished he could plug his ears and poke out his eyes. Master Augustus seemed invigorated by his cries. Franky called out to Stank, asking him to help him, to reason with their Master. Stank had become the machine his father had trained him to be.

He turned the crank, rotating Franky one quarter to the right after Augustus had completed paring away a section of skin from his friend's body. Stank focused hard on an unseen point on the wall, compressing his sinuses and ear passages in hopes of drowning out the sound of his friend dying. He returned to the days he'd spent with Franky and Toussaint down by the Tangipahoa River, fishing and talking on Sundays after church.

"Forget you ever saw her, Franky," Toussaint would say. He and Franky were almost the same age. Maybe Franky had been born a couple of harvests before Toussaint. "She's too young."

"I'se ain't gonna do nuthin' to her," Franky would say. He would smile, thinking of Lela. "I'se gonna make her my wife once her womanhood comes on her. I'm gonna talk to Miss Sammie 'bout it then."

Yet, Franky couldn't wait. Stank could tell Miss Lela liked him too. But she was still a young girl. She didn't understand what love between men and women involved. He barely understood himself, even after Toussaint and Uncle Teddy had sat him down and explained 'relations' to him at least three times.

Stank winced, hearing Franky's agonizing screams. He couldn't understand why Franky hadn't died yet. Stank turned the crank, rotating Franky's beleaguered form once more. He'd become a breathing corpse.

Augustus eyes lit up with the fire of judgment. Then, his eyes changed. Stank figured he'd seen a ghost. With all the folks who'd been tortured to death in the room, Stank was sure a few haints lingered. Augustus turned pale white. His hand trembled, unable to hold the knife steady. No longer able to grasp it, the knife fell on Franky, severing an exposed muscle.

Stank watched as Augustus fixated on him. His face boiled crimson. Trembling, Augustus steadied himself. "It ain't the same thing," he said. "Your mama ain't got nothing to do with this. Stop laughing at me."

Stank hadn't said anything to him, not that he would. What was he talking about?

Augustus eyes opened, a spark flashing through them. Sadness enveloped his soul, but then it hardened to flint.

"Turn him."

Stank turned the crank, rotating Franky ninety degrees. Augustus dislodged the weapon from Franky's forearm.

"I convict you," Augustus said to Franky. When Augustus pared off his fingers, Franky didn't scream.

With his fishing pole in his hand, Stank sat in the mud of the Tangipahoa River. The water wasn't water, but the blood, muscles and sinews of his friend.

This is your fault boy

I know you saw him doing it

You could have prevented this

Augustus words clanged around in his head. It was his fault. Where were the Sheddah's last night? Why couldn't they have done it for Master Augustus?

You needed to learn a lesson

Stank raised himself out of the mud. He started walking to the shore's edge. A hand stopped him. "Whatcha doin' Stank?"

"Nuthin'."

Toussaint pushed his cousin down into the mud and plopped down next to him. "It ain't your fault. You know Massa is the devil." Toussaint hugged his cousin. "His sins ain't worth your life." Toussaint excavated a pebble from the river's bank and skipped it across the water. It lost momentum and sank, disappearing from sight. "Yup. Ain't nann one of Augustus' or Franky's sins worth your life."

Hot tears rolled down Stank's face. "I'se didn't know what to do, Toussaint. I'se could see she liked him too."

Toussaint swatted away a hungry mosquito. The persistent mosquito refused to abandon his quest to taste Toussaint. Falling into rhythm with the attacking insect, Toussaint clap his hands together, crushing the adversary within his palms. He wiped the remains of the insects on his overalls. "I'se reckon she did. He'd brought her candy from his father Napoleon's, well Massa Augustus' shop off the road. Not only did Franky take his daughter, but his money too. He stole from his shop." Toussaint picked up a stick and stuck it into the mud. "Don't steal from me," he said, a little above a whisper.

"Whatcha say?"

"Don't steal from me." Toussaint threw down the stick and peered into the sky. He watched the buzzards circle the river a mile downstream. He figured they were feasting on what remained of Franky, but he didn't tell Stank. "Franky stole from Massa. He would have just beaten him within an inch of his life for the candy he'd stole to court Miss Lela. That was nothing." Toussaint swallowed deep. "But he put his hands on his daughter." Toussaint drew in his fishing line and cast it out again. "She ain't but ten years old. He shouldn't have done it. He should've stuck to his original plan and asked Aunt Sammie for her hand once she was old enough. Aunt Sammie could have reasoned with Massa."

Stank nodded, trying to understand as much as a ten-year-old could. Then he realized something. "Wait— Miss Lela is his daughter?"

Toussaint couldn't believe he didn't know, but then he could see in the Spirit he didn't. "Don't go 'round talkin' 'bout that. Aw'rite?"

Stank stared at the water, confused and bewildered by all that had happened. Something moved through the brush toward river's shore. Miss Bits emerged, panicked. "Ya'll done seent my grandson Franky? I'se cain't find him nowhere." She wrung her hands. "Ya'll please, tell me? Did he run off or sumpthin'?"

Toussaint arose from the mud and took her hand. "Yessum, he has. He's free now."

La Rose Plantation, St. Helena Parish. August 31, 1963.

LELA REGARDED THE gardens through the screen of the gazebo. That's what happened? She never could remember when it had happened. "His name was Franky."

Julian blinked, incapable of comprehending the whole thing. "You liked Franky, Grandmère?"

Lela continued to absorb the Spirit until the window closed. She inhaled, and then exhaled hard. "I thought he was a nice man. He seemed like a nice man to me at the time, from what I can remember." Lela sucked in her breath, remembering his voice for the first time in 106 years. "He'd said, 'This is the way men show they like a lady. You'se a lady." Lela began to cry. "My God, I was only ten years old."

Rage swelled inside of Julian. "Grandmère, did he?"

Lela took a glimpse out into the Spirit, but it was veiled. "My Lord, I can't see it. I'm trying, but I just can't." Lela leaned back into the settee. "I just remember I wasn't allowed to go out for a long time, not even to Maman's."

Lela chewed her lip, thinking. "But I do remember this. One day, Father had allowed me to leave the house for the first time in months. I walked home to our kitchen house and stopped outside the door, hearing Maman and Aunt Sarah talking inside. Aunt Sarah said, "Augustus did the right thang. The man gots what he had comin' to him. I kissed Lela. She won't 'members nuthin' 'bout what he did to her.""

Julian sat in silence, grinding the heel of his shoe into the floor.

"My God, it must be true. I just remember having a boyfriend, but can't remember when. I could never figure out when. Until this very moment, I could never recall his name. I just knew I had a boyfriend of sorts." Lela picked up her hanky from the side table. "Maybe that's why I never had anyone until Jamie. Everyone has always attacked me. No one ever loved me until Jamie."

Julian patted his grandmother's hand. "It sounds like you had plenty of people around you who loved and protected you Grandmère. Although, they were all kind of sinister."

"I suppose you're right." Lela said, hugging her great-grandson.

La Rose Plantation, St. Helena Parish. September, 1857.

LATE AGAIN. MASTER Augustus had told him he'd better be sitting at his feet before the clock chimed that morning. As he ran up the back stairs and entered the kitchen, he heard the clock begin to chime the hour. "Mornin' Miss Sammie," he said racing through. He could hear her reply as he ran at top speed down the hall.

Stank stopped before the door of the library and inhaled deep. Maybe Master Augustus hadn't noticed he was late. Maybe he would be drunk. Maybe if he entered the room quiet like, he wouldn't notice him. The clock chimed again. He took the golden door knob in his hand, embossed with a flower of some sort, and turned it slowly, hoping the lock wouldn't click. He was unsuccessful.

"Get in here, boy."

Defeated, he opened the door and entered.

"You're late, boy," Augustus said without looking up from his newspaper.

Lela stared at him, her eyes filled with fear. Stank sat at Augustus' feet, cross-legged. He expected him to hit him, but nothing happened. He watched Lela as she sat by the fireplace, near the corner, working on her sewing and darning. Her face melted with sympathy for him. She returned to her work without saying a word.

After forty-five minutes, Augustus continued to read the

paper. He still hadn't assigned Stank his task for the day. Maybe he didn't have anything for him to do. Augustus always had someone he wished for Stank to spy on. Bored, Stank picked at the rug.

Augustus rolled the newspaper and hit him on the head. "Stop boy," Augustus said. He unfurled his paper and flipped back to the page he'd been reading. "Goddamn Niggers tear up everything."

Stank rubbed his head. Suppressing his humiliation, his sorrow laden eyes turned to Lela. *I'm sorry, Stank*, she said to him in his mind.

Since they couldn't speak to each other while in Augustus' presence, over the years, they'd somehow learned how to 'think' to each other. They didn't realize they were even doing it at first; it all happened by accident. One day, after Augustus had passed out for the morning, Stank told himself a funny joke in his mind, *I'm gonna take some ash from the fireplace and draw a pitchfork on his forehead.* Lela had laughed, covering her mouth so she wouldn't awake Augustus.

Then they both stared at one another in shock. He then thought, "*You can hear me?*" And then he heard a whisper in his mind, "*Yes.*" His eyes bugged out. She nodded with her mouth open, amazed by the phenomenon herself. Since then, they'd communicated in that fashion.

Stank wondered what Augustus was reading about in

the paper. He'd hardly touched his bourbon. Normally, Lela would have made two more for him by now. His shoulders slumped, realizing he wouldn't escape Augustus anytime soon.

The two children turned to the door, hearing a light tap, and then silence for a minute, and then another two quick taps. Lily had given Lela her signal. Augustus lowered his paper and listened. Hearing nothing, he reached for his glass and drank more bourbon. Augustus uncrossed his left leg from over his right. He raised the paper, blocking his field of vision. He crossed his right leg over the left and shifted in his chair, settling in.

Lela stood up and stretched, adjusting the bodice of her dress. She froze. Augustus' newspaper closed and then opened in a flash, turning the page. Stank assessed the amount of liquor remaining in Augustus' glass. Almost empty. He turned to Lela, finding her making her own assessment of the tumbler's contents. Soon, Augustus would need a refill, reminding him of his daughter's existence. She held her finger to her mouth and then snuck out, closing the door to the parlor without a sound. Stank wished he could sneak out with her.

The right side of his newspaper collapsed. Augustus reached for his drink. He lifted the tumbler to his lips and drank. The small sip which remained evaporated before it hit his lip. "Lela, get me a bourbon." Augustus looked up from his paper when he didn't hear the crystal stopper click against the lip of the decanter. "Where's that Nigger?"

Stank stood up. "She left, suh."

"Who told her little ass she could leave? You do it."

Damn. Lela always fixed his drinks. Stank walked over to the bar cart and picked up a decanter. He guessed it contained bourbon, since it was his master's drink of choice. He felt a breeze pass him. He turned to find a woman standing next to Augustus, placing a drink on the end table. Augustus picked up the tumbler and downed half of the beverage.

"You'se done killed Franky to cover your sins against Nicka."

Hearing the voice of the one he despised, Augustus scanned the room, but could not see her.

Stank saw her. Aunt Sarah bent over and whispered into Augustus' ear. He turned red.

"That Nigger deserved to die. He put his hands on my Nigger."

"Your daughter?"

Augustus thrashed about in his wing chair. "Stop saying that. She's my little Nigger and can't nobody touch her. I'm her master. Only I can judge and punish her."

Sarah conjured up the condemnation of heaven and hell in her eyes. "As was your li'l ole Nigger, Nicka. But you'se didn't mind makin' her your concubine. Why'se that, Augustus? Then you'se keeps her progeny wit' you to do your biddin'?"

Sarah grabbed him by his throat. "Although you'se seek to corrupt this child, he can never be like you. None of your chil'ren can ever be as evil and corrupt as you is." Sarah released her brother, leaving him gasping for air. "You'se gonna burn in hell for what you done did, Augustus."

Augustus swung out into the emptiness of the room, hoping to strike Sarah. His fist flailed in the air, failing to connect with anything either visible or invisible. "Me? You ain't no better than me, Niggah."

Stank saw Sarah materialize on the opposite side of his chair. Augustus' head jerked from left to right, searching for her.

Sarah considered his words. "You'se right. I'se ain't. But at least our daddy asked me first. I'se agreed."

Running to the fireplace, Augustus grabbed the poker. He smashed a table and two nearby vases. He punctured the couch. Stank ran and cowered in a corner of the room, avoiding him.

Coming to a portrait of his father, Emmanuel, he stopped. "This is your fault. You made me this way, and then you leave." Augustus slammed the poker into the heart of the man in the portrait and pulled downward, slashing it.

Before his eyes, the slash closed.

From his corner of the room, Stank watched the eyes of the portrait glare at Augustus. He heard the portrait speak.

"I will not curse my seed."

Stank gasped in horror. He watched his master. Augustus covered his ears. "You've already done it, Papa. You're the reason I am what I am." A shadow box opened in the Spirit. Stank saw an old White woman appear in the box with wispy hair, rocking back and forth in a bed before a window, patting her elbow, worn raw. "Maman," Augustus said, crying out. "It's you, Papa. I curse you and send you to hell where you belong. You did it. You started this!"

Augustus dropped the poker and inhaled deep. "Fuck you, fuck you, fuck you." He collapsed to the floor, exhausted by all of them. He coughed and then crawled to the end table. Reaching up, he grasped his tumbler, spilling some of its contents. Struggling, he brought the glass to his lips, ingesting what remained. He leaned against the pedestal table, knocking it over. He fell back against it, dropping his empty crystal tumbler, shattering it on the cypress floor. "Fuck you, Papa."

"You're the one who'se fucked, Brother."

Augustus searched the floor for his dagger, which had fallen out of his ankle holster.

Sarah stood by the door, laughing at him. Stank saw Augustus blink hard, seeing her. His master covered his ears, blocking out her never-ending laughter.

Spotting the dagger, Augustus grabbed it. Taking aim, he threw it at the heckling Black witch standing before him. She glowed and dissolved into a white light.

Augustus wiped his eyes and then massaged his temples. "I'm going to shut your mouth once and for all, bitch." Steadying his vision, Augustus found the weapon embedded in the door. With great effort, he arose from the floor and walked to the doorframe. He dislodged the dagger. No blood stained it.

Chapter 6

La Rose Plantation, St. Helena Parish. February, 1859.

The beat of the drums intensified. The crowd moaned.

"I love the Lord..."

"He heard my cry..."

The worshipers repeated the words of the leader, singing in a slow, mournful dirge.

"He heard my pitied groan..."

Toussaint closed his eyes and raised his head toward the night sky. He hoped the White folks couldn't hear them, but they were so deep in the swamp near the Tangipahoa River, he couldn't see a way they could. In any case, he knew God had made Master Augustus' ears deaf to their worship with bourbon.

His mother Sarah appeared within the midst of worshipers. She held up a child with a crown of gold on his head. The pitch of worship intensified, becoming feverish. The child vanished.

Bits sang with her aged, soprano voice, ringing out into the night sky. *"Got on my travelin' shoes..."*

Lawrence answered, *"Got on my shoes, Lord."*

Everyone danced around the mourners, waiting to receive the baptism of the Holy Spirit. Those who received it would be baptized in the Tangipahoa River the next day, on Sunday.

Toussaint stood amongst them and outstretched his arms. "Father, you're so good. Thank you, Father." He grasped Sarah's and Lawrence's hands, now standing side by side.

Toussaint felt the Holy Spirit enter his body through the crown of his head. The air flowed through him, going down to his feet. He felt as if he would fall, but he didn't. Did the air keep him standing on his feet? He smelled a strange smell, like the new oil called kerosene Master Augustus burned in his lamps, which vented through the windows of the plantation house at times. After a few moments, the air backed out of him the way it had come. It retreated, but it didn't turn around. It pulled out of him.

The women and men shouted.

"Toot, what do you mean?" Sarah's eyes filled of tears, unable to believe the prophesy relayed through her son.

Joy beamed from Lawrence.

"What?" Toussaint spoke, but not of his own volition.

"Men with guns, all dressed the same, is gonna come here and set us free. Massa Augustus gonna spit, but he cain't stop them."

One of the worshipers stepped forward. "We'se ain't never gonna be free." Others joined in, denouncing the vision.

"Doncha listen to them, chile," Miss Bits said, patting his shoulder. Others in the group gathered around Toussaint in silent support, accepting his words. Toussaint lowered his head.

Stank stood at his brother's side. "The Lawd done told ya'll the truth. If ya'll cain't believe it, then ya'll callin' the Lawd a liar."

The crowd stood around in shocked silence. How were they to believe the word of Nicka's bastard son, Stank? Yet, Stank protected and watched over Toussaint. Everyone knew how much Stank loved Toussaint and would do anything for him.

The worshipers emitted a collective sigh, confused. If Stank's little evil ass could believe what Toussaint had prophesied, how could they not? They each departed the meeting ground, one by one, considering all that had happened.

Once all had left, only Toussaint, Stank, Sarah, Teddy, and Lawrence remained in the clearing of the meeting place. Lawrence kissed Toussaint on the forehead and left for the plantation house. His brother Stank patted him on the back and left, headed for their cabin.

Teddy and Sarah embraced their son. "The devil is a liar. Believe what God done showed you, Toot," Sarah said, comforting her son.

Inserting the padding into the steaming water, Missy stirred the pot. The linens still appeared a bit dingy to her, but she trusted the bleach and saleratus would extract the gloom from the white garments. Only she laundered master's white items, for he'd once commented to Bonnie the housekeeper that Missy's whites were whiter than anyone else's. Bonnie came to her one day and said, "Gal, how you'se git them sheets so white?"

Missy blushed when questioned by her idol. "I'se don't rightly know. I'se just soak them in boilin' water, bleach, and saleratus."

"You'se been puttin' Massa's bicarb'nate in wash?"

"Yessum. Aunt Sammie says I should."

Bonnie let it go. If Sammie was okay with it, she wasn't going to say anything. The sheets sure were white. Bonnie watched Missy stir the pot. "Well Gal, Massa likes what you do." She turned and left.

Missy stirred the pot, remembering the day. Hooking a sheet on the end of the paddle, she raised the steaming mass from the water. "Still ain't white e'nuff." Missy lowered the paddle, returning the sheet to its bath.

She spotted a pillow case floating near the top of the wash. She removed it from the pot with her paddle and submerged in another large pot filled with cool water. She swirled it around, cooling it down. She reached in and grabbed the pillow case, wrung it out and tossed it in a wicker basket. She would hang it up to dry later. She shook her hands. They stung. She dried them on her apron, intensifying the pain.

Although the harsh chemicals made the skin on her hands crack and bleed, it was better than enduring the heat of the day working in the fields. Her Aunt Sammie would steal away a little lard, giving it to her to rub on her hands. It seemed to help, healing the lesions. She couldn't wait to finish the day's wash, so she could apply some. There was no sense in doing so while work remained. The lard was too precious to wash away.

"Hi, Missy."

Missy found her little brother sitting on the stool near her cauldron. However, he wasn't little anymore, but a grown man. It didn't matter; she still treated him like he was five years old. "Boy, whatcha doin' outta the fields this early?"

"I gave the overseer the slip," Toussaint said with a smile. He put a bit of apple in his mouth.

"Toot, where you'se git that fruit from? Massa gonna tan

your hide good." Missy reached for the fruit to destroy it, but Toussaint gobbled it up before she could do so.

"Massa ain't gonna miss it. It ain't bourbon."

Missy eyes flashed to the left and then the right. "Keep your voice down, boy."

Toussaint could care less. Everyone on the plantation knew Augustus was a violent drunk. What did he care about missing food? Food wasn't his primary concern. He only cared about drinking and killing folks.

Toussaint watched his sister stir the pot. He saw a greater purpose for her. She was a lady. She should be attired in fine silks, receiving callers like the White ladies, in a fine home. Yet, she had been condemned to stirring and wringing out scalding hot sheets.

Yet, he could see his sister enjoyed her work. Missy took pride in her job, believing she produced the whitest laundry in the parish. If Missy detected the smallest speck, she would rub the stain with fierceness until it released itself from the garment.

After washing on Monday morning, Missy would hang the laundry out in the afternoon. On Tuesday morning, she would remove the laundry from the lines. She would then starch and press the sheets, along with any other white linens and shirts. Toussaint found them to be the most pristine items he'd ever seen. Bonnie the housekeeper said Missy's sheets could stay on the master's bed for two weeks, but they changed them every few days anyway. Missy washed the master's sheets on Mondays and Thursdays.

Toussaint noticed Missy's attention divert from her laundry. Kinky walked by, having returned from the fields early. Toussaint watched Kinky smile at his sister as he passed. So, the rumors were true. They were courting in secret.

Stirring her pot, Missy forgot her brother, waiting for Cupid to shoot her with his arrow.

"Why him?"

Missy looked up from her laundry. "You'se knows it, huh?"

"Everybody knows."

Missy pursed her lips a bit. She tossed a long braid out of the way, over her back. "I'se reckon they'se do." Missy stirred the pot. "What's wrong wit' Kinky, Toussaint? Why doncha like him?"

Toussaint crossed his arms. "His name is Kinky. What you gonna do with a man named Kinky?" Toussaint didn't believe the man to have any potential other than his current profession. He wasn't very good at it, either. "What about Bradford? He's smart."

Missy dug her paddle deep into the pot. She didn't want to miss anything small, like wash clothes or pillow cases. "You'se so highfalutin' Toussaint." Missy smiled at him.

"Anyhow, Bradford's courtin' Pauline."

It was true. In the Spirit, Toussaint couldn't see the lovers breaking up anytime soon. They would marry. Toussaint made a mental scan of the other eligible men in the slave community. "Napoleon's a good man. He has a mind for numbers. He runs Massa's general store."

Missy considered her brother's suggestion. Napoleon was alright, but he was old and had never jumped the broom. She wanted someone closer to her own age. Napoleon was nice. He would stop by and give her flowers. He smuggled cream to her, for her hands, from master's general store.

With dreamy eyes, Missy gazed at the sky. She loved Kinky. When Kinky would smile at her, she would melt. She loved seeing him return from the fields, covered with sweat, glistening. He would smile his broad grin, rapturing her soul. Missy smiled, thinking of her love. Yes, she would marry Kinky.

Toussaint wanted to spit. What was it with girls? Napoleon was the obvious choice, but she wanted Kinky. Kinky was dull, with big muscles and brute strength his only redeeming attributes. His sister could be dumb at times. "I'm going home," Toussaint said.

Missy stirred the pot, lost in love. "What? Oh, aw'rite Toot. I'll see you'se later."

Toussaint stepped down from the stool, just in time to

see dense Kinky strutting over to talk to Missy attired in his overalls with no shirt. At least he had gone home to wash off. Toussaint had to admit his arm muscles were enormous. He considered his own puny arms. What girl would want a man with puny arms? Apparently, being smart wasn't enough to win the heart of girls. If his own sister didn't like smart men, why would anyone want him?

To be honest with himself, Toussaint didn't believe Kinky was dumb. He possessed a mechanical knowledge. He always fixed the cotton gin. He understood how to best utilizes the plows, work animals and such. However, he didn't possess book learning, as did Toussaint. While Missy complimented Toussaint on his book learning, she never sought out anyone educated for herself.

Toussaint pulled off his boots, the soles worn away, and entered the house. He sat at the table.

"Go wash yo'self, boy." Sarah poured some water from the kettle into the washbasin. Lawrence had given it to her, along with the matching cracked pitcher. Yet, it still held water.

Toussaint took the lye soap and lathered it. Their family was blessed. Most of the slaves didn't have soap. His mother had told him tales of the time before Augustus took over as master of the plantation. Back then, the slaves were a community. They traded their wares and goods amongst themselves and lived in decency. They lived as a people. Now, they all dressed in rags.

His mother spoke from time to time of her sisters whom Augustus had sold off. One had been a seamstress, and the other a candle stick maker. He could never remember their names. Toussaint splashed hot water on his face, and then took the ragged towel and dried himself.

"Sallie and Sylvia."

Toussaint nodded and finished washing up. He walked over and sat at the table, ravenous. Sarah placed a bowl of collards, kale, and mustard greens, seasoned with salt pork, before him. "Why are we having a feast today, Maman?"

"The Lord provides. Eat your food for it gits cold."

Toussaint dug in. Sarah sat at the table. "Did you'se say grace boy?" Toussaint stopped eating. Sarah said the blessing. Toussaint dug in, scooping collards and salt pork into his mouth. His mother watched him, allowing him to eat his fill for a few moments. When she figured he'd satiated his hunger pangs, she spoke. "Why doncha like your sister's beau, Toot?"

She had ruined his appetite. Toussaint rested his spoon in his dinged tin bowl. "He's stupid."

Sarah raised an eyebrow. "Is your daddy stupid?"

Toussaint pushed away his dinner, unfinished. "Papa is

the smartest man I know. He can do anything. He's brave. He can hunt. He fixes thangs. He charms the overseer, cajoling him into seeing his way of doing things. The overseer believes he came up with the idea by the time Papa gets through with him." Toussaint folded his arms and smiled with pride for his father. Soon his smile mutated into a frown. His mother had tricked him.

"So, what's wrong wit' Kinky? Sounds likes to me he's got a lot of the same thangs goin' for him as your Papa does."

Toussaint shut his mouth. He hated it when his mother convicted him with his own words. He desired Missy to have a life of ease. Napoleon could give it to her.

"Boy, no one knows what the Lawd has in store for them. Napoleon could drop dead tomorrow. Then what? He's an old man tryin' to court a young gal like Missy. Ain't gonna happen." Sarah resisted the urge to ignite the old man upon his bed.

"Let Missy, me, and her Papa choose her mate. Stay out of it, Toussaint. You'se a man, but you'se still young." Compassion and mercy for Toussaint welled in Sarah's heart. "But you'se picked well for your sister. Ifs you'se could see a little better, you'se would choose different." Sarah walked over to where her son sat and took him in her arms. She kissed him on the forehead. "Well, finish your dinner. You'se still hungry?"

His mother's faith in him restored his appetite. His dinner was still warm. He shoveled a few spoonfuls into his mouth while his mother returned to the fire, checking on the corn bread she'd made for his father. She always made his papa cornbread. He adored the treat.

Hearing voices, Toussaint left his meal and went to the door. He found Kinky sitting on the porch with his sister. Kinky took his sister's blistered hand in his, patting it. She blushed. "Those sheets you washed sho' look fine, Miss Missy."

Toussaint watched his sister blush, yet again. *Sap.* "Thank you," his sister said.

The couple sat in silence for a few moments. With the lightest touch, Kinky grazed the bleeding and swollen lesions on Missy's hands with his fingertips. "Do your hands hurt you much?"

Missy rubbed the skin on her cracked hands. They were too raw to scratch. "I'se manage."

Kinky reached into the pocket of his tattered overalls and extracted a jar. He removed the lid. "Mistah Linus had some lard he'd been savin'. I traded some cotton I'd been savin' wit' him. His wife gonna spin the cotton and weave it to make a patch for his britches." Kinky dipped his rough fingers into the oil, extracting a glob. "Do you'se thank Miss

Sarah would mind if I'se rubbed a li'l on your hands?"

Toussaint saw his sister's body relax. "I'se reckon it's aw'rite."

Kinky took her blistered hand in his. Gazing into her eyes, he massaged her hands, working the lard into her open cuts and sores. Once finished, he removed straps of cloth from his other pocket. He wrapped her hands. He kissed her bandages, and then left.

Toussaint returned to the table and sat down. Sarah sat on the stool, before her washbasin, never looking his way. He scooped cold greens and salt pork into his mouth and swallowed. The nourishment and love encapsulated in the meal smoothed over the lump in his throat.

La Rose Plantation, St. Helena Parish. December, 1859.

HE HAD TO admit it; he liked flowers. It was a girly thing, but he could appreciate all of them, having been created different in every way to praise the Lord. Toussaint loved the roses. They were magnificent; yet, dangerous at the same time. One couldn't just grab them without taking a great level of care and respect. He found it better to appreciate the flower with his eyes. It was the best way to avoid bloodshed.

"You'se right 'bout that, boy."

Toussaint turned to find his mother standing behind him. He hadn't seen her in a while. He guessed she'd just returned from escorting the enslaved to liberty and freedom somewhere in the world.

The sun had begun its mission to set on the Earth. Toussaint felt a chill rush through him. "Whatcha doin' foolin' 'round in Augustus' rose garden?"

Toussaint cast his eyes downward. "I was just taking the long way home from the fields." He didn't tell her he'd hoped to see the master's Negro daughter. Sometimes she passed through the rose garden in the evening, taking a detour from the mansion to her mother's kitchen house. He never knew when he might catch sight of her. She didn't leave the big house often. From time to time, folks would spot her in the square with the master's daughter, Lily.

"That ain't gonna happen no more," Sarah said.

Toussaint scoured the Spirit, but it was veiled. He could feel terror. "What happened, Maman?"

Sarah removed a rock from her pocket and threw it across the walkway. "Augustus done shot his White daughter. He was aimin' to shoot Lela, but the White daughter jumped in the way, sparin' her."

Toussaint stood frozen before his mother. He'd failed in some way he didn't understand.

"It ain't your time yet to protect the Rose, but it's comin'. Don't rush it." Sarah heard something fall in the garden, screams of agony, and then a curse. She snickered. "Here comes your brother."

Brother? Toussaint spotted a rose bush rustle in the distance. Much to his surprise, his master arose from it grips, scratched and bleeding. "Nigger bitch," Toussaint heard the master say.

Finding the path, Augustus staggered over to where they stood. He pitched a haphazard punch at Sarah, but missed. Toussaint commanded himself to jump the man, but he found himself frozen and unable to move. He only could move his eyes.

He watched his mother reach into her pocket, remove her corn cob pipe and light it. She inhaled deep and then blew smoke into Augustus' face. "I'se done told you'se before. You'se cain't go 'round hittin' on me, brother."

Toussaint shifted his eyes to his master.

"You've been meddling in my business again, bitch," Augustus said. "You didn't have nothing to do with my business with Lily's murderer, Marion Clemens. He was mine."

Sarah nodded, considering his words. "Naw, he's the Lawd's, just like all the other folks on this here place and this Earth. But you'se don't git that. You'se thanks all folks should bow to you. You'se a fool Augustus." He lunged at her, but she disappeared, reappearing behind him. "Besides, I'se didn't do nuthin'. The Lawd sent your li'l ole gal, Lela, out there to warn him. I'se just backed her up. Marion wasn't listenin' to her. I'se helps him see that he should."

"Fucking bitch," Augustus said. "I swear I'm going to put you in your grave before it's all done. Stop messing with my family."

Sarah tapped her pipe on her shoe, knocking out the remaining tobacco. "So you'se finally admits it, Augustus?"

"What?"

"You'se claiming Lela as your daughter?"

Augustus stood before them both, motionless. He pulled his gun and then aimed it at Sarah. His eyes glassed over, glistening in the twilight. He holstered his weapon, turned and walked away.

Toussaint's paralysis left him. He took off running, but tripped and fell. "Where's you'se runnin' to, boy?"

"To kill him."

Sarah walked over to where he lay on the crushed pebbled path. She lifted him to his feet by his arm. Melancholy overcame Sarah, seeing the future. "Not yet, baby. The time ain't here yet." Taking his hand, she smiled at him.

Sarah led Toussaint back to their cabin. She could see the defeat in her child's eyes. She could hear his thoughts, wishing to be a conqueror. Instead he was a boy, still learning how to become a man who protected those he loved, and most important, good judgment. It would all come to him in time. "It ain't your time yet, boy. Listen to Maman." He hung his head. She hit him on the back of then neck. "Doncha ever hangs yo' head boy, as long as you'se be Negro like the Good Lawd made you." Toussaint sat at the table. She gave him a cool drink.

Chapter 7

La Rose Plantation, St. Helena Parish. August 31, 1963.

Lela crossed her legs at the ankle. "Augustus never learned. I guess none of us ever do."

Startled, Julian jumped in his chair. He'd caught a chill. The sound and cadence of her voice had changed abruptly, jolting him out of his trance, for lack of a better word.

When his grandmère relayed the past to him, she spoke in a soft whispery voice, strong, not weak. Her speaking voice was forceful and authoritative, but feminine. Now lucent and speaking in the present, her eyes focused on him instead of an indeterminate spot in the distance. "Why do you say that, Grandmère?"

Lela patted his thigh. She stood up and stretched. She had begun to sweat. "I don't know how much longer I can sit out here in this heat."

Julian noticed the perspiration soaking the bodice of her dress. "We can go in, Grandmère."

Lela walked over to the bar cart and poured some cold water into her glass. "Not yet," she said. "I enjoy being mistress of this plantation. I recall being locked in the mansion all the days of my youth," she said. "I was a slave, but I wasn't. I was beaten, but I wasn't. I was loved by my White father, but I wasn't. I was an anomaly of sorts, caught between two worlds." Lela turned red with rage. "Why am I still angry? These events occurred over one hundred years ago, and I'm still outraged." She walked over to where Julian sat on the upholstered window bench and plopped down, frustrated. "I'm still mad. Why, Julian?"

Lela allowed her gaze to fall upon the white roses in the vase on the wrought iron table. The roses, absorbing her energy, bloomed. Its thorns grew sharp. "I must let the hurt go." She peered through the screen of the gazebo into the late morning sky. "It's over and in the past." She nodded in agreement with the outcomes God had brought forth.

"But you know what Julian? Talking to you about all of this is making it better. Everything I tell you is a release for my soul. I've never shared the details of my life with anyone, neither with Jamie, Leelee, nor Toussaint. Lily, and later Suzette, lived through much of it with me."

She stood from the window bench and removed a rose from the vase. It withered and died. "Yes, the past is dead, but it continues to live on within us, tormenting us. Well, if we allow it to do so." Lela tossed the now dead rose in the waste basket near the settee. "Yes, my darling. We must forgive ourselves and those who played their roles in our lives; otherwise, we fail to go forward and live."

Julian nodded. He remembered his grandmère's story from a couple of days before, accounting Lily's death. "Marion Clemens left the country, didn't he?"

Lela nodded. "Yes, darling. He moved to France. I didn't see him again for many years." Lela smoothed her dress. "The Lord saw fit to send each of us to France at the appointed time, to heal, grow, and to come into our own, so to speak. We all needed to regroup and find ourselves."

Lela sat on the bench with her great-grandson. Her mind ricocheted through the past, considering it all. "Augustus had made an enemy of his brother that day, in the garden. Yet, Augustus and Toussaint persisted together for a time upon the Earth, before they crossed paths again."

La Rose Plantation, St. Helena Parish. December, 1860.

WITH HIS BROTHER, Mammon, safely imprisoned, Lawrence could now leave the house from time to time, to visit with his little ones. In the Spirit, Lawrence could see Mammon's incarceration would be short-term. Mammon continued to slaughter the innocent, seeking the Rose.

Lawrence peered through the eyes of Heaven, seeing all.

Mammon had discovered the Rose lived in chains during her current incarnation. Therefore, Mammon had instructed his minions to slaughter slaves across the Americas. He'd hardened the hearts of slave masters', encouraging them to be even more sadistic and vicious than normal.

Yet, the Good Lord still veiled the location and identity of his Rose from Mammon. His brothers laughed at Mammon, finding the Lord had hidden her in his own garden. The entire angelic community could see it, both the holy and the fallen alike, except for Mammon. Even his fallen brethren refused to tell him of the Rose's whereabouts, for they hated and envied him. Lawrence found it all to be sort of comical in a way.

Walking down the road, he waved at folks sitting on their porches, seeking relief from the heat of the day. He came to Sarah's cabin. Ah, Sarah. He'd loved her since the beginning of days.

Sarah sat in her rocking chair on the porch smoking her pipe. Lawrence decided to join her. She usually wore her strange little straw hat. He rejoiced, for on this day, her gray, dread-locked hair flowed down her back, uncovered. She was still fine.

"You'se fine for eternity. I'se an old lady now."

"Quit your foolin', woman." He sat in the rocker next to hers, enjoying the humid, early morning breeze. "How's

Teddy?"

Sarah took a drag on her pipe and exhaled, the smoke gathering beneath the roof of the porch. "He's just fine. He's out in the cane fields by now, I'se reckons. His back been botherin' him again. Goddamn overseer works him too hard. I'se thanks evil ass Augustus tells him to do so."

"Sarah—"

"Doncha Sarah me. You'se knows he does it. Augustus cain't get me, so he's figures he's go after my love." Sarah's gray eyes turned to stone. "He's been evil since Marion got away from him. He blames me. So, he punishes me by makin' life hard for Teddy."

Lawrence noticed the grass on the side of the cabin dry up and ignite. He picked up the pail of water sitting on the porch and threw it on the burning grass, extinguishing the impending flames. Lawrence sighed and returned to his seat.

"Augustus should be on his knees ev'ry day thankin' the Good Lawd for the hedge he done put 'round his old evil ass." Sarah looked out, seeking his end. It was veiled.

"Vengeance is mine, saith the Lord," Lawrence whispered, comforting her.

"Yeah, I'se knows it," she said. Yet at the same time, she wished the Good Lord would share a bit of his ability to mete out vengeance with those who loved Him. She realized she could never be a just judge. But the issue of justice wasn't a stumbling block when it came to Augustus. Everyone in Floridian Louisiana knew him to be a hellion and wanted him dead for one reason or another, Negro and White folks alike.

"You'se sayin' you'se knows better than the Most High?" Lawrence asked, horrified.

"Stop listenin' to what I'se thankin', boy," she said with a sexy grin. She had to stop flirting before Teddy messed around and caught her. She gave Lawrence a little smile anyway. His ole fine self. Lawrence flashed his toothy grin at her, seducing her. The man was shameless. Sarah curtailed her thoughts. "And naw, I'se don't know no better than Him."

He reached over and patted her hand. "I'se gonna stop by after dinner and put my hands on Teddy's back. He'll be aw'rite." Sarah nodded, saying nothing.

Lawrence could feel the rage radiating from within her. Not only did the husband's excessive toil enrage her, but that of her people. Hundreds of thousands languished within Satan's grasp. But the believers trapped in bondage all hoped in God, and in God would be their salvation.

Lawrence rubbed Sarah's shoulders. He admired the slaves so. He'd kept watch over his fair share of slaves since Abraham's time until that moment, but the institution of slavery was different for Africans in America.

In times past, it hadn't been the mission of owners to

annihilate the minds and souls of their chattel. It had been more of jail sentence of sorts. One did their time and once completed, the captives had been set free, at least in most instances. It took a strong spirit and soul to endure the endless, generational hopelessness of American bondage. What torture and humiliation hadn't the African slave endured? But Lawrence encouraged himself, for he could see the end.

"Yessuh, you'se right," Sarah responded to Lawrence's thoughts. "Soon, we'se gonna leave this here place and never looks back."

"Yessum, you'se right," Lawrence said. "The time is short for ya'll."

Sadness filled her, for she could see Lawrence wouldn't be permitted to leave the land until ceased to exist.

A movement in the distance caught Sarah's eye. She squinted to focus on the moving form, unable to accept the sight her eyes perceived. "What in the world!" Sarah placed her pipe on the side table, watching her son race by. She'd mistaken him for his father at first. She began to dematerialize, but Lawrence stopped her. "What?"

Lawrence sat her down in her rocker. "I'll go. You'se stays here." Sarah tried to arise from the chair, but an invisible force prevented her from doing so. "Trust me, Sarah. Trust God. It'll be fine." Tears sprung forth in her eyes. "Darlin', God always protects his Seed." Lawrence trotted down the porch steps and fell into a light jog, headed for the mansion.

Toussaint had seen it happening while in the fields chopping cotton. He'd dropped his hoe and ran. The overseer tried to run after him, but couldn't catch him. Toussaint ran to where he'd seen them in the Spirit, sequestered in one of the rear, formal gardens. He stopped once he came near, finding Hanzel Johannessen with Lela backed up against a tree.

He ran back to the terrace of the mansion. Lawrence would help him. Much to his surprise, he found Master Augustus, having mounted his horse and prepared to leave. Toussaint ran and stood before the animal, blocking its path. The horse reared back, for Toussaint had spooked him. Lawrence stood on the terrace, watching. "Whatcha want li'l Niggah," Augustus asked him.

The master terrified him, but Toussaint found his voice. "Massa Hanzel's out back wit' Lela, suh."

Augustus jumped down from his horse. "Show me."

Running through the garden, Toussaint led him to a little wooded area and stopped before a garden gate concealed by the bosquet. Augustus opened the gate and found Hanzel ready to force himself on Lela.

Augustus put his finger to his mouth. Toussaint nodded. Lela's screams deafened him.

Toussaint watched Augustus tip toe across the small lawn with stealth ease. He grabbed Hanzel by his shirt collar and threw him against a tree. Hanzel staggered, disoriented, as he tried to button his fly.

Augustus slammed the boy to the ground and beat him. Toussaint heard Hanzel's nose crack, his cheek bone snap. Augustus stood, having taken his full due. Augustus misstepped, causing his foot to come down heavy on Hanzel's left arm. The sound of the bone shattering beneath Augustus' boot reverberated throughout the garden like glass breaking in a heavy towel.

Augustus kicked him, trying to kill him. Yet, he stopped himself. Toussaint wasn't sure why. Why not kill him? Hanzel was filth, but even more so, the boy was Satan.

Panting for air, Augustus spoke. "Listen here, little Cloggy. I don't give a fuck if Josef is your daddy, boy. Let me catch you near one of my slaves again. I'm gonna take you where nobody can hear you scream." Hanzel lay before him, crying and broken. "Now get from 'round here."

Dragging himself up from the ground, Hanzel locked his eyes with Toussaint's, while holding his broken arm. "Nigger, you're going to learn about crossing me."

Augustus punched him in his kidney, returning him to the dust. "What I tell you about messing with my Niggers? You don't own shit on this place, boy. Hell, your broke ass

Daddy don't own shit on ya'll place." He watched the boy turn red. "Now get your ass in your buggy and go home. Don't let me catch you 'round here again." Hanzel staggered away.

Augustus turned to Toussaint. "Look at me, boy." Toussaint raised his head and met his master's eyes. They were wet. "Go home, li'l Nigger."

Toussaint stole a glance of Lela standing riveted to the tree, terrified and bruised. He turned and ran home.

Chapter 8

La Rose Plantation, St. Helena Parish. August 31, 1963.

Julian stood from the window seat and stretched, while his grandmère still traversed the fringes of those times. He didn't get her. Why did she always believe someone was trying to rape her?

Julian walked over to the bar cart and removed the lid to the ice bucket. "Good. There are a few left." Before he could grab the tongs to secure the last remaining ice cubes, they melted. The water in the bucket steamed and boiled until all the liquid evaporated. He could feel heat on the back of his neck. He turned around.

"I don't cry rape." Lela glared at him. "Why don't you ask me to explain instead of accusing me? You still accuse me instead of embracing me, even after all these years."

Julian stood before her in stunned silence. He spoke against his will. "I never accused you of lying about it, gal."

"Yes, you did," Lela said.

Julian marched around the gazebo. He rushed toward

her, with his hand raised. He stopped, his eyes darting from the left and then to the right, from the present to the past.

Lela took his hand. "Oh Lord, forgive me." *He's not Augustus*, Lela told herself. *He is Augustus, but he is not.* "Mon fils, Grandmère is sorry. I apologize."

Julian nodded. He rubbed his temples and sat on the window seat, confused. He shivered, trying to sort it all out. For a split second, he wasn't himself. He saw himself standing in the garden with his grandmère, filled with hurt and disgust because she'd allowed Hanzel to touch her. The vision faded as fast as it had descended upon him, finding his grandmère before him. "I'm sorry. I don't understand."

Lela took him in her arms and comforted him. "Let it go, Julian. It is well," she said, burrowing into his red eyes. She smiled at him, reassuring him. "Let us call indoors for someone to come and freshen up the bar, yes?" Julian nodded. Lela walked over to the intercom and depressed the button. "Lawrence, please ask Nanette to bring out some ice."

A few moments later, the box emitted a string of crackles. "Madame, why don't ya'll come indoors? It's hot out there."

Lela turned to Julian. "Would you like to go indoors, mon fils?"

He nodded, relieved. He could no longer endure the heat of the day and the madness of his grandmère's story. Locking his arm with hers, Julian escorted her down the steps of the gazebo and across the lawn. Hearing a chopping noise, Julian searched the sky. "I thought I heard a helicopter."

Lela crooked her neck to capture a better view of the horizon. She spotted the helicopter. Overjoyed, she clapped her hands and then broke into a childish skip along the stone path to the terrace. Julian had to run to keep up with her. "It's here!"

"What?"

"Our fish order," she said to him. "What have the fishermen selected to delight us with today? Maybe oysters or mussels? I hope they sent some salmon, halibut, and sea bass. Oh, maybe they sent trout for dinner." Lela furled her brow. "Well, I guess the fishermen on La Rose can catch trout in the river, along with some catfish too."

Julian shook his head, unable to fathom his grandmère's insatiable appetite. "Hey, wait a minute, Grandmère. You have your seafood flown into La Rose?" His anger surged, realizing the truth.

Lela stopped, winded. She patted her forehead with the back of her hand. "Well, of course. How else would we receive it?"

Julian scrutinized the terrain, trying to figure out where a helicopter would land amongst the forests and cultivated fields.

"Oh, we have a helipad and landing strip two miles away," Lela said.

"What?"

"Well, yes darling. The nearest airport is in Baton Rouge. Back in the 1940's, your Aunt Leelee had tired of the long car rides out here to the plantation. So, Toussaint had the airstrip built," she said, not understanding the basis of her grandson's confusion.

Julian boiled with rage. "What are you saying? You own jets and helicopters?"

Lela shrugged her lips. "Yes, I do. How else am I to get around?" She patted her forehead with the back of her hand again. She had no doubts her face appeared as an oily mess. She needed her compact. "I'm too old to fly commercial."

"Why did we drive here?" Julian suppressed his urge to yell.

Lela pinched him on his forearm. "Watch your tone, boy." Lela leaned in hard on him, growing weary in the heat. "We're only fifty to seventy-five miles from New Orleans. Why shouldn't we drive? Besides, I wanted to visit the Harris'."

Julian said nothing more, quickening his steps to escape the heat. Climbing the stairs of the terrace, he found the French doors open. They escaped into the coolness within.

***

Lawrence entered the drawing room carrying a gold tray loaded with a crystal pitcher of iced tea, a crystal ice bucket and variety of other items. Nanette followed with a gold tray filled with tea cakes, finger sandwiches and an assortment of nuts and sliced fruit. She arranged the snacks on the buffet while Lawrence placed the tea on the table before his mistress. Lela frowned.

Lawrence left the room, returning a few seconds later with an ancient bottle of brandy. Lela smiled. Lawrence placed a few ice cubes in the highball crystal glass, and then filled it a quarter of the way with brandy. Lela frowned. Lawrence continued to pour. Lela smiled. Lawrence stopped pouring and topped off the concoction with iced tea. He bowed and turned to leave.

"What about my drink?"

Lawrence closed the door behind him. Julian sat on the sofa, pouting. His grandmère lifted the glass to her lips, sipping it, careful not to smudge her lipstick. *Lush.*

"There was a time when I was a drunk. When I first began my career as a prostitute, I drank heavily to deal with the psychological pressures of my new business as a Madame. Hell, I drank to cope with my new life. Jamie had left me." Lela's eyes misted. "Anyway, once I became acclimated to the profession and released the past events which had led me to that point in time, I stopped drinking to get drunk. Since that time, I only drink sociably."

"Whatever, Grandmère." Julian leaned forward to make his drink.

Lela considered him, remembering his earlier comment. Although his former incarnation as Augustus had spurred the comment, the belief still dwelled within his soul. She shifted toward him on the sofa, her knees together and legs crossed at the ankle. She smoothed down her dress as she considered her words. "I don't think men are always trying to rape me, Julian," she said, biting her lip. "The Devil doesn't want the Seed to find a place to rest."

Julian dropped his glass on the table. "What?"

She assaulted his soul via the orbs of his head. "The Lord's Seed must find a place to rest. If the seed rests, it will take root, grow, and become incarnate into the world. What would Satan do, if the one who can throw him into the Lake of Fire returns to Earth once more, this time mounted upon a White Horse?"

Julian sat beside his grandmère, his brain deadlocked. He knew she believed a lot of things, but this statement was incredible. What exactly was she trying to say?

Lela grasped his wrist, bruising it. She relaxed her grip, sliding her hand into his, and then clutching it. Her gaze settled into his, becoming one with his soul. She watched his spirit flutter with fear. "Just what I said, Julian. I didn't stutter."

Lela released him. She picked up her glass from the table and sipped her tea. "Throughout history, Chevalier women have been routinely and systematically attacked by Satan. Either he tries to kill us outright to prevent the Lord's seed from taking root and flourishing, or he rapes, wishing to infuse his own seed into us. He tried to destroy Livvy."

Who was Livvy? Julian combed his memory of her tales. His grandmère had mentioned her. He didn't remember her from *La Rose Family History.* Julian sat still.

"Grandmère," he began, but stopped. His grandmère's laser beam glare affixed to a spot on the coffee table. It began to smolder and then a small flame shot up. Grabbing the seltzer bottle, he extinguished the hotspot. Her hair had turned gunmetal gray. The lines on her face funneled into the abyss lodging at the corners of her mouth. "I allowed you to win Mammon. You cannot defeat me."

Julian swallowed hard. "Mammon?" The heat radiating from his grandmother made him sweat. She didn't seem to notice him. "Grandmère?"

Lela arched an eyebrow and turned to him. "The devil."

Julian was sorry he'd spoken, for she diverted her rage to him. He held his tongue. She couldn't be serious. What did the devil even look like?

"Like you and me, Julian. He looks just like you and me,

for he's our ancestor. I was married to him in the thirteenth century. At that time, he was Olad, and then changed his name to Ilad after he executed my Michel."

The rug beneath the sofa table ignited. Julian jumped up from the sofa and searched the room for an extinguisher. Why would they have a fire extinguisher in an ornate drawing room such as this? Nevertheless, he located one encased in a gold and glass box.

He broke the glass, grabbed the extinguisher and ran to the sofa. Within a few moments, flames surrounded his grandmère. Yet, the flames failed to consume either her or the furniture. She sat in the mist of the inferno upon her sofa, smiling. The energy of her smile fed the flames, causing them to reach up toward ceiling.

The paint from the ceiling's mural flaked and rained down upon them, becoming little sparks, meeting the sparks soaring up from where Lela sat, burning. She puffed out staccato bursts of air.

"You used me to bring forth your filthy seed."

Julian cowered in the wake of Lela's sinister laugh.

"In the end, I'm going to force you to do some things you don't want to do, Mammon. I can't wait. I can't wait for Judgment. Little devils. I bore your little devils." The fire surrounding Lela flashed.

Julian depressed the lever on the extinguisher, but nothing happened.

"Jamie was his progeny." Lela sighed, feeling the burden of her 116 years. She rubbed her temples and curled her brow in anger, thinking. "I'm his progeny too. The blood of the scum of Heaven dwells within me as well."

Julian stared at her, horrified. Lela took another sip of her iced tea, more so brandy. "Well, the blood is so intermingled at this point, I guess I have God and the devil within me too. It has come to past. The seed of the holy and the profane have merged into one."

Julian gulped down his scotch, suppressing his fear of his grandmother. She seemed to have calmed down. The room appeared normal. Nothing had happened. Maybe the room hadn't been engulfed in flames a few moments before.

He inhaled deep. He smelled wood burning in the fireplace; however, when he glanced over, it was cold. Well, the room contained a few fireplaces, perhaps someone had lit one of the others. A chill ran through his bones, telling him it wasn't the case. "Grandmère, are you warm?"

Lela placed the back of her hand against her forehead. "A little, perhaps. Why?"

Julian sat on the sofa, staring at her. The hall clock chimed. "Grandmère, would you like to return to the gazebo? It may have cooled a bit. I'm sure it's cooler out there, than in here."

Lela considered his suggestion. The room had grown warm. "Well, perhaps. If the staff doesn't mind bringing out some refreshments, I will join you."

Julian pulled the cord next to the French door. Soon, Lawrence entered drawing room. "Ma'Dame needs to go outside for a while, huh?"

Julian knew they were all crazy. "Yes."

Lela stood from the sofa. "Oh Lawrence, did I see the fish order come in?"

"Oui, Ma'Dame. The truck should be arrivin' in a few minutes, if it ain't already here."

Lela rubbed her hands together. "Do you think they sent oysters?"

"Prob'ly so. I'll send some out. What kind of wine would you like?"

Julian extended his hand to her. Lela blushed, for his chivalry reminded her of Jamie. "You decide." Lela placed her hand in Julian's, allowing him to lead her outdoors.

Chapter 9

La Rose Plantation, St. Helena Parish. January, 1861.

The triangle bell clanged in the square, sounding throughout La Rose's fields. He stood up from his crouched position and straightened his back. He could see the top of his father's tattered straw hat a few rows away. In the weeks which lay ahead, the fields would be turned over in preparation for the next growing season.

Toussaint placed the hoe on his shoulder and began his journey home. Although the sun had set a bit in the sky, the humidity exhausted him while the cool winter air provided rejuvenation. His straw hat, dotted with holes, did little to shield him from the late afternoon sun. A hole had developed in the front brim, creating a periscope, allowing a beam of sunlight to shine into his right eye. Maybe his Maman could fix it.

He plotted his course for future. *I will never work the fields again. I will never work the fields again. I will never work the fields again.* He inhaled. "I will never work the fields again."

Teddy placed his arm around his son's shoulders. Toussaint jumped. His father laughed, for he knew he'd caught his son by surprise. "You sho' won't. You'se gonna be free, Toot." Toussaint stared straight ahead, his eyes fixed on his future. "You'se gonna be more than a field hand." Teddy smiled with pride, his eyes set on heaven. "Yup, sho' is. God done told me 'bout it the first minute I'se holds you in my arms."

Toussaint released the vision and turned to his father. He didn't look up at him anymore, for they were now close to the same height. "Really, Papa? You can see it too?"

Teddy rubbed the back of Toussaint's sticky, sweat drenched neck. "Yessuh, it's true. Your Maman done seent it too."

Reaching the water boy, father and son waited their turn for a drink. The child offered them each the ladle, dripping with warm water. They wiped their mouths with their shirt sleeves, in unison, and then began the mile journey home.

After dinner, Toussaint left the cabin. He saw his sister sitting on the porch of a neighboring cabin, talking with her friends. He admired her so. She was tall, slender, midnight dark, and shapely. Toussaint dreamed of a lady loving him as beautiful, if not even more so, than his sister.

Stank had told Toussaint he'd heard Miss Bits grandson,

Kinky, was sweet on her, which Toussaint already had figured out. Everyone waited for them to announce their plans to jump the broom. Toussaint heard giggling. He knew Missy and her friends discussed her plans to wed.

Finding a small opening in the brush, Toussaint passed through, leading to the fields. After walking another half mile, he turned off through a small opening in the overgrowth bordering the cotton field. He walked another quarter of a mile in the darkness. He didn't need a light for his journey, having emblazoned a map of the trail in his mind. He came to an abandoned hunting shack. He opened the door and lit the lamp.

He sat on a pile of hay shaped into a chair of sorts, upholstered with burlap cotton bale sacks. He relaxed for a moment, dreaming of his future. "I will own businesses. Papa won't have to work the fields anymore." His mother never did work the plantation. Toussaint lit the old oil lamp on the crate he used for a table. He let the lamp burn low. He didn't know when he could get his hands on a new supply of oil.

Initiating the routine he'd established four years before, Toussaint pried up the floorboard and extracted a tin box. Removing the lid and then its contents, he laid out his future before him.

First, he took out his lesson book. He wasn't sure how

his mother had come into possession of it, but she had. After four years, Toussaint could read. He'd taught himself. The book said *8th Grade Primer* on the cover. He opened it with reverence. Toussaint began his reading lesson. Once finished, he opened his arithmetic book and worked the problems beneath the dim lamp light.

Having completed the evening's lessons, he next removed a bundle of pamphlets. The pamphlets motivated him to be disciplined and diligent in taking his lessons. Turning up the oil lamp, he admired the etched image on the cover of a Negro man with bushy gray and white hair, sporting an untamed beard. The caption beneath the portrait read Frederick Douglas.

His mother had given him many articles on the man. He would always ask, "Maman, how did you get these?" She would respond, "You'se knows I'se travel, boy." Then she would say, "Boy, I'se gonna make sure you'se gits your learnin'. When I'se take refugees to the North, I'se pick up these books for you. You'se used to go travelin' wit' me when you'se was small, remember?" Toussaint would nod, indicating he did.

Toussaint returned his attention to the article reporting the suffering of Negroes. He never ceased to be amazed by the phenomenon of Negroes and Whites in the North working together to free slaves. He would never have believed kind White folks existed, if it hadn't been for the articles. He'd believed most White folks behaved as Master Augustus.

After he completed his lessons and meditations, Toussaint replaced his primer and the pamphlets in the tin box, returning them to little place beneath the floor. He snuffed out the lamp and left his sanctuary, latching the door.

Toussaint decided to take the long way home, walking through the Slave Quarter. The shuttered, pseudo area of commerce inspired hope within his soul for a day when Negroes would have their own towns with self-sufficient economies, independent of White folks.

He closed his eyes, and saw visions of Negro women attired as ladies, carrying parasols and dressed in finery, accompanied by their husbands, dressed in their business suits. He then envisioned the farmers with their wives wearing calico dresses and bonnets. The farmers wore heavy starched overalls and clean white shirts. These families drove their wagons into the Negro town for the day to do their shopping. Their little girls wore dresses with at least one petticoat and their boys paraded down the street in their starched overalls, like their fathers.

He admired the families strolling the boardwalks of the imaginary Negro towns, going in and out of the shops owned by other Negroes, buying their needed wares. The farmers would bring produce and goods from their prosperous farms to sell to the shop owners, who would then sell the goods to others in the community. No one dressed in rags. Everyone worked hard and prospered. The White folks left them alone. No one hunted the Negro people.

Toussaint could see in the Spirit these towns would come into existence in the years to come, although Satan would do all he could to destroy these utopias. He could see the White mobs destroying the towns. Why would they do such a thing? The Negroes weren't bothering them.

The Spirit revealed to him the White folks needed Negroes to be dependent upon them. The success of the Negro raised fear in the collective hearts of the White folks. For if allowed to flourish, the White folks feared the Negro people would overtake them. Toussaint's muscles contracted and shuttered from the screams of the Negroes, echoing in the Spirit, being burned alive in their homes and businesses. Their only crime would be thriving and prospering without the help of White folks.

Passing the stable located at the northern edge of the square, the piercing screams inundated his being once more. Light seeped through the planks of the barn door. Toussaint stopped cold, realizing what he heard didn't stem from his vision, but from an event happening at that moment. He ran to the doors and looked through the cracks. He found a

Negro woman bent over a bale of hay, screaming.

Missy

Toussaint opened the door. He fell to the hay strewn dirt floor.

Toussaint awoke to find himself hog-tied. He lay before his sister, facing her. "I told you I was going to get you back, Nigger. You're going to learn to mind your own business," Hanzel said, his voice even more shrill than normal.

The devil assumed a place of prominence in Hanzel's soul. "James, why don't you give it a go," he said. "You're going to the Citadel. Go there as a man. Here, have a poke." Hanzel spread apart the cheeks of her behind, revealing her vagina. He couldn't resist the urge to slap her buttocks, watching the fullness of her behind jiggle.

He stuck his finger inside and extracted it with a bit of effort, placing the finger in his mouth. It was dry. He'd hoped James wouldn't take his turn. His dick was hard with the anticipation of ripping her. He hadn't believed a bitch Nigger of her age could be a virgin.

Straining his neck, Toussaint turned to find a timid man standing in a corner of the barn behind him, mortified. The young man could see in the Spirit. *Stop him!* Toussaint called to him with his mind. The young man covered his ears. He ran for the bolted doors. Lifting the bar, he opened the door and fled the barn.

"Nigger lover," Hanzel said as he took his position behind Missy. James has always been a Nigger lover. Like she was a real woman. Hanzel tossed her skirt up over her head, shielding her desperate eyes from her brother.

He thrust himself inside of her. She was bone dry. Hanzel feared she'd rip the skin off his cock. He labored, pulling in and out. Her screams, coupled with the screams of her brother, strengthen his resolve and heightened his pleasure. It seemed to go on for an eternity, his orgasm just beyond his reach. Her blood lubricated him, making it easier for him to pull in and out.

After some time, his body began to shudder. He had taken his fair share of women, but none had been like this one. The crescendo of her voice, harmonizing with her brother's, took him to a place he'd never imagined. Unable to bear the rush of it all, Hanzel chimed his hellish aria with their oratorio of desolation. He ejaculated with a force unknown, never ceasing. He collapsed atop her. He bit her neck, savoring her blood on his dry lips.

Hay snowed downed upon them all, dislodged from the rafters by Missy's inconsolable screams, her agony ripping her vocal cords in two.

Chapter 10

Hell. La Rose Plantation.

She'd never walked to the edge of the formal garden. Sarah passed the lewd statue in the fountain of the one she sought. She continued her eastern journey along the grand axis of the garden. The darkness deepened the further she traveled. There was no light in the East.

The bosquets gave way to the forest, emitting little light for her journey. She could have walked with her eyes closed, there was no difference. However, Sarah was fortunate. She didn't need the light to see. After walking for miles, Sarah stopped before running into the ancient weathered pine door, having surrendered its patina to a rough-hewn, rotted gray surface.

Sarah kicked the door down.

Eternity. La Rose Plantation.

SARAH THE SLAVE gazed out into the openness of everything and nothing. Infinity radiated with an artist's hasty mixing of colors, swirling together the hues of a peacock blues, green golds, and metallic reds, and then smearing the sum of it across his palette with a wet brush. However, the rebellious colors retained their independence, amid being forced to assimilate.

Cherubim placed her halo on her dreadlocked head, allowing it to float above. She stood before creation, covered in thick, milky honey.

With nothing below her feet or above her head, before or behind her, to her left or to her right, she inspected the nothingness. "You cannot hide from me."

Sensing a presence behind her, in the seven o'clock position, Sarah levitated in the direction. She heard a door close. "He can't run forever, Barachiel. This time, he's going to pay."

Barachiel revealed himself to her. He adjusted the belt of his tunic. "*Ma Reine L'Abeille*, Heaven grieves for our little girl."

Exiting the honey combs of her locked hair, a grand army of drones spread out across Eternity. "Find him and bring him to me." The insects radiated out from their Queen in circle formation, searching. Pulses of light flashed in the distance; the drones clearing the spirits they encountered as good and clean.

Barachiel placed his arm around her, or at least tried to do so. One of her drones attempted to sting him. "Stand down," L'Abeille commanded him. The drone fell back into ranks with the others left behind to guard their Queen, circling her head.

Barachiel never did care for the drones. The only souls the hostile insects loved were their Queen and Christ. Barachiel found them to be more vicious than any attack dog in Heaven or Hell. One could reason with the dogs. "Ma Reine, this horrible thing has been allowed." Barachiel raised his wing tip to his hand, pruning his blood feather. Although it gave him the same feeling as hearing nails scrapped across a chalk board, he found it less painful than looking L'Abeille in the eye. "*Je suis profondément désolée.*"

"You're sorry?" The buzzing surrounding her intensified. "This is my flesh, as well as yours, Barachiel. You allowed this happen?"

"La Rose," Barachiel whispered. The bees circled L'Abeille's head, filled with fury. Their buzzing deafened Barachiel.

She consulted the Spirit. "Oh, I see. It was either La Rose or my child. So, to save the Rose, the Throne decided to allow my Missy to be sacrificed. No one thought to ask me my thoughts on the matter?"

"You're banned from attending Throne, L'Abeille. You

know this."

L'Abeille released a low-pitched buzz. "No one died. I'm not sure why I've been made the example. Besides, it all happened eons ago." Recalling the near deaths of Lucifer and Mammon at their collective hand, not long after the Fall, L'Abeille plopped down on the nothingness. Her dread locked hair cocooned her, as she considered all that had transpired. How did she always forget? They had been cut in half, creating The Rose and the Bee.

Never again had the women been allowed to walk the earth together as adult, seeing women. Maybe their lifetimes would overlap from time to time; however, once one of the women had gained their sight and power, the other would have to vacate the Earth. Even in Eternity, their contact together required supervision. "That was unfair. Why did the Most High separate us? We were one. We are one. La Rose and L'Abeille are one." L'Abeille wiped colorless honey from her eyes. "They'd plotted to sacrifice our Little One. Perhaps we allowed our emotions to best us for a moment."

A mother protecting her child was a dangerous thing. Barachiel knew this fact first hand from dealing with La Rose and L'Abeille. Even though the Most High had neutralized the situation by splitting the soul of La Rose, thus creating L'Abeille, they both remained dangerous spirits. "Soon the time will come when you will be assimilated again as one,"

Barachiel said. "As one, you are dangerous. Dare I say even mon Frère Michael avoids you?"

L'Abeille censored her response. If Michael feared her and La Rose, that was his problem. "Humph. In any case, I've been told for eons I'll be assimilated. I'm not convinced. But we must maintain our faith, n'est-ce pas?" Buzzing distracted her. Her drones returned from the distant void of the horizon. They had arrested no one. "Where have you hidden him? Why do all of you continue to protect him?"

"It has been allowed." Barachiel stretched his wings. "My question to you, L'Abeille, is why can't you accept it?"

"He has rendered my daughter desolate."

Barachiel tucked his wings behind him. "Is she not a child of the Most High? Was not Christ the Son of the Most High God as well?" Sarah took on the glow of a furnace, dripping molten honey. "Is it not true?" Barachiel watched her float away, followed by her army of drones. She passed the shattered pine door leading back to the garden.

Raguel and Sealtiel flew over to where Barachiel levitated. "Oh, now you two come."

"I wasn't dealing with that," Raguel said.

"She hot like oven. I might burn," Sealtiel said. "She has right. See what devil did to her child? Too much devil in the Holy Line. Look at Keyholder. Now more devil to dwell in girl child to come from union."

Raguel peered into the void. "He's right, Barachiel," Raguel said. "With one as evil as the Doctor, there is no telling what the progeny will become."

Barachiel crossed his wings behind him, thinking. "As you both know, it has been allowed." They nodded, casting their eyes downward into the Abyss. "It will be well. All will come to pass according to notre Seigneur's will."

La Rose Plantation, St. Helena Parish. January, 1861.

VOICES AWOKE HIM. One was enraged, seeking vengeance. The other pleaded for a level head. Toussaint sat up on his pallet, unsure of what was going on. He had a nightmare about Missy, but he couldn't remember it.

"They'se can tar and feather me if they'se wants to," Teddy said, yelling and crying at the same time. "That li'l piece of White trash ain't gonna git away wit' this!" Teddy wiped his eyes. He breathed in deep and then exhaled, causing the corner of his mouth to turn up. "Won't nobody ever find him no way."

"Yeah, that may be so, Teddy. But they'll find you," Sarah said, grabbing him by his shoulders and shaking him. "What's I'se gonna do wit'out you? Missy needs you'se now. Toussaint needs you. Thank how'se the chil'ren gonna feel."

It hadn't been a dream. Toussaint pulled on his britches and ran from the cabin. Hanzel still had to be on the place. Toussaint ran down the road, leading from the slave cabins to the plantation house. He heard his mother calling him. He panted.

Toussaint had decided how he would dispose of Hanzel's body. His mother could take him away to another place once he buried Hanzel. He had a spot in mind, on the edge of the swamp. There was no need to kill him first. A lack of food and oxygen would cause him to die a natural death.

Reaching the front drive of the mansion, he could see Hanzel in the Spirit, running. Toussaint's parents called him, but he ignored their cries.

Charging the plantation house, Toussaint hit an invisible wall and fell backwards. Out of sorts, he sat up from where he lay the ground, finding three men. A petit White man stood in the center, with tall a Negro standing to his left, wearing a king's attire constructed of gold thread. A short man with narrow eyes stood to right of petit White man, attired in emerald woven silks. The White man spoke. "Where are you going, mon fils?

Overcome with rage, Toussaint took no consideration of the White man. "To kill Hanzel," Toussaint said. "He raped… He raped Missy."

"We know, my son. We saw it." The Negro man picked him up from the road, dusted him off and patted his cheek. "The Most High God of Heaven and Earth, along with his

Son, Jesus the Christ saw it as well." The Black man snickered. "'The Lord laughs at wicked, for he knows their day is coming.' In the meantime, what do you propose to do?"

Toussaint broke away from his grasp, but found he couldn't move. Giant magnets anchored him to the road.

The White man lit a cigarette and blew its fumes into Toussaint's face. He collapsed. The Chinese man caught him. "Protector full of rage. Perhaps we allow him justice."

"You know it is not allowed," the Negro said to his blood thirsty brother. "Satan hasn't completed his reign of terror on this line."

The White man threw down his roll up and extinguished it. "Let us take him to his mother."

Teddy rubbed Sarah's back as she sobbed. Missy lay upon her pallet, weeping. She hadn't stopped crying since they found her earlier that morning. However, Sarah preferred her cries, for then, she knew Missy's soul battled against insanity. However, when she stopped crying and her eyes went blank, Sarah watched her child retreat to a place in the Spirit world where even she couldn't find her.

Sarah removed a tattered handkerchief from her pocket and wiped her eyes. How would she stop Teddy and Toussaint from hunting down Hanzel and taking him to Augustus' Shed? Now, Toussaint had escaped. Looking out into the Spirit, she couldn't find him.

"Here he is."

Teddy yelled out, surprised by the three men who appeared out of nowhere. A man with slanted eyes held their son in his arms. "Who'se ya'll?" Teddy asked.

"It's not important," the White man responded.

Sarah glared at him. *Keep your mouth shut.*

He cleared his throat. "I found him on the road," the White man said. "What has happened here?"

"You'se knows what that li'l bastard did," Sarah said to the White man. "He raped my Missy, and made her brother watch!"

The men bowed their heads. Toussaint stirred in the Chinese man's arms. "Allow us to take him to a place where he will be safe."

Sarah arose from her chair at the table and put her face in the White man's. Teddy grabbed her arm, but she shook him off. "You'se ain't takin' my baby off this here place."

Taking Toussaint from his comrade, the petit White man rocked Toussaint in his arms, filled with sadness. He admired the young man's sleeping face. Toussaint stirred, but settled down. "You won't have a son if he stays."

Teddy couldn't believe his words. "Toussaint ain't done nuthin'."

The White man nodded. "This is true. However, Toussaint has a bit of a temper and a need for revenge, much like his father." Teddy turned his eyes to the floor. "Do you not agree your boy has an important mission in life?"

Teddy found it incredible this White man could see his son's purpose. "Yessuh."

"Then allow him to leave with us."

Teddy considered the situation. His wife's eyes pleaded with him to deny their request. "What's the Massa and the Overseer gonna say?"

"Nothing. They won't notice him missing."

Teddy wiped away a tear, conceding. Sarah screamed. "He'll return to us, Sarah. I'se promises you," Teddy said to her.

For the first time in her life, Sarah felt powerless. She turned to her ravished daughter, battling insanity.

Seeing her angst, the Negro king walked over and knelt where Missy lay. She whimpered, her eyes darting to and fro, seeing the terrors of Hell. "Sleep my child." He touched her between the eyes. Missy fell into a deep sleep. The Negro wept for her. "She will be well for a time."

"Whatcha tryin' to say, Albertus," Sarah asked before she could stop herself. "Heal her!"

"Jesus heals, not me."

Teddy considered the four of them. "You'se knows them, Sarah?"

Sarah ignored her husband. "All thangs is possible…"

The Chinese man patted Sarah's cheek. "Try give her will to live. Then Christ heal her. She must want to live."

Sarah lost hope, knowing her daughter didn't have the resolve. *I can raise hope in her*, Sarah told herself. She melted into tears within the comfort of her husband's arms.

The White man looked down at Toussaint, resting in his arms. The three men left the cabin, taking Toussaint with them.

Chapter 11

Chevalier Château, Fargniers, France. February, 1861.

Why would they ask him now? He didn't know what to do. This matter should have been addressed in thirteenth year of the young man's life.

Claude Hicks watched Toussaint toss in bed, tormented by injustice. Peering into Toussaint's soul, he could see the rape of not only his sister, but of Toussaint's very soul. "Perhaps it would help." Claude left his bedside, walking down the hall to a small salon. He sat with the men, awaiting him. "Has he regained consciousness since arriving in France?"

Emmanuel raised an eyebrow and took a sip of his cognac. "No."

Claude leaned back against the gold damask George III sofa and closed his eyes. "Father, guide us." He relaxed, allowing all stress to leave his flesh. Soon, an image of the Rose appeared before him with Mammon's minion, the Doctor, making his move against her. A clock sat suspended in time above the two, its hands spinning around with great speed. Claude opened his eyes. "The time approaches for the wicked Doctor's final solution," he said.

Albertus adjusted his gold ring with the Ark of the Covenant upon it. "There is some time in the human realm. For us, it will happen before we know it."

Claude took a sip of his cognac. "Let it be done." Claude considered the torment Toussaint endured with the memory of his sister's violation. "Maybe we should wait until his twenty-first year. I'm not sure if he can handle the revelation the Blood will bring. Give him time to accept what has happened."

The men nodded in agreement. "So shall it be," Li-Zhan said. He waved his *Ju-i* with care and then returned the wand to its resting place upon his lap. "As you wish, *mes Frères.*"

Chapter 12

Montmartre, 18th Arrondissement, Paris, France. November, 1862.

Squeezing the sponge, the water rained down onto the scarred corpse. Toussaint's heart filled with sorrow as he considered the layers of filth upon her skin. The poor child hadn't enjoyed the opportunity to bathe often during her short, brutal life. Toussaint rubbed the grime away from her shoulders and then her neck.

Was the girl even fifteen years old? Toussaint guessed no. He was sure she'd been a prostitute. All the victims from the killings which had occurred over the past few weeks had been prostitutes. Why did women demoralize themselves like this? Couldn't they sell flowers? He dabbed away the white crystallized salt from the corners of her eyes with his towel, the final remnants of her tears of agony. "I won't hurt you, Mademoiselle. No one will ever hurt you again."

She's already dead

With vigor, Toussaint shook his head in his feeble attempt to dispel the voice he'd been hearing since arriving in

France. In any case, he would treat her remains with respect. He would prepare her as he would the remains for any paying family. This child had no family, no one to mourn her. As he examined her butchered remains, he noticed another wound. The animal had bitten her neck.

Toussaint covered the corpse with a shroud and busied himself with ordering his instruments. With each victim, he found it more difficult to perform his duties. He walked over to window, streaked with coal residue from Paris' chimneys. Looking down on the dim streets, he reflected on the recent changes in his life. He wasn't sure how he'd arrived in Paris. His last memory, before awaking in Claude's home, was at La Rose. He'd been hunting Hanzel and had planned to bury him alive.

After sleeping for what felt like an eternity, he'd awakened in a small room above his benefactor's funeral parlor in an area of Paris' 18th arrondissement called Montmartre. Toussaint liked the neighborhood. He could see the *Sacre Coeur* cathedral from his bedroom on the third floor.

He never imagined Negroes could live in such a fashion. In Paris, he was a man. Sure, he encountered some stares from the French from time to time, due to his midnight skin. Yet, he was respected.

His benefactor, Claude Hicks, tutored him in French, accounting practices, and other lessons. But most importantly, he taught him mortuary science. After a few months, Toussaint had demonstrated his acuity for the profession. An unknown benefactor had secured a position for him at the *Hôtel-Dieu.* Toussaint visited the hospital three times a week, observing doctors while on their rounds. However, his primary job was to assist in the morgue.

Toussaint watched a man pass on the street. His back stiffened. "He is here." He searched the street, but the man had disappeared. "It must be him. He's the killer." But how would he prove it? He had to find Hanzel and kill him.

It is not for you to do, mon fils

Toussaint frowned and returned to his work. In recent days, spirits, both good and evil, spoke to him more than the living. He chatted with physicians and co-workers at the hospital. He dined with Claude and his wife every evening. That was it. He was alone with his ghosts.

Toussaint removed the shroud from his client. He could see Hanzel standing behind her, violating her. Violating Missy. Just a baby. The child lay before him with her neck gapped open. Rape alone no longer satisfied Hanzel. He placed his hand on the wound, patting it. He could stop the bleeding and the pain.

They all looked like Missy to him, bleeding from every orifice, ripped open without mercy. "You're fine now." He massaged the wound to make it better. Her frozen, terrorized eyes stared back at him. Lifeless. A chill shook him.

The wound oozed. *"Pardon moi, Mademoiselle."* Taking his needle, he sutured the wound. "I cannot heal the dead." Once finished, he knotted and cut the thread.

Claude had arranged with the sisters at the *Couvent de Saint George* to bury the rash of rape victims in charity. So far, there had been four nameless women. The one laying before him was number five.

"The Doctor will rest for a time, once you drink the wine. All will be well. He will return to hell."

He turned around, but found himself alone. "Who said that?" He scanned the preparation room. Finding no one, Toussaint covered the corpse and picked up his scalpel. He turned around to find a man standing before him.

Toussaint's heart pounded. He knew this to be the one he'd heard in his thoughts. Studying the man, he recognized him, but from where? Perhaps Toussaint had seen the petit man in a dream? Maybe he'd seen him at La Rose. Yes, he had seen him there, but when?

"Mon fils, the better question would be, when haven't you known me?" Toussaint scrutinized the man's words. "Do you wish to remember me, mon fils?"

Toussaint didn't know what to do. His natural curiosity shouted yes, but the cautionary side of him encouraged him to run. Although the man wasn't physically imposing, wickedness lounged in his eyes. "Do you expect an answer now?" Toussaint asked. "I don't know you."

"As you say. But yes, if you have an answer, I would like it." The man walked over to the cooling table and removed the sheet. "Excellent work. The Doctor had been particularly brutal with her. He seeks to the scar the soul and the flesh, rendering his victims unpresentable to God and the world for all time." The man replaced the sheet, smirking. "But then again, God knows, as we all do, the devil is a liar."

"The devil?"

"Oui, mon fils, the devil. You have called her attacker as much, yes?" The man removed a cigarette case from his breast pocket. He opened it, extracted one and lit it. "You can hear him, feel him here in Paris, can you not?" Toussaint nodded. "He steals flowers from the notre Seigneur's garden. Yet, he doesn't put them in vases, but dashes them against the fence and the rocks of the garden, knocking away their petals. He will continue to do so until he finds the Rose. It is her he seeks."

You are her protector, he heard his mother whisper to his soul. "But why?" Toussaint asked.

The man threw down his cigarette and stomped it out. "The seed must not find a place to rest."

Toussaint walked over to the window and beheld the urban scene before him. However, he didn't see a city, but a garden. Before his eyes, the soil trembled. A green tender shoot sprung forth. It grew into a towering bush, bringing forth the most magnificent, crimson red blossom.

The blossom opened, revealing a woman standing within its center with a boy child. The child left her arms and walked down the bush, growing into a man. Once reaching the garden, he mounted a white horse that awaited him. He lifted his sword and rode away. "Le Baton."

The man arched his brow. "You know of him?" The man watched Toussaint labor to understand his knowledge of things he shouldn't know. "There aren't many people who know that name. Why do you know it, mon fils?"

Toussaint placed his hands against the small, rectangular glass panes of the window. He searched for the garden, but only found the surrounding neighborhood with it bustling streets. He could still see the image of the garden in his mind's eye.

"What you have seen is true."

Toussaint faced him. "Who are you?" The man didn't reply. Toussaint peered into his eyes. He had a vision of looking down on the man from a lofty place in his La Rose Plantation cabin, standing next to his maman. The man had admonished and loved him at the same time, proud of Toussaint's tenacity.

"You were a good boy." The man nodded. "I am your

relation, your cousin. I am Claude's father."

Toussaint hadn't realized Claude was related to him. He wondered how. He'd never seen him on the plantation before.

"He is from another plantation, in Virginia. *La Pivoine.* It's a bit complicated," the man said, taking hold of his pocket watch. The time had drawn near. "Have you made a decision?"

Toussaint closed his eyes. He could see the bodies piling up around Paris. The Doctor bruised the flowers' petals. "I will."

The man snapped his pocket watch closed and placed it in his breast pocket. "Bon! I had every confidence you would."

Toussaint shifted the corpse from the cooling table to the special dumb waiter, able to accommodate bodies up to seven feet in length. Pulling the chain, he lowered the body to the cellar.

Once the dumbwaiter hit the bottom, Toussaint secured the chain and hurried down the narrow steps to the cellar, where they kept bodies until the services. Thirty minutes later, Toussaint returned upstairs, finding the man waiting for him. "I'd thought you'd be gone."

"Not without you."

Toussaint turned down the lamp in the preparation

room. He opened the door and left, with the man following him to his living quarters on the third floor. Since the man wouldn't leave, Toussaint invited him inside. "Would you like a cognac?" The man nodded, taking a seat in the chair near the window. Toussaint prepared the man's drink and handed it to him. "What is your name, Monsieur?"

After sipping his cognac, the man lit a cigarette, crossed his legs and leaned back in his seat. He exhaled, filling Toussaint's room with smoke. "I am Emmanuel Chevalier. But I am your cousin, your relation. Please, call me Emmanuel."

"Toussaint."

With heavy eyes, he rolled his head from side to side. His spirit curled within his flesh, like cigar smoke in an enclosed room. There was no destination, no past or present. Being. "Oui?"

"Do you wish to stop? You do not have to do this. It is not necessary. I will love you, regardless. You are a great man with or without this. It is a hard life and a long one. I wish for you to reconsider."

Toussaint heard the voice float across the ages to the distant land where he sat in a garden filled with beautiful roses. Wolves prowled the perimeter. He stood in the center of the garden, watching the wolves and the roses. Some of the plants had budded, others were in full bloom.

There was one rose, the most beautiful of all, a red rose just beginning to unfurl her petals. He knew this was his rose, La Rose, his to guard and protect. It sat atop a strong bush, with little buds lounging in her shelter, beneath her leaves, awaiting their time to bloom.

A flower had been pruned away. Where was it? Who had pruned his flower without his knowledge?

Toussaint turned, searching the garden for the missing blossom. He spotted a wolf with the stem in his mouth, attempting to run with it, but the thorns bit his tongue. He dropped it.

Sarah stood beside him, with the severed stem. "I'll plant her, next to *vos fleur*," she said to him, in a whisper. With her hands, Sarah burrowed into the soil, scooping out a hole. She inserted the bare stem, and then filled the hole with soil. Toussaint watched the stem take root and grow with vigor, generating several blossoms of its own. "Now you have two, my son. Guard them," Sarah said to him.

Toussaint eyes popped open. He burned with fever. "I accept."

Claude smiled and frowned all at once, now knowing what his son must endure. "Bon," he whispered and walked away.

***

Toussaint's feet left the earth. Swaying in nothingness, several hands touched him, steadying him. Looking down, he watched the faceless men wrap him with a golden rope, beginning at his ankles, working upwards, stopping beneath his chin. He couldn't move.

His head drooped down, watching those below look up at him. Silence. His ascension halted. He floated.

His head bobbed in the darkness. Below, he noticed an altar with six candles on either side, illuminating a wooden cup.

The candles didn't give off enough light to see those standing in the darkness. Although silent, he felt the presence of many. They lowered him, but his feet never touched the floor. He felt himself being secured to a stand or a tree. Two women appeared before him, suspended somewhere between heaven and earth. Their albino white faces before his, the women peered deep into his eyes, searching him, looking past his suffering and pain. "Are you in agreement?" One woman asked the other. "Is it him?"

"Oui. I am in agreement with you," the other responded. "*C'est vrai.*"

The first woman turned her back to him, as did the other. His pain intensified, causing him to cry out. "Stop questioning and the pain will subside. Stop fighting," one of the women said.

"Your number has reached thirty," the other woman announced to those standing below. "There are three remaining. They will not come for some time." The women turned to Toussaint once more. "Will you die for the Blood of Our Lord, Jesus the Christ?"

The question astonished him. He began to weep. Something welled up from deep within him, a love which he had never known, a consuming passion. "Yes."

"Will you protect La Rose and destroy her enemies at all costs, even to the point of yielding your own life?"

"Yes," he said, mourning the life of the One who had departed and the One yet to come.

One woman peered into the eyes of the other. "Do you accept and receive the validity of his testimony?"

The other woman kissed Toussaint, searching out his depths, swimming through the waters of his very soul, verifying his identity one final time and the sincerity of his response. She kissed him again. Toussaint felt a spirit, a force, enter his body. The spirit traveled throughout his being, cleansing him.

The woman inhaled, her mouth covering his. The spirit left him, leaving him spent and weak. The woman stepped away from him and spoke. "I am in agreement with you, sister. I accept and receive his testimony." Descending to the floor, the women returned to the altar, standing to either side of the chalice.

"Christ reigns, the line is sure. Love reigns. The Word has been proven true," they said in unison. "He has chosen the Way, being of the Way, having walked with Our Lord."

They faced one another, and then turned to altar. They knelt. Two men came and veiled the women. Wispy, fervent voices floated up to Toussaint. The two voices melded into one, speaking a language he couldn't understand.

They pierced him.

Toussaint could feel his life vacate his flesh. The volume of the Sister's feathery voices increased, in unison, speaking the same words.

Wood pressed against his bottom lip, encouraging him to open his mouth. He drank.

Toussaint sat in the garden wounded, confused, and enraged. Sarah comforted him. "Be strong, my child. This is the purpose for which you have returned."

Toussaint heard a blood curdling scream, begging for mercy. It was his voice. The burden was so hard to bear; it was too heavy. He was cold and alone. He was all alone.

You are never alone

I am always with you, my son

The women stopped praying. Hooded, silence covered Toussaint.

He floated.

Chapter 13

Chevalier Château, Fargniers, France. December, 1862.

He could feel the soft sheets beneath his fingertips, first. Then, sensation returned to his arms, legs and torso. Next, he perceived a cloth under his chin, descending the length of his body, covering his feet. Warm sand weighted down his eyelids. He could feel. Yet, he couldn't move his body. He feared someone had entombed him in a clay vault.

"Monsieur?"

Toussaint managed to open his eyes and catch a glimpse of a man standing above him. He closed them again. He listened. Feet walked away from him. He heard a door open and close. Time passed. A door opened. Several pairs of feet approached him. They surrounded where he lay. "You said he was awake?"

"Oui, Monsieur. He had opened his eyes."

Toussaint listened to the muffled sound of a hand slipping into some sort of cloth bag, maybe a pocket. His nostrils burned; he couldn't stop coughing and sneezing. He could feel liquid running down his face from his nose. Someone applied a cool cloth to the affected area. "He has returned to us. Allow him time to regain his strength. He has slumbered for thirty days." Many feet walked away. "Drink this Monsieur," said the voice who'd spoken to him before the arrival of the others. The liquid moistened Toussaint's lips.

With effort, he sat up in bed. Every muscle in his body ached, as if a butcher had beaten him with a mallet. He swung his legs from beneath the covers and sat on the edge of the bed, holding his head. The image in his eyes multiplied and cascaded downward like cards shuffled from one hand to another. His perspective of the room shifted to the right. Without warning, everything steadied, all views of the room uniting into a single image within his brain.

The drapes were open, allowing entrance of the morning's gray gloom. He walked over to the writing desk, finding a newspaper. *January 12, 1863*. 1863? Toussaint combed his memory, trying to recall what had happened. He remembered preparing a prostitute for burial. A petit White man had visited him.

Toussaint scrutinized the grand room. "This isn't Claude's home." He was in some sort of castle. "Château?" Yes, it was a château. He'd heard of them, but had never visited one. Yet, he knew he'd been in the room before.

A crescent shaped canopy crowned his bed, mounted on the wall near the top of the twenty-four-foot high muraled ceiling. Gold moiré bed curtains cascaded down from the fixture. The bed was larger than any he'd ever seen. His entire family could sleep on it and never know the other was there.

He heard knocking. Toussaint crossed the room and opened the door, which led to a room lined with small coves where suits of clothes hung. A large, round settee sat in the center of the space. The room was filled with bureaus, armoires, and variety of other furnishings to storage the multitude of hats, coats, shoes, cravats, canes, and miscellaneous apparel.

The knocking continued. He left the room and opened another door to a room with a wash stand, a golden tub, gold racks loaded with soft, white towels, each monogrammed with a scripted "C". Within the room he found a second door, opening to room paneled with a fragrant wood. Toussaint sniffed the wall. "Cedar." Large stones had been stacked atop a pyre stand of some sort.

The knocking persisted. Toussaint left the washroom. There were at least three doors remaining, which he'd yet to open. "Yes, come in," Toussaint said, exhausted.

A man entered, followed by servants taking hot water

into the room with the wash stand. "I am Jeffery, the butler of La Château de Chevalier."

"Chevalier?" Toussaint panicked. "Has Augustus found me?" None of it made sense. If Augustus had found him, he would've been suspended from hooks in the barn.

"Oui. Monsieur Augustus is related, but he isn't the one who brought you here." Jeffrey considered the boy. He thought he would have remembered more by now. It had been two months.

"You will find suits in your dressing room, through the first door you opened." Toussaint's mouth fell open. "Once you have dressed, one of the servants will escort you to the dining hall."

His words confused Toussaint at first, but then he remembered the room filled with clothing. "What, those clothes are for me?"

Jeffery shrugged. "Who else would wear them?" He opened the door, allowing the staff to leave first. He bowed to Toussaint and left.

Toussaint returned the bed and sat there for a few moments in stunned disbelief. Confidence and joy surged within his soul. He jumped up and ran to the wash room to prepare himself for his day.

The magnificent staircase leading into the grand hall presented the warmth of a prison, accented with thirty-foot-tall golden statues of angels of damnation, standing guard. The limestone fortification had been decorated over the years to give a more 'homey' feel.

Following the manservant, Toussaint descended the stairs. His eyes locked on the coats of arms and weapons mounted to the limestone walls. Looking down into the foyer, an army of armor suits stood at attention on either side of the entryway, cautioning guests to behave. There were no windows or skylights. However, he did notice slits along the front façade, one-foot wide, eight feet tall, spaced every twenty-four feet perhaps? "God, no one could enter or exit this place without permission."

"Oui, Monsieur," the manservant replied. Reaching the ground floor, the manservant escorted him across the vast open space. It seemed more like an enclosed courtyard where executions had once occurred. Toussaint noticed the red blotches on the stone floor in an area near the wall. He could hear voices crying out to him. It was the blood.

Why could he hear the blood? In fact, the place reverberated of voices, screaming for mercy. Not justice, but mercy. Why didn't the blood cry out for justice?

"They were receiving justice when their blood was spilt, mon fils," the manservant said. Toussaint smelled smoke and turned around, but found nothing. "My question would be why don't these souls repent and ask for forgiveness? Not one ever has done so," the manservant said, filled with wickedness.

Toussaint wondered if the man had been an executioner at one time.

"Perhaps."

The muted screams resonating from the bowels of the château caused Toussaint to cover his ears. How could anyone live in the place? An ear-piercing gong rang out the hour of the morning. The wailing intensified.

Searching the area to determine the source of the noise, his attention riveted to the wall. His eyes crept up to find an enormous clock face mounted within its stone surface. It couldn't have been a wall, but the side of a mountain, incorporated into the château.

The gong sounded again. Toussaint scrutinized the clock's face. It had no hands. The clock's face had been constructed of some sort of quartz mixed with mother of pearl, giving it a translucent surface. Something bumped against a clock's face from within, causing the milky quartz to part and swirl about. The roman numerals shimmered upon the time piece's face like lily pads on a pond.

Toussaint dropped his hands from his ears, no longer overwhelmed with the clock's eardrum shattering gong. He stood before the clock, immobilized, unable to comprehend what was going on behind the clock's face. The gong blared. Another dark figure came forward to the face of the clock and then disappeared within. A few seconds later, a human face, etched with horror, pressed against the surface, pleading to him. An unseen forced yanked him away. The soul vanished.

The chime of the hour ended. Toussaint blinked, finding the clock's hands had reappeared in their appropriate place, indicating one minute past eight o'clock in the morning.

"Are you ready to proceed, Monsieur?"

Toussaint couldn't believe the manservant's indifference to the clock. "Didn't you see that?"

"Pardon, Monsieur?"

Toussaint turned back to the clock and then to the manservant. "There are souls trapped in that clock. Is that what they are?"

"Oui, Monsieur."

Toussaint's eyes bugged open wide. "Why don't you release them?"

A bewildered look arose on the manservant's face. "That is where they belong, Monsieur." He could see Toussaint didn't understand. "Perhaps Monsieur Chevalier can explain it to you. Follow me, s'il vous plaît." They continued their journey across the grand hall.

***

The manservant signaled to the guards to open the doors. He stepped aside, bowed and extended his arm, inviting Toussaint to enter the room. Toussaint stopped at the door. A room was a poor description of the space. It was enormous. The table stretched on forever, able to accommodate many guests. But who would come to such a place, having to pass through the executioner's hall, stained with blood?

"In the fifteenth century, I would have one of my servants cover the clock with a tapestry emblazon the Chevalier crest. He then would cover the blood-stained stone floor with fine rugs." A snort reverberated throughout the dining room. "Mortals don't hear the voices or see the blood as you do, my son." Toussaint heard the laughter of many men.

"And in response to your question to my manservant, he is correct when he says the souls belong there. They claw one another for the opportunity to approach the clock face at the appointed time. Let us say, it's their window to the land of the living. They hope one will hear and free them. I am sad to say, it has yet to happen. And it won't."

Toussaint stood in the doorway, amazed. Who had spoken to him? The room was empty.

"I am standing before you, my son."

Toussaint blinked. Servants stood along the far wall. He

found a petit, finely attired man standing before him smoking a cigarette. He felt a force clutch his heart within his chest. "Guillet."

Emmanuel raised an eyebrow. "Guillet, eh?" He extended his hand, inviting Toussaint into the sumptuous, gold gilded dining room. Enormous paintings honoring the mighty conquerors of the Chevalier family adorned the walls of the great hall, intermingled with landscape paintings of the surrounding countryside.

Emmanuel sat at the head of the table, inviting Toussaint to sit at his right. A servant opened the door, admitting Claude. He sat at Emmanuel's left. "What is this place," Toussaint asked, amazed.

"The dining room," Claude said. He and Emmanuel laughed. "You're at the Chevalier Château. We are north of Paris, in Fargniers," Claude said.

The servant placed Toussaint's first course before him, croissants and marmalade, and then poured a cup of coffee for him. Ravenous, Toussaint ate. "Hungry?" Claude asked.

"Why, yes. I feel as if I haven't eaten in weeks."

"You haven't," Emmanuel said.

Toussaint stared at the man, trying to place him. He knew he'd seen him before. "What is your name, Monsieur?"

"I told you, it is Emmanuel. I am your cousin. Do you not remember meeting me at Claude's mortuary? I enjoyed cognac with you in your room."

Toussaint peered out into the Spirit. "Yes, I remember now. In fact, it's the last thing I remember."

Claude and Emmanuel said nothing, continuing to consume their meal. The waitstaff removed the first course and presented the diners with yogurt and fruit. Claude considered the meal before him. "I want eggs." The waiter covered his plate with the silver lid and then uncovered it, now offering eggs, along with American cut bacon and sausage.

"Claude, you're almost a centenarian now. You should begin to watch what you eat. You won't be a youth forever," Emmanuel said.

Claude ignored him, enjoying his meal.

Toussaint sat in awe. "Monsieur, at what age do you consider a person old?"

Emmanuel screwed his lips, thinking. "I'm not sure. Everyone is young to me. There is no mortal as old as I."

His soul a sponge, Toussaint soaked up Emmanuel's words. The statement bounced around in his new state of consciousness. An unfamiliar sensation surged throughout him on a molecular level. Toussaint felt different, but he couldn't identify how. He could now see in the Spirit on a deeper level, observing dimensions never imagined.

He felt wood pressed against his lower lip

Toussaint sat erect in his chair, electrified. The sensation surged throughout his body, again. The liquid he'd accepted from the cup, took the initiative to enter his mouth. The thick, bittersweet pudding glided over his tongue and down his throat like quicksilver, traveling into his depths of its own volition, crashing into the pit of his stomach. It lived. The substance blossomed in his gut and migrated throughout his body, permeating every cell.

Claude stood up from the table, watching Toussaint's orbs glow white hot within their sockets. "He's reliving it," Claude said.

Toussaint stared at Claude, seeing him. "*Haute Chevalier*," Toussaint said. He turned to Emmanuel, seeing him. "Archangel Barachiel, Holy Patron of the Rose." Toussaint slumped back in his chair.

"He has remembered too much too soon," Claude said, hurrying over to where Toussaint sat. "Is he dead?"

Emmanuel left his place at the head of the table. Standing over his son, he lit his cigarette and exhaled. "I wouldn't worry, Claude. He will be well."

Refreshed from his bath and shave, Toussaint finished dressing. He tied his cravat, and then inserted the diamond and ruby studded tie tac, fashioned into a dagger stained with droplets of blood. "I'm never going back to Louisiana," he said to reflection in the mirror.

Toussaint descended the stairs, wondering what delights awaited him in the dining room. As he crossed the foyer, the imprisoned, tortured souls screamed out to him, pleading for release from their torment. Yet, their cries weren't as fervent as when he first arrived. Now, the souls, twisting in their eternal hellfire, would silence themselves, once they recognized Toussaint. They knew he held no mercy in his heart for them.

From the center of the grand hall, Toussaint saw a man speaking with his cousin in front of the dining room's double doors. He believed he recognized the man, but never caught a glimpse of his face. Toussaint consulted the Spirit. "You're the one!"

The man turned to him. Toussaint could see recognition and fear in his eyes. The man walked away, quickening his step. He raced out the front door, which Jeffrey held open for him.

"Wait," Toussaint yelled at him.

The man escaped his view. Toussaint ran through the open doors past Jeffrey; however, before he could descend the steps of the château, the man had entered his awaiting coach. The driver popped the reigns, spurring the team of black horses to spirit him away at top speed, taking the sharp curve on two wheels. The coach disappeared.

Toussaint stood on the narrow steps, wondering how the

coward had escaped him. He closed his eyes and listened. Transported back to the barn on La Rose Plantation, he listened to Hanzel's shrill voice.

James, why don't you give it a go?

"James. That's your name." Toussaint returned inside. Jeffrey closed the doors.

Montmartre, 18th Arrondissement. Paris, France. February, 1863.

THE CRUELTY OF man never ceased to horrify him. How could one crush another's skull to rob him of a few *centimes?* Wasn't a man's life worth more than that? Apparently not. But the injustice wasn't Toussaint's concern. His mission was to make him presentable for burial. The widow had insisted on an open casket funeral, but could Toussaint find a way to mask the disfigurement of the man's face?

Toussaint placed his scalpel on the tray and considered the challenge which lay before him. "I could reconstruct his skull, but with what?" Toussaint considered the situation a few moments more. "Tin."

Running to the shed located at the rear of the town-home's courtyard, he rummaged through the scrap metal in a crate under a workbench. He found a piece of tin that might do the trick. He returned to the preparation room. Studying what remained of the man's skull, he considered how the left side of his skull would have appeared.

Taking a small mallet, he pounded out an image of the right side of the man's face. Once satisfied, he reversed the profile to mirror the left side of the head. Toussaint then rolled back the skin on the corpse's face and removed the shattered bone. He slid the tin mold into place.

Judging the fit, he removed it and then made his adjustments. Once finished, Toussaint inserted the metal plate. He found the fit better complimented the shape of the corpse's head. Toussaint removed it once more, excavating openings for the eyes and ears, as well as shaping a bridge for the nose. He inserted the completed tin mold into position.

He rolled the skin back into place, pulling it tight. Toussaint utilized the finest invisible stitch he'd learned from Claude to suture the skin at the hairline and down the side to the ear. Pleased with is work, he then packed the seams with wax. It wasn't a customary technique, but one of Claude's trade secrets. Satisfied with the continuous surface he'd formed, Toussaint applied a pancake makeup of sorts, concealing the scars.

After hours of tedious work throughout the night, Toussaint admired his handiwork. "I don't want the wax to soften too far in advance of the services." He took the body to the cold cellar.

Claude said a prayer and then opened the casket. He

hadn't checked the corpse beforehand. He had to trust his apprentice. Once he saw the body, he wept.

The widow approached the coffin, apprehensive. The monsters had destroyed her love, beating him with clubs. She'd found him behind their little home on the rue, a bloody pulp.

Stopping next to Claude, she grasped his hand for support. She closed her eyes, and then turned away, unable to look on him. Yet, something in her soul stirred, giving her the courage to gaze upon him.

Her love slumbered in the coffin.

"This is impossible," Madame said with tears streaming from her eyes. "There's nothing amiss with him." She reached in and lifted his head to kiss him. His head dropped forward, lifeless, rigor mortis having passed. The coldness of his flesh chilled her hands, radiating to the core of her being.

She allowed his head to drop and then collapsed into Claude's awaiting arms.

Once the services ended and the mourners had vacated the mortuary, Toussaint remained in the chapel to pray for the soul of the deceased. He crossed himself and rose from before the Lord at the small altar. Yet, he couldn't focus his prayers on the man's soul.

He saw the one who suffered. Although she suffered in this age, in a time to come she would be crowned a queen. He always saw her face when he prayed. She reminded him of the master's Negro daughter on La Rose Plantation, but she was different. The woman in his prayers was a lady, not a slave. Yet, she was a slave. He brushed it off. Toussaint rubbed his aching knees and left.

Papa. Toussaint now had two fathers. Each man had loved him unconditionally and educated him in a variety of disciplines. Teddy had given him practical skills and common sense. Claude had built upon Teddy's foundation, providing him with a formal education and a vocation. He could feel a shift; a change approached him he couldn't avoid.

Toussaint walked down the hallway to the parlor, which could accommodate the wide loads of caskets being wheeled to the various chapels. Although the room had been designated for funeral services, Claude and his wife, Sophie, would use the room as personal living space. He heard laughter, and then Maman Sophie scolding someone in her hot, peppered French. *Cousin!*

Opening the door, cigarette smoke billowed out. Toussaint's soul filled with joy. "Emmanuel, what are you doing here?" Toussaint hugged him tight. It had been a couple of months since he'd last seen him.

"To visit my little ones." Emmanuel extinguished his cigarette. "How have you been, Toussaint?"

"I'm well." Toussaint smoothed his lapels and adjusted his shirt cuffs. If he'd known his cousin had come to call, he would have checked his appearance first. "Papa said I'm ready. I'm no longer an apprentice, but I've graduated to a mortician."

"Bon!" Emmanuel exclaimed. "You've completed your work here, but there's still much for you to learn."

Madame Sophie clapped her hands together and hugged her son, overwhelmed by the love she held for him. In all their years of marriage, the couple never had a child. However, when Claude brought Toussaint to their home two years before, he'd become the son for which she'd prayed.

At the end of the day, Toussaint would sit with her in the upstairs parlor and talk. He would listen to her concerns and comfort her. He would even run errands for her. The best thing about Toussaint was the hugs and kisses he showered on her. She remembered the first day he'd called her 'Maman.'

"Mon fils," Sophie said, her voice trembling. Rising to the tips of her toes, she patted his cheek.

Toussaint took her in his arms and rubbed her back, loving her.

Sophie burst into tears. She turned to Emmanuel, burrowing into his soul with her rage. "You wicked little man, taking mon fils from my arms." Sophie rushed from the room and ran up the stairs.

The men jumped when they heard her bedroom door slam. They stared at the floor, refusing to embrace her raw emotion. Emmanuel crossed his legs and smoothed his pants leg. "It's time for you to return to America, Toussaint."

Toussaint's hands balled into fists. Yet, he couldn't be mad, for he'd known it was coming. "I'm happy here. I have no desire to return."

"Yes, this is so." Emmanuel removed an invisible speck of lint from his trousers. "Yet, your sister slips deeper into insanity. Your niece is in danger."

Toussaint believed he'd lost his voice. "Niece?"

Emmanuel invited Toussaint to sit beside him, but he didn't move. Rising from the sofa, Emmanuel tapped his index finger between Toussaint's eyes, causing him to collapse upon the settee. After a moment or two, he regained his wits.

"Your sister Missy bore a child. Her name is Claret. She is now two years old," Emmanuel said. Toussaint sat before him, expressionless. "When your sister looks at her, she sees her attacker. You must save the child."

"Is she White?"

Emmanuel sneered at him. "No, she is dark, as are you and your sister."

Toussaint wept. How could God be so cruel as to allow Missy to bear the child of her rapist?

His face stung.

Emmanuel shook off the pain in his hand from striking his son. He only felt pain when correcting his flesh and those he loved. "Do not question the purpose of the Most High." Emmanuel lit another cigarette and exhaled. "The child is holy, and you must protect her. Her mother seeks the child's life."

"Why must Missy suffer? Why not Hanzel?"

Emmanuel punched him in his mouth. Tears filled his eyes, but he held them back. Taking a drag, Emmanuel exhaled as Toussaint inhaled, filling him with trepidation. "Always remember Toussaint, 'The Lord laughs at the wicked for he knows their day is coming.' Remember the scripture whenever you consider seeking vengeance, young man." Emmanuel patted his son's thigh.

"I understand your need for revenge. Claude and I have sought revenge from time to time throughout our lives. In times past, you have done so as well." He watched confusion skate across his son's face.

It amazed him how remembrance dallied in returning to the young man's spirit and soul. It was well. "However, we've learned when we seek to execute vengeance based on our own understanding, it never turns out well. You would be wise to learn this now, but I can see you won't." Emmanuel extinguished his cigarette. "Leave your things with your Papa and your wardrobe at the château. They won't be of use to you on the plantation."

"I have to go back?" Toussaint sat before him, panicked. "I'm no longer a slave."

Emmanuel felt sorry for his child. He'd wished to immerse him in Parisian life, as he'd done with James. However, their paths were different. It would have been detrimental to his purpose. He sighed, patting Toussaint's shoulder. "This is true. But you must lead your family out. You will create a life for them outside of bondage."

Chapter 14

La Rose Plantation, St. Helena Parish. February, 1863.

Fourth watch. Sarah despised awaking during the time night, for it never yielded a good revelation. Although she had no clock, she could sense the time.

Sarah arose from Teddy's side on their little straw mattress and lit a candle. Opening the cabin door, she found a star hanging in the dark blue sky at a forty-five-degree angle from where she stood. Three o'clock in the morning. She closed the door. Returning to bed, she felt a presence.

"It cain't be."

In the dim light, Sarah found her son, now a man, lying on the pallet next to his sister. For the first time in years, her daughter hadn't cried out in the night. Now she understood why.

Sarah returned to bed and blew out the candle. Claret, laying between her and Teddy, opened her eyes. "Grandmère?"

"*Oui, ma petite fille?*"

"Oncle's home. Grandpère sent him home?"

Sarah kissed her little one on the forehead. "Yessum. Grandpère done sent him home."

Nothing had changed on the plantation since his departure. Toussaint spotted folks he'd known all his life. Tatters. Everyone wore rags. However, the slave community still managed to take pride in their appearance. The seamstresses would mend their neighbors' dry rotted clothes to the best of their abilities, decorating the dead parts of dresses, slacks and shirts with multicolored patches, well any sort of scraps they could get their hands on. One could tell what seamstress had made which mends, for each possessed a signature stitch, a unique patch design, or an embroidered symbol of some sort, to give status, pride, and style to clothing so desperate and rudimentary.

Toussaint tipped his hat to Miss Betty, carrying a basket on her head filled with potatoes. His father had given him the old hat once he returned, worn out and beat up by the sun. He put his fine French wardrobe out of his mind. It was the past. He had to move forward.

As he entered the square, he could hear a sizzling noise, a fire hissing from being splashed with water. Toussaint walked toward the wash house. He could see Missy standing at her cauldron, stirring the boiling water like a madwoman. She beat the hot water, forcing the demon she saw within to stay submerged in the pot. Little Claret sat close to the pot. The scalding water splattered her. The child screamed and cried.

Toussaint broke into a run. He watched his sister divert her rage from the demon in the pot to her little daughter. "Stop it," he heard Missy say. She snatched the child from the ground. "You'se cain't do it to me again. Stop laughin'!"

Toussaint ran faster.

"I'se gonna stop your laughin' once and for all." She held Claret above the pot by her neck. Piercing screams ranged throughout the square, compelling people to look up from their work.

Toussaint pulled Missy from the edge of the pot with one hand while grabbing Claret with the other. "Vos oncle is here, little one," Toussaint said, jostling the child. He scanned the square. The others had turned away, returning to their toil. "Maman wants you, Missy. C'mon, let's go."

"Massa's sheets gonna burn."

Toussaint suppressed his tears, forcing a jovial, carefree nature. "You can check on them a little later." He led his sister and niece home.

Teddy sat on the porch, rocking his grown daughter in his arms. He remembered rocking her as a little girl, before Toussaint's birth. He would rock her to sleep, letting her know she was loved. He'd wanted her to know her Papa would always love and protect her. Teddy rocked her for the same reason now. She drifted off to sleep. He hoped his tears wouldn't awake her. He muffled his cries, clutching his child tighter.

Teddy wanted to find the White boy who'd done this to his daughter. Teddy had fantasized for years on how many ways he could kill him. The boy had disappeared.

Stank had come home late one night, two weeks after the rape. He and Master Augustus had been searching for Missy's attacker, but couldn't find him. The next day, Stank had heard at the general store the Johannesen's had sold off some land to get Hanzel out the country. "What did Massa want wit' him?" Teddy had asked him.

Stank scratched his head. "I'se wondered the same thang. Ain't like he got no love for Niggahs." Teddy frowned at him. "Sorry Uncle Ted, it slipped. Anyway, Massa said Hanzel stole from him and was gonna make Hanzel pay him his due. Well, you know what that means, Uncle Ted." Teddy nodded.

"Yup, Massa said, 'now my sheets is dirty and that gal ain't in her right mind to clean them proper,'" Stank filled with sadness. "I'se ain't never seen Massa so ready to 'collect a debt' as he was wit' that Cloggy. It seems to me like it was personal for him."

***

Missy whimpered in her sleep. Teddy kissed her forehead and rocked the chair. A little cool breeze surprised him, soothing them both. He patted Missy's thigh, humming a little song he'd sung to her as a five-year-old, the night Toussaint was born. Sleep reclaimed her. Teddy looked down the lane, spotting his friend.

Lawrence stepped up on the porch. "Suh."

"Mistah Lawrence," Teddy whispered.

Lawrence picked Missy up from where she rested on Teddy's lap. He kissed her forehead. A cup materialized in his hand. "Drank this, honey."

A little child, Missy awoke and sipped the hot drink in the cup. Within seconds, she fell into a deep sleep. Lawrence carried her in the house and put her on the pallet. A few moments later, Lawrence returned to the porch and sat in the chair next to Teddy.

Teddy focused on the plantation house in the distance. "She's gonna mess 'round and kills my grandbaby," Teddy said. "I'se don't know what to do for her. Some days she's fine. Others, she's likes this." Teddy let go of the pain and anguish, sobbing before his friend.

"I'se 'clare 'fore God she was gonna put my grandbaby in the pot today. Thank the Lawd Toussaint came along. He stopped her." Lawrence patted him on the back. "I'se don't know what to do no more." Teddy put his head in his hands and cried.

Teddy rubbed his back. "Pray. God's the only one who can help both your babies now." Teddy nodded. Lawrence arose from the chair and left, returning to the mansion.

Everything was peaceful down on the Tangipahoa River. The water fowl circled, searching for their breakfast. One dived into the murky water, captured a treat, and then retired to the river's edge to enjoy it. Another bird swooped down and captured its meal. Toussaint watched it soar to the high branch of a pine tree, the fish wriggling in the grasp of its beak. Squinting a bit, Toussaint watched the bird land in its nest. He guessed the meal would nourish the bird's little ones.

Toussaint placed his crate in the mud at the river's edge and took his seat. He couldn't sit in the mud anymore, since returning from France. He figured he didn't want to muddy his fancy clothes. "Those are just a memory."

Placing a worm on the hook, he cast out his line. A pair of eyes glowered at him from the water and then submerged. Toussaint figured the alligator had decided to cruise down river to find his breakfast. The sun warmed him, instilling strength in Toussaint's heart to endure and persevere.

Hearing rustling in the brush, Toussaint turned around. "Fuck." He didn't swear often, but the one approaching brought the worst out in him.

"Hey, Toot."

"Kinky."

Kinky sat in the mud beside Toussaint, wearing old overalls without a shirt, allowing his muscles to glisten in the morning sun. They sat together for thirty minutes, in silence. "I'se still loves your sister. I'se never stopped." Kinky wiped his eyes.

"These years done been rough on ev'rybody, since that Cracker… Well, since she got attacked by that White boy." Kinky turned his eyes upward, studying the careless and wispy clouds. "She screamed for a year. The church folks would pray for her ev'ry Sunday. She'd stop for a week or so. Then the devil would git back in her.

"I'se went to see her after it happens." Kinky bit his lip, suppressing his rage. "I'se always thanked the Lawd they'd sent you away, Toot. You'se wouldda found that White boy and killed him, seein' how bad off your sister was," he said, wringing his hands. "I'se would try and hug her. I'se told her I still loved her and wanted to jump the broom wit' her. She didn't know me or nobody else no more."

Kinky stopped talking, sitting in the mud, crying. "Your Pappy stopped me from comin' 'round, 'cause Missy would go crazy. She would see him when she seent me. She seent that White boy in ev'rybody 'round here. And when that sweet li'l ole Claret was born, well that done did it for her. She was gone. That baby came out wit' her red hair and that did it."

Toussaint cast out his line. He hoped for a bite.

"Miss Sammie kept the child for a long time. Claret couldn't be in same room wit' Missy wit'out her tryin' to kills her. Finally, when she got older and her skin darkened up, Missy would allow her to stay 'round for a spell. Thangs seemed to git better for a while. I'se told her I still wanted to marry her and take li'l Claret for my own daughter. She looks at me likes I'se a stranger. She said naw."

The men sat on the bank in silence for a time. The water was still, not a ripple. "Massa surprised me."

Toussaint turned his focus from the water, finding his voice for the first time. "How's that?"

Kinky thought about how he wanted to say what he wished to share. "He was huntin' for that White boy. He had me and Stank helpin' him search for him." Kinky scooped up some mud from the river bank, formed a ball and pitched it out into the water, causing water to torpedo up into the air. "I'se thanks he was mad 'cause Hanzel had put his hands on his property. Massa hadn't touched her, so it pissed him off the Cloggy had done it. Folks said the White boy's pappy sold off some land to git him out of Louisiana."

Kinky dislodged a pebble from the damp soil and threw

it into the river. "I ain't never touched her either, Toot. We'se was waitin'." Kinky stood up. "Well, I'se just wanted you'se to know I'se didn't turn my back on your sister. You'se can ask your Pappy and Stank if you'se don't believe me. They'll tell you."

He walked away, but stopped. "I'se still loves her and wants to take her for my wife. But that devil done took hold of her senses. She cain't be wit' nobody right now, but if she lets the devil go, I'se here. I'se ain't far off." Kinky disappeared into the brush.

Toussaint dropped his pole. He put his head in his lap and wept for his sister.

Chapter 15

La Rose Plantation, St. Helena Parish. August 31, 1963.

The fan blew hot air. On second thought, it wasn't blowing air, although the blades were going around. Julian hooked his head to the right to catch an off-kilter glimpse of the thermometer through the window screen, held in place by a little wrought iron angel. One hundred one degrees. "It's too damn hot." Lela had fallen asleep with her head on his shoulder. She'd sprawled her body across the window seat with her legs gapped open. She'd kicked off one of her high-heeled shoes.

The heat, two dozen oysters, an aged vintage of white wine, chased by brandy, had done her in. Such a lady. He'd only eaten maybe five oysters out the bunch. Little piggy. And then Lawrence had brought out smoked salmon, mussels, a relish tray loaded with olives, cream cheese, a variety of toasted breads, and other pickled treats. Julian surveyed the carnage left behind on the empty platters. Not one sliver of fish remained.

The old broad had eaten all the hors d'oeuvres, drank all the wine, and emptied half the bottle of brandy. Meanwhile, Julian was starving. Every time he'd reached for a treat, she would give him a dirty looked veiled with a smile. God, what grandmother didn't want their children to eat? Not her, especially when it came to oysters, mussels, olives, and liquor. He watched his sleeping great-grandmother drop an olive she'd held captive between her fingertips, which rolled beneath the table. Only it had survived.

Lela snored, causing every organ within her body to rumble. How could she have fallen into such a deep sleep within a few seconds? He remembered the empty wine bottle. She'd been talking for hours; however, once the temperature hit one hundred degrees and the humidity had soared through the roof, her grape-based sleeping aids activated. Lights out.

She snored again. He wondered if her throat hurt? Julian was sure somewhere on the plantation, a cow had started walking back home to its barn. He felt saliva run down his shirt, pooling in his breast pocket. "Lord help me," Julian said.

Lela coughed and smacked her lips, burrowing her head into his armpit. "Sue… *Merde*, Suzette! You laced me too tight." Lela coughed, turned, and snored even louder. What the hell? Now she talked in her sleep about her corset. Julian leaned forward, stretching to reach the intercom button.

"Yes?"

"Where is Lawrence?"

"I'm right here."

Julian jumped in his seat. Lela stirred, rolled over and snored. "It's noon. I'se figured it done got hot out here by now." Lawrence walked over to where Lela slumbered on Julian's shoulder. "She looks just like she did when she was a baby."

"What?" Lawrence held no compassion for Julian's torment. He could only idolize upon his sleeping queen, remembering her old ass as a child.

Lawrence scooped Lela up. She appeared as a little girl in his long, gangly arms. Julian guessed the man to be at least seven feet tall.

"You'se 'bout right. I'se seven feet, five inches."

Freak. Julian followed Lawrence back to the house, carrying his grandmother in his arms.

Why couldn't he eat without his grandmère being present? It was now half past one o'clock in the afternoon and she still hadn't awakened from her nap. Julian left the sofa in Augustus' library, searching for the kitchen. It had just occurred to him he didn't know where it was. "I'm surprised Lurch isn't hovering around." Julian hadn't thought of the comic strip in years. Lawrence was the Black Lurch from the

Addams Family cartoon strip in *New Yorker Magazine*. Julian giggled, leaving the library.

Crossing the foyer, Julian headed toward the northeast section of the mansion. He stopped in the center of the grand hall, atop the mosaic rose in the center of the floor. Hmm, the dining room was on the south side of the house. Shouldn't the kitchen be there as well? When he'd eaten there earlier, he couldn't remember the staff bringing in food through concealed doors.

Sammie stood against the wall. Lawrence led her away.

Julian batted his eyes, picturing his grandmère's earlier stories in his mind. "She stood there," he said, pointing to the northern wall of the hall. Why did he know where his grandmère's mother had stood on the night of Augustus' wedding to Emmie Sue?

Walking beneath the colonnade, he stopped before a painting above a demi-lune table. A very dark-skinned woman with beautiful eyes wearing a large scarf tied upon her head into a turban of sorts, stood behind a little White girl in a white chiffon dress constructed of many petticoats. The child sat on a chair constructed of a dark wood, carved with roses, and upholstered in red velvet. Her skirts, fanned out upon the chair, gave her the appearance of a princess. The little girl had the strangest eyes, wise beyond her years—kind, but cunning and dangerous. The Black woman who stood behind the child wore a gray dress with a white lace collar and cuffs. Her eyes were haughty, sporting a self-assured smirk on her face.

"Grandmère," Julian said in a whisper. The little girl was his grandmère.

"Yup, sho' is."

Julian jumped. Why did the spooky people working for his grandmère always surprise him?

"Didn't mean to scare you. I'se was in the salon hangin' them portraits."

"What portraits?"

"Of the descendants," Lawrence said. Julian stared at him with blank eyes. "Them pictures Miss Lela had made of the former slaves and their chil'ren."

Julian could care less and returned his attention to the portrait.

Lawrence stood with him, admiring the painting. "Miss Lela was just a li'l ole thang when her Pappy had this picture made. Sammie had been pesterin' him 'bout havin' it done. Don't know how she got him to do it, but she did. Sammie had a way with Massa Augustus. She wasn't scared of him, that's for sho'."

Lawrence held his stomach with both hands, leaning back and laughing deep. His voice boomed throughout the grand hall. "Lawd, I'se believes Massa was scared of her. No suh! He never did back talk her much." Lawrence hooped and hollered.

"Lawdy, I'se remembers the day. Massa came in the kitchen half drunk, as usual. Sammie said, 'Lela's gittin' old. She's gonna be six years old next year. I'se wants our portrait painted.' What slave tells her Massa what she wants done? *And to have a portrait made?* She didn't stutter either.

"Augustus figured he was gonna act tough 'cause I was standin' there. He said, 'Look woman, I told you to stop worryin' me about havin' that little Nigger's portrait made. It ain't happenin'. Ya'll Niggers. Decent White folks don't have portraits made of their Niggers.'" He left the kitchen. I'se turns to Sammie. She didn't look my way or say a word. She continued to snap the beans she'd been preparin' for supper.

"Later that evenin', Massa came into my little butler's pantry. Now, it's the li'l office near the front door. Anyway, he handed me a couple of letters. 'Have one of the older Niggahs get on one of the mares and run this down to New Orleans for me in the morning. And don't send that Nig-ger Ned. He's likely to run off. I ain't got time to hunt him down.' I'se took the two letters from him. One was a pass for whoever was takin' the note to New Orleans. The other was a letter.

"I'se cain't read, suh," I said to Augustus. "Who'se I'se gonna tell the boy to deliver it to?" Lawrence held his breath for a minute and exhaled. "Boy, ole Massa turned beet red. He said, 'Jacques Amans, in the French Quarter.' He finished his bourbon, slammed the empty glass on my desk and went upstairs to his room.

"I'se don't know what Sammie did, but she sho' got after his ass. That painter was out here to the house the followin' week and got the portrait did 'fore the end of the month.

"Incredible," Julian said. "I've seen pictures of his work while in school. He painted portraits for a number of planters across the South." Julian studied the work. The portrait possessed the life-like brilliance of Amans' works. "Now I understand the smug look on Sammie's face."

"That's right, boy," Lawrence said. "Sammie held the power in this house and she knew it. Ma'Dame Emmie Sue never had it, and she knew it too. I'se figures that why she hated Sammie so."

Lawrence shook his head, remembering the silent war which persisted between the women. "Augustus had stayed out of it, for the most part, daring either one to bring their troubles to him. When Sammie told Augustus to do sumpthin', she expected it to git done. She wasn't gonna take too much of his shit for too long, 'specially when it came to li'l Miss Lela."

Lawrence opened the drawer of the large demi-lune table. "You wanna see something, boy?" Julian nodded. "Well,

Miss Sammie didn't know nuthin' 'bout it at the time, don't suspect she ever found out 'bout it either, but Augustus paid Mis'sur Amans to make this one too."

Julian took the small portrait from Lawrence. The White man with the dark curly hair had to be Augustus. He could see the hardness of his heart; however, when Julian considered him, he could detect a haughtiness and pride in his eyes.

He held a little girl on his knee, the mirror image of him. The little girl wore the sweetest smile Julian had ever seen. She wore the most delicate sheer chiffon dress with layer upon layer of petticoats. It was the same dress his grand-mère wore in the picture with Sammie. He wiped away a tear. "She looks like a doll," Julian said, overcome with love. "Is this Grandmère?"

"Yup, that's li'l Lela. Cutest li'l ole thang." Lawrence sat the picture on the demi-lune below the portrait of Lela and her mother. "Funny thang too. Jeffrey, he's the butler for the Chevalier Château over there in France, sent the dress here six weeks 'fore Sammie put the hammer down on Augustus to have the portrait made. Jeffrey included a note, 'I hope this is what Madame Sammie desires.'

"I'd showed the dress to Miss Sammie. I'd always figured Manny, Monsieur Emmanuel's tailor, had made it for her. He likes to dally in dressmakin' from time to time, especially when the Rose is walkin' wit' us. He always wants to make her a li'l ole special occasion dress. Anyways, Sammie didn't seem surprised at all when the package arrived. She removed the dress from the box and held it up in the sunlight.

"She was so happy. Miss Sammie smiled and twirled around in the kitchen wit' the dress, settin' the petticoats a flight like kites. 'This is what I'se been dreamin' of for my baby. Tell Mis'sur Jeff I'se said thanks.'"

Looking back, Lawrence found himself amazed by the entire scenario once again. "I'se didn't even know she knew him. I guess Miss Sammie was more able in the Spirit than either me or Miss Sarah knew. I guess li'l ole Lela compelled her to spread her spiritual wings."

Lawrence wiped away a tear. "I don't reckon neither Lela nor Sammie ever saw this picture. I've kept it in this drawer for 110 years."

The picture fascinated Julian. It should've been in a museum. "Hey, did Augustus display this picture of Grandmère and her maman here, back then?"

Lawrence thought for a moment, rubbing his chin. "Not at first. It had to dry once the Mis'sur Amans completed it." He scratched his beard. "Yup, he sho' did. It pissed off Ma'Dame Emmie Sue too. I'se remembers them fightin' one night. He'd told her, 'If you'se can hangs your portrait of that li'l bastard Lily in the Grand Hall, I'se can hang this one of my li'l Lela here beneath the colonnade.'"

"Ma'Dame tried to destroy the portrait a few times. She tried to slash it, throw paint on it. She could never harm it. It's been hangin' there ev'ry since. Even after Miss Warren shamed Massa 'bout Lela, he never took it down. Some nights I'se see him standin' before it for hours, just starin', 'specially after ev'rythang went bad. Once in a while, I'se hear the drawer to this li'l demi-lune open. Then several minutes later, I'd hear it shut."

Julian stood before the picture in silence, considering a family which could never be together in public. "I don't understand why he didn't just move them all to France," Julian said, suppressing the lump in his throat. "We should have moved."

Lawrence arched an eyebrow. He patted the boy's back. "Well son, it wasn't meant to be. Cain't go livin' in the past. Won't change nuthin', no way." Lawrence patted him on the back again. "You'se ready for lunch, boy?"

"Oh, God yes. I'm starving," Julian said.

"Reckoned you'se would be. Ma'Dame wasn't in the mood for sharin' the snacks." Lawrence chuckled. "Your grandmère woke up. Sue gittin' her ready for lunch."

"Getting her ready? How?"

Lawrence removed his polishing towel from his apron pocket and swiped it against the portrait, removing a few specks of dust. He adjusted the vase of fresh roses on the demi-lune table below it. "Oh, you'se knows how women-folk can be. She's prob'ly just powderin' her nose and brushin' her hair."

Julian nodded and headed for the dining room. "Oh Lawrence, where's the kitchen?" He turned around. "Dammit." Lawrence had vanished.

At least his head had stopped hurting. Julian sopped the salad bowl with the last piece of romaine lettuce. Someone placed a bowl of soft rolls before him. He grabbed one and tore it open, allowing the steam to escape. He smeared it with the vibrant, yellow butter. Julian bit in. Euphoria.

"You couldn't wait for me to join you?"

Julian couldn't believe his grandmère. She stood before him in some sort of white lace pencil dress with a deep, boat neckline. Her cleavage threatened to spill out. However, he doubted if it would, weighted down by the massive platinum and diamond multi-tiered necklace. She wore a matching bracelet and chandelier earrings. It surprised him her earlobes didn't rip from the weight of the stones.

"These are clips," Lela said.

Lawrence pulled out Lela's and then Suzette's chairs. As Lela sat, Julian waited to hear a seam burst in her tight dress. "Where are you going, Grandmère? Do you have a hot date?" The waitstaff brought in Julian's main course along with the ladies first course of salad.

"Of course not," Lela said with a slight blush. I'm here for lunch, darling. Why do you ask?"

Lawrence removed the cover of Julian's dish, revealing the salmon. Julian rubbed his hands together and picked up his dinner fork. "Your diamond studded cleavage is blinding me. You appear as if you're out on the prowl, wearing your tight lace dress. I figured you had another engagement."

Lela picked at her salad. "You don't care for what I'm wearing?"

"I think you would look great, if you were twenty-five years old. Although you present yourself as such, we all know to multiply the number by five or six for your true age."

Lela pushed her plate away. "Suzette, be a darling. Run upstairs and get my calico housedress and hemi-walker. We don't wish to make Monsieur uncomfortable."

Suzette nibbled on her romaine lettuce. "Oui, Madame." She speared a tomato with her fork and ate it.

Oh Lord. "Grandmère, I think you look great. I didn't mean anything by it."

"No, no. I'll change. You always complain about the way I dress and I'm tired of it," Lela said. Suzette passed Lela a monogrammed hanky, so she could dab her eyes.

Drama. Julian arose from his seat and kneeled before his

perfumed grandmère. "You're beautiful, Grandmère. I just don't want people checking you out."

Lela raised an eyebrow. "You're never happy. You'd be horrified if I came to dinner in the alleged house dress I own." She resumed eating.

Julian returned to his seat. "How many carats?"

"What?"

"Your jewelry. Where did you even get that?"

Lela munched her salad. "Oh this? It's very old. My love, Jamie, gave it to me. I'm not sure where it came from," Lela said. "Monsieur and Madame Cartier had dined one night at our home in Paris. Oh, what year was it Suzette?"

"1888, *probablement*, Madame."

I believe you're correct. Anyway, I was wearing this ensemble that night…"

"You wore your new Worth dress which had arrived the day before, Madame. The yellow one," Suzette said.

"Oui, you're right, Suzette. Jamie loved that dress."

Julian choked on his salmon. "Grandmère!"

"Well, he did." Lela placed another bit of romaine in her mouth. "Anyway, I believe your Uncle Toot was visiting that summer. Oh yes, the jewels. I'd thanked Monsieur Cartier for having designed the piece for me. He said, 'Madame, I didn't design this.' He removed his loupe from his pocket. He always carried one on his person. With my permission, he examined my necklace."

Julian placed some mashed potatoes on his fork. "I guess you didn't take the necklace off first."

Lela cocked her head to the side. "Strange, Jamie had said the same thing. Why would I take it off? He's a professional."

"You are correct, Madame."

"Thank you, Suzette." Lela didn't understand the men in her family. "Anyway, he'd said, 'Madame, this piece has the mark of Pierre de Montarsy.' I'd never heard of him. Monsieur turned to Jamie. 'Monsieur Roberts, where did you acquire this ensemble? It is at least two hundred years old, a piece designed for the royal family.'" Lela wiped her eye. "Jamie said, 'It was in the vault. The family has been saving it for our queen, my Lela.'"

Suzette dabbed her eye.

"That's a hustle, Grandmère. I bet he got some that night."

"And then some."

"Ugh!" Julian thought he might vomit.

"You put it out there. Besides, what did I say that was improper? What have you been doing to provoke such a reaction, young man?" Everyone at the table turned to him.

"That's none of your business, Grandmère. Anyway, this is about you."

Lela placed her fork on her plate. The waiter removed her salad plate and served her salmon. "Don't come around here selling wolf tickets, young man. I'm going to buy each and every one you have to sell."

Flaking away a piece of salmon, she placed it in her mouth and closed her eyes. "Lawrence, please tell chef this is delightful," Lela said. Lawrence nodded.

Lela placed her fork on the plate. "Oh yes. Anyhow, most of my jewelry is very old. It has been in our family for centuries." She smiled. "Much of the collections remains at the Roberts and Chevalier Châteaux in France. This is simply my everyday jewelry."

Julian shook his head. Who wore millions of dollars in diamonds and a variety of other precious stones as everyday jewelry?"

"Madame does," Suzette said. "Would it be better enjoyed in the vault?"

Julian let it go. He placed a forkful of mashed potatoes and asparagus into his mouth. His attention diverted to the portrait above the fireplace. A flamboyant French man in a powdered wig, wearing stockings and red heels, sat on a settee amidst a harvest, surrounded by buxom maidens. He leered at them and the fruits of the harvest they held in their baskets. He held a peach in his hand, waiting to take a bite and savor its juices. Each time he considered the portrait, the scene depicted seemed different. Only the petit man remained the same. "Pervert."

Following his gaze, Lela considered the painting. "Oh, are you speaking of Emmanuel? He's not a pervert. He's the patriarch of the family."

"Yeah, I'm sure he is. He looks like the statue in the fountain."

Lela thought for a moment. "Oh, the large fountain at the center of the gardens? Is that the one you speak of?" Julian said nothing. "It's a statue of our family's patron, the Archangel Barachiel. It's a lovely monument."

"You like his pecker."

The room became silent.

"What are you saying, Julian?"

Julian finished his salmon. "Oh, come on, Grandmère. You're not blind. Anyone with eyes can see the statue is lewd."

Lela put her fork down. Once again, her great-grandson had ruined her appetite. "Are you ashamed of your body? The statue is a piece of art, reflecting the artist's interpretation of his subject."

"Was it carved by Hugh Heffner?"

"Julian, the human body is a beautiful creation by God. If the artist had made the focal point of his work a woman with huge breasts, would you have an issue with it?"

"Not at all. Breasts are meant to be appreciated by men," Julian said.

The waitstaff left the room.

Lela pushed her plate away. "And 'peckers', as you so maturely put it, are created to be appreciated by women." Suzette put her head down. "Being a prostitute for many years, I've sampled my fair share of 'peckers.' I've learned size is nice, but it doesn't matter.

"Peckers are like cars. Everyone should know how to work their own stick, no matter how short or long." Lawrence, standing next to Lela, massaged his temples. "Trust me, young man. I like sticks, and can drive any stick with ease you put in my hand. So, in my garden, you may find male statues of variety of different 'gear shifts.' The artist who created the fountain's statue designed it with his Rose in mind.

"If the angel's pecker makes you uncomfortable, you should review how you relate to your own. The statue is beautiful, as is every other nude in my garden." Lela patted her forehead with the back of her hand. "Why conceal what is beautiful? We all are glorious, as the good Lord created us. We should share our beauty with the world. So, if you have a problem with it, place a blindfold over your eyes. I'll give you a cane, so you don't run into any peckers you can't handle."

Julian sat before her, ashen faced. Who discussed dick

size and sex with their great-grandmothers? He heard Lawrence's slow laughter in the background.

"You walked into that one boy," Theo said.

Julian hadn't even notice Theo join them. "Shut your old ass up. No one is talking to you."

"Come here, Julian," Lela said.

Julian gulped. "I apologize, Theo. I was out of line."

Theo grunted and picked up his fork, eating his salad.

Lela didn't wish to scar her child. "I say this to teach you, Julian. Enjoy life and be free, as God created you to be. Cherish the form in which he created you. Appreciate the form in which he created others. We're all beautiful, as the Lord created us. And if we free our minds, we can reach levels of unknown ecstasy." Lela surveyed those gathered around the table. No one would look at her. Perhaps she'd gone too far. Even her friends weren't prepared for her ideals on sexual and physical freedom.

I am

"Hush, Toussaint."

"What did you say, Grandmère?" Julian asked.

"Nothing." The waitstaff served them their crème brûlée. "Eat it while it's hot. Cold custard never does anyone any good." A little embarrassed, Lela dipped her spoon into her dessert.

***

He should call Jannette. His conversation with his freaky grandmère made him think about his love even more than he had over the past few days. Julian wondered if Jannette enjoyed making love to him. Sure, she did. How could she not? He knew how to use what God had given him, at least her screams for satisfaction told him so. But, he had to wonder after his conversation with his grandmère.

Julian sunk into the comfort of the goose down sofa in the main parlor, near the grand front entrance of the home. The piece had to be as old as the mansion itself, but remained pristine. The sofa could be in the Smithsonian. His attention turned to another gigantic portrait of his ancestor, Emmanuel Chevalier. He didn't mind having portraits made of himself, that was for sure. In this portrait above the fireplace, Emmanuel's eyes seemed alive, mocking and laughing at him. He sported his powdered wig, short pants and stockings. If Julian hadn't known better, he would have thought the portrait's subject to be Louis XIV.

"Asshole."

Julian loved saying the word to every image he saw of him. On a molecular level, Julian wanted to let the dead man know he wasn't fooled by him. He didn't understand his urge to do so. Nevertheless, Julian didn't feel right if he failed to address the man by the name of asshole.

"He was a great man, Julian. Stop calling him that." Lela took a seat in the winged chair near the sofa. Lawrence bought in a snifter of brandy for her and left.

"What about my Glenlivet?" Julian asked. Lawrence exited the room and closed the double doors to the parlor. "I don't understand why I can't get a drink around here." Julian went to the bar cart and prepared a beverage. He returned to the sofa.

"I apologize, mon fils."

Julian choked on his drink. "Why, Grandmère?"

Lela sipped her brandy. "I went too far earlier. I'm Victorian. People of my era were sexually repressed. Everything happened behind closed doors and in secret, making the physical expression of love dirty in some way. I just don't want you to feel that way."

She never ceased to surprise him. Julian nodded and let it go.

Lela sauntered back through the years. "Toussaint was very Victorian. Matters regarding more tawdry subjects shamed him. Maybe that's why he couldn't deal with Missy's situation. He sought to vindicate her, instead of telling her she was innocent and what had happened wasn't her fault. In his quest to vindicate her, he continued to victimize her." Lela swirled her drink in the snifter. She pursed her lips, searching for the words.

"In the Spirit, I can see Toussaint staring at Missy, very intense, burning a hole in her. In his heart, he was frustrated because he couldn't find Hanzel and exact justice. Every time he saw Missy, it reminded him of his failure to protect and avenge her.

"Missy felt his hostility, thinking it was directed toward her. Already in a compromised emotional and mental state, she believed Toussaint hated and found her disgusting. Coupled with his leaving without notice following the rape, her misconstrued rejection of her by Toussaint made her even more desperate."

Lela considered the lilies in the crystal vase atop the sideboard, their fragrance setting her at ease. "She needed to hear her brother attest to her innocence. Missy needed Toussaint to hold and protect her, telling her everything would be alright. Instead, Toussaint could only focus on avenging her. He never said anything to make her feel less dirty. He never told her she was good. But who knew to say such things back then? Hell, people don't understand how to say them now.

"In any case, things didn't improve for my cousin.

Chapter 16

La Rose Plantation, St. Helena Parish. 1863.

He hated Emmanuel for sending him home. He hated the plantation. Toussaint stood from his bale of hay and stretched. "Time to go." After replacing his pamphlets beneath the floorboards, he blew out the lamp. Toussaint left the abandoned hunting shack and started for home. It was late, probably second watch.

After a forty-five-minute trek, he arrived at his family's cabin. Toussaint stood on the ramshackle front porch and picked the twigs and burrs from his clothing he'd picked up while walking through the woods. He wished he still had his fine wardrobe he'd enjoyed in France. Sometimes, France seemed like a fantasy. If his mother hadn't told him it had been real, he may have believed all of it to have been a dream.

Muffled sobbing filled his ears. He hadn't heard it at first, but now it flooded his being. Toussaint opened the door. His mother sat on the floor against the wall, her face covered with tears. He'd never seen her cry so much. She'd always been so strong, but since Missy's rape, she couldn't stop crying.

Toussaint watched his father sleep on the mattress. He was sure his mother had stuffed his father's ears with some sort of supernatural cotton, so he couldn't hear her.

Sarah looked up at him. "Sammie's dead."

"What?"

Taking the hem of her apron, she blew her nose. "She done saved Lela. She sent her away wit' Augustus' son to New Orleans. Your evil brother done strangled her for it."

Toussaint burst out of the cabin, deaf to his mother's cries. They weren't real tears. She could have stopped him if she'd wanted too. Toussaint ran for a mile before reaching the grand French garden behind the plantation house. The only Negroes allowed in the garden were the gardeners.

Toussaint walked another mile searching for Augustus. He could hear him there, his rage and tears filling the universe. Approaching the grand fountain centered where the garden's eight axes met, Toussaint searched the Spirit for Augustus' imprint. Not finding him, Toussaint wondered if Augustus had chosen to spend his rage in the Shed torturing a slave who'd disobeyed the overseer.

"What are you doin' in my yard, Nigger?"

Toussaint's heart beat fast, filling with fear. Rage entered and married with the fear. The man who'd killed his Aunt

Sammie would die that day.

"I ain't dying today, Nigger. But you will."

Toussaint hadn't believed someone as ignorant as Augustus could hear in the Spirit. However, the devil could, so why shouldn't Augustus?

With inhuman speed, Augustus arose from where he lay drunk. He leveled Toussaint, knocking his legs from beneath him, sending him to the ground. Toussaint could feel a sharp object against his Adam's apple. Augustus blew his bourbon saturated breath into his face. "This here, boy, is my favorite knife. It's a Bowie. I cut Liddy's tongue out of her mouth with this here knife for tormenting and lying on my Sammie."

Augustus coughed in Toussaint's face, raining spittle on him. "I got one of them witches in her grave. Now I only have one to go." Augustus gritted his teeth. "Your Mama helped her. They stole Lela. Now I'm going to kill that bitch. I should've killed her years ago, but I can't ever catch her. But I will. I can feel it. I'm going to catch her ass and shoot her."

Toussaint punched his master, freeing himself. The men struggled on the ground. In his inebriated state, Augustus was too loose and fast for Toussaint. "You think you can best me, boy?" Augustus said. "Not in this lifetime."

A peaceful, controlled rage swept over Toussaint. He felt

like a hunter with a wild animal in his sights. He knew at that moment he would put Augustus in his grave. "You touch her, I'll touch you. And I swear you won't recover from my touch. Yup. I'll put you in the grave for one thousand years."

Augustus freed himself from Toussaint grasp and jammed his knife into his chest. Toussaint didn't cry out, which seemed to further enrage him. Augustus stood up and kicked him. He drew his revolver from his ankle holster.

Fishing around in the breast pocket of his waist coat, Augustus removed a silver bullet and held it up to the moonlight. "I was saving this for your mama, but you will do." Opening the chamber of his new Smith and Wesson revolver, Augustus dumped out the bullets. He inserted the silver bullet and spun the chamber.

He sunk to his knees on top of Toussaint, where he lay bleeding. Augustus placed the nozzle of the weapon against Toussaint's left temple. "Tell you what. We're gonna let the Good Lord decide. In fact, I'll give him three tries to figure out what he wants to do."

Toussaint met Augustus' death glare. He didn't shudder with fear, cry out, or plead for his life. Infuriated, Augustus pulled the trigger. The hammer released, but a bullet did not leave the chamber. The satisfaction of murder eluded him. Augustus pulled the trigger again, and then once more.

Defeated, he staggered to his feet. He threw the gun

at Toussaint's head. The nozzle struck his left temple, but failed to discharge.

"Cheat," Toussaint said, losing consciousness.

Augustus spat on him. "You can't hold me in a grave for one thousand years, boy. God can't do it either." Augustus coughed. His chest felt tight. "Ain't gonna happen." The image before his eyes multiplied, finding three Toussaints lying before him. Sammie and Sarah stood over two of them, protecting him.

"Sammie." Augustus blinked. Only one Toussaint lay before him, alone. Augustus searched the flowers of the garden. Finding his crystal decanter, he removed the stopper and turned the bottle up, allowing the bourbon to cleanse him. He walked away, forgetting his heartache and rage.

Toussaint sat up, clutching his stab wound. "Yessuh, Massa Augustus. We'll allow the Good Lord to decide how long you'll rot in the grave." Toussaint laughed, causing his chest to ache and blood to gush forth. "But the Lord has spoken. I'm putting you in your grave. Don't touch my maman." With much effort, Toussaint managed to rise to his feet and stumble home.

La Rose Plantation, St. Helena Parish. 1864.

MOST OF LA ROSE'S slaves had run off, once they heard of President Lincoln's Emancipation Proclamation. Toussaint had overheard at the general store the president had signed the proclamation the year before. Yet, word of the emancipation had only reached the plantation a few months ago. Some left that night, taking their chances. They never returned. Toussaint figured either they'd been successful in their efforts to escape or had been murdered by the slave patrols.

Sarah had become Toussaint's wartime correspondent, giving him news from a variety of battlefields and skirmishes. The war and the liberated slaves leaving southern plantations had proven to be a good distraction for Sarah from her troubles with Missy. Her travels left Teddy and Toussaint to deal with her.

Many times, she took Claret with her. She possessed some of the same abilities Toussaint had enjoyed a child, but not as strong. She could levitate pretty good; however, she couldn't fly about as Toussaint had been able to do.

Sarah immersed herself into her wartime work, spending her days assisting former slaves walking off plantations across the South. Even though slavery had been abolished, it didn't stop the slave patrols, or paddy rollers, from capturing the liberated slaves and returning them to bondage.

Some of the liberated slaves had joined the Union Army. No longer an impossible dream or the subject of spirituals sung during Sunday meeting, former slaves now had the chance to fight for their liberty. While many found themselves in a state of servitude to the Union soldiers, other liberated warriors realized the joy of combat on the battlefield.

Toussaint placed a few articles into a burlap bag. He'd given up on trying to reason with his papa. He couldn't understand why he refused to leave the plantation. "Papa, if we leave, perhaps Missy will get better. Being here isn't helping her."

Teddy ran his fingers through his hair. "Son, you'se don't know what it's like out there," Teddy said. "They'se killin' Negroes just as soon as look at them. How we'se gonna run wit' Missy like this?"

Toussaint couldn't look at his sister, whimpering on her pallet in a fitful sleep. "We can pray over her. She will be alright."

"Oh yeah? What if sumpthin' spooks her out there in the brush? She starts screamin' and we'se cain't git her to settle down? Dem paddy rollers would find us wit'out a doubt. I'se 'clare they would." Teddy mopped his wet face with the sleeve of his shirt. "Them White bastards might hurt your sister again." Teddy gasped, suppressing the lump in his throat. "Or worse."

Toussaint considered the Spirit. He could see his father was right. "Then what are we going to do Papa?"

Teddy began to cry, unable to hold in his grief. "You'se go on 'head, son. You'se strong. You'se can make it. We'll stay here. You can send for us once you'se gits settled."

Toussaint wished he was back in France. Where was his cousin? Surely, he could help them. But he hadn't seen him in the Spirit since returning to the plantation. Sometimes, Toussaint wondered if he'd ever lived in France. It must have been a dream.

"It's true, boy," his father said. "Trust me. You'se was gone from here a long spell." His father hugged him, comforting him.

"Your mama gonna be mad, but go. If'se that's what you thank you'se should do, then go. I'se trust your judgment, son."

Toussaint stood before him, torn. Falling into the Spirit, he beheld a vision of himself standing on the road, extending his hand to the passersby. "I don't have the money to run, Papa."

Teddy grunted, and then smiled. "Didn't you'se bury our family's 'fortune' when you'se was a li'l ole chap?" he asked. Teddy smiled at his weeping son. "You'se 'member where you'se put it?"

"Yes, Papa. But I was going to leave it for you all."

Teddy patted his son's cheek. "We'se can make it wit'out it. You'se takes the money, son. It's yours." Toussaint opened his mouth to speak. "No backtalk, boy. Take it." Teddy kissed and hugged his son. He left the cabin, sat outside on the porch, and cried.

Once his father went to the fields the next morning, Toussaint tossed his books in a burlap bag. He planned to take only the clothes which he wore. He had a few gold coins, which had been in his pocket when he returned from France. However, they were French coins. Being Negro, he couldn't go to the bank and exchange them. He had fifty cents in cash.

Toussaint felt cold like death. Missy slept for once. He went over to her pallet and kissed her forehead. He then went to his parents' pallet where Claret slept. He kissed her on the forehead and turned to leave.

"Goodbye, dead man."

He whirled around, finding his niece sitting up in bed, staring at him. She held the doll his mother had made for her from black burlap, with red yarn for hair. "What?"

"You're about to die. I love you. Goodbye."

Toussaint couldn't turn his eyes from the emotionless child sitting on the hay mattress. She laid down and returned to sleep.

Toussaint left the cabin and pulled the door closed behind him. He walked through the slave quarter and then into the brush, heading north. The brush grew thick. He'd traveled the land a thousand times before. Why couldn't he find his way? He ran into something. He yelped, but silenced himself.

"Where you'se goin', Toussaint?"

He sighed. His mother. "To freedom."

"To death," she said. "You'se should listen to your niece." Toussaint began to cry, frustrated. "You ain't like the others. Don't run."

"Why not, Maman? There's nothing for us here."

Sarah poked him between the eyes, right above his nose. "Ain't nuthin' here for them who'se runnin'. You'se a different story." She peered into her son's eyes. He should be able to see better, but youth, male pride and rashness consumed him. "Boy, your inheritance is on this here land. You'se walk away now, you'se gives it all up. We all turn to dust. Is that what you'se want?"

"No, Maman."

She kissed him. "Now git your ass back in the house for somebody sees you." Toussaint turned and walked back to the house, followed by his mother.

Once they reached the cabin, Sarah made some tea out of some herbs she'd gathered from the land. She poured the hot liquid into a tin cup and went out on the porch, where

Toussaint sat. She gave him the cup. He drank from it. She could see the tea awake his mind and spirit, reuniting him with the anointing he'd received in France.

Toussaint's sight cleared. All that had happened in the past mingled with the present, bringing the future into focus once more. He placed his head in his hands. He'd almost misstepped.

"You'se still young boy. You'se don't know no better yet."

Toussaint leaned back in the chair, watching a child play in the road. "You'se don't know what's happenin' to folks out there, Toussaint. The devil is busy."

He finished his tea and then sat the tin cup on one of the porches worn, weather planks. "What's happening, Maman?"

Sarah removed her pipe from her apron pocket and lit it. She closed her eyes and exhaled. "Folks leavin' the land finds themselves in slavery all over again. In some cases, they'se worse off than they was on the plantations. White folks ain't lettin' us folks go and live in peace. They'se lynchin' us, tarrin' and featherin' whole families. I'se cain't bear it all."

"What? How can that be so? We're free. The president said so."

Sarah rocked her chair and closed her eyes. She grasped Toussaint's hand in hers while puffing on her corn cob pipe. "A piece of paper don't mean nuthin' to mobs of angry White folks." She patted his thigh.

Sarah rocked her chair. "Both the Confed'rate and Union armies is makin' freed folks do hard labor in the army camps, workin' on construction projects, cleanin' up, doin' the soldiers laundry, whatever they don't wants to do themselves. It ain't always in a bad way though.

"When I'se went up to Corinth, Miss'ippi to a… What do they'se call them now? Oh yes, contraband camp. That's the name. Since the soldiers, and I'se guessin' the gov'ment too in some way, still considered the freed folks as the property of their former masters, they'se calls them that.

"To them soldiers, the freed folks were like errant sheep who'd done escaped their pens, just wanderin' the roads and cities of the South. Since nobody can figures out who they'se belonged to, the soldiers done herded them all up and put them into holdin' pens 'til White folks can figure out what to do wit' them.

"Corinth's a little different, though. Boy, now these was some motivated Negroes. They'se just needed a safe place to help themselves. They'se got up in that there camp, started buildin' houses and a church for themselves. They'se got to plantin' crops, and buildin' roads. And they'se weren't shuckin' and jivin' when it came to gittin' their learnin', either. Those folks set up schools and got to learnin' themselves on readin' and 'rithmitic. It was beautiful. Some missionary folks came in to help them out wit' their learnin' too.

"I'se showed up in the camp, not long 'fore the end came. I'se don't thank the orders had come down to the officers yet, but the Lord had done told me the military was goin' to move out of the camp. I'se tried to git some of the folks there to go wit' me, but they'se wouldn't. Why would they? Hell, I wouldn't have either. They'd built lives for themselves. Within months of being free, they'd hit the ground runnin' to make themselves a legitimate, thrivin' community. I was so proud of them folks.

"Corinth was lovely. These here were some Negroes at their best in such fucked up conditions. 'Scuse my language mon fils, but I'se cain't thank of no other way to put it. Ain't like in the Bible when the Good Lord led the Children of Israel out of bondage. Sometimes I'se feels like the Good Lord just unlocked the front gate for us and said, 'Ya'll go on 'head now and git. Watch out for them White folks if you'se can. But I'se gots faith in ya'll. Ya'll can overcome the devil'."

"Maman!"

Sarah patted his hand. "I'se wrong for that, Toot. I'se really is. The Lawd's been good." Studying the afternoon sky, Sarah attempted to sort it all out in her heart and mind. "Anyways, I'se came across an old timer in Corinth. I'se could see in the Spirit he was 'bout ninety years old. He was pickin' up trash and sweepin' up. I'se asked him why he was doin' it. Wasn't nobody forcin' him to do it.

"You'se know what he done told me?" Sarah wiped away a new crop of tears. Her throat tightened, but she breathed in deep, releasing her emotions. "He says, 'This here's work for freedom. I'se gittin' paid wit' my freedom for workin' here.' The man began to cry. 'I'se reckons this here is the first time I'se ever work for sumpthin' for me and my youngin's in all my days. Ain't for the massa, but for me and mine.' I'se pat him on the back and told him he was right."

With some effort, Toussaint merged his soul with the Spirit. All he could hear were moans and suffering. He turned to his mother, terrified by the vision.

"I'se see what you'se done seent, Toussaint. I'se shouldn't have given you the tea. Now your sight is razor sharp and clear, not shaded by the desire for revolution. I'se wants you'se to hold in your heart the spirit of hope and the motivation to overcome fear. What you'se done seent might kills it."

"It's not like that Maman," Toussaint said. "We must face to the truth, if we're to change our lives."

Sarah nodded and puffed on her pipe. "Well, I'se can see you done looked to the south, to Natchez. The devil done taken his hold there." They both sat in silence, watching the prisoners in the Devil's Punch Bowl waste away and die. They saw folks with shovels, digging trenches and then tossing the dead into them. They covered them with dirt. The living slept next to the graves. Soon they would join their fallen. Peach trees sprung from where they lay, marking their graves. "You'se know what Toot? For the first time since helpin' them runaways, I'se cain't deal wit' it all. I'se cain't deal wit' what I done seent there in the Devil's Punch Bowl."

Toussaint couldn't turn away from the Punch Bowl in the Spirit. How could men be so cruel to his fellow man? But then he realized this was the source of the problem. Those being allowed to starve to death and die in the Punch Bowl weren't viewed as human. They were less than dogs to the soldiers who'd imprisoned them there. "Lord, the Union Army did this," he whispered. Toussaint scrunched up his eyes to break the vision's hold on him. "Maman, can't you get them out?"

His words caused Sarah to wail even louder. Her sobs subsided after a few moments. "Toot, the Lord wouldn't let me. I wasn't allowed."

"What do you mean, Maman?"

She wasn't sure how to explain it to him. "The Lord has allowed Satan his due. The Good Lawd done did this before, throughout time. This here is one of them times. The Punch Bowl is the worst of the camps, but it ain't the only one, mon fils. The Union and Confed'rates has camps like the Punch Bowl set up across the South." Sarah puffed on her pipe, thinking about it more.

"Hell, they done even set up some camps like this for their own White Folks. Once, I'se came to rest from the Spirit outside a prisoner of war camp called Andersonville. Them rebels done set it up for the Union soldiers they'se done captured. It was plumb awful too, and that was for White folks." Sarah took another puff on her pipe. "I don't thank White folks gots no respect for nobody's life. If you'se ain't on their team, you'se the enemy, whether Negro or White."

Sarah wiped away her tears with the hem of her skirt. "Anyways, at the Devil's Punch Bowl, I'se was tryin' to git in. Every time I would fade into the Spirit to cross over the walls, I'se gits knock back by the devil's minions. I'se tells them ole devils, 'Step aside, ya'll ain't got no dominion over me.' They'se wouldn't bow.

"Finally, Archangel Michael appeared to me durin' the fourth watch one night, outside the Punch Bowl in the woods surroundin' the place. Lawd, the swamps of Louisiana don't even compete wit' them. He tolds me, 'Leave here Sarah. It has been allowed.' He left and returned to where ever he was to begin wit'. So I'se did. I'se left hell on Earth." Grief welled up in her soul again. "I'se guessin' them folks who done died there are all up there under the Lawd's altar wit' all the other martyrs, 'till the End of Days."

Toussaint grasped Sarah in his arms, hoping to comfort her. "First the devil takes Missy. Now this? Lawd, what is

I'se good for?" Sarah wept on her son's chest, releasing all the bitterness trapped within her soul. Toussaint rocked her in his arms. "I'se wants you'se to have your freedom, son. But I'se done seent what's happenin' out there. If you walk off this place wit'out the Lord wit' you, you'se gonna end up in the Punch Bowl. I'se ain't tryin' to frighten you. I'se just tellin' you'se what is." She clutched her son in her arms. "Toussaint?"

"Yes, Maman?"

Sarah bit her lip, gazing into her son's eyes filled with desperation. "Whatcha gonna do?"

Toussaint clutched his mother even tighter. "I'm going to stay and see where the Lord leads me."

Chapter 17

La Rose Plantation, St. Helena Parish. 1864.

Sunday was the best day of the week. No fields, no overseer. Toussaint could be free for twenty-four precious hours. His mind drifted back to his days in France. Although he'd worked hard, studying with tutors and working in Claude's mortuary, every day was a free day. He had attended parties and receptions with Emmanuel and Claude. He'd met new and interesting people. He wore fine clothes. Toussaint considered his ragged overalls. At least he had overalls to wear. "I will rise from this place," he told himself.

He watched his sister sleeping on her palette. Claret lay with his parents on their palette, asleep as well. The sun had yet to rise. He slipped out the cabin and pulled up the door behind him, careful not to make a noise. Avoiding the squeaky floorboard in the porch, he grabbed his fishing pole and headed out into the pre-dawn night.

Toussaint allowed the Spirit to guide him through the

darkness. He could have closed his eyes as he walked, it was the same difference without the moon to light his path. But the Spirit led him along his way. Smelling the river, he lit his lantern he'd been carrying. He'd chosen not to light it for the journey. Toussaint laughed to himself. Perhaps he'd wished to hone his trust in the Lord to guide him through the darkest night.

Finding his crate concealed in the brush, he sat it at the river's edge. He cast out his line, hearing the weight plunk into the water out in the distance. He smelled the latent stench of a decaying body. He guessed it lay some distance downstream from where he sat. Toussaint had grown immune to the smell of death, between helping his father gather the dead corpses from the river's bank in his youth, and from his profession as a mortician.

Toussaint wanted to open a mortuary of his own in New Orleans. He dreamed of an honorable business, catering to the Negro community. He would be a respected businessman, helping the impoverished to bury their dead with dignity and respect, instead of opting for the pauper's grave.

How would he do this? He had no money, no inheritance. His cousin Emmanuel had money. Perhaps if he wrote a plan for his business and sent it to him, he would consider loaning him the startup money.

He had to get free first.

Toussaint had dreamed of taking his family to France to live with his cousin. How would they travel there? He hadn't heard from his cousin or Claude since leaving France. Feeling a tug, he pulled in the line. He raised his lantern to examine his catch. "Shucks," Toussaint said. He'd caught a water lily and some piece a cloth, maybe from a pants leg. He shuddered, wondering what he'd snagged, submerged in the river. Toussaint sat on his crate and fished a worm out of his bucket, baited his hook and cast it out.

He heard a rustling in the brush. He grabbed his hunting knife he'd 'found' in the barn and stood up. "Who's there?"

The brush rustled again. A figure exited. "Don't hurt me, Toot."

Toussaint sat on his crate. His peaceful morning had just ended. "Hey man."

Kinky walked over and sat next to him. "How'se you this mornin', Toot?"

"I'm fine, Kinky." Toussaint cast his line out. The two sat on the bank of the Tangipahoa River in silence for a while. A faint glow appeared above the horizon of trees, easing the burden of the night upon the Earth. Toussaint turned down his lamp to conserve oil.

"I'se runnin' off to join up wit' the Union Army, Toot. I'se gonna fight for our freedom."

Oh Lawd. Toussaint jerked the line, hoping to spur interest in the fish. They should be hungry.

"Once we'se whip these Rebels, I'se comin' back for Missy and Claret." Kinky put his thumb in his mouth, gnawing on a hang nail. "I'se done heard of a city in the north called Cinc'natti, in a state called Ohio. You'se ever hear of it, Toot?"

Toussaint nodded. "Yessuh, I have."

Kinky became excited. The stories he'd heard were true. "Well, my'se plan is to move Missy and li'l ole Claret there. We'se gonna be happy." Kinky bit his lip, afraid to ask. "Do's you thank Mistah Teddy will give us his blessin'? You'se thank he's gonna let me wed Miss Missy and take her away?"

A nibble? Toussaint popped the line. Nothing. "I guess he would allow it. I'll talk to him for you, if you like."

"That sho' would be a mighty fine thang for you to do, Toot. Sho' would 'preciate it." Overcome with emotion, Kinky hugged him.

Toussaint patted his back and hugged him, praying for his soul.

Chapter 18

La Rose Plantation, St. Helena Parish. 1865.

Toussaint walked from his cabin to the main house in the twilight, amazed and confounded by what he saw. More so by what he didn't see. Where had everyone gone? Very few of his co-workers remained. He watched his neighbors return from the fields, what was left of them.

A few months ago, hundreds trudged their way back to the slave quarters within an hour of the evening bell clanging in the square. Now, less than fifty made the journey. He could see rebellion and escape simmering in the eyes of those who lingered on the plantation. He figured they would make their journey soon, as well.

His vision from long ago had come to pass. Freedom for Negroes was in reach, even a reality, for many of La Rose's slaves. The dream had ceased to be an endless prayer.

One night, Stank and Toussaint sat out on the porch of their cabin. Stank had told him Augustus had sent slave catchers after his escapees. Once his contraband had been returned, Augustus would bring the chained runaways into the Shed for 'Plantation Re-orientation'. According to Stank, Augustus seemed to have lost his passion for torture. "Man, it's like he knows he done lost the battle," Stank had told him. "I'se don't even know him no more. He would only hit them a few times wit' the whip and then send them back to their cabins, tellin' them don't run off no more."

Toussaint couldn't believe his cousin's account of Augustus' change of heart. When had he ever accepted defeat? Toussaint searched the Spirit and found it to be so. At the same time, he saw the men and women who'd endured the Shed had retained their resolve to obtain their freedom. The spirit of 'what is' surpassed their fear of Augustus. Many of the recaptured slaves did make a second attempt to escape, never to be seen again.

Reaching the mansion, Toussaint continued his journey to the stables. Why had Augustus commanded him to join him? This was Stank's job, not his. He should have run off when he had the mind to do so. But he had heeded his maman's words and remained.

He spotted Augustus loading crates into the wagon. "You're late, Nigger. Get over here. Put those crates in the wagon."

Toussaint sucked in his breath, spotting twenty crates. A few were already on the wagon with about fifteen remaining to be loaded. What was all of this? However, he knew better than to question Augustus. He set about his work, helping his master load the cargo in the darkness. After about an hour, they finished.

"Get on, boy," Augustus said.

Toussaint mounted the servant's bench on the rear of the wagon. "Giddy up." Toussaint twined the leather straps around his wrists as the team of horses galloped away. Augustus drove the wagon like a mad man. He feared the wagon's load would spill over and crush him with a sudden stop.

Toussaint held on tight. The rutted road threatened to toss him, but he maintained his balance. He was grown man, now twenty-four years old. Why should he be subjugated to such a humiliation? His mind drifted back to France when he rode in grand carriages with Emmanuel and Claude. He longed to return to his life as a man.

Toussaint ricocheted up, almost falling off the narrow plank deemed a bench. Although he'd thought twice about going anywhere with Augustus, he found he didn't really have a choice.

Toussaint's thoughts drifted back to his first day on the plantation, after returning from France. Seeing Augustus for the first time had been strange.

He'd feared Augustus would snatch him and take him to the Shed. Instead, he'd scrutinized at him, as if awaking from a dream. Augustus said, "I've been looking for you, Nigger. Where have you been?" Toussaint hadn't responded. "Don't matter no way. Come with me."

Toussaint couldn't remember what Augustus had tasked him with that day. Yet, he could never get over how Augustus knew he hadn't seen Toussaint; yet in his master's mind, it had only been a few days instead of years. Toussaint knew his cousin Emmanuel and his mother had something to do with Augustus' memory lapse.

Over a year had passed since their encounter in the garden after Sammie's murder, but Augustus didn't seem to remember it. In fact, a few days following the incident in the garden, Augustus had passed him in the field, surveying the work of the remaining slaves on the plantation. Augustus had looked directly at Toussaint that day, but he hadn't seemed to notice him. Instead, he turned his horse around and rode back toward the mansion, without incident.

The wagon jerked to the left and then to the right after the rear wheel hit another rut in the road. Augustus was drunk, as usual. With his haphazard driving, he'd almost thrown Toussaint from rickety servant's bench, yet again. He wished Augustus would watch where he was going.

In recent months, Augustus never failed to bring Toussaint along on all his covert missions, instead of Stank. Toussaint had seen more than he wanted to see, done more than he wished to do. He felt corrupted, knowing Augustus would one day try to either blame one or all his murders on him. Who would believe a slave? He knew he could do nothing to protect himself against Augustus' lies.

A tear in his ragged shirt caught on a rusty nail protruding from the wagon. He could feel blood oozing from the cut. The ragged cloth of his shirt sleeve matted to his arm.

Toussaint contemplated the star littered sky, remembering the life he'd enjoyed in France and the fine attire he'd sported. "I'll never dress in rags again," he said. Toussaint gripped the bench and its straps, the wagon hitting a shallow ditch in the road. The ride leveled off again.

The wagon stopped, and Toussaint hopped off the bench, rounding the vehicle to where Augustus sat. Augustus tossed a small sack down to him. He could hear coins clinking within. "Go down to the river. There's a rock ten paces down the river's edge. Put this sack underneath it and come back. Don't mess around and dally down there."

Toussaint nodded and ran down to the river's edge. He almost skidded in the slick mud, but he maintained his balance. He walked off ten paces and located the rock to his right, well the only rock. With much effort, he tilted the rock up. He thought he would need a stick for leverage, but he managed. He placed the sack beneath it and ran back to wagon. Toussaint hopped on the servant's bench. Augustus popped the reigns and the wagon pulled away.

Toussaint knew his master well enough to know the money was payment for some sort of backwoods assassin to handle a situation for him. In recent weeks, many bodies had been found floating in the Tangipahoa. Many of those found dead had disputes with Augustus. Due to the war, there were few law enforcement resources available to investigate the string of murders or 'mysterious deaths', as he'd heard some folks in town describe the occurrences.

Toussaint soon figured out why so many men were turning up dead. Most of the dead were poor farmers whose lands bordered La Rose Plantation. Once the deceased had been buried, Augustus sent his lawyer to visit the widows and offer them next to nothing for their acreage. He knew they were desperate and would take anything.

Only a few women had resisted, vowing to make their farms work. All had failed except for one lady. The others had crawled back to Augustus to accept his offer.

In most cases, the value of the land had fallen due to the war, per Augustus' appraiser. The widows had been forced to sell for even less, eighty-five to ninety percent below market value in most instances. La Rose's acreage increased for pennies on the dollar, sending many families to the poor house. Augustus seemed happier with each day that dawned.

The heavy-laden wagon turned the bend, creaking and groaning. Toussaint could hear gunshots in the distance. Pulling onto a hidden road, they continued for another one-half mile and stopped. Augustus put the brake on, jumped down from the driver's bench and put on his work gloves.

"C'mon boy," Augustus said. Toussaint followed him. Once they reached a small clearing between two trees, Augustus stopped. "Them Yankee's are about two to three days from here. Word came yesterday they've made it from the Red River to Alexandria." Toussaint put his head down and prayed. Augustus kicked him. "I know you ain't praying they come here?"

"Naw suh."

Augustus threw a shovel at him. "Start digging."

Daylight crested the horizon as Augustus eased the wagon to a stop before the barn. Augustus jumped out the wagon and walked away. Toussaint led the horse into the barn, where he unhitched the wagon. Grabbing the mare's reigns, he walked her over to the stable. He watered and fed her, and then led her to her stall. Returning to the wagon, he unloaded the tools and put them away. He went home.

Toussaint opened the door and found his maman sitting

at the table. Sarah jumped up and enveloped Toussaint in her arms, praising God. She hadn't been able to see him in the Spirit. Augustus possessed latent spiritual abilities. Without his conscious effort, he'd blocked Sarah's view of their whereabouts. "What that devil have you out there doin' all night?"

Exhausted, Toussaint didn't feel like answering his mother's questions. At least he didn't have to go to the fields, for it was Sunday. "We were burying stuff."

"Buryin' stuff?" Sarah asked.

Teddy entered the cabin, having 'found' some eggs for breakfast. It wasn't like the old days, before Master Augustus, when the slaves kept their own hens. "What ya'll been buryin'?" Teddy placed the eggs on the table.

Sarah set about the task of preparing them. She grabbed an old, chipped ceramic bowl from the shelf Teddy had built above the fireplace. Although a large crack ran through it, the bowl still held it liquid contents.

Toussaint stared off into the distance, over his mother's shoulder. Closing his eyes, he peered inside the crates and trunks they'd buried, unable to believe it. "Gold, Maman. Bars and bars of gold."

Teddy sat at the table and pulled his whittling out, waiting for Sarah to prepare breakfast. "Gold," Teddy said in a shout, but then he lowered his voice. "Sarah?"

Sarah's mind began to click. "What else?"

"Some heavy stone-like coffins. I don't know what was in them." Toussaint closed his eyes, using the Spirit to peer inside the containers, to no avail. "But I heard stuff clanking around in them, so I don't think they were bodies." Toussaint couldn't figure it out. "Why would he do that, Maman?"

Sarah patted her son's cheek. "Fear is a killer, son. You'se remembers that. He done heard news of the Union comin' through here soon. He's hidin' his valuables." Sarah looked from Teddy to Toussaint, seeing the future and liking what she saw.

"That gold's yours, boy. Once the war done ended and Augustus done forgot 'bout it, you'se go back and git it. A little at time, though. You'se don't wanna raise no suspicions. Once he's dead, you dig it all up. It'll be aw'rite by then." Sarah kissed her son's forehead. "There's a kettle on the hearth. Goes and git washed up for breakfast."

La Rose Plantation, St. Helena Parish. January, 1866.

THE SOLDIERS CAME to a halt before the steps leading to the grand cypress doors inlaid with stained glass windows. The lieutenant knocked. A few moments later, Lawrence opened it. "Where's your master, boy?" Lawrence stepped aside, allowing Augustus to step out from behind him. The lieutenant smirked at him, presenting Augustus with a piece a paper. The soldiers stood with their rifles ready.

Augustus read the ragged sheet of parchment the lieutenant had handed him and spat, just missing the officer's boot. "What? Ya'll going to loot my place now?"

The lieutenant appraised the plantation house and its lands. He would love to rape the place. He could only imagine the riches which lay within. Many of the farms and plantations the troops had encountered on their march through Mississippi and Louisiana had been thread bare. No crops, no animals. Perhaps a few slaves had remained.

The men would take whatever hens and pigs they could find, any dry goods left in the homes, root vegetables in the field, and keep it for themselves. After bringing a few southern belles to the understanding they would have to surrender their virtue to the troops as ransom for their lives, each one had suddenly remembered where a gold watch or a few coins had been buried.

Now, he stood before the El Dorado of the South. The lieutenant spat at Augustus' boots, returning the favor. "No, sir. We got orders from Washington, D.C. not to touch this place." He spat again. "You must have some sort of angel looking out for you."

Once more, the lieutenant leered at the golden goose he couldn't touch. The Secretary of War had been very clear, sending word down through the ranks. Looting La Rose

Plantation of St. Helena, Louisiana wasn't worth dying of starvation in Andersonville. He'd heard rumors the camp had been cleared out and closed at the war's end, but he didn't want to find out first hand. "Now, let your Niggers go." Knowing the rich planter had lost his slaves comforted the lieutenant. He would suffer as the lieutenant had due to the war.

Augustus descended the steps of the plantation house and peered down the driveway. He spotted Toussaint standing near the hedges, watching. Augustus walked over to him and spat in his face. "You're free, Nigger. You and your people get the fuck off my place."

Chapter 19

La Rose Plantation, St. Helena Parish. August 31, 1963.

Lela watched her great-grandson as he sat on the sofa. He said nothing, but she could hear his thoughts. *Cracker. He had it coming.*

Lela found it funny how reincarnation could change a soul. She shook her head and adjusted the position of her Cartier watch on her wrist, so she could see the dial. She squinted. Old age was something else. At times, she had perfect vision. At other times, everything was a blur. She searched the coffee table and the sideboard across the room for her readers, and then remembered. "I left them upstairs," she said.

"What?"

"My reading glasses, Julian. I left them in my bedroom on the nightstand."

Julian groaned. "I'll go and get them for you."

Lela raised her eyebrow. *Lazy boy.* "Don't trouble yourself, Monsieur. I will get them myself."

"Grandmère, I don't mind," Julian said.

"It's fine, Julian." Lela arose from the wing chair. "I need to stretch my legs anyway." She felt pressure in her bladder. "I'll attend to a few other tasks as well. I will return soon."

Leaving the parlor, she heard the hall clock ticking. She hadn't heard the clock chime, so she walked over to find out the time.

Lela considered the clock's face and gasped in wonder. "I'd never noticed." She'd always believed the gilded clock had been constructed of wood. She ran her fingertips along the belly of the clock. Gold. As a child growing up in the mansion, she'd seen little for what it was. Now as an old woman, she could see everything and everyone with clarity and understanding.

The mystery of the clock unfurled before her. The clock concealed the body of an angel, cast in gold. The face of the clock sat upon the acanthus breast plate, leading to a smooth stomach area with a navel (where the key would be inserted for winding), descending into a fluted base.

She circled it and examined the ornate floral moldings on the side of the clock. It all flowed together to form an enormous wing. She ran to opposite side, finding another concealed wing. "But it doesn't have a head." She noticed the smooth triangular area, topped with a volute, at the top of the clock. "Lawrence."

Lawrence left his little office and joined her. "Yessum?"

"Do you have a ladder?"

Following her gaze, Lawrence smiled. "Don't need one." He picked her up, hoisting her above his head.

Lela giggled. "Now don't you steal a peek under my dress," Lela said. She could feel the heat of Lawrence's blush on her leg.

She stopped breathing. Viewing the top of the clock for the first time in her 116 years, Lela found a sinister golden face staring back at her, its head adorned with a nemes. Lapis lazuli striped the nemes, topped with a winged creature. A long, phallic beard descended from the face's chin, the volute of which could be seen from the floor. With his piercing lapis lazuli eyes and garnet lips, the sculpted face attempted to seduce and rapture her soul. "Not on your best day, Monsieur," Lela said. Unable to resist, she winked at the face. The corners of the face's jeweled lips twinkled. "I've seen enough."

Lawrence lowered her to the floor. "I'se was wonderin' if you'se see'd it this time, Ma'Dame. You'se couldn't see as good when you'se was last here for a spell in the '40's."

Lela shook her head. "There isn't a modest bone in his body. I know Barachiel is behind this. Where… Lord, when did he have this clock constructed? I'm guessing his ego is the inspiration for this clock?"

"Oui, Ma'Dame, it is. Reckon he had it made back over in Egypt during the First Dynasty. Naw, that ain't right." Lawrence rubbed his chin, searching the millennium. "I'se remember now. Pharaoh Menes had it made to honor him." Lawrence scratched his head, thinking. "I'se guessing he had the clock added later, when he was in the King's court over there in France? Must've been 'bout the fifteenth century."

Lela shook her head. The angel's pomposity never ceased to amaze her. "Lord help us." Lela heard footsteps approaching. She turned to find Julian leaving the powder room. "Could you come here for a moment, darling?" He joined Lela and Lawrence before the clock. "Darling, what do you see?"

Julian shrugged his lips. "What do you mean?"

"This." Lela extended her hand. "What is it?

"A clock made of gold." Julian checked the time. "It's getting late. I'm going to rear salon. Lawrence, send us some refreshments." Julian left, crossing the grand foyer and hall. His shoes made a muffled, clicking sound as they struck the gold and mosaic tiles.

Lela returned her attention to the clock. "Well, he knew it was gold. It didn't surprise him, either."

Lawrence laughed in a low, deep voice, agreeing with her. "If that boy cain't see nuthin' else, he can spot him some gold. It's what the Keyholder is supposed to do, I'se reckons," Lawrence said.

Lela shrugged. "I guess you're right, Lawrence." Lela patted his hand. "Oh my! The powder room!" Lela walked across the foyer with her thighs together, making it to the restroom just in time.

Nanette arranged the gold utensils on the buffet. Lela appraised her work. "Ma fille, you didn't have to go through all this trouble," Lela said, rubbing her back while admiring the magnificent spread. She grabbed a shallow, rose embellished bone china bowl, packed with ice, and placed within it one-half dozen oysters. "We just had lunch."

Nanette blushed. "Well, Mistah Larry said ya'll might be hungry, so Miss Almedia and Chef Mario put a few thangs together for ya'll," she said.

Lela scanned all the delights on the table. "Who made the caramel cake?"

"Miss Almedia."

Lela ran to where Julian sat, placing her plate of oysters on the coffee table. She skipped back over to the buffet and cut a large slice of cake. "Is there milk?" Nanette poured the iced contents from the golden pitcher into a crystal glass. "Thank you, darling," Lela said, taking it from her. She returned to the sofa and plopped down like a little girl.

Julian watched her in amazement. He was still full from

the lunch he'd enjoyed an hour and a half earlier. His grand-mère was a bottomless pit. She slurped down the half-dozen oysters, chasing it Vouvray. She rested for a moment, and then drained her misted goblet of ice water. Without warning, his grandmother wolfed down the cake and then gulped down the milk. Once she'd devoured the treats, she leaned back against the sofa, expelling a burp on impact. "Please excuse me, darling."

"Oh, you can save it," Julian said, popping an oyster in his mouth. Lela gave him a dirty look. "Such a lady, scarfing down oysters and cake, and then wishing to stab me with your tiny little seafood fork because I ate one of your oysters."

Lela rubbed her stomach, leaning back against the couch, immobilized.

Suzette entered the salon with Nanette to assist with refreshing the buffet. Mario followed with another platter of oysters, along with smoked salmon, soft cheeses and a garnish plate. Hearing a burp, Suzette opened her mouth to chastise Julian. She stopped once she considered her red-faced mistress sitting on the sofa. She rushed to her side. "Madame, what have you done?"

"M'Lady just enjoyed one-eighth of the caramel cake and chased it with a big glass of milk," Julian said.

"Milk?"

"Yes, the perfect topper for one-half dozen oysters and wine," Julian said.

Lela looked away, rubbing her stomach.

"Madame, you know you aren't to drink milk," Suzette said.

"Leave me alone," Lela whined, rubbing her tummy.

A ball of fear arose in the pit of Julian's stomach. "Why not?" Lela seemed puffy and uncomfortable to Julian. Her stomach swelled before his eyes, causing her to appear pregnant in her white lace pencil dress.

Suzette frowned and wagged her head. "You will find out. I must go." Suzette opened all the French doors leading to the gardens and then returned to the grand hall, closing the doors behind her.

Lela burped again. "Suzette thinks she knows everything." Lela adjusted her position on the sofa. She eyed the oysters Mario had just brought out, but then decided to wait.

"Why is she concerned about the milk?"

Her stomach rumbled. She'd hope Julian hadn't heard. Lela's face twisted, revealing her internal conflict. "No reason," Lela said. "Darling, please bring me some soda water from the bar." She willed the discomfort building within her to subside.

Julian went to the bar and poured a glass of soda water for her. Returning to the sofa, he handed her the beverage.

She sipped it.

After a few moments, his grandmère let out a small belch. Julian held his breath, but not before inhaling the sour air steeped with traces of oysters and sour milk. He said nothing, trying to ignore it. He didn't wish to offend her. "So Grandmère, did Toussaint and his family leave the plantation that day?"

Lela grimaced and altered her position on the sofa. "No, of course not. Once Sarah heard what Augustus had said, she took her own sweet time packing up. She had been saving a few items she'd transported from around the country for their new home, for she'd already seen in the Spirit Negroes would soon be free. In fact, she'd already found a place for them to stay in New Orleans, a nice building." Lela turned green.

"Ugh!" Julian hopped up from the sofa. "Grandmère, I know you didn't just let out that putrid smell. That is the absolute worst gas I've ever smelled in my life. And trust me; I've smelled some bad farts, living in the Alpha house at Morehouse."

Julian fanned the air with his hand, to no avail. "Even after a night of heavy drinking, my frats didn't let out gas this bad." Julian covered his nose and ran for an open French door. He stood in the doorway inhaling deeply. "So, this is the reason why Suzette scolded you for drinking milk?"

Lela's eyes filled with tears. "Pardon, mon fils."

Julian could see he'd hurt her feelings. How could her feelings be hurt? Couldn't she smell it too? But he knew she had tried to hold it. "Grandmère, it's okay. It's not that bad." He sat beside her again and patted her hand. She released another round. "Do you need to excuse yourself, Grandmère? I can wait for you."

Lawrence entered the salon with bowls of potpourri, scented candles, and a can of aerosol air freshener. "Ev'ry since you'se was a li'l ole gal, milk never did sit well on your stomach." Lela glared at him. "Well, I guess this too shall pass."

"Funny."

"Sho' is, Ma'Dame. Do ya'll want to sit outdoors?"

Julian opened his mouth to say yes. "No, Lawrence. It's too hot out there," Lela said.

"Aw'rite, then." Lawrence rushed for the door. "Well, I'll be in the front of the house. Call me if ya'll need me."

Julian wished he could escape to front of the house with Lawrence. The salon smelled like the toilet. His grandmère appeared as if she would cry. Julian softened his face and held her close. Lela hadn't run from him when he was ill as a child; he wouldn't run from her now due to a bad case of gas. "It's okay, Grandmère," he said. A tear rolled down her face, but she nodded, accepting his comfort and loyalty. "So, tell me, what happened next?"

Lela pushed, forcing out more gas. She'd hoped Julian wouldn't smell it, but the expression on his face told her otherwise. Oh well.

Chapter 20

After the soldiers departed the plantation, the Bailey family left La Rose for New Orleans a month later. It was a hard journey, but they made it through. Every time Missy saw a White man, she would go into hysterics. Along the way, Aunt Sarah would give her some sort of tea to make her sleep.

In any case, I think the Baileys arrived in New Orleans in March, 1866. Prior to leaving St. Helena Parish, Toussaint had dug up some of the gold he'd helped Augustus bury a few years before.

The bustling city amazed the family. Only Sarah had visited the town before. They witnessed gangs of freed Negroes with nowhere to go, gathered in vacant lots. Some White men stood on milk crates talking to the masses, telling them of a better life on this plantation or that, promising them a wage and somewhere to stay.

Toussaint continued to drive the two mares through the

chaos, following his mother's directions. "Stop here, boy," she'd told him. Toussaint stopped the wagon and applied the brake. "There it is."

Toussaint told me many years later he'd never seen such a grand building. Well, he had in Europe, but for him to own such a property? He'd allowed such dreams to die once he returned to La Rose.

Toussaint had purchased the property from the owner for a sack of gold coins. I think Toussaint anticipated trouble, being a Negro, but there wasn't any. I wonder why? Maybe the owner needed to unload the property and didn't care who purchased it. Looking back, I think the owner had been so desperate for money, Satan could have brought it and he wouldn't have given the matter a second thought. In any case, your Uncle Toot embarked on his life as a free, prosperous Negro in New Orleans.

New Orleans, Louisiana. March, 1866.

TEDDY SLID HIS arm around Sarah's waist, watching Toussaint stand on the ramshackle porch of his new home and business. The building needed a lot of work, but they'd lived under worse conditions. "Son, we'se need to git to work on unloadin' this wagon," Teddy called to him. "It's gittin' late."

"We'se ain't stayin' here tonight, Teddy," Sarah said.

Toussaint walked down the stairs. "Then where are we staying, Maman?"

Sarah allowed a little grin to course across her face. She'd been saving the surprise for some time. "Well, I'se done found us a temp'rary place to stay while you'se and Teddy's fix up this here place," Sarah said. "I'se been livin' in the dust all my life. I'se ain't doin' it no more."

Teddy should have known his wife had other plans. "Where's this here palace you'se talkin' 'bout woman?"

Sarah kissed her husband. "On St. Ann Street."

The heavy-laden wagon eased to a stop before the shuddered townhome. She hadn't believed Toussaint would be able to follow the map in her mind, but he did. She wished the boy would focus more on developing his spiritual abilities, but concerns with the physical world distracted him.

The door of the townhome opened. "Lawd, this cain't be!" A man ran from the house and lifted Sarah from the rear of the wagon, twirling her around in the twilight. "Sarah! How is you, gal?"

Sarah kissed him on the cheek. *Still fine*. Time had passed him by.

"Shucks, time don't mean nuthin' to me, gal," he said hugging her once more. He noticed a man standing behind her, having jumped down from the driver's bench. He seemed a little hostile. "Is this here your husband, Teddy?"

Sarah blushed, her husband's jealousy turning her on. "Yessuh, it is." Sarah took Teddy's hand. "Maurice, this here's Teddy."

Teddy didn't move. "Go on now. Be nice," Sarah said. Teddy shook Maurice's hand. "Maurice is an old family friend."

Teddy suppressed his rage. "Good to meet you, suh."

Maurice watched the others exit the wagon. "This here's Toussaint," Sarah said. Toussaint shook his hand. He didn't seem to remember Maurice. The boy was spiritually lazy. "And this here is little Claret."

Maurice stooped down to face her. "You'se a blessed one, ain't you gal?" Claret clutched her grandfather's leg with one arm while holding her rag doll in the other, never breaking her glare on the man. Maurice backed away, afraid she might kill him.

"Be nice, gal," Sarah scolded the child. She smiled at the man, obeying her grandmother's command.

Maurice stood up and walked over to the young lady still in the wagon, clutching the railing. She stared out into the abyss, swimming there. "Come out the water, gal," Maurice whispered to her.

Missy shuttered and looked around. "Where is we?"

Teddy began to cry. It was the first lucid statement she'd

uttered in years. He could see she was in her right mind. "We'se in New Orleans, baby," Teddy said to her, weeping.

"Why we'se here, Papa?"

Teddy sobbed, standing on the sidewalk before the group. Toussaint grabbed him for support. He regained control of himself. "We'se free now, honey," he said. "I'se reckons you is too."

With each passing day, Missy seemed to improve. When Sarah would enter the parlor, she would find Missy sitting in a chair watching Claret. Peering into her daughter's heart, Sarah observed her child trying to figure out her feelings for her daughter. Slowly, Missy's aversion for her flesh melted away, granting her the ability to see the child as her own daughter instead of constant reminder of her rape.

Later that night once everyone had gone to bed, Sarah left her bed, headed for the kitchen. She needed some water, for her throat was dry. As she walked down the hall, she noticed Missy's open bedroom door. She stopped and checked on her.

Maurice sat on the edge of Missy's bed, stroking her hair. Missy closed her eyes. She began to weep, but then settled down, emitting a pitiful whimper. At last her body relaxed, surrendering to a restful sleep. Maurice hummed a little song Sarah couldn't identify.

He left the room and closed the door. Finding Sarah standing outside, he patted her cheek. Sarah resisted the urge of materializing a dagger in her hand to stab him to death. "I'se would never hurt her like that White devil did. You'se knows that, right?"

Sarah turned her eyes to floor, ashamed. He'd detected her desire to kill him before she could suppress it. "Yessuh, I'se knows. Sorry. It's a reflex, I'se reckon."

He led her downstairs to the kitchen. Removing a match from the cast iron box mounted on the door frame, he struck it and lit the lamp. He extended his arm, inviting Sarah to have a seat at the table. Taking a pitcher from the icebox, he poured Sarah a glass of water and handed it to her. She drained its contents.

"I'se help folks to heal and release their troubles. You'se knows that 'bout me, right?" Sarah nodded. "Then doncha you'se worrys 'bout me wit' Missy. If I'se didn't want you'se to see it, you'd still be asleep. Ain't that so?"

"I'se reckons you'se right. I'se sorry, Maurice."

Maurice went to the counter and got a little piece of praline out the canister. He gave it to her.

Sarah gobbled it up. "This reminds me of Mickey's pralines, back on La Rose."

Maurice poured her another glass of water. "Who'se that?"

Sarah hadn't thought of him in years. "He was my sister Sallie's man. He would always bring us girls pralines."

"Humph." Maurice stood from the table and walked to the door, followed by Sarah. "Now ain't that sumpthin'?" He blew out the lamp.

After the men left for work, Sarah went downstairs to the parlor. She found Missy sitting on the rug playing dolls with Claret. The two chatted like childhood friends.

She backed out the room before they noticed her. She walked across the courtyard, finding Maurice in an opulent office tidying up. "Maurice, you'se ain't gonna believe it."

He finished polishing the gold lamp. "What's that, Miss Sarah?"

"What's goin' on wit' Missy?"

"Whatcha mean?"

"She's in her right mind, on the floor playin' wit' Claret." Sarah fiddled with the fold of her dress. "It's like nuthin' ever happened to her. I'se don't thanks she remembers none of it now." She began to cry, unable to accept the unbelievable. "I'se thanks I'se gots my baby back, but I'se afraid to claim it."

Maurice laid his polishing cloth on the desk. Taking Sarah's hand, he led her to the settee. "I'se guess she just needed her some rest."

"Rest?"

"Yessum, rest." Maurice patted her hand, easing her fears. "That gal needed some rest from her troubles. Gittin' off La Rose is the best thang that could've happened for her." Maurice stared out the window into the Spirit. "She needed to git away from the spirit of that White devil who done vi'lates her. He lurks on that place, even when he ain't there."

Maurice stood from the settee and returned to the desk. "As long as ya'll stays here, she's gonna be aw'rite. I'se coverin' her here." He picked up his cloth and rubbed away a blemish on the golden lamp. "Maybe's you'se and Teddy should thank 'bout her stayin' here wit' me."

Sarah thought about it. Every day Missy got better. She could see that limited contact with her father and brother, along with staying at the townhouse, had done wonders for her daughter. Yet, she knew Teddy would never agree to it. She could see her husband didn't care for Maurice. She wasn't sure of the reason why.

"Well, I'se guess that settles it, then," Maurice said. He crossed the room to dust the buffet and fill the decanters.

Sarah wiped away her tears, shutting her eyes to the future. She would enjoy today. "You'se expectin' visitors, Maurice?"

He topped off the cognac and replaced the stopper

in the decanter. "Yeah. Maybe's the one I'se sweet on may come and stay a spell wit' me after ya'll gone."

The next day Sarah awoke, refreshed. She dressed and rushed downstairs, hoping she'd hadn't missed breakfast with her granddaughter. She entered the dining room and stopped at the door.

"Maman loves you, my li'l Claret."

Claret nodded, her mouth filled with oatmeal. Some dribbled down her face. Missy wiped it away.

Stunned, Sarah forgot her breakfast and went to the parlor. She sat there for a while, unable to process what she'd just seen. *Missy told Claret she loved her.* "Lawd, help me to convince Teddy." She didn't want her child to leave the house, yet she knew her husband would never allow her to stay.

Claret burst into the parlor with her mother in hot pursuit. They ran around and around the room, making Sarah dizzy. Finally, Missy caught the child and fell on the floor, punishing her with tickles. "Who loves you?" Missy tickled the child mercilessly.

"You do, Maman!"

Missy smiled at her mother sitting on the sofa, weeping. "And who else loves you?"

Claret noticed Sarah on the sofa, seeing her for the first time. "Grandmère!" The two rolled on the floor. Claret won the struggle, sitting atop her mother. "She loved me when you couldn't, Maman. Is that alright?"

Missy, cognizant of the world around her for the first time since her child's birth, allowed her tears to fall. "Yessum, she did. Maman's grateful for it. Maman loves Grandmère too."

Sarah left the sofa and dropped to the floor with her children, engulfing them both in her arms.

Life became a dream to Sarah, each day bringing new blessings. While Teddy and Toussaint spent their days working at the building, Sarah, Missy and Claret enjoyed spending time with Maurice and the household staff.

"It's music day!" Claret ran into the parlor and bounced on the sofa, her ruffled skirts flaring out around her.

Missy entered the parlor behind her. "Just 'cause it's Wednesday don't means it's gotta be music day. Maybe they'se don't feels likes playin' today, baby."

Maurice gave Claret a little piece of rock candy. "Ifs Miss Claret says it's music day, then that's what it is." The musicians entered the parlor. One sat at the piano and another removed his violin from its case. After tuning up for a few minutes, the two played a waltz.

"I want to dance!" Claret ran over to Maurice. He bowed to her and she curtsied, as he'd taught her to do. They began to dance around the room. Tired of dancing, Claret stood on Maurice's shoes, allowing him to whisk her about the floor.

Sarah walked in and sat next to her daughter. "That gal done shucked and jived Maurice into her Wednesday dance."

The women smiled, watching them go around the room. "Papa."

Sarah leaned into her, unable to hear her over the music. "You'se say sumpthin', Missy?"

The corners of her mouth turned up a bit. "He reminds me of Papa, Maman."

Sarah kissed her daughter on the forehead. "Sho' does, baby." She smoothed down her daughter's hair. "You'se wanna dance wit' me?"

Missy arose from the chair. Sarah grasped her tight, never wishing to let her go. Taking her hands, they danced around the room with Maurice and Claret, floating on the notes of love.

Chapter 21

New Orleans, Louisiana. February, 1869.

The miracles of the Most High never ceased to amaze Sarah. He'd returned her daughter to her. Sarah sat in the courtyard, watching Missy and Claret skip rope. Joy radiated from her daughter's face, as well as from her granddaughter's. They stopped, with Missy taking Claret in her arms. "Let's go on inside and see if there's some ice cream," Missy said to Claret. Hand in hand, they disappeared into the parlor doors.

The doors from the street opened. Teddy and Toussaint walked in dusty and tired. "What ya'll doin' home so early?"

Teddy and Toussaint sat their leather satchels containing their work tools on the bench inside the front door. "Aren't you glad to see us, Maman?" Toussaint walked over to where she sat and kissed her.

Sarah perspired in the heat of the day. "'Course I is, boy." Teddy followed behind his son and kissed his wife. "Ain't even dinner time. I'se was just wonderin'."

Teddy continued his way to the side stairs, leading to the balcony bordering the second-floor bedrooms. "Cain't men-folk 'round here come home early and git some rest? You'se women just wanna work us into an early grave," Teddy called down to her, leaning on the balcony. Everyone present burst into laughter. "Naw, we'se called it quits early. We'se almost finished," Teddy said, filled with pride and excitement.

"You is?"

"Yessum, we is," he told his wife. "'Sides, feels like we'se ain't seent Missy and Claret in years," Teddy said.

"It would be nice to see them awake for a change," Toussaint said, headed for the stairs.

"Me and Toot gonna wash up and have dinner wit' ya'll," Teddy said, smiling down on her. He entered his bedroom and Toussaint entered his.

Hearing the doors close, Sarah's eyes affixed on the near-by Camilla bush in a pot. The blooms wilted; the petals fell to the ground.

Sarah lit her corn cob pipe while sitting with Teddy, waiting for him to dress for dinner. She'd laid out his good overalls she'd starched for him that morning. After all the years they'd been together, he still looked good and had a great body. He slipped on the white starched shirt, and then stepped into his overalls, buttoning the straps to the bib.

"What's wrong wit' you, gal?"

Sarah puffed on her pipe. Had she smoked it since moving to the townhouse? "I'se needs to talk to you, Teddy."

He stood at the mirror, straightening the collar of his shirt. "What 'bout?"

"Missy."

He turned to her and could see something troubled her. He walked over and sat on the side of the bed next to his wife. "She done got worse?"

Sarah fiddled with the fold in her fine cotton dress. "Naw. She's better."

Teddy's eyes lit up. "She is?" He couldn't believe it. He'd thought they would have to put her away, or keep her locked in her room at best. "How so?"

Sarah bit her lip, staring at the fold in her dress. "Well, she's talkin' now. She's playin' wit' Claret. She even told the child she loved her."

Teddy fell back on the bed pillows. "For really?"

"Yessuh, it's true."

Teddy lay there thinking. "The Lawd is good. She done finally got past what that White devil did to her."

Sarah grabbed Teddy's hand. She pierced him with her glare. "I'se wants you'se to listen to me good, Teddy. Doncha mention it to her. Let her be."

Teddy took her hand in his and patted it. "Why'se you'se

worry 'bout it? She's fine now." Considering the concern on his wife's face, he conceded. "Aw'rite. I'se won't say a word 'bout what happened."

Teddy took his place at the head of the table as the wait-staff and footmen stood about, waiting to serve them. The footman came forward, presenting a platter of ham. The next came along with rib roast. It seemed raw to him, but he took some anyway. He could eat the edges. "Lawd, we'se ain't White. Why cain't they just set the food on the table and we'se git what we'se want?"

Upon his command, Maurice instructed the staff to place the platters in the center of the table. Teddy smiled, serving himself. Toussaint rubbed his temples.

Missy walked in holding Claret's hand. She placed the child in the chair next to hers, equipped with a booster seat, and then took her seat.

Teddy stopped loading his plate with food, unable to believe the sight of his daughter. Her hair had been upswept into a head wrap. He believed the Creole women called them tignons. He'd seen some of the high yella women around town wearing them. She wore a fine dress. He looked into her eyes, finding them clear and lucent. "Lawd, you'se sho' is beautiful, Missy."

Missy bowed her head. Uncomfortable, she fiddled with

the lace collar of Claret's dress. "Thank you, Papa."

Sarah swallowed hard. "Say grace, Teddy."

Once the prayers had been completed, they dug into dinner. "This sho' is good, Maurice. You'se gotta thanks Miss Tildie for us."

Maurice nodded.

"Grandpa!"

Teddy smiled at Claret. "What's got you all excited, gal?"

Claret giggled. "Maman skips rope with me every day! She sits with me during my lessons too," the child said, placing a sweet potato in her mouth.

"For really? Well ain't that just fine!" Teddy finished his ham. "Your Maman is doin' just fine."

"Hush, Teddy," Sarah said.

He sipped his brandy. "What I'se done said, Sarah? I'se just said the gal's doin' fine. I'se cain't tell her that?"

Missy fidgeted in her chair. "Thank you, Papa."

He smiled at her daughter, full of pride. "You'se welcomed, gal. Papa's proud of you, that's all."

Teddy rolled over in bed. His stomach burned. He knew better than to drink whiskey so close to bedtime, but he couldn't resist. He wanted to celebrate with his son. Not only would the construction on the building be completed within the next few weeks, but his daughter was in her right mind. He'd prayed so long the good Lawd would heal her. Now he had.

Acid surged from his stomach into his throat. "Dangit! Sarah?" She rolled over, asleep. He wondered if she was having a nightmare, because she whimpered. "Sarah?" She wouldn't wake up. "I'se guess I'se gotta make my own tonic for my stomach."

Lighting a candle, Teddy left their bedroom and entered the hallway. He noticed the door to his daughter's room open. He went to close it, but spotted a figure sitting beside her on the bed. He sat the candle on the floor and burst into the room, jumping on the figure, beating him without mercy.

"You'se ain't gonna take her again, White devil," he said, pummeling him. Someone hemmed his arms up behind him.

"Papa, stop!"

"Let me go, Toot," Teddy said, wrestling in his arms.

Sarah came in with the candlestick. "Teddy, whatcha doin'?"

Teddy began to cry. "What ya'll doin'? Cain't you'se see that White devil Hanzel tryin' to ruin my gal again? She's in her right mind now after what he done did to ruin her, and he's comes back?"

Missy screamed and wouldn't stop.

"Papa, look!" Toussaint turned his head to the bed. Sarah held the candle to the face of the figure, so her husband could see. "Papa, it's Maurice."

Teddy's face melted.

"Baby, he comes in here and prays for her at night. He's been helpin' her git better." Sarah sat the candlestick on the table. Sitting on the bed, she grasped her daughter in her arms and stroked her hair to calm her. Maurice lay on the floor, wounded.

Teddy resisted the urge to spit on him. "Stay away from my daughter. You'se ain't gonna ruin her too." Breaking free from Toussaint, he left the room.

New Orleans, Louisiana. March, 1869.

TEDDY DECIDED THE time had come for his family to leave the townhouse. Although their departure date had been scheduled for two weeks later, he refused to stay in the house one more night. "I'se gittin' my baby outta this place, Sarah. It's bad e'nuff that White devil vi'lated her. I'se ain't allowin' this Nigger to do it too."

Sarah slapped him. She'd never struck him before. She'd done so before she could stop herself. "Doncha use that kind of language 'round here Teddy. You ain't no Nigger and neither is he!"

Teddy gritted his teeth, suppressing the urge to hit his wife. "You'se aw'rite wit' him puttin' his hands on our daughter?" With all his might, he resisted the desire to beat

Sarah. He'd never thought of doing such a thing. Never even dreamed of it. But he figured the woman could use a good ass kicking now.

Sarah could see rebellion in his eyes. "I'se sorry for strikin' you. I'se shouldn't have done it. But I'se 'clare 'fore God if you'se lays one finger on me I'm gonna strike you'se dead where you stand."

Teddy walked away, running his fingers through his kinky gray hair.

Sarah gathered her words. "Maurice is a good man, like Lawrence."

"He ain't nuthin' like Lawrence."

"Baby, he's exac'ly like him. He would never hurt our baby," Sarah said. Teddy stood at the window, silent. Sarah gathered her courage. "I'se wants her and Claret to live here wit' him."

Teddy laughed. "Woman, you'se done lost your mind."

Sarah walked over to him at the window and faced him. "I'se ain't. But Missy gonna lose hers if she leaves this here place." Sarah inhaled deep. "She's gonna lose her mind livin' in the house wit' you'se and Toot. Ya'll gone ruin her for good."

Teddy didn't know the woman standing before him. "I'se her father! I'se loves her. It was me, Toot, Stank and Kinky searching for that White trash wit' Massa Augustus.

We risked ev'rythang to vindicate her. Doncha remembers that?"

Sarah began to cry. "Yessuh, I'se do. You'se know I'se do. But vengeance ain't helpin' her!" Sarah took her husband's face in her hands, peering into his eyes, attempting to guide his soul through the spirit to the truth. "You'se saw her! Love done brought her back to us. Not vengeance! Ya'll keep tellin' her she's ruint. She ain't ruint! Stop tellin' her that."

Teddy wiped away his tears of rage. "That trash put his hands on her. He made her no good. She had done lost her mind."

Sarah couldn't hold her tongue any longer. "You'se and Toot made her feel like trash."

Teddy held up his hand to strike her. It went numb. "Now you'se gonna put your voodoo on me, woman?"

Sarah stood before him, frozen. "That's what you'se thanks 'bout me, Teddy? You'se need to be right 'bout this so bad you'se gonna call me a witch?"

"Baby…"

Sarah adjusted her dreaded hair, her eyes locked on her husband. "Let it be as you'se done said. Missy's blood is on you. Her blood gonna stop your heart." Sarah felt dead inside. She left the room.

The day had come for the Bailey family to leave Emmanuel's townhome on St. Ann Street. Sarah toured the rooms. Defeated and discouraged, she departed the townhouse for the courtyard. She sat in her favorite wrought iron chair. She watched as her husband led Missy to the wagon. Hot tears filled her eyes and rolled down her cheeks. She refused to cry.

"We'se cain't save ev'rybody Miss Sarah. God saves. We'se can only do what we'se can. Even for our own chil'ren."

Sarah scowled into the Spirit, filled with bitterness. "Teddy bein' bull-headed. He's don't know what he's doin'!" Sarah buried her face in her lap, more enraged than hurt.

Maurice appeared before her. He sat on the cobblestone and stared up at her. "At least your baby had some peace. She gots to know her daughter."

"That ain't e'nuff."

"Well, I'se reckons its gonna have to be e'nuff, since that's all the Good Lawd done allowed." Maurice pulled a young sprig of grass, growing up between the cobblestone pavers. It couldn't survive there for long anyway. A fresh stream of tears fell from Sarah's eyes. "I'se guessin' your li'l one is like this here blade of grass."

Sarah stood from the chair. "My'se baby's gonna make it."

Maurice said nothing.

Sarah walked away and stopped at the open front doors.

She turned around and faced her friend. "I'se wanna thanks you, Maurice." Sarah began to sob, but stopped herself. She straightened her back and dried her tears. "You'se been good to us." Sarah began to cry again, but stifled herself once more. "My daughter knew peace whiles stayin' here. My granddaughter knew the love of her mother. I'se guess that's more than I'se figured on when arrivin' here." Sarah inhaled deep, turned and walked out the door.

Maurice walked to the front door. He arrived in time to see the wagon pull away, loaded with the family's belongings. He could see they would neither need nor utilize most of the items. "Humph," Maurice said. "We'se always hold on to the stuff that no longer suits us." He closed the front door, barring the townhome from the world, for a time.

Chapter 22

New Orleans, Louisiana. March, 1869.

The house took her breath away. No longer a run down, ramshackle hovel, the two-story building in the Ninth Ward of New Orleans had been painted yellow. Its missing siding had been repaired. Fresh gingerbread trim bordered the eaves of the home. The windows appeared to be brand new, having received fresh glazing and a good washing. Although she couldn't read well, she could pick out a few words on the sign above the second-floor windows. *T. Bailey and Son Mortuary.* A grin encroached upon her face.

Sarah entered the building. Toussaint and Teddy stood to the side near the oak coat stand, accented with a hat rack and mirror. They cast down their eyes, awaiting her inspection and approval.

Sarah walked through the first floor. What Negroes had a fine house such as this? "Ya'll did this?"

Toussaint raised his eyes from the floor, furling the brim

of his straw hat in hand. "Yessum, Maman. We did this for ya'll."

Sarah nodded and continued her tour of the house, admiring its fine furnishings. She came to the kitchen, showcasing a large cast iron stove. "Lawd, where ya'll git this? We'se ain't gotta cook in the fireplace?"

"Naw," Teddy said. "The fireplace is just for heat, not that you'se cookin' for us men day and night won't do the trick," Teddy said with a laugh. Toussaint hit his father on the arm.

"Well, ain't that just fine," she said. She opened the back door leading to the rear yard. She scanned the area, finding a space had been sectioned off for a garden. A few collards, onions, potatoes and carrots had been planted. "My garden?" Her husband and son nodded.

Facing the house, she noticed a stairwell leading down into the earth, beside the stairs descending from the kitchen. "What's that? The root cellar?"

"Yeah, baby," Teddy said. "That's where we'se works on preparin' folks for burial."

Sarah nodded. Claret toddled into the yard. She didn't toddle anymore, Sarah had to admit to herself. She walked like a grown woman. She led her mother by the hand. "Look at our new house, Maman!"

Missy's eyes skated to and fro. "Where's my pot?"

"What, Maman?"

"My pot. It's Monday. I'se needs to git to work on Massa's sheets."

Feeling Sarah's glare on him, Teddy turned away. His daughter had spiraled into insanity once more. "Missy baby, let's take you'se upstairs to your room."

"I'se gotta work, Papa. Kinky gonna stop by soon. I'se wanna be finished wit' my chores."

"Okay, Missy," Toussaint said. He smiled and kept the mood light. "But let's get you settled first."

Missy wrung her hands, unsure. "Aw'rite, Toot. If's you'se thanks that's best."

They returned indoors and then walked up the rear stairs. Reaching the second floor, Sarah admired the rug running the length of the hallway, the pictures on the wall. Toussaint walked ahead of them all, stopping at a door. "Missy, you'se want to see Claret's room?"

Recalled from the fog of her mind, she reunited with the present. "She sleeps with Maman and Papa."

Toussaint patted his sister's cheek. "Not anymore." He opened the door to Claret's room.

Negro children don't live like this. Sarah squelched the negative thoughts. She stood in the doorway, awestruck.

Claret burst into the room and jumped on the bed. "Look, Maman," Claret said, jumping on the bed. Her mother remained in the hallway, staring into the darkness of her spirit. Sarah grimaced, watching her daughter slip into insanity, yet again.

She gathered her wits, leaving behind the pain and impending doom concerning Missy. Sarah walked into the room and sat on the bed with Claret. She worked between her fingers the lace bordering the top sheet. They were the softest linens Sarah had ever felt. Sarah admired the carpets to warm little Claret's feet.

Leaving the bed, Sarah opened the armoire, finding it filled with dresses fit for a princess. She turned away from the armoire, taking in the grandeur of the boudoir. Claret had the most beautiful room she'd ever seen, filled with lace curtains and artwork depicting fairytale and nursery rhyme characters. Dolls Toussaint had ordered from France lined the shelves. Exquisite doll houses and carriages had been arranged around the room. "I purchased them from a friend who owns a shop in the French Quarter," Toussaint told her.

Sarah breathed in deep, unable to accept the magnificent home. "Toot, how's you'se do all this?"

Toussaint cleared his throat. "It's from our inheritance."

That's a lie. She knew he'd dug up some of the gold he and Augustus had buried out near the Tangipahoa River before the war's end. She watched in the Spirit as Toussaint and Stank dug up the gold during the third watch of the night. The slave patrol had been all around the place, but never spotted them. She thanked God and her evil father, Barachiel.

You are welcomed, my love

She wished to cry. Sarah could have only dreamed of such a beautiful home. After spending her life as a slave living in a drafty one room shack on La Rose Plantation, her most fantastic dreams had come true.

Leaving Claret's bedroom, Toussaint led his parents to their own room. The couple stood in the doorway, unable to speak. In the center of the room, placed between two windows was a big, mahogany bed with a feather mattress. Sarah heard Teddy suck in his breath. This was a real bed, not the straw mattresses they'd endured their entire lives.

Nightstands had been placed on either side of it, with ornate kerosene lamps adorning each. A mahogany wash stand stood in the corner of the room, with a porcelain basin and matching pitcher, decorated with blue flowers.

Sarah's rocking chair from La Rose had been placed in the opposite corner of the room. "I was going to fix it up for you, Maman, but me and Papa decided to leave it as is." Sarah nodded, her eyes filled with tears.

"There's more," Toussaint said. Taking his sister's hand, he led Missy, and the group, to see her bedroom. Sarah stayed behind, absorbing the grandeur of her first, private bedroom. She sat in her rocking chair. Removing her pipe from her apron pocket, she lit it and relaxed. She exhaled, thinking of her brother, Les. She wondered about him. Maybe she still had the strength to go to Canada and visit him. She'd grown old and tired.

T. Bailey and Son Mortuary. Sarah and Teddy were honored when Toussaint named the enterprise after his father, taking on the role of his apprentice. But once Sarah saw how Toussaint laid his clients out, she realized he was the master and her husband was the apprentice. She didn't know what Claude Hicks had taught him in France, but every one of Toussaint's clients appeared to be sleeping before their loved ones, no matter how gruesome an end the deceased may have endured.

Few had died of old age. Most had fallen victim to race riots, Klansmen, or mobs seeking to annihilate the Negro menace from their streets. The White man perceived the Negro as the source of their suffering and lack of employment. Many days, Toussaint and Teddy refused to allow Sarah to bring lemonade to the root cellar, for the room reeked of the charred flesh from their latest tar and feather client.

Sarah placed the last pin in her bun of locked hair, and then tied her new tignon about it. It was a little old fashioned, but then again, so was she. She'd always told herself once she became free, she would sport her tignon like New Orleans' *gens de couleur libres*. The head dress was a badge of honor to her. She intended to wear it for the rest of her days.

Her brother's face flashed before her soul. "It ain't your time yet, Augustus," she said to her reflection in the dressing table mirror. She could see Augustus snort in his library on the La Rose Plantation. *Fuck you.* Sarah rubbed her hands together, nervous.

"You'se ready, baby?"

Sarah leered at her husband. She had to admit, he looked fine in the suit of clothes Toot had ordered for him from France.

Manny

So that's who made Teddy's suit of clothes. "Merci," Sarah said.

In the Spirit, Manny nodded and returned to the cutting table in his workroom.

Teddy adjusted his lapels and then his cravat. "You'se thankin' me for lookin' fine?"

Puffed-up rooster. Sarah left her dressing table and stood before her husband. She cuddled him with her left hand, promising him joys to come. It was a blessing to have their own room and not have to go out into the fields or the woods to be alone. "You'se still is fine to me, even in a barrel wit' some straps tied to it."

"You'se better git on wit' all that talk, gal."

Sarah kissed him. "Do we'se have to go?"

Teddy gripped her tight. "I'se reckons. Toot gots sumpthin' he wants to tell us."

Sarah shrugged her lips. "Why'se can't he tells us here?"

"Woman, I'se don't know. Let's just go to that fancy Negro restaurant and find out."

Sarah frowned, for the Spirit veiled the news. She gave up. "Stank's here to keep an eye on Missy and Claret?"

"Yeah, baby. He's downstairs." He adjusted the rose lapel pin his son had given him earlier. "I'se thank he knows Toot's news, but he won't give it up."

Sarah tightened the knot on her tignon. "That boy always knows. It's his business to know other folk's business."

Teddy nodded. He took his wife's hand and escorted her downstairs to the wagon.

The décor of Negro restaurant on St. Claude Street, Chez Louise, enchanted Sarah. The owner had chosen yellow curtains to dress the twelve-foot windows, played against the red interior. The walls running the length of the establishment boasted murals of the Louisiana countryside. Such a nice restaurant so close to home! Now she and Teddy would have somewhere to go for supper on Sunday's. They could stroll the streets afterwards and focus on life outside of their children.

Sarah had never been in an establishment as fine as the restaurant. And to think Negroes owned the restaurant! Her stomach growled, ingesting the savory smells flowing from the kitchen into the sumptuous dining room. Heavy starched cloths dressed the tables arranged in two rows upon the waxed, checkerboard floor.

"Would you care to have a seat, Madame?"

"Oui." Sarah sat in the chair as the *maître'd'* pushed it in for her.

Teddy adjusted the gold ring on his right middle finger, which his son had given to him. Toussaint was trying to make a gentleman out of him and he didn't mind one bit. "Is my boy here yet?"

"I think I saw him in the lounge, Monsieur. I'll let him know ya'll here." The maître'd left them and disappeared into the rear of the establishment.

"Lawd, I'se ain't never seen nuthin' like this Teddy," Sarah said.

"Welcome to our new life, baby." Teddy sipped his glass of water. "This here life is our reward for survivin' Li'l Massa and all his shit."

"Watch your mouth." Sarah grinned. She sipped her water, following Teddy's example. She almost choked, spotting Toussaint approaching them with a lady on his arm. He stopped at the head of the table. *"Bonjour Papa et Maman."*

Lawd, he's talkin' Franch. "Bonjour," Sarah said.

Toussaint stood before them, shy and meek. He seated the lady to his left and then took his seat. Once the waiter arrived, Toussaint ordered for the entire party. The waiter bowed and left. "So, Toot. Who's this?" Teddy asked.

The young lady blushed upon hearing his nickname, but Toussaint ignored her. "Papa, Maman, this is Jannie Walker." He faced his parents who sat in silence, waiting for him to continue. "Well, you both know I went to Covington on the Parish retreat in conjunction with Union Normal College's men's retreat."

"Yessuh," Teddy said, arching a brow.

"Well," Toussaint sipped his water. "I met her at the church picnic. I think she's beautiful. She's smart too, Maman. She's going to be a teacher. She wants to make sure our Negro children receive a good, solid education."

Sarah nodded.

The waiter presented Toussaint with a bottle of wine. Toussaint nodded. The waiter turned over his wine glass and poured a taste. Toussaint swirled the wine around and then ingested it, allowing it bouquet to fill his mouth and sinuses. "This will do. Merci." The waiter served everyone and left.

His parents watched in amazement. Following Toussaint's example, they tasted the wine. Teddy leaned over to

Sarah and whispered, "I'se thank strawberry wine got this beat." Beneath the table, Sarah hit his leg.

Toussaint began to sweat. His parents didn't care for the wine. "Jannie is planning to open a library here in New Orleans for Negroes." Jannie blushed, looking away.

Sarah smiled. "For really, Miss Jannie?"

"Yes ma'am."

"Well, ain't that just fine! Our folks needs to gits their learnin'. I'se proud of you."

Toussaint grasped Jannie's hand, relieved his parents approved of her. How could they not? Toussaint cleared his throat. "Well, I've asked her to marry me." Teddy and Sarah stared at him. "She's agreed to become my wife."

Sarah began to cry. Jannie was beautiful. Gazing into the Spirit, she could see the young lady would prove to be an excellent wife. Sarah left her seat, walked over to Jannie and hugged her. "*Bienvenue, ma fille.*" She kissed her on both cheeks and then peered into her eyes. "Be faithful and persevere."

"Persevere?"

"Oui, ma fille. Persevere."

La Rose Plantation, St. Helena Parish. August 31, 1963.

THE SALON HAD grown hot. The fragrance of sulfur filled the air. Julian turned to his grandmère. Her platinum bun had kinked up, turning into a loosely curled afro. She continued to stare into Eternity. "Grandmère?"

After a few moments, Lela realized he'd spoken. "Oui, mon fils?"

Fear engulfed him. "Are you well?"

"I'm fine. Don't interrupt me," she said.

Julian sat in silence, waiting for her to continue. As always, his grandmère had consumed everything provided for their enjoyment. He captured a cracker topped with Gruyère cheese and popped it into his mouth. It wasn't often he could enjoy snacks with his greedy grandmère.

Munching on the cracker and cheese, Julian realized something. He couldn't remember his Uncle Toot ever being married. "When did you say Uncle Toot married and what happened to his wife?"

Lela raised an eyebrow. She spotted a renegade olive on the platter. She devoured it. "She died of consumption in the 1920's, once Toussaint returned from France. I guess they married in 1868 or something like that. Maybe 1866. I don't recall. Oh. It was 1869."

Julian nodded and then it occurred to him. "You have nothing else to say? No long, drawn out story on how they met?

Lela continued to stare into Eternity. She blinked and then returned her focus to Julian. "No."

Julian began to laugh. "Are you jealous?"

Lela grabbed another olive from the platter and ate it. She spat the pit on the floor. "No. I just don't have a story about them. Why would I be jealous?"

She was jealous. Julian could see it. "Were you in love with Uncle Toot?"

Lela shrugged. "He is my family. Of course, I love him."

Julian let it go. He'd learned his lesson about questioning old folks on topics they had no desire to discuss.

Lela surrendered. She wanted to enlighten the boy and to encourage to him to ask questions, furthering his edification about their family. She took an apple slice and scooped some brie. She thought better of it and returned it to the platter. She was barely managing her indigestion.

"Toussaint was a handsome man. He loved his wife." Lela opted to eat another olive instead of the cheese she desired. She spat out the pit, just missing Julian's head.

Why couldn't she manage her temper? The boy had done nothing wrong. He'd only asked a question. "Pardon mon fils. I'm not sure what came over me." Julian scowled at her.

Lela reached for a slice of *cantal vieux fromage* and consumed it, chasing it with a Kalamata olive and sip of brandy. Her shoulders slumped, exhausted by it all. "No, Julian. I don't have insight into Toussaint's marriage, because I don't care to know. I didn't have a lot of insight into Jamie's first marriage. Why? I don't care to know. Jamie should have never married Melissa. He could see. He knew that bitch, pardon, he knew the lady wasn't me. Yet, he married her ass anyway. She died. End of story. He belonged to me. I can't understand why he married her." Lela could feel her hair curling at the edges, but she couldn't stop. "Toussaint knew his place and purpose. It was to be with me."

Although afraid to speak, Julian took a chance anyway. "But Grandmère, you were married to Grandpère."

Lela's eyes went blank. "What does that have to do with anything?"

Julian said nothing else.

Lela exhaled. "Well, that's all I have to say. Toussaint married Jannie and had a relatively happy life, although she was dull. I'm sure there were others. End of story."

Julian bit his tongue, but it didn't do any good. "Did he have another after his wife died?"

"Another what?"

"Love."

Lela peered into Julian's eyes. "Do you remember him having a love?"

Julian sipped his scotch. "Yes, Grandmère. I do."

Lela pursed her lips. "Really? Who boy?"

Julian opened his mouth to speak and decided against it. Sometimes it was better to let things go.

Lela patted her great-grandson's cheek. She had promised to answer his questions, even those concerning Toussaint's sorted affairs. "I will tell you what I know."

Chapter 23

New Orleans, Louisiana. November, 1874.

No grandchild. Sarah ground the coffee beans in the new Burns Mills grinder her son had purchased. She couldn't deny her boy was frugal; however, when it came to his coffee, money didn't matter. She couldn't imagine how much he'd spent on the contraption. Sarah had to admit, the machine produced beautiful ground coffee. She inserted three scoops of beans into the grinder and turned the wheel. Once finished, she stopped and appraised the outcome. Toussaint liked his coffee strong, so she added another scoop of beans.

Next, Sarah added some chicory. Jannie had roasted it the day before. She ground it. Removing the bin from beneath the grinder, Sarah mixed the chicory and coffee grounds together.

She didn't care for the additive, but Toussaint loved it. Augustus had drunk coffee on occasion (when not drinking bourbon). He would have Sammie add chicory to his coffee.

Toussaint must have acquired the taste for it during his covert expeditions with his half-brother.

Sarah filled the tin filter of the pot with the grounds. Toussaint had been married for some time, but no grandchild. Her son dawdled. Without a doubt, the couple put forth their best effort. She and Teddy had endured many nights of listening to their son and his wife consummate their marriage through the thin walls. Nevertheless, they'd failed to produce a grandchild. Sarah placed the coffee pot on the stove.

Little girl footsteps. Well, she wasn't a little girl anymore, although she remained so in Sarah's heart. Sarah could hear her grandbaby walking from room to room upstairs. She grabbed a bowl from the shelf and put some oatmeal in it, topping it with butter. The child loved butter. She listened to the child's footsteps, now descending the stairs.

Moments later, Claret entered the kitchen and sat at the table. She picked up her spoon and dug into her oatmeal. Sarah poured more milk on it. She knew her little one liked soupy oatmeal. She noticed the child's face was wet. "What wrong wit' you, gal?"

Claret turned from her meal to Sarah, with tear filled eyes. "You don't want me either."

Sarah sat beside her on the kitchen bench, engulfing the child in her arms. "Doncha ever say nuthin' like that. You'se my joy."

Claret nodded.

"What makes you'se say that?"

Claret stirred her oatmeal. "You're always wondering when Uncle Toot will have a child."

Sarah kissed the child on her forehead. She took the spoon from Claret and mixed the oatmeal to the child's liking. "I'm not a baby anymore, Grandmère." Taking the spoon from her grandmother, Claret took a scoop and put it in her mouth.

Sarah bit her lip. "Parents is funny like that. They'se wants to see all their offspring 'fore the Lawd calls them home. Just 'cause they wants to see those who ain't here yet, don't mean they'se don't love and cherish the ones the Lawd done already blessed them wit'." Sarah smoothed Claret's hair. "You'se my baby and my joy. I'se thanks the Lawd for you."

Claret began to cry. "Maman doesn't."

Sarah held Claret close. "Your Maman gots troubles. It ain't 'bout you. Grandmère wants you to trust her on that, okay?" Claret nodded. "Besides, don't you wanna meet your cousin one day?"

A spirit came over the child unbecoming to a thirteen-year-old. A chill ran through Sarah. "I think I will know my cousin quite well one day, Grandmère."

Sarah started to chastise the child, but she held her tongue, seeing in the Spirit what was to come. "Maybes you'se might."

She peered into Claret's eyes once more, finding the innocence and ignorance of a sheltered thirteen-year-old girl. God always protected his seed. Wouldn't it all work out according to his plan? Sarah kissed Claret's forehead. "Your Grandpère almost ready to take you to your lessons. Git your slate."

After an hour of re-arranging the gurneys in the cold storage room, he'd finally created enough space for another client. He returned to the freight elevator and rolled the gurney into the room, squeezing it into the space he'd created.

Teddy returned to the elevator and stepped inside. "I'se can take the stairs." He hopped out and closed the doors, hitting the release button so it could be returned to the preparation room.

Toussaint amazed him. How could he afford such things? The elevator had been a blessing, that was for sure. Before, he and his son had to lug the coffins down the narrow stairs. Now, they could just wheel the gurneys onto the elevator and push a button.

It still spooked him. He put on a strong face for his son, but the contraption terrified him. "Well, ifs that's all I'se gotta fear in this ole life, that ain't half bad," he said, entering the preparation room.

"What you say, Papa?"

"Nuthin', boy."

Toussaint placed some instruments in the sterilization solution. He noticed the elevator button, glowing red. "How did you get up here, Papa?"

Teddy sat at the desk and poured the last of the water into his glass. "Sarah!"

"Maman's out in the yard, Papa. Don't change the subject."

Teddy drank his water. "I'se walked up the stairs. I'se needs to git me some exercise. I'se gittin' soft."

Toussaint let it go. He could see his father feared the elevator.

Teddy grunted, ignoring his son's disapproval. He looked at the wall clock. Half past two o'clock. "Ain't Jannie home yet?" he asked, opening the appointment book. "Maybe she can fix us sumpthin' to eat." He put on the spectacles Toussaint had purchased for him. When Toussaint had begun to teach him and Sarah how to read, his son noticed he squinted. Toussaint took him to have his eyes examined by a Negro doctor the next day.

"She's at her library," Toussaint said.

Teddy smiled, filled with pride for his daughter-in-law.

"That gal sho' is determined. She's doin' triple duty, with teachin' school, takin' care of home, and runnin' the library. Been doin' so for a year. But she got that place open. Didn't think she would." He watched Toussaint order his instrument tray. "Maybe you'se can help her out down there." Teddy removed his glasses and polished them with his handkerchief. He noticed his son hadn't replied to him. "You'se don't care for it?"

Toussaint removed his instruments from the sterilization solution and rinsed them in the sink. "It's fine, Papa. I just think it can be more."

"More?" Teddy shook his head. His son always had grand ideals. "Sometimes you'se gotta let womenfolks work thangs out for themselves and do thangs the way they'se feels they should be done. I'se did it wit' your Mama," Teddy said, drifting off. "I'se shouldda listened to her more, 'specially wit' you'se chil'ren."

Teddy swiveled in the chair, finding Toussaint focused on his work. He exhaled, releasing it. "Well, you'se should talk to her."

"She satisfied with it as it is."

Teddy nodded. "Try makin' suggestions instead of tellin' her what to do. A little honey can go a long way." Teddy laughed, thinking of all the times Sarah used 'a little honey' to convince him of her way of doing things. He thought of the time she didn't. His eyes filled with tears. He wiped them away.

"Well, ya'll gonna work it out." He flipped through the book. In addition to Toussaint's lessons, Claret tutored them in the evenings. The girl was tough. Every night, he and Sarah studied in bed to avoid Claret's unforgiving scowl of disapproval at lessons the next day.

Pride welled within him as he examined the book. He could read the names and meeting times. God was good. "Lawd, we'se double booked, Toot. Did you'se see this?"

Toussaint walked over to the table and read the book. He smiled down on his father, full of pride, but he concealed it from him. "I think you're right, Papa."

Teddy closed the book and leaned back in the chair, thinking. "Why'se doncha git you one of them boys down at the parish school to help out 'round here? They'se could keep track of folk's services and burials, help you move these bodies to the cold room…"

Toussaint laughed before he could stop himself.

"Whatcha laughin' at boy?"

"Nuthin', suh."

Teddy ignored him. So what if he was afraid of the elevator? "Well boy, the Good Lawd done blessed you wit' all this learnin' and this here trade. Ain't it right to train up somebody on how to do these thangs? I'se won't always be here to help you, son."

Toussaint patted his father on the back. "You'll prob'ly outlive me, Papa."

Teddy patted his son's hand, resting on his shoulder. "You'se may be right, but you'se could be wrong 'bout that. Just in case, you'se should thank 'bout it. Elijah had Elisha. You should git you an Elisha too."

Toussaint kissed his father on the forehead. "Alright, Papa." Toussaint's stomach growled, prompting him to look at the desk clock. "It's almost three o'clock. Maman hasn't brought us our sandwiches."

Teddy stood from the chair. "Well, you'se know how your Maman git when she's out there in the yard. It's coming along right nice, too. Cain't wait for them collards to come in." Both men nodded in agreement, dreaming of a pot of greens simmering on the stove. "Anyways, she thanks she's only been out there thirty minutes, when three hours done passed." The men couldn't stop laughing. "I'se gonna head on upstairs to see what the holdup is wit' the chow."

"Don't let Maman hear you talking like that."

Teddy rubbed his stomach. "She'll be aw'rite."

Missy coughed to clear the hay dust from the back of her throat. She coughed harder. Her mouth filled with a salty substance. She spit out the red liquid.

Spikey, shrill laughter grated her eardrums. She rammed the stick into her ears to make it stop. She couldn't get the hay off her face. She scratched her face, but she couldn't scrap it off. She stopped, examining the bloody clumps beneath her fingernails. Peering closer, she didn't find any hay under her nails. The hay was still on her face.

She searched the room, hearing the barn door slam. Maybe he'd left. No, he was still there, laughing. He was laughing with his orange hair spiraling up from his head like horns. The devil. No more. She saw the knife on the bench. The Lord had provided her with the means to protect herself. She lunged for it. The devil laughed. Missy threw him down on the floor. "You'se won't do it no more."

"Missy!"

She knew her brother hated her. He found her to be dirty. But, could he want her to remain the devil's slave? To be free, she had to free herself from her brother.

The angels began to sing, high and loud.

Freedom.

The white light surrounded her, clearing her vision. She stood still.

Cherrie was a good mare. He'd just purchased her from the Negro breeder in New Orleans, who'd 'inherited' the mare's mother from his former owner. Toussaint assessed the smooth glide of the animal, her hind quarters shuddering with each powerful step. He would breed her in the spring.

The clopping of her hooves on the cobblestone compelled him to think of the future. Although tempted to believe his family had reached its end, he knew it not to be true. Things had to improve. God always protected his seed.

Toussaint was glad he'd purchased the small buggy a few months before. It had been a present of sorts for Jannie. They'd used it once, one day opting to drive to Mass instead of walking. Now, it proved useful to transport Missy to her new home, the New Orleans Insane Asylum. He feared the doctors would transfer her to the East Louisiana State Hospital for the Insane.

He hoped it would be a short stay, maybe three months. They would assess and rehabilitate her, and then send her home. His father's butchered and bloodied body eluded to an alternative ending. In the Spirit, he could see his sister would die within the hospital's walls.

Missy had turned into some sort of insane monster, lunging at his father. Claret had heard his screams and raced into the kitchen. Missy went after her instead.

Papa had saved his granddaughter. He stood between Missy and Claret. Missy carved him up instead, the butcher knife severing his heart in two. Claret had told him later Missy had called her the devil.

Toussaint girded himself, unwilling to allow himself the luxury of emotion. He had to think, to keep Missy from hanging and to keep Claret safe.

He'd never seen his mother so terrorized. All she could do was yell, "Git Missy outta here. Git her out!" Sarah sat on the floor clutching Claret, beside his Papa's corpse, her gray skirts soaked with her husband's blood. Toussaint feared she'd go mad as well, but he knew his Maman would hold on for Missy's and Claret's sakes.

Toussaint had taken Missy out to the barn and tied her up, to keep her from hurting herself. He could hear her growling, snarling and shouting at her tormentors throughout the night as he prepared his father for burial in the preparation room.

Toussaint stopped the buggy and applied the break. Missy jerked her head from left to right, following an invisible being with her eyes. "Are you ready to see the doctor?" Tears ran down his face, his sister having taken on the temperament of wild, caged animal, being transported to the zoo. It wasn't short of the truth.

It would be more merciful to shoot her.

Toussaint took her to the door of the hospital. Two orderlies met them. He knew they would abuse her; he could see the lust for her in their eyes. What could he do?

Lawrence appeared in his mind's eye with tears streaming down his face, shaking his head in despair. Toussaint remembered La Rose Plantation and his friend. Maybe he could take her to Lawrence. He would be able to help her. "You want to go to La Rose, Missy?"

Her eyes focused. "Kinky?"

Toussaint closed his eyes and prayed. He could take her there. The orderly reached out to take hold of her. "I've changed my mind." Toussaint yanked her away, leading his sister to the buggy. Yes, he would take her home.

Eternity, La Rose Plantation.

Inserting the key within the depths of his brother's navel, he turned. The clock gears tightened with every twist. Lawrence watched the wagon approach with a sorrowful and desperate spirit marching before it, announcing the arrival of the desolate, devastated one. Heaven's little light had been snuffed, although it had resisted being extinguished.

The clock's gears locked.

Lawrence wiped his eyes and walked away. Perhaps she would gather her will to go on within his care.

"Make her comfortable. Greatness has sprung from her womb."

Lawrence turned, finding Albertus standing behind him. Albertus leaned against the hall clock, constructed in the image of his brother, Barachiel. Throughout the centuries, they'd trusted the mechanism to chime the hour of man. Without the instrument, only eternity existed for them. He turned his sorrow laden eyes to the floor, destroyed.

"Take heart, my brothers. Her fruit will ripen and mature, bringing forth others."

Hope and goodwill filled Lawrence's heart. Winslow Hempsworth stood before him, smartly attired in a yellow and green plaid suit with red undertones, finished off with a yellow top hat. Lawrence couldn't think of many men who could pull off the look, or would desire to do so. "Lawd, I'se ain't seent you in a thousand years. At least it seems like it." Lawrence shook his brother's hand.

"Rightly so, I'm afraid." Hempsworth gave his brother the grip, filled with joy. A full length gilded mirror appeared before him. He checked his appearance. He never transitioned well from his heavenly garb to earthly apparel. Spot on. The mirror disappeared. Hempsworth walked over to the hall stand, deposited his umbrella and hung his hat on the hook above. "It is a might humid here. Are you expecting rain?"

"Rain is eminent. It's just a matter of when," Albertus said.

Lawrence searched the centuries, attempting to recall the last time he'd seen Hempsworth. The court of Henry VIII. That must have been the last time.

"Henry?" Hempsworth removed his gloves and placed the pair on top of his hat. Not proper etiquette, but it would do in the casual company of his brothers. "I do believe you're right, good fellow. That bloke tried the patience of God. However, the Keyholder always does."

Hempsworth removed a sterling box from his breast pocket, enameled with roses. He dipped the contents from within, placing it between his gum line and inner lip. Lawrence placed a spittoon near him.

Such a pity to spit tobacco into a solid gold pot, but what was he expected to do with it? Spit it on the floor? Hempsworth dabbed the corner of his mouth with his handkerchief. "I tried to convince the chap to be sensible in those times, but he refused reason, even then. And now, the household of the Keyholder is troubled once more. Nevertheless, I am here to resolve it. What has happened?"

Snuff. Albertus watched his brother dip it. During the third century, he'd picked up the habit from Barachiel. The tobacco substance wasn't in wide-spread use at that time, but Barachiel had supplied them with the herb. It had taken him three centuries to stop. "The Doctor has ravished the daughter of Sarah the Slave." Hempsworth looked at him, confused. "L'Abeille."

"Good Lord," Hempsworth said, wagging his head.

Albertus massaged his temples. "Now, an evil spirit has

taken hold of the child. She has slain her father."

All which had occurred crystallized before Hempsworth in the Spirit. "Bloody hell. It amazes me the Most High allows savages such as Satan's minions to trouble his little ones," Hempsworth said. "Sarah is a good old girl. She's cross, but I suppose she will get pass it." Hempsworth smoothed his lapels. "In any case, I shall bring the child with me to jolly old London Town."

"Sarah ain't gonna let you do that," Lawrence said.

Hempsworth turned his attention to the mural on the ceiling of the dismal French pastoral lands, thinking. He could feel his wretched brother, Barachiel, glaring at him. "For God's sake, man! They are French pastoral lands, not the British Isles. Why would you expect me to find solace in them, Barachiel?"

The head of the clock, hidden from the face of man, began to rise.

Lawrence shook his head. "Barry, let it go. You'se knows he's just antagonizin' you."

The clock relaxed, returning to its inanimate state.

"I'm afraid, my good man, she won't be able to stop me," Hempsworth said. The unfamiliar emotion of melancholy overtook him. Hempsworth found it a rare occurrence to experience the strange phenomenon of emotion. Through-out Eternity, from praising the Lord in his Throne Room to defeating Lucifer and casting him out of Heaven, it had been his duty to set things right in a rational matter. His brother Barachiel had chosen to embrace human emotion, to his downfall. In fact, the fellow seemed to relish the psychosis.

"I won't take the precious little urchin today. Her grandmother still has much to teach her. However, once Sarah has returned to the Most High, I will come to claim her. Agreed?" Lawrence and Albertus nodded. "I find it quite odd our brother isn't here to meddle in the welfare of my tiny waif. Has he been detained in a brothel?"

Lawrence heard the host of heaven laughing. "Naw, mon Frère. He just hates you. That's all."

The clock surged in height, crashing into the baroque ceiling, raining plaster down on those below. The clock retreated, returning to his former height of twenty-four feet.

Hempsworth snorted and dipped more snuff. "I suppose he couldn't withstand the man with a wardrobe superior to his own. Does he still employ that Manny fellow? Good Lord, when will he ever learn?"

The clock creaked, lifting its Egyptian head to face its subjects standing below. Hempsworth smiled. "Well, there you are, good fellow. Jolly ho! You just couldn't stay away from our little soirée. Is it not what you would say in grand old Paree?"

Smoke streamed from the clock's nostrils.

"It isn't important, I suppose," Hempsworth said. "I guess you have eavesdropped on our conversation to your own satisfaction. Claret is coming to England, not your wretched France, to learn good judgment and common sense. It has been settled. There is nothing you can do." Hempsworth returned to the stand to retrieve his umbrella. Lawrence handed him his top hat. Good morning." Hempsworth glowed white, leaving them.

After the earth trembled for a bit, the clock reclined its head to face the ceiling once more, concealed from men of average height. "Good Lawd, those two. They'se the biggest peacocks in Heaven."

Albertus nodded in agreement. "It is to be expected, mon Frère." Albertus observed the Spirit. "Toussaint has arrived with our little one."

Lawrence's countenance sank, faced with the reality of the world he'd agreed to endure. "Well, let's go out and git the child and put her to bed."

"Is Augustus here?"

Lawrence had forgotten him. "Well, he lives in the bottle now. He won't know she's here." Lawrence thought for a moment. "I'll put her in his Madame Camille's room. He never goes in there." The men opened the front doors, exiting the mansion to receive their charge.

Chapter 24

La Rose Plantation, St. Helena Parish. August 31, 1963.

Lela sat on the sofa, lost in the pain of the past. Sensing a presence before her, she found Lawrence standing there. He handed her a small snifter of brandy, bowed and left. She could see the irritation on Julian's face, for Lawrence had neglected to prepare a beverage for him.

Once Lawrence closed the door, Julian prepared a drink for himself and returned to the sofa, plopping down and crossing his legs. Lela patted his shoulder. "He's trying to antagonize you, darling. Do not allow him to do so."

"It's working,' Julian said. Sipping his drink, something occurred to him. "Why didn't he take Missy to the guy in the French Quarter?"

Lela furled her brow. "Who?"

"You know, the butler at the townhouse."

"Maurice?

"Yes, Grandmère. Him. Missy seemed alright there."

Lela stared into the mirror across the room. She'd never considered the option. Looking back, it was a logical choice. "Darling, I don't know!" Lela peered into the Spirit. "The thought never entered Toussaint's mind. Teddy despised Maurice, so Toussaint considered him as untrustworthy, I suppose."

Julian grimaced. "That sounds like Uncle Toot." Anger surged in his heart. "She may have been alright if he'd taken her there, instead of allowing his hatred to guide him."

His words dumbfounded her. As Augustus, he'd imprisoned her in the house for years. Now as Julian, he's appalled by his uncle's behavior. Lela let it go, chalking it up to personal growth. "I supposed you're right, Julian."

"I am."

Lela closed her eyes, allowing her temper to subside. She sipped her brandy. "Anyway, Missy seemed to improve after a few months. Lawrence had been serving her tea three times daily; I can't tell you what. She began to go out and wander the old slave quarters where she'd once labored. While visiting here in the 1940's, Lawrence told me he would find her standing beside her empty cauldron, where she once cooked Augustus' sheets brilliant white."

Lela opened side table's drawer and grabbed a crisp, white handkerchief, monogrammed with a 'L'. "She would search for Kinky. Every evening she would go to the wash house and stir her empty cauldron, waiting for Kinky to come and court her.

"One day, Lawrence found Missy sitting alone on the porch of their old cabin, taking to the girlfriends of her youth. It was all quite desperate and sad." Lela inhaled deep to suppress her emotions. She dabbed her eyes. "Missy never mentioned Claret. She didn't seem to remember her."

Lela stood from the sofa and stretched, arching her back, and then relaxing, falling forward to touch her toes. She had been sitting for far too long. She sat and refreshed herself with a sip of brandy. "Before your Uncle Toot left me, he would speak of Missy from time to time." Lela swirled her brandy in the snifter.

"Toussaint told me he would visit Missy every month at first, accompanied by their mother, Sarah. They never took Claret with them." Lela looked to the floor. "Missy didn't know them, blocking the existence of her family from her conscious mind. She only remembered Kinky. She recognized Lawrence at times. But she searched for Kinky. Her life had ended, waiting to take Kinky's hand. She truly loved that man."

The parlor doors opened. Lawrence. He had perfect timing when it came to interrupting Julian's inquiries. "Ma'Dame?"

"Yes, Lawrence?"

"It's done cooled off a heap outside. Why don't ya'll go out there for a spell and relax?"

Lela nodded in agreement. She arose from the sofa, a little wobbly, and followed Lawrence. "Aren't you coming Julian?"

"Do I have a choice?"

Lela raised her eyebrow. "No."

The steaming atmosphere hadn't realized its grip upon La Rose Plantation. Julian couldn't understand why Lawrence had suggested they return outdoors. The sun sat low in the afternoon sky; however, the heat persisted in its mission to torment the inhabitants of Floridian Louisiana.

The bottle of brandy had worked its magic on his grandmère, once again. She now snuggled into him, her human pillow. At least she hadn't started slobbering yet. He considered her face. Her strange, youthful appearance endured, although a centenarian.

Yet upon further consideration, it wasn't youthful. Her face was eternal. It displayed some of the expected deep lines which occurred with age; yet, she didn't have any wrinkles. Her skin reminded him a kid skin gloves, soft and smooth to the touch, traced with the deep lines where the fingers moved. He stroked her chin line. The corner of her lip turned up in acknowledgment. She gurgled and retreated into a deeper sleep.

Maybe she wasn't asleep. Her eyes moved to and fro beneath her eyelids. He imagined her sorting out which tales to tell him during her slumber, in her endeavor to bore him for days to come. However, time seemed to have no tangible boundaries when his grandmère spoke. They'd toured eternity together, with abandon and without concern.

Julian smoothed her hair. She was a doll to him, at least when her mouth was closed. She could be maniacal, always seeking to put him in his place. Well, putting him in his place seemed to be her goal, but no one had ever been able to do so.

Now, Aunt Nancy had been a different story. He missed Nancy, even now. Somehow his grandmère, who'd spoiled him as a child, had picked up Nancy's mantle to call him out on his antics. However, his grandmère drilled deeper into him than Nancy ever had, challenging him on the issues concerning his spirit and soul.

Lela stirred, burrowing her head into his chest. "Augustus shot her in the middle of Marais Street. He shot her dead." Lela's face converged into swirl of hard lines.

"What?"

She returned to sleep. Julian allowed his focus to wander, focusing on the land and its endless garden.

His grandmère left his arms.

Julian's body felt like concrete. With great effort, he commanded his head to move, turning it toward his grandmère. Her eyes were open, devoid of her soul. Julian wished to speak, but couldn't. Lela shuttered her eyes without closing them. The shutters vanished. Julian peered in, a mirror into the Spirit.

An old time talky movie played before him, but in color. He felt like a haunt hovering in the upper corner of a room, watching the living. He saw Toussaint tidying up the preparation room of his mortuary. He could see him looking around, ill at ease. Jannie, his wife, came in with a tray loaded with lemonade, some sort of tea cakes and a glass. She sat the tray on his desk and left.

Toussaint poured a bit of lemonade into a glass, taking it with him to the root cellar. Julian could see the shrouded bodies, three in all. Toussaint stood at the stairs and looked upward to the preparation room. Julian could hear a girl crying. He could hear Toussaint's wife yelling and weeping. Toussaint ascended the stairs.

Lela closed her eyes and then opened them. In her eyes, Julian found Toussaint alone, standing amongst a constellation of bees. The bees swirled in hurricane formation around him and the woman laid out on the cooling table. Intoxicated with their sonata, Toussaint listened as the bees praised and mourned their Queen. The drones formed a crown about Sarah's head, standing guard over her spirit and her flesh.

Toussaint covered his mother's body with a shroud, pulling it up to her neck. Julian watched a man materialize beside him. "Les," Julian managed to say. He'd never seen him before, but recognized him from his grandmère's stories.

The men lifted Sarah's barge, with roses and sunflowers surrounding her. The constellation of bees fell into their battalions. They came to rest upon the flowers which covered her.

TThey carried Sarah's corpse up the narrow staircase to a flower laden wagon parked in the driveway. Toussaint and Les marched in time to the dirge sung by the bees. They came to a halt before the wagon.

Four enormous men appeared. Julian could see they weren't men. The four men relieved Toussaint and Les of their duties, taking hold of the barge. They slid the barge onto the wagon's bed. Once finished, the men assumed their positions, standing guard.

Julian spotted Toussaint's wife, Jannie, sitting on the driver's bench holding the stoic Claret to her bosom. It seemed to Julian that Jannie couldn't see the twelve-foot-tall guards with their swords outstretched, standing watch at the four corners of the wagon.

Toussaint stepped up onto the driver's bench. Les appeared in the bed of the wagon, sitting next to Sarah's corpse, now covered with bees. Her dread-locked hair surrounded her face, taking on the appearance of an Egyptian nemes. Toussaint popped the reigns, driving the team. Her guards walked with the wagon, two before the wagon, and two bringing up the rear.

Julian became lost in the mirror of his grandmère's eyes, watching the mourners arrive at La Rose Plantation. Lawrence met the group in front of the plantation house. The four twelve-foot-tall beings, who'd escorted them to the plantation, presented their swords, touching their noses with the weapons.

Lawrence signaled for Toussaint to follow him. Snapping the reigns, Toussaint drove the team of horses to the slave cemetery and stopped before the gate. The angels, who'd before been invisible, materialized into the realm of the living. Jannie released a sudden gasp, although Claret didn't seem surprised.

The living exited the wagon. Sarah's army, now awake from their slumber upon their Queen's funeral flowers, took flight. The insects fell into the formation of a canopy, leading from the wagon to the grave. The four angelic pallbearers removed Sarah's barge from the wagon, marching in time with elongated strides.

Standing in the background, Lawrence held Missy's hand.

Julian could see she didn't understand what was happening. Lawrence prayed and thanked the Lord for the visitation of their Queen. Stank stood behind them.

"Carry on, good and faithful servant. The Good Lawd loves you," Julian heard Lawrence say.

Les materialized beside Toussaint, draped in a fur coat constructed of white wolf pelts, the wolf's head crowning him. He placed his hand on Toussaint's shoulder, comforting him.

Les took Claret's hand. "Carry on the work of your Grandmère, little one," he said to the stoic child. She kept her eyes focused on her grandmère's barge.

The mourners followed the pallbearers, marching in time to the dirge of the drones. Arriving at the open grave, the pallbearers placed the barge in a glass coffin. The army of bees filled the coffin, resting atop her. They died.

Claret closed her eyes and prayed.

The hand of God lifted the glass coffin from the grave side, floating it up toward the heavens. The pallbearers assumed their positions at each corner of the grave. They sang the most beautiful hymn.

Jannie saw it and passed out in Toussaint's arms.

As the chorale floated up to heaven, Sarah's glass coffin descended into the iron box inside of the grave. Once inside, an iron lid materialized above the vault and covered her.

The pallbearers extended their swords to heaven and then planted them into the earth.

"Amen," Lawrence said.

The pallbearers removed the swords, now shovels, and returned the earth atop Sarah the Slave, at rest, beside Teddy. Julian saw a man standing in the distance observing the burial.

"Asshole."

Julian blinked, breaking his bond with his grandmère's eyes. She closed and then opened them. The Spirit had closed the window, her eyes now blank.

Julian yelped.

Lela shuttered and shook her head, returning to the present. "What's wrong, darling?"

Julian removed his jacket, finding a bee with its stinger lodged in his arm. The wound began to swell. Lela leaned over to examine the wound, surging in size. She plucked the bee away, but the stinger remained, continuing to pump venom into the wound.

Lela left the terrace and returned indoors, running down the hall to the parlor. She rushed over to the appointed place of her youth in the corner near the fireplace, where she'd once darned her father socks. Finding her sewing basket where she'd left it one hundred years before, she grabbed the pin cushion and returned to the terrace. Removing a needle, she used it to dislodge the stinger. "Are you allergic to bee stings?"

His blood burned in his veins. "I've never been stung before, not that I remember, anyway." Julian's tongue swelled.

The wound turned blue, the swelling and discoloration traveling up his arm. "Lawrence!" Lela ran into the great hall, but found no one. She returned to terrace. She needed to take him indoors, but Julian was too heavy for her to move. She covered his body with her own, hoping to shield her child from bees, now beginning to gather around them. "Stay back," Lela yelled. Some heeded her command, while others seemed inspired to defy her.

Stretching to reach the intercom on the end table, Lela depressed the button. "Lawrence? Is anyone there?" Receiving no response, she left Julian and ran into the mansion again, finding the house empty. Where had everyone gone? "Most High God, please have mercy." Lela returned to the terrace and found herself alone.

Eternity, La Rose Plantation.

HE'D SET THE Niggers free, now they'd robbed him. Julian walked the empty mansion, devoid of all furnishings, adornments, and gold. Only a shell of the house remained, stripped down to the brick and lathe work where ornate plastered walls and moldings once resided.

It didn't matter. He would rebuild. It had been a long day, living an entire lifetime within it. Julian felt like an old man, but like a youth at the same time. He stopped in the center of the grand hall, standing atop the rose mosaic. "Humph, only you remain," Julian said, considering the glass and jeweled ornament.

His eyes veered to the right, falling upon the place where his freedom had come. Emmie Sue. Every time he thought about her skull cracking against the marble floor his dick got hard. Freedom and vengeance were beautiful things.

At last, he'd achieved his greatest goal in life, killing Sarah. His could still feel the tingle in his temples and cheeks, traveling down his neck to his forearms. The sensation of pulling the trigger pooled in his fingertips. He would never forget it.

Julian swatted at the buzzing insect. Goddamn bees. They wouldn't stop stinging him. The savage insects had even followed him to Jean Charles' home earlier in the day. He should have put a bullet in his son's head. Weak ass bitch. Jean Charles' family dies and he disintegrates into a mess.

Julian ascended the stairs, opting for the right flight of the bifurcated staircase at mid-landing. The swarm of bees followed him, taking turns stinging the back of his neck. He was too tired to run anymore. He'd tired of running.

His blood burned in his veins. "Goddamn bees." Intoxicated, Julian grabbed the bannister to steady himself. He surveyed the grand hall filled with wedding guests. "I stood here." Beneath the colonnade in the grand hall, his love stood against the wall in maid's attire, ashamed.

"Jannette?"

Julian shook his head and looked again. "Sammie." He expelled thoughts of her from his mind and spirit, for today was a day to rejoice. Sarah was dead.

"I'se ain't as dead as you'se was hopin', brother."

Julian stood in awe of the woman who had materialized before him, glowing bright white in her drab slave dress. Her locked hair rose into the air forming large 'U' shapes. A halo of bees surrounded her head in the most brilliant yellow, overjoyed to crown their Queen. Fire flies. But Julian knew the truth. Goddamn bees.

Sarah the Slave hovered just above Julian's head. "Even the grave ain't enough to soften your heart, Massa. You'se ain't changed one bit."

Sarah raised her right hand. Angry warrior drones exited the hole in her chest, the fatal wound gifted to her by Augustus. The insects surrounded him. "Once she returns to Earth from the Most High, you'se ain't gonna treat my Queen Bea like you'se treated folks on this here place, Augustus."

The bees tightened their ranks around him. Julian shuddered, his spirit shifting between the past and the present.

This is 1963. "My name is Julian."

Yellow rays of light beamed from her eyes, permeating Julian, searching his soul. "You'se hidin' out as Julian now, but you ain't him. You'se Augustus. You'se can't fool me." Glee filled Sarah. "It's your time, Augustus. C'mon and take your due."

Sarah raised her skirts, in the throes of childbirth. A babe slipped out. Sammie washed him. He grew into a man. The albino sisters clothed him. Lawrence handed him a rope outfitted with a hangman's noose. The man was black, not brown, with white hair. He grinned at Julian. "Uncle Toot?"

"I told you, Augustus. I'll touch you if you touch my Maman." The warrior bees eased their ranks around Julian, creating an Arc de Triomphe for Toussaint to pass through. "You're the bitch, Augustus, if you think I'm going to allow you to gun down my Maman in the middle of Marais Street and not do anything about it. You're a goddamn fool."

"Uncle Toot, I never knew your Maman," Julian said.

Toussaint punched him in the stomach, disabling him. "You can't run from me, Augustus. God has passed judgment on your soul this night, anointing me as your executioner." Toussaint hit him again, but Julian didn't feel the blows.

Toussaint touched his chest, raising his blood covered hand for Julian to see. "You think you're allowed to stab me to death? I told you Augustus, you're mine." Toussaint hit Julian once more, knocking him to the floor. He placed the noose around his neck.

"Uncle Toot," Julian said.

No more than a sack of shit to him, Toussaint flung Julian over the banister. The insects buzzed around him. He could hear them laughing through their incessant buzzing as he descended deeper into the bottomless heart of hatred.

Julian continued to free fall, never stopping. The rope caught.

La Rose Plantation, St. Helena Parish. August 31, 1963.

"WELL, MADAME. THE antidote seems to be working." Dr. Jerry Barry closed his bag. "That was a close one. I thought we might lose him."

Lela dried her tears. "I'm grateful you could come here so quickly, Dr. Barry."

He checked Julian's temperature with the back of his hand. "Well, I was down the road. It wasn't a problem for me to come." He considered the young man lying on the bed, drenched in sweat. "My, my, my. You've escaped destruction twice in two days, mon fils." Dr. Barry tapped him on the center of his forehead three times. "Perhaps in the years to come, you should take more care in your thoughts and actions toward others."

Julian couldn't remember what had happened. Bees. A bee had stung him. His throat and neck were sore. He'd felt himself falling and grabbed the side of the mattress. When had he retired to his bedroom?

"Madame Chevalier, be sure to keep him hydrated. He may not be able to talk for a few hours, until the antidote takes its full effect." Dr. Barry smirked at Julian. "Perhaps during his recovery, he will reconsider the adage to treat others as one would himself."

Lela scowled at Dr. Barry.

"I have overstepped what is proper. My apologies, Madame." Dr. Barry removed his hat and bowed to her, passing his hat before him in a sweeping, downward arc, bringing it to rest on his left shoulder. Lela nodded. "I will leave instructions with Lawrence on what's required for Julian's care."

"Lawrence? Where is he?" Lela's face twisted into a scowl. "I searched everywhere for him, but couldn't find him."

Dr. Barry shrugged. "He opened the door for me. I'm guessing he's in his butler's lounge. Would you like for me to go and check?"

"It won't be necessary Dr. Barry. I will chat with Lawrence later."

Dr. Barry arched his brow. He felt sorry for Lawrence. "As you wish, Madame." Dr. Barry picked up his bag and tipped his hat to Lela. "Bonjour." Dr. Barry left the room, closing the door behind him.

Taking a seat in the chair beside Julian's bed, Lela wondered how long they should remain at La Rose. The visit didn't seem to be helping the boy, but instead, hurting him. The Spirit world attacked him, barraging him with memories of his past life. The Spirit continued to propel Julian into the past not only psychologically, but physiologically. Lela couldn't blame the Spirit. It was the souls residing there who held a grudge against her baby. She placed her head in her hands.

"Grandmère?"

Lela found Julian staring at her, his tears crashing onto the damask duvet cover. His voice seemed so weak. She wouldn't have heard him if she'd shifted her weight in her chair at that moment. "Oui, mon fils, what is it?"

Julian struggled to move his tongue and to utilize his vocal cords. "Did Uncle Toot murder me?" He tried to swallow and suppress the lump in his throat.

Lela closed her eyes and focused, choosing her words with care. "Mon fils, Uncle Toot executed his brother, Augustus Chevalier."

Leaving her chair, Lela sat on the bed next to her child. She kissed away his tears, and then she kissed his forehead. "You, my darling, are Julian Charles Chamberie. Uncle Toot did not, and would not, ever kill you. *Comprends-tu mon cher?*"

Julian nodded, accepting her words. He pulled the covers up to his chin, afraid. "In my dream, I told all of them I was Julian, but they called me Augustus."

Lela scowled. Toussaint and Sarah could be vindictive at times. "Well, I think both the living and the dead are now clear on who *is* whom. And if they're not, all residing in Eternity should listen to me, NOW."

Lela stood from the bed and stretched her arms toward heaven. "I proclaim this before all Heaven and Hell to hear. You, *my child*, are Julian Charles Chamberie. You are no other but Julian." Lela's face twisted into the most terrorizing scowl he'd ever seen in his life. Julian cowered in fear. "And to all souls and spirits, living or dead — you all had better not lay a finger on him."

Julian would have laughed if he could. His grandmère had just scared off every boogey man and woman in the Good Lord's creation. He was glad, too. Julian closed his eyes and slept.

Chapter 25

La Rose Plantation, St. Helena Parish. August 31, 1963.

Julian twisted in bed. His hip was stiff. "Grandmère?"

Lela opened her eyes. She'd fallen asleep in bed with Julian, guarding her little boy. She couldn't believe Sarah would do such a thing, but at the same time, she remembered her Aunt's need for the last word.

She heard Julian speak her name again. The swelling in his tongue and throat had subsided a great deal; she could understand him. "Oui, mon fils?"

"So, was Uncle Toot a murderer?"

Lela sat up in bed. She patted her forehead with the back of her hand and then smoothed her hair. "What? Why would you say such a thing? He'd only avenged his mother's death." Lela reconsidered her words. "Well, only when required. He didn't just go around killing people; however, when the lives of those he loved were in danger, people did seem to go missing."

Julian's mouth was dry. "Grandmère, may I have some

water?" He watched her walk across the room to the bureau to pour a glass.

She sat down and handed it to him. "Do you want to know anything, mon fils?"

Julian emptied the contents of the glass and then sat it on the table. "Well, I know how Augustus died, that's for sure," he said rubbing his throat. "Did Uncle Toot have to go to jail?"

Lela shrugged. "Why would he go to jail?"

"Well, because he killed a White man in the South."

Lela patted his hand and then clutched him in her arms. Everything was black and white to him. He'd yet to learn the hearts of White folks. "Darling, Toussaint had done the community a favor. I think the official report concerning my father's death had been suicide. No one questioned it. In fact, it was celebrated.

"The day of my father's death was, and still is, a parish holiday. June 26, 1875 is Augustus Chevalier Day." Lela smirked. "In fact, in later years, it was the finale of the Juneteenth celebrations for Negroes. By 1877, even the White folks had joined in celebrating the day's festivities with the Negroes.

"It was strange, seeing Blacks and Whites coming together, playing music and dancing. They always roasted several pigs and a hog. Whoever won the shooting contest had the honor of cutting the ear from the boiled hog's head and eating it before everyone present. It was a strange custom which persisted until the teens of this century.

"Then the awful movie came out called *The Birth of a Nation*. If my memory serves me, Lillian Gish starred in the film." Lela shook her head, recalling the hate-mongering epic.

"It must have been about 1915. It wasn't safe for Negroes to be out on the streets in the rural areas or in the cities. Lord, I remember them burning down Black Tulsa in '21. Negroes had created a utopian economic center of commerce there.

"We, as a people, had turned the economic and social corner, and then the jealous White—" Lela stopped. She didn't wish to instill and facilitate a spirit of hatred and racism in her seed. Those things had occurred in the past. He needed to know, but she couldn't tell him from a place of anger and hatred. Yet in her heart, she understood the White folk's collective mentality to destroy and suppress any group whom they feared would suppress and overtake them. "Things changed for the worst in our little corner of the world. Now, we had a Midwestern town full of Augustus'. Well, not only there, but across the nation.

"I digress." Lela smiled on her grandchild, smoothing his hair. "Toussaint had to atone for the passing of his brother, in a way.

The murder of his brother. Julian said nothing, allowing her to continue. He rubbed his neck.

Lela allowed his thought to pass without comment. She understood the source of his anger toward Toussaint. "In any case, the Lord made him face what he'd done."

Julian relaxed upon his pillow. His grandmère stroked his forehead, relaxing and encouraging him to enter the Spirit with her once again.

Chapter 26

La Rose Plantation, St Helena Parish. June 26, 1875.

A bright, hazy light, filtering through the dew of the morning, awoke Toussaint. Even after freedom, the old family cabin on La Rose Plantation still felt like home. Standing up and stretching, he rubbed his neck, hoping to coax the crook into releasing its grip on him. No luck.

The old cane back chair. Toussaint snickered. Why had they'd left it? Oh yes, it was broken. One of the back legs was shorter than the others. He couldn't stop himself from laughing.

Kinky had come to call on Missy one day. Wishing to impress his girlfriend, Kinky leaned back in the chair, balancing it on two legs against the cabin wall. He'd folded his arms behind his head, flexing his enormous muscles.

The weight of the chair caused a small section of the floorboard to give way. Without warning, one the legs fell through the hole, snapping off the bottom. Kinky lost his balance, nearly falling off his seat.

Missy had been so concerned, asking if he was alright. Kinky had shrugged it off saying, "Gal, it's gonna take a lot more than a chair leg breakin' to knock me off my block." Missy blushed, falling in love with him more than before. The family had called it Kinky's chair ever since.

Toussaint's smile faded. Their family was happy then, despite the hardships of bondage. Sure, they hated their situation, but they'd loved one another. Now that love was buried in the slave cemetery.

He left the cabin and began his walk to the plantation house, not sure of what he would find there. Guilt attempted to take hold of him, but he rebuked it. "God has not given me a spirit of fear…" he said to himself, walking down the road. The house came into view over the tree line. His heart jumped in his chest.

He stopped before the granite steps. "There is nothing to fear." He climbed the steps. The cypress doors opened, allowing him entrance. Toussaint searched for Lawrence, anyone, but found no one. He walked to the center of the grand hall and looked up.

No one had touched the corpse of the evil one. Augustus hung suspended, swaying neither to the left or the right.

Dead.

***

Word of Augustus' death reached town by late morning, prompting a visit from the sheriff. He didn't ask too many questions. "Where did ya'll find him," the sheriff asked. Lawrence stood behind Toussaint, placing his hand on his shoulder. The sheriff opened his little flip pad, waiting for Toussaint's answer.

"He's in the grand hall, hanging from the balcony, suh," Toussaint answered with downcast eyes, full of humility.

"Show me."

Lawrence walked to the grand hall, followed by Toussaint and the sheriff. He looked up to the second floor. "Lord Jesus," he said, scribbling notes on his pad. "You'se reckons he hung hisself, boy?"

Tears welled in his eyes. Lawrence patted his shoulder, encouraging him. "I reckon so, suh." Toussaint swallowed. "I…" Lawrence patted his right shoulder. Toussaint silenced himself.

The sheriff nodded, noting Toussaint's account on his pad. He removed his hat to smooth down his greasy hair. "Guess there ain't no figurin' in this. No wonder he killed hisself, after all the decent White folks he sent to the grave. I guess the Good Lord finally made him take his punishment." The sheriff completed his notes on his notepad.

He smiled at Toussaint. "Ain't you Aunt Sarah's li'l ole

chap?" Toussaint nodded. "Our family thinks a heap 'bout Aunt Sarah. She saved my cousin's mule. It was the only animal he had to plow the field he rented from Mr. Chevalier. Cousin was already in debt to Mr. Chevalier. If that ole mule had died, my cousin's crops would've died along wit' him.

"Dang mule got himself bogged down out there in the bottom, south of the river's bend. Aunt Sarah came strollin' by out of nowhere. She whistled to the beast and he walked on out, like he was on dry land."

The sheriff bent over, overcome with laughter. "Lawd, you'se wouldda thought Jesus hisself had come down and pulled that critter out the mud, the way my cousin went on and on 'bout it. Aunt Sarah told him, 'Maybe one day you'se can shows mine some kindness if they'se needs it.' My cousin told everyone in the parish what she'd done did for him. He couldn't stop singin' that Nigrah's praises.

"Cousin made his crop that year, and every year thereafter. Mr. Chevalier was mad as Satan. He'd even told my cousin he wouldn't bring in the harvest, but he did. My cousin is still down there on his place to this day."

The sheriff nodded, validating his cousin's good fortune. "Well, I'll put ya'll account in the report. No need in wastin' the parish's time on this here matter no way. We got bigger problems in Amite than dealin' with Chevalier hangin' hisself."

The Sheriff removed his hat and scratched his head. A little white bug fell out. "There's been a bunch of lynchin's and some tar and featherin's goin' on since they tossed them Niggers out the state legislature. We ain't got nowhere to bury all of them Niggers."

Toussaint shook his head. "If you need assistance, I am a mortician by trade. I can assist those families who have been victimized… I mean, bury their dead."

The sheriff didn't hear him, lost in his memories of Sarah the Slave and the blessings she'd bestowed on his family. He shuttered, reuniting with the present. He found the Negro staring at him, awaiting direction. The sheriff cleared his throat. "You'se a good Niggah just like your mama. Stop by the station tomorrow. We got them dead Niggers stacked up in the shed out back. Lawd, they'se startin' to stink to high heaven," the sheriff said.

Leaving Toussaint's side, Lawrence materialized at the front door by the time the sheriff and Toussaint arrived. He opened the door. "This sho' is a fine place. I ain't never seen nuthin' like it! Looks like Chevalier wouldn't have been as mean and hateful, havin' money like this. I know I'd be sweet as pie." Before he could stop himself, he tipped his hat to the Negro men. "Afternoon ya'll." The sheriff exited the house.

Lawrence shut the door. Toussaint couldn't understand how ignorance and wisdom flowed with ease from the same mouth. Lawrence patted Toussaint's shoulder. "It's the Lawd's way. All thangs is possible," he said.

Later that afternoon, Toussaint brought the wagon around, easing it to a stop before the front door. It had been left to Toussaint to bury his master and tormentor.

Entering the mansion, Toussaint walked up the staircase to the second floor. He found two women and a man standing across the way, silent and watching. He mistakenly blinked, finding them gone.

His family.

It didn't matter. Taking his hunting knife, Toussaint cut the rope from which Augustus hung, allowing him to plummet to the foyer. Augustus hit bottom like a sack a wet shit.

Toussaint descended the stairs and walked to where Augustus lay. "God laughs at the wicked, for he knows their day is coming." Toussaint wrapped the corpse in a tarp and then bound it with rope. Resisting the urge to spit on him, Toussaint wound the loose ends of the rope around his hand and began to drag his brother away.

"You'se needs help takin' him out to the wagon, Toot?"

Toussaint found Lawrence standing behind him. "Lawrence, I didn't even know you were here," Toussaint said.

"I'se just got back." Lawrence considered the bound body of his little evil one. He hadn't seen anything like it since his Egyptian days. "You'se shouldn't have treated him like that."

"Like what?"

Lawrence said nothing for a time, considering Augustus' remains. "I'se ain't gonna say he didn't have evil ways, but doncha do him like this."

Toussaint wished to confute him, but couldn't.

"You'se gotta a box for him?"

"I haven't ordered one yet. How could I've known he planned to die?"

Lawrence frowned. "You'se sho' 'bout that, boy?" Lawrence left the foyer. Toussaint followed him.

Arriving at Toussaint's wagon, Lawrence let down the tail gate. Toussaint stood in awe, finding a golden casket inside. The casket had been crafted of solid gold, adorned with roses and angels at war with one another. A baby with a crown upon its head, topped the casket.

The heat of the day brought to a boil the pains and trials Toussaint had bottled up within his soul since the beginning of time. He balled his fists. Why honor a monster?

"That's your kin, your brother. Treat him wit' respect. He ain't no dead dog on the side of the road. He's holy like you and Queen Sarah is."

Toussaint's face twisted in a scowl. "How can you defend him, Lawrence?"

Lawrence re-configured the knot Toussaint had tied around the corpse into a bow. He patted it down, securing it into a place of honor and respect. "Cause I'se knows who he is."

Placing his enormous hands on Toussaint's face with love, Lawrence drew him close and peered into his eyes, traversing the young man's soul. "You'se done sips the cup of the Most High. You'se should know who he be, too." Toussaint pursed his lips and shut his heart. "It's aw'rite. I ain't gonna press you 'bout it." Lawrence patted Toussaint's back. "C'mon, I'se helps you wit' him." Lawrence removed the casket from the wagon, alone. Remembering Toussaint's presence, he asked him to help.

He considered the room, awashed in sorrow and revelry. How many Negroes had he prepared in the room? He remembered the bodies, many of them field hands with the life worked out of them on La Rose Plantation, their remains twisted with arthritis and rheumatism, their skin scarred by the lash. Others who had arrived on his table had been the victims of Augustus' Shed, their bodies mutilated in the final throes of death, crying out for their lives.

In the Spirit, Toussaint could see some had been falsely accused. Some had been tortured by Augustus out of boredom when he had nothing better to do. Yet still, others had met an unspeakable end because Augustus wanted something they possessed. Only a few had deserved the punishment they'd received.

Toussaint recalled how his cousin Emmanuel had tortured many souls. But that had been different. Those souls deserved the punishment they'd received. Emmanuel had convicted and executed on divine direction and justice, while Augustus had only done so out of self-indulgent sport and vengeance.

He smiled, listening to the souls of Augustus' victims singing from beneath to the altar of the Most High God. "All of you have been vindicated. Rest." Toussaint removed the shroud from Augustus' body. "Heaven rejoices." Taking Teddy's old scalpel, Toussaint made the first cut. Joy arose within his soul.

"Did you ever dream of satisfaction such as this, mon fils?"

"No." Realizing the Spirit of the Most High hadn't spoken to him, Toussaint turned to his right to find a man attired in black, adorning a curly, platinum colored pompadour wig with coarse strands of hair. The wig appeared to be very old, reminding Toussaint of portraits he'd seen from centuries past at the Chevalier Château in France. "Emmanuel?"

Extracting a gold case from his breast pocket, the man removed a cigarette and placed it in the holder. He struck a match on the bottom of his boot and lit it. "Hello, son," Emmanuel said.

Toussaint didn't care for the smoke.

"Hypocrisy is a sin."

Toussaint ignored him and returned to his work. He didn't smoke, not enough to count.

"Treat your brother with respect."

"I don't have a brother. Well, Stank is my brother, rather my cousin. He's the only brother I have." Toussaint shook his head, clearing his mind. "Why are you here? You wait until now to come?" Where had he been when Hanzel violated his sister? When Augustus had killed his mother?

The man pitched his exhausted, rolled cigarette to the floor and stomped it out with the tip of his boot. "One of my sons and one of my daughters have died. I've come to pay my respects." Rising to the tips of his toes, he stood nose to nose with Toussaint. "And I did come for Missy. I came and saved her brother from destruction. Have you forgotten?"

Toussaint burned with indignation. Confuted, Toussaint let it go. He returned his attention to the corpse before him. "Augustus was at least seventy years old. His father would've been at about ninety years of age. Cousin, you can't be any older than forty years old."

A gilded mirror materialized on the wall behind Toussaint's worktable. Emmanuel ran to it and checked his face for wrinkles. He found himself perfect, as always. "You are mistaken. I still appear as a man in his twenties. I look no older than you." The mirror disappeared. "You are slow in the Spirit. While you visited me in France, I told you no mortal is older than me." Emmanuel patted his wig. "However, I keep up my appearances."

"But not your wigs, I see."

The man laughed. He would not kill his son today. "Enough about me. I see the Lord has allowed you the victory. You slew the man who'd struck down his holy one, L'Abeille, your mother. Take satisfaction.

"However, you've disrespected his flesh and soul in your preparations for his burial. Well, allow us now to say, one will arise who'll disrespect you." Toussaint didn't respond. "Intern him in the sarcophagus I've installed for him in the mausoleum. Think of him no more, and pray. You have struck down your brother."

Toussaint looked out, but could see little in the Spirit. Yet, he knew his benefactor's words to be true. Although his mother had implied Augustus was his brother, as well as her own, he never understood it. "How is he my brother? Theodore is my father and Sarah is my mother."

Emmanuel patted his cheek. "Mon fils, you are my son. One day, you will understand this. You are my own."

***

The rooster crowed. Jannie sat up in bed, rubbing the sleep from her eyes. Her husband tossed back and forth, trapped in a fitful sleep. "Toussaint, what is it?" His contorted, tormented face concerned her. "Baby, wake up!"

Toussaint's eyes popped open. He sat up in bed and scanned the room in fear. "Teddy isn't my daddy?"

Jannie yawned. "Of course, he is. What are you talking about?"

Toussaint lay down in bed. "Nothing, darlin'. Just some foolishness I was dreaming about."

Chapter 27

La Rose Plantation, St. Helena Parish. November, 1875

White face. Red hair. White face. Red hair. Hay. Screeching laughter. White face. Red hair. Hay. Horn blaring. Deafening. Hay. Knives. Hay. Cleaver halves chicken. Pain. Hay. White face. Red hair.

Twisted in the covers, she searched for a way out. *Out.* She pulled. The grip tightened. *Out.* She pulled. Legs bound. She pulled. Arms.

"Gal, whatcha doin'?"

Missy sat up in bed, bewildered. "Where is I?"

Lawrence exhaled. The morning ritual never changed. "You'se at La Rose, honey."

Missy brow twisted, her eyes scattered. "This ain't our house."

Lawrence folded the sheet from which he'd freed her. "I'se knows it, baby. I'se thought I'd let you'se stay here. It's nicer."

Missy stared out the window.

Lawrence went to the dresser and brought her a cup of tea. "Here, drank this. It's gonna make you'se feel better." Missy continued to stare out the window. "Well, I'se gonna leave it here on the nightstand. You'se drank it when you'se gits ready." Lawrence wiped away his tears and left her alone, closing the door softly behind him.

Hearing the door close, Missy jumped. "Kinky?" She scanned the room. A white dress hung on the hook of the open armoire door. Wedding day. It had come. "I'se need to git them sheets done, ifs I'se gonna jump the broom." Missy ran from the bed.

She pushed. It seemed harder to do than before. "I'se gonna git my dress dirty." She pushed harder. Finally, the rusted casters creaked, giving way to her strength. She pushed, finally reaching the pump.

"You need some help?"

Missy head snapped from left to right. Nobody there. Devils.

"I'm right here."

Missy squinted. A girl in a white lace dress stood before her, with the head of White man with red hair. "Git from 'round here, devil."

"I'm not the devil. I'm your child."

Missy blinked. The head of the white man was gone,

replaced with the head of a brown skinned girl with red hair. "Whatcha want, devil?"

The girl clutched a little handmade doll, made of black burlap with red yarn for hair. "I'm here to help you, Maman."

"You'se cain't. You'se haints need to stay 'way from me." Missy turned her back on the child and pumped, filling her cauldron with water.

Toussaint covered his client and wheeled him to the elevator. It had been a busy morning. There was never a slow period in the mortuary business. He'd signed three new clients that morning.

You'se need an Elisha

Toussaint couldn't deny he needed help. "Yessuh, Papa. I will look for a helper." He closed the elevator door and pushed the button, descending to the cold room.

Twenty minutes later, he returned to his preparation room. "Time for some coffee." When his mother was alive, she would bring sandwiches and coffee for him and his father while they worked. Now, he had to fend for himself. His eyes misted, missing them both.

Toussaint walked up the stairs and opened the door leading to the backyard. A young boy stood there, prepared to knock. "May I help you?"

The boy snatched his cap from his head and clutched

it in his hands. "Hello, Monsieur Bailey. My name is Allen Pruett." He twisted his cap in his hands. "Father Pierre said you was looking for someone to help you around the yard?"

Toussaint didn't remember talking to Father Pierre about the matter. "Oh, he misunderstood. I'd just mentioned to him my workload. I'm not looking for help, son." Toussaint passed him and walked up the stairs to the kitchen.

"But I can cut the grass for you, sir. Maybe clean up after your mare? I can do anything, just tell me what you need, Monsieur."

Toussaint opened the kitchen door. He gave the boy a second look. He was persistent, that was for sure. "You're willing to cut the grass?"

"Yes, Monsieur."

Toussaint considered the boy. He consulted the Spirit, but it was veiled. He considered the tall grass in the yard. The dogs barked. "I forgot the feed the dogs."

"I can do it, Monsieur."

Toussaint fished a coin out of his pocket. "Alright. I'll give you a nickel to feed the dogs and chickens, clean the coop, cut the lawn, and feed my mare, Cherrie. Feed her first. You'll find what you need in the stable."

"Thank you, Monsieur! You won't be disappointed." He ran to the stable to begin his work.

***

She leaned on the side of the pot to catch her breath. The girl sat on the ground playing with her doll.

"You're almost finished. Why did you stop?"

"I'se tired."

"Don't you want rest, Maman?"

A tear fell from her eye into the pot. "Yessum."

Toussaint raised his coffee cup to his lips as he read the paper. Having a helper may just work out for him. It had been ages since he could afford the time to read in the afternoon. Normally, he would have been doing chores.

"I guess I can stand another cup." Toussaint went to the counter to pour another, but thought better of it. He didn't want to hear Jannie's lecture about how coffee kept him awake at night.

He decided to take a pass on the nagging. Toussaint went to the sink to rinse the cup. He pumped vigorously, encouraging the water to surge into the porcelain cup. The water pooled within, circling, sinking deeper. The water disappeared into a black hole of nothingness, engulfing the cup, the sink and then the counter. He fell in.

Toussaint dropped the cup. It shattered in the sink. He grabbed his jacket from the coat rack and ran out the house to the stable.

Cherrie munched her oats as the Allen brushed her. Toussaint pushed him aside, threw the feed bucket against the wall and jumped on Cherrie. "Yah!" He bolted out of the stable.

Missy wiped her brow with the sleeve of her dress. "This too heavy."

The little girl laid her doll in the mud. "Don't worry, I'll help you." With all their might, they pushed the heavy caldron.

"I'se cain't do it."

"Just try. You can, if you try."

Missy nodded. With everything she had in her, she pushed. She and the little girl pushed the pot to the wash house.

"Careful, you don't want it to fall into the pit."

Lining up the wheels, they pushed the caldron over the fire pit. Missy collapsed to the ground, gasping for air.

"You dirtied your dress."

"What?" Missy stood up and looked down at her pretty white dress, covered with mud. "I'se cain't marry Kinky lookin' like this."

"Who'se Kinky?"

Missy blushed. "My'se intended."

"Can't you wash it away?"

Laughter ranged in her ears. The little girl stood before her with the head of a White man. He laughed at her. He wouldn't stop. Missy covered her ears and closed her eyes. "I'se cain't git clean!"

The laughter stopped. She opened her eyes, finding the little girl with a brown, little girl's head.

"You washed Master's sheets clean. Can't you wash this away too?"

Jannie walked up the side drive of her home, tired. Her eyes perked up. "Toussaint cut the grass!" In fact, everything looked great. The porch, the walkway and side drive had been swept too. Her husband must have had a busy day. She remembered seeing mourners in the parlor when she'd left that morning, waiting to arrange services for their loved ones.

Reaching the back door, she found one of the students who attended St. Maurice sitting on the steps. The kitchen door was open. "Allen?"

"Good afternoon, Madame Bailey," he said, jumping up from where he sat as he snatched his cap from his head.

"What are you doing here?"

He gulped. "Father Pierre suggested I come by and ask Monsieur Bailey if he needed help."

Jannie removed her gloves and walked up the stairs. "Alright…"

"Well, Monsieur Bailey hired me for the day. I was in the barn finishing up with Cherrie, when he bolted in, pushed me down, jumped on Cherrie and rode away."

Jannie felt a sinking feeling in the pit of her stomach. "Did he say where he was going?"

"No, Madame. He didn't even saddle Cherrie," Allen said. "Well, I didn't want to leave with the door open, so I decided to wait, after I finished my chores. I figured you'd return home from school soon."

Jannie patted his cheek when she realized something. "Why weren't you in school today?"

Allen swelled up, trying to hold in his tears. He coughed. "My papa lost his job. Mama's sick and can't work. I figured I would try and earn some money today by finding some work around the neighborhood. We're running low on food, Madame." Allen buried his face in the crook of his arm.

Jannie hugged the boy. "Well, we have plenty of food here. Come inside and I'll pack a basket for you." She stroked the boy's head, comforting him. "All will be well. Do not worry." She patted his cheek. "Come inside and help me."

Missy inhaled deep. The fire smelled good to her. The smoke made her feel good. She was good when working with the fire and water. She was good.

The little girl returned to the pot from the wash house with a stool. She sat it next to the pot and stood on it. The water churned and boiled. "Will this clean your clothes?"

Missy considered the boiling water. "Naw. I'se needs to git the lye." Missy ran to the wash house and returned a few moments later with two cans. She poured both into the pot. The smell rejuvenated her. She felt good. "Where's my paddle?"

"Do you need it?"

Missy figured she didn't. She watched the water churn. White bubbles formed on the water around the edges of the pot. "Kinky gonna come in from the fields soon. I'se cain't let him sees me dirty. He's gonna knows I'se dirty."

The little girl hopped down from the stool. "Well, wash up."

Missy looked down at the little girl, and then into the pot. She stared out across the square, searching the horizon for Kinky. Down the road leading to the fields, she saw a speck in the distance, surrounded by a cloud of dust. "I'se ain't got e'nuff time. There he is, far off."

The little girl smiled at her and then returned her attention to her doll, arranging her hair. "Well, you'd better hurry."

***

Toussaint kicked the mare hard. She could go faster if he continued to kick her. He held tight to her mane. He could see smoke rising in the distance. He kicked the mare.

A white kite soared up and then fell from view.

"Cherrie, go darlin'."

Fifteen minutes later, Toussaint reached the wash house. He ran to the pot and found a little girl standing beside it. The little girl matured into a young lady. "She's better now." She flashed white and disappeared.

His eyes remained locked on where the girl once stood. Toussaint turned toward the pot. He moved one leg. He focused, and then forced the other to move. He repeated the process until he reached the vessel.

A white dress floated surrounded by hair and fat.

Toussaint reached into the scalding water and pulled her out. She melted, dripping down his arms, her flesh falling in clumps to the ground. He walked with her, the path behind him flowered with puffs of dust from the road, receiving her flesh. Cherrie followed behind, neighing.

La Rose Plantation, St. Helena Parish. August 31, 1963.

"I'D ALWAYS WONDERED how Lawrence didn't see it happen." A hummingbird fluttered against the closed window and watched them. He flew away. "I guess the Lord has been known to block the vision of angels as well as men."

The bee venom had vacated his body, relieving the swelling in his face and tongue. Julian felt sorry for Missy. She'd suffered such pain.

Lela sobbed, reaching out to her great-grandson. He took her in his arms. "How could she do it? Who boils themselves? Hanging? Okay. A gunshot to the head, I get it. But to jump into a pot of boiling water and lye, who does that?" Lela wailed, overcome with the tragedy. "I guess she sought to cleanse herself of her defilement for all time."

Lela's eyes widened with understanding. "My God, she wanted to make herself clean, as white and clean as Master's sheets. She'd always succeeded in removing blemishes from the laundry. Maybe she believed she could remove the stains upon her soul in the same fashion." A sob escaped Lela. "It wasn't her fault," Lela said, weeping for her lost cousin.

Julian patted his grandmère's shoulder, comforting her. Why would God allow her cousin to endure abuse from the devil?

Lela stopped crying and kissed his forehead. "Resist the devil and he will flee from you." Lela left the bed and sat in the chair.

"Can we prevent bad things from happening? Not necessarily. The only thing we can control is our reaction to these tragedies. It's difficult, but it isn't impossible. I speak from experience. During the tragic times of my life, I didn't want to go on. However, the Lord had blessed me with loved ones who presented me with the truth. I had to choose whether the accept the truth or the devil's lies. Eventually, I choose truth and love. I survived.

"Missy didn't have that. She didn't want it either. She'd been violated and could never release the pain of the event. Trust me, it is hard to do. The spirit of victimization is a seductive lover. You desire to submit out of desperation and hopelessness, to give up. You feel as if there is nothing better. I'm not sure if I can describe quite what it's like.

"In any case, not long after Missy's passing, Albertus located Kinky's body. He'd been buried in a mass grave for Negro soldiers fighting for the North. I believe either Albertus or Lawrence had mentioned Kinky fought for the 5th United States Colored Troops out of Ohio. He fell at Fort Fisher in North Carolina in December, 1864.

"Albertus exhumed his body and brought his remains back to La Rose. He and Lawrence buried him beside Missy." Lela sucked her teeth, looking back. "At least he hadn't died in one of the White folk's camps for liberated slaves. He'd made it pass the Devil's Punch Bowl in Natchez. He saw combat. He conquered. Yet, he died in a prison camp, nonetheless."

Tears streamed down his red face. Julian sat up in bed, but he felt dizzy. He slumped down beneath the covers. Falling back into the vision, what he saw confounded him. It could not be true. "Grandmère?"

"Oui, mon fils?"

"The little girl… Was that Missy's daughter?"

Lela turned away.

Julian continued to replay the scene before his eyes. "Are you saying her daughter killed her?"

Lela stared straight ahead, unresponsive.

"Grandmère?"

Lela inhaled deep. She returned to bed and sat on the side, smoothing his hair. "Claret was in New Orleans, I would imagine."

Julian thought back through her story. "But she could move about, like Sarah?"

Lela nodded.

"So, let me rephrase. Did she assist and encourage her mother to kill herself?"

Lela stood from the bed and pulled back the covers. "It's time for you to get up, mon cher." She kissed him on the forehead. "Let it rest."

Chapter 28

New Orleans, Louisiana. February, 1876.

The house seemed empty with both Teddy and Sarah gone. Jannie missed her in-laws. She hadn't realized the fullness they'd brought to her life while they had been with her. Now that they were gone, she could do nothing but think about them.

Toussaint seemed to have moved on, busying himself with a variety of business and civic projects. At times she wondered if he was relieved, now free of his difficult family life. Jannie shook her head as she put away the last plate. She knew Toussaint's heart ached, although he didn't show it. She dried the last plate and placed it in the cupboard. She smiled, hearing the kitchen door open.

"Hey, darlin'."

Jannie opened her arms, hugging and kissing her husband. "You're finished, already?"

Toussaint smiled. "I didn't work today. I had an errand to run."

"Oh." Jannie returned to her chores. Her husband's clandestine ways irritated her at times.

Toussaint put his arms around her waist. Jannie smiled, releasing her irritation with her husband. She noticed he concealed an object in his hand. He smiled at her and unfurled his fingers, revealing what lay captive within his grasp. "Oh, my Lord. Toussaint!"

He kissed her and then slid the ring on her finger. "Happy anniversary, darlin'."

Jannie stared at the ring on her hand, the most brilliant diamond she'd ever seen. "Toussaint, I can't wear this out," Jannie said.

"Why not?"

"Well, someone might rob me."

Toussaint laughed at his pragmatic wife. "Trust me darlin'. No one will ever lay a finger on you. Ever."

A cold chill ran through her. She nodded, accepting his words. "Toussaint, how can you afford such a fine ring?"

He kissed her again. "Maman left me an inheritance. I thought I'd buy you something nice with it, since I didn't give you a proper ring when we married."

"I love the ring you gave me, Toussaint. The ring didn't matter. Only you."

Toussaint blushed. "Well, I love you too. That's why I brought you this ring. Do you like it?"

Jannie held out her hand, admiring it. "Of course I do, honey." She'd never imagined owning such nice things. Since his mother's death, Toussaint had made several extravagant purchases, which embarrassed her. What would the neighbors think? "Toussaint?"

"Yes, baby," he said, kissing her.

"How much money did Maman leave you?"

Toussaint eyes went cold, but he quickly softened them. "Baby, don't worry about it. Just know we'll never starve." He could see the anger boiling up inside of his wife. Why couldn't she trust him? He took her in his arms. "I will always care for and watch over you. Why do you choose to worry about such things?"

Jannie melted within his embrace, his sultry black eyes seducing her.

New Orleans, Louisiana. April, 1876.

ONE MONTH REMAINED before the dedication, and the library was still a mess. Although she'd opened the library nearly two years before, they'd never celebrated the occasion.

Looking around her office, she remembered the library as a small storefront with one bookcase, half full. She'd worked hard, appealing to parishioners at church and patrons of the school to donate their old books. Cash donations had been welcomed, as well. For the first year, she counted it as a good week if she had ten visitors.

Once Toussaint's parents died, he seemed lost to her. She wanted to get his mind off their deaths and had asked him to talk to some of his friends about donating to the library. She hadn't seen such a broad grin on his face since they'd first met, at the church picnic.

Within a year, Toussaint had purchased the entire city block of storefronts on either side of the library, and had converted it all into a single space. He'd taken over her project.

Jannie sorted the mail. "Maybe I should go and do something else." She leaned back in her chair, allowing her mind to clear. "Father, help me focus on what is important." Allowing God's peace to fill her, she removed the mail from her brass inbox. She opened envelope after envelope. Checks. They were all checks for thousands of dollars, francs, and English pounds. There were some Yen and Ethiopian currency, also.

Having exhausted the stack of mail, Jannie swiveled in her chair to the parcels stacked behind her desk. Taking her sterling silver scissors, she cut through the string and paper. The boxes contained a variety of currency, filled with rubles, rupees, and wén. Jannie couldn't understand it. Why would people from all over the world fund a little Negro community library in the upper Ninth ward of New Orleans? She also wondered why a person would send large amounts of money through the mail.

Jannie moved on to the large envelopes stacked beside the boxes and crates, detailing shipping instructions for collections from around the world. "Where will we storage all these books?" Her little idea had ballooned out of control.

Jannie stood and straighten her back. Her corset had bunched up on her. She walked over to the plans for the library, framed and hanging on the wall. The library they'd built didn't resemble the drawings in the least bit. In fact, the drawing was much grander than the library. She didn't recognize any of the rooms detailed in the floor plans. In fact, the library only had two floors, while the plans dictated three floors, with sub-basements. Jannie shook her head and walked away. "Be careful what you ask for," she said, leaving her office.

Jannie entered the reading room, filled with crates. The library had received book donations from all over the world, many from London, Paris, Brussels, and Shanghai. They'd even received many books from collections in Africa, as far away as Ethiopia.

"What will we do with all of these books? Lord, with everything?" Despite her worries, she knew they would find a way to accommodate the donations. Toussaint had contracted an army of librarians to construct and organize the stacks.

She watched a man, a few feet away, open one of the crates from Africa and walk away. Once he left, she walked over and peered in, finding volumes wrapped in muslin. She removed one and unwrapped it. Jannie gasped, finding the cover encrusted with jewels. Placing the heavy book on the table, she opened it. A sparkled dust soared up from the pages and then disappeared. "What in the world!"

The book appeared to be an ancient, holy text. With care, she turned the vellum pages, stopping at a plate depicting the Ark of the Covenant, crack in two. A man stood before it with his hands outstretched to Heaven. The book shut.

Startled, Jannie looked over her shoulder to find the librarian who'd accompanied the crates of books from Ethiopia. An extremely tall man with smooth, dark caramel skin, he sported a kind smile. Surely, he was a king in his homeland. "Madame, the contents of this book will be revealed in a time yet to come." He picked up the book and walked away, taking the volume with him. Workers appeared with hand trucks and wheeled the remaining crates away to a special vault designated for the Ethiopian collection.

***

With stealth assuredness, Claret stood on the bottom stair, watching. She kissed her doll and entered the preparation room, stopping behind her uncle. Her uncle possessed little awareness of what was happening around him. *He doesn't know we're here*, she said to her doll in her mind. She watched him as he sutured his client. Allen wheeled in a gurney. The men moved the corpse from the table to the gurney, prepared to transport him to the cold room. "Has his murderer hung?"

Toussaint jumped. Once he saw Claret, he placed his hand on his heart, hoping to dissipate the heavy thumping. "What?"

Claret adjusted her doll's hair. "Did she hang for his murder?"

Toussaint grabbed a shroud from the shelf. "He died in his sleep, Claret," he said, irritated. "What are you doing down here, anyway?"

"Are only boys allowed here?"

Toussaint didn't feel like arguing with his niece. "We're busy, Claret. Go upstairs and study."

"I've completed my studies. My new texts have yet to arrive from my tutor."

Toussaint covered the body with the shroud. "Who's your tutor?"

Claret kissed her doll. "It doesn't matter. Allow the murderer to go free and bury the body."

Allen turned to Toussaint, confused. Toussaint sighed. "Why do you say he's been murdered, gal?"

Claret smiled at him. "Don't call me gal, boy."

He resisted the urge to slap her. "Show me."

Walking over to the gurney, she reached beneath the shroud and removed his hand. "He was poisoned. Look at his fingernails. See this discoloration?"

Toussaint examined the hand. He ran to his desk, found his magnifying glass and returned to the body to take a closer look. "My God."

"You're welcomed, Uncle." She left the room, returning upstairs.

Allen swallowed deep. "Is it true, Monsieur?"

Toussaint went to his desk and wrote a note. "Saddle Cherrie and take this note to Commander Thomas, downtown. Tell the desk sergeant I sent you. You shouldn't have any problems."

Toussaint watched Allen leave.

He despised his niece.

With a little tug, she was able to lock the library's double doors. She couldn't believe her dream had come to pass. She'd dreamed of establishing a library since her youth. Every day after school for the past two years, she would stop by the library to manage the project. Fortunately, Sarah had taken care of home in her absence, feeding the family and keeping the house tidy. "Now doncha worry none, baby," she'd told her. "I'se a old woman. You'se young. Go builds your dream, so our li'l ones hungry minds can have a place to feast."

Her eyes teared, thinking of her mother-in-law. At least working on the project had eased her pain. However, she still missed her.

After twenty minutes, Jannie pulled her buggy into the driveway. Her heart leapt in her chest. "The police?" Once the wagon pulled away, she hopped out the buggy, ran up the stairs, and rushed in the front door. "Toussaint!"

Toussaint walked into the living room. "Everything's fine, Jannie."

She panted, catching her breath. "Why were the police here?"

Toussaint sat on the sofa. "Claret said one of my clients had been murdered. And she was right."

"What? How? Why was she even down there?"

Toussaint frowned. "Trust me. I didn't invite her."

Jannie sat next to her husband, confused. "You let her examine the body?"

Toussaint snorted. "Of course not. Not after the last

time I caught her down there conducting a dissection on one of my clients." Jannie stared at him, mortified. He'd forgotten he'd decided not to tell her. Oh well. "Today, she'd been standing there watching me work. Neither Allen nor I knew she was in the room. The girl walks like a cat," he said, although he knew she hadn't 'walked' into the room.

"She'd noticed a discoloration around the man's fingernails, pointing to poisoning over a long period of time." Toussaint patted his stunned wife's thigh. "And she was right. The police are looking into it. I cannot bury him until they make the arrest." He peered into the Spirit. "I suspect his wife. I've heard rumors he wasn't very kind to her."

"My Lord," Jannie said. "The child is gifted. She reads these text books, but I don't know who gave them to her. Toussaint, these are books intended for medical students."

A chill went through him. "She mentioned today she had a tutor. Have you met him or her?"

"No!" Anger surged within her. "The child is secretive. I never know what she's thinking." Jannie wiped a tear from her eye. "She doesn't care for me, Toussaint."

Toussaint patted her hand. "She hates everybody. It isn't just you, darlin'. You should see how she treats Allen. I think she's jealous of him." Toussaint stared into the Spirit. "No, he's just immaterial to her." Toussaint swallowed hard. "The only person she has ever loved was Maman. I don't think she'll ever love another with her whole heart, again."

"Toussaint!"

"It's true, darlin'." Toussaint kissed her cheek and left for his office.

Jannie rubbed her temples. Exhausted by Toussaint's family, she went to the kitchen to prepare dinner.

"My God," Jannie said as she closed her book. She'd been reading slave narratives as of late, to better educate her students. Their parents hadn't shared with them their stories of bondage, so she thought it would be a good education for them. She decided to read to them over the next few weeks, *Our Nig: Sketches from the Life of a Free Black* by Harriet E. Wilson. She placed the book on the night stand and turned off the light.

Toussaint snuggled into to her. "I thought you were asleep."

He kissed her neck. "Naw, darlin'. I was waiting for you."

Jannie smiled. "Oh really? You were waiting for me?"

"Yes," he said, kissing her. "Also, I was thinking about the library. How are things going over there?"

Jannie sat up in bed. "Toussaint, it's too much. I wanted a small, neighborhood library with modest collections, supplied by the community."

Toussaint bit his tongue, regretting he'd broached the

subject. "Who in the community has books to donate, Jannie?"

She thought about it, surrounded by the darkness. "Well, we could continue to solicit the Negro colleges and parishes for donations."

"They're just starting up themselves," he said. "Do you remember the three shelves of books you started with?" Toussaint sighed, knowing he'd hurt his wife's feelings. He'd belittled her accomplishment. "Darlin', don't take my comment the wrong way. I think it was great. You did a great job." She nodded and looked away, hiding her tears. He kissed her hand. "Honey, I know people. Allow me to help you?"

"Alright." Jannie laid down in bed, with her back to her husband.

Toussaint felt bad, but not really. Jannie had great ideas, but limited vision. "Darlin', don't be mad."

"I'm not mad, Toussaint. I just want to go to sleep."

Toussaint sat up in bed and lit the lamp. "Darlin', we have the opportunity to do something great here. You had a great idea. I don't think you realize its significance."

Jannie sat up in bed. Toussaint took her hand in his.

"Darlin', this library is only the start," he said, his eyes sparkling with excitement. The new library…"

"New library? We haven't finished this one, Toussaint."

"Just listen to me, darlin'," he said. She sighed and relaxed. "The new structure will be a monument to the Negro community, containing many fire and water proof vaults for special collections. You've seen what has been delivered, haven't you?" She nodded. "They can't survive over the long run in the rooms. The benefactors who sent them are working together to plan a more permanent structure. It will rival the Louvre."

Jannie brow twisted. "How will we pay for this? Who are these people, Toussaint?"

Toussaint patted her hand. "I told you, I met them while living in France. I sent a letter to my patron, and he has made many of the arrangements."

Jannie nodded, not understanding.

Toussaint enveloped her in his arms, kissing her. "Now, don't you worry, darlin'. The Lord will provide. All we must do is conceive and believe all is possible if we hope in Him."

New Orleans, Louisiana. May, 1876.

"YOU'RE BEAUTIFUL, MRS. Bailey."

Looking into the mirror at the hairdresser, Jannie nodded at her, uncomfortable. She couldn't believe Toussaint had hired her to come to their home to style her hair and to do her makeup. Jannie couldn't remember if she'd worn makeup before.

"I'm finished, Mrs. Bailey."

She stood from the chair. Another woman entered the room. "Are you ready to dress, Mrs. Bailey?"

"Yes, Gladys. I'm going to bedroom, now," she said. Gladys followed her. "Thank you, but I can dress by myself."

Gladys stood before her, confused. "But…"

"Jannie, allow her to help you."

Jannie turned to find Toussaint dressed in a Parisian morning suit. "Toussaint, where did you get that suit?"

He walked over to his wife and kissed her. "I had it made. Why?"

She patted his lapels. "Nothing, I was just wondering."

Toussaint decided not to allow his pragmatic wife to ruin his day. "You look beautiful, darlin'."

"Thank you, Toussaint," she said.

"What are you wearing?"

Why did he care? "My blue dress I wear to Sunday Mass."

Toussaint smiled at her. "No, you're not. Follow me. And Gladys, you come too."

Irritated, Jannie followed her husband to their bedroom. Why couldn't anything ever be simple with him? He opened the door and stepped aside, allowing her to enter.

The most beautiful dress she'd ever seen sat upon a dressmaker's form. She'd only seen drawings of dresses such as the one before her in *Godey's Ladies Book*. "My God. Toussaint!"

He blushed. "Do you like it, darlin'?"

Jannie circled the dress, admiring it. The dress had been made with silk, the fabric patterned with narrow, blue diagonal stripes on a white background. The designer had constructed the dress where the diagonal pattern met at the center of the bodice, giving the appearance of arrows pointing down. The skirt was solid white, while the diagonal fabric had been used for the bustle. Glass buttons flowed down the bodice, from the neckline, stopping just above the waistline of the dress.

"Those are diamonds, darlin'."

"What?"

"Just kidding."

Jannie returned her attention to the dress. "Toussaint, this is too much. What will people say if I wore such a grand dress? We're a poor community, Toussaint, and people are struggling."

Toussaint took his wife in his arms and kissed her. "Well, maybe you will provide them hope, darlin'," he said. "Once they see you, they will know without a doubt that all things are possible, with God."

Where had all the people come from? Jannie's guest list totaled maybe seventy-five people. However, she estimated at least three hundred in attendance, including people from the neighborhood, as well as many she didn't know. She watched workers bring out additional chairs for the over-flow of attendees. She didn't have five hundred chairs, yet the slew of workers continued to bring them out from the library. Everyone seemed to find a place to sit.

Toussaint admired the crowd who'd gathered for the dedication. Taking his wife's hand, her trepidation surround-ing the event flowed into his spirit. Why couldn't she think on a grander scale? Maybe he could calm her. "Some of our benefactors traveled here from afar for the dedication, dar-lin'."

"Toussaint, how can that be? If they traveled from over-seas, it would have taken weeks or months."

Claret stood next to them fiddling with her doll. "I as-sure you, Aunt Jannie, their travel required but a twinkle of an eye."

"What are you saying, Claret?"

"Nothing, Aunt." The child frowned. "Here comes some of our travelers now."

Toussaint scowled at the girl. He extended his hand to the three men. "Jerémèy, Albertus, and Zhan. Welcome! I'm glad you could join us today."

Jerémèy shook his hand. "The devil in hell couldn't have kept me away," he said, frowning at Claret.

"Well, I'm glad to see your comrade allowed you to attend today, Monsieur," Claret replied. Albertus and Zhan stared at the child, in shock.

Jannie blushed with embarrassment. "Claret! Watch your mouth, young lady. Why would say such things? You haven't met this man before."

"You don't know whom I know, Aunt." She walked away to find her seat.

Jerémèy watched the child as she walked away. He laughed, thinking of how his brother, Hempsworth, had goaded him about Augustus. Every dog shall have his day, as Minnie would say. His brother's day had come. "My, my, my. She is the little spitfire."

Toussaint frowned at the girl. "That she is," he said through gritted teeth.

Albertus patted his shoulder. "Be patient, son. And persevere."

"Yes, you bring princess thus far. She be well. She grow to be great and powerful woman, a genius. The mother of many. Take heart," Zhan said.

Jannie found the men to be strange, but kind. "Thank you all, for your kind words. We are very proud of Claret, although she can be a handful."

"Quite," Jerémèy said. "We will leave you now," he said, shaking Toussaint's hand. "You, Mrs. Bailey, I will see in a few moments," he said with a comforting smile. The men bowed to her and left.

"Who are they, Toussaint?"

"Some of our donors, darlin'. Haven't you seen Albertus at the library? He donated the collection from Ethiopia. He traveled here to manage its installation at the library."

Jannie's eyes brightened. "Oh yes, I remember him now. How could I have forgotten him? He is very tall and regal." Her nerves took hold of her, once more. "I can't speak before all these people Toussaint."

He patted her hand. "Sure, you can. Just imagine you're at Mass, doing the reading." He led her to their seats.

"Ladies and Gentlemen. Thank you for joining us today to dedicate this beautiful monument to God and to the community — *La Bibliothèque pour les Gens de Couleur.*" The audience applauded.

Jannie listened to the petit man named Jerémèy drone on with his heavy French accent about many of the collections which had been donated to the library from the corners of the world. She wrung her hands. Toussaint placed his hand upon hers and smiled. Jannie relaxed, returning her attention to the presentation.

"Many literacy programs, as well as vocational programs, will be sponsored from these halls under the direction of the library's founder." The audience applauded. "I am sure I have bored all of you long enough."

"I am glad you finally realized it."

"Claret!" Toussaint pinched her thigh. His fingers went numb, the electric current racing to his heart. Claret smiled and returned her attention to the speaker.

Jerémèy veiled his desire to incinerate the girl with a smile. "I'm glad to see I have one who agrees with me. It is a rare occurrence, indeed."

The gallery laughed.

"Without further delay, allow me to present to you the founder of La Bibliothèque pour les Gens de Couleur, Mrs. Jannie Bailey."

The audience stood and applauded her. Toussaint glared at his niece, still sitting in her seat fiddling with her doll. "Stand up, gal."

"Don't call me call gal, boy." Claret stood.

God, I can't stand her. Toussaint escorted Jannie to the podium and kissed her cheek, leaving her alone. Jerémèy kissed her hand and then bowed to her. He stepped back.

Taking the podium, Jannie inhaled deep. *I can do this. I must do this.*

"Ladies and Gentlemen, thank you for coming." Jannie inhaled deep. "A little more than twenty years ago, our Father in Heaven released us from bondage, many without homes or finances. We had nowhere to go. But the Lord has blessed the works of our hands, bringing us here, today."

The audience applauded. Claret sat disinterested, fiddling with her doll. Jannie refocused and walked over to the shrouded figure to her right. "I would like to thank our many donors from around the world, sending not only financial donations, but their collections as well, to our little library here in the Ninth Ward." The audience applauded. "I especially would like to thank my husband, Toussaint Bailey, who was instrumental bringing to fruition this institution for our community, creating a source of hope in and resources for our lives, for years to come."

Jannie smiled at the well-wishers before her. "My mother-in-law was passionate about this project, putting aside her personal desires to attend to the daily needs of our home, thus affording me the time to supervise this project." She watched the audience bow their heads. "In remembrance of Mrs. Sarah Bailey, on this day, the one-year anniversary of her death, I would like to make this presentation, in her honor."

Jannie nodded to the two men standing beside the shrouded object. They removed covering.

Toussaint stood from his seat in awe and wept.

Claret stood, clutching her doll to her chest.

A bronze, life-size image of Sarah the Slave gleamed in

the morning light.

Standing tall, her eyes searched the horizon. The artist had captured her very essence, portraying a prophet and a judge with long, locked hair secured within a tignon. The statue held a staff in her left hand with a satchel slung across her midsection. A small boy sat on her shoulders, his eyes shining and filled with the freedom of God. With her right palm outstretched upward, a large bee sat upon it, his wings in position to take flight.

Toussaint left the audience and stood before the image of his mother. He touched it, feeling the energy of her spirit. "How did you do this, Jannie," he asked, entranced, with tears streaming down his face.

She took his hand. "One of our patrons from France, commissioned it. In fact, the emcee. Jerémèy is his name?" Toussaint nodded. "A few days ago, he was here directing the workers who installed the statue." Jannie's brow curled, remembering. "We talked, but he didn't mention his name. Anyway, he'd told me he had commissioned the work. He said he knew of your mother. Funny, I didn't recognize him when you introduced us."

Toussaint looked over to Jerémèy, who chatted with Albertus and Li-Zhan. Jerémèy smiled at him. *You are welcomed, my son.*

Overcome with joy, Toussaint stepped up onto the base

of the statue, fashioned into a hilltop, and kissed the face of the bronze statue. He leaned his head on the statue's shoulder and cried. Once he'd spent his emotion, he jumped down and took Jannie in his arms and kissed her, encouraged by the applause of the gallery.

New Orleans, Louisiana. November, 1876

JANNIE HALTED THEIR buggy before the library. Each time she beheld the structure, her heart filled with pride. Support and patronage of the institution continued to grow. Toussaint had established a foundation, equipped with a board of directors, to manage its finances, organize fundraisers and to manage programs offered to the community. He'd appointed Jannie as Chairman of the Board.

"Aunt Jannie, aren't we going in?"

Jannie frowned at her. Sometimes she didn't care for the child. "Come along."

The ladies escaped the heat of the day, entering the library filled with patrons. "Find somewhere to settle down, honey."

Claret stared at her, confused. "I think I know how to do that, Aunt Jannie." She walked away, in search of an empty reading room.

Jannie removed her gloves, irritated. How could she love and despise a child at the same time? The child must have taken on her father's personality. She hadn't known Missy before she went mad, but the stories she'd heard from Sarah and Teddy indicated Missy had been a carefree, loving soul in her youth. Jannie let it all go, headed for her office.

She opened the door and frowned. She felt ill at ease in the space. Toussaint had created a sumptuous office for her, filled with walnut paneling and a fancy desk, accented with gold and kingwood. He said it had been donated by a European patron. The style of the desk was bureau plat, or something like that.

Jannie longed for simpler fare, such as her pine teacher's desk in her classroom at St. Maurice Parish School. However, Toussaint had convinced her they must employ finer furnishings because their potential sponsors and patrons were accustomed to luxurious lifestyles. The opulent office would ease any latent concerns they may have about donating to the library.

Jannie placed her parasol in the stand and walked over to the wall, where the plans for a new library hung. Toussaint mentioned a member of the foundation had donated land for the project, somewhere in New Orleans, near the Garden District. When she protested, Toussaint assured her they would maintain the current location for the community.

Having completed her tasks, Jannie left her office. She

needed to return home to start dinner for her family. Jannie scanned the reading room, but she didn't see Claret at any of the tables. Walking to the far side of the library, she searched each of the private reading rooms. Near the rear, Jannie spotted her red-headed niece in the second to last room through the side light, receiving instruction from a man in a garish suit. She opened the door. "Claret, is everything alright?"

Claret didn't look up from her lesson, continuing with her studies. "Yes, Aunt. Why do you ask?"

Jannie grabbed the child's hand, pulling her from the chair. "Who are you, sir?"

The man stood. "I am Winslow Hempsworth." He adjusted the rose in his lapel. "I am a patron of this library, hailing from England."

Jannie drew Claret closer. "I haven't met you before."

"Quite so. However, I have met your husband, Toussaint Bailey. I was fortunate to make his acquaintance at the château of his cousin, Emmanuel Chevalier, in Fargniers, France, while on holiday one year. Such a quaint little place. In any case, Chevalier finds the place comfortable, I suppose. To each his own."

Claret giggled.

Hempsworth winked at the child. "Several months ago, I asked my secretary to contact your husband. He responded to my note and is aware of my arrival. Has he failed to advise you of my visit?"

Jannie gritted her teeth. "Yes."

"Pity." His eyes fell upon Claret. "Such a brilliant child, your Claret. She has an uncanny ability to absorb the sciences. How has she performed in school?

Jannie massaged Claret's shoulder, unsure if she could trust the dapper man. He was quite handsome, rather tall with blonde hair boasting white highlights. His chiseled facial features completed his distinguished appearance. His suit of clothes disturbed her. What man wore such bright colors and patterns? "Well, Claret is an excellent student. She has out-paced the curriculum of our parish school. I am working on her admittance to one of the local colleges."

"Humph," Hempsworth grunted. He removed his spectacles and cleaned them.

"What does that mean?" Jannie asked.

"I'm afraid there is no school in the Americas equipped to educate a brilliant mind such as hers."

Jannie clutched Claret to her breast. The child struggled to free herself. "What do you mean, Mr. Hempsworth?" A shadow at the door's sidelight distracted her from her inquisition.

Toussaint entered the room and hung his hat on the stand. "Mr. Hempsworth, how are you?" Toussaint shook his hand.

"Old chap! Jolly good to see you again. You appear to be in good health."

Jannie's mouth fell open. "You know him, Toussaint?"

It was going to be a long evening. Toussaint hadn't expected Hempsworth to arrive in New Orleans so soon. He couldn't lie. Toussaint knew in his heart Hempsworth would arrive on time. He just wanted to avoid a confrontation with Jannie regarding Claret's future. Now, his poor decision had returned to bite him. "Well, of course, darlin'. He's an old friend from Europe."

Claret flounced her skirts, allowing them to cascaded back into place. "Aunt Jannie, has Uncle neglected to share with you he's shipping me off to London with Mr. Hempsworth to be educated?"

"What?"

"Now baby, calm down," Toussaint said reaching for his wife. She dodged his embrace. Claret escaped Jannie's hold and ran to Hempsworth. Toussaint and Jannie frowned at the child.

"Yes, Aunt. He's my new father now. I will be attending Oxford straight away upon my arrival in England. I will board at university during the semester and then take holiday with Mr. Hempsworth at his estate."

Jannie stood before them all, astonished. When had the

girl developed a British accent? How long had she been meeting with the man? Had Toussaint known about it? Jannie began to cry. "And you're alright with this, Toussaint?"

"Baby, I didn't expect him arrive here so soon. I was going to tell you."

Claret smiled, filled with wickedness and indignation. "Trust me, Aunt. Uncle is overjoyed with the news of my departure. He cannot wait." Claret walked over to Toussaint and stood before him, triumphant. "God is good to you, Uncle. Now you don't have to think of your unfinished business with father every time you look at me." Claret toyed with the lace on the sleeves of her tea length white dress. "Take heart, Uncle. Good things come to those who wait, does it not?"

Hempsworth closed his eyes. The girl would prove to be a genius and a handful, while in his care. He could hear his brothers laughing in the Spirit. He was the Lord's General, his champion. He'd conquered his brother Lucifer, expelling him from Heaven. Surely, he could manage a little girl in a lace, tea length dress and ruffled pantaloons. He considered the girl's cold, indifferent eyes. Maybe he shouldn't have goaded Barachiel about Augustus' unruliness. "Perhaps we should all go to dinner and talk this over?"

"Have you forgotten we're Negro, Mr. Hempsworth? Where do you suggest we go?" Claret asked.

Hempsworth weighed the challenges of American society. The same challenges existed in the Empire, but not to the same degree. "During my afternoon walk, I noticed a lovely restaurant down the street. Chez Louise, I believe was the name. It's not elegant dining, but I'm sure it will be pleasant, all the same," Hempsworth said, put off by the child's bluntness.

Jannie's stomach turned. "I'm not well, Mr. Hempsworth. My apologies. However, I'm sure you will enjoy your meal with Toussaint and Claret." Jannie glared at Toussaint, her eyes brimming with tears. "Why involve me now?" Jannie left the reading room.

"Jannie!" Toussaint listened to the clicks of her heels fade in the distance, punctuated by the library's front door slamming shut. Toussaint scowled at his niece. "Why would you do that, gal?"

Claret sauntered over to Hempsworth, sliding her hand into his. "I told you. Don't call me gal, boy."

Hempsworth's jaw dropped.

"And what did I do? I never disclosed if either you or Mr. Hempsworth told me about my impending relocation, to a land across the sea." She laughed, twirling around, overcome with whimsy and joy. She picked up her doll from the table and kissed her. "I was quite happy when Grandmère visited me in my sleep, telling me all about it."

Claret signaled for Toussaint to bend down. She placed her lips close to his ear. "God laughs at the wicked, isn't that what you say Uncle? If God is good, I won't see your face again until it's time for me to leave this Earth." Tears filled Toussaint's eyes. "Mr. Hempsworth, when are we scheduled to depart?"

Sadness flooded his being at the sight of the child's cold heart, unbecoming a girl fifteen years of age. "When do you care to leave?"

Claret removed her parasol from the stand and kissed her doll. "In the morning. I have my doll Grandmère made for me when I was a child. I require nothing else." Claret left them both standing in the private reading room, leaving behind her sordid origins.

Chapter 29

La Rose Plantation, St. Helena Parish. August 31, 1963.

The crickets soothed her nerves, as the sun set on the plantation. Dusk having descended upon them; the mosquitos began to invade the sanctum of the terrace. "Leave at once," Lela said. The twilight sky cleared.

Julian watched the swarm leave, creating a perimeter around the edge of the terrace. He was too tired to be amazed, still groggy from his earlier attack. Lawrence brought him a cup of tea and left. He drank it and felt better.

Lela stared at the predatory insects surrounding the terrace. How could Toussaint have been satisfied with such a dull woman? She had no adventure, no oomph, as Leelee would have said. "To each his own."

"What did you say, Grandmère?"

She sighed, letting it go. "Nothing. Just thinking about Toussaint's marriage to Jannie. I can't see what he saw in her."

Julian laughed, holding his sore throat. "Why? Because

she wasn't you?"

She wanted to scold him, but laughed instead. "Be quiet, boy." She arose from the sofa and went indoors, followed by her great-grandson. The mosquitos breached the invisible perimeter, failing to taste their flesh.

New Orleans, Louisiana. January, 1877.

BOY, AIN'T YOU *gonna git that gold Augustus done buried?*

Sarah disappeared into the bull rushes.

Toussaint sprung up in bed. The gold. After digging up a few cases to fund their move to New Orleans, he'd forgotten it. He shook Jannie.

She jumped up, startled. "What is it?" Reaching for the clock on the night stand, she squinted to see the time in the moonlight. "It's three o'clock in the morning, Toussaint."

He kissed her. "We're going to remodel this place, baby. I got it all figured out."

"How?" Jannie rolled over and snuggled into her pillow.

"Don't worry baby," Toussaint said. "I'll take care of it."

The next day at dusk, Toussaint and Allen drove out to Tangipahoa Parish, near the river. "What are we doing here, Monsieur?"

Toussaint handed him a shovel. "Start digging. I'll explain later."

After two hours of hard work, the men unearthed fifteen wooden crates and four heavy trunks. It took them another hour to load the cargo into the wagon. By dawn, they'd returned home. "I want to thank you for helping me, Allen," Toussaint said.

He nodded and turned to walk home.

"Allen?"

"Yes, Monsieur?"

Toussaint chose his words with care. "Do you understand the term, plausible deniability?"

He thought about it for a moment. "Kind of."

"Well, I will tell you. Sometimes it's better not to know the details. You helped me with dig up some items. That's all you know, if anyone ever asks."

Allen bit his lip. "Did we do something illegal?"

"No. However, the less you know, the better." He patted the boy on his shoulder. "Your aid will not be forgotten, son. In fact, it will be rewarded in the years to come."

Allen smiled and headed for home.

He had to be prudent. He didn't want to squander his new-found wealth. God had already shown him he would be successful in his business enterprises; however, Toussaint planned to save eighty percent of the gold as a nest egg for Jannie, only using a small fraction of it as seed money for his business ventures. He also put away a portion for Claret, Allen, and his cousin, Stank. Toussaint purchased the lots on either side of his property, demolishing the structures standing on the land.

Much to his good fortune, Toussaint met a freedman who'd managed numerous construction projects for his former master. Together, the men had scoped the renovation of his property. Now eight months into the project, the tradesmen's progress astounded him.

At six o'clock in the morning, the workmen arrived. Toussaint took pride in the all-Negro workforce, comprised of master carpenters, masons, plumbers, and laborers. Toussaint had designed their sumptuous second floor living quarters, choosing to restore the existing plaster molding, in addition to adding new molding to rooms lacking the adornment.

Taking a chance, Toussaint decided to install pipework for indoor plumbing, emulating some of the grand hotels he'd read about on the East Coast. However, New Orleans hadn't developed the sewer systems East Coast cities enjoyed. As a result, he installed a cistern on the property, in addition to an invention called a septic tank. Toussaint had met its inventor, John Mouras, at a reception while living in France. In any case, he hoped New Orleans would commission the water and sewage projects for their grand city, in time.

Now that the building had been outfitted with plumbing, Toussaint upgraded the home with bathrooms, including porcelain tubs and sinks. He also updated the kitchen with running water. Jannie protested, so he allowed the old-fashioned pump to remain.

On the first floor, the plumber installed two water closets, one toward the front of the building for their mortuary guests and another off the rear of the kitchen for the family. The plumber had told him in a few years he could install one upstairs, once advancements in the trade and the city's infrastructure had been developed.

Progress on the renovation of the mortuary's three chapels and salons on the first floor surprised Toussaint. He'd ordered the latest Victorian furnishings to decorate the spaces, which the maker had just begun to deliver that week.

Toussaint went to the preparation room to check the progress. "Bon!" Toussaint appraised the room with pride. His workspace was now state of the art, complete with all the contemporary tools available to their trade. Inside the cold room, he added a walk-in refrigerated unit. His root cellar remained the same; however, he'd commissioned an extra level to be excavated beneath it, concealed by a secret door. He'd paid the foreman an undisclosed amount of money to forget the unplanned, waterproof cellar.

Within a few weeks of completing the renovation project, New Orleans' prominent Negro families, as well as its
poor (both Black and White), began to flock to his mortuary.
He charged the wealthy Negroes twenty-five percent above
market rate, providing them with the lavish services which
their opulent means dictated. However, many of the poor
he buried in charity, with the help of gifts from associates
in his business and fraternal organizations who sought to
save their souls by building up good works to atone for their
respective, concealed indiscretions.

Peace and pride washed over Toussaint, his work giving
him an even greater joy in his renovated space. Secluded in
the preparation room, he tested his new tools, elevating his
art of preparing the dead for burial to an unanticipated pinnacle of excellence. With the addition of the refrigeration
unit, Toussaint no longer had to bury the dead haste. How
had he worked without it in the past? He still used his cold
cellar for short term clients, only utilizing the refrigerated
unit for longer term guests.

He pulled the shroud over his latest client. He'd considered hiring one of the students at the mortuary school to
help. The workload had become too much for him. Toussaint heard the bottom stair leading to the space squeak. He
waited for his angel to appear, who had sounded the alarm.

"Toussaint?" Jannie glided into the preparation room.

He covered his client, not wishing to distress her. "Yes, darlin'?"

"Monsieur Hamil has come to call. He's waiting for you in the parlor."

"Who is he?" Toussaint asked while washing his instruments in the cleaning solution.

"He's from Normal University." Jannie turned away, unable to fathom what lay beneath the shroud. She wouldn't be able to eat her dinner later and she knew it. She still couldn't stomach her husband's macabre profession after many years of marriage.

Toussaint could see his wife losing her constitution. "Seat him in the parlor. I'll come upstairs in twenty minutes."

Jannie nodded and hurried from the preparation room. Reaching the sanctity of the kitchen, she rushed to the sink and turned on the faucet, which spewed water heavy laden with sediment. She turned off the faucet and used the pump instead. Cupping her hand beneath the cool, clean water flowing from its depths, she allowed it to course across her lips, suppressing her urge to vomit.

Twenty minutes later, Toussaint appeared before his caller in the comfort of the parlor, accented with new furnishings in keeping with the current Victorian fashions.

Jannie served their guest. He didn't wish for his wife to serve anyone, for his mother never had. Yet, Jannie served their guests with pride. She would be insulted if he denied her the honor of doing so. The Lord Jesus had served the sinners of the world with love; he would allow his wife the joy of following the Lord's example. Toussaint adjusted his cravat. "Bonjour, Monsieur Hamil."

"Bonjour, Monsieur Bailey." The men shook hands. Toussaint invited his guest to retake his seat on the sofa. Accepting a cup of tea from Jannie, Toussaint reclined into his wing chair.

The gentlemen discussed a variety of topics for the next hour, everything from the nation's repeal of the Reconstruction Act, national politics, and the overall welfare of Negroes in the wake of slavery. Former slaves had found few opportunities for advancement, unless they'd been favored by their former owners with land bequeaths or other monetary gifts. The men sat in silence for a time. "I read an article in *La Tribune de la Nouvelle-Orleans* concerning the phenomenon of a former, unconnected slave who had managed to prosper," Toussaint said.

Hamil nodded, and then he remembered something. "Why, the fellow's son and daughter attend Normal University."

"Really?"

"Yes, they do. They're doing quite well. When they arrived at the school, the children possessed a command of rudimentary math, reading, and writing. In their short time at the University, the children have excelled at quite a quick pace. We expect them to graduate next year."

Toussaint reached forward and retrieved his cup and saucer, tasting its tepid contents. "Well done."

"Merci." Monsieur Hamil sipped his tea. "We're aware of your studies in France under the Negro mortician Claude Hicks and your internship at Hôtel Dieu." Toussaint seemed uncomfortable to him. Monsieur Hamil cleared his throat. "We would like for you to accept an adjunct professorship at the university, teaching Mortuary Science. We would pay you a stipend. You may take a course for your own enlightenment in business and accounting, free of charge." Toussaint seemed cool toward the offer. "I don't expect an answer now; however, I ask you to consider the opportunity."

Toussaint's mind raced, thinking of all he could teach his students about Mortuary Science, as well as, the business and life skills required for a Negro man to be successful in the South. Many young adults of the new generation had never known slavery and didn't possess an intimate understanding on how to deal with Whites. "I must discuss this with my wife."

"They're the bosses of us all, I'm afraid." Both men

laughed.

"I'll have an answer for you by the end of the week."

"*Bon. Très bien.*" Monsieur Hamil arose from the sofa and shook Toussaint's hand.

Toussaint picked at his roast, unsure how to broach the teaching opportunity with Jannie. He didn't believe she would object; however, it would require more of his time, leaving less for her. Although Jannie had her students and the library to keep her busy, he understood she expected him to spend a certain amount of time with her on a daily basis.

"What is it, Toussaint?"

Toussaint placed a succulent slice of roast in his mouth. Excellent. "Monsieur Hamil offered me the position of adjunct professor at Normal, teaching Mortuary Science."

Jannie left her chair and raced to her husband, sitting on lap. He poked her inner thigh. "That's wonderful. You're taking the position, right?"

He gawked at her. "You want me to?"

"Of course. Why wouldn't I?"

"Well, I would be gone much of the time. Who would maintain the yard?"

Jannie pinched his cheek. He yelped. "You must think I'm stupid."

"What?"

Jannie couldn't stop laughing. "Little Allen Pruett from down the street cuts the lawn."

Toussaint kissed her neck. "I'm glad Father Pierre sent him. He's been a big help with keeping things up around here."

Jannie nodded. "Yes, he has." She gazed into her husband's eyes. "I'm sure your students at Normal will love you. You can't deny them an education. You should accept the appointment." Jannie arose from Toussaint's lap. "And you should take consideration of Allen as well, Toussaint. He has more potential than cutting the grass, cleaning up behind Cherrie, and feeding the dogs." Jannie patted his cheek and then cleared the table of the dinner dishes.

New Orleans, Louisiana. November, 1877.

TO SAY NEGROES had received their emancipation the decade before, Toussaint couldn't help but admire the interior of New Orleans University, although most people still referred to it as either Union Normal School or Straight University. Beginning as only a two-room house, it had swelled to two stories with over twenty rooms, accompanied with several other buildings on Esplanade Avenue.

Toussaint had to admit, his first two semesters of instruction had been rewarding. He worked with those in the medical department to build a robust curriculum for the

Mortuary Sciences, while incorporating into the required coursework Liberal Arts, Biology, Chemistry, Philosophy, Business and Theological Studies.

Monsieur Hamil had been appointed Dean during the semester. Much to his surprise, Toussaint received an invitation from Dean Hamil to meet that afternoon. He guessed Dean Hamil wanted to discuss how to improve the new science discipline he'd implemented.

Toussaint waited in the outer office several moments for the Dean. After ten minutes, the gentleman exited his office and shook Toussaint's hand. "Welcome, Professor Bailey," Dean Hamil said. Extending his arm, he invited Toussaint into his office.

Toussaint sat in the leather banker's chair and accepted a cup of coffee from Dean Hamil. After a few moments of discussing the progress of Toussaint's labs and lectures on Mortuary Science, as well as the progress of his students, the Dean came to the point. "I would like for you to go to the rural areas of Louisiana and recruit students, with a focus on those who exhibit not only the promise to excel in academics overall, but also the acumen for the mortuary curriculum as well."

The new opportunity excited Toussaint. Traveling the back roads of Louisiana concerned him, but he knew he could overcome any adversity he may encounter along the way. "I'm honored," Toussaint said.

Dean Hamil lit his pipe. "You've done excellent work with the students here, Professor Bailey. Your students excel across the board, in both their core subjects and their degree coursework. Your students possess some of the highest grade point averages in this institution." Toussaint nodded. "That's why I would like you to accept this opportunity. You have a knack for selecting high achievers." Dean Hamil opened the ledger. "We've received some generous grants which have been earmarked for scholarships."

Toussaint was unsure of what to say. Maybe he should discuss it with Jannie first, but he knew she wouldn't want him to pass up the opportunity. "I accept, Dean Hamil."

"Bon!" Dean Hamil reviewed his desk calendar. "I would like to have at least five new students by the time classes resume in January. So…" The Dean flipped through the calendar. "Please plan to leave by the semester's end."

Toussaint's eyes grew large. "That's next week."

The Dean stared at him. "Well, if you can't do it, I understand."

Toussaint knew Jannie was going to have a fit. "I will discuss it with my wife. I'm sure the timing won't prove to be a problem."

***

Toussaint placed his head in his hands.

"Next week? You're leaving next week?"

Toussaint tried not to sweat. "You don't want me to do it, Jannie?"

"You know I do," Jannie said. "But Thanksgiving and Christmas are coming." Jannie shoulders slumped. She couldn't, in good conscious, deny him the opportunity. "Will you return home by Christmas?"

Toussaint scooped her up, spinning her around the room. "You know I will, baby." He kissed her, sealing the deal.

"Where are you going?" Jannie asked.

"Tickfaw."

La Rose Plantation, St. Helena Parish. August 31, 1963.

HEARING A CLICKING sound, Julian opened his eyes to find his grandmère leaving the room. "Where are you going?"

"To the bathroom." Lela continued to the door, her hair curling into tiny ringlets, growing tighter. Her heels sunk into the parquet floors, leaving a forged trail. Her dress was damp with perspiration. Lela opened the door to leave.

"Grandmère wait," Julian said. She turned to him. Her makeup had mutated into war paint. "Aren't you going to tell me what happened?"

"What do you mean?"

"What happened in Tickfaw?"

"Nothing important." Lela pursed her lips. "Mon fils, like I told you earlier. I don't care to know what happened in Tickfaw." Lela closed her eyes. The flushed red hue of her face retreated down to her décolletage. "I'm tired, Julian. Would you mind if I retired for the evening?" Julian nodded. Lela left the parlor, closing the door behind her.

PART III

Chapter 1

La Rose Plantation, St. Helena Parish. September 1, 1963

Walking the crushed pebble path, Julian admired the fountains, lawns, and gardens. If he didn't know better, he would have believed he strolled the gardens of Versailles. However, the punishing humidity kept him grounded in the reality of Louisiana. Even at eight o'clock in the morning, Julian inhaled the atmosphere of a steam room.

The gardens went on for at least three miles, fading into the horizon. Misery lay beyond the garden's edge, concealed by fir and box trees. No one would think fields of cotton, indigo, tobacco and sugar cane lay beyond the curving walls of the eastern border, where hundreds had toiled, suffered, and died at his own hand.

"I am not Augustus."

Although he repeated the affirmation to himself, it did little to dismantle the truth within him. Peering down the center axis, Julian could see a geyser of water shooting up over the tops of the bosquets. Julian didn't wish to be violated by the sight of the lewd statue in the fountain. Instead he turned, strolling down a small allée lined with palissades on either side.

After a short distance, he came to the *pate d'oie*, discovering yet another fountain. A marble angel stood within its center, its arms and wings extended upward, his eyes filled with longing for his former home of heaven. Roses sprung forth from his chest. One rose, the largest rose he'd ever seen, surged past the others into full bloom, pointed upward like a trumpet. Its stem was covered with thorns. An apron, emblazoned with symbols he'd never seen before, covered the angel's groin.

"How about that? Modesty." Julian sat at the baroque fountain's edge. He leaned over and ran his fingers through the hot water. He'd expected it to be cool.

"It should be. However, it's already eighty-five degrees and it is only eight o'clock. The water may reach its boiling point soon."

Julian grabbed the edge of the fountain to prevent himself from falling in. The creepy gardener he'd met when he had first arrived at La Rose stood on the walkway, edging grass which didn't need edging. "Bonjour, mon fils," the gardener said.

"Good morning."

The gardener placed the clippers in his holster and walked over to the fountain, sitting beside Julian. "Did you enjoy your stay?"

"It was fine." Julian didn't understand his need to confide in the man. "Well, it was a bit stressful."

"How so, mon fils?"

Julian thought about his experience. "I wasn't myself, but at the same time I was. But then, I learned my other self wasn't me after all." Julian dislodged some crushed pebbles from between the granite paving stones with the toe of his shoe. "At times, I thought I was the racist Augustus Chevalier. But I'm not him. I'm Julian. I'm not a racist."

The gardener nodded, considering his words. "No, you're not. But perhaps you have a superiority complex like the former master here? Perhaps you think you can control and manage everyone you love?" The gardener removed his towel, wiping away water which had splashed onto the fountain's edge.

"I am no one. I am just the gardener here. However, I will say this." The gardener peered into Julian's eyes with love and compassion. "Forgive yourself. Love yourself. If you do these things, you can love others around you as you love yourself. I borrow my words from the true Master and Teacher, Jesus Christ. His words are true. What our Savior has said is true. This I do know." He watched the boy sit in silence, tormented by his inner conflict. "Well, think about it another day. I'm guessing Madame and the lovely Suzette are packed and ready to leave."

"Where are they going?"

"Back to New Orleans. You're going with them. Didn't you know?"

Julian admired the Louisiana sky. He didn't wish to leave. He belonged on La Rose. Yet, La Rose had corrupted him.

"You are correct. However, La Rose is where you found your salvation as well." He patted his thigh. "It's time to go."

Julian nodded. "Thank you for talking to me—" Julian found himself alone. "Now I know, for sure. You're the sanitation guy from New Orleans." His family was crazy. Julian left the fountain's edge, prepared to face his life once more.

"Where's Lawrence?" Irritated, Julian opened the massive, heavy front door of the mansion. "Dammit!" He'd almost tripped. He found his grandmère's luggage lined up, along with Suzette's, and Theo's. He snickered as he ascended the central stair. His grandmère never went anywhere without the ancient set of Louis Vuitton luggage. He had little doubt she'd known the founder and he'd custom made the set for her. Turning the gold door knob, Julian entered his room.

He checked the dresser drawers and found them all empty. Walking across the room, he entered the closet, which was the size of very large living room. Everything was gone. "Where in the hell are my things?"

"I'se packed them for you, suh."

Julian turned to find Nanette standing behind him in a simple floral dress, staring at the floor. "Thank you," he said. Nanette turned to leave. "Wait," Julian said. She stopped, but didn't turn to face him. "Is my attaché case still here?" She turned and walked over to the Edwardian desk and retrieved it. She handed it to him. Julian placed it atop the desk and opened the lid. Finding the depression point, he opened the secret compartment and removed a gold coin. "I want you to hold this for me."

Nanette examined the coin. "This here is gold." She turned to coin between her finger tips. "This here man on the horse is trying to kill something." She turned the coin over to find a crest of some kind, reminding her of the many crests lining the walls of the plantation house. "Why'se you givin' me this?"

Julian didn't really know why. He felt bad for how he'd treated her when he'd first arrived. However, he didn't feel bad enough to give her the coin. His father, Robert, had given him the coin before he left San Francisco to attend school at Morehouse. He'd said to Julian, "Slay dragons and take their gold."

He signed a deed and handed it to the trader. Julian stared at the young lady. *Nicka.* A chill ran through him. He shook it off. He'd been listening to his grandmère's stories too long. "You may have to battle a dragon one day. Here's your charm for the battle." He watched Nanette stare at the coin. "It's called a Sovereign; it comes from England. This is an image of St. George battling a dragon." Julian gave her hand a quick pat and turned to leave. "Just hold it. No back talk. Close my case and bring it to the car." Julian left the room.

"Lawd, I'se sho' is gonna miss you Ma'Dame," Lawrence said. Tears streamed down the enormous man's face, reduced to a child whose mother was leaving him behind to tour a foreign land, unsure of when he'd see her again.

"Please stop, Lawrence. You're going to make me cry," Lela said.

Lawrence considered the young girl who now resided in the body of a centenarian. Lela was still beautiful, attired in a white sateen dress with a full skirt and matching hat. "Next time we'se sees each other, I'se hopes you'se won't leave me ever again." He kissed her on the cheek. "And you too, Miss Sue."

"*Mon Ange*, we will meet again."

"Reckons we'se will. But you'se knows you won't know me right off," Lawrence said, grinning slick. "*Oui, ma chere?*"

Suzette blushed. "Stop it."

Hearing a floorboard creak, they all turned their attention to the central landing of the grand staircase. Julian descended, with Nanette following behind. Lela waited at the foot of the stairs to meet him. Still a king, he descended the stairs with majesty. All he was missing was a crown.

Lela admired her child, having defeated his demons at the grand home. La Rose still reminded Lela of the Opera Garnier in France. In fact, the staircase of La Rose's grand hall resembled the central stair of opera house a great deal.

Julian appeared an angel, attired in his white linen suit. The whole scene took her breath away. Lela would remember the day forever, the day he took control of the terrors and heartaches lurking within his soul since the beginning of time. She knew these damning spirits would rear their heads again, but now he was conscious of their existence. She and the Good Lord had prepared him for the life-long battle.

Reaching the bottom of the staircase, Julian stopped before her and bowed. He saw Suzette dab her eye. Sap. "Are you ready, Grandmère?"

"Almost," she said. "Nanette, would you come here, please?"

The young girl approached her queen, honoring her with an informal curtsy. Lela kissed the child on the forehead. "Lawrence?"

"Yes, Ma'Dame?"

"Has all been made ready?"

The staff filled the grand hall. Lawrence went to his office and returned a short time later with a gold box. He presented it to Lela.

Lela thumbed through the envelopes in the box, coming to the one she searched for inscribed 'Nicka'. She removed the envelope and handed it to Nanette. "This is for you, my child."

Nanette opened the manila envelope and removed its contents. She began to cry. "What's this you'se givin' me, Ma'Dame?"

Lela smiled at the photo. "My God," she said, appraising the group standing before La Rose's cotton gin. At one time, it had been the only gin in the parish. Her father had charged the neighboring farmers a fortune to gin their cotton. "Well, I'm guessing the woman on the left is your great-great-great-grandmère, and my sister, Nicka." Lela dried her eyes with her gloved hand. She'd never laid eyes on her sister before. "Who are the other people in this photo, Lawrence?"

Lawrence walked over and appraised the picture. "This was right before you'se left for France wit' Mis'sur James. 'Members, you'se had that high yella boy come out here and take pictures. What was his name?" Lawrence thought about it for a moment. "Solomon Phillipe. Sho' was!"

Lawrence began to laugh, patting his heart. "That fella was the most uppity man I'd ever met. He didn't care for takin' pictures of the staff 'round here. I'se guess he only took pictures of Creoles and society folks in New Orleans." Lela shook her head. "Well, you musta paid him a heap of money to do it."

Lela put on her reading glasses. "Jamie compensated him handsomely. He photographed the Roberts Plantation and the staff there as well." Lela sighed. "Such a hateful man. How unfortunate."

"Sho' was. But he did take fine pictures." Lawrence pointed to a person in the photo. "That's Nicka's daughter, Tabby, her grandson Saul, and her great-granddaughter, Carrie. Ya'll knows Stank, Nicka's son. He came on back home when he heard Ma'Dame was havin' folk's pictures made." The joy and happiness of the time enveloped his heart. "And that's me, with my arm around Nicka." Lawrence eyes filled with tears, admiring the photograph.

Lela noticed the big, broad, smile on Lawrence's face in the photo, his eyes fixed on Nicka who stared straight ahead, emotionless, with her arms crossed. Lela could see Lawrence's love for Nicka in his eyes. "Lawrence, I never knew Nicka had another child."

Not hearing Lela, Lawrence shuffled to the next photograph. "This here's Carrie and her little girl Sweetie, who'se

I'se holding. Sweetie is Nanette's mama." Lawrence placed his arm around Nanette's shoulder, holding her tight. He kissed her on her forehead. "Yup, sho' is," he said. Lawrence fell silent, appraising the beautiful young girl before him. "You'se just like Nicka. I'se 'clare 'fore God you is!" He hugged her tight, unable to let her go.

Lela smiled, seeing the truth. So, he'd had a love too. Nannette was his child with Sweetie. Happiness surged into Lela's heart, observing the love Lawrence held for her. "How did Sweetie die, Lawrence?"

The tall dark man turned red, but then he suppressed his emotions. "Miss Sweetie died givin' birth to this precious li'l thang here. I'se remembers the day. The birth was real hard on Sweetie. There wasn't nuthin' I'se could do to make it better.

"When li'l ole Nanette left her maman, we'se didn't even have time to clean her up." Lawrence inhaled deep. "We'se wrapped Nanette in a blanket and placed her in her maman's arms. Sweetie kissed her baby and closed her eyes. She'd smiled the strangest smile I'se done seen in years." Lawrence wiped his tears and turned away.

Nanette couldn't break her gaze with the photograph. "Can I'se have this, Ma'Dame?"

"Of course. I had copies made of all the family photos for not only you, but everyone," Lela said, addressing the staff gathered around. She could hear a few of the older members gasp, for the only image they'd maintained of their loved ones was in their hearts. "All of you should know what your ancestors looked like, what they did here at La Rose, and how they loved each of you without ever knowing you. If you understood how they suffered here," Lela stopped herself, redirecting her focus to love's joys and fruits.

"I didn't have the chance to make the formal presentation to all of you as I'd planned, but I wanted each of you to have the photos. During the 1920's, a lady named Dorothea Lang visited La Rose. One of my patrons at the house in New Orleans had known Dorothea and arranged for her to visit. She was just embarking upon her career as a photographer. My client believed photographing former slaves would be a good experience for her. Miss Lange gave me the negatives and the photos. I don't believe the world even knows these photographs exist."

Nanette studied the photograph. Although she'd seen the photo of her mother and Lawrence from time to time, she'd never seen the Lange photos before.

Wandering across the great hall, Julian stopped before her and snatched the photo from her hand. He glared at it, unable to take his eyes off Nicka. Julian returned the photo to Nanette and walked away.

"Doncha pay him no mind, honey," Lawrence said.

Nanette patted his hand, choking back her emotion. "He don't bother me no more," she said. "Well Mistah Larry, I guess I'se should git the rest of these pictures passed out."

Lela handed her the box, containing envelopes inscribed with each ancestor's name. "I would like to thank Lawrence and Suzette for organizing all of this," Lela said, addressing all those present. The La Rose staff applauded, filling the great hall with praise. Lawrence blushed.

"I did nothing, Madame. Lawrence did all the work. I only inscribed the envelopes with the names he told me," Suzette said.

"I'se couldn't have done it wit'out you, Miss Sue. I'se don't writes so well."

Lela couldn't believe Lawrence had fixed his mouth to make such a statement. In heaven, he'd written incredible sonnets on love, inspiring some the Earth's greatest poets and authors. He just wanted to spend time with Suzette. Lela knew he'd always been sweet on her.

Lawrence winked at Lela.

"Are you finished, Grandmère? I'm ready to go."

The boy had a low threshold for love and sentiment; however, Lela could feel his heart had softened. She let it go. Lela gave her impatient great-grandson a curt nod.

Julian extended his arm, creating a triangular shape. Filled with the enamored genteel sentiment of a débutante,

Lela placed her hand upon his arm, allowing him to lead the way.

"Bonjour, Mis'sur Julian."

"Lawrence."

Reaching the massive doors ahead of the party, Lawrence swung them both open in one motion and stepped aside, allowing them to exit. The staff, at least one hundred people, lined both sides of the drive.

Theo opened the Cadillac door, awaiting his royal family. Julian assisted Lela into the car. Once he found her to be comfortable, he opened the passenger door for Suzette. He ran around the vehicle and entered, sitting next to his grand-mère on the back seat.

The rev and then the hum of the engine relaxed Julian. He admired the household staff in their formal attire, the gardeners and field workers, along with the tradesmen and women, in the best overalls and dresses, holding the instruments of their trades. The household help stood in ranks with them in their formal attire. Emotion and a new-found admiration for them all welled in Julian's heart as the Cadillac circled the drive and descended hill, leaving La Rose Plantation.

"This is going to take forever."

"What was that, Julian?"

"Nothing, Grandmère." If he'd known La Rose had a landing strip, he would have insisted on taking the jet. What the hell? There had been no reason to drive. He hated driving.

Julian's grandmère looked out the window, her eyes affixed on Floridian Louisiana's landscape. Although he would never tell her, he believed his grandmère to be the most elegant woman in the world. The full, white skirt of her iridescent dupioni silk dress fanned across the back seat, her bust showcased in the V-necked bodice. He loved the three-quarter length sleeves with turned up cuffs, converging into a soft 'v' beneath her elbow, accented with a pink rose appliqué.

Who would wear so many jewels on a car ride through the backwoods of Louisiana? Yet, his grandmère did. On the lapel of her dress, she wore a diamond pin set in platinum, depicting a dagger topped with a rose. Little rubies dripped from the tip of the diamond dagger. Julian guessed the rubies represented the blood of the wicked. Grandmère had some of the creepiest jewels.

Her hat was fabulous, with a full, oblong shaped brim. Lela removed it, and then placed it on the seat between them. She removed her gloves and smoothed her platinum colored hair back into her bun.

He wondered what portion of his grandmère's fortune Madame Chanel had gleaned from her over the years? But as he considered the ensemble she wore, it didn't appear to be Chanel. It troubled him he could recognize Chanel's designs. What man was cognizant of women's fashions unless they were a designer or some type of sissy?

"Watch your mouth, Julian. Do not dismiss or be cruel to others because they're different. Love everyone."

"I didn't say anything."

"You didn't have to."

Julian turned red. "I am not the Allen & Burns radio show. Stop listening to my thoughts."

"No, you are the Julian Charles Chamberie Show. I can hear you, if I chose. I've told you before, control your thoughts." Lela removed her Cartier compact from her purse and checked her face. Satisfied, she closed the compact and replaced it in her bag.

"Oh, and by the way, Gabriel didn't design this for me. You are correct when you say this isn't her style," she said. "You've been surrounded by her designs all of your life. I would be shocked if you couldn't tell the difference. She designed your mother's wardrobe for years."

Lela fluffed her skirt, allowing it to cascade down upon the seat. "Monsieur Dior designed this for me years ago. I haven't purchased anything new since before you left in '53." Lela patted his hand. "I guess I should make some calls and place some orders. Oui, mon fils?"

Julian nodded. "Always keep it fresh, Grandmère. But you still look incredible in your old clothes."

Pompous little peacock. Lela admired her great-grandson's linen suit. "Your suit doesn't appear to be off the rack."

Julian smoothed his lapels and adjusted his wristwatch. "Of course not. I have a tailor. He makes everything for me, down to my socks and boxers."

Lela smirked. "Do tell? And who is this master tailor?"

"A gentleman named Manny," Julian said. "He was trained in France. He has shops in San Francisco and Washington D.C." Lela shook her head. "In fact, when I picked up this suit and other items suitable for the Louisiana climate, he gave me a card with the address for his shop in New Orleans. Who would have believed he would have a shop in New Orleans?"

"My goodness, Julian. That is unbelievable," Lela said. "It's as if he follows you everywhere you go." Suzette snickered from the front seat.

"I know. It is." Julian considered the strange coincidence. "Well, as you can see, he is very convenient. He always has shops wherever I am. He's available whenever I need him. Manny implied he maintained an exclusive clientele."

Suzette grunted.

"Something stuck in your craw, old woman?"

"Oui, mon fils. I always choke on *naiveté.*"

Evil old biddy. "Anyway, he made my wardrobe before going away to Morehouse. Nice sweaters, slacks, shirts. He made my tennis clothes. He even has a cobbler who made my shoes. He is very accommodating. And his prices are great. With his experience and quality of work, he could make as much as the top designers. Yet, he is satisfied maintaining small shops for an exclusive clientele, selling his apparel at reasonable prices." Julian shook his head in disbelief. "Grandmère, he undercuts what the department stores charge for sub-standard articles. He's a find, that's for sure. I'm lucky he accepted me as a client."

"Oh really? And how did you find him?"

"Well I…" Julian combed his memory. "Funny I can't remember. I must have seen an ad in the paper. Maybe Monpère told me about him." Julian thought about it further. "No, I was walking through the Presidio area in San Francisco. He had his shop door open and I went in. The samples he presented impressed me. I've been with him since then."

"You would have been the first in centuries not to," Suzette said in French.

"I would have been what, Suzette?" Julian asked, not fully understanding her.

"You would have been a fool not to choose him."

"Well, we all know I'm not a fool." Silence ranged throughout the car. Julian looked out of the window on his grandmère's side of the car, when the light pinged off her unsettling brooch. "What's with the creepy pin?"

"What? Oh." Lela stroked it. "Your grandpère gave it to me. He was trying to atone for his sins." Lela reclined into the seat and grinned.

"He cheated on you?" Julian asked.

"I wish to forget those days," Suzette said from the front seat.

"It wasn't that bad, Suzette," Lela said. She shifted in her seat to face Julian. "Your grandpère enjoyed carousing with your Uncle Toot."

"Perhaps Toussaint had been compelled to carouse with Monsieur, Madame?"

"Well, I don't remember exactly, Suzette. In any case, I had tired of it. So, I left him."

Julian couldn't believe it, although she'd mentioned the event for the second time. "You actually left your husband, Grandmère?"

"Oui, mon fils. I did."

Suzette grunted. "If that is what you wish to call it."

"Hush, Suzette," Lela said. "In any case, I'd made my point. After he'd begged for my forgiveness, I returned to our home in Paris with him. When I entered his bedroom (we had separate rooms back then), I stopped breathing. On the bed sat the largest gold jewelry box I'd ever seen, about the size of one of my large steamer trunks. I opened it, finding it filled with jewels.

"The box itself was beautiful, embossed with enameled roses, angels and the family's crest on top. It had a chalice molded under each handle. There were strange scenes depicted on the side of the case. I can't recall the images right at this moment." Lela closed her eyes, hoping to picture the scenes in her mind's eye. She gave up. "Humph, I haven't thought of the box since Toussaint installed the vault in my bedroom. Where is it, Suzette?"

"It's in the attic with the rest of your things, Madame."

Julian's mouth fell open. "The attic? You've stored a solid gold jewelry box the size of steamer trunk in the attic?"

Suzette tucked a red curl under her hat. "Oui. Where else would we put it?"

Lela nodded. "We need to go through the attic, Suzette."

"One day, Madame." Suzette knew it wouldn't happen. Lela had been planning to clean the attic for fifty years.

"Theo, see if you can contact Allen Pruett. Perhaps he can help us."

"Aw'rite Ma'Dame."

Lela didn't feel like going through the attic. She had too many things. Maybe Julian hiring an auctioneer wasn't such a bad idea. Lela looked out the window. *I'm not selling a damn thing,* she said to herself. "Well anyway, this was one of my gifts. Isn't it beautiful?"

"Yes, Grandmère. It's beautiful." *They are crazy*. His family regarded gold as tin.

"Gold is plentiful, Julian. Why, is there a shortage?" Lela asked. "What? Should we invest in another fortified building to keep our things? I'm tired of paying for them. Our things can stay in the attic. It's free."

Julian sighed. There was no sense in trying to reason with the insane. He turned his attention to the passing scenery. Broken down shack. Old barn. Cow. Grass. Trees. Telephone lines. Country store with old men sitting on the porch reading the newspaper. Train tracks without a train. Julian looked at his Rolex watch. They'd been driving forever. "I'm bored. How long before we arrive in New Orleans?"

"Boy, stop whinin'," Theo said. "We ain't been in the car forty minutes. We'se gonna git there when we git there. Now stop worryin' me."

Julian crossed his arms and looked out the window. If Theo drove more than thirty miles per hour, it wouldn't take two days to return home. He caught sight of an upcoming speed limit sign. Forty-five miles per hour. He craned his neck to see around the driver's seat in front of him. Theo was pushing thirty-seven miles per hour. A Packard and a pickup truck came into view, passing their car on the left. "The speed limit is forty-five miles per hour. Drive faster."

"*Je vais l'étrangler. Je promets,*" Suzette said. Theo patted her hand.

"Julian, you're getting on everyone's nerves. Suzette is ready to strangle you." Lela said. "Stop complaining and look out the window."

"Besides, we just left Tickfaw, boy. The speed limit in town is thirty miles per hour. I'se cain't just go speeding through their town, now can I?" Theo checked his speedometer. "You'se should learn to appreciate the ride, boy. That's how you learn what folks are all about. You'se can see how they live, where they shop, and what they grow."

Nobody asked you, Julian retorted within. Theo slowed down to thirty-five miles per hour. What the hell?

"Besides, the highway men are rough 'round here," Theo said to Julian.

Julian resolved himself to the fact he'd be in his thirties by the time they reached New Orleans. If he had his Maserati, he would have arrived in New Orleans thirty minutes ago. "You can at least turn on the radio," Julian said.

Theo reached for the radio and turned the dial. "If I'se remembers right, we'se can pick up that radio station out of New Orleans." The station crackled, going in and out. Theo fiddled with the dial.

"You drive. I will try." Suzette adjusted the knob for another three minutes.

"Oh God, I'm going crazy," Julian said. He heard his grandmère sigh. The radio came in clear. "Thank you, Grandmère," he said. She nodded and returned her attention to the passing scenery.

Theo blew the horn. Julian looked out the window on the passenger's side and saw an old Black man, on a mowing tractor, wearing a straw hat. He seemed to wave out of courtesy. As their car passed, the man on the tractor recognized them. He removed his hat and waved at them, excited. It surprised Julian that Theo didn't stop the car, so they could visit for the next two hours.

"You know who'se that was, Ma'Dame?" Theo said. "Lawd I'se thought he wouldda been long dead by now."

"Who, Theo?"

"You prob'ly knew his mama's people. That's Brenda Mae's boy."

"McAllister?"

"Naw, not that Brenda Mae. Brenda Mae Pegues."

Lela combed her memory. "You're right. Mon Dieu, I haven't thought of them in years. What was his name? He was one of Peter O'Bannion's and Stank's friends."

"Yeah. Friends," Theo said. "His name is Bobby Pegues. That boy used to run so many books in New Orleans the Feds were lookin' for him. Peter had to send him on 'vacation' for a while." Theo wiped the tears from his eyes as he suppressed an onslaught of uncontrollable laughter. "I used to carry Josephine out here to his mama's honky-tonk."

"Josephine was coming out here? The way she used to complain about Brenda Mae cutting into the house's business?"

"Jo knew they weren't competing with us. I'se don't even know why she would fix her lips to say that." Theo grabbed a stick of gum out of his pocket. He fumbled with the wrapper as he drove. The car drifted toward the left, into oncoming traffic.

"I will open it," Suzette said. She partially removed the foil and gave it to him. Theo returned the car to the proper lane, avoiding an oncoming pick-up truck.

"Thanks, Sue."

At least we didn't die. Now I must listen to him smack on the gum. Julian looked out the window.

"I'se ain't gonna kill you, boy." Theo smacked on the gum. It was sticking to his dentures. "I'se thank I was ridin' Jo 'round in that pretty Duesy back then. Anyway, one night we were down there to Brenda Mae's havin' a good time. I'se was shootin' dice out back wit' Bobby and the boys while Jo was dancin' and socializin' with the fellas inside. They'd left their poker game to dance wit' her." Theo frowned. "She never did want to watch me shoot dice. Anyway, ole Henry Gouch came up in the joint wit' his shot gun, mad as hell.

He accused Bobby of sleepin' with his wife again." Theo shook his head.

"Well, you know Brenda Mae didn't care for no shit goin' down in her place. She came out there on the back porch wit' her hunting rifle, cocked and ready. As soon as Henry made a move to raise his weapon…" Theo happened to look back in his rearview mirror. Lela had arched her eyebrow so hard it rose like a mountain peak above the rim of her sunglasses. "Well, I don't reckon I'se saw ole Henry after that night. I'se guess he moved away."

Julian scrutinized his grandmère and Theo. "You left something out."

"Like what?" Theo said. He returned his attention to the road. "Well, we'se almost to Hammond. Ain't gonna be long now."

"Yeah, only another few days before we reach New Orleans," Julian muttered under his breath. "Ow! Why did you pinch me?" Julian rubbed his thigh.

"I asked you to stop complaining. Take a nap," Lela said.

Julian looked out the window. Grass. Trees. Cows. Cotton. Weeds. Passing truck. Trees. He consulted his watch. Twenty minutes had passed, and they still hadn't reached Hammond. Julian peered out the windshield, there had to be traffic. There was no one on the road.

Julian heard a faint whine approaching their car from

behind. Theo stared at him in the rear-view mirror, and then diverted his eyes to the road behind them. Julian turned around in his seat to the back window. The color drained from his face. "Are you speeding Theo?"

Theo continued to stare into the rear-view mirror. He watched the patrol car speed toward them, the sirens growing louder. "Naw, I'se ain't."

Fuck. Now this. Julian turned to his grandmère. She removed her cat eye sunglasses, inserted them in their case, and placed them in her purse. Fishing around inside her handbag, she removed a pair of large, round, black sunglasses, the size of headlights. She put them on and returned her attention to the passing scenery. Julian could hear the siren close in behind their car. The approaching vehicle didn't pass. Theo pulled the car over.

A White deputy appeared at Theo's window with the largest beer belly Julian had ever seen. His skin was red and shiny from spending too much time in the sun. "You'se in a hurry, Nigger?"

"Naw, suh. I'se ain't."

The deputy leaned over to look inside the car, resting his belly on the door. "Is this here your employer, boy?"

"Yessuh, she is."

The deputy scrutinized Suzette, sitting in the front, and the two sitting in the back. "Why them Mulatto, Creole, hell whatever these highfalutin' Niggers call themselves, sittin' in the back while this White lady is up front with you, Nigger?"

"She's our employer. That's her great-grandson."

"Humph. Ain't this some shit?" The deputy spit tobacco on the road. "All ya'll git out the car."

"The ladies will remain inside. We will get out," Julian said.

"Yella Nigger, who asked you?"

"You better watch how you talk to me—"

"*Tais toi*, Julian!" Lela opened the door and exited the car, followed by her entourage.

The deputy snickered. "So, you'se some ole fancy Creole bitch from New Orleans?" He looked down at her hands. "Are those rings real, gal? They'se looks like diamonds. You'se steal them?"

Lela arched her eyebrow, undetectable to the deputy.

Julian noticed a second squad car pull up. A deputy got out of the car, drawing his night stick. *I'm not going to allow them to kill my people on this road.*

We will be fine.

Julian frowned at his grandmère, but held his tongue. The second deputy walked up. "What we got here, Deputy Charlie?"

Deputy Charlie spat again, just missing Lela's shoes. "I done caught these Niggers speeding through here in this stolen Cadillac. The White Nigger there is wearing stolen jewelry, Jonesy."

Deputy Jones assessed the group of travelers, stopping before Lela to examine her jewelry. "Ma'am, will extend your hands for me? And please, remove your sunglasses."

Lela moved her glasses to the top of her head. She presented her hands to deputy, extending her fingers.

The deputy locked eyes with her, and then a force he couldn't explain caused him to fixate on her hands. On her left hand sat a diamond larger than any he'd ever seen in his entire life. He couldn't even guess the size of it. Her right hand horrified him. On the ring finger, she wore a solid gold ring emblazoned with the letter 'C', with a rose trellising around it. "Where ya'll coming from, Ma'am?"

Lela sneered. "St. Helena."

Deputy Jones panicked. "Call in their license plates."

"Naw, Jonesy. We can handle this thang here ourselves." He got up in Julian's face.

Deputy Jones panted, trying to catch his breath. "I know you don't listen to me because you outrank me. But if don't ever listen to me again, listen to me now. Call the station and have them run the plates."

Deputy Charlie had never seen fear in his subordinate's eyes. He decided to humor him. "I didn't want to trouble the sheriff with this, but I'll do it." Lumbering back to his car,

Deputy Charlie reached in through the open window and grabbed the speaker. "This here Car 16, come back ya'll."

The radio crackled. "We'se copy ya'll."

"Run this here plate for me. Louisiana LCR0214."

The radio went silent for a few minutes. "This here is Sheriff Howard. Who'se you got pulled over, Charlie?"

Perspiration burst forth on Deputy Charlie's forehead. The sheriff never got on the radio. "Some Niggers with a red head White gal. She's old as hell. Damn, all of them are, except for the young Nigger who the driver said is the old Creole bitch's great-grandson."

The line reverberated with silence. "I'll be there in five minutes."

"The station is ten miles away. How you gonna do that, Sheriff?"

Four minutes later, the sheriff sped up and screeched to a stop beside them. He jumped out the car and ran to where they all stood. "It is you."

"Pauley," Lela said.

Red flushed Deputy Charlie's neck. "You know them?"

"Shut the fuck up, Charlie," Sheriff Howard said. "Madame, I'm sorry for how you were treated here today. Please, continue on your way. I'll have Deputy Jones escort ya'll back to New Orleans."

"Do all Negroes traveling through your Parish require an escort, Pauley? Oh, I see. A good word or a nod from someone in authority is required for Negroes to pass safely through these parts?" The sheriff lowered his eyes, staring at the road. "I remember your family's name before your maman married Monsieur Howard. It was Salvatorie. I knew your grandfather, personally. Benito was a good friend of mine, Pauley. When Benito needed a friend, did I ask questions?"

"You'se a Dago, Sheriff?"

Sheriff Howard removed his hat to wipe away the sweat. "I'm trying to help you, Charlie. Shut the fuck up." Sheriff Howard remembered his manners. "Sorry, Madame Lela."

She nodded.

"Who in the hell is this Nigger and why you kowtowin' to her?"

Sheriff Howard accepted the fact Charlie couldn't be saved. "You picked the wrong one today, Charlie." Sheriff Howard ran his fingers through his hair. "You've pulled over Madame Lela Chevalier. A lot of folks, powerful folks, like and respect her not only in New Orleans, but across the country."

Confusion skated across Charlie's face. Sheriff Howard could see he hadn't heard of her. Deputy Jones lowered his head. Sheriff Howard could see Deputy Jones knew of the family and had probably told Charlie's dumb ass to run the plates. "She's the daughter of an old planter from up in St. Helena named Augustus Chevalier. Madame Chevalier still owns half of St. Helena and Tangipahoa Parishes, each." Sheriff Howard turned to Lela. "You comin' from there, Madame?"

Lela adjusted her signet ring. "Should it matter where we're coming from Sheriff Howard? What laws have we broken? Must White travelers endure the same treatment in this parish, coerced into presenting their travel itineraries to law enforcement agents?"

"What's an itin'rary?"

Ignoring his subordinate, Sheriff's Howard heart thumped hard. What if word of this got back to his family? Growing up, he remembered Madame Chevalier to be a kind woman with a brutal heart toward those who embraced hate. "Madame, we try to be fair, but I can't control everyone," Sheriff Howard said.

"What does 'being fair' have to do with anything?" Lela refused to go into a rant about treating others with respect and decency. "So, you're telling me you weren't aware of Deputy Charlie's treatment of Negro travelers through *your* parish?"

Shame consumed him. "It won't happen again, Madame," he assured her, his eyes cold. "The matter will be handled."

Lela nodded, satisfied. "Bon."

"And Deputy Jones?"

Lela shrugged her lips a bit. "He treated me with respect."

Jones clutched his chest with tears in his eyes, relieved. "Thank you, Madame. Thank you!"

Lela nodded.

"Jones, escort Madame Chevalier to her home in New Orleans. Charlie, go 'bout your business."

Jones ran to his squad car and pulled it in front of the Cadillac. Julian opened Lela's door for her to enter, but instead, she walked over to Charlie. "What?" Deputy Charlie asked.

Lela spoke to him in a language none of them could understand. Once she finished, she put on her sunglasses. "I am ready, Julian." She entered the car and they pulled away, led by Deputy Jones.

"Uppity Niggers," Charlie said. He spat out the remnant of tobacco lodging in his mouth.

Sheriff Howard pitied Charlie, too stupid to get a clue. At times, he couldn't understand the persistent, unrelenting ignorance and stupidity of men. Hell, anyone should be able to figure out when they shouldn't screw with a person. "You're the dumbest, most ig'nant specimen of White trash

I done ever met in my entire life, Charlie," Sheriff Howard said. He returned to his squad car and sped away.

"We'se back," Theo said, opening the door. Jimmy hurried into the entry hall, followed by the younger boys who continued out to the car to bring in the luggage. Theo relaxed, enjoying the cold air filling the room from the new window air conditioner they'd installed prior to Julian's arrival.

Lela sat on the sofa, allowing the arctic breeze to cool her neck. "Where is everyone?"

"We just walked in too, Grandmère. How should we know?" Julian said. He found it strange no one other than Jimmy and the boys had greeted them. Usually, Sissy and Isabel bounced around at the door like little puppies waiting for their mistress to return.

"Haven't you learned anything, Julian?"

"About what?" Julian walked through the house to the solarium, where he found Isabel, Sissy, and Mario riveted to the television set. When had he returned? Julian let it go. "Watching your stories?" Julian went the bar cart and poured himself a drink.

"No, mon fils. Today is Sunday. Our stories don't air on Sunday." Isabel left the sofa to adjust the antenna. The picture had become fuzzy once Julian walked in. Not surprising.

"We're watching the midday news," Isabel replied.

"What, did some shrimp and oysters go bad down on the docks?" He cracked himself up sometimes.

"Naw. The Law out there on Route 51 done found an empty squad car. They can't find the deputy. They'se gittin' ready to search the area," Sissy said, tossing a nut into her mouth. She propped her elbows on her knees, resting her head in her hands. "I'se wonder if they're going to bring out the dogs for him, like they do with Colored folks?"

Julian bent over for a glimpse of the television set. Car 16. The color drained from his face.

Lela walked in and sat in her favorite chair. Mario prepared a drink and sat it on the end table for her. "Mon Dieu, Julian. You look like you've seen a ghost. What's the matter?"

He pointed to the television screen. Lela arched a brow, watching as five squad cars pulled up with their dogs yelping in the back seats. "As you Uncle Toot would say, "The Lord laughs at the wicked, for he knows their day is coming.""

Chapter 2

New Orleans, Louisiana. September 1, 1963.

He gripped the armrests and prayed.

"*…and the pitch,*"

Julian jumped in his seat. A foghorn sounded. He scowled at his grandmère. Slobber ran from the corner of her mouth. She continued to snore, growing louder with every breath.

"*It's all over folks. St Louis Cardinals triumph over the Phillies in beautiful Philadelphia. The final score: Cardinals 7, Phillies 3. Thank you for joining our broadcast today. Stay tuned…*"

Julian walked over and turned off the television set. His grandmère's snoring had distracted him from the last out. Throughout the game, she had sounded her foghorn at every important play.

Julian checked his watch. Four o'clock. God, how long was she going to sleep? Julian plopped down on the couch. "Such a lady, asleep in your pretty dress with your legs gapped open, shoes kicked off and snoring like a lumber-jack. What the hell is this?" His grandmère turned her head to the right, hunkering down into her three-hour nap. "I bet you'll sleep like a baby tonight, too."

Suzette entered the solarium and placed a shawl around Lela. She mumbled baby talk in French, grinned, and then returned to snoring. Suzette kissed Lela's forehead and turned to leave. "Why are you sulking, mon fils?"

He didn't feel like fighting with Suzette. "Why can't she sleep in her room?"

"Why not here?"

"I'll tell you why," Julian said. "She sounds like motor-cycle with an extra loud muffler. I've missed the whole ball game." Julian burned with frustration. "And then, she can't just snore. She has to talk in her sleep."

"Your grandmère is old. She needs her rest."

"Whatever." Julian glared at his grandmère. "Look at her. She looks like a corpse."

Suzette considered slapping him. "She is 116 years old. She relaxes her body when she slumbers. If you cannot tol-erate her, leave. This is her home. Why should she be in-convenienced by you? Theo will come in and sit with her." Suzette left the room. "Theo," he heard her call, walking down the hallway.

"His old ass is probably napping somewhere too." Julian

left the solarium for the garden. It had cooled off a touch, but not much. He sat on the wrought iron bench. Hearing wings fluttering, Julian looked up to find every branch of the tree lined with doves, in ranks, prepared to attack. "Goddammit!" He left the bench and exited the rear gate.

Julian walked down Fourth Street. He remembered playing on the street with his friend, Joey Francoise. Joey was Tara Simon Francoise's son, his mamère's best friend. They would travel from Metairie every month to visit.

He rounded the corner at Coliseum, continuing down the block. Commander's Palace! His mother and Aunt Tara would always take him and Joey there for ice cream. His mamère seemed to have been friends with the owner. He needed a drink. "I guess I'll stop in for a minute." Reaching the establishment, Julian entered and went to the bar.

It was the slow time of the day for most restaurants in New Orleans, between the lunch and dinner hours. There was no one at the bar but him. A man wearing an apron came out, gawked at him, and returned to the back room. "I can't believe this shit," Julian said. He stood to leave. He had forgotten he was in New Orleans and not Washington D.C., although it wasn't much better.

Another man entered the bar from the back room. "Is it you, Julian?"

"Yes. Who are you?"

The man's eyes teared up. "I'm the bartender here. I've been so for years. Your mother brought you here often when you were a child. God, you look just like her."

Julian sat down. Perhaps he'd misjudged. "How is Madame?" the bartender asked.

"My mother passed ten years ago," Julian said.

The bartender cast his eyes downward. "Yes, I remember. When your mother died, it was a civic day of mourning for New Orleans." He removed his handkerchief and dabbed his face. "However, I was speaking of Madame Lela. Is she well? She hasn't visited us in some time."

"Yes, she's fine. She's napping right now. I thought I'd come out for some fresh air and stumbled upon this place." Julian sat thinking for a minute. "When I was a child, it seemed we would walk for blocks to come here. Now as an adult, I discovered this restaurant is right around the corner."

The bartender nodded. "Things always seem larger in size and of greater distance as children. Once we become adults, we discover things are closer and smaller in size than they seemed before. We're now the giants of time." He swiped the bar with his cloth. "So, now that you're big boy, I'm guessing you don't want vanilla ice cream topped with strawberries and whipped cream?"

Julian laughed hard. "You're right. I've graduated to

Glenlivet. I'd like a double shot, no ice."

The bartender prepared his drink and sat it before him. "Tough day with the family, yes?"

"You can't even imagine."

The bartender walked away. Julian sipped his scotch. It was good. The bartender must have given him 40-year-old pale.

"What are you doing here, man?"

Julian swiveled on the barstool. "Man! Richard? What the hell?" The men embraced and sat down at the bar. "Sir, please give him what I'm having."

Richard held up his hand. "Do you have any tea?"

"Tea?" the bartender said. "We have shelves of 'tea'." Julian and the bartender laughed.

"No, I mean Darjeeling."

The smile disappeared from the bartender's face. "Sure," he said, recouping his jovial mood. "I'll send out to the kitchen for some."

Richard Mison was such a square. He never drank. While attending Morehouse College, he would say he'd have a beer, but would nurse it all night, never drinking it. Liar. "So, how's things been going for you, Richard?"

"Very well. I've been attending to business here in New Orleans."

"Really?" Julian sipped his drink. "I thought you'd returned to D.C."

"I intended to do so; however, I've been delayed. I'm still hoping I can pull a real estate deal out of the toilet." Both men laughed as the bartender returned with Richard's beverage. He placed his cup of tea before him, along with sugar, cream and lemon. Richard added nothing to the drink and sipped it. He spat it out. "My tea is cold," he said.

The bartender stared at him, amazed. "My apologies, sir." The bartender placed his hands on the cup. "Sir, this is very hot, at least to the touch."

"Make the water hotter," Richard said, dismissing him. The bartender returned to the kitchen. "So how is your grandmother?"

"Great."

Richard stared at the kitchen door, waiting for his tea. "Did you arrange the sale of the house?"

"No."

"Why not?"

"I decided against it."

Richard patted Julian on the back. "Old people can be very persuasive, sucking those they love into their fantasies."

Julian sipped his drink. "Well, Grandmère is fine. She has plenty of help around the house and she's happy. There's no reason to sell and put her in a nursing home, at least not yet."

Richard nodded, considering Julian's assessment of the

situation. "You shouldn't allow emotion and affection to temper your decision on doing what's best for her. You were resolved to make the hard choice before leaving D.C., Julian."

Julian slammed his glass on the counter. "Why the fuck do you care? Goddammit, you act as if my decisions regarding my grandmother affects you in some way."

"That's not it, Julian." The bartender returned with his tea, the water still boiling in the pot. Richard poured the water into the tea cup. The tea bag sizzled. He drank it straight down. "I once hesitated on making decisions about my family, and it cost me. I finally strengthen myself and made the hard decision. I was much happier. Good thing I did too. My family members died soon afterwards. If I'd waited, I would've lost money and opportunities."

Julian stared at his friend. "You need to shut the fuck up talking to me about my grandmère. I'll do with her as I see fit. Unlike you, I don't need her money. I have my own. If her old ass croaks tonight, I'll put her in the grave and do what is required. Until that time, I'm going to allow her to live her life."

The bartender returned from the back room to check on them, but a new patron distracted him. He smiled, beaming with joy. "Julian, you never said Madame planned to join us tonight!" He ran from behind the bar to the entrance of the restaurant, where Lela stood with Suzette.

"She is glorious," Richard said.

Julian turned to him, incredulous. "What the hell you just say?"

"Is that your grandmère?"

Julian wished he'd grabbed his revolver before leaving the house. "I know you're not trying to check out my grand-mère."

"No, not at all. She's a beautiful woman. Her looks have persisted throughout her years," Richard said. He couldn't help but admire her. Just then, Lela's glowered at him. Richard began to sweat.

"Man, you're bleeding," Julian said.

Richard swiped his brow with the cocktail napkin. "It's not blood. I went to Lake Pontchartrain today. Perhaps I had too much sun."

Julian wasn't sure why he maintained his friendship with his best friend, the liar. "Julian." He turned to find his grand-mère beckoning him.

Julian walked over and kissed her. "Awoke from your beauty sleep, I see?" Julian had to admit she appeared as a fifty-year-old, glorious in her pink chiffon dress.

"I'm an old woman. I need my rest," Lela said, blushing.

"No one would know if you didn't advertise it, Madame," the maître'd said. The bartender nodded in agreement.

"You may be correct," Lela said, bestowing him with a little flirt. The maître'd left to instruct the waitstaff to dress the best table in the restaurant for them. "May we sit in the garden?" Lela asked as he rushed away. The maître'd stopped and gave her a curt bow. He hurried away to redirect his staff.

Lela appraised the restaurant. It was still glorious. She hadn't visited the establishment since before Toussaint's departure. She remembered something. "Who were you having drinks with Julian?"

"His name is Richard Mison, my best friend from college." Julian turned to the bar to call Richard over. "Hmm, I wonder where he went?" Julian scanned the restaurant, but didn't see him. "He's probably in the men's room."

"Probablement, mon fils," Lela said, patting his hand.

The maître'd returned to escort the party to their table.

The gate squeaked as it swung open. Julian allowed Suzette and Lela to enter. Walking through the backyard, they entered the solarium door. Lela sat on the sofa, tired and stuffed from the tremendous meal they'd enjoyed. "Madame, would you care for a coffee?" Suzette asked.

"Don't make a fuss Suzette. I know it's past your bedtime."

Suzette listened to the hall clock chime half past seven o'clock. "As it is yours, Madame."

"You're correct. I think I will relax in the parlor before retiring. You should go to bed. I can prepare it myself."

Suzette curtsied and left the room. Julian considered the two. After so many years, they still behaved formerly with one another.

"It's her choosing, not mine," Lela said. "When she is working, it's work. When we're relaxing, we're friends. It's strange."

Julian assisted his grandmère from the sofa and escorted her to the front parlor. She sat on the sofa, exhausted. Julian turned on the air conditioner and then went to the buffet to prepare a brandy for her and a scotch for himself. He placed the drinks on the coffee table and sat beside her.

He considered all that had happened, their visit to La Rose, the traffic stop, seeing Richard. He felt different. He felt at peace in some ways, but agitated in others. Julian leaned back into the sofa and relaxed. He sipped his drink. "Grandmère?"

"Yes, my love?"

Julian blushed. "I shouldn't bring this up. But what happened after, well you know. After Hanzel?"

Lela had hoped he would have forgotten the story, but he never could let anything go. She'd planned to tell him; she just didn't feel like talking about it now. She'd eaten too much.

Considering her great-grandson's eyes, Lela found love and concern for her welfare, coupled with the desire for understanding. She conceded. There was no way around the story. The time had come for her to face the past. "My hell was just beginning. But sometimes we must walk through to the fire to obtain our reward."

Chapter 3

New Orleans, Louisiana. March, 1883.

Nancy wept for her ward. It never changed. At least in this lifetime, Hanzel hadn't succeeded in violating her Rose. The Johannesens, or their spirits, had always tormented the Lord's line, jealous and envious of the Most High God's holy ones. Their disdain for the family had boiled over into the current age, attempting to destroy them all.

Taking Lela's limp, lifeless hand in hers, Nancy tried to lead her out. Lela remained affixed in her stance, unable to break her gaze on James. Although their physical bodies were in the room, their spirits had departed to another dimension where the lovers convicted each other for crimes against their respective hearts. Heaven wept for them, lost in the wasteland of fear and heartbreak.

Nancy couldn't understand James' decision to invite the doctor into the house. She knew he'd drunk from the cup while France. She hadn't believed the blood would allow him to do so. However, it had happened. No matter the degree of anointing upon a soul, it could be difficult for a person to process catastrophic events.

The moment Hanzel stepped in the door of the Chevalier mansion, Nancy had recognized him as the devil. James had to have seen it too; yet, he'd allowed the devil to corrupt his home, his life, and his love. She couldn't understand it. There was no sense in crying over it now. She had to redirect her focus and save the future.

Nancy tugged on Lela's hand once again, but her spirit hadn't return to her flesh. She had to break their connection. Nancy placed her right hand over Lela's eyes. "C'mon, honey," Nancy said. She led Lela away like a little lamb, her eyes cloaked.

Once outside of the bedroom, Nancy hollered downstairs. "Jimmy!" Thank the Lord, he'd returned. He'd showed up out of nowhere the week before. She hadn't seen him since Madame Red's, after the fire. He didn't say much except, "I'se back now. I'se gotta watch the door." Nancy had let him in and gave him a room over the stable.

He came running at top speed. "Yessum, Nancy. What's the matter wit' you?" He gawked at Lela. "What's wrong wit' Miss Lela?"

"Jimmy, just trust me honey. Don't ask me no questions. Just do what I'se tells you, okay?"

"Yessum. Tells me whatcha need."

"You'se goes outside and git on that mare and bring Mis'sur Bailey back here as fast you'se can. Now git!" Jimmy ran down the hall and out the rear door.

While putting Lela to bed, she heard two horses galloping up to the house at top speed. Before she knew it, Toussaint stood with her, staring at Lela. "Here, give her these."

Nancy went to the lavatory and pumped some water, filling a glass. Returning to Lela's bedside, she popped the pills into her mouth. "Drink this, honey." Like a little child, Lela took the glass and drank the water, swallowing the pills. "Lay down, baby." She obeyed. Nancy tucked her into bed. "I'se steppin' right outside the door, I'se ain't goin' nowhere." Lela lay in bed, unresponsive. Nancy closed the door.

"What happened, Nancy?" Toussaint said, afraid to ask. He'd had a bad feeling all morning, and now he understood why.

"Hell done broke loose up in here today, Mis'sur Bailey," Nancy said, wringing her hands. "Now 'fore I'se tells you'se this, I'se givin' you'se the chance to walk away. What happened here today could bring trouble on you and yours. So, if you'se don't want no parts of this mess, leave now." Her eyes involuntarily filled with tears. "But we'se sho' could use your help."

He knew whatever had occurred in the house had been catastrophic. *Mon Dieu, what should I do?*

Help them and I will help you

"Show me, Nancy."

"You'se sho' 'bout this, Mis'sur Bailey? Once I take you downstairs into Mis'sur Chevalier's room, there ain't no turnin' back."

He placed his hand on her shoulder to reassure her. Nancy's tears rolled down her face. "Show me, Mademoiselle Nancy," he said to her in a soft voice.

She led him down the stairs to Jean Charles' bedroom, stopping outside of the closed door. "Mis'sur, this is your last chance to walk away. If you'se turn back now, you'se still innocent and clean."

"Mademoiselle, please. Open the door."

Distressed, she peered into Toussaint's soothing and comforting eyes. Gratitude and relief swept through her. Nancy opened the door.

Toussaint stopped in the doorway, unable to move. "Mon Dieu! What is this place to which you've sent me, My Lord? The depths of hell?" With the shock wearing off and curiosity taking control, Toussaint entered the room. At his left sat a man at a small writing table, trapped in some sort of trance, maybe having suffered a mental collapse. A crossbow lay at his feet. "Monsieur," Toussaint called to him. Hoping to rouse him, Toussaint placed his hand upon the man's shoulder. He didn't respond.

His attention diverted to the horror which lay upon the bed. "My God." A chill ran down his back. He couldn't figure out what had happened. One man, facing downward, lay across another man's body tucked into bed in a customary fashion. An arrow shaft protruded from the center of the man's head lying on top of the one beneath the covers.

Toussaint walked around the bed for a better look at the man shot with the crossbow. Considering the broken arrow protruding from his head, he walked across the room to the window frame, finding the arrowhead lodged in the framework beside the drapery. He pulled it out with ease.

Returning to the bed, Toussaint found himself captivated and mystified by the corpse's open, sharp blue eyes. Forever frozen as they had been when he died, Toussaint could see the hatred and malice in his soul. His cold blue eyes fueled the fury of the red hair atop his head. The corpse's pants straddled his knees. His suspenders hung as nooses on either side of him, touching the floor. His eyes drifted to the dead man tucked into bed.

"Mis'sur Chevalier done been sick for a very long time," Nancy said. Toussaint gaped at her, and then he nodded. "This other man on top of him is Mis'sur Roberts friend."

"Who?"

"That's him over there at the table."

"Oh." He couldn't believe what he was seeing. How? Why would the Lord bring him here? He made a second appraisal of Roberts and then Chevalier. Roberts? Something clicked in his mind regarding the men before him; however, he couldn't quite make the connection.

"Lets me tell you," Nancy said. "This man here on top of Mis'sur Chevalier is Hanzel Johannesen. He's their friend, a doctor from Natchez who came here to tend to Mis'sur Chevalier. He's been jealous of his friends all their lives. He came here wit' plans to steal Mis'sur Chevalier's money and Lela too."

Johannesen? The veil rolled back, revealing all to Toussaint. *Oh no, it can't be*, he marveled to himself. He turned to Roberts, and then to Johannesen. Now he knew with certainty, but he said nothing. "What does Lela have to do with this?" Nancy turned toward James, who sat at the table in a daze. He understood. "Oh my."

"That's right, Mis'sur. Johannesen figured out Lela and Mis'sur Roberts loved each other. Johannesen, wantin' to hurt Mis'sur, decided he was gonna take ev'rythang that was precious to him, includin' Mad'selle Lela, along wit' Mis'sur Roberts' freedom and his life."

Nancy became lost in what had happened. "I saw Mis'sur bust in the front door like a madman, lookin' 'round, searchin'. He grabbed that crossbow from over the fireplace and ran up them steps. I'se follows him. Mis'sur kicked open this bedroom door to find Johannesen wit' Mad'selle bent over her dead brother fixin' to rapes her. He shot him on the spot, dead center in the head."

"Did he?"

"Naw, he didn't. She's aw'rite, just beat up some. You'se done seent her."

"Yes, but she's not alright. However, she will be." He stood there in the room for some time, considering the whole situation. He knew if he didn't handle this situation carefully, they would all hang. *Mon Dieu, what should I do?* He stood there for a few minutes with his eyes closed. He opened them and then clapped his hands together. "Alright, Nancy. Let us get to work."

Wrapping Johannesen's body in a bed sheet, the two carried him to the cellar. Once they had concealed his body, Nancy and Toussaint returned to the bedroom to find James still riveted to his chair, lost. "Monsieur," Toussaint said to him, tapping him on the shoulder. He couldn't allow him to sit there. James had to snap out of it. "Monsieur!"

"Maman—" he muttered. "*Pourquoi*, Maman?" Tears streamed down his face. "Why?"

"Monsieur," Toussaint said, shaking him. "Monsieur

Roberts, can you hear me?"

"Lela." James stared straight through Toussaint, speaking to a person not present. "Lela, *je t'aime*. Why? I tried. I tried—"

"He thanks Lela's dead?" Nancy asked.

"I don't know," Toussaint said. "Monsieur Roberts, Lela is alive. You saved her. Nothing happened."

James directed his trance toward the voice which had spoken to him. "No, Monsieur. He did kill her. See, the blood runs down her neck?" He pointed toward the bed at an invisible figure. "I couldn't save her. She couldn't stay with me. Love me."

What is he talking about? God gave him understanding. "Oh God. Monsieur, you're a man now. She's not your Maman." Toussaint turned James toward the bed where now only Jean Charles remained. "Look. Look and see! Your Maman isn't here."

James saw the bed for the first time. Confusion ran across his face, for the scene he now perceived with his eyes contradicted the vision which played before his mind. He began to reconnect, startled by Toussaint's presence. "Who are you? Get away from me!" He punched Toussaint.

Nancy jumped on James' back. He had the strength of ten men. "Stop it. Stop! This here's Mis'sur Bailey. He's here to help us."

Ignoring Nancy's cries, James swung at Toussaint again, this time missing him. Toussaint grabbed James' arm and hemmed it behind his back. "Look," he said. "Look at it!" Toussaint turned James in the direction of the bed forcing him to look; however, James refused. Nancy grabbed James' head and steadied him, compelling him to do so.

His eyes locked onto the bloody bed where his friend lay dead. "What?" he muttered, falling limp in Toussaint's arms. "Is he? Jean Charles, is he?"

"Oui, Monsieur. He has slipped away," Toussaint said, letting him go.

Unable to make sense of it all, James refocused his attention on Toussaint. "Who are you and why are you here?"

"This here's Mis'sur Bailey, the undertaker," Nancy said. "He done come here to help us."

James shook his head, trying to clear his thoughts. When had there been time to send for the undertaker? "Not to be rude Monsieur, but I don't think it would be proper or acceptable," he blurted out.

Toussaint's eyes flashed with fury. "What, for me to bury a White man?" Some things never changed. He'd involved himself in this mess and Roberts had the nerve to say it isn't proper for a Negro to bury a drunk, violent White man? Toussaint turned for the door.

"Mis'sur Bailey, wait," Nancy said. She grabbed James

by the shoulders. "I'se the one who called him to helps us, Mis'sur Roberts. We'se can trust him to fix this mess."

"What are you saying, Nancy? Come out with it," James said.

"Mis'sur, you'se done killed Johannesen!" Nancy pointed to the crossbow propped against the chair.

Without warning, the day's tragedy came flooding back to him. James could see the arrow leaving the bow, whizzing across the room, hitting its target. "Oh God."

Toussaint checked his anger and tried to be understanding of Roberts, against his better judgment. "You saved Lela's life, Monsieur. She's fine and is resting upstairs."

James' face converged into a scowl. *Lela. Why would she do it, and with Johannesen?*

Nancy heard his thoughts. She watched the confusion and the betrayal skate across his face, twisting it. "Mis'sur Roberts, Mis'sur Bailey has a plan. And we'se better git started or else we'se all gonna hang."

Nancy and Toussaint worked for the remainder of the afternoon and throughout the night cleaning the bedroom. Toussaint shrouded Jean Charles corpse and moved him to another bedroom. He checked him for blood splatter, only finding a few needle-point sized drops. He wouldn't have to change his bedclothes. He covered him and returned to the bedroom.

Nancy had just finished stripping down the bed. Now he understood why Jean Charles had so little blood on him. Standing on the opposite side of the bed from Nancy, they both stared at the blood-soaked mattress. "We must cut out the soiled section of the mattress and burn it," Toussaint said.

Nancy left the room and returned a short time later with a butcher knife. She stabbed the mattress, causing a gush of down feathers, some white, others pink, and a few red, to soar into the air, covering everyone and everything within the room. "Oh Lawd! It's gonna take days to git all these feathers up," Nancy said.

"One crisis at a time, darlin'," Toussaint said, reassuring her. "We'll get it all done."

Nancy nodded. She finished cutting an oval shape into the mattress. Grabbing a pillow case, she and Toussaint scooped out the bloody feathers. "I'll take this back to the mortuary with me." They stuffed the hole with rags.

"We'll get rid of the mattress later. We just need to make this room presentable for the undertaker," Toussaint said.

"Nothing will be amiss," James said, sitting at the writing table. He gulped his cognac to settle his nerves.

After Nancy made the bed, Toussaint brought in Jean Charles' body and laid him down. Nancy placed a Battenberg lace coverlet over him and then combed his hair. Once Jean Charles had been laid to rest, Nancy dampened a dust mop and gathered the renegade feathers scattered about the room. Appraising her work, Nancy decided she would go over everything with a damp feather duster later, gathering any remaining bloody feathers.

Completing his visual inventory of the bedroom, Toussaint found everything in order except one thing. He scowled at Roberts. "Give me the bow. I'll take it with me."

"What? Oh." Half drunk, James handed Toussaint the weapon. "Why are you doing this?"

"Do you find it wise to leave the murder weapon lying around?" Toussaint asked, disgusted. "You did kill Johannesen with this crossbow, did you not?" James turned away from Toussaint, distressed.

Hearing the Lord's admonishment, Toussaint soften his stance with James. The Lord revealed to Toussaint James' desire to know why he wished to help them to conceal the murder, not hide the crossbow.

He exhaled, releasing his anger. "Lela and Nancy are my friends," Toussaint said, filled with coldness. "I help my friends. Besides, *Notre Dieu* directed me to help. With His blessing, I know all will be well." Toussaint watched James wince at the mention of Lela's name. Yet he nodded, seeming to understand Toussaint's motives.

"Now, I want you to go to every undertaker in this city. There are at least five who are considered as acceptable to prepare for burial a man of Chevalier's rank. They'll all turn you down because of Jean Charles' despicable reputation. Then, you'll hire me. Trust me, you'll pay me handsomely to handle this 'burial' for you."

"Do as you see fit. I'll pay you whatever you ask," James said.

"I'm sure you will. I'll take care of Johannesen's body as well. No one will ever find him."

Hanzel's name burned in James' ears. "I don't care what you do with him." He thought for a moment. "Oh God, he has a family. Surely, his wife will search for him after a period of time."

Wickedness sprung into Toussaint's eyes, frightening James. "The Lord has revealed a plan for that matter as well." He left the room, followed by Nancy and James.

Chapter 4

New Orleans, Louisiana. March, 1883.

On Monday, Monsieur Roberts implemented his part in Toussaint's plan. Just as Toussaint had told him, none of the reputable undertakers who traditionally serviced their class would take the job. They were either too busy, overbooked or taking an unforeseen holiday. At last, James went to T. Bailey and Son Mortuary to hire Toussaint as the undertaker.

The majesty of the Chevalier Mansion didn't compare to La Rose Plantation. But somehow, the opulence of the plantation house had never made an impression on him. It had been the habitat of his bondage. He'd never entered the house until Augustus' death. He'd only visited the plantation's French gardens once, maybe twice. As Augustus would say, 'If that Nigger ain't tending the grounds, they'd better not let me catch them back there.'

Before he could turn the corner at Fourth and St. Charles

Streets, he could see the slate, mansard roof above the tree line. The Chevalier Mansion had to be the grandest home in the Garden District. "Whoa, Cherrie." He sat on the driver's bench of the hearse, admiring the gardens surrounding the home. The mansion sat on two acres of land. What home had two acres of land in the Garden District? He saw the one who'd purchase the land in the city's infancy, lounging in the Spirit. Emmanuel.

Toussaint and Allen disembarked the driver's bench and stood before the home, awestruck. "Folks live like this, Monsieur?"

"Oui, mon fils. They do," Toussaint said. The home appeared to be three stories high. However, Toussaint suspected it to be four, the highest floor concealed by the mansard roof. The family most likely utilized the attic space for storage. The grand balconies, one on every floor except the fourth, were supported by white columns. Everything was white, with angels and *fleur-de-lis* accenting its façade.

Toussaint saw James standing on the front walk with Michael Salley, talking to Father Pierre from St. Maurice the Moor Parish. Toussaint had asked his own priest to perform the services, since Jean Charles wasn't a member of a parish. Father Pierre had been happy to oblige, since he'd performed Last Rites for Jean Charles that past Sunday evening, praying with passion for his tormented soul.

Toussaint and Allen joined the group and stood in silence as Father Pierre spoke. "We all lose our way, but God loves and forgives us," Father Pierre said. The men removed their hats and bowed their heads, reflecting upon the priest's words.

After an appropriate moment of silence, Toussaint put on his hat. "Monsieur Roberts, I wish to review with you the itinerary for today's services, if you have a moment."

"Yes, of course."

The men left the group and spoke privately. Once finished, Toussaint nodded at Allen, signaling for him to follow him. The two returned to the hearse. Toussaint opened the rear glass doors, revealing a large, beautiful mahogany casket, appointed with gold hardware and silk linings.

Obeying the words of the Holy Spirit, he'd ordered it a few weeks before. At the time, he couldn't understand his need for it, but now all was clear. "Allen, grab the tarp in the side compartment near you. I want to cover the coffin to ensure we don't damage it." They spread the tarp over the coffin and removed it from the hearse.

Carrying the casket to the side door of the home near the kitchen, Toussaint raised his knee to support it. Using his free hand, he opened the door, swinging it wide. The men entered, navigating the narrow flight of stairs leading to the cellar. Much to Toussaint's amazement, they managed to move the casket without incident. The prior evening, Toussaint had placed four wooden crates in a rectangular formation, creating a platform. The men placed casket upon it.

Toussaint exhaled, placing his hand on the coffin for support. "Allen, I wish to present you with a choice before we continue any further."

"What is it, Monsieur?"

He paused, considering what he wished to share. "Something horrible has happened in this house, in addition to Monsieur Chevalier's death. Before I involve you in this, you must choose. If you don't wish to dirty your hands by involving yourself in this crime, you should leave now and wait for me outside."

A blank expression covered Allen's face, unsure of what to make of Toussaint's statement. "A crime, Monsieur?"

Toussaint removed the tarp from the coffin. Extracting a soft cloth from his pocket, he polished the vessel. "Yes, Allen. A crime has been committed here. That's all I'll say about the matter." Toussaint folded his arms and leaned on the coffin, peering into Allen's eyes. "Allen, you're a bright young man with your whole life ahead of you. You don't have to agree to assist me. In fact, I would prefer if you refused."

"But why are you involved, Monsieur?"

Toussaint turned his heart toward to heaven, praying for

the truth. "When first confronted with this matter, I prayed and asked the Lord what I should do. He instructed me to help Lela and Nancy."

Allen considered Toussaint's response. "If notre Dieu told you to help them, then I'll assist you, for I'm under your charge."

"I want you to—"

"I have," Allen said. "If this is what the Lord has instructed you to do, then I'll follow your orders. Elisha wouldn't walk away from Elijah, and I won't walk away from you. I'll do whatever you direct me to do, as in any situation. There is no difference for me."

Toussaint patted him on top of the head, suppressing his tears. Teddy's smiling face appeared before his eyes. *Looks like you done found your Elisha, boy.*

He realized at that moment Allen was no longer the young boy who cut his grass and fed his animals. He'd matured into a young man, his apprentice. "Oh Father, please don't allow me to take this young man down the path to destruction."

He will be fine, as will you, My Son

Toussaint walked over to the croaker sacks of flour and sugar, stacked against the wall. Allen watched Toussaint move aside the fifty-pound bags with ease, burrowing down to an unknown destination. "Monsieur, may I help you?"

Toussaint continued to move the sacks of flour and sugar.

Nearing the bottom of the pile, Toussaint lifted a bag. Its contents poured out on the dirt floor.

"Wait, Monsieur. The bag," Allen said.

Toussaint stopped. The flour continued to spill from the croaker sack, red at first, and then the contents streamed pink, and then finally white. A wicked grin arose on Toussaint's face.

Filled with horror, Allen's eyes fell upon what lay beneath the bag. He gasped, finding a dead White man lying face down upon a croaker sack of flour with an arrow protruding from the back of his skull. The hair surrounding the wound was matted with dry blood. Allen yelled out before he could stop himself.

Toussaint dropped the croaker sack and ran to Allen, covering his mouth. "Keep your voice down. They may hear you outside." Once he felt the boy calm down, he released him.

"I know this is shocking. But rest assured, this man got what he deserved," Toussaint said. "'The Lord laughs at the wicked, for he knows their day is coming.' Trust me, his day has come, and the Lord has collected his due."

Toussaint went to the casket and opened it. Removing all the pillows and bedding, he laid them upon the tarp once covering the casket. Reaching into the casket, he removed another tarp, and then covered the bedding to prevent it from becoming soiled with the dust and flour floating in the air.

Grabbing his tool bag from a crate near the coffin, which he'd brought in the night before, Toussaint fished around for a screwdriver. Finding it, he returned to the casket and proceeded to pry open the false bottom, revealing a secret compartment.

"Mon Dieu, I would have never known it was there," Allen said.

"If you've changed your mind, Allen, you may still leave," Toussaint said.

"No, Monsieur. I'm fine. It surprised me, that's all," he said. "What would you like me to do?"

"Help me put the body in the coffin." The men walked over to where Hanzel's contorted body lay upon a sack of sugar. Together they lifted the corpse, still somewhat frozen with rigor mortis. They carried the thin body over to the casket, placing it inside the secret compartment.

"Oh, merde." Toussaint ignored Allen's surprised expression, for the boy had never heard him swear. "This is my fault, due to hastiness. I should've taken care to lay him flat. We were in such a rush the other evening."

Toussaint considered his options, the body having molded to the shape of the croaker sack it had come to rest upon.

"Let us lift him out and place him on the floor." Together, the men removed Johannesen's half nude body and placed him on the floor.

"You may wish to look away, Allen," Toussaint said. Allen continued to watch. "Very well, as you wish."

Toussaint lifted his foot and slammed it down on Johannesen's neck, snapping it. The air escaped his windpipe, making a whistling noise. Allen flinched, but he didn't turn away. Toussaint proceeded to break every rebellious bone in Hanzel's body, snapping his twisted arms and legs, his contorted torso. After all was done, Toussaint broke away the arrow shaft protruding from the base of his skull.

Appraising his work, Toussaint found Hanzel's form satisfied him. "He should fit comfortably now. Let's give him another try," Toussaint said.

Lifting him, Allen found his body felt like oranges in an old silk stocking, with the clumps of bone and flesh shifting beneath the skin.

They threw the corpse inside. "He's a good fit," Toussaint said.

Allen stared at the corpse's half-naked body. "Monsieur Bailey, what happened?"

"The less you know—" Toussaint reconsidered. Allen deserved to know what had happened. "When he died, this man was attempting to rape Mademoiselle Lela," Toussaint said. "Monsieur Roberts burst into the room and shot him with the crossbow. Hanzel didn't succeed in violating her."

"My God!" Although horrified, Allen felt better about their mission, justified even. Reassured, Allen continued his work with a new conviction.

The men began to reinsert the false bottom when Allen remembered something. "Monsieur, the crossbow."

"Oh, yes." Retrieving the weapon from the corner of the cellar and the pillow case filled with bloody feathers, Toussaint returned to the coffin and placed the items beneath the corpse's legs. The crossbow reminded him of a few other items on his 'to-do' list. Toussaint removed the arrowhead from his pocket and tossed it in, along with the broken shaft.

"Alright, now the cover." The men lowered the false bottom into the coffin; however, it faced the wrong direction. Walking in a half circle around the coffin, they re-inserted the false bottom. "There should be just enough room." Forcing it a little, the men locked the panel into place. "Bon! Now let us replace the bedding and the pillows." As they replaced the coffin's contents, Toussaint smiled at Allen. "Good job, remembering the crossbow, well with everything," Toussaint said. Allen nodded, attempting to conceal his grin of pride.

Toussaint and Allen checked each another for any telling signs which could betray their activities. Allen found quite a bit of flour on the right side of Toussaint's suit. He went to the worktable and found a rag. Although little dirty, it would work. He dusted off his mentor, removing every trace of flour.

Toussaint extended his arm and leg, inspecting Allen's work. "Bon." He in turned checked Allen. The boy didn't have anything on him.

The two men exited the cellar. As they returned to the hearse, Toussaint spotted Lela sitting in the garden, lost in thought. "Allen, I'll return shortly."

"Oui, Monsieur," he said, climbing onto the driver's bench.

Toussaint could see her face as he approached, racked with trauma, agony, and pain. Lost in her own personal hell, she fixated on the cracking earth, hinting at the splendor of flowers yet to come.

"Lela." She continued to stare straight ahead, not hearing him. Toussaint placed his hand on her shoulder.

"Stop," she screamed, balling her fist, prepared to pummel her attacker. "Oh, Monsieur Bailey." Lela relaxed and scooted over on the stone bench, making room for Toussaint to sit with her.

"How are you holding up?" Based on the dark circles under her eyes, he already knew the answer.

"I'm managing." Without warning Lela began to cry, no longer able to contain her pain. "I viewed Jean Charles' body before the others arrived," she said. "I've decided not to attend the burial."

"You may ride with Allen and me instead of Roberts and Salley, if you prefer."

Lela flinched at the sound of James' name. "No," she said in a low voice. "I've said my goodbyes." She wailed, but quickly regained control. "I don't wish to continue on. I wish Monsieur Johannesen had killed me," she said, tears streaming down her face. "I've lost everything. I have lost…" Lela drifted off, unable to say the rest.

"Monsieur Roberts? Is he the one of whom you're speaking?"

A tear, larger than any raindrop, rolled down her cheek. "Yes, I've lost him."

"Has he told you this?"

"He doesn't have to. I can see it in his eyes. He thinks—" She fell silent, not wishing to reveal their relationship.

"Lela, you can talk to me," Toussaint said. "You must talk to someone. This will destroy you if you don't." Lela continued to stare at the earth beneath her feet. He could feel her heart closing, determined to dwell in grief and heartbreak.

Toussaint looked across the gardens to find Father Pierre, James, and Salley exiting the house. Salley stopped at the hearse and chatted with Allen. "I must go now, but if you ever need to talk, please know you can always talk to me."

Lela didn't hear him, her stare affixed upon James. In the distance, James turned and walked away, never seeming to notice Lela sitting in the garden. Toussaint patted Lela's hand and arose from the bench, leaving her.

"Monsieur Bailey." Allen hopped down from the driver's bench. "Messieurs Roberts and Salley will travel to St. Helena today, expecting to arrive there late tonight. They would like for us to have the body at La Rose no later than eleven o'clock in the morning for burial."

"Very well. Let us begin." The two men went to the cellar and retrieved the coffin, taking it to the parlor where Monsieur Chevalier rested, in repose. Toussaint considered Jean Charles, filled with sadness regarding his unfortunate end. "May God rest his soul."

The men lifted Jean Charles from the white silk and lace draped cooling table and placed him in the coffin, closing it. Piercing Allen with his stare, Toussaint communicated with Allen without speaking. *We cannot appear to strain as we move this coffin. Nothing can appear out of the ordinary.* Allen nodded, hearing his mentor's telepathic instructions.

Both men silently counted to three and lifted the coffin in unison, bearing the immense load. They navigated the room's furniture, the hallway, the narrow door and side stairs with great care, leading them to the side drive.

Reaching the funeral hearse, they sat the coffin on the lip of the tailgate, gliding it inside, and then closing the etched glass doors. The men walked around to the side of the hearse, facing the street. The two leaned against the glass window, catching their breath. "Beautiful coffin," Toussaint heard Salley comment in the distance, as he and James walked to their carriage.

After a few minutes, the heartbeat of each man normalized. "Let's prepare to leave, Allen." Following his apprentice to the driver's bench, Toussaint sat and took Cherrie's reigns. The animal neighed, the eight black plumes atop her head shimmering in the sun. Looking past it all, he spotted Lela sitting on the stone bench in the garden, in the same place he'd left her at least a one-half hour before. She continued to stare at James. Surely James could feel her longing for him, Toussaint surmised. However, he never looked her way.

James entered the awaiting carriage, followed by Salley and Father Pierre. The men drove away. Lela's gaze remained affixed to the spot where he once stood, devastated.

"Mon Dieu, help us all," Toussaint prayed.

Chapter 5

New Orleans, Louisiana. March, 1883

Forty-five minutes later, Allen and Toussaint arrived at his mortuary. Toussaint slowed the hearse, so he could make the sharp turn onto the inclined side drive. "Whoa, girl," he said to Cherrie.

Ignoring her master's command, Cherrie pulled the hearse up the drive and stopped in the appropriate spot before the cellar door. The men unloaded the coffin, taking it to the cellar.

Toussaint clapped his hands together, dispelling any imaginary dust upon them. "Allen, you have done enough for one day. You may go. Thank you for your assistance."

"But Monsieur!"

"No 'buts' Allen. Thank you for your help today." Toussaint could see his dismissal had hurt the boy, implying a lack of faith and confidence in Allen's ability. "Allen, some things you just don't need to see. Some things should remain confidential between a man and his God." Toussaint placed his hand on his shoulder. "Go home, Allen," he said, smiling at him, filled with kindness and thankfulness. "Please, go home."

"Oui, Monsieur. I'll go."

"Merci, bon ami."

Allen was honored Toussaint considered him as a friend. "I'll see you at first light, Monsieur Bailey."

"Very good, Allen. I'll see you then," Toussaint said. Allen closed the door.

Toussaint ordered his instruments on the table. Tired, he decided he would work later and went upstairs. Stomping his feet on the mat, he opened the kitchen door and entered his home, breathing in deep the sweet smells of dinner. Pot roast? "Hey, darlin,'" Toussaint said to Jannie, standing at the stove. He walked over and stood behind her, wrapping his arms around her small waist and enjoying the comfort of her behind against him. He kissed her neck, inhaling her soft, flowery scent.

"How did things go today, baby?" she asked with a sad smile.

"All went well, just sad. But then again, I've never been to a happy one," he said. "Oh, Nancy and Lela send their thanks for keeping an eye on Willie."

Jannie removed a plate from the cupboard. "It's my pleasure, baby," she said, spooning pot roast and potatoes on the plate.

"How is he?"

Jannie poured water into a glass and sat it on the table. "He finally fell asleep. I had to read to him four bedtime stories."

"That little buster! I'm sure he conned you out of some ice cream, too."

"Sure did," she said, hiding her guilty grin. "Two."

"Two?" Toussaint sat at the kitchen table. He loved the boy with all his heart, as if a son of his flesh. He could see Jannie loved the child also. "You just don't have a back bone when it comes to Willie, do you?"

"He's a sweet child, Toussaint," she said, her smile fading.

"Come here, baby." He guided her onto his lap, hugging her tight and then kissing her. "Baby, it isn't too late. We can still have a child." She wept, unable to contain her heartache. "Don't lose hope, alright?" She nodded in agreement, overcome with emotion. "I'm just gonna have to put my back into it!" He leered at his beautiful wife, tickling her.

"Boy, stop. You're so nasty."

"What's wrong with a little nasty in your life?" He kissed her neck. "I love you, Jannie." Finding her soft lips, Toussaint kissed her long and deep, allowing his hands to explore the treasures hidden beneath her long skirts.

Jannie jumped up. "Willie, what's wrong?" She ran over to the child, taking him in her arms. Toussaint's heart pounded. He had no idea the child had been standing there.

"I had a bad dream. I dreamed the house was on fire."

Both Toussaint and Jannie sighed. The horrors of the Madame Red fire still haunted the child's sleep. It all seemed to have happened a lifetime ago, in light of recent tragedies. Jannie sat in the chair across from Toussaint. "Come here, honey." Jannie scooped the boy up into her lap. "Baby, you're safe now. The fire is over."

Tears bubbled up in his eyes and cascaded down his cheeks. "My Uncle Nate must have died in the fire. I always hoped he'd come back home." Willie began to cry, staring at the floor.

"I know baby, I know. We did too," she said. Toussaint watched his wife rock him, while singing softly to him. Her love flowed into Willie, so natural and easy. Willie snuggled in, hugging her tight. Within a few moments, the child had fallen asleep.

Toussaint's heart broke. Jannie needed a child, but for some reason, she hadn't become pregnant, not even once, during their fifteen years of marriage. She loved children so much. For a reason he couldn't figure out, guilt and remorse flooded Toussaint, watching Jannie stand and carry the child upstairs to bed.

***

Toussaint finished his dinner, savoring the last bite of his pot roast. Jannie made the best roast. He knew if he tried, he could eat an entire thing by himself. Drinking his water, he felt hands slip around his neck, and then arms embrace him. He jumped, but relaxed, ingesting the essence of her love. Jannie kissed him behind the ear. "How's Willie?"

"He's sleeping, but it is a fitful sleep," Jannie said. She bit her lip. "Baby, do you mind if I sleep with him tonight, just so I can be nearby and keep an eye on him?"

"Not at all, darlin'. You do what you believe is best for him. He's been through a lot in his five years."

"I know," she said. "Nate did a great job with him. Nancy has done wonders for that boy." Jannie removed Toussaint's empty plate from the table, placing it in the galvanized wash pan. She avoided washing dishes in the porcelain sink. She didn't want to scar it with marks from pots and pans.

"Willie is worried about his Mama Lela. He told me since Monsieur died, she cries all the time when she doesn't know he's nearby. As soon as she sees him, she stops and then smiles as if nothing is wrong." Jannie shook her head, returning to the table. "Willie is a little afraid and very confused by everything that has happened."

"I know."

Jannie fiddled with Toussaint's shirt button, undoing it.

"You know, I don't mind keeping Willie for a while until things settle down over there, if Nancy and Lela don't mind."

Toussaint followed Jannie's slender hands with his eyes, watching her work loose the next shirt button. "I think that's a wonderful idea, baby." Toussaint arose from his chair and kissed her. "Although, he has a bad habit of showing up at the wrong time," Toussaint said. He smiled slow and broad, devilment filling his eyes.

"Well, we're all alone right now." Jannie said. She'd run out of shirt buttons. Her fingers moved on to the next group of buttons on his trousers. "You need to learn how to use the time which you are given wisely."

Toussaint led Jannie by the hand into his office and locked the door.

He descended the stairs to the cellar with a smile on his face. Jannie had put him a few hours behind, but he didn't care. It had been a few days since they had made love. For the life of him, he could not figure out why he couldn't give her a child. He feared he may be sterile. "God is a God of miracles. He can bless us with a child despite our physical shortcomings," he said.

Toussaint put on his leather apron, tying it at the waist first, and then the bib around his neck. He opened the casket. "Jean Charles Chevalier, did you ever think in your wildest dreams I would be the one to lay you to rest? Humph. Who would have believed it?" He stared at the man whom he'd watched from afar as a child on La Rose Plantation.

Lifting Jean Charles from the casket, he placed him on the embalming table. Toussaint had become strong from working alone for so many years. He could lift three hundred pounds of dead weight alone, if required.

Toussaint patted Jean Charles' cold arm and then covered his remains with a shroud. Returning to the coffin, Toussaint removed the pillows and bedding, placing the items in a trunk he'd brought downstairs from the bedroom. He closed the trunk's lid and returned to the casket.

He removed the false bottom.

Standing before the Johannesen's mangled remains, he inhaled deep, savoring the full bouquet of retribution marrying with the putrid odor of decomposition. He turned the casket on its side, dumping the corpse onto the floor.

Tying a rope around Johannesen's neck, he dragged his lifeless body down the stairs into the root cellar. With a bit of work, he found the location the trap door leading to the private room he'd excavated years before. The contractor had done an excellent job concealing the entrance. He'd believed it to be an extravagance at time, but he was now thrilled he'd listened to the Good Lord. Money well spent.

Opening the trap door, he tossed in the corpse. Hearing

the thud of the corpse hitting the dirt floor below, Toussaint descended the ladder. He closed and bolted the hatch door above him. Lighting the lamp, warmth filled his heart, finding Johannesen's broken body lying in a heap on the dirt floor, on trial before Heaven and Hell.

"Vengeance is mine saith the Lord," he said, whispering to the corpse. "And today, the Lord has blessed his servant." Toussaint sat down on a wooden chair which he kept in the room and lit his cigarillo, laughing to himself. "Who would have ever thought it, Hanzel? I had no clue the Lord would bless me by helping sinners. It is true. God does help those who help others. Wouldn't you agree, Hanzel?

"Oh, but I guess you wouldn't know much about helping others, would you?" He kicked him in the ribs from his chair, his long legs stretching across time and space to strike its target. "The Lord sent me to help the refugees of the Madame Red fire. I know you knew the place well.

"You know, Hanzel, I hate— Well hate is a strong word. Let us say I have an aversion to whorehouses and to whores in general. Missy believed herself to be one after you hurt her."

He paused and refocused, so he could relish their last few moments together. "So, when Commander Thomas contracted me to retrieve and bury the dead from the fire, how could I ever have known? God used a string of sad and horrible events to lead me to my heart's desire."

Toussaint took another puff on his cigarillo, flicking the ashes and coals on the corpse. "When Nancy sent the house boy to fetch me, could I have ever foreseen our day of justice had arrived? Imagine my joy, my elation, when I found you dead, with an arrow through your head, ass and dick out, and your eyes staring back at me from hell."

Toussaint exhaled, recalling the heartwarming scene. "Of course, Roberts doesn't remember me, being so out of it, and understandably so. But then again, why would he remember me or my family? But I remember you and Roberts.

"You know Hanzel, you dirty motherfucka, I couldn't have asked for more. I really couldn't have. The Lord told me to wait on him, and I listened. God has given me justice." Toussaint extinguished his cigarillo on the corpse's penis. "No, he has given Missy justice." Toussaint inhaled deep, sucking down his pain.

"God is good. I'm his instrument to exact his vengeance, even though Roberts' received the lion's share of the spoils in this case." Toussaint fantasized for a moment about having Hanzel in sights, and then releasing the arrow, watching as it pierced his tiny, under-developed head. He refocused. It was getting late and he had a lot of work to do.

"I won't complain, for the Lord blessed me with Augustus." He got on the floor, hovering above Hanzel's body at an awkward angle to peer into his clouded, inanimate eyes. "You believed you'd escape your sins, didn't you Hanzel? You truly believed you could get away with all you'd done. But the Lord laughs at the wicked, for He knows their day is coming." He dissolved into hysterics. "But not only has God laughed at you, but he has spat upon you."

Toussaint stood up, his laughter mutating into tears and then exploding into a rage which had been suppressed for over twenty years. Toussaint kicked Hanzel. He kicked him repeatedly, the coagulated blood oozing from every hole which he stomped into Hanzel's corpse. Toussaint collapsed to the floor, exhausted.

"Did you not say a Nigger could never win justice over a White man? But you stupid motherfucka, '*His ways are higher than our ways, and His thoughts are higher than our thoughts.*'

"We got you so completely. No one will ever miss your evil ass, ever. The Lord has given you to me."

Toussaint began to wail. "You stole my sister's life! I watched her slip away from us, while at the same time watching Claret grow up beautiful and strong." He grimaced at the thought of Hanzel's blood flowing through Claret's veins.

Sobbing, Toussaint walked over to the corner of the cellar to retrieve his father's double-head ax. "Papa and Missy, as I promised you, the Good Lord has delivered Satan into our hands this day." A vision of Missy's face twisted in terror and excruciating pain catapulted him back to the horrific night in the barn on La Rose Plantation, years before.

You'll think twice next time Nigger. You'll think twice before you ever cross me again.

Toussaint hadn't realized he had swung the ax. Hanzel's head rolled for a bit, coming to rest near the far wall of the room. Through his pain and tears, he thanked the Lord for Missy's justice.

He proceeded to hack Hanzel up into small pieces with the ax. Once he separated his penis from the body, Toussaint picked it up and sat it on the small table. For this portion of his anatomy he'd planned a special event, but he hadn't quite determined what.

Toussaint dragged his chair over to the table, where he'd set up the meat grinder earlier in the day. He'd purchased the professional grade grinder from a friend down at the slaughter house for five dollars. It was the best five dollars he'd spent in his life.

He gathered up the small pieces of Johannesen's body strewn across the dirt floor, stacking the parts in a mound next to the table. Taking his seat, he selected a chunk, caked in mud and blood. It was small section, most likely from an arm, cut right above the wrist.

He dropped the first piece into the grinder and turned the crank. Toussaint watched the blades of the grinder turn, consuming Hanzel's flesh with ease, offering its fruit to the galvanize tub. Smaller bones were no match for the sharp blades; no need to remove them.

Time escaped Toussaint, lost in the ecstasy of reducing the devil to ground chuck. However, his ground meat consisted of multiple cuts; not just one superior cut of meat. It was all garbage to him anyway.

Toussaint shrugged off his need for quality control and dropped in another piece, a bit larger. He couldn't turn the crank. "Merde." Even though Hanzel had been a thin, puny man, a thigh bone still proved to be a thigh bone. Toussaint pulled it out of the grinder and cut away the remaining meat. He threw the bone on the floor.

"Where is it?" He searched around the dim lit cellar, spotting the blood covered ax lying on the floor between an arm and the neck. Toussaint picked it up and chopped up the thigh bone into smaller pieces. He couldn't run the risk of jamming the meat grinder. He had too much work to do. He reinserted the rebellious piece of bone and turned the crank. The grinder consumed it with ease.

Once he finished with the larger cuts of meat, he ground the organ meat. He picked up a lump from the floor. "The heart?" He tossed it up and down in his hand. "How small." Toussaint dropped in the grinder, watching it pop between the blades like a hen's egg. He scooped up another piece of meat.

"Liver." Toussaint smiled, thinking of Jannie's meal of liver and onions the week before. She sure could cook. "I will ask Jannie to pick some up from the butcher for dinner tomorrow." He dropped it in, followed by the kidneys, pancreas, lungs and a variety of other parts.

He surveyed the room and smiled. "Finished!" Toussaint stood from the chair and massaged his arm. Turning the crank had made his muscles sore. "Lord, look at all of this meat." He'd lined up several five-gallon galvanized tubs of it against the wall. It would take some time to get rid of it all.

Toussaint took a shovel and scrapped up a good six inches of the dirt floor. He placed the dirt in croaker sacks, which he would dump in the river over the course of the next few weeks.

Exhausted and covered in blood, he sat down on the wooden chair to rest. However, he couldn't, invigorated by grinding the flesh of his enemy into mush. Spotting Hanzel's penis on the table, he picked it up and studied it. He couldn't figure out what to do with it. How could something so small be used to destroy his sister? In any case, he didn't plan to keep it as a trophy.

Grabbing Hanzel's head from the floor, he climbed the ladder to the root cellar and then walked upstairs to the preparation room. He stood before the fireplace. Watching the flames dance within, he felt peace flood his soul and his heart. He threw Hanzel's penis into the fire. He then threw in Hanzel's head.

The flames engulfed it, first incinerating his hair and then reducing the skin to charred crackling. Hanzel's skull whistled. Toussaint believed he heard it cry out 'No,' once the hellfire consumed it. Remembering a few items from the mansion, Toussaint retrieved the bag of feathers and the arrow shaft, sitting near the door. He threw it into the fire.

"Oh yes, Monsieur Hanzel Johannesen. God gives justice to Niggers, because men never will."

Toussaint stripped off his clothes and threw them into the fire. Before he'd begun his work, Toussaint had bought down a wash pan, filled with water and bleach. He dipped his fingertips into the water, now almost cold. He washed himself. Next, Toussaint washed his apron and hung it to dry on the coat rack. He wrung out the wash towel and then threw it into the fire.

He dumped the bloody water down the drain. Thank God for indoor plumbing. He dried himself and then went to his chifforobe, removing fresh slacks and a shirt. He dressed. Toussaint removed a clean leather apron from the coat rack and put it on, tying the ends at his neck and waist.

Toussaint stood before his client and bowed. "Monsieur Chevalier, pardon me for keeping you waiting. Allow us to begin."

Chapter 6

New Orleans, Louisiana. March, 1883.

Allen rubbed his eyes, walking up the drive. Half past five o'clock in the morning. He hoped Monsieur Bailey wouldn't be upset with him for being late. Once he thought about, Toussaint hadn't given him a specific start time.

The screen door squeaked. He made a mental note to oil it once they returned from the burial. Entering the kitchen, he found Toussaint sitting at the table reading the morning paper. "Bonjour, Monsieur."

Toussaint folded his paper. "Bonjour, Allen. What a lovely day. Would you care for some coffee?" Allen nodded as he sat at the table, while Toussaint went to the cupboard to get a cup and saucer for him. "Watch out. Jannie was a little heavy handed with the chicory this morning."

"I heard that, Toussaint," she said from the parlor.

Toussaint's good mood surprised Allen. He decided he wouldn't question it. Taking a sip of Jannie's eye-opening coffee, Allen's concerns regarding the previous day's activities got the best of him. "Is everything in order, Monsieur?"

"Oui, Monsieur. Everything is now decent and in order," Toussaint said. He winked at him.

After finishing their coffee, the men went to the backyard to prepare for their journey to La Rose. Toussaint fed the dogs and then skipped down the steps to the preparation room. "Allen, aren't you coming?"

Standing at the stairs, Allen watched the dogs eat their food, captivated. "Yes, but the dogs. They're fighting each other for the food." Allen stared in awe at the hounds growling, snarling, and snapping at one another, in some instances drawing blood.

Toussaint unlocked the cellar door. "I guess they're hungry."

La Rose Plantation, St. Helena Parish. March, 1883.

HE FELT A knot tighten in his throat, beholding the place of his suffering and youth. He couldn't take his eyes off the plantation house sitting on the hill and the winding path leading to it. "La Rose."

"What?" Allen said.

"La Rose. Beautiful to behold but painful to hold." Toussaint wagged his head in sorrow. He popped the reigns. Cherrie commenced her slow trot up the hill.

He remembered the day his family left the plantation. He

remembered burying his parents. He remembered the day he came and pulled Missy from the laundry pot and buried her. He remembered the day Augustus swung from the second floor. He'd cut him down and buried him. Death always brought him home to the land of bondage and misery.

The hearse hit a little rut in the road. Toussaint heard the casket side back and forth. He exhaled, releasing the memories of the past. Toussaint had been joyous back then to escape the beautiful place called hell, which housed its horrible family and their wicked friends. Now he would rejoice when remembering the plantation, for never again would he need to concern himself about one friend of the Chevalier family. Whenever his thoughts would drift to Hanzel Johannesen, he would smile, vindicated.

Good things come to those who wait, does it not Oncle?

He saw a young woman standing in the field, some distance from the road.

Go home, he whispered to Claret's mind. A light flashed in the distance. She had seen what had happened in the Spirit. It worried him. He let it go. He couldn't do anything about it.

They continued their journey up the winding road, and then turned off onto a little side drive, passing the old slave quarters. Much to his own surprise, Toussaint's eyes lit up a little when he laid eyes on the family's cabin. He'd figured it would have turned to dust by now.

Cherrie trotted through the open gates leading to the white, marble mausoleum, constructed in the style of a Greek temple. Without guidance from her master, she stopped and then drifted to the side of the road to munch on the tender grass. Toussaint pulled the brake and exited the hearse, followed by Allen. "The services will begin in about one-half hour," he told him.

Toussaint glanced across the lawn to the Chevalier mausoleum, finding its doors open. He could see Jean Charles' white marble sarcophagus had been installed between Lily's and Cindy's, awaiting his arrival. "Stay here," Toussaint said. Allen nodded while admiring the sprawling plantation in awe. Toussaint crossed the grounds.

He stood inside the mausoleum's door. The tomb had grown crowded. Camille. Emmie Sue. Both Lily Chevaliers. Augustus' gold sarcophagus sat in the center of the structure. One would think he'd been a pharaoh of some sort. The sarcophagus bore his likeness, complete with a crown upon his head, embellished with diamonds and rubies. His hands clasped a blood red rose at the center of his chest. Toussaint walked over for a closer look. The flower appeared to be real. He sniffed it. The fragrance intoxicated him, forcing him to lean against the sarcophagus to steady himself.

Once his head cleared, Toussaint scanned the mausoleum. "There." He walked to the rear of the structure to the trap door. For centuries, the Chevalier family held a superstition, or paranoia, about being entombed alive. As a result, they never bolted down sarcophagus or coffin lids. Also, the family had adopted the extra precaution of installing a secret escape route for the deceased, in case they proved to be undead.

He opened the trap door and found a shallow hole, maybe two feet deep. "I guess these are only for show, now." Toussaint unbuckled his pants and removed a bag tied to his waist. Opening the bag, he dumped Hanzel's ashes, which he'd gathered from the fireplace, into the passageway to freedom which led to nowhere.

Satisfaction

"Yup, you'se should be at ease for a while, boy."

Toussaint turned around. "Lawrence." He hugged the massive man, rivaling the height of any giant California redwood tree he'd heard tale about.

"How'se you, son?"

"I'm doing just fine." Toussaint looked back at the escape door for the undead. "Why do you say I should be at ease for a while?"

Lawrence grimaced as he patted Toussaint's shoulder. "Well, there's a blessin' and a curse on this blood, the Chevalier blood," Lawrence said. "Some of Emmanuel's children suffered more than others, I'se suppose."

"I'm not Emmanuel's child."

Lawrence raised his eyebrow and opened his mouth to speak, but closed it. "Reckons that may be so," Lawrence said. "But in any case, after this whole mess here is put to rest, I'se wants you to enjoy the love of life. Life's about love, not all this here heartache." Lawrence dusted away some of Hanzel's ashes which had adhered to Toussaint's suit. He opened his hand to Toussaint, displaying a few specks of ash. "One day, you'se gonna come across this devil again. We'se call him the Doctor."

"What?"

"Doncha worry 'bout it now, Toot. Ain't no sense in worryin' 'bout it. But when he comes back, you'se gonna see him and deals wit' him then. You'se gonna git your share for Missy and for those you'se ain't met yet." Lawrence blew the specks of ash into Toussaint's face as he inhaled, compelling him to ingest the incinerated flesh of his enemy. "Yup, this here's only a taste of vengeance."

Toussaint had learned to trust Lawrence over the years, accepting his words as true. He found himself alone. Toussaint left the suffocation and desperation of the mausoleum.

Across the lawn, he watched Monsieur Roberts greet Allen near the wagon. "Bon, you're here," he heard him say. Toussaint was glad James had decided to leave the comfort of the plantation house and attend to business, instead of running from unpleasant matters. "Shall we get started?" Toussaint heard James say.

Within an hour, the services had ended. The mourners gathered outside while the groundsmen closed the tomb and sealed it with wax. Toussaint hadn't seen the procedure performed before, but somehow it seemed familiar to him. Placing the key in the lock, the grounds men secured the tomb and left. All bowed their heads in a moment of silence.

Salley lifted his eyes towards heaven and crossed himself, having completed his prayers. He replaced his hat on his head. "Well, I'm not far from here, as you may remember James, so I'm heading home. I sent word last evening for my driver to pick me up at half-past eleven o'clock this morning."

Looking past the Chevalier cemetery and the slave cabins, Salley saw a carriage coming up the road. "Ah, as we speak, he comes." The men stood in silence, watching Salley's carriage saunter up the road. "I'm surprised Hanzel missed the visitation, funeral, and the burial. Have you received any word from him, James?"

Regret and concern overcame James. "No. I'm quite concerned myself. I've attempted to contact him for several days now, without success. I'm not even sure if he knows Jean Charles has passed on."

"Pity." Salley's carriage arrived, easing to a stop before the men. "Where is your carriage, James?"

James bowed his head in humility. "Father Pierre has decided to remain in St. Helena for a while and visit with former parishioners now living in the area. I allowed him to use my carriage."

"Good man, James," Salley said. "The Lord will bless you for your kindness to his servants."

James nodded, saying nothing.

"I can have my servant drive you back to New Orleans after he takes me home, if you like."

"I'll be fine," James said. "If Bailey doesn't mind, I'll ride back to New Orleans with him." James removed his pipe from his pocket and lit it.

Toussaint averted a scowl, maintaining his professionalism. "That will be fine, Monsieur. You're welcomed to ride with Allen and me."

"Then it is settled." Salley clapped his hands together. "*Bon voyage, mon ami!*" Salley hugged James. He walked to his carriage and allowed his driver to assist him with entering the vehicle. The driver closed the door and mounted the driver's bench. He pulled away, the horses taking on a slow trot, anxious for the journey which lay ahead.

"Merci, mon ami," James said to him. They watched Salley ride off, descending the hill.

Chapter 7

New Orleans, Louisiana. September 1, 1963.

Julian harbored a new respect for his Uncle Toot and his great-grandpère. They understood how to make a man disappear. He felt laser beams burning into the side of his face. He turned to find his grandmère frowning at him. "What?"

"Nothing."

"It's always something with you, Grandmère," Julian said, rising to pour himself another Glenlivet. "What type of hocus pocus are you spinning now?"

"As I told you before, I am not a witch. In any case, I would like a brandy, if you care to pour one for me."

Julian poured another round for his grandmère. She sure can toss them back.

"I'm not an alcoholic. However, there was a time when the addiction nearly consumed me. But once I took control of my life, the demon recoiled."

"Demon? Oh, never mind. When did this happen?"

Lela traversed back through the years and exhaled, wearied. "I will tell you later. I'm not prepared to discuss it at this time," she said. Lela considered her great-grandson. "What do you desire to do in life, Julian?"

"Why do you care? As long as I decide not to commit you to a nursing home, you should be happy."

Lela smoothed her hair, resisting the urge to cut his tongue out of his mouth. "I'm not self-centered as you are, mon fils. Tell grandmère."

He sat beside her on the sofa. She relieved him of her drink. "I enjoy investments and finance."

Lela concealed her smile. "I see. I would be surprised if you didn't have a passion for it. From your infancy, you demonstrated a passion for gold." Lela watched him sip his scotch. "So, why are you working in the Civil Rights movement?"

Julian mouth dropped open. "They're trying to destroy us, Grandmère. Every Black in America should be up in arms." Julian stood from the sofa and paced the floor. "Our generation must take action now, or risk our descendants being enslaved to White America for generations to come."

"Oh, I see." Lela didn't know whether she should be amused by his theatrical passion for the movement or irritated by his unstated insinuation previous generations had done nothing to further the cause of Negroes. "How do you serve in the movement?"

"I organize protests and demonstrations."

Lela raised a curious brow. "Really? How is that working out for you?"

He knew she already knew. "Not well."

"Why not?"

"Apparently, others in the movement don't respond well to direction. They hate me," Julian confessed.

"I can't understand their dislike for you. Why is that?" Lela swirled her brandy in the snifter.

"They're jealous and won't submit to my leadership. They refuse to do as they are told. When I try to correct them, they run to the area coordinator, defaming me."

"Ah. So, how do you currently fair in the movement?" Lela sipped her brandy.

Julian twisted his mouth. "I've been removed from my position. They've requested I only attend events, not coordinate them." He couldn't believe he'd told her the truth. He hadn't even shared the news of his demotion with Jannette. "I know you have something to say," Julian said.

"No."

"Yes, you do, Grandmère. What?"

Lela finished her brandy and sat the empty glass on the table. "The area coordinator did you a favor, Julian."

"How so?"

"That isn't your calling. It isn't your passion. You only did it to make your own life easier." Lela watched as Julian considered her words, his heart pulled in three directions by his passion, his civic duty, and his inflated ego.

Julian stopped pacing. "We all participate in movements for our own benefit."

Lela nodded, acknowledging his words. "Perhaps. However, there are people who volunteer simply for the joy of helping others, not to benefit themselves."

Lela extended her arm. Julian sat and laid his head on her shoulder. Lela stroked the hair of her little school boy, too proud to admit he'd lost a fight on the playground. "Darling, your talent lies in your passion. You should follow it. Your passion won't lead you astray. You're not cut out to work in the movement. You should leave it to those who are."

Julian turned red, angered by her passivity. "If everyone had your attitude, the movement would go nowhere. There are too many complacent, okie-doke Negroes sitting on their hands, afraid to immerse themselves in the fight for freedom."

Lela found Julian's words to be true. "Yes and no. Many of us who desire to fight do so in alignment with our skills and gifts. Some fight on the front lines. Others raise money. Still others use their influence to persuade those in power to become more sympathetic to the cause. Others send supplies to the activists or provide them with lodging while working in their towns. There are many ways to help. Coordinating events isn't your forte, Julian," she said. Lela burst into laughter, but stifled it. "You aren't a people person, so to speak."

"What is that supposed to mean?"

"You're an asshole, Julian," Lela said, watching shock overtake her great-grandson. "I'm sure you've driven away many volunteers."

He almost choked on his drink. "Grandmère!"

"It's true and you know it. How many volunteers abandoned the cause under your watch?"

Julian stared at his hands. "Thirty percent, according to the area coordinator."

Lela took her great-grandson's hand in hers. "Darling, coordinating volunteers isn't your calling. Perhaps you should have offered to advise them on their financial concerns, manage the books, etcetera." Julian nodded, understanding. "Support the movement, I encourage you to do so, but do not interact with or attempt to lead the other volunteers. You will kill the movement."

Julian scowled. "Well, it doesn't appear as if I have a choice in the matter."

"No, you don't," she told him. "You should give Alexis Micheaux a call. I'm sure he could use you at SR Holdings."

"No thanks," Julian said. "I don't want to work for the family."

Lela snorted. "As you wish. But you will traverse that way."

Retrieving the misted glass from the table, Julian took a sip, attempting to subdue his indignation. "Stay out of my business, old lady." He got up and poured himself another drink. "What else do you wish to bore me with? I would like to go out tonight."

God help me. I cannot kill him, Lela prayed in her heart.

New Orleans, Louisiana. March, 1883.

ALTHOUGH ONE WEEK had passed since Jean Charles entombment, James felt as if it had only been hours. He had become a machine working in a fog, with each day slipping away without meaning or event. He would awake, attend to the business of the Chevalier estate and go to bed. Life had no meaning. He had died with Jean Charles, yet he couldn't understand how.

He exited the carriage and entered the Bank of New Orleans to meet with Monsieur Charles du Montel. He hoped the man would be ready to receive him, for on most occasions, he had to wait fifteen minutes past their scheduled appointment to be received.

Entering the bank, the cool breeze of wealth and ease

met James. He found the interior of the bank stunning, its high ceilings accented with gold gilding, plaster fleur-de-lis surrounded by wreaths of acanthus leaves. James crossed the marble lobby to the Private Banking area, where the bank serviced its wealthier clientele.

The receptionist smiled at him once he opened the etched glass doors. "Please have a seat Monsieur Roberts. I will let Monsieur du Montel know you're here," she said. James nodded and sat near the window.

After a few moments, she returned. "He will see you now, Monsieur." James followed her to his office.

"Bonjour, Monsieur Roberts," du Montel said, shaking his hand vigorously. "How are you? It's been a few weeks since you've been in to see us."

"It is good to see you as well," James said. Du Montel extended his hand, inviting James to sit. He opened his humidor, offering James a cigar, but he refused. "Sadly, I cannot say all is well. Monsieur Jean Charles Chevalier passed away over a week ago, peacefully in his sleep."

"Mon Dieu, I had no idea," he said.

"Yes, it is a pity. His passing has devastated me." James paused to regain his composure. "In any case, I'm here to begin the process of executing the terms of the agreements previously arranged regarding his estate." Placing his attaché case on the desk, he removed the relevant files. "Here are the documents we've been working on for the past several weeks in preparation for this horrible day."

"But, Monsieur," du Montel began.

"Yes?"

"Monsieur, your attorney withdrew all of the funds from the trust account yesterday. His paperwork was in order, with the required signatures. I don't understand."

"Attorney Silas Jacobson was here? I didn't know he had returned to New Orleans from France."

Du Montel felt his chest tighten. "Well, no Monsieur. It was his associate, Attorney Johannesen."

"Hanzel Johannesen?"

"Oui, Monsieur. That was the gentleman's name," he said, relieved James knew the man.

"What credentials did he present to you, Monsieur, considering you had never met him before, which convinced you to execute such a transaction for him?"

"Well, he had all of the trust documents and an authorization to release the funds executed with your and Attorney Jacobson's signatures."

James ran his fingers through his hair. "Place a stop-pay order on the certified check immediately."

Du Montel gulped. "That would be impossible, Monsieur."

The veins sprung forth at James' temples. "What credentials did he present to you, sir?"

"Please, lower your voice Monsieur Roberts," du Montel said.

"I will, once you tell me what credentials he presented to encourage you to give him $15 million?" James' face mutated into a purple hue, threatening to explode across the room.

"Monsieur Roberts, du Montel, is there a problem?" The bank president entered the office and closed the door behind him, hoping the other bank patrons hadn't heard the yelling.

"Yes," James said. "It seems Monsieur du Montel has released the Chevalier estate, totaling in excess of $15 million, to an impostor, without verifying the man's credentials."

The blood drained from the bank president's face. "Is this true, du Montel?" Du Montel stood before them stark white and speechless. The bank president knew from his silence the charges were true.

"Monsieur Roberts, we apologize for this error. I'm certain this man hasn't had the opportunity to negotiate a cashier's check of that size yet. So, we will place a stop order on it and return the funds to the trust."

James pursed his lips, causing the ends of his handle bar mustache to twitch. "Tell him why it won't work, Monsieur du Montel," James said. Du Montel stood before him, silent. "Cat has your tongue, Monsieur? Very well, I shall tell him.

Du Montel gave him cash."

The bank president turned to du Montel, amazed. He should have never allowed his sister to convince him to hire her husband. "Oh, that's impossible. The bank does not keep that amount of cash in the vault. Even if we did have the cash on hand, it wouldn't be available for withdrawal." Both men awaited his explanation.

Du Montel gasped for air. "A little over a week ago, the gentleman, Johannesen, came in and requested the withdrawal. I told him we didn't have the amount in cash. We would have to order it. I told him it wouldn't be available until Monday, which was yesterday."

"Who signed off on the paperwork for the cash order and the release of funds? $15 million would require my signature and I know for certain I didn't fucking authorize it!"

"Well Monsieur, Attorney Johannesen was in a hurry. You weren't here, so I— I—" du Montel swooned and passed out. The two men watched him hit the floor. The bank president threw a glass of water in his face, but it didn't revive him. He turned blue.

"I think he may be having a heart attack," James said, retaking his seat. "You may wish to send for the doctor."

"In a minute," the bank president said. "Let us see if the Good Lord will have mercy on him and take his life now. I assure you, he has nothing left to live for," he said. "I will fully investigate this matter. Please accept my apologies for this inexcusable error. I hope we will not lose your other accounts due to his foolishness."

"Merci, Monsieur." James closed his attaché case and left the office.

Chapter 8

Lela

I fought back my tears as I passed the library. Jamie hadn't spoken to me at length since Hanzel's attack. I knew what he believed about me and Hanzel. I'd never had the chance to tell him all his 'friend' had planned to destroy him.

Now, I was merely his servant. Nancy prepared his meals and I brought them in to him. He thanked and dismissed me without any further acknowledgment, never looking up from whatever he worked on at his desk in the library.

Once James had returned from Jean Charles' burial, I ceased to exist in his world. I had become the equivalent of a human automat for him. He discontinued all conversation with me, sending his requests via another servant. A servant would come to me and say, "Mis'sur said for you'se to pick up some cigars at the store today, Miss Lela." One day, he sent me another message. "Mis'sur Roberts says to tell Miss Nancy he wants duck for dinner."

New Orleans, Louisiana. March, 1883.

STANDING OUTSIDE THE kitchen, Lela inhaled deep. She'd tired of dealing with James' indifference toward her and dreamed of leaving New Orleans. Where would she go? She could return to La Rose, but she couldn't figure out which life would be the most intolerable. "I guess I don't have a choice," she said.

Lela strengthen herself and went to the library to serve James his duck. She placed the silver serving tray on the floor and rapped on the door.

"Yes, what is it?"

"I have your dinner."

"Bring it in, please."

Lela opened the door. Stooping down, she picked up the heavy tray and entered the room. She found him sitting at the desk reviewing the household accounts, as always. He pointed to a table at his right, without diverting his eyes from his work. When she didn't move, he spoke. "Over there."

In a confused state, she walked over to the small table near the window. "Here?"

"Yes," he said, maintaining his focus on his work.

She placed the tray on the table and returned to the desk, standing before him once again. He continued to work, without acknowledging her. After several moments he said, "That is all. You may go."

Lela's eyes welled up with tears. Her face flushed red from the emotion erupting within her, ignited by the continued hurt and heartache she'd suffered due to his coldness. She ran from the room, slamming the door behind her. Running up the stairs to the third floor, she collapsed outside of her bedroom, wailing so loud the other servants in the house heard her.

One of the maids went to the kitchen. "Miss Nancy, I'se thanks Miss Lela's upstairs cryin'."

"What?"

"Somebody's upstairs cryin' in the hallway," the maid said.

"Lawd, ain't we seent e'nuff heartache in this house?" Nancy dried her hands and ran upstairs. Reaching the landing, she found Lela slumped on the floor. She didn't need to ask her what was wrong, for she already knew. "C'mon chile. Let's git you in the bed."

James jumped in his chair, startled by the hard knock on the door. "Who is it?" he said, finding himself little afraid.

"It's Nancy, Mis'sur. I'se comes for your dinner tray."

He didn't wish to be bothered with Nancy. She never left the kitchen, unless she was going to her room, to the market to pick up a few items for a meal, or to Mass. He knew she only wished to lecture him. "Never mind, Nancy. Lela will take them tomorrow morning."

"No suh, she won't. Lela won't be here in the mornin'."

He massaged his brow, unwilling to deal with it all. "And why is that, Nancy?"

"I dunno suh. Just said she ain't gonna be here."

James knew he couldn't escape the looming conversation with her. "Come in, Nancy."

Gliding across the floor, she made her way to where the dinner tray sat on the table. She retrieved the napkin, placing it along with the plate and the utensils on the silver tray, and then covered it all with the lid.

Once she completed the cleanup, Nancy walked over to the desk. She leaned down, coming eyeball to eyeball with him. "If'se you'se wanted her dead, you'se shouldda lets Johannesen, your slimy li'l friend, rapes and kills her."

"You are out of line, Nancy."

"No, you'se the one who's wrong and you'se bein' selfish." Remembering she had left the door ajar, Nancy went to close it and then returned to the desk. "She went to the wall for you. She wouldn't deny you, no matter what Johannesen tried. Your friend was gonna turn you over to the sheriff so you'se could hang for killin' Mis'sur Chevalier."

"What?"

"That's right. Your bosom buddy was plannin' to destroy you," Nancy said. "He wanted to enslave all of us. But what he had in mind for poor Lela was just plain cruel." Nancy studied him. "How you'se thank all that got cleaned up?" She noticed James' body stiffened.

"You'se busted in this house, grabbed that crossbow from over the mantle and ran up them stairs like a ball of fire. I'se followed you. We'se went into the room and that evil li'l man had her—"

"Enough!"

"No, not e'nuff, 'cause you'se don't 'members it all," Nancy said, unwilling to back down. "You'se kicked in the door and found your friend wit' your woman bent over, 'bouts to fucks her."

"Shut your goddamn mouth and get out, Nancy."

"Naw, suh. Not 'tils you'se 'members all of it and not just the parts you'se can stands," Nancy said. "Doncha remember runnin' up them stairs? We'se could hear Lela screamin' murder from down the hall, beggin' for her life and for your ole sorry ass life too."

"No." James leaned back in his chair. Covering his face with his hands, he sobbed. *I don't want to remember.* Nancy droned on in the background of his nightmare, forcing him to relive all of it.

Nancy walked around the desk and stood before him. "What he been tellin' you, Mis'sur? Been messin' wit' your mind 'bout Lela? Did he tells you she wanted him? 'All Niggah bitches the same. They'se go wit' anybody. If you'se wasn't 'round all the time, she'd go wit' me.' Is that what that bastard been tellin' you?" James sat before her, red faced.

"'Cause I'se knows he's a dirty, foul, cruel, sadistic man. Hell, Ma'Dame Red told him not to come back to the house no more 'cause he cut up one of the gals. He was gonna do the same to Lela. I'se could see it. He was gonna take her outta here to a place where nobody could hear her scream and do just God awful thangs to her. So, when you'se saw them, he was ready to git started."

Tears ran down James' face. Nancy's voice narrated a scene only he could see. "No." Shaking his head, he yelled out in pain.

"Look," she said. "What do you'se see? What's really happenin'?"

"No," James said, seeing for the first time the actual events.

Scream

Now you will be at the ready for me

Silence

Whimpering

"Lela."

"What you'se sees, Mis'sur?"

James slid from his chair, coming to rest on the floor, weeping. "Now I'se knows you'se done seent the truth,"

Nancy said. "She fought him. Lela didn't want him. But he wanted to rapes her to hurt you. He wanted you'se to see it, too. Johannesen wanted to best you'se and Mis'sur Chevalier, to make ya'll pay. When ya'll was young, you'se and Mis'sur Chevalier had everything. He felts like he had nuthin'."

James continued to sit on the floor. Looking back, he always knew Hanzel disliked him, but this much? But he knew it was true. Hanzel never missed an opportunity to either humiliate or intimidate him. Now, he'd allowed Hanzel to influence him to the point of doubting his love. "How could I think she wanted him, Nancy?"

"She didn't wants him. I'se 'clare she didn't, Mis'sur."

"Did he?" Jamie couldn't ask the question.

"Naw, suh. He didn't vi'lates her. You'se killed him 'fore he could. You'se saved her. Wit' you, God answered her prayers."

"Lela." For the first time, James thought of her as a victim and not as a willing participant. "Oh, God. What have I done?"

Nancy tried to feel sorry for him, but she couldn't. He had cut a wound so deep in Lela's heart, she wasn't sure if it would ever heal. She wanted Lela to leave and never turn back, but she could see it wasn't to be. "You'se killin' her worse than Johannesen ever could. She needs you now, but you'se treatin' her like trash. She told me, 'I'se wish Johannesen wouldda killed me. It wouldda been better than Jamie killin' me now.'"

Nancy's words cut open his heart. "Where is she, Nancy?"

"Let her be, Mis'sur."

"Nancy…"

She gave in. "Lela's in her room, Mis'sur."

James bolted from the floor and ran up the stairs to the third floor. His old fears attempted to overtake him once again. However, he rebuked them, strengthening himself. He could no longer believe in the lie. Jamie could hear Lela sobbing from the other side of the heavy cypress door. He knocked.

"Who is it? Nancy?"

"No, Lela. It's me."

Silence answered his response for several minutes. "Come in." She'd spoken so softly, he'd almost missed it.

Entering the dark room, James could see a slight figure lying in the bed. The moonlight outlined the edge of the heavy drapes, tightly drawn, attempting to bar the light's admittance into a room overrun with grief and heartbreak. However, the light rebelled, cutting a small beam through the opening where the panels met, coming to rest upon Lela. "May I come over and talk to you, Lela?" After a few moments of silence, he heard her whisper yes.

James stood above where she lay in bed with her face buried in the pillow. The errant beam of moonlight revealed her red, tear stained cheek. Spotting the faded, deep purple bruises on her neck, left behind by Hanzel's grip, James suppressed the anger welling up inside of him. How could he have ever believed for one single moment she could have desired him?

With caution, he sat beside her, ready to spring up at the slightest objection. However, it never came. She continued to weep while hiding her face. He examined the wounds on her arms, scarred from her gallant defense of all their lives.

James listened to Lela cry. He reached out and stroked her hair, moving it away from her cheek. He began to cry as well, mourning what Hanzel had done to her and for his own sins against her as well. "My darling, I'm so, so very sorry for bringing him here. I'm sorry for his brutality against you." James paused, unable to contain his regret. "But I'm most sorry for my own cruelty toward you. Darling, I'm sorry."

Lela turned to him, her face scalded from hours of nonstop sobbing. She righted herself, pulling her knees up to her chest, protecting herself from whatever lay ahead.

"Please, Lela. I was wrong. Please ma chere, don't shut me out," he said, extending his hand to her. "Please, don't shut out love, as I foolishly did." She didn't move. "I am a fool. I am a fool. I'm a fool!" Lela allowed his hand to hang there. Realizing she wouldn't take it, he allowed it to fall in defeat.

"How could you think I wanted him, James?"

God, she knows. "The truth is, I never truly thought—" He stopped, frustrated. He didn't wish to make all which had transpired about him, instead of Lela. "I never believed you wanted me," he confessed.

"How could you not know I loved you, James? What would make you think I didn't?"

His given name burned in his ears. "Because it would mean I'm somebody. My every boyhood and adult dream would have become my reality. My Lela loved me too," James said. Moonlit teardrops streamed down his face. "I'd failed you. I had failed my one and only true love, the only one for whom I would gladly die. I found it easier to accept the lie of you wanting him than to admit to myself I couldn't protect you from him. So, I blamed you," he said.

Lela's face remained stoic and unforgiving.

"I'd thought… I'd thought I was too late. I thought he was ra— raping—" He paused to catch his breath and to summon the courage to say the unspeakable. "I thought he had raped you.

"I stood there helpless, powerless, gripped with fear, and unable to help. Like, like with Maman. When Hanzel's father killed Maman." He slipped years into the past, once again a scared boy. "He— He—" James gathered his resolve. "He cut her throat for denying him."

Jamie sat next to Lela, frightened to death. "You know, I saw him do it. The knife passed before Maman, gliding by her like a silk scarf, so smooth. I thought he'd missed, but then a ribbon of red began to flow in a 'u' shaped formation down her neck, welling up in the neckline of her dress.

"Father had said she was a whore and got what she deserved. But—" A light went off in his head which triggered horror in his soul, devastating him once again. "Oh, God. He raped her too, or he tried to. Maman kept saying, 'No. I told you no!' Josef became enraged. Oh, Maman!" James melted into the horror of the night long ago.

"You know, after Josef, well after he killed Maman, Papa wouldn't even bury her in the family plot on the plantation. Instead, he buried her at St. Roch, here in New Orleans. He'd planned to bury her in a pauper's grave, but I begged him not to do so. He said 'Well, she was your maman. I will mark the grave.'"

Although wearied by it all, she couldn't suppress the compassion, love, and sympathy which still smoldered in her heart for him. "That was a great burden for a boy to bear," Lela said.

"Yes. Yes, it was." James stared at the rug, still lost in the past. "It still is." His grief drained from him in a slow procession of tears.

Returning to present, he pleaded to her with his eyes. "I can't lose you too. I don't know how to keep you." James couldn't say what was in his heart. How could she ever accept him? Heartbreak compelled him to try. "Lela, I'm so very sorry."

A little more than frightened children, two devastated souls clung to one another. They cried themselves to sleep upon Lela's small bed on the third floor of the Chevalier mansion. The moon lit their path, so they could perhaps return to each other once again.

By eleven o'clock in the morning, Nancy still hadn't seen any sign of either Lela or James. At first, she decided not to disturb them, but then she thought better of it. "Maybe they'se hungry. I'll take them some breakfast." She placed the croissants and coffee pot on the serving tray. They were cool, but still soft and flaky.

She retrieved a jar of her pear preserves from the pantry, which she had put up the prior fall at Madame Red's. When packing the kitchen house, she'd found the six jars beneath her bed. She and Willie had almost starved, with jars of preserves under the bed, forgotten. "Well, ifs I'd remembered them, then I'se wouldn't have found Miss Lela."

Opening the jar, the fragrance of autumn's sweetness

enveloped her, reminding her of Nate, who had assisted her with the canning. Not that he knew how, but the process fascinated him.

"Man, you ain't ever watched your mammy jar before?"

"Yeah, but Mammy didn't look like you. Her fruit wasn't sweet and juicy like yours is," he said, leering at Nancy. "Naw ain't ever wanted to eat my mammy's fruit and sap up the juices like I'se gonna do wit' yours." He towered over her, allowing his formidable presence to dominate her.

"Boy, you'se nasty." She shoved him away. He bent down and kissed her neck. The steam of the stewing pears mingled with his breath, tickling her. Entranced, she lost interest in canning. "I'se... I'se gotta put these pears up."

"Let's me put your fruit up first." He slid his arms around her. He kissed her, his tongue dancing inside of her mouth as his hand slipped inside of the bodice of her dress. His other hand, equally as fast and agile with her full skirts, found what it searched for. "Yeah, girl. Your fruit's much sweeter than Mammy's ever couldda been."

He picked her up. Nancy wrapped her legs around him. Headed toward the pantry, he tantalized her with his kisses, growing with passion, heat rising. Nancy could hear the lid on the pot rattle as her pears began to boil, searing hot and sweet. The fury of cherished love taking its course, he kicked open the swinging door, and laid her down upon the croaker sacks.

"Boy, folks hafta eat this flour!"

"What folks don't know won't hurt them," he said, followed up with a deep growl. "'Sides, what's wrong wit' a li'l bit of lovin' in your biscuits?"

"Nate!"

"C'mon girl." He cooed in her ear, seducing her all over again.

It was too late to stop anyway. Nancy grabbed his dick, so big and hard. She just liked to hold him in her hands. Burning, her body arched and contoured to the flour sacks, ready to receive him. "C'mon boy," she said in a tortured voice. "Doncha make me beg for you."

"Not yet, gal." He growled at her. A sinister smile crept across his broad face. "I'se gonna makes you'se want it."

Nancy awoke from her revelry with tears streaming down her face. "Nate." She sat down on the bench he'd made for her and cried for what seemed like a hundred years. "Why Lawd? Why'se would you'se takes my love from me? After so many years of me bein' by myself, I'se given up on love. Then you'se sent me my Nate, and I'se thought my lonely days were gone. And then you'se burns him up?" Nancy wailed for her love.

"Father why? It wouldda been better to kills me." She put her head in her hands and wept, allowing the bottled-up pain to flood out. She felt a gentle touch her shoulder.

"Aunt Nancy, don't cry. I miss him too."

Nancy found Willie standing before her, hurting. In her grief, she'd forgotten the child had returned home from the Baileys.

"C'mere, honey." She opened her arms and he collapsed into her. Nancy enfolded him in her soft embrace.

"Chile, the Lawd done gave us each other. You'se got an Aunt and I'se gots me a nephew. That's more than either of us done figured we'd ever have." They both sat on Nate's bench crying, hugging and comforting each other.

She stopped before Lela's door. Hearing nothing, Nancy entered the bedroom and sat the tray on the bureau. She glimpsed at the bed, where they lay entwined in each other's arms, sound asleep. "Lawd, lets them find their way together," she said. "They'se both still here on this Earth. Be merciful, and let them find their way."

The soft click of the closing door awoke Lela. A little disoriented at first, her body soon registered the sensation of James' arms around her once again, protecting her from every danger.

She turned over and peered into his sleeping face. So

lovely. But in her heart, she knew the end had come for them. "How will he ever get pass this," she said. "Lord why? Why can't I be happy for once in my life?" She regretted her ungrateful attitude. She thanked the Lord for the short time she'd been happy before Hanzel's arrival.

Maybe she'd ruined it by doubting what the Lord had given her, a precious love such as her Jamie. She twirled the tip of his handle bar mustache between her fingertips. The corner of her lips perked up, but she suppressed the smile of joy before it could materialize.

James awoke, feeling Lela's eyes on him. He found tears running down her face, cascading over the bridge of her nose. "What's wrong?" he asked, his voice still deep and heavy with sleep.

"Nothing. Just thinking."

"About what, ma chere?"

For some reason, Lela decided to tell him the truth. "About losing you and what my life would become as a result," she said, stoic. "I'm wondering how I could go on without you."

James caressed her cheek, wiping away the tears falling from her eyes. "You will never lose me, Lela."

"How are you going to get pass all of this, Jamie?"

"I don't know," he said. In his heart, he didn't know if he could.

Lela decided to be direct with him. "Do you still believe I wanted him? Do you believe I was willing to give to him what is yours alone, my love and my body? Do you still believe I could do such a thing?" She searched his eyes for the truth. Lela feared his answer; but at the same time, she had to know.

Her bluntness knocked him off kilter. "Well, no. I now know you never desired or encouraged his advances. Han— Han—" James steadied his soul. "He was an evil man, manipulating everyone around him. I understand that. But—" James stopped, put off by her silence. "How do I say this to you? I can't get the image out of my mind. And I don't know if I can."

Lela received the words she knew were coming. At least he'd told her the truth. *Well, there it is,* she thought to herself. *I'm damaged goods.*

"Oh."

The truth hung between them. A gavel had been sounded, pronouncing judgment over their relationship. "Well, I can't take the image out of your mind. I have images in my head as well, like him raping me, killing you, or better yet, the State of Louisiana executing you for something you didn't do. I prayed to the Lord to save us both, and he did."

Lela broke down, sobbing. "That motherfucka had me by my goddamn neck, treating me worse than some folks treat their dogs. Yet, I hoped you would save me from him. I hoped you would take me in your arms and say, 'Darling, I'm here now. Everything is alright.'"

James turned away. With hardened eyes, she'd sentenced him. Her verdict was irreversible and final. She'd condemned him.

"The Lord answered a portion of my prayer, I guess," Lela said.

"I love you with all of my heart. I think you know that, but maybe the image of seeing me on the brink of rape is stronger than the reality of you saving me from destruction." Lela's tears dried without warning. "Jamie, you saved us both; but, I'm sure all of it is more than you can bear." Lela turned away, unable to accept her new status with her only love.

He knew his feelings were wrong, but they were true. He just couldn't get the image out of his head. He knew that whenever he would lie with her, he would see Hanzel standing over her with his little prick, ready to take what didn't belong to him. Lela belonged to him and Hanzel knew it.

James shuddered, realizing the truth. In his eyes, Lela had been handled by another, regardless if by force or not. Hanzel had left his mark on her. *Am I really this shallow*, he wondered? Did he ever truly love Lela if he only regarded her as his property, his woman? *His property?*

He struggled with the reality he was no better than Hanzel, perhaps even worse. Even now, with this great revelation, he still didn't feel any compassion for her and for what she'd suffered. She'd risked death rather than deny him, and this was the only repayment he could grant her. "You deserve better than me, Lela."

Weary and tired of crying, she stared pass him, over his shoulder, to the draperies. They'd been drawn tight like her heart, shutting out the light of the sun. "Jamie, did you ever love me?"

James stared at the bed, not knowing what to say. Lela arose from where they had lain together. She grabbed her robe from the modest cane back chair and put it on, barring herself from all. "Nancy brought up some breakfast. The croissants are cold, but perhaps you may still enjoy them."

Chapter 9

Atlanta, Georgia. March, 1883.

James unlocked the door and stepped into the refreshing coolness of his Atlanta home. He walked up the stairs. His only desire was to fall into bed and sleep. He heard a click. "It's me, Sallie."

Sallie walked down the hall to the foyer. "Boy, whatcha doin' here? I'se almost shot you." She uncocked the shotgun and leaned it in the corner, near the grandfather clock. Walking over to the staircase where her son stood, she opened her arms, welcoming him. James ran down the stairs and dove into her love and comfort, melting. *Oh Lawd*, she thought to herself, feeling her son's pain.

"I'm sorry, Ma. I should've wired you."

Sallie frowned at him. "Yeah, 'cause ifs I'd known you'se was comin', I'se wouldn't have given ev'rybody the next two weeks off for Easter. Now you'se here and there ain't nobody left to care for you."

"I'm not a child, Sallie."

"So you say." She picked a strand of hair from his jacket. "C'mon upstairs. Where's your thangs?"

"They will arrive later."

"Well, I'll send some of the boys to help wit' them. Sam didn't go on vacation, so he can help me wit' you." She placed her hands on his shoulders, peering into his eyes. James looked away. "Let's git you settled in."

James attended to business for the next week in Atlanta, visiting his old haunts and lady friends. He returned to his bachelor's life as if he'd never left it.

Stepping out of his carriage, he traveled the carpeted, canopied walkway. The doorman opened the door, allowing him to enter. James spotted the concierge, who'd waved at him. "Mr. Roberts. I'm glad you've returned."

"Thank you, Simpson. Has seating for dinner begun yet?"

"No, sir. It hasn't. Why don't you relax in the club room? The chimes will sound once we begin."

"Thank you," James said, handing him his hat and cane. Adjusting his cuffs, James smoothed the lapels of his tuxedo and made his way to the lounge.

"Would you care for something to drink, Mr. Roberts?"

"Yes, a cognac," he said, taking a seat in the supple, leather wing chair. The waiter nodded and rushed away to fulfill his request.

James lit his ivory pipe, carved with swords intertwined with roses. He reclined into the chair, taking pride in the strides which the Civic Club of Atlanta had made in such a short period of time. The chimes sounding, he watched the club members make their way toward the dining room, escorting their wives with pride and grace.

Sorrow overcame James, knowing he could never entertain Lela at the club. What if someone discovered she was Negro? Surely the members would lynch them both, despite the hundreds of thousands of dollars he'd donated in furnishings and money. Landowners and businessmen from across the South comprised the club's membership. As if many of them didn't have Negro lovers of their own! However, he guessed these individuals weren't trying to marry their Negro women. James knew there wasn't another in all eternity he desired to marry. He simply wished to honor his wife as they all did, not only at the club, but before society and the world.

The waiter placed the snifter of cognac on the side table, along with a napkin and a silver bowl of assorted nuts. "Thank you." The waiter bowed and left. James scowled, remembering. He'd lost her. Lela would never forgive him.

The trauma of Hanzel's attack had begun to subside in James' psyche, allowing his love for Lela to take hold of his heart once more. Witnessing her in a compromising position didn't matter anymore. All that remained was his desire to make her his wife. How could he have been so foolish?

"Pride is the downfall of us all, mon fils."

James scanned the area, finding no one. The Holy Spirit had spoken to him. He took a gulp of cognac and returned to his misery.

"All isn't as you believe. It is well. She's your wife, or will soon become so. Why do you worry?"

"We can't marry here." Realizing another had verbally addressed him, James looked up. "Guillet, how did you gain admittance?"

He smirked, removing his gloves. "No man can bar me from anywhere I wish to go on this Earth," he said. "By the way, my name is Jerémèy in this time." He took a seat on the chair near James. "*Ma petite fille est très belle, n'est-ce pas?*"

"Oui, mon père."

Jerémèy appraised the spiritual progress of his child. James' sight had grown immensely since reuniting with the Rose. He hadn't addressed him as Guillet in centuries. Well, after he'd first drunk from the cup, he'd called him Guillet off and on for a while.

James sat before him, troubled. Jealously and possessiveness dogged his child's soul, at first with Sallie, and now, Lela. Jerémèy understood why. Richard had scarred him with his wicked little Doctor. Well, Richard had scarred the Seed in the thirteenth century as well, but Jerémèy wasn't sure if James remembered the time. "What prevents you from marrying her?"

"Well, she has shut me out because—" James stopped, unable to speak the words. "As she has declared time and again, miscegeny is illegal in the United States. I could never bring Lela here or anywhere else as my wife. They will find out. Lela is right. We can't live here in love, only as master and servant." James wiped his brow with his handkerchief. "I can't protect her."

Jerémèy wished to slap the boy, but decided to be patient and allow him to talk out his feelings. "Why would you say such a thing?"

"Grandpa, how can you ask me that?" James wept, his eyes flashing to the left and then the right, hoping no one had noticed them.

Jerémèy concealed his joy. The boy had remembered him as his grandfather, but it had been many centuries before. "They can't see you, mon fils."

James began to shudder. "Richard, Well Olad…"

"Release it."

James wept, inundated by the horrific memories of his wife's death, resurfacing in his heart and soul without warning. "Well, you know what Richard did to Melissa." James blinked in quick staccato bursts, scanning the room from side to side filled with terror. He hoped the devil wouldn't hear him speaking of the incident.

So, he does remember. Jerémèy could see James' love for Lela had released the memories. So, maybe he didn't remember the thirteenth century. However, James' soul remembered Melissa, which was bad enough. "She wasn't la Rose. God protects his Seed."

"But the child was my seed, Guillet. The child was Richard's grandchild. How could he do it?" James stiffened with terror, seeing before his eyes his wife's death for the first time in years.

'*I cut too deep. He's not the one*'

'*I will take the next child*'

Jerémèy touched James between his eyes.

James rubbed his temples, reconnecting with his whereabouts. "Oh, Jerémèy. What were you saying?"

"You shouldn't feel guilty about what happened to Melissa. She died in childbirth. It wasn't your fault."

James nodded, out of sorts. "Yes, I guess I do harbor some guilt over the whole matter. I felt helpless, unable to help her." James grimaced, confused by all that had happened. "But with Lela… Well, we're older. We won't have any children." James felt the pain of despair deep within his stomach. "Oh, yes. She hates me now," James said. "Yet, even if she would consider me, we cannot be married."

To say the boy was bright and had a seeing eye, he could be blind when it came to his Rose. In the boy's defense, the Lord had shut his eye after he'd defied him regarding Sallie, but this? He'd only begun to regain his sight in recent years.

Yet, Jerémèy could see James' fear of Richard decimating his family again was the source of his blindness and inability to act with the strength of God. "Is the world comprised of this one continent alone, this single nation?" James' eyes brightened with his words. "Mon fils, consider returning to your homeland once again. Have you forgotten the home you've built? Rather the home I've built for you?"

With everything that had happened over the past few months, James had forgotten it. "I hadn't fully considered the option."

"At times, we all suffer from tunnel vision," Jerémèy said.

Hope returned to him. How could he have forgotten? "It is done," James said. However, new doubts sprouted in his heart. "She will never leave the Queen Mother."

Jerémèy raised an eyebrow. James had recognized her. "Nancy? Trust me, she will. But first, you must atone for your deplorable treatment of Lela."

"Lela will never forgive me," James said.

"Talk to her. Confess your heart. Have you spoken to Sallie concerning the matter?"

"I don't wish to discuss it with her. She may beat me."

Jerémèy smiled as he lit his cigarette. "You may not have a choice, but to accept her punishment."

James finished his cognac, conflicted. "How could Lela…"

"You know she didn't. Why do you continue to embrace the lie?" Jerémèy said. James wiped away a tear. "You're behaving like your father. But, you are more than him alone, mon fils. You are…" Jerémèy censored his words. "You are Emeline's child, as well. Embrace your heart, James. The blessing for Earth must come through you. Don't allow fear, lies and distrust to hinder it."

James nodded. "I'm not sure if I can."

Jerémèy slapped him. He stretched his hand, hoping to alleviate the pain. "You can, and you will." Jerémèy watched as one of James' associates walked toward them.

"James, how are you?"

"I'm well, Armistead," he said, rising from the chair to shake his hand. "Samuel Armistead, please meet my cousin—" James turned to find Jerémèy gone. "He must have stepped away. Where is your lovely wife?"

"Chatting with some of the other ladies," Armistead said, pointing to a group of women. "James, you don't have a wife?"

"I'm a widower. But soon, I will take another wife," he

said. "Satan will prove powerless in his attempts to steal my love from me."

"Good man. Maybe you could wed here?"

James smiled with pride, surveying the grandeur of the club. What hadn't the members accomplished? He considered the fine works of art gracing the walls, many of which he had donated from the Roberts Château in France, along with the elegant furnishings, some of which he'd donated and others he'd purchased for the club.

James nodded, proud of the establishment they'd all worked together to build. Yet, at the same time, he knew Lela would never be allowed to cross its threshold. "Perhaps. But I believe it would prove a blessing to our union if we returned home to France and married there," James said.

Armistead's face slackened, filled with melancholy. He'd wished for the couple to marry at the club. "I believe you're right, sir. Follow the path which the Good Lord has laid out before you." He patted James on the shoulder.

The men watched as Mrs. Armistead approached them. "Honey, you remember Mr. Roberts?"

Her eyes flirted with James. "Yes, I most certainly do. It's a pleasure to see you again." Mrs. Armistead extended her hand for James to kiss.

"The pleasure is all mine. You are beautiful, as always."

Mrs. Armistead batted her eyes, blushing a bit. "Thank

you, Mr. Roberts."

The dinner bells chimed. Taking her hand, Mr. Armistead led his wife to the dining room. James dreamed of
his Lela on his arm, presenting her to the French court and
society. He followed the happy couple, overjoyed.

Sallie lit the lamp and then tied her robe. Holding the
lamp, she navigated her way down the grand staircase. She
glanced at the hall clock once she'd reached the ground floor.
"Four o'clock?" she muttered. "Nuthin' but trouble rangs at
four in the mornin'," she said.

The doorbell chimed again and again. "Sam?" She wondered where he was and why he hadn't answered the door.
"Who is it?"

"It's Sheriff Lucas."

She opened the door and found Sheriff Lucas, accompanied by two patrol officers holding up James. "Lawd! Sheriff
Lucas, what happened? Is he aw'rite?"

"He's fine, Aunt Sallie. Just drunk. He got into a bar
fight."

"A fight? What on earth for?"

Sheriff Lucas considered his drunken friend, filled with
pity. "I'll let him tell you about it. Where do want us to put
him?"

Sallie lifted James' chin and searched his eyes. He had

succumbed to alcohol. "You'se can take him upstairs and put him to bed, if ya'll don't mind."

"Please, darling. Don't cry. Forgive me. I'm sorry!"

Sallie refreshed the wet compress and placed it on his forehead. "Wake up, honey."

James' eyes fluttered opened in the darkened room. He placed his hand on his head, attempting to sit up. He fell back onto the soft mattress. "What time is it?"

"Two o'clock in the afternoon."

He tried his best to remember what had happened the night before. He'd taken care of business all day. He dined at the Civic Club. Then what? Oh yes, he went by the gentleman's club. He had a few drinks with his lady friend. Someone called Lela a Nigger.

"Lela."

Sallie's eyes grew big. "What's this gots to do wit' Lela, Jamie?"

"What?"

"You'se said Lela."

He rubbed his head. His jaw was sore. Had he been in a fight? When had he returned home? He didn't remember coming home.

"Jamie?"

"Yes, Sallie?"

"What's troublin' you, baby?" Sallie sat on the bed beside him, taking him in her arms. "Why you'se here?"

"I live here, Sallie."

She smoothed his matted hair. "Yeah, this is your home, but it ain't were your heart is," she said. Sallie took him in her arms, rocking her little boy.

"Stop, Sallie. I'm not a child anymore."

She kissed his cheek. "I'se knows you'se ain't. You'se a grown man, but you'se stills my li'l boy. Always will be, I'se reckon."

James broke down and wept, unable to stop.

"What happened in New Orleans, Jamie?"

"I lost Lela."

"How?"

"I caught Hanzel—"

"Oh Lawd, no. Did that low life—"

"No, but he tried Ma! He almost did, but I killed him before he could."

"Well, thank the Lawd for that. He's truly merciful," Sallie said, relieved. "They'se were filthy, wicked folks. Always was. Sarah told me what Josef did to your mama."

"Ma, please!"

Sallie let it go. She began to think. "What happened, Jamie? After it was all over?"

James started to cry, but stopped, wiping away his tears.

"I blamed Lela for what had happened," he said.

Sallie stared at James, not recognizing him. "James Roberts, how's on earth did you'se do that? After what your low-down Daddy did to your mama, you'se turn 'round and do the same thang to poor Lela?"

He began to sob. "I couldn't deal with it, Ma. I just couldn't. It was just easier—"

"To blame her?"

"Yes."

Sallie never could understand the psyche of the Roberts men. They were insane. "So, when Lela needed you'se the most, you'se turns your back on her? Is that what you'se tellin' me?"

James stared out the window. He couldn't bear to face Sallie. "I can't get the picture of Hanzel out of my mind, standing over Lela."

"You'se actin' like your daddy, Jamie."

James glared at her, full of anger, but then it subsided. Sallie was right. "But, he put his hands on Lela, Sallie! He knew I loved her, and he tried to take her—"

Sallie slapped Jamie's face, hard. "Boy, what's wrong wit' you? He didn't take your ball on the playground. She's the woman you'se claims to love, not a toy to keeps to yo'self. This ain't no comp'tition 'tween you'se and Hanzel.

"Lela is a woman, a livin', feelin' human bein' who your

wicked li'l friend almost vi'lated. How'se you'se thank she's feelin'? You'se thanks she's hurtin', haunted by what that li'l motherfucka tried to do to her? But all you'se can thank of is yo'self. Hanzel took your toy wit'out your permission. What the fucks wrong wit' you? I ain't raise you like this, I'se 'clare I'se didn't. Your evil ass daddy is comin' out of you on this."

James sat before her in stunned silence. In all their years together, Sallie had never talked to him like this, filled with disgust. Sure, she had whipped him from time to time, but nothing serious. But now, he feared she would disown him. "I'm sorry, Sallie."

"Why'se you'se apologizin' to me, boy? I'se ain't the one you'se done disgraced." Sallie glanced out the window. "You know, I'se understands who you'se is and what you'se been through. I'se knows why you'se do the thangs you do." She massaged his hand.

"Lela don't knows you. She don't know why you'se would blame her when all she did was love you. Then you'se pack up your thangs and leaves her like trash in the street. You've always loved that gal, but now when bad thangs happen, you'se blames her? Is that how you'se love somebody, Jamie?"

James slouched over, defeated. "I do love her, Sallie. You know I do!"

Sallie glared at him, threatening to whip him the spot.

"Then git your ass on that railcar and take yo'self back to New Orleans and fix this thang wit' her, boy," she said to him. "Don't lose love 'cause of the devil's ploys."

Chapter 10

New Orleans, Louisiana. March 31, 1883.

James returned with all his trunks in tow. Lela watched him. The man behaved as if all was well. Lela stood in the hallway when he crossed the threshold, appearing dapper and refreshed like he'd just returned from vacation. He passed her, along with the other servants. Lela stood at attention in her formal maid's attire, not noticing him. And she didn't.

"Hello, Lela."

Lela nodded, but avoided his eyes. Why look upon a man, a White man even, who'd humiliated her? *Keep on walking. Fuck you.*

Saddened, James walked down to the hall to the library and closed the door.

The show now over, Lela departed for the kitchen. "Pardon," Lela said as she passed one of the maids, directing several house boys carrying James' trunks, luggage and parcels. She walked in and sat on the bench near the window.

Nancy stood at the counter, humming and singing, preparing James' meal. Why was she so happy he'd returned? As far as Lela was concerned, the devil had returned from his vacation in hell.

Her friend turned and faced her, drying her hands on the kitchen towel. "You'se don't love him no more, baby?" Lela curled her lip, refusing to answer. "Doncha let the devil stir up a hard heart in you, Lela."

Nancy sat on Nate's bench, beside her. "You'se just a woman and he's just a man. We'se all got stuff to deal wit'. We'se all afraid of love." Nancy wiped away her tears, choking back the pain of her own heartache. "Your love is still on this here earth. You'se cain't find it in your heart to forgive him?"

Lela turned away from her, torn.

"He's only a man. He's frailer than a woman is 'cause he's gots him a man's heart. Lord didn't give menfolk a forgivin' and understandin' heart likes he did to womenfolk. But you-know what's special 'bout Jamie? He's tryin' to make thangs right. You'se gonna make it impossible for him?" Lela stared out the window. "Well, that's your decision. That's 'tween you'se, Jamie, and the Good Lawd."

Following Nancy's lead, Lela went to the stove. Nancy took the bacon and eggs off the hearth and put them on a plate. Lela sneered, placing the plate on the tray and covering it with the lid. She wished to spit in his food, but she didn't.

Lela hoisted the tray to her shoulder and left the kitchen, walking down the hall to the library. She placed the tray on the floor. Standing there, her hatred for the one who lurked on the other side bubbled to the top of her heart. She smoothed her dress and then patted her hair, tucking an errant curl beneath her little cap. She blotted her face with the back of her hand. Now ready to face the devil, she knocked.

"Yes?"

"I have your breakfast, Monsieur."

"Come in."

Ignoring him, Lela entered and walked over to the small table. She placed his breakfast there and then turned to leave.

"Lela," he said to her, his voice brimming with hesitancy.

"Oui, Monsieur?" She faced him and diverted her eyes to the floor, as custom dictated.

He winced. "I'm returning to Atlanta in a few weeks. There is no need to unpack all my trunks. Just have the maids put away the items in my suitcases."

His statement hung in the air. She said nothing, indifferent. Why would he lug all his things back to New Orleans when he intended to return to Atlanta in a few weeks? *Wasteful.* "Oui, Monsieur," she said, turning to leave. She placed her hand on the doorknob and opened it. The door slammed shut.

"Lela." James stood behind her, his mouth close to her ear. She began to feel him, but then she strengthened herself, determined not to do it all again.

James sensed her reaction to his closeness. Not from any visible movement, but from the energy which she radiated, the heat of the love which still smoldered somewhere deep inside of her. "Lela, I'm sorry. I'm sorry for the way I've treated you. I know I've hurt you deeply. I didn't mean to, I didn't want to, but I couldn't lie to you, either. You would've known if I had lied. You would have known."

James refused to release her until he said what he had been building up the courage to say for weeks. "Lela, I do love you with all of my heart. I'm still in love with you. I want to be with you."

James felt Lela's defenses break down. Backing away from her, he allowed her the freedom to leave if she wished, but he held his stance. She didn't leave, but continued to face the door in silence. "I guess, well I think I behaved like Papa, when Hanzel's father attacked Maman. I told you about it."

Lela didn't reply, listening.

"I didn't want to do it, I was just being selfish. Well, that's not true. I was scared. I wanted to shield myself from it all, even at your expense. I guess, oh Lela I don't know." They both stood together in silence as he sorted his feelings.

"I'm territorial like Papa and Hanzel knew it. He knew I

couldn't tolerate him touching what I held precious. Besides, I still believed you didn't want me, so in a strange way, I surmised you wanted him. I know, we've been over all of this, but why me? Why would… How could you ever want me? Who am I?"

Lela turned and faced him. "James, why wouldn't I want you? You're all I ever wanted." Lela found herself wearied by it all. "Although I tell myself I hate you, and that isn't far from the truth, I love you. You're all I desire, James."

Her rage spiked. She wished to spit on him. "You just walked away. You turned on me?" Lela wagged her head filled with indignant disbelief. "I don't know if I can forgive you."

Terror gripped James, fearing he'd lost his life and purpose on earth. "Please darling, forgive me. I'm only a man, a damaged man at best. I know what I did was wrong, I admit it, but I'm afraid. I'm afraid of being loved. Who could ever want me?"

"A damaged and corrupted soul such as me."

Lela damaged? James laughed it off. He searched her eyes, seeking forgiveness. "It's difficult for me to trust women. I tell myself I won't be the man my father was. However, when something goes wrong, I immediately blame the woman for the occurrence, especially in the case of infidelity. It's wrong and I know it, but I still do it. I don't know if I can ever stop."

Lela pondered the hopelessness of their situation. "Why are you telling me these things now, James?"

The sound of his formal name stung his ears. Lela never uttered it unless she was cross with him. He'd heard Lela say his proper name more in the past few minutes than he ever wished to hear again. "Because I don't want to leave things as they are between us, Lela. I don't want to lose you. I want you to understand why I behave as I do," James said.

His pride gone, James began to cry. "I love you, Lela, and I want to be with you." He looked down at the floor, bashful and afraid. His teardrops splashed against the polished leather of his shoes. "I want us to be man and wife."

Lela's mouth gaped open. "Jamie, miscegeny is illegal in this country."

Hope welled in his heart. She hadn't called him James. "But not in France." James took her hand with child-like innocence. "If you will marry me, we could move to France."

The turn of events overwhelmed her. Could she enter a room hating someone and leave loving them, ready to marry them? "Jamie, I don't know."

"You'll never have to work again. In France, you will be a lady of high society," he said, enticing her to take the step. "In France, they don't have the same laws or beliefs concerning Negroes. We would be free to love one another and to be in love, publicly. We could be married."

"What about this house, Nancy, and Willie?"

"They can stay here and take care of the place or come to France with us, whatever Nancy chooses to do. Attorney Jacobson will take care of the legal and financial matters. Do you have any other family here, Lela?"

"Just Nancy, Willie, and you are my only family," she said before she could censor her words.

With her confession, James knew she still loved him. Regaining his strength, he rushed over to his desk. Opening the drawer, he retrieved a flat, velvet box. "I didn't plan to do this today," he said. James inhaled, gathering his courage. "During my initial journey here to check on Jean Charles, I purchased this in Chicago at Fields and Leiter." He cast his eyes to the floor, bashful. "I'd purchased it in hopes of finding you here." James handed her the box, a gift unworthy of a queen.

Confused, she opened it. Inside, Lela found a gold locket, encircled by small gold beads. Lela opened the locket to find an 'L' engraved on one side and a 'J' on the other. She gawked at him, attempting to make sense of it all.

Taking her hand in his, James knelt on one knee. "Lela, will you forgive me for how I've treated you?" he asked with glassy eyes. Lela began to cry and laugh a little at the same time. James laughed too, through his insuppressible tears.

"Will you, my darling?"

"Oui, mon cher."

"Will you grant me the honor of becoming my wife?" he said, now hopeful, but still unsure if his greatest desire would come true for him, at last.

Lela beamed with joy. "Yes," she choked out between her sobs of joy. "Yes, my darling!"

PART IV

Chapter 1

New Orleans, Louisiana. September 1, 1963.

At dusk, the sun radiated its final rebellious glow. Taking its cue from the departing star, the moon rose to its predestined place of dominance in the evening sky. Although the orb projected its fledgling light, Julian found the parlor dim, dark even, in its illumination. He left the sofa and walked over to the to end table next to his grandmère. Julian turned on the lamp, flooding the room with light. Outside, the crickets tuned up their legs to begin the nighttime concert.

The lamplight shadowed Lela's ancient face, revealing time concealed within. Joy radiated from her, the vertical folds of her face marrying with the now prominent lines around her eyes. Oblivious to the current century and time, she smiled, reunited with a love past.

He tried to suppress his disgust about his grandmère's love for his White great-grandfather. How could she love this White man? Yet at the same time, Julian wondered how he could despise his ancestor.

He watched her fiddle with her locket. Could it be the same locket his great-grandpère had given her in the story? He'd never noticed it before, but now knowing the story behind it, he realized it had been around her neck the entire time. Julian watched her raise the locket to her lips and kiss it. She opened it and kissed each side, and then snapped it closed again.

"My darling, yes. I will love you for all time. I await your return," Lela said. "I won't allow the sun to set on me before I hold you in my arms once more." She closed her eyes, as if receiving the affections of her dead husband. Julian could see she would never release him. She was still in love with him.

The hall clock's faint chime drifted into the parlor. Lela jumped where she sat. Gaining her bearings, she yawned, as if awaking from a long slumber. Remembering the past, Lela smiled, giddy in love.

Julian sat down and placed his arm around her. "Jamie asked me to marry him and I said yes." Julian patted her shoulder, allowing his grandmère's spirit to return to present. After a few moments, she sat up from his embrace still holding the locket between her tiny fingers.

"Are you alright, Grandmère?"

Lela nodded. She could see his concern as well as his

prejudice. She patted his thigh. "Yes, darling. I just didn't wish to leave him, yet again."

Julian nodded, saying nothing.

"God remembered us and interceded on our behalf, reuniting us despite insurmountable obstacles." Lela nodded, thinking. "Sallie and Nancy were instrumental in bringing us together. God always sends his angels, both human and otherwise, to unite those he desires to be together."

"How's that?"

Lela slid the locket back and forth on its chain. "I'm not sure, my darling. It just works out that way. He did the same for Nancy."

"Really?"

"Well, yes. She'd lost her love. Whereas I was a basket case when Jamie spurned me, Nancy continued on after her loss, never revealing her suffering to us. But God saw the pain in her heart and refused to allow her to suffer any longer."

"Whom was she missing?"

His question shocked her, but then again, why would he remember? She had told him so much. "She'd lost Nate in the fire."

"Oh!" Julian had forgotten. Grandmère could never finish one story without beginning another. "So, what happened to him?"

Lela pursed her lips. "The devil was busy," she said. "But, so was God and his angels."

Chapter 2

Lela

Although none of us, meaning Toussaint, Jamie and myself, had ever met him, we all knew him. We recognized him in Nancy's eyes, in her muffled pain. She never displayed any outbursts, but it was there. Nate and the pain of her loss could be found lodging in her pear preserves. It covered the porcelain dishes decorated with blue flowers upon which she served meals from time to time. It could be heard in the whistling of her pots, boiling on the hearth. The pain walked with her every day.

Yet, none of us noticed it. We were selfish beings, each of us consumed with the traumas and challenges of our own lives. We never took much concern of Nancy, except on how she could fix our problems, which she did without hesitation. Once our challenges had been resolved, we noticed the twist of bitterness in her jaw, the glistening of her eyes.

Toussaint noticed it first.

New Orleans, Louisiana. December, 1882.

REGAINING CONSCIOUSNESS, HE sat up. *Where is I?* He squinted his eyes. The bars came into focus. The law sat at the table outside his cell, playing cards.

Nate cleared his throat. "Why'se I here?"

One of the officers gathered the cards, shuffled, and then dealt. The men studied cards as they drank whiskey and smoked cigars.

"Why'se I here?"

The deputy threw in his hand and left the rickety table, walking toward Nate with indifference in his eyes. He opened the cage.

Nate stepped back, bumping into the brick wall behind him. The five deputies entered the cell, crowding him. The thunder of clubs striking him filled the cigarette and cigar infused air of the jailhouse.

Sitting at his desk, the sheriff aimed his spent tobacco for the spittoon. He hit his mark, dead center. The sheriff chuckled and turned the page of *The Picayune*, tuning out Nate's cries.

The guards brought him in, shackled. Nate remembered being shackled once before, when he'd been sold to the plantation in Louisiana. He couldn't find any difference between that time and his current predicament.

They led him to the defense table. "Stop, Nigger. Stand here."

Nate stood before the bench in the half empty courtroom, watching the clerks enter and leave through a door to the right of the judge's bench. Several minutes later, the judge entered the courtroom.

"All rise," the bailiff said.

The judge sat and nodded to the bailiff.

"All may be seated."

Nate began to sit until the deputy jabbed him with his nightstick. He remained standing.

A man entered the courtroom and approached the bench. He handed the judge a folder and left. The judge flipped through the papers in the file and closed it. He folded his hands. "What's your name, boy?"

"My'se name is Nate, suh."

"You have a last name?"

"Yessuh. It's Johnson. My'se name is Nate Johnson."

"Very well," the judge said. The court clerk handed him additional documents regarding Nate's case. The judge skimmed them and tossed the papers aside. "Do you have representation today?"

"Re—preee—sant…"

"Representation," the judge said, irritated. "Do you have a lawyer, boy?"

"Naw, suh. I'se don't."

"Well, the court will appoint one for you." The judge skimmed down the sheet of paper the clerk had just handed him. He tapped his finger below a name to his liking. "Is Attorney O'Malley in the courthouse today?"

"Yes, sir. I'll send a deputy to locate him," the clerk said. The judge called for a recess.

One-half hour later, Attorney O'Malley arrived in court. He was a short man, middle aged and somewhat overweight, reeking of vodka and garlic. Attorney O'Malley took one look at Nate and sat down.

A few moments later, court reconvened. "All rise," the bailiff commanded. The judge entered the courtroom and took his seat on the bench. The bailiff signaled to the gallery to take their seats.

"Who is representing this boy?"

"I am, your Honor," O'Malley said with the voice of a sleepy frog.

"Have you had enough time to review his case?"

"Yes, your Honor," O'Malley said. "I've seen enough."

Nate gawked at him in disbelief. How could he know anything about his case?

"Very well, then. In the case of the State of Louisiana versus Nate Johnson... Nate Johnson, you are charged with one count of arson, fifteen counts of murder in the first degree, and ten counts of attempted murder, resulting from the Madame Red fire. How do you plead?"

"Not guilty, suh! Not guilty," Nate said. "I'se didn't set no fires!"

"Order! Order," the judge said, pounding his gavel. "Look here, Attorney O'Malley. You'd better get control of that wild Nigger or I'm going to hold him in contempt of court."

"Yes, your Honor. I'll do what I can," O'Malley said. He shifted in his chair, his glassy eyes focusing on Nate after a few seconds. "Sit down and shut up if you want me to defend you. Your case is a lost cause," he said, oozing his garlic-tainted breath into his face. "You're making it worse with these outbursts."

"But I'se didn't do it," Nate said. "I'se was tryin' to save folks, not kill them, suh!"

"I didn't ask you all of that," O'Malley said, spitting in Nate's face as he spoke. "I told you to shut up."

Enraged and defenseless, Nate wanted to cry. "Lawd, please help me."

The State presented its case to the court, filled with circumstantial evidence. The prosecutor entered into evidence a sworn affidavit from an unidentified individual who placed Nate at the scene. The witness claimed he or she had seen Nate running in the back door of Madame Red's. The witness stated Nate was a violent man who wanted to kill the whores and their customers because Madame Red's was a 'Whites only' establishment; therefore, denying Nate admittance.

Nate leaned over to O'Malley. "That's a lie, suh. I worked there. I'se was Ma'Dame Red's driver."

"Didn't I tell you to keep your mouth shut, Nigger?"

It took the prosecution all of five minutes to finish presenting their case. O'Malley required even less time to present Nate's defense. "My client states he didn't do it. Mr. Johnson claims he worked for Madame Red as her driver and was in the process of saving the patrons and whores when apprehended." Attorney O'Malley sat down.

"That's…" Nate silenced himself once he saw the bailiff walk toward him. O'Malley shot him a cold glare.

Once the prosecution finished their closing arguments, the judge folded his hands, his eyes set on Attorney O'Malley. "Closing remarks, Counsel?"

"Oh, yes," O'Malley said, rising to address the court. "Nate Johnson states he didn't commit these crimes against the People." O'Malley sat down and fished inside his pocket for his watch. He opened and then snapped it shut, waiting for the bench to rule.

After considering both arguments, the judge informed the bailiff he was ready to make his ruling. He hadn't bothered to retire to chambers for deliberation.

"Will the Defendant rise?" the bailiff said.

The judge stared at Nate, condemning him without compassion. "Nate Johnson, this court finds you guilty of arson, murder in the first degree, and attempted murder, as charged. I sentence you to life in prison. You are to be immediately remanded to the Louisiana State Penal Farm, where you will serve out your sentence on the chain gang detail."

The guards walked over to Nate and grabbed him, leading him away. "Your Honor! You'se got the wrong man. I'se innocent. Innocent!" The guards removed their clubs from their belts and beat Nate about the head and upper back until he passed out.

Pinching. The earth pitched to the front and down, and then backwards, hard, without warning. "Where's I?" Sitting up, Nate became dizzy, his head falling backwards over to the side of the vehicle. The wagon jolted, waking him once more. Nate opened his eyes. Straining to move his neck, he focused his eyes on his wrists. He had been chained to others.

The wagon hit another deep rut, causing Nate to knock his head against the side of the wagon. Already weak from the earlier beating at the courthouse, he lost consciousness. A dog tore into his right leg. Nate awoke, screaming in agony.

"I said git out the goddamn wagon, boy," the prison guard said. After the dog finished his job of ripping out Nate's shin muscle, the guard called off his beast. Nate crawled from the wagon with the other prisoners. Once the men lined up in the camp yard, a red colored man appeared before them, his skin leathered by many days in the unforgiving Louisiana sun.

"I'se Warden Jaden and I'll be keepin' a close eye on ya'll boys. I don't care if any of you'se lives or dies. I'se just wants my work done." Jaden scrutinized each of his new prisoners. "Each day, ya'll gonna git up at first light, eat your chow, work, break for a fifteen-minute chow at noon, and then work 'till sundown. Then ya'll gonna do your chores around this here camp, and then hit ya'll bunks. This is ya'll new life," he said. "Ya'll understand?"

The prisoners didn't respond, hanging their heads in despair. The guards' whips sang out against the tired flesh of the captives, causing them all to cry out.

Nate hadn't felt the lash in many years. Colors swirled before him, mingling into a macabre dirge with the chords of anguish. Heat and pain.

Sho' Nancy, I'se help you'se wit' your cannin'. Mammy's fruit was never as sweet as yours

Warden Jaden droned on in the background of Nate's

dwindling consciousness. "When I'se ask ya'll a question, ya'll says, 'Yessah, Warden Jaden.' Understand?"

"Yessah, Warden Jaden!"

Nate sat in the kitchen, watching Nancy can pears. Arising from the settee which he'd made for her, he kissed and hugged her, loving her, making love. They played with one another, joyous in the love with which God had blessed them.

The whip snapped to the left of his head, echoing with a staccato end. The side of Nate's face opened, the tip of the whip wrapping around his back, licking him like hot coals, and then returning the way it had come. Nate hit the hard, unforgiving ground of the prison camp, his blood spilling forth and curdling in the hot Louisiana sun.

New Orleans, Louisiana. March, 1883.

THRASHING ABOUT, HE defended himself. He couldn't move his hands. He couldn't run. The pain in his leg crippled his soul.

Jannie sat up in bed. "Baby, what is it?"

Entangled in the covers, Toussaint freed himself and sat up in bed. "No, Father. Mercy!"

"Toussaint, you're scaring me," Jannie said.

Releasing the vision of the night terror, Toussaint squinted in the darkness, working to identify his surroundings. Still groggy, he sweated, unable to release the dream. "What?" Light flooded the room. Toussaint squinted and covered his eyes. He cried out, but then realized Jannie had lit the lamp. He relaxed and opened his eyes. After a few moments, he reunited with the present. "Oh baby," he said, clutching Jannie in his arms. He kissed her, never wishing to let her go.

"What is it, honey?"

"Nate."

Jannie's heart skipped a beat.

"Darlin', he's alive."

Chapter 3

New Orleans, Louisiana. April, 1883.

Nancy washed out the last pot, pumping water into the pan to rinse it. She heard footsteps behind her, but she didn't need to turn from her work to see who had entered the kitchen. Toussaint. In her mind's eye, she watched him steal a slice of bacon from the pan on the table, crunching its salty goodness between his teeth. She knew he only did it to irritate her, and it had worked. She wasn't in the mood for his shit.

Drying the pot, Nancy turned and scowled at Toussaint. Although she loved him, she had to be on guard with him at all times, because Toussaint never tired in his quest to pick her pocket, in the Spirit. "What's wrong wit' you, boy?"

Toussaint went to fireplace. Taking a towel, he picked up the coffee pot and poured some of the scalding hot liquid into a cup. The white cup turned dark brown from the lethal beverage. Judging from the look on her face, Nancy had heard him talking about her coffee in the Spirit. Oh well. "Is

Lela sure? I don't advise this marriage," Toussaint said.

So, he'd seen it happen. Nancy knew no one had told him, because no one knew of the couple's plans but her. "Why? 'Cause he's White and she's Negro?"

"That's the least of her problems, especially if they move to France or almost anywhere in Europe, as planned." Toussaint sipped his coffee, possessing the same bang as dynamite. "Lela doesn't know anything about the Roberts family."

"They'se all dead, so what diff'rence does it make?"

"What makes you think they're all dead, Nancy? Who told you that? Besides, the Roberts are, well, they're not kind people. In fact, they can be quite cruel."

Nancy's eyebrow arched. "How you'se know so much 'bout them? You'se knows Mis'sur Roberts 'fore now?"

Toussaint shut down the window in the Spirit before Nancy could see the truth, but he suspected he'd waited too long to do so. "We don't know each other. I've just come into possession of third party information regarding the family from reliable sources." Toussaint kept a straight face, but he knew she didn't believe him. "Some of the parishioners in my Parish were once slaves on the Roberts Plantation. They shared with me memories of the Roberts family and their cruel and brutal treatment of their women and slaves."

"Oh," she said, retreating on the subject. She knew he wasn't telling her the whole truth. *Yes, Lawd. I know*, she told

God in her heart. Well, there was her confirmation he withheld information to the point of lying.

Toussaint knew she knew he was lying. However, since she didn't challenge him, he would let it ride.

"Spit it out, Mis'sur. What's the problem wit' them gittin' married?" Nancy knew he could see it too. *Let's see if he will tell it.*

"It will end badly. This shouldn't come to pass," Toussaint said.

"Well, if it ain't supposed to be, then it won't. What's your point, Mis'sur?"

Trying to test me, huh Nancy? "They're adults, free to do as they please, at least in France. It's no concern of mine. I have no say in the matter. I'm not Lela's blood," Toussaint said.

Humph! Not her blood. Nancy considered him, seeking to view the desires of his heart. The Lord revealed some things, while concealing others. *Protector of the Rose.* Although he was still a fledgling, Nancy could see it. Her Aunt Sarah had mentioned it during her visits to Mississippi, when Nancy was a child. She accepted what had been revealed. "Well, the Good Lawd will let it play out accordin' to his master plan. I'se ain't tryin' to stop nuthin'. I'se gonna help that girl find her happiness."

"There won't be any happiness for Lela with James Roberts," Toussaint said. "At least not for very long."

Nancy perused the Spirit. Hay fell as snow. Screaming. So, he was hiding something. The veil came down on the vision. "Look Mis'sur, either stop your hexin' and hipoxin' over that gal's weddin' or go home. You'se decides."

Toussaint and Nancy faced off, having come to an impasse. "So, you approve of this marriage?"

"Yessuh, I'se do. I'se thanks they'd be good for each other."

"Well, let it be as you see it," he said.

"Oh, and it will be. I'se can guarantee you'se that, Mis'sur." She walked over to the stone oven and grabbed the bread paddle leaned against the wall. Opening the riveted cast iron door, she removed three loaves of brioche, baked to perfection. Nancy placed them on the kitchen table to cool. Frowning at Toussaint as she passed him, she reached up in the cupboard for the pear preserves; however, Nancy stopped herself and grabbed a jar of strawberry jam instead.

Watching Nancy, Toussaint searched the Spirit. His heart broke for her. He could now see the hole her love Nate had left in her heart. "I should probably stay out of this."

"Then you'se should follow your own advice," she said.

So, it was true. Things were not as they seemed with Nate. His dream was true. Toussaint heard her heart groan, *'Well, I'se ain't gonna go crazy thinkin' 'bout him.'* He watched Nancy throw dirt on Nate in her heart, allowing him to remain in his grave. "Nancy…"

"Let it rest, Mis'sur. I'se 'bout tired of your goddamn lip this mornin'. I'se said let the shit be, so let it be. Damn, you'se should know when to shut the fuck up sometimes."

Placing the jam on the tray with the brioche, bacon and eggs, Nancy grabbed the serving tray. She left the kitchen, taking it upstairs. "Doncha wants me to take that up for you, Miss Nancy?" Toussaint heard the houseboy ask her in the hallway.

"Naw, baby. I'se gonna do it myself," he heard Nancy tell him, trudging up the stairs.

"Nancy just cussed me out," Toussaint said to himself, stunned. The Lord had told him Nancy's heart ached. Yet, she'd always been so strong. She'd helped everyone else, never seeming to be in need herself. Perhaps she had the greatest need of all.

Fifteen minutes later, Nancy returned. "Mis'sur Bailey, I'se so sorry. I'se just high-strung wit' this weddin' and all. I'se gotta git on that boat and go 'cross the sea. I'se just at my wit's end."

Toussaint rubbed her back. "It's alright, Nancy. I'll just pull this harpoon out of my heart. Could you apply some pressure to stop the bleeding?" Toussaint fell backwards, feigning death.

"Boy, you'se just horsin' 'round and makin' fun of me." Removing her dishtowel tucked in her apron, she twined it up with lighting speed, popping Toussaint hard on his thigh.

"Ow! Watch out with that towel, woman." Toussaint staggered around the room rubbing his thigh.

Nancy watched him limp around the room, making a joke of it all, angering her once again. "Look, we'se both knows what the other's got. The Lawd done showed both of us the hearts of men and of thangs that ain't yet happened. So, don't act like I'se don't know what you'se doin', 'cause I'se do. I'se sees the same thangs you'se do and the same thangs is blocked from me too. Doncha come up in here tryin' to work me, boy.

"You'se gonna learn wit' age. Just 'cause you sees it don't mean it's there for you'se to fix. The Lawd done seent it too, but He loves us e'nuff to let us choose and to walk our own paths. We'se got to do as the Lawd does. Let them two do what they'se goin' to do and STAY OUT OF IT!" Nancy threw her dish towel on the wooden workbench. "And stay outta my shit too."

Chapter 4

New Orleans, Louisiana. April, 1883.

"The community will miss you, Madame Louise La Croix," Toussaint said to her vacant shell. He removed her clothing and washed her. Madame La Croix had been a generous benefactor to St. Maurice le Moor School and Orphanage for many years. No one knew how she'd come into her fortune. However, Father Pierre had confided in him she'd left the school and orphanage a sizable endowment in her will.

Toussaint walked away from the remains. He couldn't work on her now, thinking of her awful, elitist grandson. Solomon Philippe had become infamous in the Negro business community for discriminating against Negroes and Creoles of dark skin. Solomon's photography studio walls were lined with the genteel portraits of light-skinned Negro Creoles, whose lineage could be traced back to either French or Spanish ancestry. All of his subjects were les gens de couleur libres, comprised of the freed concubines and the mixed heritage offspring of New Orleans' European elite.

Solomon had limited his association with his own grandmother, not wishing to remind the community of his relation to the dark-skinned woman. Rumor had it that she was the Negro descendant of the Spaniard Señor Miguel Escobar, who'd purchased lands south of New Orleans during the mid to late 1600's.

Toussaint washed his hands and dried them, throwing the towel on the sink's edge. How could Solomon deny his own grandmother, especially one as loving and well-respected as Madame La Croix? Toussaint silenced his heart, remembering the goodness and vengeance of God.

Unbeknownst to Solomon, he'd lost the respect of both the Negro and White communities in New Orleans due to a Creole matron catching him treating his grandmother with coldness after Mass, bordering on disrespect. The lady wasted little time informing others, sharing tales of his cruelty with her lodge sisters and church members.

Soon, a quiet disdain for Solomon had blanketed the Negro community; however, no one ever said anything to him. His grandmother had heard of the bad talk concerning her grandson and squelched it. Out of respect for Madame La Croix, the Negro community held its collective tongue. Solomon would've been devastated to know the community only tolerated him because of the respect they held for his dark-skinned grandmother.

He had been cruel to Jannie when she'd begun her campaign to establish the library. At first, Solomon wouldn't receive her. But once he'd saw her name in the Negro paper, listed with other prominent citizens from New Orleans' elite cosmopolitan society, he stopped by the library and offered to donate his photography services to document the plethora of fundraisers, socials, and galas.

Jannie had started to refuse his gift; however, Toussaint had whispered in her ear, "Remember his grandmother, Madame La Croix." Jannie accepted his offer with a strained smile. Toussaint had never seen his wife put on a false face in the history of their marriage.

Having harnessed his emotions, Toussaint returned to the remains of Madame La Croix. He fantasied about how the Negro community would shun Solomon, now that his grandmother had passed. He suppressed the vengeance in his soul and redirected the attention of his heart to the departed Madame La Croix. "How many orphaned hands of former slaves did you hold Madame, wiping their faces, filling their bellies, and clothing their bodies? God has blessed you in your new home in Heaven, more than you could have ever dreamed of on Earth."

Toussaint kissed her forehead. "Your grandson should learn from you." He didn't wish to speak ill of Madame La

Croix descendant while preparing her for her final rest. Yet, he couldn't resist. "Honor thy Father and Mother." Toussaint inhaled, releasing his hatred for Solomon. He made his first incision. Toussaint jumped.

"Hey man," Stank said, his face full of laughter. "How'se it goin'?"

"Stank? Man, you're going to mess around and get cut doing stuff like that." Toussaint embraced him. It had been some time since he'd seen his brother, rather his cousin. In fact, Toussaint couldn't remember the last time. "You see I have this scalpel in my hand."

"Man, you can't cut no movin' targets. Yours got to be as stiff as board." The two men burst into laughter. "How you been, Toot?"

"I've been alright," he said, his laughter subsiding. "A lot of trouble going around, though."

"Oh really?" Stank hung his hat on one of the coat rack's empty hooks. He took a seat on the stool near the embalming table, where Madame La Croix lay. Stank turned his head out of respect for the lady. She was a good woman. He'd even helped out once or twice at the St. Maurice soup kitchen after she'd shamed him for shooting dice behind the church.

Watching Toussaint place his instruments on the tray, reverence filled Stank. He could hear his brother pulling the shroud over Madame La Croix's corpse. Stank relaxed, knowing her remains had been concealed. "What's going on?"

Toussaint removed the towel hanging from the bar on the embalming table. "You remember the fire late last year?"

Stank thought for a moment, and then he remembered. "Yeah, I can't forget it. You're talkin' 'bout the fire at Madame Red's whorehouse over there on Baronne Street?" Toussaint nodded. Stank shook his head in despair. "Yeah, I knew the spot well. I spent many a night in that house."

Toussaint decided not to comment on his statement. In fact, he would've been surprised if Stank hadn't been a regular patron. "How well did you know the workers there?"

"Pretty well, I suppose. I heard some of them died in the fire. Some of the bodies were so burned up, folks couldn't tell who they were."

"Yeah, I know. I was the mortician on the fire."

Stank caught himself, for he'd almost fallen off his stool. "Shut your mouth! I didn't think you'd dirty your hands wit' sinners like them," Stank said. "Hell, I cain't hardly believe we're friends."

Toussaint smiled at his cousin. "Well, I pray for your ole dirty soul every day at Mass."

"Watch out, man," Stank said.

Guiding the table onto the elevator, Toussaint loaded Madame La Croix, taking her to the cold room. He'd yet to find an effective mechanism to keep the room cool enough. It didn't matter in her case, for she would be buried early the following morning. No need to place her in the refrigerated unit, although he believed he should do so out of respect. He heard her voice. *I'm going in the ground in the morning. There's no need.* Toussaint nodded and placed her in the cellar. He returned upstairs and closed the door. "Hey, do you remember a fella named Nate? He was the driver over there."

Stank's eyes brightened. "Yeah, I know Nate! That's my Nig…" He caught himself once he saw the frown encroach upon Toussaint's face, prompting him to modify his word choice. Toussaint didn't allow any cussing or the use of racial slurs in his house, or in his presence for that matter. "My boy. Yeah, Nate's my guy." Stank watched a mournful spirit creep across Toussaint's face. "Aww, naw. Not Nate, man! Aww shit. That's a god… motherfuckin' shame." He'd barely dodged the bullet of taking the Lord's name in vain. 'God-damn' was the only word worse than 'Nigger' to Toussaint.

"He was so in love with Miss Nancy. They were a beautiful couple. I would always tell him I hoped to find a woman like Miss Nancy someday, a good-hearted woman, like her."

Stank's admiration of the couple's love shocked Toussaint. Everyone desired to be loved, he reasoned. "I don't believe he's dead."

"Really? What makes you think that?"

"The Lord showed him to me in some sort of prison, injured."

"Oh, yeah?" Stank stroked his goatee, thinking. "What else did God show you?"

"I saw the word 'Innocent.' I saw death standing outside of where he lay, but far off. Death walked toward him though, but very slowly."

Stank shook his head, pitying his friend. "What can I do, man?"

Toussaint went to the sink and pumped some water into the galvanized pan. He washed his hands. He needed to have plumbing installed in the preparation room, but he liked the pump. He frowned, thinking of how he'd talked about Jannie for wanting to keep the pump in the kitchen. "Ask around and see what you can find out. Let me know what you discover."

"Not a problem, man." Stank thought for a moment. "Why are you so concerned about him, Toot? You ain't never had no concern for sinners."

Stank's words cut him; however, they were true. "Well, I guess the Lord has changed me," Toussaint said, ashamed of his past convictions. "First, Jannie shamed me into taking the Madame Red job. Then one night while reading the scriptures, the Lord directed me to Jesus' reply to the Pharisees. He said something like, 'I came to save the sinners, not the righteous.'"

"But the final call came from Mademoiselle Nancy. I've never seen heartbreak like hers. She loved Nate so much. There she was, helping all the fire victims and she'd just lost the love of her life. If she could have compassion and love for 'sinners' and she's a God-fearing woman, why shouldn't I?"

Three weeks later, Stank dropped in on Toussaint, finding him embalming a client. He sat on his favorite stool. "They set my boy up, man."

Shrouding the corpse, Toussaint could see in Stank's eyes the news was bad. He sat at the small desk he kept in the room. "What happened?"

Stank removed his hat and placed it on his knee. "There's been a war going on in New Orleans even I didn't know about." Stank lit his pipe. He knew better than to smoke in his house and business; however, they both realized Toussaint would let it go. "Some Dagos from New York been tryin' to take over the New Orleans crime operations."

"Watch your mouth."

"I'm sorry man, it slipped. Anyway, they'se called the… dang, what's the name? Bon… Bono…"

"Buonoguidi?"

"Yeah, how do you know that?"

"I'll tell you later. Go on."

"Man, how do you know?"

"I said I'll tell you later."

Stank resisted the strong urge to bust Toussaint in his self-righteous, authoritative mouth. Why couldn't he just tell him? Sometimes Stank believed Toussaint didn't trust him, but deep down he knew it wasn't true. Toussaint had a staunch 'need to know' policy. In his mind, everyone didn't need to know everything, for their own protection. However, Stank surmised it simplified the process of elimination. If confidential information was leaked, there would be a short list of suspects. "Well, here it is. Bono…"

"Buonoguidi."

"Yeah, him. He's been rolling over all the New Orleans crime rackets: loan-sharking, gambling, and especially prostitution. The clamor is he's even opened an opium den on the waterfront, near the docks. They sell funny weed and sumpthin' called cocaine too."

"Cocaine? That's a prescribed drug."

"Yeah man, and so is heroin. He sells all that shit to the White folks. Anyway, folks been turnin' belly up in Lake Pontchartrain and 'round the docks. Word is, the deceased wouldn't roll over to the Ben'gedies.

"There's this low-life, White trash, umm, White man named Smitty who's been helpin' the gangsters roll the hometown rackets. Ben'gedie promised him a high position in the organization if he helped them. That dumb mutha… uh, that so 'n so. He's gonna take a swim in Lake Pontchartrain too once Ben— well you know." Stank gave up on pronouncing the name. "Anyhow, Smitty's a loose cannon with even looser lips. He'll turn on them Ben'gedies in a minute if the law ever caught up wit' his ass and offered him a deal. Shit. I mean shoot! Man, you're killin' me with your holy rules."

"God's house, God's rules," Toussaint said. He knew Stank wasn't cocky enough to challenge God, no matter what kind of life he lived. "Well, what about Nate?"

"Yeah, man. Well Genovese, he ran Madame Red's for the boss. I think he's out of Chicago. Anyway, Genovese refused to cave for Ben'gedie. Business was too good. Genovese had all the big wigs and high rollers patronizing the house.

"Ben'gedie couldn't take no for an answer because if Genovese didn't roll, none of the other ho' houses would either. So, he ordered Smitty to torch the place. However, Ben'gedie told him to wait until after half-past five o'clock in the morning after all the Johns had left. He didn't wanna draw no heat from the law. But, like I said, Smitty does whatever the fuck, I mean, whatever he wanna do. He goes and toss a flamin' bottle filled with gasoline through the window at ten o'clock at night."

"Lord have mercy. How stupid and cruel can he be?"

"Damn stupid. Oh, sorry," Stank said.

"Go on man," Toussaint said, tired of trying to correct his cousin.

"As you well know, a bunch of folks got killed. One of them was the mayor's nephew, the city controller. Couple of other folks from City Hall were there too, celebrating the controller's birthday. They all got burnt bad, one of them dyin' the next day. The other folks are still in bad shape, even after all this time. This one fella, they say every day is agony for him. The doctors just keep him on morphine to ease his pain."

"Mercy," Toussaint said, a little above a whisper.

"Anyhow, Nate carried a bunch of folks out of the fire. He rescued two folks at once by himself. One person was on fire, but Nate rolled him around on the front lawn to put out the flames. Then he ran back in. Smitty and Ben'gedie's other guy stood there watchin' him. When he didn't come out again, they ran 'round back and found him lyin' on the lawn with a kid. I guess he got up to go back in. That's when Smitty and the henchman grabbed Nate and took him away."

"But why?" Toussaint asked, although he knew.

"To frame him for the fire. If the mayor knew the Ben'gedie's had set the fire, he would run them out of town on a rail and the New Orleans market would be closed to them. Instead—"

"They present Nate as the sacrificial lamb, becoming heroes in the mayor's eyes, thus guaranteeing their hold on the New Orleans market while at the same time keeping the whole matter quiet. Mon Dieu." Toussaint sat in silence for a moment. But he encouraged himself, remembering the Lord had called him to help Nate. "Where's Nate now?"

"He's on a chain gang down in one of the gulf parishes, man. They gave him life. They're down there beatin' the shit outta him."

Toussaint didn't hear his cousin's profanity, lost in conversation with the Lord. "I think I have a plan on how to free him."

Stank smirked and stood from his stool. He put on his hat. "I figured you would, wit' your ole evil self," he said. "People think you're all holy, but they don't know you like I do. I would never want to get on your bad side, that's for sure." Toussaint cut his eyes at his cousin. "Hey man, you never said how you knew Ben'gedie."

"I know." Toussaint left his desk and went upstairs, followed by Stank.

Once Stank left, Toussaint went to his office and opened the safe, retrieving the cigarette case he'd recovered from the controller's rib cage. He examined it with disgust. Toussaint's first inclination had been to throw away the filth. The voice of the Lord had directed him to keep it.

Now, he knew with certainty the identity of the corpse which he still held in the refrigerated unit. With everything that had happened, he'd never buried the body. Toussaint had believed the family would claim him. He read *The Picayune* daily, combing the missing person inquiries; however, he'd never found any advertisements. Now, he knew the reason why.

"Those low-lifes." Toussaint turned the object between his fingers, examining it. How could the family be more interested in protecting their reputation and their political dynasty than in the burial of their own dead?

Toussaint left his office and walked out the kitchen door, stopping on the rear steps. "Allen, could you come in here please?" Allen had been out in the stable tidying up, as he did every day after school. "It's good to have an apprentice," Toussaint said with a chuckle.

Allen left the stable with a cloud of dust and hay following him. "Oui, Monsieur?"

Toussaint wagged his finger, beckoning the boy to come. Allen trotted across the yard, and then followed Toussaint into the preparation room. The faint aroma of horse manure clung to him. Toussaint concealed his amusement. "Go upstairs and freshen up. I need you to run an errand for me."

Twenty minutes later, Allen returned dressed in fresh clothes. Toussaint raised an eyebrow, recognizing his slacks, shirt and suit jacket. Jannie always dressed the boy in Toussaint's clothes after returning from stables, her clandestine hint that Toussaint should be doing the work himself.

"What can I do for you, Monsieur Bailey?"

"I would like for you to call on Monsieur Philippe." Toussaint sat at his desk, finishing his note and then inserting it into an envelope. "Please give him this letter. Also, tell him I would appreciate his discretion by not discussing this appointment with anyone."

"Oui, Monsieur." Allen wondered why his employer would have need for Monsieur Philippe, but Allen knew better than to ask. He found it better not to know Monsieur Bailey's plans.

"Saddle Cherrie and ride over there. You have watered and fed her, right?"

"Oui, Monsieur Bailey," Allen said, a bit insulted by the question.

"Bon. And please, don't dawdle."

By early evening, Toussaint heard a noise outside. He peeked out the kitchen window. Monsieur Philippe had arrived. Toussaint walked out the back door as the man applied the brake on his wagon, loaded with photography equipment. "Solomon. How are you, my friend?"

"I'm well."

Toussaint suppressed his dislike for the man. Solomon Philippe owed him several favors, one of which he intended to collect that evening.

The men carried Solomon's equipment down the narrow stairway leading to the preparation room, and then another short flight of stairs into the root cellar. Once they'd brought in the final load, Toussaint stood next to a table covered with a tarp, near the earthen wall. "Solomon, I need your help."

Solomon opened a crate containing photographic plates. "Yes, my friend. What is it you need?"

Toussaint waited in silence beside the shrouded table until Solomon turned his attention from his work, focusing only on him. "I need for you to take photographs of this." Toussaint snatched away the sheet and revealed the charred remains of what seemed to have been a human body.

Solomon screamed in horror. "What in God's name!" Solomon continued to bellow in terror while covering his mouth and nose to shield himself from the stench.

"These are the charred remains of a patron from the Madame Red whorehouse fire, which burned to the ground late last year."

Solomon couldn't disconnect his eyes from the atrocity. "My God, man! Have you gone mad? Why is it still here? Aren't you going to bury it?" He backed away from the monstrosity, bumping into the wall behind him. He turned around to see who had attacked him. His panic reflexes redirected his focus to the body upon the table.

"I don't know what this mound of flesh is. I know they are human remains. That, I do know." Toussaint circled the gurney, considering the deceased. "I don't know if this person is male or female, Negro or White. No one has ever inquired of a missing person, disappearing on the horrible night. It's a pity, really. Can anyone be so unloved they wouldn't be missed for so long?" Toussaint walked around the corpse once again, scrutinizing the charred remains.

Solomon's chest heaved up and down. "Why pictures?"

Toussaint stroked his chin, thinking. "They will assist me in my efforts to identify the body. Then this poor soul, or rather its shell, can then be laid to rest, hopefully with his or her family members."

"Why me? Why not call the police?"

Toussaint avoided laughing at the insanity of his inquiry. "Be reasonable, Solomon. They would ask too many questions. They may send me to prison because I didn't report the death. The fact I've held the body for many months wouldn't help matters, now would it?"

Toussaint tapped his chin, analyzing different scenarios in his mind. "No, that wouldn't work. Besides, they would toss him in an unmarked grave. That wouldn't do at all. However, I may have some leads on this person's identity." Toussaint removed a silver case from his breast pocket and handed to Solomon.

Praying for the horrible evening to end, Solomon examined the case. Squinting a bit, he was able to make out the engraved initials. "These could be the initials of any number of people. How can you identify anyone based on this?"

Toussaint pondered Solomon's question. "Yes, Solomon. What you have said is true. However, when we open the case, we find out a bit more." Toussaint opened the case. Depressing a button, a concealed lid popped open from inside the front cover, revealing a secret compartment containing miniature tin types. He removed them and gave them to Solomon.

"They're too small. I can't see them."

Toussaint handed him a magnifying glass from his worktable. Solomon sighed, holding it above the small tin types. The first image was of a thin White man, having his penis sucked by a shapely Negro woman as another woman, White and very thin, licked her. The next photograph depicted the same man, this time receiving oral sex from a man on all fours while engaging in bestiality with a horse.

Solomon viewed another tin-type, depicting a man rap-ing a young girl, a little older than thirteen years perhaps, with a baseball bat, his penis fully erect. He wore a clown's mask with a wicked smile, which he'd removed from his face and now rested atop his head.

Solomon noticed the same man appeared in all the tin-types, a strangely familiar man. In the next tin-type, the same man played the role of a vampire, sucking a woman's blood from her neck. "Bailey, what are you trying to pull here? Is this a joke?"

Toussaint crossed his arms and grunted, filled with dis-gust and disdain for the man in the tin-types. "Unfortunate-ly, no. I pried this case from the rib cage of this corpse." Toussaint returned to the corpse, scanning the carbonized outer shell. "Look. Right about there."

Removing a pointer from his workstation besides the embalming table, Toussaint directed Solomon to the spot. "You can see the depression left behind in his chest cavity by the cigarette case. Ah, yes. Here it is," he said. The flesh reminded one of seared steak; however, it still resembled flesh. The remainder of the corpse had fossilized into lava rock, glassy black.

Solomon removed his handkerchief from his pocket and mopped his brow. "I'm sorry, Bailey. I cannot do these photographs for you," he said, unwilling to involve himself in the horrible, macabre situation. What kind of man was Toussaint?

"That is unfortunate Solomon, to deny this person's family the peace of closure by knowing the fate of their loved one. No peace, no rest. But you wouldn't understand that, would you Solomon? Your family has never experienced this sort of agony, of not knowing, or even of not receiving justice for a crime committed against one of your own. It's good to get satisfaction when a wrong has been committed against you, n'est-ce pas, Solomon?"

"What?" Fear gripped Solomon's heart. "Bailey, that was different."

"No, Solomon. By all means, call me Toussaint," he said. "Mary was so very young. So young," he said.

"You leave Mary out of this, Toussaint," Solomon said.

Toussaint placed his hand over his heart, grieved by it all. "No one could find her. How long was Mary gone, Solomon?"

Solomon wiped away his tears, standing before him, immobile. "For nearly one year."

Toussaint retrieved an instrument from the tray and began to pick at the corpse's charred flesh. "At the end of eleven months of sheer hell, whom did you seek for help?" Toussaint awaited a response, but none came. "You came to the Negro quarters of the Ninth Ward to consult Aunt

Sarah, to see if she had a vision of your child." Toussaint stood before Solomon, recalling the incredulous occurrence. "Imagine, that. A high-class Creole man of your station, visiting the Negro quarters to consult a medium. How bizarre.

"But you were desperate to find your precious Mary, as any father would be. In fact, should be. But Aunt Sarah wouldn't give you a vision, for she wasn't a voodoo priestess. She was a prophet and a judge." Toussaint labored to contain his outrage. "Yes. She was a prophet of the Most High God, but the Lord wouldn't reveal to her Mary's whereabouts.

"The Lord instructed Sarah to direct you to her son, a man whom you had hated and harassed since establishing his business in New Orleans. Why did you hate him so? Because he was of brown complexion and a former slave. Forget the fact he attended Mass at the same parish church you did. That didn't matter, because he was still only a Nigger to you. But now, God, being a righteous judge, had placed this man whom you hated without cause between you and your young daughter."

Solomon swung on Toussaint, wishing to silence him for all time. Toussaint pinned him against the earthen wall. They stood close, sharing the breath of hatred. "God sent you to me.

"You wanted to walk out of our home, but where else could you go? So, mustering as much kindness as you could, you asked me, 'Toussaint, can you see my Mary?'

"I responded, 'Only the Lord sees Mary. If I have favor with the Lord, he may reveal her whereabouts to me.'"

Solomon struggled in Toussaint's restraint. "You smug motherfucker."

"Don't swear in God's house." Toussaint said. "So, then you asked, 'Will you please ask the Lord where is my daughter? Hopefully, He will favor you this day.' I immediately responded, 'He has. I will take you to Mary.'

"So, we loaded into the wagon and set out to find Mary. After nearly two hours of riding through the back country, just south of Hammond near Ponchatoula, we came to a decrepit little shack next to a creek. The shack appeared to be abandoned. You accused me of deceiving you, implying I wished to pay you back for all those years of torment you were kind enough to oblige me with when first moving to New Orleans. But I know God. He never lies."

Toussaint reconsidered his comment. What man knows God? "I climbed over the bench into the wagon bed and removed the hatchet from my toolbox. I jumped down and then walked up to the door of the shack. When I kicked it open, the stench rolled out as if from the depths of hell." A wicked grin coursed across Toussaint's face. "And it was."

"You shut your fucking mouth, Toussaint Bailey!"

"Temper, Solomon," he said. "And please, control your

mouth in the Lord's house."

"You smug little…" Solomon gritted his teeth. "THIS IS NOT THE HOUSE OF THE LORD!"

"Oh, bon ami, you're mistaken. God dwells in the hearts of men, not in temples, masques, synagogues, or cathedrals. The Lord lives in the hearts of men who love and obey him. I do whatever the Lord tells me to do; no matter if it may seem right or wrong, or what the outcome may be."

Solomon saw something flash in Toussaint's eyes, stirring fear inside of him. He glared at Toussaint, but he couldn't confute him.

"Ah, yes. Back to our sad tale. Once I kicked open the door, what did I find? That sick, perverted man atop your pretty little girl. I took the hatchet and struck him dead center in the back of his head, his blood spilling all over poor little Mary, who'd already suffered so much. Truly the sins of her father had fallen upon her."

"You bastard!" Breaking free of Toussaint's restraint, Solomon lunged at him. Toussaint caught Solomon by the throat with one hand, constricting his grip on Solomon's windpipe. Solomon tried to choke out his curse, but Toussaint tightened his grip a bit more, rendering Solomon unable to complete his statement. He turned blue. Toussaint released him. Solomon fell to the floor, gasping for air. He massaged his throat to ease the pain.

"Now, mon ami. I've asked you not to swear in the Lord's house. But you never did receive direction very well from those whom you consider as beneath you, now did you?"

Sadness and remorse filled Toussaint's heart for little Mary. "In fact, on the day I, well we, rescued Mary, I insisted you stay outside of that hell hole. I begged you to allow me to go in and bring her out to you. However, after I kicked in the door, you rushed past me and found the horrific scene."

Toussaint reconsidered all that had transpired between the men. "But, you're correct. I'm not righteous. I don't always obey the Lord as I professed earlier," Toussaint said, reviewing his sins in his heart. "After I split the awful man's head open like an overripe fruit, the Lord whispered to me, 'and now the son.' But I rebelled saying, 'He's only an infant, perhaps a month old.'

"So, I spared him, leaving him to fend for himself. I assumed he would die without his mother to nurse him. But it wasn't to be. Now, I must suffer, witnessing his actions in the Spirit, for they are more heinous than his father's."

Solomon turned white with fear.

"I believe I later learned the child's father's name was Obadiah Purvis." Leaving Solomon on the floor, Toussaint returned to gurney where the corpse lay. He picked up a scalpel and planted it into the decomposed skull.

He repented. "You're correct. I am disobedient to the

Lord as well." Tears flooded Toussaint's eyes. "Others have suffered because of my disobedience. One who is yet to come will suffer most of all at the hand of your grandson, to the point of her destruction."

"That baby wasn't my grandson," Solomon said.

Not hearing him, Toussaint reflected on his folly, lost in his confession before the Lord. Toussaint gathered his wits and exhaled, releasing it. "So, you see Solomon, this is why I can come to you, because I know I can trust you. Why? Because you have trusted me when you needed assistance. No one knows about Mary's past. Once we returned with Mary to my mortuary, Aunt Sarah prayed for her and the Lord removed the memory from her heart and mind."

He removed the scalpel from the corpse's head. He dropped it, sending a muffled, clanging noise throughout the room. "Your daughter believes herself to be a virgin, an innocent, correct?" Toussaint bent down to pick up his instrument. Solomon scowled at him.

As Toussaint went to the counter and placed the scalpel in the sterilization bath, he remembered a bit of good news he'd heard. "Isn't she about to wed? Oh, now what is the eligible young man's name?" He tapped his chin with his index finger as he looked to the ceiling, hoping to jog his memory. "Ah yes, Antoine Chamberie. Now there's a family who is very particular about their pedigree."

Toussaint's laughter and joy filled the preparation room with a sadistic glee. "I buried Antoine's mother, Madame Celia, close to a year ago. Monsieur Victor... You know him, right? Antoine's father? Well, he and I hit it off very well.

"See, I'm good enough to be his acquaintance, but I could never marry into the family. I'm just a tad dark for the Chamberie stock." Toussaint's face brightened, recalling something he'd forgotten. "In fact, I believe the time has come for our monthly luncheon."

Toussaint watched Solomon massage his temples in disbelief, hearing him think, '*Why would Victor Chamberie ever associate with the likes of Toussaint Bailey?*' Toussaint snickered. "Why, I'se don't rightly know, Mistah Solomon," Toussaint said. "I'se guesses he likes us common, low-class Niggahs just a li'l bit mo' than you'se do, suh."

Solomon glared at Toussaint

"I wonder what we should talk about at lunch, Solomon?" Toussaint stared at him, his face blank. "Any suggestions for small talk?"

"I hate you, Toussaint."

Solomon's declaration hurt Toussaint. "Well, I don't hate you, Solomon, mon bon ami. You're my friend. I trust you as you have trusted me. We help each other, n'est-ce pas?" Solomon didn't reply. Toussaint returned to the corpse. Solomon arose from the floor of the preparation room. "Well, let's get to work."

Chapter 5

New Orleans, Louisiana. April, 1883.

Although it had been a few weeks since Solomon had taken the photographs, Toussaint still hadn't received them. He knew Solomon avoided him. "Either he can give me the photographs, or his Mary can become a spinster. It's up to Solomon. Either way, I win."

Remember Nate

"Alright, mon Dieu. Alright!" Toussaint would give him one more chance to comply. If Solomon refused, he would inform Monsieur Chamberie of his soon to be daughter-in-law's less than pristine past. Toussaint sighed, considering he may have to find another way to get Nate out of prison.

Allen arrived at work on time after school, like always. As routine dictated, Allen went to the stable to brush, feed, and water Cherrie. At three o'clock sharp, his apprentice knocked on the office door and entered.

"Good afternoon, Allen," Toussaint said, completing his letter. Toussaint inserted the note into the envelope. He hated using the sponge, housed in the small crystal bowl of his desk set. The envelope's glue always became either too wet or dry. If too wet, the water would soak through the envelope and wet the letter, causing the ink to run. If too dry, Toussaint would wet it over and over, in the end wiping away the glue. Then he would have to begin the process again with a new envelope, and perhaps re-write the letter.

Frustrated with the whole process, Toussaint had retired the tiny sponge, now sealing his envelopes the old-fashioned way, with his tongue. He always took extra care not to cut his tongue. He'd done so once. Strangely enough, he'd always remembered the pain. "How was school today?"

"Great, Monsieur. I received an 'A' on my advanced Algebra examination."

"Très bien, mon fils!" He beamed with pride over the strides the young man made to educate himself. "Did your instructor offer any suggestions on what you could do better or differently?"

"Well, now that you mention it," Allen began, but then stopped, ashamed.

Toussaint set the letter aside and opened his desk drawer, searching for a postage stamp while waiting for Allen to continue. Jannie hadn't refilled the stamp dispenser. "Yes, what is it?"

Allen skipped his left foot along the floor, and then

crossed it behind the right foot. Finally, he returned the foot to its proper position of rest. "Well, Monsieur St. Luc asked me to say behind after class."

"Well, what did he want?" Irritated, Toussaint closed his desk drawer, causing a faint, slamming noise to echo throughout the office. He remembered he didn't need a stamp, anyway.

"Well…"

"Allen, spill it for goodness sake." Toussaint couldn't endure dawdling in the conveyance of news, whether good or bad.

Allen inhaled deep. "Monsieur St. Luc told me I had exceeded his expectations for this level of Algebra. He shared with me his plans to speak with Ma and Pa about sending me to Union Normal to study math on a college level. He said he would speak with my other instructors as well. If all agree, he plans to recommend to Monsieur St. Clair I skip my last year of prep school and begin coursework at Union Normal in the fall."

"St. Clair?"

"He's the headmaster at St. Maurice, remember?"

Toussaint stared at him, not understanding at first. Comprehending the boy's words, he jumped out of his seat and gave Allen a bear hug. "Excellent. Excellent! I'm proud of you son," he said, beaming with pride. So many opportunities awaited him. "Have you told your parents yet?"

"No, Monsieur. Not yet. I came here right after school."

Toussaint walked in a circle three times before his desk, planning his course of action. Perhaps he should resume his adjunct professorship at the institution to ensure Allen received proper instruction in Mortuary Science. Had he declared Mortuary Science as his course of study? Toussaint stopped pacing and considered the boy. Of course, it would be Mortuary Science. What else would he consider studying?

Jannie. Toussaint started pacing again. How would he convince Jannie to allow him to return to teaching? She'd had enough after he stayed too long in Tickfaw recruiting students back in '77. He didn't make it home for Christmas that year. She'd never forgiven him for it, either. He knew better than to revisit the subject with her.

Coming to a decision, Toussaint stopped pacing and went to the safe. He turned the combination lock. "Tell you what I'm going to do," Toussaint said. Hearing the tumblers click into position, he turned the safe's handle and opened it. Reaching toward the back for his strong box, he removed and opened it.

Toussaint extracted a coin and returned to his desk. "I would like for you to deliver this letter to Monsieur Philippe, and then take the remainder of the day off, with pay." Toussaint handed him the coin. "Go home and share the good news with your parents. Then maybe, you might consider calling on Mademoiselle… What is her name? Ah yes, Tamara Sils from church. Maybe you could take her for ice cream," he said, revealing a sly, knowing smile. "I've noticed her making eyes at you during Mass."

"Monsieur!"

"She's a wonderful girl, Allen." Toussaint closed the lid to the strong box and placed it in the safe. Closing the door and then spinning the dial, Toussaint's countenance grew serious. "I see her becoming an excellent wife for you some day." He peered over Allen's shoulder into his future. "Yes, she would make a great wife for you. Both of you would be very much in love and enjoy a wonderful home."

Allen considered his advice. He did like Tamara, but he'd avoided talking to her. She seemed to like him. She would always smile at him and then conceal it behind her little fan. Yes, perhaps she did like him. Maybe it was a good day to call on her. He fiddled with the coin in his hand, causing him to look at it. "Oh, Monsieur," Allen said.

"Yes, son?"

"You gave me a twenty-dollar gold piece. My salary is only twenty-five cents per day."

Toussaint regarded his young apprentice. "I know what I gave you, boy. I'm never mistaken about what I give to people, especially those for whom I care." Toussaint patted

Allen on the shoulder and then hugged him. "Now go on, before the afternoon escapes you." Allen bolted toward the door. "Wait Allen, the letter."

"Oui, Monsieur," he said. Hurrying back, Allen grabbed the letter, and then ran out the door.

With a few tucks of the heavy cotton cloth, Toussaint finished shrouding Madame LeMarche's body. He wasn't ready to embalm her and didn't wish for her to lie on the table, exposed. "You shall be as modest in death as you were in life, Madame." Toussaint saluted her, bowing. Madame LeMarche had been a wonderful teacher at St. Maurice parish school and a staunch volunteer in the parish's soup kitchen.

Toussaint ordered his instruments on the table, preparing for his work on Madame LeMarche. The tingling bells caused him to look up the stairs. It never failed. As soon as he would enter the cellar once Jannie left for school, someone would chime the bell. Toussaint ran up the cellar steps, up the steps to the kitchen door to enter the house, and then made a final sprint to the front door.

Reaching the door, Toussaint parted the curtains and peeked outside. The one standing on the porch had been worth the run from the preparation room. He had to admit, he was pleasantly surprised. "Bonjour, Solomon," Toussaint said, opening the door to greet his longtime enemy with a smile. "*Comment allez-vous ce matin?*"

Solomon ignored his greeting and walked in the door.

"What is it? Aren't you well this morning?"

Solomon threw the package on the floor at Toussaint's feet. "I'm going to make you pay for this, Bailey."

Toussaint picked up the envelope and examined its contents. "*Les photos sont superbes*, Monsieur. You still do beautiful work. I thank you for your services. Oh, and what do I owe you, Solomon?"

"Your life." Solomon turned red, trembling.

"Threats? Tisk, tisk, Solomon. If you know nothing else, you should know never to threaten me." Toussaint wagged his pointer finger at him, chastising him.

"Oh, it isn't a threat. You will die for what you're attempting to do to me and my daughter. That's a promise."

Toussaint peered into Solomon's eyes and flirted with his fragile soul, purged on the edge of perdition. "Yes, I may die eventually, you're correct in what you say. However, it will not be at your hand or as a result of your plotting.

"Yet, you will die as you have planned to murder me. Yes, now this is true." He lingered in Solomon's future, nodding his head in agreement with what he saw. Leaving his trance, Toussaint pitied Solomon. "Oui, bon ami. You will fall into the hole you have dug for me."

Solomon suppressed his urge to kill Toussaint in the entry hall of his home. He would get him later. He could care less about the witchcraft Toussaint attempted to spin over him.

Toussaint opened the door and stepped to the side. "Bonjour, Solomon Philippe." Solomon marched passed him. Toussaint closed the door.

Chapter 6

New Orleans, Louisiana. September 1, 1963.

The hall clock chimed the hour. Nine o'clock in the evening. Although past his grandmère's bedtime, she didn't seem tired. Why would she be, after all the naps she'd enjoyed throughout the day?

Rising from the sofa, Julian stretched and then went to the bar cart to refresh his drink. "I'll have another too, darling," Lela said.

I'm tired of serving you. He considered setting the bottle beside her, allowing her free access. She drank too much.

"Storytelling dries my mouth, mon fils. The story flows much better with a bit of brandy."

Alcoholic. Julian pulled out the cork and poured. A drop fell into the brandy snifter. *Lush.* Julian went to the intercom and depressed the button. "Isabel?"

A few moments later, she entered the parlor. "Oui, mon fils?"

"Our resident drunk has drained the bottle. Bring in another one."

An invisible force held Isabel's open hand at her side, preventing her from slapping the boy. "It was the last bottle," Isabel said and left the room.

He could see it coming. "Grandmère, choose something else. You're out of brandy."

"I only drink that vintage. You'll have to go to the liquor store and buy another bottle."

His grandmère was insane. "You're kidding, right? It's late. Besides, you have a cellar full of wine and liquor. Choose one of them," Julian said, taking a seat next to her.

Isabel brought out a tray of sharp cheeses and olives, along with sliced hard salamis, breads, and crackers. Lela clapped her hands together with joy and thanked her child. Isabel curtsied and left.

After admiring the heavy-laden platter, Lela extracted a tooth pick from the gold holder and speared two helpless Kalamata olives. She inserted them into her mouth, savoring their saltiness. After downing another six olives, she smacked together her salt-cured lips. Now she really wanted her brandy. Lela shifted on the sofa, facing her grandchild with sad eyes. "I've been drinking brandy all day. I don't wish to mix my alcohols. I may get drunk."

You are drunk.

"I assure you I'm not," Lela said. Isabel returned and

placed a napkin across Lela's knee, to catch any errant drips or crumbs. "Isabel darling, get some cash from the safe. Give it to Julian so he may purchase my beverage."

What is the point in protesting, Julian lamented within.

"None," Lela said. Isabel removed a rose scented note pad from her apron pocket and handed it to Lela. Fumbling for her glasses suspended from her neck on a diamond studded platinum chain, Lela placed her spectacles on the tip of her nose.

"My goodness," she said, untangling her locket chain from the eyeglass chain. Freeing it, she kissed the locket quick and allowed it fall. Lela jotted down a note and handed it to Julian. "This is it. Château de Laubade Bas-Armagnac, 1912 vintage," Lela said, removing her reading glasses.

"Where am I going to find this? You must buy this from a dealer."

"Well, there's one in the French Quarter. He should still be open, if you hurry. Theo knows where to go. He will take you."

The establishment seemed as old as New Orleans itself. He had to admit the cypress plank floors were beautiful, although they creaked quite a bit. The runners, some sort of Turkish carpet, muffled the sound of the aged floors. Julian admired the rich mahogany shelving, the cornices engraved with flowers and grapes. The brass chandeliers had to have been there since the 1700's. The fixtures illuminated the store with a soft, yellow light, creating a subdued, somewhat dark, ambience.

Julian went to the counter. The storekeeper busied himself with dusting ancient bottles on the shelves behind the counter. He didn't seem to notice Julian's presence in the store. The man must have heard the creaking floors, announcing him. Julian cleared his throat. "Do you stock Château de Laubade Bas-Armagnac, 1912 vintage?"

The smartly attired storekeeper turned around to face him, arching his eyebrow. "Is this for Madame?"

Madame? Another spooky person. "Lela Chevalier?" Julian asked.

The storekeeper nodded, turned on his heel and rushed away. Julian could hear a door slam in the rear of the store and the sound of feet trudging downstairs, or so he assumed. It didn't surprise him the owner knew his lush of a grandmère. He had no doubts Lela's tab had put the man's children through college.

While waiting for the owner to return from the cellar, Julian browsed some of the bottles behind the counter. He found nothing priced under fifty dollars, based on the vintages he spotted. He would bet his last dollar the proprietor didn't sell malt liquor in the place.

The door bells chimed, prompting Julian to glance at the front door. He couldn't believe whom he saw before him. The man browsed the merlots. "Richard?"

The man looked up, surprised someone had called his name. "Julian?"

"Yeah."

The men embraced. "What are you still doing here?" Julian asked.

"Well, my plans changed. I wanted to say hello to an old friend, but she hasn't been available."

Julian nodded, irritated. He'd picked up a tone in Richard's voice for which he didn't care. "Yeah, I get it," Julian told him. "I plan to leave soon, maybe in a few days. When are you planning to return to D.C.?"

Richard removed a bottle from a bin, examining a label. "I'm not sure, maybe in a couple of days. Hey, we should go out and take in the local delights," Richard said with a sly grin.

"Maybe some other time. I have to finish up my business here, so I can leave this horrible town."

Julian's remarks surprised Richard. "You don't like New Orleans?"

"I grew up here. What is there to like?"

Richard patted his friend's shoulder. Julian flinched at his touch. Richard sighed. "Well, it's great town. If you would experience the city as a tourist, you'd like it."

"Can't do it. I know better," Julian said.

The storekeeper returned from the basement with the case of brandy. He sat the wooden crate on the counter and walked to the front of the store, where Julian and Richard chatted. "Bonjour, Monsieur." The storekeeper greeted Richard with a smile. "And what do you desire on this day?"

Richard began to sweat, but regained his composure.

"I ran into my friend while browsing the vintages," Julian said.

The storekeeper considered the two. "Friends, eh? Are you his friend, or is Julian yours, Monsieur?"

Richard said nothing.

"You enjoy merlot, do you not? May I interest you in this vintage?" The storekeeper walked over to a nearby bin. He removed a bottle and presented it to the men.

Julian eyes popped from his head, reading the label. However, there were no words, only a silver, blood stained lance mounted on the bottle. There was no year on the bottle. The strangest wax sealed the neck of the bottle, entwined in thorny vines. An unusual seal had been placed just below the shoulder of the bottle, with a cup of some sort impressed upon it. Fear surged in Julian's heart.

The bottle and its contents were dark. Something hit the side of the bottle, bouncing around within. In fact, there seemed to be a lot of activity within the bottle. Julian shook his head. He squinted his eyes for sharper focus. He thought he'd seen a little face, twisted in agony, pressing its nose against the side of the bottle. The figure peered out. Something ripped him away, disappearing within the depths of the bottle.

The storekeeper outfaced Richard with his omniscient eyes. "I'm not sure of the vintage. We've had it forever. It is very dry and very bitter."

Richard glared at the storekeeper.

"You agree, yes? Well, I will just have it sent to your home, Monsieur. I'm guessing you still reside at the same address?" Richard stood before him, silent. "I'll take that as a yes. By the way, I recently received another case. I'm not sure of its vintage either," the storekeeper said. "Maybe we should call the vintage, 'Eternity.'"

Richard left them and went to the counter. Julian followed, saying nothing. It seemed as if the storekeeper and Richard knew each other; however, they never addressed each other familiarly. Julian stood before the counter, ready to pay. Richard opened Julian's crate and removed a bottle. "Wow, nice vintage," Richard said. "You have good taste."

"Yes, I do. However, it isn't for me, but my grandmère."

Richard eyes grew bright. "Really? The lady from Commander's Palace?"

Julian stared at him. He'd forgotten he'd seen Richard earlier that day. "You disappeared before I could introduce you, so how would you know? Why do you care?" Julian reached into his back pocket and removed his wallet.

Richard scratched his head. "No reason. I guess I take an interest in you, since you're my best friend. It isn't important. I didn't mean to pry."

Julian felt a little bad, but not really. Richard had always been nosy. "It's okay. Yes, that was her."

Richard nodded. Julian handed the cash to the storekeeper. Feeling a little bad, he decided to be kinder to Richard. He really didn't want him around his grandmère for reasons he didn't understand. Whenever Richard asked about her, Julian had the unrelenting urge to kill him. "Hey, you want to come by this evening for a nightcap? Grandmère is still awake."

"That's nice of you man, but no. I'll allow you to enjoy your evening with your grandmother."

Julian noticed the storekeeper hadn't taken his eyes off Richard. He handed Julian his change. "It is for the best, Monsieur. Madame hasn't seen her great-grandson in many years," the storekeeper said.

Julian placed the bills in his wallet. "How in the hell do you know?"

The storekeeper patted Julian's hand. Looking down, Julian noticed he wore the same rose embossed pinky ring as the sanitation worker at the trolley car stop. *Freak.*

"I speak to your grandmère quite a bit. She speaks of you often and had hoped, for quite some time, you would return to her." The storekeeper closed the cash register drawer. "I see her prayers have been answered."

Julian started to press the storekeeper, but he decided not to do so. Richard seemed nervous. Julian didn't wish for his friend to meet his crazy family anyway.

Richard had a way, unlike no other, of making him feel guilty. Jannette could do so too, but not like Richard. The less Richard knew about him and his family, the better. He already knew too much. Although Richard was his best friend, Julian didn't appreciate his constant questions about his feelings and his life. *Deceiver.*

The storekeeper arched his brow. *You are correct, mon fils.*

Julian thought he'd heard the storekeeper say something; yet, he found him writing a receipt for his order, not paying attention to him.

"Well, I'll be on my way. Have a good stay here, man," Richard said, headed for the exit.

"You're not buying anything?"

"No, I changed my mind."

"Okay. See you in D.C.," Julian said to him as he walked out the door. Richard never looked back, instead waiving his hand above his head as he walked out.

The storekeeper handed Julian his receipt. "Interesting fellow. You're best friends, yes?"

"Yes."

"How did you become friends, if I may ask?"

Julian closed the crate of brandy Richard had left open. "In college."

The storekeeper nodded. Removing his hammer from beneath the counter, he secured the lid with a couple of tacks. "Your grandmother mentioned you attended Morehouse College in Atlanta, yes?" Julian nodded. "My apologies, but I didn't realize Morehouse had integrated."

Julian's mouth fell open. "I never thought of it like that," he said. A subdued laugh escaped him. "Yes, I must say there aren't many Whites attending Morehouse. In fact, Richard may have been the only one."

The storekeeper nodded while checking if he'd adequately secured the crate's lid. "You should watch him."

"Why?"

"Madame would desire you to do so," the storekeeper said.

Julian considered the man further. He reminded Julian of the gardener at La Rose. His thoughts became fuzzy, unable to make the connections. "What is your name, sir?"

"Why is it important? I'm just a man working in a liquor

store." Knowing he wouldn't accept his answer, the store-keeper submitted. "My name is Jerémèy Andrews."

Mind fuck. Saying nothing in response, Julian grabbed the crate of brandy and left the store.

Chapter 7

New Orleans, Louisiana. September 1, 1963.

The bright light faded, disintegrating into a gray and opaque horizon. Despair persisted. A vacuum ingested the void of nothingness, whirlpooling the darkness into a being of rebellion.

The eternal adversary stood before her

"I am where you are, my Queen"

"You will not seduce me again"

"We live through you

…through all of you

…through you and your flowers"

"I resist you"

The adversary departed

Her patron enveloped her

"He is one with us

…he is of the kingdom

…fallen though he may be

…he is a part of this"

Lela sat up on the sofa. The wispy tail of the dream spirited out the open window; yet, before it could, Lela stretched out her hand and grabbed its tail. The dream struggled in her grasp. Lela closed her eyes, absorbing its message. It stung her and flew away.

Lela awoke and found Julian preparing her drink. "What year is it?" Lela picked up the newspaper from the coffee table. September 1, 1963. She'd been dream hopping again. Since she'd turned one-hundred, she had experienced the phenomenon with increasing frequency. It tired her.

Julian sat with his grandmère on the sofa, placing the drink before her. Lela blotted her forehead with the back of her hand and then smoothed her hair. She patted her great-grandson's thigh. "I'm glad to see the storekeeper had a few bottles left. I will have Isabel place an order tomorrow."

"You cleaned him out?"

She ignored him. "Did you meet anyone interesting at the store?"

Julian gulped his drink to avoid choking. Her spooky ass had seen it all. He knew it in the core of his soul. "As a matter of fact, I ran into my friend, Richard."

"Really? Is he from New Orleans?"

Julian thought for a moment. "I'm not sure where he's from. He never talks about his family. But he's nosy, though.

He always inquiries about mine. I tell him very little."

"Why? Are you ashamed of us?"

Julian suppressed his laughter. "Of course, I am. But that's not the reason why." Lela scowled at him. "He wants to know too much. I don't trust him."

"You trust no one."

"Yes, and with good reason, wouldn't you say, Grand-mère?"

Lela reviewed in her mind all possible heirs who could complete the task ahead. There was only Julian. She had to control herself. "You're going to make me kill you."

"You should do as you see fit."

Lela let it lie and changed the subject, sipping her brandy. "Allow us to continue."

"Now that you're liquored up, I suppose we can."

New Orleans, Louisiana. May, 1883

"C'EST UNE BELLE *journée!*" Monsieur Jerémèy Andrews strolled down Saint Charles Street. Concerned about the time, he extracted his gold Patek Philippe pocket watch from his waistcoat. "Half-past eight o'clock? Bon!" He would have enough time to stop at the café.

Ordering a café au lait and croissant with orange marmalade, Jerémèy took a seat at an empty table near the window. Daydreaming about the future, he could see God's Creation before him, all that had come to pass and everything yet to come. He sipped his coffee, watching as passersby rushed to reach their destinations by nine o'clock.

A stickler for punctuality, Jerémèy left the café at eight minutes before nine o'clock and walked the remainder of the way to Gallier Hall. Entering the door at four minutes to nine, he opted to walk up the two flights of stairs, entering the office at precisely nine o'clock.

"May I help you, Monsieur?"

"Oui, Mademoiselle," he said with a sultry smile, seducing her. "I have a nine o'clock appointment with the mayor. I am Jerémèy Andrews."

Scanning her appointment book, she located his name. "Oui, Monsieur. The mayor is expecting you. Please have a seat and I will announce you."

Taking a seat, Jerémèy admired his reflection in the window. Always impeccably attired and well groomed, he changed his clothing at least twice per day, in accordance to the time of day. Certain suits of clothes were appropriate prior to noon while others were only suitable in the afternoon. Still others he reserved for the evening and then others for formal events. Finding his appearance satisfactory, he relaxed and waited for the mayor to receive him.

By a quarter after the hour, Jerémèy had become irritated. He couldn't understand why people weren't prompt in keeping their scheduled appointments.

"The mayor will see you now," the secretary said.

Seventeen minutes past the hour. Jerémèy arose from his place of rest and followed her.

Entering the office, Jerémèy arched an eyebrow. The room had been renovated since his last visit. The mayor's office had become a grand space, regally appointed with mahogany paneling. The ferns spread their fronds, perched upon their marble-topped Corinthian corniced pedestals.

The decorator had upholstered the stylish Victorian furnishings in hunter green silk damask, while constructing the drapes of a heavy, reddish burgundy silk taffeta interwoven with gold accent threads. Jerémèy found the design of the office to be very smart, even by his standards.

The mayor, a round, jovial man in appearance, arose from his desk to greet him. "Monsieur Jerémèy!"

"*Bonjour monsieur le Maire. Comment allez-vous?*"

"*Bon. Ça va très bien.*" The men sat and attended to civic business. Lost in thought, Jerémèy's attention drifted away from their discussion. "Is something troubling you, Monsieur?"

Jerémèy stared out the window. "Mayor, we're friends, yes?"

"Oui, of course."

Jerémèy paused for several minutes, picking at a strand

of imaginary lint on his trousers. "Mayor, please tell me truthfully…"

"I won't withhold anything from you, Jerémèy. You know this," he told him. The mayor valued Jerémèy as a trusted friend of his family and his administration. Not only had Jerémèy financed city projects, but he also had the uncanny ability to correct any delicate situations which arose from time to time.

Jerémèy removed and then re-inserted the red rose boutonnière into the button hole of his lapel. He slapped both hands upon the mayor's desk, causing the man to jump in his seat. "Bon. Mayor, where is the controller?"

Anguish contorted his face. "I don't know for certain," he said.

Jerémèy removed a large envelope from his attaché case, placing it before the mayor. "A man whom I don't know gave this to me last week in a French Quarter bar." The mayor reached for the envelope, but Jerémèy placed his hand on top of his, stopping him. "I must warn you Monsieur, the contents of this envelope are, well, disturbing. I just wish to warn you prior to your review."

"Oui." The mayor inhaled deep, gathering his resolve. He removed the contents. "Photographs?" His expression soon turned from one of curiosity and concern to one of horror and fury. "Mon Dieu."

The mayor stared in disbelief at the pictures depicting bizarre and explicit sexual acts, the rape. Once he saw the photograph of a charred corpse, he knew. "Oh no." Shuffling back through the pictures, he now recognized the man in the each of the photographs. "Oh God, no." He arrived at the last picture of the silver cigarette case, engraved with a monogram. "This can't be."

"Mayor, I will ask you again. Where is your nephew?"

The mayor fiddled with the feather of the quill pin sitting in its holder. "A man named Anthony Buonoguidi informed me my nephew had been killed in the whorehouse fire a few months ago."

"Is this your nephew in these pictures? Is that his cigarette case?"

Defeated, he leaned back into his chair. "Yes. The case belonged to him." The mayor began to weep, but regained his composure. "Who gave you these photographs?"

Jerémèy adjusted his four-in-hand knot and then his cufflinks. He missed his cravat. "As I previously stated, neither do I know the gentleman nor had I ever seen him before."

The mayor studied the photographs spread out across his desk. "Well, what do you think? Is someone trying to blackmail me?"

"Perhaps. They want something. I found this in the envelope with the pictures," Jerémèy said.

The mayor took the letter from Jerémèy, opened it and began to read. "Who are they?"

"I conducted a little investigation of my own, prior to bringing this matter to your attention." Jerémèy withdrew his solid gold cigarette case from his breast pocket. The mayor placed the crystal ashtray to the outer edge of the desk. Jerémèy lit his cigarette and inhaled, slowly and deeply, as he considered the tale. "Have you ever heard of the O'Bannion Family?"

"O'Bannion? Who in the hell are the O'Bannions?" The cigarette smoke filling his office mingled with the impending scandal, making the mayor's patience short.

"The O'Bannion Family is a gang out of Chicago."

"Chicago?"

"Yes," Jerémèy said. He took a drag from his cigarette. "They've been in New Orleans for at least two years now, working to consolidate the New Orleans' rackets under a single, cohesive umbrella. They have succeeded for the most part, doing it quietly and without bloodshed. They are a very discreet operation.

"However, one should not mistake their subtlety as meekness. They're a very dangerous and territorial gang, having caused their fair share of turf wars in Chicago. In fact, the 'competitive' Chicago and New York markets motivated the outfit to trail-blaze new operations in larger southern cities.

"Typically, they enter a new market unnoticed and invite local rackets to join their operation, giving them ownership in the O'Bannion organization. If the local gang chooses not to join, all is well. The O'Bannion's simply establish their own racket, undercuts the competition, and eventually forces the competitor out of business," Jerémèy said. "They're very corporate in their actions."

"You're kidding me?" The mayor had never encountered gangsters who behaved as businessmen. He'd always considered them as glorified street thugs.

"It's quite true." Jerémèy said. "Neither you nor I have heard of them. We still deal with the same individuals we always have." Jerémèy extinguished his cigarette.

Relieved, the mayor left his desk to open a window. He smoked cigars, not cigarettes. Disgusting.

"But now the Buonoguidis have come into the New Orleans market, moving in on their territory. The O'Bannions don't care for it. Buonoguidi has stepped on a water moccasin and he doesn't even know it. A very bloody and vicious war may result."

"What kind of war?"

"A turf war," Jerémèy said. "Buonoguidi has stolen from the O'Bannion's. Peter O'Bannion, he is the founder and leader of the organization, fully intends to retake what is his," he said with a snicker. "In any case, Madame Red's whorehouse belonged to him. Peter O'Bannion was particularly fond of Madame Red. Some say they were in love."

"Mon Dieu." The mayor picked up the letter and read it once again. "Who is this Nate fellow?"

"He was Madame Red's house man and driver. He also drove for O'Bannion whenever he was in town. The rumor is Buonoguidi framed him for the fire. I believe my sources are correct. I doubt if Nate would burn down his boss's investment."

"Oh God." When he'd approved Nate as the scapegoat for the fire, he had no idea of the Negro's close affiliation with the phantom gangland boss. "Well, if this Nate man didn't burn down the house, who did?"

"Buonoguidi, of course. He didn't know the house belonged to O'Bannion. He hadn't vetted the local competition. If he had asked a few questions, as I did, he would have known. But Buonoguidi is not the picture of due diligence. He believed O'Bannion's operation to be a local organization he could crush with little or no effort. He was wrong."

The mayor's head began to pound. He went to the door. "Do we have any Eclectric Oil?"

"Yes, sir. We do," his secretary said. She handed it to him with a spoon. He closed the door and returned to his desk. "So, you mean to tell me Buonoguidi started the fire?"

"Of course not. He ordered his henchman, Smitty, to

torch the house."

"Smitty? Who in the hell is Smitty?" Placing the cap of the bottle between his teeth, he twisted it. Loosened, he screwed it off and then gulped from the bottle.

Jerémèy smirked but said nothing. "Smitty is a small-time thug and hustler, recruited by Buonoguidi. Buonoguidi had ordered him to burn down the house between five and six o'clock in the morning, after all the patrons left. Sadly, Smitty takes little direction and utilizes poor judgment as well. He made an executive decision to carry out his boss's instructions during peak hours at the house."

"My God." The mayor left his desk and walked to the window, searching the streets for a man he didn't know. The pounding in his head intensified. He pictured his nephew burning to death because of this man's insolence and incompetence. "Is Smitty still in New Orleans?"

"Yes, your Honor."

"Get him."

Jerémèy smoothed his tie into the security of his waistcoat without unbuttoning the garment. "He will be in my custody within the hour. However, there's still the question regarding Nate. O'Bannion wants his man back. Now."

He began to perspire. "I have no idea where he is, or if he's even still alive."

Jerémèy reached down to retrieve his attaché case. Placing it on the mayor's desk, he fastened the buckle. "I suggest you find out where he is, and you should pray he's still alive. As we speak, O'Bannion is on his way to New Orleans to find his man and to deal with those responsible for the loss of his property. He also wishes to chat about Madame Red's death."

The color drained from the mayor's face. "How do you know this?"

"A different source alerted me. I'm sure he has relayed to O'Bannion what I told him regarding Buonoguidi's involvement in this matter. O'Bannion was unsure before, but not anymore. And I promise you, he will not come to town alone."

The mayor stared at Jerémèy in disbelief. He spiraled into panic mode, his mind working to spin the story to hide his involvement. "I'm not going to take the fall for this. I won't tolerate some sort of gang war in my city, either. I'll give him Nate, Buonoguidi, and Smitty too. They lied to me," he said.

"You didn't know, Mayor. I don't blame you."

He dabbed his eye with his handkerchief. "You're a good friend, Jerémèy. Merci." The two men sat in silence for a time. "Where's my nephew's body? I want to give him a proper burial. I should've done so months ago. I only wished to spare my sister the grief," the mayor said.

"Does she know he's dead?"

"No. I told her I sent him away on business until I could figure out what to do. I didn't have a body. When he didn't return, I knew he must have died in the fire. I knew he patronized Red's. But how could I tell his mother, his wife, and children he died in a whorehouse? God!" The mayor began to cry. He mopped his face with his handkerchief.

"And you won't have to. We will explain the death. I'll see what I can do to retrieve his remains for you. No questions, alright? Just accept I can secure his remains."

Jerémèy's heart filled with compassion for the man. Although corrupt, Jerémèy could see in the mayor's heart the love dwelling there for his family and his desire to protect them from tragedy.

"Whatever you think is best, Jerémèy. I should've contacted you when this all happened."

Jerémèy arose from his chair. The mayor escorted him to the door and opened it. "It will be well," Jerémèy told him. "However, you will have to deliver Nate, Buonoguidi, and Smitty before the party will release your nephew's remains." He walked out the door.

The mayor returned to his desk and flopped into his chair, spent. "It's to be expected."

In the weeks which had passed since Jerémèy's visit, the mayor's sense of urgency had waned. He'd made a few inquiries regarding Nate's whereabouts, but no one knew anything. As for Smitty and Buonoguidi, they had disappeared from the streets of New Orleans. He guessed the two had left town and returned to the East Coast. A knock at the door interrupted his review of *The Picayune* morning addition. "Yes, what is it?"

"Mayor." His secretary slipped in the door, closing it behind her. "Monsieur Jerémèy is here with a man I don't know."

He went pale. "What is the gentleman's name?"

"Some Irishman named Peter O'Bannion." The mayor swallowed hard. "Your Honor, are you alright?"

"I'm fine. Fine!" He could see the shock and confusion skate across his secretary's face. "Really honey, I'm fine. Give me five minutes and then show them in. Alright?"

"Oui, Monsieur."

Five minutes later, the mayor's secretary escorted the men into his office. Mustering up the politician within, he arose from his desk with a smile. "Jerémèy, how are you?"

"I am well, your Honor," Jerémèy said. He suppressed his irritation with the mayor, who'd failed to reply to his numerous messages. "Allow me to introduce my acquaintance. Your Honor, this is Peter O'Bannion, the gentleman whom I spoke of at our last meeting."

The mayor put a big, welcoming grin on his face. "Mr.

O'Bannion, welcome to New Orleans! It's a pleasure to meet you." He extended his hand to O'Bannion; however, the man didn't take it. Fury seemed to radiate from the enormous man, standing a terrifying six-feet, seven-inches tall, three hundred fifty pounds (all muscle), with shocking red hair and a ruddy complexion. He found the man's stone cold blue eyes impossible to read. The mayor swallowed. "Please gentleman, sit."

Jerémèy took his seat in the leather winged chair. Once comfortable, he crossed his legs and adjusted his French cuffs. "As I previously informed you, your Honor—"

"Look, I ain't got time for this fuckin' bullshit," O'Bannion said, his complexion growing even ruddier. "Where's my goddamn Nigger, Nate?"

"Mr. O'Bannion, I assure you we've searched everywhere for him and…"

"You'se ain't looked everywhere, because Nate's ass ain't fuckin' here. Where in the fuck is he?"

Jerémèy held up his hand. "Monsieur O'Bannion, I assure you we're searching for him. But perhaps there's someone who could shed some light on the matter."

O'Bannion snorted. "Yeah? Who'se that?"

"I have in my custody a gentleman named Smitty. I believe he knows of Nate's whereabouts."

O'Bannion loosened his tie. "Now you're talkin', Jerémèy.

Take me to him."

Surely this man would kill Smitty in his attempt to ascertain the Negro's whereabouts. With Buonoguidi at large, he may become the target of the gang's retaliation. *"Ce n'est pas bon,"* the mayor said to Jerémèy. *"Il pourrait le tuer…"*

O'Bannion lunged and grabbed the mayor by the collar. He snatched him from his chair and pulled him across the desk. "Is that it? You'se thinks I'm fuckin' stupid? That I'm some dumb Mick? Is that it?"

"No! No, Mr. O'Bannion," he mumbled, losing his battle to breathe.

A blood vessel popped out of O'Bannion's forehead. *"Ma mère est française, toi connasse! Je parle français très bien, imbécile,"* he said. "I'm going to murder you, slow and easy like."

"Messieurs, Messieurs!" Jerémèy parted the two men, despite his small stature. "Monsieur O'Bannion, sit down, s'il vous plaît."

O'Bannion decided not to murder the man and released him from his grip. The mayor collapsed upon his desk, gasping for air. "Jerémèy, you'se a good guy. You've been straight with me. But this motherfucker is a liar. I'm gonna tear this town apart," he said.

He got in the mayor's face, breathing hard. "You stole my lady, my business and my Nigger. I didn't come into your town causin' no problems, I kept our operations low. Is this how you repay me?" O'Bannion turned to leave.

Jerémèy straightened his rose shaped tie-tac, for the stem had gone askew due to the scuffle. It didn't look bad, slanting to the right; however, his personal guidelines for proper attire demanded the rose stem to point straight down. He grabbed a small silver tray from the desk to check his adjustment of the jewel. Perfect. "O'Bannion, my offer still stands. Would you like to ask Smitty yourself?"

O'Bannion stopped. The mayor had pissed him off so much he'd forgotten his friend's offer. "Yeah, sure Jerémèy. Let's go and talk to Smitty." His wicked glare came to rest upon the mayor. "I'se wants Hissoner to come along for the ride."

The mayor froze, but then revived himself. "Oh, I have another appointment."

Jerémèy raised an eyebrow. "I suggest you come along, your Honor," Jerémèy said, placing his hand on his shoulder. He pulled him from the chair and guided him toward the door.

Accepting his life and political career had come to an end, the mayor's shoulders drooped in defeat. "Allow me to get my hat and cane."

After a two-hour ride south of New Orleans on a rough road through the swamp country, they finally turned off onto an even rougher road, built to accommodate only one carriage. After one-half hour, tortured by the deep ruts in the road, they came to an even narrower road with a row of weeds growing tall between the faint wheel tracks. The men continued along the road for another ten minutes through a jungle teaming with mosquitoes. "Merde," the mayor said, swatting away the insects. "What is this place, Jerémèy?"

"Hell."

Jerémèy stopped the carriage before a rough-hewed plank house with a rusted tin roof. "Let us begin."

The mayor and O'Bannion left the carriage and headed toward the shack. "No, this way Messieurs," Jerémèy called to them. The men followed Jerémèy to the rear of the shack, and then through the thick, overgrown abandoned field for one-quarter mile. Jerémèy stopped. "We are here."

O'Bannion and the mayor scanned the area, seeing nothing. "What? Are you mad, man?" the mayor asked, hot, tired, sore, and mosquito bitten. "There isn't anything here."

Jerémèy pitied the man for his ignorance. Without a reply, he reached down and removed the overgrowth. Lifting the wooden hatch door, he unhooked the ladder secured to the side of the wall and lowered it. Once secured, Jerémèy descended into the black hole. Hesitating at first, the men decided to follow him.

Arriving at the bottom, Jerémèy moved aside, allowing

the men to step off the ladder. He extracted a match from his trouser pocket, struck it on the bottom of his shoe and lit the kerosene lamp on the rickety table.

The men focused their eyes, adjusting to the dim light. The mayor gasped. There, tied spread-eagle to stakes pounded into the earthen wall were both Smitty and Buonoguidi, nude.

"My God, are they alive?" the mayor asked. His nostrils filled with the essence of burning, rotting flesh entrapped within the earthen walls, a millennium of despair and suffering. He cowered near the wall.

O'Bannion stroked his chin, impressed. He'd misjudged Jerémèy, believing him to be a soft, prissy French man, unwilling to get his hands dirty.

"Oui, your Honor. They're alive." He moved the ladder away from the trap door, much to the mayor's horror. Jerémèy picked up the bucket of water he kept in the bunker, in case of fire, and threw half in Smitty's face, and then the other half in Buonoguidi's face. The men revived, coughing. "Messieurs, you have visitors *aujourd'hui*."

"Who's there?" Smitty asked with a hoarse, tortured voice. The light from the lamp blinded him.

"It doesn't matter. Where is Nate?"

"I already told you, I'se don't know what they did with that Nigger." Smitty coughed out the water he'd taken on from Jerémèy's wake-up call.

Jerémèy walked over to the small wood burning stove in the corner of the room. Finding a few live embers, he inserted the iron poker. Taking a log from the wood pile, he threw it in and closed the door, as much as the poker would allow. He returned to the men. "O'Bannion, would you like to persuade them?"

An evil grin crept across his face. "Sure Jerémèy. I'll give it a crack." He reached into his trouser pocket and extracted a set of brass knuckles.

"What are you going to do?" The mayor watched the scene unfold, horrified. If Jerémèy freed the men, they would be able to identify him.

"I'm gonna see what they know." Gripping the brass knuckles, O'Bannion reached back and propelled his fist into Buonoguidi's face. The sound of brutal hit from the brass knuckles fell dead, muffled by the bunker's thick, earthen walls. Buonoguidi screamed out in pain, aroused from his state of near unconsciousness. His jaw sagged, blood gushing from his mouth. "Where's my goddamn Nigger, you no good fuckin' Dago?"

Buonoguidi wagged his head, attempting to clear the blood from his swelling eye. He focused on the man before him. "You! What the fuck you doin' here? This ain't got nuthin' to do with your potato diggin' ass, O'Bannion."

O'Bannion gritted his teeth, channeling all his energy into the hit. He shattered Buonoguidi left jaw. "Now that's no way to say hello, Buonoguidi." O'Bannion hit him again. "You'se thought you could cut me out of my business, eh? Not now, not ever. You're a dead man."

The mayor broke out into a cold sweat. O'Bannion would surely kill the man. He inched the ladder toward the hatch door leading out of the bunker.

"You're not contemplating leaving us, are you, your Honor?"

Jerémèy's voice grated the mayor's nervous system, causing him to shiver.

"You're as much a part of this now, as we are." Jerémèy smiled at him.

The mayor wondered if he'd befriended Satan, finding evil lodging in his eyes.

"We're doing this for you and your family, not our own." Jerémèy grabbed his hand and returned to the group.

O'Bannion continued to pummel Buonoguidi's face, exposing what remained of his cheek bones. "Wuck woo, Wanyon!"

He lost his enthusiasm, for he knew it would take days to break him. Tony Buonoguidi had come up the hard way, just as he had, and wouldn't be easily defeated.

Irritated and bored, Jerémèy was ready to leave. "O'Bannion, allow me to end this please."

"By all means." He slung the brass knuckles several times, flicking away the excess blood and clumps of flesh. With his clean hand, he removed his handkerchief from his pocket. He wrapped his brass knuckles in it, soaking the cloth with blood, and then shoved them in his pants pocket. O'Bannion stretched his fingers and chuckled. "I don't wanna bloody my Franch cuffs anyway, Monsieur."

Jerémèy walked over to the pot-bellied stove and removed the iron poker, glowing red-hot. Bypassing Buonoguidi, he charged the semi-conscious Smitty. He rammed the poker into his bare groin. Smitty released a blood curdling scream for fifteen minutes, his penis left hanging from a sliver of flesh. "Where is Nate?" Jerémèy asked Buonoguidi.

"You sick son of a bitch! What the hell's wrong wit' you, you goddamn Frog?"

"I'm tired," he said. "I've been asking you both the same question for the past few weeks. The two of you have insisted on withholding the answer. Today, I demand the answer to my question." He returned to the stove and buried the poker beneath the coals.

While waiting for the poker to reheat, Jerémèy leaned against the dirt wall. Why couldn't people just tell the truth? It would make his life so much simpler. But instead, the wicked seemed to enjoy the drama of trying to deceive him.

Now he must spend his day torturing liars for a confession of guilt instead of admiring the Lord's blessing for all men, women. They were the true angels in his opinion, perfect in every way.

He extracted a cigarette from the case and placed it on the stove's hot exterior. The afternoon seemed to drag on forever. "My suit," he said. Jerémèy stood away from the dirt wall, finding dirt on his sleeve. Manny had just completed the suit for him. Now he must return it to Manny so that he could take it to his launderer. Manny had told him the fellow had developed some sort of method to clean wools without water. Jerémèy believed the man would become wealthy from this yet unknown process for cleaning garments.

After enjoying the last, deep, satisfying drag of the cigarette, Jerémèy threw what remained into the stove. He walked over to Buonoguidi and exhaled the smoke into his face. "You're next, Monsieur. You have, allow us say, ten minutes to remember Nate's whereabouts."

Fear engulfed the heart of the hardened street criminal. He glanced over to Smitty who had fallen unconscious, his cock burnt off. He probably would have bled to death if the hot poker hadn't seared off the wound. For the first time in his life, Buonoguidi experienced the sensation of terror.

Jerémèy extracted the poker from the stove, and then returned to Buonoguidi. "Would you like to do this?" He extended the poker to O'Bannion.

"Naw, you'se go ahead," O'Bannion said.

O'Bannion's unwillingness to extract the truth from Buonoguidi surprised him. "Humph." Jerémèy stood before his prisoner and proceeded to caress his nude body with the red-hot poker without touching him, the hot metal passing fractions of an inch above his bare flesh. The intense heat burned him anyway, leaving red welts in its wake. Jerémèy's eyes made love to his captive's, seducing and taunting him all at once.

Buonoguidi winced in pain, but he didn't cry out.

Jerémèy left him and reheated. Ten minutes later, he extracted the sparking, glowing poker from the fire. It appeared molten.

The mayor turned away, sickened at the very thought of the events about to unfold.

Jerémèy charged the poker toward Buonoguidi's groin, stopping short of making contact. "I will ask you once more, Monsieur. Where is Nate?"

Peering into his eyes, he found the devil staring back at him. Buonoguidi knew the sadistic motherfucker would love nothing better than to burn his dick off. "He's in St. Bernard Parish on a chain gang, you sadistic Frog!"

"Where? I don't have time to figure it out."

"He's out on Route 5."

The poker married itself to his left cheek. "Near?"

"He's just south of Poydras, I swear to God!"

"We looked. He's not there," Jerémèy said, irritated by his lies. Jerémèy jabbed the still hot poker into Buonoguidi's stomach.

"He's there under the name of William Smith."

O'Bannion's mouth fell open in disbelief. Jerémèy amazed him. In Chicago, his gang either shot people or just beat the shit out of them until they confessed. In Louisiana, he'd observed a level of sheer torture and terror they'd never delved into up North. This guy was sick, but he got results. However, O'Bannion didn't know of one man in his operation who could torture a motherfucker like this. Not even he had the stomach for it.

The mayor turned his head, unable to bear it all.

"Why did you frame my associate's hired man?"

"I didn't know that Nigger Nate was his man, I swear to God. I just thought he was some Nigger hangin' 'round the house. That's the God's honest truth!"

Jerémèy considered the matter for a moment, knowing all along what must be done. He leaned the poker against the wall, relieving everyone the torture segment had ended. Pulling up his right pant leg, he removed a hunting knife from its sheath and cut Smitty's throat with lightning speed. The blood flowed from his neck down his nude chest, appearing as a comical four-inch wide necktie, inappropriately long. He walked over to Buonoguidi.

"You son of a bitch. Don't you know who I am? I'm Anthony Buonoguidi, the whole New York—" His eyes rolled back in his head. Battling unconsciousness, he looked down at his chest, amazed to find his blood flowing down like Niagara Falls.

His eyes locked on Jerémèy in disbelief, his fingertips and toes twitching. His eyes went blank.

Hearing a dull thump, O'Bannion and Jerémèy turned to find the mayor passed out.

Smoke arose from the ground in the middle of nowhere as the three men rode away from the little shack, destined for New Orleans. "Your Honor, have Nate released from prison first thing tomorrow morning, s'il vous plaît."

"Yes, of course, Monsieur," he said. The mayor passed out and remained unconscious for the remainder of the ride to New Orleans. The mosquitoes allowed them to pass in peace, satiated from their morning feast.

Chapter 8

New Orleans, Louisiana. September 1, 1963.

He thought he would be sick. Julian held his crotch. Lela sipped her brandy. It wasn't often she shared the story, but men always found it disturbing. She and Nancy could never understand it. They'd found the story to be hilarious. Nate would smile, but by the end of the story, they would notice he would've crossed his legs, spurring another round of laughter from her and Nancy. "They had it coming, Julian."

Isabel entered the room and placed a glass of seltzer water on the table before Julian. He grabbed it and gulped it down, almost choking on the carbonation. He coughed and cleared the bubbles from his throat. "I realize that, Grandmère," he said, his stomach settling down. "But what man could do such a thing to another man?"

Lela's smiled waned. "The propensity for cruelty and deception abound upon this Earth, in the hearts of both men and angels alike. I'm not sure which being has proven to be more sadistic and cruel throughout the millennium." Lela sipped her brandy and then placed the glass on the table. She stared out the window. A thin, dark rim outlined the moon.

Atlanta, Georgia. April, 1883.

HE SLAPPED THE back of his neck. "Merde!" The insects continued their relentless attack on him. Feeling movement beneath his shirt collar, he scooped in his hand, removing the insect and then smashing it between his fingertips. Anton Lamont Trouvier removed his top hat and sat it on his lap, eliminating a hiding place for the pests. Did the passenger line offer first-class? He then remembered he couldn't afford it anyway.

La vieille sorcière, sitting to his right, sneered at him. She seemed to be in mourning, dressed in black and wearing a small *chapeau* with wilted flowers springing forth, even more dead and decrepit than her. Her husband had probably willed his own death to escape her. Anton had no doubts about it.

The old lady snorted and then turned her attention to the window across the aisle, peering out. She'd wanted his window seat. Although he would have preferred to sit on the aisle, it had been his pleasure to deny her, putting the spoiled old Southern belle in her place. The creaking wooden floorboards spurred Anton to look up. The frail waiter stopped before their seat. "I'se sorry, sir. We don't have any cognac, only bourbon," he said.

Anton closed his eyes and then opened them. *These are a backward people*. "That will do. Merci."

"Mercy?"

"Thank you." The waiter asked the old hag if she cared for a refreshment. She grunted and gave him a curt nod. The man continued down the aisle to check on the other passengers, the floorboards creaking with every step he made. The sound grated his nerves. He needed his drink; however, Anton had no idea when he would receive it. How far were they from Atlanta? Anton put on his top hat and looked out the window.

Anton despised the American South, having little patience for American society over all. Everything was primitive. At least New York City had proven to be civilized, to a certain degree. He'd considered hiring a man to drive him to Atlanta, but decided against it. He could only imagine the wild animals and people he would have encountered along the way, let alone the untamed terrain.

Prior to leaving France, American expatriate associates had warned him to steer clear of the Poor White Trash, Red Necks and Hillbillies that littered the American South. They'd referred to the groups as *Nègres Blancs* and had advised him against traveling by coach through the back country, for they would rob and kill him. From what he'd seen from his train window, Anton was glad he'd heeded their advice. As far as he was concerned, these sub-classes of the White race should be kept in cages too. They were a disgrace and an embarrassment.

Besides, his benefactor had given him only fifty francs for expenses. He couldn't have hired a driver anyway. The man had been kind enough to book him third-class passage on a freighter for his voyage to America. Cheap bastard.

Staring out the window, Anton could see nothing but green as the train passed through a narrow lane canopied by trees on either side of the single track. He wouldn't even be on the train riding through the wretched back country if his father, the drunkard, hadn't squandered away the fortune *La Famille de Trouvier* had labored to build for over eight hundred years. Now, Anton would have to rebuild what his father had lost.

"Sir, we'll be pulling into Atlanta in about fifteen minutes," the waiter said, handing him the bourbon. Anton nodded, dismissing him. He should have chosen to relax in the train's rustic café car, but he couldn't afford to tip the waiter. He should've retired to the car anyway and not tip the man. La vieille sorcière frowned. He determined his consumption of alcohol offended her sensibilities.

Anton saw blood streaming from a sharp cut to her throat. He blinked and it was gone. He sipped his drink. "I hope your journey was enjoyable, Madame," he said, breathing alcohol into the woman's face.

The old hag covered her nose and held her breath. Anton mocked her with his eyes. She shoved the needlework she'd busied herself with during the train ride (when not despising him) into her bag. She signaled for the porter, who assisted her to the front of the car. A man stood and gave her his seat.

Anton grunted. He'd hoped the train would stop abruptly, flinging her across the railcar to her death. He returned his attention to the passing scenery.

Leaving the jungle of the Georgian countryside, the landscape became peppered with dilapidated shacks, and then livestock grazing in fields. Soon warehouses, both wooden and brick, lined the outskirts of the train yard. "Welcome to the great city of Atlanta," the conductor announced in the car.

Anton finished his green bourbon and sat the empty glass on the floor.

He waited in line to disembark the train behind a herd of old men and women, heavy laden with luggage. Another delay, but it didn't matter. While standing in line, Anton realigned his career goals. His mind focused on the fortunes he could glean from the naïve businessmen of the South.

At last, his turn had come. He skipped down the narrow stairs, freeing himself from the wretched train car. He bumped into the old lady, who had sat beside him during the ride. She fell on the platform. Anton stepped over her and continued to the street, where he searched for a coach to take him to the home of his host. Soon, he spied a slave standing next a coach with an old mare. The Negro held a bucket of feed to her mouth, allowing the animal to gorge herself. He walked over to him. "How much?"

The driver removed the bucket from the mare's mouth. The animal grunted. "Two bits."

What was a 'bit'? Anton reached in his trouser pocket for a coin and removed it. Although unfamiliar with American currency, he didn't believe it to be worth a great deal. "You will take me to my destination for this amount." He placed the coin into the man's hand.

"That ain't e'nuff, suh." The driver's eyes locked with Anton's. Fear gripped him. He opened the door to the coach, allowing Anton to enter, and then placed his bags on the overhead rack. Once he secured the luggage, the driver mounted his driver's bench and pulled out into the busy street. "Where to, suh?" he asked.

"Thirteen Peachtree."

"Yessuh," the driver said.

Looking out the window, Anton's stomach turned in disgust. "This is a squalid place." The war had ended many years ago, yet the city still bore its scars. Slaves littered the streets, selling their wares and standing in line for food. He saw a sign with 'Jobs' inscribed on it. What *Nègres* worked without a whip to drive them? Before his father squandered the family fortune, Anton had refused to have Africans in his employ.

Anton watched the poor little… Oh, what was the English word he'd heard in France? *Niggers.* That was it. He watched the little Niggers play in the gutter lining the tracks. Worthless creatures. Anton snorted, spotting well-dressed Negroes. Perhaps they still labored for their masters, but he didn't think so. They had a certain air of success and self-sufficiency about themselves. The Negro man escorted the woman (his wife?) up the plank stairs, entering the feed store. Anton sensed a strong spirit of freedom, love, pride, and affluence from the two.

He dismissed the happy couple as an exception to his truth, soon spotting a couple of old Confederate soldiers still wearing their uniforms, each missing a limb or two, standing on the street corner hoping someone would place coins in their cups. "They must be the White Trash my associate spoke of." Disgust welled up inside of him, as it had when he encountered urchins begging on the streets of Paris. "I'll never be like them," he said.

The coach turned the corner and drove past vacant lots marked with surveyor's stakes and ribbons, awaiting a new life. Anton wondered who was the developer and if he could invest in his venture.

Stay focused

Anton averted a growl. He despised the voice in his head, the voice of his benefactor. It had to be his imagination; nevertheless, he listened. He had to focus. The voice was right.

The coach stopped. "We'se here, suh." The coachman opened the door.

Smoothing his jacket, Anton stepped out of the coach and appraised the grand home before him. Yes, it was a home, not a hovel, like the ones he'd passed earlier. He walked up the granite steps to the welcoming porch and ranged the bell. He hoped he hadn't perspired in the humidity.

The door opened, revealing a distinguished Negro man with salt and pepper colored hair, attired in a tuxedo jacket with tails. He'd heard there were civilized Negroes in America who understood their place in society, excelling in their roles of servitude to Whites, as allotted them by evolution.

"I believe your owner is expecting me. I am Monsieur Trouvier."

The butler raised a brow, but said nothing. "I will announce you." The butler stepped aside and allowed Anton to enter. He didn't close the door behind him, as if he expected to shove him out upon his master's refusal to receive him. The butler disappeared into the coolness of the house.

Anton admired the mahogany paneling. He hadn't believed such places existed in the Atlanta in the aftermath of the gut-wrenching war. Through the door left ajar, Anton watched the driver carry his bags to the rear of the house.

"Mr. Armistead will receive you."

The butler must have been some sort of ghost. Anton had neither heard nor seen him return. He followed the butler to the parlor and suppressed his surprise upon entering. The portraits of hunting scenes, in what he presumed to be the Georgian country side, took his breath away. He recognized the artist, but he couldn't recall the name. He believed him to be a British artist. The walnut paneled walls and leather furnishings rivaled any fine British manor. Without a doubt, his ancestors weren't of French descent.

"Welcome, Mr. Trouvier," Samuel Armistead said. "Did you have a pleasant journey?"

Anton suppressed his tongue. "It was. Thank you for welcoming me into your home, Monsieur Armistead."

"I'm honored to have you as my guest." Armistead signaled to the butler to prepare drinks. "You appear to be a cognac man to me." Anton nodded. "I brought a case of this vintage while me and the Missus toured your fair land last year."

The butler presented the bottle to Anton for his consideration. He couldn't believe his good fortune. He hadn't enjoyed a cognac of such high quality in years. Anton nodded. The butler bowed to him, and then left the men to uncork the bottle. Anton could smell the spirit's sweet essence fill the room. The butler returned with the beverages on a sterling silver tray. Anton accepted his drink as the butler made a slight bow. Once finished, the butler returned to his post near the parlor doors and stood at attention.

Armistead sipped his beverage. "I hope you'll find your stay here pleasant, Mr. Trouvier."

"I am sure I will. You have a wonderful home, Monsieur, pardon. Mr. Armistead," he said.

Anton walked around the room, admiring the paintings and furnishings. He stopped before a painting of a plantation house and its lands.

"I suffered some losses during the war. Yankee's burned down the house you're looking at in the painting. Thank the Lord I fared better than many of my associates."

Armistead expelled a laugh tinged with melancholy and reflection. "I knew better than to give the South all my gold. I gave them plenty, though. Ended up giving them my Niggers too, I mean my livestock. Every one of them defected to the Union Army. I went to the Yankee general to get them back. He said, 'Sorry, they're contraband of war.' That's bullshit. They stole my property."

Anton sipped his cognac.

"So early on, I took the Missus to France, to take her mind off the war and our sons who'd enlisted in the Confederate Army." Armistead drifted off, his eyes watering with emotion. "Sent four, got two back." He nodded. "Hell, that ain't bad. Most of my friends lost all their sons and kin.

"Anyhow, while in Paris, I met Monsieur Richard Roberts. He seemed to have an intimate understanding of the South's plight. I think he said he owned a plantation somewhere in Louisiana. Anyhow, he told me he would send help once the war ended. Sure enough, he sent me a wire advising of your visit and here you are."

Armistead patted Anton on the shoulder. Before he could stop himself, Anton sneered at him. Yet, he repressed the urge to tell the greasy man to keep his hands off him. Apparently, he hadn't noticed his aversion to his touch, for his host invited him to sit in the wing chair. Armistead took a seat in the chair to his right.

"I am happy to assist you, Mr. Armistead."

"Thank you, Mr. Trouvier." Armistead snapped his fingers. The butler came and refreshed their drinks, and then returned to his post. "If you're feeling up to it, I would like to lunch today at the Civic Club of Atlanta," Mr. Armistead beamed with pride. "It's a newly formed club for business-men here in the Atlanta area, of which I'm a charter member. I hope to introduce you to some of my colleagues and acquaintances."

The corner of Anton's mouth perked up. "I would be honored, Mr. Armistead." He pasted a smile on his face, hoping to hide his dissatisfaction. Anton desired to service European interests with longstanding wealth and aristocratic status. American clients didn't interest him; however, business was business.

The opulence of the club astounded Anton. Although newly formed, it did have a European air to it, coupled with Southern charms. The men had arrived at the club a little early, finding their table not yet ready. "Would you care to relax in the clubroom?" the maître'd asked. "We'll call you once your table is ready."

"Thank you, Matthew. That will be fine," Mr. Armistead said, following him to the clubroom. Upon entering, the men found all the tables and sitting areas occupied. "Let's sit at the bar," Armistead said.

Anton sat on the leather stool, astounded. He found the room to be magnificent, appointed with rich mahogany paneling, high ceilings, and ornate wood moldings. To say the club had been formed just a short time ago, they seemed to have acquired many comforts in a brief period. Trouvier took note of some of the works of arts which adorned the walls. "These paintings are stunning."

Armistead swelled with pride, leaning against the bar. "Thank you, Mr. Trouvier."

"They appear to be the works of European masters."

"Yes, many of them are. They were donated to the club by one of our members, as were much of the furnishings here," Armistead said. The bartender served their drinks. "We have a few very wealthy members."

Trouvier decided perhaps he'd underestimated the caliber of Atlanta's businessmen. "Excuse me for a moment, Mr. Trouvier. I see a few gentlemen whom I wish to greet," Armistead said, leaving him at the bar.

Trouvier sat alone a few moments finishing his drink, irritated Armistead had left him alone while he networked. "Mr. Trouvier, would you please come with me? I have some folks whom I'd like you to meet," Armistead said.

He followed Armistead to a seating area where three men lounged, smoking cigars while enjoying their drinks. "Gentlemen, please meet my financial manager, Mr. Anton Trouvier." The men smiled and greeted him. "Mr. Trouvier, this is Robert Mills, James Roberts, and George Echols."

Trouvier greeted each of the men, shaking their hands.

"Please, sit and join us Mr. Trouvier," James Roberts

said.

His mind worked frantically. Could this be the same James Roberts who had made a fortune in munitions during the Civil War? If so, he would be the primary heir of the Roberts fortune in France.

He'd made James' acquaintance at a Chevalier ball back in the '60's, although he could see Roberts didn't remember him. If he remembered his history of French families, the Roberts and Chevalier families were close relations. In fact, Monsieur Richard Roberts had shared as much, admonishing him to remember James.

Perhaps my fortunes have turned. Just then, Armistead leaned over to him and said, "Roberts is the member who donated much of the artwork and furnishings which you find here in the club room."

"I see," Anton said, a little above a whisper.

James smiled at him. Anton could see he'd impressed the man. "Monsieur— Pardon me, Mr. Trouvier," James said.

Anton raised his eyebrow. So, his suspicions were correct. "*Monsieur, vous avez raison,*" Anton said, telling James his assumption was correct.

"*Ah, c'est vrai. Vous êtes de la maison Trouvier en France, n'est-ce pas?*"

Anton nodded. "*Oui. Je le suis.*"

"I thought so," James said. Their acquaintances gawked

in amazement. They hadn't identified James to be of French descent. "Gentlemen, this is my countryman. My family immigrated to America from France in the late 1700's." The men nodded in understanding. "The House of Trouvier in France has an outstanding history in investment and financial management. They are an aristocratic family of the highest rank."

Anton couldn't believe his good fortune. Perhaps James hadn't learned of his family's recent status, much to his relief. If he knew of the scandal, he didn't make mention of it.

"Well, the Roberts' have a stellar aristocratic history in France as well," Anton said. "The family possesses large land and business holdings in France, as do the Trouviers."

"It is so." James began to think of the future, of his life with Lela and the family they would raise together. Perhaps this Anton would be the ideal person to organize his financial holdings in a way that would best benefit his darling Lela.

James blinked. He'd met the man before, but couldn't remember where. Perhaps he'd met him in France? He scratched his left hand. "Monsieur Trouvier, I would like to meet with you prior to leaving Atlanta," James said, exhaling a hardy puff of cigar smoke. "Perhaps tomorrow?"

"That would work well for me, Monsieur Roberts."

Chapter 9

New Orleans, Louisiana. September 1, 1963.

Her soft comfort soothed him. He found himself lost in her warmth and peace. He had just finished eating, receiving her nourishment, and was ready to return to his dreams. His stomach settled. He could hear the man. He called himself Monpère. The man cooed to him. He could feel him playing with his fingers. He loved them. They made him feel safe.

The woman called Mamère allowed him to fall asleep. He opened his eyes when he felt her pass him to another. Monpère's face came into focus. Monpère made a funny face. He closed his eyes.

He opened his eyes. He saw his mamère's friend. She called herself Sissy. She left.

He closed his eyes. He awoke in the thing. They had laid him down. He hated it. Hold me. He whimpered. His stomach rumbled. He wailed.

"Are you hungry, Julian?"

He cried. Monpère left his sight. He cried. Monpère picked him up. He cried and wiggled. Monpère cuddled him. Monpère put something in his mouth.

I hate this.

He screamed. Monpère rocked him. Monpère put something in his mouth. He suckled. He spit it out. Bad.

He screamed.

Monpère felt hot. Monpère rocked him. Monpère hummed.

He screamed. Give me the one called Mamère. Mamère stop rumbles. Mamère's stuff tastes good.

"Your mamère can't always nurse you, Julian. You must learn to take the bottle."

He screamed. His throat hurt. Salt rose into his mouth.

He opened his eyes. No name man stood before him. He hated no name man. The man handed him a toy. He liked the toy. It spun around. He closed his eyes.

Julian sat up on the chaise. Too much Glenlivet. He presumed his grandmère had taken a nap too. She'd probably knocked back an entire bottle of brandy.

"I'm right here, Julian."

He spotted her sitting at the desk reading a book.

"You shouldn't drink if you can't handle your liquor," Lela said.

Julian rubbed his face, disoriented. *I'm not an alcoholic like you.* He saw her raise an eyebrow and return to her book. He read the cover. *Their Eyes Were Watching God.* He'd read the novel during his undergraduate studies at Morehouse. Good book. Why was she still awake? Just then, the hall clock chimed ten o'clock.

Julian stood up, stretched, and walked over to the window. He saw the darkness pinwheel in the starlight. He remembered his dream. He'd held a spinning object, a toy. Julian left the window and sat before his grandmother's desk. He remembered her story of her grandfather placing a rattle in her father's hand before he died. It had spun.

"What is it, Julian?"

He rubbed his eyes, unable to shake the drowsiness. "Do you remember from your story when your grandfather took the rattle to Brussels?"

"What?" Lela continued to read her book.

"The rattle, old woman."

He'd now gained his grandmère's full attention, much to his dismay. After a few moments, she responded. "Yes. What about it?"

"I dreamed I was a baby and a man gave it to me."

Lela said nothing, returning to her book.

"You said your grandfather stated it would only spin for your father."

Lela continued to read her book.

Julian ran his fingers through his hair, fretting over the dream. Did he really remember it, or was his subconscious fusing her story with his dreams? A name sprung into his mind. "The Keyholder. Who is he?"

"Who?" Lela turned the page of her book.

"Dammit, Grandmère. Listen to me!"

Lela put her book down and arose from her desk. "Don't curse me, Julian."

He shrank back, scooting his chair away from her desk.

Lela calmed herself and moved to the wing chair near her great-grandson. "We all have dreams, Julian. Sometimes they reveal the angst within our hearts. Dreams reveal our hopes. At times, they can reveal the future." Lela returned to the desk and opened her book. She finished the chapter. To mark her place, Lela inserted a gold chain weighted with rubies on each end. She closed the book. "Are you ready to continue?"

Julian couldn't believe she'd ignored his question. *Mind games.* "You're not going to tell me?"

Her child wearied her at times. "Darling, what do you wish for me to tell you?"

Julian felt like crying. Nothing could ever be simple. "Am I your father?" He inhaled deep. "Am I Augustus?"

Lela sipped warm water from the glass. She folded her

hands atop the desk. "Darling, I can't tell you who you are." She left the desk and sat on the arm of his chair. She stroked his curly head, compelling Julian to lay his head upon her breast. "My darling, you must reveal to the world whom you are. It's the only way for you to become *you*. Every man and woman must tell the world their own truth. Oui?"

Although dissatisfied with her answer, it made sense. He nodded in acceptance.

"Good. It's late. The day has escaped us. Allow us to continue." Lela returned to the sofa and sat. Julian sat beside her, laying his head upon her breast. She stroked his hair.

Chapter 10

Lela

Although I still labored in the Chevalier Mansion, things were different. Jamie's love had returned to my life. He'd forgiven me for a sin I never committed, but to which I'd fallen victim. I should've left him, yet I didn't. I loved him and understood the man on a deep level. I allowed him to come to terms with his issues, while I came to terms with my own.

He no longer managed the household, transferring all to me. "Darling, I want you to learn how to do this," he'd told me. So, I did. I controlled the finances. I wrote checks, kept the books. I went to the bank on Mondays, Wednesdays and Fridays.

The first time I went to the bank (Jamie refused to go with me), I thought I would be arrested. Much to my shock and surprise, no one ever said anything. They treated me with respect, like a White woman, addressing as 'Ma'am.' I transacted our business at both the teller window and in the private area, exclusive to large depositors. I guess Jamie was right about my appearance. Most people saw me as White, which troubled me a great deal back then.

My duties didn't end there. I managed our many vendors who provided us with food, coal, fish, and a variety of other services. Nancy primarily dealt with the food vendors. Her negotiation skills with the vendors amazed me. She haggled with finesse, assuredness and ease, securing the best deals. She had no problem telling them what she was willing to pay. If they didn't agree to her prices, she would find another vendor with better quality goods and lower prices.

While sitting in the library reviewing the books, Jimmy brought in a wire, delivered by the Western Union man. I stopped myself from snatching it from him. Jimmy winked at me and left, closing the door behind him.

I will be home in one week

I couldn't believe it. Jamie was coming home! While he'd been away, nightmares tormented me about him consorting with the devil. In my dreams, I'd watched him being lured into the fire. But with the telegram, I shoved it all aside.

I ran to the kitchen. "Nancy, did my package arrive?"

She shook her head. "I'se put it on your bed this mornin'."

I ran upstairs and rushed into my bedroom. There it was, wrapped in brown paper. I sat on the bed beside the package, stroking it with my fingers. I dreamed of my love walking through the bedroom door. My new sheer curtains shimmered in the breeze, prophesying of joys to come.

New Orleans, Louisiana. May, 1883.

LIFE SPRUNG FORTH from the barren earth everywhere he looked. God had granted his creation another chance at happiness and joy. James noticed several magnolia trees parading their robust blossoms, ecstatic to leave winter behind and thrive once more. Several gardens showcased the grandeur of spring flowers and summer perennials, ready to live again. Hibiscus trees showcased their enormous orange-red blooms for all to see. He grinned, spotting daylilies near the street in the neighbor's garden, soaring up and unveiling their glory into the world.

He didn't allow the driver much opportunity to bring the carriage to a full stop. James hopped out and opened the white wrought iron gate, embellished with roses. He stood on the brick walk, staring at the house. He was home, at home with his love.

James entered the front yard, finding the flowers in full bloom. They seemed especially vibrant, the impatiens flaunting their tender petals under the oak tree, the anemones parading their majesty in the sunlight. Immaculately manicured, vibrant green hedges framed the yard. The camellias and the gardenias progressed at their own pace, displaying the promise of beauty yet to come.

"Mis'sur Roberts!" Li'l Willie swung open the front door, ran down the steps, and jumped into his open arms.

James kissed the boy. "Well, haven't you grown into a fine young man in just a few short weeks? Soon, we won't be able to call you Li'l Willie." He rubbed the top of the child's knobby head.

He did love the boy with his whole heart. William was sharp. Prior to his departure for Atlanta, he'd begun to instruct the boy on the household ledgers, allowing him to calculate simple entries, which the child had picked up with ease.

James admired the child's loving heart, even after enduring so much heartache. Children didn't seem to dwell on the bad things. They always reached for love and forgiveness, moving on.

"Did you bring me anything?"

"What makes you think I brought something for you, Willie?"

"Mis'sur!"

Just then, the houseboy passed with a package wrapped in brown paper and tied with string. "Son, you can give it to me," James said. The young boy handed the package to James and then returned to the carriage for another load.

"Hmm." James taunted the child with a sly grin. "Maybe this is for you."

Willie squealed with glee, grabbed the large package, and ran indoors. "Mis'sur is home. Mis'sur is home and he brought me something!" The child's voice faded as James heard him running through the house.

Nancy appeared at the door, drying her hands on her apron. "Look who done found his way home." She took him in her arms and hugged him, filled with the joy of his homecoming. "Lawd, you'se a sight for sore eyes. Boy, how'se you?"

"I'm better now that I'm back, Nancy."

"How'se Sallie?"

"She's well. She sent you a little package. It's packed amongst my things. She thanks you for all of the preserves you sent to her," James said. "Sallie said you're rubbing it in her face that your preserves are better than hers."

Nancy let out a boisterous laugh. "The Lawd is good. I'se didn't know what had happened to her. We ain't seent each other in years, since I'se was a child, I'se reckon." Nancy furrowed her brow. She'd met Sallie, she was sure of it, but couldn't remember when the meeting had occurred.

"She's my aunt!" Nancy peered into the Spirit. "Well, Aunt Sarah used to visit Mama when we still lived on Massa Mills' place in Miss'ippi. Mama would send Aunt Sallie preserves she done jarred by Aunt Sarah." Nancy stared at the brick street. I'se 'members Aunt Sarah sayin' an evil ole man owned Sallie and she didn't eat like she should." The window closed in the Spirit.

"You're related to Sallie, Nancy?" James asked. He'd wondered why Sallie seemed so surprised when he'd mentioned Nancy's name while in Atlanta. She'd held the preserves in her hands, closed her eyes, channeling the spirit of the one who had made them. Afterwards, she'd opened her eyes and asked James several questions on how Nancy looked, how tall she was. It was strange, but he hadn't paid much attention to her inquisition. Sallie always grilled him about one topic or another.

Nancy shut her mouth. She'd said too much. "Did you'se have a good trip?"

"Yes, it was productive. I took care of a lot of business while in Atlanta." He became a little solemn.

"Thank twice before frat'nizin' wit' him, James," Nancy said. She patted his cheek.

"What?"

"Nuthin'."

The veil rolled back, returning him to his early days in France. Anton, it was him! At that time, he'd declared he would never allow Trouvier to touch his money. How had he forgotten?

James couldn't do anything about it. He'd already agreed to work with him. The Spirit wouldn't allow him to correct his mistake. He wished to cry, but refused to do so before Nancy.

He knew Nancy could see his folly. Synchronizing with her spirit, he absorbed her compassion for him. She would allow it all to rest, if he so desired. Patting his cheek, she soothed him, strengthening him to walk through it all.

James decided to pick on Nancy to lighten the mood. "You're not wearing that overseas, are you Mademoiselle?" he said, feigning horror. "You will surely be attired to the height of Parisian fashion." In good humor, he jostled her, causing her to giggle.

"Shut your mouth boy 'fore I'se git your foot," Nancy said, punching him in the arm. "You'se thanks you'se funny, huh?" Nancy removed her handkerchief from her apron pocket, wiping away her tears of laughter. "Naw, Lela done had the dressmaker out here, makin' us all new clothes to wear in France. I'se even gots me a corset." Nancy breathed in deep, trying to get in front of her onslaught of laugher. "That thang there is hell on Earth, I'se tellin' you!" They both roared with laughter. Nancy patted his cheek. "Hey, Lela's in her room waitin' on you."

"Oh, is she now?" He cocked his brow, intrigued.

"Oui, Mis'sur. Why doncha go in and say howdy to her?"

James tipped his hat to her and bowed. "I think I will." He gave her a kiss on the cheek and entered the house.

"Ya'll supper gonna be ready in 'bout an hour," Nancy said.

James ran up the stairs, his thoughts far from dinner. He'd dreamed of Lela every night and day during his absence. He could smell her perfume. God, he could surely smell and taste her sweetness. How had he almost allowed her to get away? James shuddered at the mere thought of his life without her. But now, as he landed the third floor, only a few steps remained between him and his beloved.

He stood outside of her door. "Maybe I should freshen up," he said to himself. He had been traveling for some time. James removed his hat and ran his fingers through his hair, knowing it had become somewhat flat. He rapped upon the door.

"*Entrez.*"

Filled with timidness, James opened the door and peered into her room. The sunlight filtered through the white, sheer curtains creating the appearance of heaven.

He couldn't find her. Maybe he'd only imagined he had heard her reply. But then he noticed a form behind the dressing screen, outlined by the soft sunlight. He stepped into the room and closed the door. Once the latch clicked, the form glided from its hiding place.

"Mon Dieu."

There stood Lela in a satin, soft pink corset with white piping concealing the boning, matching pink ruffled panties, white silk stockings and pink velvet mule slippers. Breathtaking. She'd swept her hair up into a careless, loose bun, held in place by an ivory comb. Long ringlets of hair rained down, kissing her temples. He found himself unable to process his thoughts. She walked across the floor to him as a jaguar to its prey.

Helpless, he found himself unable to do anything to escape her mystery. She slid her arms around him, allowing her hands to go deep, and then sliding down and under. She inhaled, savoring his scent. Her breath, hot with passion and desire, caressed his ear. "*Bienvenu à la maison, mon cher*," she said to him, barely audible.

"This will not do." James removed the ivory comb from her hair, allowing her tresses to fall free. She smiled at him, her hair cascading down her shoulders, concealing her bosom plumped up by the corset. James gripped her tight, untying the bow at the base of her corset, grinding into her. It loosened, but didn't free what he desired most. He kissed her throat, moving southward, coming to the garment which thrilled and banished him all at once. Hooks. Pulling her into him, he unlatched each hook, one at a time. The restrictive garment fell to the floor, allowing her glory to unfurl before him. In her eyes, he found his joy.

James dove on her, propelling her onto the small bed.

The twilight twinkled, danced, and flirted with the iridescence of the white sheer curtains, giving them a pinkish, purplish glow. James and Lela lay in each other's arms, exhausted but fulfilled, after a day of lovemaking. She snuggled into him, asking God to allow her to always remember this single day of joy, a day of love. Lela admired the handsome face of her beloved, his handlebar mustache wilted, shadowed in the twilight.

Feeling her eyes upon him, he awoke. "*Bonsoir*, ma chere," James said, his voice heavy with sleep. "Why are you smiling so?"

"Why shouldn't I smile? You've given me ten reasons to smile."

"You're never satisfied, my little ferocious one. You're insatiable." He fell into her long, sensuous kiss, seeking to draw the very life's breath from his body.

Lela and Jamie forgot their supper.

Chapter 11

New Orleans, Louisiana. June, 1883.

James held Lela tight, watching as the carriages and wagons stopped before the Chevalier mansion. "Perhaps we need another five wagons for your things, darling."

Lela pinched his behind. "You may be right, my love. For these wagons will hardly accommodate your hats and shoes," Lela said. "You're the peacock of the family, not me."

"Well, I must always look my best for you, my love," he said in a whisper, kissing her. A large shadow fell over them. "Yes, what is it?" James asked the man, irritated he'd interrupted the moment with his love.

"Suh, we'se wants to take ya'lls trunks out first," the man said, holding his hat in his hands, his eyes cast down.

Considering the insignificance of the infraction, James released his bad feelings. He felt sorry for the man, for the facial scars he bore remained as monuments, commemorating the suffering he'd endured over the course of his life. "Of course. Jimmy?" James didn't see him appear in the doorway. He must have been busy directing the workers. "He must be busy. Go straight to the kitchen. My cook will direct you," James said, softening his demeanor.

"Yessuh," the man hobbled away, entering the house.

Lela frowned at him, hitting his vested chest with her handkerchief. Her love for him softened her wrath. She adjusted his cravat, believing the hankie swat had set it askew. "You could have been kinder to him, James."

He winced at Lela's use of his proper name. He knew she was upset. "I'm not sure why I became annoyed," he said, a bit ashamed at first. His brazen soul delved into Lela's angry eyes, igniting his intoxicated adoration for her. He felt like a naughty little boy who hadn't been polite to their guests. He hoped she would spank him. "Well, yes I am. He had the gall to interrupt my time with you," James said. Emitting a low growl, he pulled Lela close once more.

Lela pushed away from him, rushing toward the door. "Oh God!" Lela ran into the house in the direction of the screams. James bolted ahead of her with his gold-plated Derringer drawn and cocked.

"Nancy. Please God, not my best friend." Lela ran behind him. When she arrived at the kitchen, she found James standing in the doorway, confused. Peering in, Lela found Nancy enveloped in the moving man's arms, crying.

"Thank you, Lawd! Thank you, thank you!" Nancy called

to the Lord over and over, crying tears from a spring deep within her soul, overflowing with a thousand years of heart-ache. Astounded, James turned to Lela for understanding.

"The Lord is truly merciful. Her Nate has returned to her from the grave," Lela whispered with a smile creeping upon her face.

"Nancy, who is this?" James asked, not hearing Lela's explanation.

"I'se thought you'se was dead!" Nancy buried her face in Nate's gaunt chest.

"I'se was dead wit'out you," he said. He sobbed, nuzzling his chin into her soft, curly hair. "I'se wanted to die, but ev'ry time I'se gave up, I'se sees your face and tells myself, I'se gotta see my baby one more time." Nancy began to cry all over again.

Li'l Willie ran into the kitchen, hearing the screams and loud voices. Spotting the skeleton of a man hugging his aunt, he froze in the doorway next to Lela, unable to move.

Nate turned to find his nephew, big and strong, stand-ing in the doorway with tears streaming down his face. He limped toward him, but stopped. "It's me boy! C'mere," he said. Willie didn't move.

Lela knelt and took the child's hands in hers. "God has blessed you this day, answering your prayers," Lela said to him. Willie stared at her, his eyes mixed with joy and disbelief. "It's him darling. Ton oncle. Go to him."

Willie ran to his Uncle Nate with all his might, jumping into his arms. "Oh, my boy," Nate said, wailing. He clutched the child, determined never to release him. "So many nights I'se was 'fraid I'se never see ya'll again." Nate kissed Willie, and then Nancy. "The Lawd done been good to me. Yessuh, he has!"

Lela's curiosity got the best of her. "Nate, where have you been?"

Nate didn't ask who was this White Negro woman, attired in the finest dress he'd ever seen, nor did he care. He'd found his home. Nancy and Willie. "Well Ma'Dame, there was a fire over where's we'se was livin'. The police arrested me for startin' it. They'd found me out back after pullin' Willie out the fire."

Nate swallowed hard to suppress his tears. "I'se been in a labor camp, on a chain gang ev'ry since. They'se tried to kills me." Nate's eyes filled with tears, unable to stop them. "But I'se strong, I'se survived. My Nancy and my Willie kept me goin'." Nate released Nancy and wiped away his tears, kissing his little nephew again. "I'se the only blood Willie got left. And Nancy, well she's the only love I'se done ever had.

"One day, they'se just let me go. I'se don't know why, but they'se did and I'se was glad." Still holding Willie, bouncing him up and down on his left arm, he drew Nancy close with his right. "I'se had no clue on how to find ya'll, Nancy. Guess I'se just knew I'se would. And the Good Lawd done brought me here. Never figured I'se finds ya'll here, but the Lawd knew." Nate clutched his family tighter, hugging them ever so tight.

James took Lela in his arms, enjoying the happy scene. "Nate, we're all going to Paris for our wedding, mine and Lela's," he said, kissing Lela on the forehead. "Join us. I have my own frigate, so there's no need to worry about your passage."

"Naw, Mis'sur. Ya'll go on 'head. Willie and me is stayin' here wit' Nate," Nancy said.

Tears sprung from Lela's eyes. "How can I marry Jamie without you, Nancy?" Lela began to cry.

Monsieur and Madame Bailey entered the kitchen with Allen in tow. He froze in his steps. "*Mon Dieu, vous êtes bon*! You said he was alive and here he is." Toussaint surmised the man clutching Nancy in his arms had to be Nate, although he'd never met him.

Nate shook Toussaint's hand. "Nice to meet you, suh," Nate said. He looked around the kitchen, admiring the beautiful, blue floral pattern dishes displayed on the plate racks, copper pots suspended from the ceiling on hooks.

"Them those plates I'se helps you'se dig up?"

Nancy nodded. "Yessuh, they is," she said.

"What?" Nate turned his head to hear her better.

The vision flashed before Nancy, hearing a popping sound. A new crop of tears welled in her eyes, but she suppressed them. Today was a happy day. She put her mouth to his good ear. "Yessuh, they'se the ones we'se dug up. And the pots too."

Nate nodded, taking it all in. "This here's a real nice place where ya'll done landed, Nancy. Sho' is." Willie wiped away the tears covering Nate's face, causing everyone to laugh through their own tears. "While I'se was out there on that gang, the Lawd told me ya'll was just fine and he would bring me home to ya'll. Now here I'se is." Nate placed Willie on the floor, but the child clung to his thin, sore leg, refusing to let him go. "If ya'll gotta go, I'se gonna be here when ya'll git back."

"I'se just got you'se back. I'se ain't leavin' you," Nancy said.

"Please Uncle Nate, come with us." Willie began to whimper.

"I'se only been on this here job for three weeks, son. I'se cain't leave it." Nate scratched his head. "I'se couldn't find my old boss. If I'se had, then ev'rythang wouldda been aw'rite. I'se could go."

James began to sweat. Conflict was imminent. Although he'd never witnessed the two women utter a cross word to one another, a war of wills loomed. Both women took up their embattlements, strapped on their armor, and prepared go to war in their efforts to convince the other to submit to their wishes.

"Nate, be my valet and my chauffeur," James said. "I'll pay you triple whatever your current boss is paying you. Just agree to join us." James couldn't endure Lela moping for an eternity because Nancy wouldn't come. But more importantly, he wished for his beloved Nancy to experience the same joy with Nate in France he was destined to enjoy with Lela.

"Well suh, I'se guess that would be aw'rite," Nate said.

"Then it is settled. Once we arrive in France, I'll purchase some suits for you. Oh damn," James said. "You don't have a passport." Everyone's countenance dropped. "Don't worry. I have quite a few friends at both the French and American consulates. By the time we arrive at the Port of New York, they will have your paperwork in order. I'll send the telegram once we arrive at the docks."

Nate, Nancy, and Willie hugged each other tight, rejoicing in the unexpected blessing the day had gifted them.

"You didn't tell us it would be a double wedding, Lela," Jannie said laughing, with everyone joining in.

Chapter 12

Eternity, New Orleans, Louisiana.

The waiter cleared the table, placing the angels' after dinner beverages before them. He returned a bit later for the finger bowl. "Leave it," Richard said. The waiter fled them in terror.

"Good job, Richard."

He sipped his tea, ignoring his brother. "Oh, I'm not finished."

"Yes, you are," Albertus said. "Your efforts are pointless. The Seed will rest."

Richard stirred his tea, considering the Spirit. "He will not. She will not give him a home. There are many in line between La Rose and Le Baton. I will destroy them."

Looking out, Li-Zhan could see it. He stood from the table and drew his sword. "You will not do this thing," he said. Zhan searched Eternity, assessing the trials and tribulations of their little ones. Tears filled his eyes, but he suppressed them. He placed the blade of his sword to Richard's throat.

Richard mocked him, daring him to cut him. What was the point of resisting? Zhan positioned himself, taking the proper stance to behead his brother, but the Lord whispered to him. Confused, he turned to his brother. "Jerémèy?"

He sighed. "It has been allowed."

Chapter 13

New Orleans, Louisiana. September 1, 1963.

The hall clock ticked, levitating Julian somewhere between his consciousness and his dreams. The ticking morphed into a gentle tocsin heralding a new day, growing louder, finishing with delicate chimes and fading into a soft tremble. Fifteen minutes to midnight. He sat up on the sofa, acclimating himself to the present. "Grandmère." He couldn't find her. Feeling movement, Julian found his grandmère sitting next to him.

Lela rocked back and forth, lost in her fairytale, grinning and laughing. Julian returned to his chair and sat. "Well, that worked out."

Lela jumped, her great-grandson's voice plummeting her into the present. Her head ached. She reached for the glass of water on the side table. Bringing it to her lips, she sipped it and then leaned back, allowing her mind to settle.

Time had captured her. She felt old and could feel herself aging. She regained control of her flesh, halting the process.

She closed her eyes and opened them, allowing her glare to fall upon Julian. "What do you mean by that young man?"

"Your perfect little life, tied up with a pretty little white bow. You live happily ever after, finding the great White prince you'd hoped for, marrying and then moving with him to the garden of dreams, Paris. Congratulations."

Had she told the story for her health? Well yes, but with a purpose. The Lord reminded her of the child's hard heart, closed to joy and love. It would take more than a few days to soften it. "You understand nothing, boy," she said, suppressing the urge to collapse all his internal organs.

She understood his angst, but it didn't quell her anger. He needed to fight to be free. "That 'White man' is your great-grandfather. I never had hopes of marrying anyone. He chose me, not the other way around. Love chooses us, when we are fortunate, if God smiles upon us. It would be foolish to turn away love when it calls."

Julian sipped his scotch and then placed the glass on the coffee table. "Especially when love is a house built of solid gold. Gold is easy to embrace. Just couldn't stay true to the struggle, huh? Johannessen was right. Go for the gold, well white gold in your case, Grandmère."

He never saw her move. Boiling with anger and outrage, Julian removed his handkerchief from his pocket to dab away the blood flowing from his busted lip. Unable to suppress his emotions, he began to cry.

"Stop looking at life through hatred and look with love," Lela said. "I understand your feelings, based on the current social and political movements in this nation, but you must always look with love, Julian. If you don't, love will walk away from you."

Lela picked up her handkerchief from the side table and wrung it in her hands. "Are you with Jannette because of her beautiful chocolate skin? Does she make you feel more real? More… what is the term, Afro-American? Does she certify you as a legitimate, card carrying Negro, justifying your high yella complexion, testifying to all your commitment to and membership in the Negro community?"

"No, it isn't like that." Julian suppressed his passion and insult, returning to his cold exterior. "How do you even know what she looks like?" Julian waved her off. "Forget it. I forgot. You're some sort of sorceress. Besides, we are Blacks, Grandmère."

"Blacks, Negroes, Coloreds. For the love of God, we're people, Julian. We are people, just like the Jews, Italians, Irish, Greeks, Chinese, and Mexicans. We are all people." Lela allowed her rage to dissipate, considering her great-grandson's words.

"But you're right, we are different. Few of us know of our true homeland. We don't know if our ancestors were brought here from Ethiopia, Kenya, Ghana, Botswana, the Congo, or some other country in Africa. In any case, we all assume we're from the African continent for it is what the slave masters told us.

"We've been raped of our identity, our camaraderie, turned and pitted against one another by our slave owners in their efforts to control us. They used our physical differences to build distrust between us, favoring one group over the other. They were successful, still controlling the psyches of our people over three hundred years later.

"Our ancestral identity was stolen from us. Nearly every other race of people in this world has retained their history. For us, our history begins four hundred years ago, built upon a lie. As you'd say, we have been mind-fucked."

Julian grinned, impressed with her use of profanity.

"I'm not sure if this generational curse will ever burn itself out of our people. It has become a part of our very souls. Capture the mind and soul of the people, infiltrate their minds and you'll have slaves for life. Not his exact words, but a good paraphrase of Satan's most loyal servant, Willie Lynch.

"He taught his fellow slave owners how to break our people, to divide and conquer us, to play upon our differences, to compel us betray the other, controlling us forever, without controlling us. Unconsciously, we instruct his lesson to our children. Centuries later, the curse still works. It's self-fulfilling. We oblige the curse, initiating the scripts ourselves, and then passing the destructive thoughts along to the next generation. Only God can break the curse. I pray every day he does. But, I've shared all of this with you the other day.

"I talked to Martin about it. He doesn't have a solution either. All we can do is address the issues at hand. All we can do is enjoy this time of solidarity amongst our people. It's a beautiful thing, but it won't last long. It will be two score years before we see it again.

"Even in those times Willie Lynch's curse will wield its head, spewing its damning accusations and slanders from the mouths of some of the Negro community's most distinguished and celebrated leaders. But they won't be able to defeat the one to come. In that time, it won't be the solidarity of the Negro people alone, but the brief unification of the nation as a whole, race and creed irrelevant, rising above its ingrained racism, for a brief moment in time, to do the impossible."

Julian stared at his grandmère, flabbergasted. He didn't know what to say. "What are you talking about? The future?" She nodded, still lost in the vision. "Who is Martin, Grandmère?"

Recalling herself to the present, she found her

great-grandson awaiting her response. "Oh. Martin. I'm speaking of Reverend King, darling."

"You know him?"

"Yes. I've met him a few times through a few of his family members I've known discretely, over the years. Why?"

He should've known. Julian wagged his head in defeat, but stopped, hoping his grandmère hadn't noticed. "I didn't think the Civil Rights Movement concerned you."

Lela could see his asinine thoughts. "Why, boy?"

"Because you're White. Why would you care? It doesn't concern you. You can travel freely and do whatever you wish."

Lela couldn't believe him. Only a few hours before, they'd been called to task because of race on the road to New Orleans. Lela grunted, remembering the man referring to her as an 'old Creole bitch.' "You haven't listened to one word I've told you today, have you?" Julian turned red with anger. "What is it, Julian?"

"If Monpère hadn't loved Mamère, I would look like you."

She couldn't believe it. "Is that what you desire Julian? Truly? For I will tell you truth, my life here in America has been pure hell, especially here in Louisiana. People accepted me because I demanded respect, after I came into the business. At first, they all knew me as Augustus' slave daughter. I was 'Negro,' but not. Then once they forgot where I'd come from, I lived in fear of them remembering. So, I would declare who I am to avoid being accused of deceiving anyone.

"In spite of the pressures placed on me by society, I love who I am. I love my Maman, for she was beautiful like Josephine; however, I believe she was closer to Isabel's color." Lela dabbed her eyes, remembering her mother. "I've always envied her appearance. Always did.

"All of that is unimportant," she said with a wearied sigh. "You're so handsome Julian. How could you think otherwise? Is that what you truly believe?"

Julian's shoulders slouched, confused. Where had the discontent with himself come from? Yet, he had to admit, he'd always desired to have his grandmère's and monpère's complexions. It made them special and exotic in some way. They possessed a magical pedigree, filled with intrigue and indiscretion. People always seemed fascinated with those of mixed pedigree. Julian pictured his face in his mind's eye. He was handsome and special, but not like his ancestors.

"Your skin color doesn't define you darling, but your spirit and your soul," Lela said. "There are many pedestrian souls who appear as I do, as your monpère. But the world will remember you for what's in here," Lela said, tapping his chest.

Julian nodded, accepting his grandmère's visceral truth

deep within his soul. "I'm very handsome, Grandmère. I'm not sure what I meant by the comment." Julian said. "I love my looks. Could God ever improve on a face and body such as mine?" Julian adjusted his tie.

"I just want to be free. Sometimes think of all I could achieve if I was White like you and Monpère. Money and connections would gravitate to me. I would be granted inroads into select groups and clubs, like Monpère. I can only imagine the fortune I could amass if race didn't play a role, the power which I could possess. But dammit Grandmère, all those things are irrelevant. Blacks shouldn't have to fight to drink from a water fountain, to use the bathroom, to vote. These are just things all people should have the right to enjoy. We are people, Grandmère."

"Yes, darling. I know."

Julian sat before her enraged, his mind unable to process the injustices all Blacks were forced to endure for no reason. "They hate us."

Lela couldn't deny his words. "Yes, some do. Many do not. It's just the times we have come through, the masses bending to the will of the few. Not every White you meet is racist. Now, do they have prejudices inside of them? Yes, for Willie Lynch and Jim Crow have trained us both. It doesn't make them bad. It just is.

"But these prejudices will subside in the consciousness

of America, becoming less prominent. As time wears on, America will collectively become more tolerant of different ethnic groups, but not. No longer will overt racism and discrimination be tolerated, after a time. Heck, there are other groups defined by sexual preference who will gain acceptance and respect, in time."

"Sexual preferences?"

Oh Lord, I've revealed too much. "Yes, Julian. Are you aware of homosexuality?"

Julian spit out his Glenlivet. "What? Perverts?" He gawked at her while coughing to clear his esophagus of liquor. "Grandmère, they're going to Hell. It's disgusting."

"As are you in the eyes of White folks."

Julian clinched his fists. "I was born Black, Grandmère," Julian said. "They have a choice in with whom they copulate. I can't alter my skin color."

Lela nodded, accepting his words. "Is it in you to go with a man?"

"Never considered it. That's not me."

"Well, imagine if you are you, but it is in you to do so. Yet, society desires you to be with women. Women disgust you, but you are forced to be with them in obedience to the law."

Julian boiled with rage. "It's not the same, Grandmère."

"Biblically, no. In the heart and spirit of people, yes.

White people see you as a human chattel. You're here to tote their bags, plow their fields, and clean their homes. Yet, you have a mind and are very intelligent. You can manage money. Nevertheless, this is not your assigned role by man." Lela ingested the remainder of her brandy. "Go and weed the garden, Julian. According to White folks and the Bible, you're a slave. Submit to your master."

Julian sat before her, flabbergasted. He understood. He still didn't care for the practice.

"It's whom they are, Julian. Just as you are whom you are. You don't have to like it, but don't deny them their God given right to exist as humans. Not your call. Love them as you love yourself. Love all people as you love yourself. That's all I'm trying to tell you. Allow the Lord to judge, for he is the only one who can do so with love.

"But always remember there is a little seed of prejudice inside of us all, Blacks and Whites alike, waiting to flower and explode without warning."

Julian nodded, accepting her truth. "I apologize for what I said, Grandmère."

Lela suppressed her surprise. Perhaps the boy's heart had softened. "It's alright. However, you do believe it. You have embraced your militant teachings, but it is well. You need them to do your work. But my darling, always put love first. James and I managed to love one another at the height of racial injustice. Yes, we were fortunate enough to be able to flee America and to live in love in France. My darling, only love matters.

"Sometimes, when one departs a locale to live their dreams, they're taking a stand. It forces those whom they've left behind to regard themselves and their beliefs, wondering why friends, neighbors, and love ones would feel the need to escape them to be whom they are."

"I'd never considered it before."

Lela wandered through the revelation. "Neither had I, darling." Lela looked up to the ceiling mural of angels and nude maidens in a garden surrounding a fountain. "Humph. Michael Salley. I ran into him many years later, after Jamie passed. We talked." Lela returned her attention to her great-grandson. She picked up the glass of water from the side table and sipped its warm contents. "Well, I'm getting ahead of myself."

Crazy old woman. She always baited him with bits of a tale and then withdrew. Dammit, just tell the story. "Grandmère, I do love Jannette. I loved her on sight. I don't believe I chose her to make a political statement."

"I know you didn't. I just wished for you to understand. Darling, we all have our idealized mate. I would've never pictured myself with Jamie, based on his physical appearance. But based on his heart and the love he held for me, I couldn't have imagined myself with anyone other than him. I couldn't have chosen anyone better. You should learn from that."

Julian nodded, accepting her admonishment. He stood and stretched. A cool breeze made its stealth entrance through the open French doors, soothing him, freeing him of his doubts regarding his own value and worth as a Black man in America. His hardness of heart toward his family began to crumble. While he still considered them as a band of whores and supernatural psychic freaks, he found he cared for them too.

He screwed his face, seeing his mother's smiling face in his mind's eye. He smelled her perfume. He shook it off, realizing he'd smelled his grandmère's fragrance. They both loved the perfume, Chanel No. 22.

Walking over to the table, he picked up the book, *L'Histoire de la Famille de Rose*. Flipping through book, he considered the photos of his grandmère's life in what he assumed to be the late 1800's. Her life had become a whirlwind of parties and joy. He spotted a picture of his great-grandpère holding a pretty little girl. "Where was this picture taken, Grandmère?" He sat with her on the sofa. "Who is this little girl?"

Lela leaned over just a bit to see the photo. Her face flushed and her eyes welled with tears. "That is your great-grandpère, as you already know," she said, the color draining from her face. "The child's name is Samantha."

"Who is she?"

"I thought I'd told you." She attempted to recall her story. Maybe she hadn't. "My daughter."

After several moments of silence, Julian became concerned, for his grandmère had failed to rattle on about the photo. He found her stiff, unable to move. "Grandmère, what is it?"

"He…" Lela gasped. "He… My baby." Lela slumped over, falling from the sofa to the floor, just missing the coffee table.

"Grandmère!" Julian scooped her into his arms and rushed her upstairs. Kicking open the door, he carried her over to the bed.

Suzette rushed in from Lela's dressing room, hearing the ruckus. "Mon Dieu. What happened?"

"I don't know, Suzette. I asked her about a picture of her husband and a little girl he held in his arms. She passed out. Before that, she'd muttered something like, 'He… he… My daughter'. Call the doctor."

Suzette placed her hand on Lela's forehead. "There is no need. She will be fine. Allow her to rest, mon cher."

"She could be having a heart attack. Do as you're told."

Suzette resisted the urge to grab him by his throat. "I

have been in service to your grandmère since 1883 when your great-grandpère brought her to the Roberts Château in France. I know when Madame requires medical attention." Suzette folded her arms beneath her chest. "The 'he' Madame spoke of destroyed her, or so he tried. But your grandmère is strong, stronger than you yet know."

Suzette went to the bathroom and returned with a soft, damp cloth. She placed the towel beneath Lela's nose. Lela coughed. Suzette handed her a glass of water, which she sipped, reviving her. "Merci, Suzette," Lela said.

Suzette nodded and left, scowling at Julian as she departed.

"Grandmère, are you alright? We should take you to the hospital."

Lela appeared to have aged beyond her 116 years of age. She righted herself in bed. "I'm well, mon fils. There's no need for the doctor," she said, releasing her terror. "I must apologize." Lela began to cry, but curtailed her tears. "Yes, I'm fine. Remember when you said you believed I had lived a life of immense wealth and ease?"

"Yes, but I never said it. You'd read my mind." *Freak.*

Her countenance disintegrated, recalling the past. "Well, I have not, as I told you earlier. While in Paris, I played in paradise, but then Satan forced me to walk through hell."

"I don't understand," he said, sitting beside her on the

bed.

"I know, but you will. However, allow us to talk later."

Lela leaned back, surrendering to the comfort of the feather pillows, releasing her hold on the past. Downstairs, the clock began its carillon, serenading midnight, disintegrating into lover's waltz within Lela's heart. Lela found herself enveloped in the arms of James, who swept her around a palace's ballroom on some long-ago night in Paris. She opened her eyes and smiled. Her great-grandson sat before her, waiting. The clock struck its final chime. Midnight.

"I'm now tired, mon cher. Perhaps we can continue tomorrow, if you have time?"

Julian blushed. "Yes, Grandmère. I have time."

Epilogue

Her entourage stood before her as she waited to enter the Throne Room. Giddy, she anticipated basking in the presence of her Love. The Most High God had summoned her. She had been more than happy to return home for a time, allowing her body, on Earth, to rest. Her caretakers would guard her flesh.

The doors opened. The call of the herald angel soared throughout heaven. "All bow and praise God Most High. All praise and glory be to Savior of Mankind, Jesus the Christ." Heaven's host cheered, singing hallelujah. "With great humility, I call forth his holy one, the Rose of the Most High God. The mate of Our Lord has returned."

"All Hail to the Rose!" The heavenly host praised her.

The light of God blinded La Rose for a bit, until her eyes adjusted. The hymns of heaven caused her to swoon, but she righted herself. The white rose buds which adorned her gown blossomed, revealing their glory to the Most High. New flowers continued to bud, opening without delay to praise the Lord. The vines budded and bloomed, forming a train behind her. Her gown, now a garden praising her husband, flourished.

The Protector of the Rose took her hand, escorting her to the Throne. The Savior sat upon his throne, grinning as she approached. He stood once they reached him.

The Protector knelt before the Savior of Mankind. "*Mon Roi*, I present to you, *Sainte Mère*."

"Merci." Jesus, the Son of God, took her hand and guided her to her throne constructed of gold roses, to the right of his own. He bowed to his mother and kissed her. La Rose sat upon her throne, the light of her husband resting upon her. She tingled at the touch of him, her love.

The heavenly host sang and rejoiced.

La Rose admired the throne room of her love, as if seeing it for the first time. Although she had spent Eternity in the room, prior to accepting the mission to dwell on Earth with Creation, she could always find something new to adore. Her husband had good taste, which she'd seen duplicated by artistic geniuses on Earth in some of the grandest halls and cathedrals of Man.

Still, interpretations of the throne of God on Earth didn't compare to the real thing. The walls of the throne room had been constructed of metals yet to be discovered on Earth. The closest comparison she could think of was white platinum. The floors had been constructed of a stone man would construe to be a brilliant white marble, but it was not. Man had yet to drill beneath the mountain which housed the stone.

Yet, one metal existed in heaven which man possessed. Gold. But the gold of heaven exceeded anything which had been mined on Earth, by most men. Abraham had mined it, upon the mountaintop where he'd sought to sacrifice Isaac. The Children of Israel kept possession of it, throughout their bondage. Once released, they'd taken heaven's gold with them upon leaving Egypt. The gold which hadn't been used in the construction of their idol (and thus destroyed), was used to build the Ark of the Covenant. Solomon had mined the gold which existed in heaven, location unknown. No man had discovered its reserves since his time. It wouldn't be revealed again, until the end of time.

The Rose could see, in the Spirit, Barachiel, Raguel, and Sealtiel had mined much of heaven's gold on Earth, storing it in the storehouses of the Lord. Even the human made eternal, Joseph of Arimathea, had laid eyes upon it. Yet, he didn't hold any of it in his vaults scattered across the earth.

Sealtiel had adorned the jade altar of her little one yet to be released from Eternity, Le Baton, with some of the heavenly gold. Her husband had permitted it.

La Rose straightened her back, ready to receive the presentations. The guardians of the Most High's children, arch-angels agreeing to walk with men, lined up, ready to present their concerns and praises to the Most High and the twenty-four elders seated around the throne. Each elder sat upon a throne, forming an arch on either side of the Savior's throne, twelve to the left and twelve to the right.

The Sisters went first, praying with fervent energy to armor the Children of Israel with the strength of the Most High. They wailed for torments the Children had yet to suffer, still lodged in Eternity, waiting to manifest on Earth. Those beneath the Lord's altar stirred, making room for those souls yet to join them.

It is well

Next, Raguel, the guardian of Ethiopia, the continent of Africa, the holy land of God, and the Middle East, stepped forward. He presented his update on the state of the Lord's Ark and those who sought its whereabouts. He next told the Lord of the atrocities suffered by those who dwelled on the continent; the sons and daughters who had been stolen from the land. Raguel wailed for those who rested at the bottom of the sea, refusing to submit to Satan's bondage.

He wailed for those who would endure the inhuman enslavement in a new land. He pronounced their rise from their lowly state. He bewailed the nations that would fall to foreign rulers from the North, seeking to pillage the continent of its riches. He wailed for the millions massacred by the Enemy through men who had embraced his lies. He thanked God for their eventual release. The altar rumbled. The souls who'd sacrificed their lives rejoiced and then returned to their rest.

It is well

Sealtiel stepped forward and advised the Lord of the inhabitants of the East, attesting to their future achievements while praying for peace. He wailed for those to be lost at the hands of Satan, the occurrence still resting in Eternity, yet to be manifested on Earth. The altar stirred again, the inhabitants making room for those yet to come.

It is well

Michael stepped forth, revealing to the Lord the plight of those who languished in the North continent, resisting the laws and precedents of kings who sought to circumvent the laws of God. He told the Lord of a child, a female child, who'd come into his care who would one day shape the lives of his Rose and her descendants. Although he'd chosen not to fall, he still watched over his little ones.

It is well

Raphael stood before the Lord. He'd chosen not to fall.

Barachiel frowned at his rival. Raphael should have joined them in their mission to guard the Lord's little ones, but he understood. His belonged in the presence of the Most High.

Raphael told the Lord of the plights of his children, re-siding in Central and South America and other lands rav-ished by the thrones of the Northern continents. They'd surrendered their gold — The gold of Heaven — to the Beast. They'd surrendered their lives and kingdoms.

Yet, they thrived and pressed on, accepting the God of their conquerors, the Most High God. Hadn't all transpired according to God's will? Although despised by many who encountered them, at the End of Days the people would be honored and praised. These people were a great people, for they held within their collective hearts an undying love and faith for the Most High. The leader of the church would come from them and rule for a time, humble and meek. Ra-phael praised the Most High.

All is well

Several presented their reports to the Most High regard-ing their wards. So much torment, yet joy and achievement, always arose from it. La Rose found the reports of those who watched over Australia and Europe to be particularly interesting. The reports from the angel protecting the free nation, troubled her the most.

While their constitution presented its inhabitants with unheard of freedoms, she could see where it would lead. Their liberties would grant Satan free reign in the future, enabling him to promote his own agendas. He would claim it to be every man's right, as proclaimed by the nation's founding fathers. The Creation dwelling in the free nation would truly have to choose between good and evil. Evil would prevail in most instances, yet at the same time, it wouldn't.

Jesus had died, his blood securing liberty and atonement for all men and women. Little could be considered a true sin when covered by his blood; however, not much would prove to be beneficial to her little ones, as the saint named Paul had testified. She watched him sitting upon his throne. He smiled at her.

She knew it would be well. She had to allow her children to find their own way.

Barachiel stepped forward and stood before the Most High. He'd always been handsome and flamboyant to La Rose. La Rose found she could never resist flirting with him. She fluffed her afro, using discretion to adjust a few roses growing from within. She grinned at him, releasing a loose petal she'd dislodged from her hair.

Surprisingly, Barachiel never passed up an opportunity to flirt back. He knew how jealous the Most High could be. Risking incineration, he winked at her. Scoundrel.

Barachiel admired his queen, the Rose. He curbed his thoughts. Her brown skin seemed golden to him, adorned with a gown of white roses. The roses continued to grow and bud, vines of roses trellising from her dress and afro, running across the throne room floor, down into the area where the angels stood. Her breasts were glorious, her gown just able to conceal them. Barachiel had to focus. He knew the Most High had heard his thoughts.

Jesus frowned at him.

Barachiel cleared his throat and prayed for forgiveness; however, not fully committed. "Mon Roi, your house is well. It has survived and will continue to survive the assaults of my brothers, Lucifer and Mammon. Yet, the devils refuse to admit defeat."

"They will never admit defeat until compelled to do so," Jesus proclaimed. "Bring them in."

Michael and his generals escorted Lucifer and Mammon into the throne room to present their report, collared and chained, as they had convinced so many men to do to their brothers and sisters on Earth. Yet, haughtiness and pride radiated from them. "*Mi Rey*, Lucifer and Mammon are present to give their report," Raphael proclaimed.

Barachiel couldn't understand why Raphael insisted on speaking Spanish. He'd thought they'd all agreed to speak French. Barachiel saw Sealtiel twine the right tendril of his mustache between his fingertips, glaring at him. So what, if he wanted everyone to speak Chinese? Barachiel let it go. Everyone wished to use the tongue of their little ones before the Lord. Barachiel smelled sulfur, spurring him to return his attention to the throne.

Rage surged within the Rose's heart. The tender vines of her hair grew larger in girth than any Redwood tree thriving in the great forests of the Americas. They extended themselves until they reached the place where Mammon and Lucifer stood, twining up their bodies, cocooning them. Golden thorns protruded from every inch of the vines, ready to pierce them.

"You would dare come to court today, Lucifer and Mammon? You have pursued my children since the beginning." The Rose's long kinky hair ignited, burning but not. The flames from her afro soared up in the throne room to a height lost in infinity.

Jesus patted his mother's hand.

Barachiel found her rage to be an exciting and titillating experience. He felt the eye of God upon him and curbed his thoughts.

"I ought to slay you right here, in the presence of my love. Why should I spare you?"

Jesus sought to calm her. Everyone believed his Father to be a harsh judge, but not like her. She possessed little patience with the wicked. "Maman, I desired to do it. You know this. It was my purpose for becoming Man." Jesus watched as the vines tightened around Lucifer. He knew his mother was still angry about the incident in the Garden, when he'd deceived her.

A golden thorn perched itself on the precipice of his jugular. "I agreed to do it for the love of Father's little ones. Your little ones," Jesus said, smiling at his hot-headed mother. "I saved each one who accepts me. We've won, don't you see?" he said. "I won, not them."

The flames leaping from the Rose's hair burned white hot. She turned to her Son, wishing to scold him as she had done in his youth on Earth, but she couldn't. His Word was true. "I know, mon fils, but still—"

"Maman, remember Father."

The flames receded upon the head of the Rose. Her vines released her captives. She wished to plunge a thorn into Lucifer, but she resisted the urge. Cocky as ever, he didn't fear her. However, she couldn't say the same for Mammon. A wet spot appeared on the front of his tunic.

Barachiel concealed his laughter.

It is well

Release them

Michael removed the collars from the necks of Mammon and Lucifer. Regaining his composure, Mammon addressed the Throne. "We are upon even ground. My seed has mixed with yours. I now have the same opportunity to sway the Keyholder and his seed, as you do." Silence reverberated throughout the throne room. "My blood has mingled with yours. I am le Baton."

The light of God filled the throne room with a violent brightness. The Rose and the Son stood from their thrones and fell upon their faces, as did all of heaven. Mammon cowered. Only Lucifer resisted, but even he found himself compelled to bow.

I am le Baton
I always protect my Seed

Acknowledgments

My first love. My true love. God Most High, Maker of Heaven and Earth, I can't thank you enough for blessing me with this story, giving my life a great purpose of which I had never dreamed. You sent your son Jesus to save us. You love me without condition. You are my companion in my darkest moments, taking my hand and guiding me. You celebrate with me; I share with you my greatest joys and accomplishments. My love, I cannot thank you enough for my life, my experience, but most of all, for your unconditional love.

I had planned to ask all of you reading La Rose to excuse my French, but there's no need to do so thanks to Mukendi Kampuku. Mukendi, thank you for taking time out of your busy schedule to review many of the French phrases peppering this manuscript. Hopefully, I sent you all the language requiring review, but I have my doubts (smile).

May all souls stamp out the pronouncements of Willie Lynch, squelching this self-perpetuating curse from seeping into the minds, consciousness and souls of our little children. He will rule the people of this Earth no more.

I wish to thank my many readers. I love and appreciate all of you. Linda, Dionne, Ramona, Lynn, Catherine, Victoria, Kristine, Bill, Rebecca, and my cousin Ericka read La Rose in her infancy. Maggie Christie always keeps me encouraged, motivated, and connected.

I would like to thank my parents Al Curtis and Bobbie Jean Ross, who loved me, who taught me how to read, and encouraged me to dream.

My sister D'mona Ross, my companion for the better part of my life, I thank you for always striving to enjoy life and your ceaseless crusade to pull me out of my reclusive shell, encouraging me to live life, not simply dream of it.

My little girl Jordan, my niece, I thank you for not only being my joy and inspiration, but taking an interest in what Auntie was typing on her laptop when you were a child. Auntie loves you.

To the great fortune of modern writers, we can access the internet at a whim, to discover answers to our questions, or to verify facts pertaining to our writings. While I browsed a slew of online articles, there are a few I would like to reference.

CITED WORKS

Lesson One Rose Anatomy. *Rose Hybridization from Texas A&M University Rose Breeding and Genetics Program Lesson Series*. Web Site. Retrieved 23 September 2013, from https://aggie-horticulture.tamu.edu/rose/rosebreeding/index.html

Goetz, Brad. Landscape Design of Andre Le Norte. *Landscape Architecture, Colorado State University*. Web Site. Retrieved 12 February 2018, from http://la.agsci.colostate.edu/people/brad-goetz/land120/landscape-design-of-andre-le-notre/

The Parts of a Flower. *The Robinson Library*. Web Site. Retrieved 01 December 2017, from http://www.robinsonlibrary.com/science/botany/anatomy/flowerparts.htm

History of United Telecommunications, INC. *Funding Universe*. Website. Retrieved 12 October 2017, from http://www.fundinguniverse.com/company-histories/united-tele-communications-inc-history/

Interstate-Guide: Interstate 55. *Interstate-Guide.com*. Web Site. Retrieved 15 September 2017, from https://www.interstate-guide.com/i-055.html

Southeastern Louisiana University. "History." https://www.southeastern.edu/about/history/

Roman Pantheon. *Your Travel Guide to Rome - Rome.info*. Website. Retrieved 12 February 2018, from http://www.rome.info/pantheon/

Oskar Schindler. *United States Holocaust Memorial Museum 2018 25. Holocaust Encyclopedia.* Web Site. Retrieved 07 January 2018, from https://www.ushmm.org/wlc/en/article.php?ModuleId=10005787

L'Ouverture, Toussaint (1742-1803). *BlackPast.org Remembered and Reclaimed.* Web Site. Retrieved 07 January 2018, from http://www.blackpast.org/gah/loverture-toussaint-1742-1803

Rosanelli, Tim (2013, August 6). *How to Roast and Grind Chicory* [Video File]. Retrieved 07 January 2018 , from https://www.youtube.com/watch?v=z9HUb6gwj74

Watts, Isaac (1719) "I Love the Lord, He Heard My Cries." *Hymnary.org.* Web Site. Retrieved 12 February 2018, from https://hymnary.org/text/i_love_the_lord_he_heard_my_cries_and_pi

Attending revival at Mt Gilliam church in Byhalia, MS as a child, the worshippers would gather around the 'mourner' and sing "Got on My Travelin' Shoes." Although they only repeated the chorus, the following is the closest rendition I found:

themanscamera (2008, August 14). *Traveling Shoes* [Video File]. Retrieved 07 January 2018, from https://www.youtube.com/watch?v=NibGaKp9yjo

Snowden, Frank (2010, February 8). The Paris School of Medicine during the Nineteenth Century. *Brewminate — A*

Bold Blend of News & Ideas. Web Site. Retrieved 07 January 2018, from http://brewminate.com/the-paris-school-of-medicine-during-the-nineteenth-century/

Lahr, John (2010, April 19). Festering: The "Addams Family" musical. *The New Yorker Magazine*. Web Site. Retrieved from https://www.newyorker.com/magazine/2010/04/19/festering

Jacques Amans. *Know Louisiana: The Digital Encyclopedia of Louisiana and Home of Louisiana Cultural Vistas*. Web Site. Retrieved 07 January 2018, from: http://www.knowlouisiana.org/entry/jacques-amans

Propert, John Lumsden (1887). *A History of Miniature Art: With Notes on Collectors and Collections* [Chapter XIV]. Page 281. Web Site. Retrieved 07 January 2018, from https://books.google.com/books?id=NCtPAAAAYAAJ&pg=PA181&lpg=PA181&dq=Pierre+de+Montarsy&source=bl&ots=Oxcd9d74rN&sig=dt-Lfk4O4g08wLygY4J4p-P1l8tI&hl=en&sa=X&ved=0ahUKEwj5he3lmMzWAhXjsFQKHQigAjgQ6AEIMjAC#v=onepage&q=Pierre%20de%20Montarsy&f=false - Pierre de Montarsy jeweler to the French crown 17th century.

University of Pennsylvania (1917). Group of Chinese Jades. *The University Museum, Section of Oriental Art*. Web Site. Retrieved 07 January 2018, from https://books.google.com/books?id=w_tEAAAAMAAJ&pg=PA3&lp-

g=PA3&dq=The+University+Museum,+Section+of+Oriental+Art&source=bl&ots=7Qi- iVQD_m&sig=luM3Gx-QvPT9q14WUoyy24T83p_g&hl=en&sa=X&ved=0a-hUKEwiVmsjyk6LZAhUH7WMKHSgkBvYQ6AEIYzA-J#v=onepage&q=ju-i&f=false – in reference to Zhan-Li's Ju-I scepter/wand

Antiques Road Show (1998, June 13). 19th Century Jade Scepter. *Antiques Road Show, Houston, TX*. Web Site. Retrieved 07 January 2018, from http://www.pbs.org/wgbh/roadshow/season/3/houston-tx/appraisals/19th-c-chinese-jade-scepter--199801A32/

Douglass, Frederick (1817-1895). *Blackpast.org Remembered and Reclaimed*. Web Site. Retrieved 12 February 2018, from http://www.blackpast.org/aah/douglass-frederick-1817-1895

Corinth Contraband Camp. *National Park Service; Shiloh, National Military Park TN, MS*. Web Site. Retrieved 22 October 2017, from https://www.nps.gov/shil/planyourvisit/contrabandcamp.htm

The Emancipation Proclamation. *National Archives Online Exhibits*. Web Site. Retrieved 22 October 2017, from https://www.archives.gov/exhibits/featured-documents/emancipation-proclamation

Never Forget: The Devil's Punchbowl – 20,000 Freed Slaves Died After Being Forced Into Post Slavery Concentration Camp. *Black Main Street*. Web Site. Retrieved 04 September 2017, from https://blackmainstreet.net/never-forget-devils-punchbowl-20000-freed-slaves-died-forced-post-slavery-concentration-camp/

Andersonville Prison. *Civil War Trust*. Web Site. Retrieved 07 January 2018, from https://www.civilwar.org/learn/articles/andersonville-prison

East Louisiana State Hospital. *Asylum Projects Reserve Preteritus*. Web Site. Retrieved 23 October 2017, from http://www.asylumprojects.org/index.php?title=East_Louisiana_State_Hospital

The Real Haunted New Orleans. (2013, August 11). *New Orleans and Me*. Web Site. Retrieved 23 October 2017, from http://www.neworleans.me/journal/detail/140/The-real-Haunted-New-Orleans - New Orleans Insane Asylum.

Missy's love, Kinky, fell at Fort Fisher in North Carolina as a soldier in the 5th United States Colored Troops of Ohio.

5th USCT History. *5th USCT*. Web Site. Retrieved 04 September 2017, from http://5thusct.net/index%20-%20 5th%20usct%20history.htm.

Lela mentions the horrible film, D. W. Griffith's *Birth of a Nation*. I've only seen clips, but that was enough.

100 Years Later, What's The Legacy Of 'Birth Of A Nation'? (2015, February 8). *Code Switch Race and Identity*

Remixed. National Public Radio. Web Site. Retrieved 01 October 2017, from http://www.npr.org/sections/codeswitch/2015/02/08/383279630/100-years-later-whats-the-legacy-of-birth-of-a-nation

Tulsa Race Riot (1921). *Blackpast.org Remembered and Reclaimed.* Web Site. Retrieved 04 September 2017, from http://www.blackpast.org/aah/tulsa-race-riot-1921

1921 Tulsa Race Riot. *Tulsa Historical Society & Museum.* Web Site. Retrieved 04 September 2017, from http://tulsa-history.org/learn/online-exhibits/the-tulsa-race-riot/

A Short History of the Septic System. *Van Delden On-Site Wastewater Systems Residential & Commercial.* Web Site. Retrieved 02 October 2017, from http://www.vdwws.com/2015/01/a-short-history-of-the-septic-system/

History of the Septic Tank System. *Newtechbio, Inc. Knowledge Base Learning Center.* Web Site. Retrieved 02 October 2017, from http://www.newtechbio.com/wiki/index.php?title=History_of_the_Septic_Tank_System

Chapter 3: Voting Rights and Political Representation in the Mississippi Delta Voting Rights Legislation And Litigation - Reconstruction. *Racial and Ethnic Tensions in American Communities: Poverty, Inequality, and Discrimination—Volume VII: The Mississippi Delta Report. US Commission on Civil Rights.* Web Site. Retrieved 07 January 2018, from http://www.usccr.gov/pubs/msdelta/ch3.htm

Dillard University [New Orleans] (1869-). *Blackpast.org Remembered and Reclaimed.* Web Site. Retrieved 04 September 2017, from http://www.blackpast.org/aah/dillard-university-1869

History of Straight University New Orleans June 26, 1869. *Dr. Bronson History Site.* Web Site. Retrieved 04 September 2017, from http://www.drbronsontours.com/StraightUniversityhistory.html

La Tribune de la Nouvelle-Orleans. *Blackpast.org Remembered and Reclaimed.* Web Site. Retrieved 02 October 2017, from http://www.blackpast.org/aah/la-tribune-de-la-nouvelle-orleans-1864-1868

Great Britain Gold Sovereign Avg Circ (Random). *APMEX Investments You Hold.* Web Site. Retrieved 03 October 2017, from https://www.apmex.com/product/17/great-britain-gold-sovereign-avg-circ-random

Barrow, Mandy. The Legend of Saint George and the Dragon. *Project Britain British Life and Culture.* Web Site. Retrieved 15 December 2017, from http://projectbritain.com/stgeorge2.html

Parkinson, Hilary. (2013, March 28). The Remarkable Story of Ann Lowe: From Alabama to Madison Avenue. *The National Archives Pieces of History.* [Weblog post]. Retrieved 07 January 2017, from https://prologue.blogs.archives.gov/2013/03/28/the-remarkable-story-of-ann-lowe-from-alabama-to-madison-avenue/

St. Louis Cardinals at Philadelphia Phillies Box Score, September 1, 1963. *Baseball Reference.* Web Site. Retrieved 04 October 2017, from https://www.baseball-reference.com/boxes/PHI/PHI196309010.shtml

Our Story. *Commander's Palace.* Web Site. Retrieved 08 February 2018, from https://www.commanderspalace.com/our-story

Godey's Ladies Book. *Accessible Archives.* Web Site. Retrieved 25 November 2017, from http://www.accessible-archives.com/collections/godeys-ladys-book/

Dr. Thomas' Eclectic Oil. *Kook Science.* Web Site. Retrieved 07 January 2018, from https://hatch.kookscience.com/wiki/Dr._Thomas%27_Eclectic_Oil

Harvard's History of Photography Timeline Viewed through Photograph Collections at Harvard University. *Harvard Library.* Web Site. Retrieved 10 September 2017, from http://library.harvard.edu/sites/all/themes/HarvardLibraryPortalTheme/timeline/index.html

Carroll, Louis. (2000). *Alice's Adventures in Wonderland.* Book Virtual Corporation. (Original work published 1865) Retrieved 12 February 2018, from https://www.adobe.com/be_en/active-use/pdf/Alice_in_Wonderland.pdf

Hurston, Zora Neale (2000, April 20). *There Eyes Were Watching God.* Archive.org. (Original work published 1937)

https://archive.org/details/TheirEyesWereWatchingGod-FullBookPDF

Wilson, Harriet. (2006, September 29). *Our Nig; or, Sketches from the life of a free black in a two-story white house, North.* Archive.org (Original work published 1859) Retrieved 12 February 2018, from https://archive.org/details/ournig-orsketches00wilsrich

Victorian Horse-Drawn Hearses, Plumes, Pomp and Processions. *Horse Canada.* Web Site. Retrieved 27 August 2018, from https://horse-canada.com/horses-and-history/victorian-horse-drawn-hearses-plumes-pomp-and-processions/

BIBLE VERSES

I reference a few scriptures throughout the novel. Below, are websites I consulted and the scriptures referenced.

Bible References. https://www.biblegateway.com

Bible References. http://biblehub.com

Genesis 5:25 "When Methuselah had lived 187 years, he became the father of Lamech"

1 Samuel 13:14 "But now thy kingdom shall not continue: the Lord hath sought him a man after his own heart, and the Lord hath commanded him to be captain over his people, because thou hast not kept that which the Lord commanded thee."

Genesis 17:12 "And he that is eight days old shall be circumcised among you, every man child in your generations, he that is born in the house, or bought with money of any stranger, which is not of thy seed."

Matthew 7:11 "If you, then, though you are evil, know how to give good gifts to your children, how much more will your Father in heaven give good gifts to those who ask him!"

Exodus 7:16 "Then say to him, 'The Lord, the God of the Hebrews, has sent me to say to you: Let my people go, so that they may worship me in the wilderness."

Psalm 37:13 "The Lord laughs at wicked for he knows their day is coming."

John 8:44: "You belong to your father, the devil, and you want to carry out your father's desires. He was a murderer from the beginning, not holding to the truth, for there is no truth in him. When he lies, he speaks his native language, for he is a liar and the father of lies."

2 Timothy 1:7 "For the Spirit God gave us does not make us timid, but gives us power, love and self-discipline."

Zechariah 2:8-9 "For thus says the LORD of hosts, "After glory He has sent me against the nations which plunder you, for he who touches you, touches the apple of His eye. "For behold, I will wave My hand over them so that they will be plunder for their slaves. Then you will know that the LORD of hosts has sent Me."

John 13:34 "A new command I give you: Love one another. As I have loved you, so you must love one another."

1 Kings 19:19 "So Elijah went from there and found Elisha son of Shaphat. He was plowing with twelve yoke of oxen, and he himself was driving the twelfth pair. Elijah went up to him and threw his cloak around him."

Romans 12:19 "Dearly beloved, avenge not yourselves, but rather give place unto wrath: for it is written, Vengeance is mine; I will repay, saith the Lord."

Isaiah 55:8-9 "For my thoughts are not your thoughts, neither are your ways my ways, saith the Lord.9 For as the heavens are higher than the earth, so are my ways higher than your ways, and my thoughts than your thoughts."

Exodus 20:12 "Honour thy father and thy mother: that thy days may be long upon the land which the Lord thy God giveth thee."

Luke 5:32 "I came not to call the righteous, but sinners to repentance."

Numbers 14:18 "The Lord is slow to anger and abounding in steadfast love, forgiving iniquity and transgression, but he will by no means clear the guilty, visiting the iniquity of the fathers on the children, to the third and the fourth generation."

James 4:7 "Submit yourselves, then, to God. Resist the devil, and he will flee from you."

Matthew 19:26 "With God, all things are possible."

Hebrews 3:8 "Harden not your hearts, as in the provocation, in the day of temptation in the wilderness"

1 Peter 2:18 "Slaves, in reverent fear of God submit yourselves to your masters, not only to those who are good and considerate, but also to those who are harsh."

Revelation 4:4 "Surrounding the throne were twenty-four other thrones, and seated on them were twenty-four elders. They were dressed in white and had crowns of gold on their heads.

1 Corinthians 10: 23 "Everything is permissible, but not everything is helpful. Everything is permissible, but not everything builds up."

Claudia Helena Ross
January 10, 2018

Works by Claudia Helena Ross

Dorothy Jones A Jazz Age Trip Through Oz
La Rose Book I Le Baton Chronicles
La Rose Book II Le Baton Chronicles
La Rose Book III Le Baton Chronicles